THE
DRIVER

MARK DAWSON

THE
DRIVER

WELBECK

Published in 2022 by Welbeck Fiction Limited, part of Welbeck Publishing Group
Based in London and Sydney
www.welbeckpublishing.com

First published in 2014
This edition published by Welbeck Fiction Limited, part of
Welbeck Publishing Group, in 2022

A CIP catalogue record for this book is available from the British Library

Hardback ISBN: 978-1-78739-703-3
Trade Paperback ISBN: 978-1-78739-704-0

Printed and bound by CPI Group (UK) Ltd., Croydon, CR0 4YY

10 9 8 7 6 5 4 3 2 1

PART I

TABBY WILSON

Tabby Wilson updated her Craigslist profile on the night she was murdered. She tweaked her personal information a little and added a new selfie that she had taken that same afternoon. It was a good likeness of her: she was wearing wispy lingerie, her skin was smooth and blemish-free, and she had on a crazy blonde wig that made her look a little like Lana Del Rey. She looked fine, she thought. Her expression was sultry and provocative, almost daring men to contact her. She was slender and had big eyes, androgynous with that alien look that was so popular on the blogs that she bookmarked and the magazines she thumbed through in Walmart or when she was waiting at the laundromat.

It was important that she looked her best. The Craigslist ad was her shop window, and as she touched up the blemishes in Photoshop, she was pleased with the results. She had perfect skin, a short bob of dark hair and those big eyes were green and expressive. She was twenty-one and had left school when she was seventeen to have a baby. She had two kids now, each with a different father, although she never saw either man. Her mom helped to bring up the kids. Until recently, she had worked in Walmart. She lived in a one-bedroom apartment in Vallejo funded by the alimony that her son's father had been ordered to pay. Apart from the fact that stacking shelves wasn't what she had in mind for her career, the alimony and her wages didn't cover all of her expenses. Things got worse when she was fired because she was always late. She got a couple of other dead-end jobs, but they didn't cut it either and she'd walked out just as soon as they had started.

Tabby liked to think that she was a positive person, so she concentrated on her ambitions. She had always wanted to be a model. There was money in that, lots of money, and she was sure that she was pretty enough and had a good enough figure to make a go of it. She created Pinterest and Instagram pages that she filled with photographs: selfies with the camera held as far away from her face as possible, others showing her in the full-length bedroom mirror, and a selection that she had culled from the shoot that a photographer friend had conducted in exchange for a night with her.

She knew that she needed to do something to get her career moving in the right direction. She spent a lot of time working on her page, and it wasn't long before she noticed the ads for modelling. She'd clicked on a site that offered free hosting for the portfolios that girls sent in. She'd set up an account and uploaded the best photos from the shoot. She'd started to see enquiries right away. She was hoping for legitimate offers and the agencies who'd replied said that they could book her for those kinds of jobs. When she'd clicked on their sites, it was obvious that what they were really looking for were hookers and escorts.

She'd started to take the offers more seriously when she saw how much money she could earn. Sex sold; she'd always known it, and now here was the proof. She couldn't really see a downside, except that she couldn't see the point of giving someone else half of the money she made.

She could do it all herself.

That was when she had started advertising on Craigslist.

*　*　*

That night's job had been booked on the phone. The john had emailed her to say that he was interested, and she had done what she always did: gave him the number of her work phone so that she could talk with him and lay out the prices and what he could expect to get in return. Insisting on a call also gave her the chance to screen the guys who had never booked her before. There were always weirdos, and she'd been knocked around by a couple. Talking to someone was better than reading an email to get an idea of what they were like. She had refused bookings with several men who had just sounded wrong on the phone. Tabby liked to say that she was a good judge of character. She was careful, too.

This guy, though? He sounded all right. A Southern accent, a bit of a hillbilly twang going on, but he'd been polite and well spoken. He'd explained to her that he was a police officer, in town for a law enforcement conference, and said that he wanted a little bit of fun. He had no problem with her charges, so she had arranged to meet him.

She was on the corner of Franklin and Turk at eight, just as they had arranged, smoking a cigarette and watching the traffic go by. She was thinking about her kids and about how she had made enough money already this week to pay the rent, pay for the groceries and maybe even take them to Six Flags for a treat. There was one at Vallejo. She was thinking about that as the Cadillac slowed to a stop beside her. Her old man had been a mechanic, and she had been big into cars when she was younger so that she could impress him; she recognised it as an Eldorado, probably twenty years old. It wasn't in the best condition. The front-right wing was dinged, the licence plate was barely attached to the chassis, and the engine backfired as the driver reached over and opened the passenger-side door for her.

He called out her name in the same redneck accent that she remembered from the phone call.

She picked up her bag and stepped into the car.

She was never seen again.

1

The grey mist had rolled in off the bay two days earlier, and it hadn't lifted yet. It softened the edges of objects within easy sight, but out beyond ten or fifteen feet, it fell across everything like a damp, cold veil. June was often the time when it was at its worst – they called it June Gloom for a reason – but the fog was always there, seeping down over the city at any time, without warning, and often staying for hours. The twin foghorns – one at either end of the Golden Gate Bridge – sounded out their long, mournful, muffled ululations. John Milton had been in town for four months, and he still found it haunting.

It was nine in the evening, the street lamps glowing with fuzzy coronas in the damp mist. Milton was in the Mission District, a once-blighted area that was being given new life by the artists and students who swarmed in now that crime had been halted and rents were still low. It was self-consciously hip now, the harlequinade of youth much in evidence: long-haired young men in vintage suits and fur-trimmed Afghans, and girls in short dresses. The streets looked run-down and shabby. The girl Milton had come to pick up was sitting on a bench on the corner. He saw her through the fog, difficult to distinguish until he was a little closer. He indicated right, filtered out of the late-evening traffic and pulled up against the kerb.

He rolled the passenger-side window down. The damp air drifted into the car.

'Madison?' he called, using the name that he had been given.

The girl, who was young and pretty, took a piece of gum out of her mouth and stuck it to the back of the bench upon which she was sitting. She reached down for a rucksack, slung it over her shoulder, picked up a garment bag and crossed the pavement to the Explorer. Milton unlocked the door for her, and she got in.

'Hi,' she said in a lazy drawl.

'Hi.'

'Thanks for being so quick. You're a lifesaver.'

'Where do you want to go?'

'You know the McDonald's in Balboa Park?'

He thought for a moment. Four months driving around San Francisco had given him a decent grasp of local geography. 'I know it.'

'That's where we're headed.'

'Okay then.'

Milton changed into first and pulled back out into the sparse traffic. The rush hour had dissipated. He settled back into his seat and nudged the car up to a steady forty-five. He looked in the mirror at his passenger; Madison had opened her rucksack and taken out a book. It looked thick and sub-stantial; a textbook, he thought. When the dispatcher had relayed the booking, she had told him to look for a blonde, although her skin was a very dark brown, almost black. Her hair was light and straightened, and Milton wondered whether it might be a wig. Curvaceous and small, she was dressed in jeans and a chunky sweater. Definitely very pretty. She read her book in silence. Milton flicked his eyes away again and concentrated on the road.

They passed through Mission Bay and Potrero Hill and continued on into Balboa Park. The McDonald's, a large drive-thru, was in the grid of streets south of Ocean Avenue. There were advertisements for three-for-two on steak burritos and cups of premium roast coffee for a dollar.

'Here you go,' he said.

'Thanks. Is it okay if we wait?'

'What for?'

'A call. We're just stopping here.'

'Fine – but I'll have to keep the clock running.'

'That's okay. I got to wait until the call comes, and then we'll be going someplace else. Is that okay with you?'

'As long as you can pay, we can stay here all night.'

'I can pay,' she said with a broad smile. 'How much do I owe you?'

Milton looked down at the meter. 'Twenty so far.'

'Twenty's no problem.' She took a purse out of her bag, opened it and took out a note. She reached forward and handed it to him. It was a hundred.

He started to feel a little uncomfortable.

'That should cover it for a couple of hours, right?'

Milton folded it and wedged it beneath the meter. 'I'll leave it here,' he said. 'I'll give you change.'

'Whatever.' She nodded at the restaurant, bright light spilling out of the window onto the line of cars parked tight up against it. 'I'd *kill* for a Big Mac,' she said. 'You want anything?'

'I'm fine, thanks.'

'You sure?'

'I ate earlier.'

'All right.'

She got out. He clenched and unclenched his fists. He rolled the window down.

'Actually,' he said, 'could you get me a coffee? Here.' He reached in his pocket for a dollar bill.

She waved him off. 'Forget it. My treat.'

Milton watched as she crossed the car park and went into the restaurant. There was a queue, and as she slotted into it to await her turn, Milton undid his seat belt and turned around so that he could reach into the back. She had left her bag on the seat. He checked that she was facing away and quickly unzipped it, going through the contents: there was a clutch bag, two books, a mobile phone, a bottle of vodka, a box of Trojans and a change of clothes. He zipped the bag and put it back. He leant back against the headrest and scrubbed his forehead with the palm of his hand.

He had been very, *very* stupid.

The girl returned with a bagged-up Happy Meal, a tall soda and a large coffee. She passed the Styrofoam cup through the open window, slid into the back seat, took the bottle of Stolichnaya from her bag, flipped the plastic lid from the soda and poured in a large measure.

'Want a drop in your coffee?'

'No, thanks,' he said. 'I don't drink.'

'Not at all?'

'Never.'

'Is that, like, a lifestyle choice?'

He wasn't about to get into that with her. 'Something like that,' he said vaguely.

'Suit yourself.'

She put the straw to her mouth and drew down a long draught.

'Madison,' Milton said, 'I need you to be honest with me.'

She looked up at him warily. 'Yeah?'

'There's no delicate way to put this.'

She stiffened, anticipating what was coming next. 'Spit it out.'

'Are you a prostitute?'

'You're a real charmer,' she said.

'Please, Madison – no attitude. Just answer the question.'

'I prefer "escort".'

'Are you an escort?'

'Yes. You got a problem with it?'

'Of course I do. If we get pulled over, I could be charged with promoting prostitution. That's a felony.'

'If that happens – which it won't – then you just tell them that I'm your friend. How they gonna say otherwise?'

'You make it sound like it's happened to you before.'

'Hardly ever, and whenever it has, it's never been a big deal.'

'No,' Milton said. 'I'm sorry. It's a big deal for me.'

'Seriously?'

'I don't need a criminal record. You're going to have to get out. You can call another taxi from here.'

'Please, John,' she said. He wondered for a moment how she knew his name, and then he remembered that his picture and details were displayed on the laminated card that he had fixed to the back of his seat. 'I can't afford this right now.'

'And I can't take the risk.'

'Please,' she said again. He looked up into the mirror. She was staring straight at him. 'Come on, man. If you leave me here, I'll never get a ride before they call me. I'll miss the party, and these guys, man, this agency I work for – they've got a zero-tolerance policy when the girls no-show. They'll fire me for sure, and I can't afford that right now.'

'I'm sorry. That's not my problem.'

'Look, man, I'm begging you. I've got a little kid. Eliza. She's just two years old – you've got no idea how cute she is. If I get fired tonight, then there's no way I'm going to be able to pay the rent. Social services will try to take her away from me again, and that just can't happen.'

Milton stared out at the queued traffic on Ocean Avenue, the glow of a hundred brake lights blooming on and off in the soupy fog as they waited for the junction to go to green. He drummed his fingers on the wheel as he turned the prospect over in his mind, aware that the girl was looking at him in the mirror with big, soulful, hopeful eyes.

He knew he was going to regret this.

'On one condition: no drugs.'

'Sure thing. No drugs.'

'You're not carrying anything?'

'No, man. Nothing, I swear.'

'No cocaine. No pills. No weed.'

'I swear it, on my daughter's life. I haven't got a thing. I'm already on probation. I got to pee in a cup twice a week, man. If I get caught with anything in my system, they'll take her away from me just like that. People say a lot of things about me, John, but one thing they don't say is that I'm stupid. It's not worth the risk.'

He watched her answer very carefully. She was emphatic and convincing, and he was as satisfied as he could be that she was telling the truth.

'This is against my better judgement,' he said, 'but, all right.'

'Thanks, John. You don't know how much I appreciate this.'

He was about to answer when her mobile buzzed. She fumbled for it in her bag and put it to her ear. Her tone became deferential and compliant. He didn't catch any names, but it was obviously about where they were headed next. The conversation was short. She put the phone back into her bag.

'You know Belvedere?'

'Don't go up there very often.'

'Full of rich folks.'

'I know that. That's where we're headed?'

'Please.'

'You got an address?'

She gave it to him, and he entered it into the satnav slotted into a holder that was suction-cupped to the windscreen. The little unit calculated and displayed the best route.

'The 101 up to the bridge,' he said, reading off the screen. 'It's going to take forty minutes. That all right?'

'Perfect.'

'You going to tell me what's out there?'

'Like I say, rich folks throwing a mad party. That's where it's at.'

2

Madison was talkative as they drove north through Sunset, Richmond and Presidio, hanging a left at Crissy Field and joining the 101 as it became the Golden Gate Bridge. She explained how her business worked as they drove. She met her driver at a prearranged spot every night. She said he was called Aaron and that he was twitchy but, generally, a stand-up kind of guy. He had let her down badly tonight. They were supposed to have met at eight at Nob Hill, but he hadn't showed, and when she finally got through to him on his mobile, he said that he was unwell and that he wouldn't be able to come out. There was a number for a taxi firm on the back of the bench she had been sitting on. She called it. It was one of the firms that sent jobs Milton's way. The dispatcher had called him with her details, and he had taken the job.

She wasn't shy about her work. She explained how she got jobs through an agency, with the rest coming from online ads she posted on Craigslist. The agency gigs were the easiest; they made the booking, and all she had to do was just show up, do whatever it was that needed to be done, collect the cash and then go. The money was split three ways: the driver got twenty per cent and the rest was split equally between the agency and the girl. Milton asked how much she made, and she was a little evasive, saying that she did okay but skimping on the detail. There was a moment's silence as he thought of the flippant way that she had given him the hundred. He concluded that she was probably earning rather a lot and then he chastised himself for his credulity. The story about the struggle to find the rent suddenly seemed a little less likely. He wondered whether there even was a little girl. Probably not. He chuckled a little as he realised that he had been well and truly suckered.

The bridge was lit up rusty gold as they passed across it, the tops of the tall struts lost in the darkness and the fog.

He heard the sound of a zip being unfastened. He looked into the mirror and saw her taking a black dress from the garment bag.

'I need to get changed,' she said. 'No peeking, John, all right?'

'Of course.'

'Don't be a pervert.'

He concentrated on the gentle curve as the bridge stretched out across the bay, but he couldn't resist a quick glance up at the mirror. She had removed her jumper and now she was struggling to slip out of her jeans. She looked up into the mirror, and Milton immediately cast his eyes back down onto the road ahead; she said nothing, but when he flicked his eyes back up again, there was a playful smile on her lips.

They crossed over into Sausalito and then Marin City.

'Done,' she said. 'You can look now.'

He did. Milton knew very little about women's clothes, but the simple black cocktail dress she was wearing had obviously been purchased in an expensive boutique. It was sleeveless, with a plain design and a deep collar that exposed her décolletage.

'You look very pretty,' he said, a little uncomfortably.

'Thank you, John.'

* * *

It was coming up to ten when Milton took the ramp off the interstate at Strawberry and negotiated the traffic circle around the tall brick spire that marked the turning onto Tiburon Boulevard. It was a long, narrow stretch of road that cut north to south right along the coast. White picket fences marked the boundaries of vast paddocks where million-dollar horses grazed. The lights from big houses that commanded impressive estates glowed from the crowns of the darkened headland to the left. They reached Belvedere proper and turned up into the hills.

The fog was dense here, and as they drove on, the vegetation closed in on both sides, the beams of the headlights playing off the trunks and briefly lighting the deep darkness within. Milton could only see fifty feet ahead of them. The flora grew a little wilder and less tended. To the left and right were thickets of bayberry and heather, a thick jumble of branches that tumbled right up to the margins of the road.

There was poison ivy, as tall as two men and thick as the branches of a tree. There was shining sumac and Virginia creeper and salt hay and bramble. Light reflected sharp and quick in the eyes of deer and rabbits. The road was separate from the houses that sat at the end of their driveways, and that night, the darkness and the fog enveloping the car like a bubble, Milton knew that they were alone.

'You know where we're going?' he asked.

'Turn onto West Shore Road. There's a private road at the end.'

He looked in the mirror. Madison had switched on the courtesy light and was applying fresh lipstick with the aid of a small mirror. She certainly was pretty, with nice skin and delicate bones and eyes that glittered when she smiled, which was often. She was young; Milton would have guessed that she was in her early twenties. She was small, too, couldn't have been more than five-three and a hundred pounds soaking wet. She looked vulnerable.

The whole thing didn't sit right with him.

'So,' he said, 'you've been here before?'

'A few times.'

'What's it like?'

'All right.'

'What kind of people?'

'I told you – rich ones.'

'Anyone else you know going to be there?'

'Couple of the guys,' she said. Was she a little wistful when she said it?

'Who are they?'

She looked into the mirror, into his eyes. 'No one you'd know,' she said, and then he knew that she was lying.

He thought she looked a little anxious. They drove on in silence for another half a mile. He had been in the area a couple of times before. It was a beautiful location, remote and untroubled by too many visitors, full of wildlife and invigorating air. He had hiked all the way down from Paradise Beach to Tiburon Uplands and then turned and walked back again. Five miles, all told, a bright summer afternoon spent tracking fresh prints into the long grass and then following them back again in the opposite direction. He hadn't seen another soul.

He looked in the mirror again. 'Do you mind me asking – how long have you been doing this?'

'A year,' she said, suddenly a little defensive. 'Why?'

'No reason. Just making conversation.'

Her temper flickered up. 'As long as you don't try to tell me I should find something else to do, okay? If you're gonna start up with that, then I'd rather you just kept quiet and drove.'

'What you do is up to you. I'm not in any place to tell you anything.'

'Fucking A.'

'I'm just thinking practically.'

'Like?'

'Like, how are you getting back?'

'I'll call another cab.'

'Back to the city?'

'Sure.'

'That's if you can find someone who'll come out this late at night. With fog as bad as this and supposed to be getting worse? I know I wouldn't.'

'Lucky I'm not calling *you*, then.'

He spoke carefully. He didn't want to come over like some concerned father figure. He guessed that would put her even more on the defensive. 'You got no one to look out for you while you're here?'

She hesitated, looking out into the gloom. 'My guy usually waits and then drives me back again. Keeps an eye on things, too, makes sure I'm all right.'

'I can't do that for you.'

'I wasn't asking.'

'I've got a day job. I need to get back to sleep.'

'I told you – I wasn't asking. *Jesus, man!* This isn't the first time I've done this. I'll be all right. The men are okay. Respectable types. Bankers and shit. A frat party – maybe I'm a little concerned to be out on my own. But here? With guys like this? Nothing to worry about. I'll be fine.'

The GPS said the turn was up ahead. Milton dabbed the brakes and slowed to twenty, searching for the turn-off in the mist. He found it; it was unlit, narrow and lonely, and the sign read PINE SHORE. He indicated even though there was no one on the road ahead or behind him and then slowed a little more.

He looked at the clock in the dash; the glowing digits said that it was half-ten.

The road ran parallel to West Shore Road for half a mile or so, and then Milton saw lights glowing through the trees. It turned sharply to the left and then was interrupted by an eight-foot brick wall and, in the midst of that, a majestic wrought-iron gate that looked like it belonged on a Southern plantation. A white gatehouse was immediately ahead. Beyond the gate, on the right-hand side of the road, a blue wooden sign had been driven into the verge. The sign said PINE SHORE ASSOCIATION in golden letters that sloped from right to left. There was a model lighthouse atop the gate. Milton considered it: a private community, prime real estate, close enough to the city, and with Silicon Valley not too far away. It all smelt of money.

Lots and lots of money.

'Through there,' she said.

'How many houses in here?'

'Don't know for sure. I've only ever been to this one. Twenty? Thirty?'

'How do we get in?'

'They texted me the code.' The glow of her mobile lit up her face as she searched for the information she needed. '2-0-1-1.'

He nudged the car forwards and lowered his window. The low rumble of the tyres on the rough road surface blended with the muffled chirping of the cicadas outside. He reached out to the keypad and punched in the code. The gate opened, and they followed a long driveway enclosed on both sides by mature oaks. Large and perfectly tended gardens reached down to the road. There were tree allées, expansive lawns, follies, knot gardens and boxwood parterres.

They reached the first house. It was a large, modern building set out mostly on one level with a two-storey addition at one end. It spread out across a wide parcel of land. There were two separate wings, each with floor-to-ceiling windows that cast oblongs of golden light that blended away into the grey shroud that had fallen all around. A series of antique lamps threw abbreviated, fuzzy triangles of illumination out across the immaculate front lawn. There was a forecourt verged by fruit trees. Milton reverse-parked in a space; there was a Ferrari on one side and a Tesla Roadster convertible on the other. Two hundred thousand dollars of peerless design and engineering. His Explorer was old and battered and inadequate in comparison.

Milton switched off the engine. 'You weren't kidding.'

'About what?'

'There's money here.'

'Told you.' She unclipped her seat belt and put her hand on the door handle, but then she paused for a moment, as if unwilling to open the door.

'Are you all right?'

'Sure. It's just—'

'You're nervous? I can take you back if you want.'

She shook her head. 'I'm not nervous.'

'Then what?'

'I'm here to meet someone, except I haven't seen him for a while, and he doesn't know I'm coming. The last time I saw him, it— well, let's say it didn't go so well, didn't end well for either of us. There's probably a very good chance he tells me to get the fuck out as soon as he sees me.'

'I'm going back into the city. It's not a problem.'

'No. I don't have any choice. I want to see him.'

'It'd be no trouble. No charge.'

'I'm fine. Really. It's completely cool. I'm just being stupid.'

She opened the door and got out, reaching back inside for her coat and bag.

She shut the door.

She paused.

She turned back to him.

'Thanks for driving me,' she said into the open window. She smiled shyly and suddenly looked very young indeed. The chic dress and stratospheric heels looked out of place, like a schoolgirl playing dress-up. She turned towards the house. The door opened, and Milton noticed a male face watching them through the gloom.

Milton wondered, again, how old she was. Nineteen? Twenty?

Too young for this.

Her footsteps crunched through the gravel.

Dammit, Milton thought.

'Madison,' he called through the window. 'Hang on.'

She paused and turned back to him. 'What?'

'I'll wait.'

She took a step closer to the car. 'You don't have to do that.'

'No, I do. You shouldn't be out here on your own.'

She liked to keep her face impassive, he could see that, but she couldn't stop the sudden flicker of relief that broke over it. 'Are you sure you're okay with that? I could be a couple hours – maybe longer, if it goes well.'

'I've got some music and a book. If you need me, I'll be right here.'

'I'll pay extra.'

'We'll sort that out later. You can leave your bag if you want.'

She came back to the car and took the smaller clutch bag from the rucksack. She put the condoms inside and took a final swig from the bottle of vodka. 'Thanks. It's kind of you.'

'Just— well, you know, just be careful, all right?'

'I'm always careful.'

3

Milton got out of the car and stretched his legs. It was quiet but for the occasional calls of seals and pelicans, the low whoosh of a jet high above and, rolling softly over everything, the quiet susurration of the sea. A foghorn boomed out from across the water, and seconds later, its twin returned the call. Lights hidden in the vegetation cast an electric blue glow over the timber frame of the building, the lights behind the huge expanses of glass blazing out into the darkness. Milton knew that the house was high enough on the cliffs to offer a spectacular view across the bay to Alcatraz, the bridge and the city, but all he could see tonight was the shifting grey curtain. There was a certain beauty in the feeling of solitude.

Milton enjoyed it for ten minutes, and then, as the temperature chilled and began to drop further, he returned to the Explorer, switched on the heater, took out his phone and plugged it into the dash. He scrolled through his music until he found the folder that he was looking for. He had been listening to a lot of old guitar music and he picked *Dog Man Star*, the album by Suede that he had on before he picked Madison up. There had been a lot of Britpop on the barrack's stereo while he had slogged through Selection for the SAS and it brought back memories of happier times. Times when his memories didn't burden him like they did now. He liked the swirling layers of shoegazing and dance-pop fusions from the Madchester era and the sharp, clean three-minute singles that had evolved out of it. Suede and Sleeper and Blur.

He turned the volume down a little and closed his eyes as the wistful introduction of 'Stay Together' started. His memories triggered: the Brecon Beacons, the Fan Dance, hours and hours of hauling a sixty-pound pack up and down the mountains, the lads he had gone through the process with, most of whom had been binned, the pints of stout that had followed each exercise in inviting pubs with roaring log fires and horse brasses on the walls.

The credentials fixed to the back of the driver's seat said JOHN SMITH. That was also the name on his driver's licence and passport, and it was the name he had given when he had rented his nine-hundred-dollar-a-month single-room-occupancy apartment with no kitchen and shared bathroom in the Mission District. No one in San Francisco knew him as John Milton or had any idea that he was not the anonymous, quiet man that he appeared to be.

He worked freelance, accepting his jobs from the agencies who had his details. He drove the night shift, starting at eight and driving until three or four. Then he would go home and sleep for seven hours before working his second job from twelve until six, delivering boxes of ice to restaurants in the city for Mr Freeze, the pseudonym of a cantankerous Ukrainian immigrant Milton had met after answering the 'positions vacant' ad on an internet bulletin board. Between the two jobs, Milton could usually make a hundred dollars a day. It wasn't much in an expensive city like San Francisco, but it was enough to pay his rent and his bills and his food, and that was all he needed, really. He didn't drink. He didn't have any expensive habits. He didn't have the time or the inclination to go out. He might catch a film now and again, but most of his free time was spent sleeping or reading. It had suited him very well for the four months he had been in town.

It was the longest he had been in one place since he had been on the run, and he was starting to feel comfortable. If he continued to be careful, there was no reason why he couldn't stay here for even longer. Maybe put down some roots? He'd always assumed that that would be impossible and had discouraged himself from thinking about it, but now?

Maybe it would be possible after all.

* * *

He gazed out of the window. He could see the glow from other houses further down the road. The nearest was another big building with lights blurring through the murk. As he watched, a sleek black town car turned into the driveway and parked three cars over from him. The doors opened, and two men stepped out. It was too dark and foggy to make out anything other than their silhouettes, but he watched as they made their way to the door and went into the house.

The dull thump and drone of bass was suddenly audible from the house. The party was getting started. Milton turned up the stereo a little to muffle it. He changed to The Smiths. Morrissey's melancholia seemed appropriate in the cloying fog.

Time passed. He had listened to the whole of *Meat is Murder* and was halfway through *The Queen is Dead* when he heard a scream through the crack in the window.

His eyes flashed open.

He turned down the stereo.

Had he imagined it?

The bass throbbed.

Somewhere, footsteps crunched through the gravel.

A snatch of angry conversation.

He heard it again, clearer this time, a scream of pure terror.

Milton got out of the car and crossed the forecourt to the front door. He concentrated a little more carefully on his surroundings. The exterior was taken up by those walls of glass, the full-length windows shining with the light from inside. Some of the windows were open, and noise was spilling out: the steady bass over the sound of drunken voices, conversation, laughter.

The scream came again.

A man was standing with his legs apart on the front porch.

'You hear that?' Milton said.

'Didn't hear nothing.'

'There was a scream.'

'I didn't hear anything, buddy. Who are you?'

'A driver.'

'So back to your car, please.'

The scream sounded for a fourth time.

It was hard to be sure, but Milton thought it was Madison.

'Let me in.'

'You ain't going in, buddy. Back to the car. *Now*.'

Milton sized him up quickly. He was big, and he regarded Milton with a look that combined distaste and surliness. 'Who are you?'

'I'm the man who tells you to fuck off. Like already, okay?' The man pulled back his jacket to reveal a shoulder holster. He had a big handgun.

Milton punched hard into the man's gut, aiming all his power for a point several inches behind him. The man's eyes bulged as the pain fired up into his brain, and he folded down, his arms dropping to protect his groin. Milton looped an arm around his neck and yanked him off the porch, dragging him backwards so that his toes scraped tracks through the gravel, and then drove his knee into the man's face. He heard the bones crack. He turned him over, pinning him down with a knee into his gut, reached inside his jacket and took out the gun. It was a Smith & Wesson, the SW1911 Pro Series. 9mm, ten rounds plus one in the chamber. A very good, very expensive handgun. Fifteen hundred dollars new. Whoever this guy was, if he bought his own ironwork, he must have been getting some decent pay.

Milton flipped the S&W so that he was holding it barrel first and brought the butt down across the crown of the man's head. He spasmed and then was still.

Another scream.

Milton shoved the gun into the waistband of his jeans and pushed the door all the way open. A central corridor ran the length of the building with doors and windows set all along it and skylights overhead. The walls were painted white, and the floor was Italian marble. The corridor ended at a set of French doors. Vases of orchids were spaced at regular intervals across the marble.

He hurried through into the bright space beyond. It was a living room. He took it all in: oak parquetry floor inlaid with ebony, a gilded fireplace that belonged in a palazzo as the focal point of the wall, rich mahogany bookshelves and fine fabric lining one wall and the rest set with windows that would have provided awesome views on a clear day. The ceiling was oak and downlights in the beams lit the room. The furnishings were equally opulent, with three circular sofas that would each have been big enough to accommodate ten or eleven people. The big windows were ajar and gleaming white against the darkness outside. A night breeze blew through the room, sucking the long curtains in and out of the windows, blowing them up towards the ceiling and then rippling them out over a rust-coloured rug.

Milton took in everything, remembering as much as he could.

Details:

The DJ in a baseball cap mixing from two laptops set up next to the bar.

The pole with two girls writhing around it, both of them dressed as nuns.

The girl dancing on the well-stocked bar, wearing a mask of President Obama.

The music was loud, and the atmosphere was frantic. Many of the guests were drunk, and no attempt had been made to hide the large silver salvers of cocaine that had been placed around the room. Milton watched a man leading a half-naked woman up the wide wooden staircase to the first floor. Another man stuffed a banknote into the garter belt of the girl who was dancing for him.

The scream.

Milton tracked it.

He made his way farther inside. The windows at the rear of the room looked out onto wide outdoor porches and manicured grounds. He could just see through the fog to the large illuminated pool, the spa and the fire flickering in an outdoor firepit. He passed into a library. Silk fabric walls blended with painted wainscoting. There was a private cloakroom and a large wood-burning fireplace. A handful of guests stood there, all male.

Madison was cowering against the wall, slowly rocking backwards and forwards.

There was a man next to her. He put his hand on her shoulder and spoke to her, but she pulled away. She looked vulnerable and frightened.

Milton quickly crossed the room. 'Are you all right?'

She looked right through him.

'Madison – are you all right?'

She couldn't focus on him.

'It's John Smith.'

Her eyes were glassy.

'I drove you here, remember? I said I'd wait for you.'

The man who had been speaking to her faded back and walked quickly away. Milton watched him, caught between his concern for her and the desire to question him.

'They want to kill me,' she said.

'What?'

'They want me dead.'

Another man appeared in the door and came across to them both. Another guard.

Milton turned his head to look at him. 'What's going on?'

'Nothing.'

'Look at her. What's happened?'

He snorted out a derisive laugh. 'She's tripping out, man. They said she went into the bathroom, and when she came out, she was like that. But you don't need to worry. We'll look after her. We're going to drive her back to the city.'

'She says someone wants to kill her.'

'You want me to repeat it? Look at the state of her. She's off her head.'

Milton didn't buy that for a moment. Something was wrong, he was sure of it, and there was no way he was going to leave her here.

'Who are you?' the man asked him.

'I drove her out here. You don't need to worry about another car. I'll take her back.'

'No, you won't. We're taking care of it, and you're getting out of here. Right now.'

'Not without her.'

Milton moved towards him so that they were face to face. The man was about the same height as him but perhaps a little heavier. He had low, clenched brows and a thick, flattened nose. He had nothing in common with the well-dressed, affluent guests next door. Hired muscle in case any of the guests got out of hand. Probably armed, too, like his pal with the broken nose and the headache outside. Milton took another deep breath. He stared forward with his face burning and his hands clenching and unclenching.

'What?' the man said, squaring up to him.

'I'd be careful,' Milton advised, 'before I lose my temper.'

'That supposed to be a threat, pal? What you gonna do?'

Milton's attention was distracted for just a moment, and he didn't notice Madison sprint for the door. He shouldered the man out of the way and gave chase, but she was quick and agile and already halfway across the library and then into the living room beyond. Milton bumped into a drunken guest, knocking him so that he toppled over the back of the sofa and onto the floor, barely managing to keep his own balance. 'Madison!' He stumbled after her, scrambling through the room and into the foyer and then the cool of the night beyond. The visibility was bad. He called out to her, 'Madison! Wait!'

She crossed the driveway and kept going, disappearing into the bushes at the side of the gardens.

She vanished into the fog.

The man outside was on his knees, still dazed, struggling to get to his feet.

Milton started in pursuit but came to a helpless stop. He clenched his teeth in frustration. He couldn't start crashing across the neighbouring properties. Their occupants would call the police, and then he would be arrested, and they would take his details. He had probably stayed too long as it was. Perhaps they had already been called. Bringing attention to himself was something that a man in his position really couldn't afford.

He ran for the Explorer, started the engine and rolled the car up the road. He turned right, further into Pine Shore, and as the headlights raked through the murky gloom, he saw Madison again, at the front door of the next house, knocking furiously. He watched as the door opened and an old man with scraps of white hair and an expression that flicked from annoyance to concern came out and spoke with her. She shrieked at him, repeating one word – 'help' – before she pushed her way into the house.

Milton stepped out of the car and then paused, impotent, as the sounds of an argument were audible from inside. Madison stumbled outside again, tripping down the porch steps. She scrambled to her feet as Milton took a step towards her, the old man coming outside after her, a phone in his hand, calling out in a weak and uncertain voice that he had phoned 911 and that she needed to get off his property. He saw Milton, glared at him and repeated that he had called the cops.

Milton paused again. Madison sprinted to the old man's fence and clambered over it, ploughing through a flower bed and a stand of shrubs, knocking on the front door of the next big house, not waiting to have her knock answered before continuing on down the road.

Milton heard the growl of several motorcycle engines. Four sets of lights blasted around the corner, powerful headlamps that sliced through the fog. He turned and looked into the glare of the high beams. The shape of the bikes suggested big Harleys. The riders slotted the hogs in along the side of the road. The engines were killed, one by one, but the headlights were left burning.

A car rolled up alongside them. It was difficult to make it out for sure, but it looked like an old Cadillac.

Milton got back into the Explorer and drove slowly up the road after Madison. It was dimly lit and he couldn't see where she had gone. He dialled the number she had used to book him earlier. There was no answer.

Another set of headlights flicked on behind him, flashing across the rear-view mirror. The town car from before had pulled out of the driveway to the party house. Milton redialled the number as he watched its red tail lights disappear into the fog, swerving away behind the shoulder of dark trees at the side of the road.

He turned the car around and went through the gate in case Madison had doubled back and tried to make her way back up towards West Shore Road. The vegetation was dark and thick to either side, no light and no sign of anyone or anything. No sign of her anywhere. He parked.

After five minutes, he heard the engines of the four motorbikes and watched as they looped around in a tight turn and roared away, heading back out towards the road, passing him one after the other and then accelerating sharply. The Cadillac followed. Five minutes after that he heard the siren of a cop car. Milton slid down in the seat, his head beneath the line of the window. The police car turned through the gate and rolled towards the house. He waited for change to it to come to a stop, and then, with his lights off, he drove away. He had already taken more risks than was prudent. The cops would be able to help Madison more than he could, and he didn't want to be noticed out here.

That didn't mean that he didn't feel bad.

He flicked the lights on and accelerated gently away.

4

Milton stirred at twelve the next day. His first waking thought was of the girl. He had called her mobile several times on the way back to the city, but he had been transferred straight to voicemail. After that, he had driven home in silence. He didn't know her at all, yet he was still terribly worried. He made his bed, pulling the sheets tight and folding them so that it was as neat as he could make it, a hang-up from a decade spent in the army. When he was done, he stared out of the window of his room into the seemingly never-ending shroud of fog in the street beyond. He feared that something dreadful had happened.

His apartment had a shared bathroom, and he waited until it was unoccupied and then showered in the lukewarm water. He ran his right hand down the left-hand side of his body, feeling for the broken ribs that he had suffered after *Santa Muerte* had stomped him in the dust and dirt outside Juárez. There had been no time to visit a doctor to fix them, but they had healed well enough. It was just another fracture that hadn't been dealt with properly, and he had lost count of the number of times that that had happened.

Milton took his razor and shaved, looking at his reflection in the steamy mirror. He had short dark hair flecked with a little grey. There was a scar on his face, running horizontally from his earlobe, across his cheek and terminating just below his right nostril. He was even-featured, although there was something 'hard' about his looks. He looked almost swarthy in certain lights, and now that he had shaved away the untidy beard that he had sported while he had travelled north through South America, his clean, square, sharply defined jawline was exposed.

His day work was physically demanding, and hefting the weighty boxes from the depot into the back of the truck had been good for his physique. His old muscle tone was back, and he felt better than he had for months. The tan he had acquired while he was in South America had faded, and the tattoo of an angel's wings across his shoulders and neck stood out more clearly now that his skin was paler. He dried himself and dressed in jeans and a work shirt, locked the door and left the building.

* * *

Top Notch Burger was a one-room restaurant at the corner of Hyde and O'Farrell. Milton had found it during his exploration of the city after he had taken his room at the El Capitan. It was a small place squeezed between a hair salon and a shoe shop, with frosted windows and identified only by the single word BURGER written across dusty signage.

Inside, the furniture was mismatched and often broken, the misspelt menu was chalked up on a blackboard, and hygiene looked as if it was an afterthought.

The chef was a large African-American man called Julius and, as Milton had discovered, he was a bona fide genius when it came to burgers. Milton came in every day for his lunch, sometimes taking the paper bag with his burger and fries and eating it in his car on the way to Mr Freeze, and on other occasions, if he had the time, he would eat it in the restaurant. There was rarely anyone else in the place at the same time, and Milton liked that; he listened to the gospel music that Julius played through the cheap Sony stereo on a shelf above his griddle, sometimes read his book and sometimes just watched the way the man expertly prepared the food.

'Afternoon, John,' Julius said as he shut the door behind him.

'How's it going?'

'Going good,' he said. 'What can I get for you? The usual?'

'Please.'

Milton almost always had the same thing: bacon and cheddar on an aged beef patty in a sourdough bun, bone marrow, cucumber pickles, caramelised onions, horseradish aioli, a bag of double-cooked fries and a bottle of ginger beer.

He was getting ready to leave when his phone rang.

He stopped, staring as the phone vibrated on the table.

No one ever called him at this time of day.

'Hello?'

'My name's Trip Macklemore.'

'Do I know you?'

'Who are you?'

Milton paused, his natural caution imposing itself. 'My name's John,' he said carefully. 'John Smith. What can I do for you?'

'You're a taxi driver?'

'That's right.'

'Did you drive Madison Clarke last night?'

'I drove *a* Madison. She didn't tell me her second name. How do you know that?'

'She texted me your number. Her usual driver wasn't there, right?'

'So she said. How do you know her?'

'I'm her boyfriend.'

Milton swapped the phone to his other ear. 'She hasn't come home?'

'No. That's why I'm calling.'

'And that's unusual for her?'

'Very. Did anything happen last night?'

Milton paused uncomfortably. 'How much do you know—'

'About what she does?' he interrupted impatiently. 'I know everything, so you don't need to worry about hurting my feelings. Look – I've been worried sick about her. Could we meet?'

Milton drummed his fingers against the table.

'Mr Smith?'

'Yes, I'm here.'

'Can we meet? Please. I'd like to talk to you.'

'Of course.'

'This afternoon?'

'I'm working.'

'After that? When you're through?'

'Sure.'

'Do you know Mulligan's? Green and Webster.'

'I can find it.'

'What time?'

Milton said he would see him at six. He ended the call, gave Julius ten dollars and stepped into the foggy street outside.

*   *   *

The business had its depot in Bayview. It was located in an area of warehouses, a series of concrete boxes with electricity and telephone wires strung overhead and cars and trucks parked haphazardly outside. Milton parked the Explorer in the first space he could find and walked the short distance to Wallace Avenue. Mr Freeze's building was on the corner, a two-storey box with two lines of windows and a double-height roller door through which the trucks rolled to be loaded with the ice they would deliver all around the Bay Area.

Milton went in through the side door, to the locker room and changed into the blue overalls with the corporate logo – a block of motion-blurred ice – embroidered on the left lapel. He changed his Timberlands for a pair of steel-capped work boots and went to collect his truck from the line that was arranged in front of the warehouse.

He swung out into the road and then backed into the loading bay. He saw Vassily, the boss, as he went around to the big industrial freezer. His docket was fixed to the door: bags of ice to be delivered to half a dozen restaurants in Fisherman's Wharf and an ice sculpture to a hotel in Presidio.

He yanked down the big handle and muscled the heavy freezer door open. The cold hit him at once, just like always, a numbing throb that would sink into the bones and remain there all day if you stayed inside too long.

Milton picked up the first big bag of ice and carried it to the truck. It, too, was refrigerated, and he slung it into the back to be arranged for transport when he had loaded them all. There were another twenty bags, and by the time he had finished carrying them into the truck, his biceps, the inside of his forearms and his chest were cold from where he had hugged the ice. He stacked the bags in three neat rows and went back into the freezer. He just had the ice sculpture left to move. It was of a dolphin, curled as if it was leaping through the air. It was five feet high and set on a heavy plinth. Vassily paid a guy fifty dollars for each sculpture and sold them for three hundred. It was, as he said, 'a big-ticket item'.

Milton couldn't keep his mind off what had happened last night. He kept replaying it all: the house, the party, the girl's blind panic, the town car that had only just arrived before it had pulled away, the motorcycles, the Cadillac. Was there anything else he could have done? He was embarrassed that he had let Madison get away from him so easily when it was so obvious that she needed help. She wasn't his responsibility.

He knew that she was an adult, but he also knew he would blame himself if anything had happened to her.

He pressed his fingers beneath the plinth, and bending his knees and straining his arms and thighs, he hefted the sculpture into the air, balancing it against his shoulder. It was heavy, surely two hundred pounds, and it was all he could manage to get it off the floor. He turned around and started forwards, his fingers straining and the muscles in his arms and shoulders burning from the effort.

He thought about the call from her boyfriend and the meeting that he and Macklemore had scheduled. He would tell him exactly what had happened. Maybe he would know something. Maybe Milton could help him find her.

He made his way to the door of the freezer. The unit had a raised lip, and Milton was distracted; he forgot that it was there and stubbed the toe of his right foot against it. The sudden surprise unbalanced him, and he caught his left boot on the lip too as he stumbled over it. The sculpture tipped away from his body, and even as Milton tried to follow after it, attempting to bring his right arm up to corral it, he knew there was nothing he could do. The sculpture tipped forwards faster and faster, and then he dropped it completely. It fell to the concrete floor of the depot, shattering into a million tiny pieces.

Even in the noisy depot, the crash was loud and shocking. There was a moment of silence before some of the others started to clap, others whooping sardonically. Milton stood with the glistening fragments spread around him, helpless. He felt the colour rising in his cheeks.

Vassily came out of the office. 'What the *fuck*, John?'

'Sorry.'

'What happened?'

'I tripped. Dropped it.'

'I can see that.'

'I'm sorry.'

'You already said that. It's not going to put it back together again, is it?'

'I was distracted.'

'I don't pay you to be distracted.'

'No, you don't. I'm sorry, Vassily. It won't happen again.'

'It's coming out of your wages. Three hundred bucks.'

'Come on, Vassily. It doesn't cost you that.'

'No, but that's money I'm going to have to pay back. Three hundred. If you don't like it, you know where to find the door.'

Milton felt the old, familiar flare of anger. Five years ago, he would not have been able to hold it all in. His fists clenched and unclenched, but he remembered what he had learnt in the Rooms – that there were some things that you just couldn't control, and that there was no point in worrying about them – and with that in mind, the flames flickered and died. It was better that way. Better for Vassily. Better for him.

'Fine,' he said. 'That's fine. You're right.'

'Clean it up,' Vassily snapped, stabbing an angry finger at the mess on the floor, 'and then get that ice delivered. You're going to be late.'

5

Milton drove the Explorer back across town and arrived ten minutes early for his appointment at six with Trip Macklemore. Mulligan's was at 330 Townsend Street. There was a small park opposite the entrance, and he found a bench that offered an uninterrupted view. He put the girl's rucksack on the ground next to his feet, picked up a discarded copy of the *Chronicle* and watched the comings and goings. The fog had lifted a little during the afternoon, but it looked as if it was going to thicken again for the evening. He didn't know what Trip looked like, but he guessed the anxious-looking young man who arrived three minutes before they were due to meet was as good a candidate as any.

Milton waited for another five minutes, watching the street. There was no sign that Trip had been followed or that any surveillance had been set up. The people looking for him were good, but that had been Milton's job for many years, too, and he was confident that they would not be able to hide from him. Satisfied, he got up, dropped the newspaper into the rubbish bin next to the seat, collected the rucksack, crossed the road and went inside.

The young man he had seen coming inside was waiting at a table. Milton scanned the bar; it was a reflex action drilled into him by long experience and reinforced by several occasions where advance planning had saved his life. He noted the exits and the other customers. It was early, and the place was quiet. Milton liked that. Nothing was out of the ordinary.

He allowed himself to relax a little and approached. 'Mr Macklemore?'

'Mr Smith?'

'That's right. But you can call me John.'

'Can I get you a beer?'

'That's all right. I don't drink.'

'Something else?'

'It's okay – I'm fine.'

'You don't mind if I do?'

'No. Of course not.'

The boy went to the bar, and Milton checked him out. He guessed he was in his early twenties. He had a fresh complexion that made him look even younger and a leonine aspect, with a high clear brow and plenty of soft black curls eddying over his ears and along his collar. He had a compact, powerful build. A good-looking boy with a healthy colour to his skin, Milton guessed that he worked outside, in a trade that involved plenty of physical labour. He was nervous, fingering the edge of his wallet as he tried to get the bartender's attention.

'Thanks for coming,' he said when he came back with his beer.

'No problem.'

'You mind me asking – that accent?'

'I'm English.'

'That's what I thought. What are you doing in San Francisco?'

Milton had no wish to get into a discussion about that. 'Working,' he said, closing it off.

Trip put his thumb and forefinger around the neck of the bottle and drank.

'So,' Milton said, 'shall we talk about Madison?'

'Yes.'

'She hasn't come back?'

'No. And I'm starting to get worried about her. Like – *seriously* worried. I was going to give it until ten and then call the police.'

'She's never done this before?'

'Been out of touch as long as this?' The boy shook his head. 'No. Never.'

'When did you see her last?'

'Last night. We went to see an early movie. It finished at eightish, she said she was going out to work, so I kissed her goodnight and went home.'

'She seemed all right to you?'

'Same as ever. Normal.'

'And you've tried to call her?'

'Course I have, man. Dozens of times. I got voicemail first of all, but now I don't even get that. The phone's been shut off. That's when I really started to worry. She's never done that before. She gave me your number last night—'

'Why did she do that?'

'She's careful when she's working. She didn't know you.'

Milton was as sure as he could be that Trip was telling the truth.

The boy drank off half of his beer and placed the bottle on the table. 'Where did you take her?'

'Up to Belvedere. Do you know it?'

'Not really.'

'There's a gated community up there. She said she'd been up there before.'

'She's never mentioned it.'

'There's a couple of dozen houses. Big places. Plenty of money. There was a party there. A big house just inside the gate. She didn't tell you about it?'

He shook his head. 'She never told me anything. Can't say it's something I really want to know about, so I never ask. I don't like her doing it, but she's making money, thousand bucks a night, sometimes – what am I gonna do about that? She makes more in a night than I make in two weeks.'

'Doing what?'

'I work for the electric company – fix power lines, maintenance, that kind of thing.'

'What does she do with the money?'

'She saves it.'

'She have a kid?'

'No,' he said.

Milton nodded to himself: *suckered*.

'She's saving as much as she can so she can write. That's her dream. I suppose I could ask her to stop, but I don't think she'd pay much attention. She's strong-willed, Mr Smith. You probably saw that.'

'I did.'

'And anyway, it's only going to be a temporary thing – just until she's got the money she needs.' He took another swig from the bottle. Milton noticed his hands were shaking. 'What happened?'

'I dropped her off, and then I waited for her to finish.'

'And?'

'And then I heard a scream.'

'Her?'

'Yes. I went inside to get her.'

He paused, wondering how much he should tell the boy. He didn't want to frighten him more than he already was, but he figured Trip needed to know everything.

'She was in a state,' he continued. 'She looked terrified. She was out of it, too. Wouldn't speak to me. I don't even know if she saw me.'

'Out of it? What does that mean?'

'She ever do drugs?'

'No way,' Trip said. 'Never.'

'That's what she told me, too.' Milton frowned. 'I went in to see her, and look, if I had to say one way or another, then I'd say she was on something. She said everyone was trying to kill her. Very paranoid. Her eyes wouldn't focus, and she wasn't making any sense.'

'Maybe her drink was spiked?'

'Maybe,' Milton said. But maybe not. He thought it was more likely that she was doing drugs. A job like that? Milton had helped a girl in the Balkans once during the troubles over there, and she had worked up a ferocious heroin habit. The way she had explained it, she'd needed something to deaden herself to the things she had to do to stay alive, and that had been as good as anything else. And Madison had kept the finer details of her hooking away from Trip, so wasn't it likely that she'd keep this from him, too? Didn't it stand to reason? No sense in pushing that now, though.

'What happened after that?'

'She ran. I went after her, but she was too quick for me, and to be honest, I'm not sure what I would've done if I'd caught her, anyway. I got in the car and drove up and down, but there wasn't any sign of her. I called her mobile but didn't get anywhere. In the end, I waited as long as I could, and then I came back. I was hoping she might have found her way home.'

Trip blanched with worry. 'Fuck.'

'Don't panic,' Milton said calmly. 'There might be a reason for it.'

'I don't think so. Something's wrong.'

Milton said nothing. He pushed Madison's rucksack along the floor with his foot. 'Here,' he said. 'She left this in the car. You better take it.'

Trip picked up the bag, put it on his lap, opened it and idly took out the things inside: her books, the bottle of vodka, her purse. 'What do I do now?'

'That's up to you. If it was me, I wouldn't wait to call the police. I'd do it now—'

'But you said not to panic.'

'I know, and the chances are that there's a perfectly good explanation for what's happened. She'll come home, and you'll just have to explain to them that it was a false alarm. They won't mind – happens all the time. But if something is wrong, if she is in trouble, the sooner you get the police onto it, the better it's likely to be.'

'How do I do that? Just call them?'

'Better to go in.'

'Yes,' Trip said, nodding vigorously. 'I'll go in.'

'You want some backup?'

'What – you'll come too?'

'If you like.'

'You don't have to do that,' he said, although his relief was palpable.

It was the right thing to do. The way Milton saw it, they would want to speak to him, and it would save time if he was already there. It would show willing, too; Milton was a little anxious that there might be questions about him driving a prostitute to a job, and he thought it would be better to be upfront right from the start. He would deny that he had known what was going on — which was true, at least up

51

to a point – and hope for the best. And, he thought, the boy was becoming increasingly anxious. He suspected he might appreciate a little moral support.

'Come on,' he said. 'You drive here?'

'I don't have a car. I got the bus.'

'I'll give you a ride.'

6

They were met in the reception area by a uniformed cop who introduced himself as Officer Francis. He was an older man with the look of a long-standing veteran. His hair was shot through with streaks of grey, his face was creased with lines, and he sat down with a sigh of contentment that said that he was glad to be off his feet. He wasn't the most vigorous officer that Milton had ever seen, but he wasn't surprised by that: with something like this, why waste the time of a more effective man? No, they would send out one of the older guys, a time-server close to his pension, someone who would listen politely and give them the impression that they had been given the attention that they thought their problem deserved, and then he would send them on their way.

'You're Mr Macklemore?'

'That's right.'

'You're the boyfriend.'

'Yes.'

'And you, sir?'

'John Smith.'

'How are you involved in this?'

'I'm a taxi driver. I dropped Madison off last night.'

'You know Mr Macklemore?'

'We just met.'

'So you're here why?'

'I'd like to help. I was one of the last people to see Madison.'

'I see.' He nodded. 'All right, then, Mr Macklemore, why don't you tell me what's happened and then we can work out what to do next.'

Trip told the story again, and Officer Francis listened quietly, occasionally noting down a detail in a notebook that he took from his breast pocket. When Trip was finished, Francis asked Milton a few questions: how had Madison seemed to him? Did he have any idea why she had run off the way she did? Milton answered them all honestly.

'You know she was hooking?'

'I didn't,' Milton said.

'Really?'

'No. I didn't. Not until we got there. It was just another job for me. I know the law, officer.'

'And you've come here without being asked,' he said, pursing his lips.

'Of course. I'd like to be helpful.'

'Fair enough. I'm happy with that. What do you think happened?'

'I don't know. Whatever it was, she was frightened.'

'Whose party was it?'

'I'm afraid I don't know that.'

'A lot of rich folks up there,' Francis mused. 'I can remember when you could buy a place with a nice view of the bay for a hundred grand. You wouldn't get an outhouse up there for that these days. Plenty of the tech guys have moved in. Driven up the prices like you wouldn't believe.'

Francis closed the notebook and slipped it back into his breast pocket.

'Well?' Trip said.

'I gotta tell you, Mr Macklemore, this isn't what we'd call a classic missing persons case. Not yet, anyway. She's only been gone a day.'

'But it's totally out of character. She's never done anything like this before.'

'That may be, sir, but that don't necessarily mean she's missing. She's young. From what you've said, it sounds like she's a little flighty, too. She's got no history of mental illness, no psychiatric prescriptions, and you say she wasn't on drugs. Just because you can't find her, that don't necessarily mean that she's missing, you know what I mean?'

'No,' Trip said. 'I don't agree.'

'Not much I can do about that, sir,' Francis said, spreading his hands.

Milton shook his head. 'I agree with Mr Macklemore, detective. I'm not sure I'm as relaxed about it as you are.'

The policeman glanced up at Milton with a look of mild annoyance. 'What do you mean?'

'You didn't see the state she was in last night.'

'That may be— I'm sorry, what was your name again?'

'Smith.'

'That may be, Mr Smith, but she wouldn't be the first working girl I've seen freak out, then check out for a bit.'

'Not good enough,' Trip complained angrily. 'It's because she's a hooker you're not going to assign someone to this, right? That's the reason?'

'No. That's not what I said.'

'But it's what you meant.'

Francis stood and held out his hands, palm first. 'Take it easy, son. If she's still not back tomorrow, you give us another call, and we'll see where we are then. For now, I'd go back home, make sure your phone's switched on and try to relax. I've seen plenty of cases like this. *Plenty*. Seriously. I'm telling you, ninety-nine times out of a hundred, they come back, a little embarrassed about the whole thing, and everything gets explained.'

'And the other time?'

'Not going to happen here, Mr Macklemore. Really – go home. She'll turn up. You'll see.'

* * *

They made their way outside and onto the street.

'What the fuck was *that*?'

'Take it easy,' Milton said.

'You think he was listening to a word we said?'

'Probably not. But I'm guessing that's standard operating procedure. And he's right about one thing – it's been less than a day.'

'You agree with him?'

'I didn't say that. And no, I don't. Not with everything.'

Milton had expected a reluctance to get involved, and part of him could accept the logic in what the officer had said; it *was* still early, after all. But the more he thought about what had happened last night, the more he had a bad feeling about it.

The way she had looked.

The way she had run.

The car speeding away.

The bikers. What were they doing at a high-end party like that?

Milton had made a living out of relying on his hunches. Experience told him that it was unwise to ignore them. And they were telling him that this didn't look good.

Trip took out a packet of Luckies. He put one into his mouth and lit it. Milton noticed that his fingers were trembling again. 'That was a total waste of time. Total waste. We could have been out looking for her.' He offered the packet to Milton.

'It wasn't,' he said, taking a cigarette and accepting Trip's offer of a light. 'At the very least, he'll file a report that says that you came in tonight and said she was missing. Now they'll have something to work with. And the clock will have started. I wouldn't be surprised if they treat it more seriously then.'

'So what do I do now? How long do we have to wait before they'll do something? Two days? Three days? When's the right time before they accept that something is wrong?'

'If she's not back in the morning, I'd call again. I'd make a real nuisance of myself. You know what they say about the squeaky hinge?'

'No.'

'It gets the oil. You keep calling. Do that until ten or eleven. If it doesn't work, and if she's still not back by then, go back to the precinct and demand to see a detective. Don't leave until you've seen one. Authority's the same the world over: you give them enough of a headache, eventually they'll listen to you – even if it's just to shut you up.'

'And until then? It's not like I'm gonna be able to sleep.'

'There are some things you can do. Do you know anything about the agency she was working for?'

'No. She never said.'

'Never mind. Google all the emergency rooms in a twenty-mile radius. There's one in Marin City, another in Sausalito, go as far north as San Rafael. That's the first place to look. If something's happened to her, if last night was some sort of episode or if she's hurt herself somehow, then that's probably where she'll be. And when you've tried those, try all the nearby police stations – Belvedere, Tiburon, the Sheriff's Department at Marin. You never know. Someone might've said something.'

'Okay.'

'Does she have a laptop?'

'Sure.'

'There might be emails. Can you get into it?'

'I don't know. There'll be a password. I might be able to guess it.'

'Try. Whoever booked her is someone we'll want to talk to. The police will get to it eventually, assuming they need to, but there's nothing to stop us having a look first.'

Trip looked at him, confused. '*Us?*'

'Of course.'

'What – you're going to help me?' He was almost pitifully grateful.

'Of course I'm going to help.'

'But you don't even know us. Why would you do that?'

'Let's just say I like helping people and leave it at that, all right?'

His time in A.A. had taught Milton plenty of things. One of them was that it was important to make amends; recovering alcoholics considered that almost as important as staying away from the first drink. It wasn't as easy for him to do that as it was for others. Most of the people that he would have had to make amends to were already dead, often because he had killed them. Milton had to make do with this. It wasn't perfect, but it was still the best salve he had yet discovered for soothing his uneasy conscience.

7

Governor Joseph Jack Robinson II was a born talker. It was just what he did. Everyone had a talent: some men had a facility for numbers, some for making things, some for language; hell, others could swing a bat and send a ball screaming away to the fences. Governor Robinson was a speaker, and Arlen Crawford had known it within five seconds of hearing him for the first time. That was why he had given up what could have been a very profitable career in law and turned down the offer of a partnership and the millions of dollars he would have been able to make. He had postponed the chance to take an early retirement and the house on the coast he and his wife had always hankered after. The governor's gift was why he had given all that up and thrown in his lot with him. That was back then, two years ago, when Robinson was governor, just starting out on this phase of his political career, but Arlen Crawford had never regretted his decision, not even for a second. It could have gone wrong, a spectacular flameout that took everyone and everything around him down too. But it hadn't, and now J.J.'s star was in the ascendant, climbing into the heavens, streaking across the sky.

Arlen Crawford had seen nothing to make him think that he had misjudged him.

He took his usual place at the back of the room and waited for the governor to do his thing. There had been plenty of similar rooms over the course of the last few months, all the way across the country from the Midwest to the coast of the Pacific: school gymnasia, town halls, factory dining rooms, warehouses, anywhere where you could put a few hundred seats and fill them with enthusiastic voters who were prepared to come and listen to what the candidate had to say.

It was like that today; they were in the gymnasium where the Woodside Cougars shot hoops, with its polished floor that squeaked when he turned his shoe on it, a banked row of seats where moms and pops and alumni and backers of the school would gather to cheer on the kids, and a scoreboard at one end that said COUGARS and AWAY, the neon numerals set to zero. A lectern had been placed against the wall that faced the bleachers with enough space for six rows of folded chairs to be arranged between the two. A poster that they had fixed to the lectern said AMERICA FIRST. A larger banner that they had pinned to the wall behind it read ROBINSON FOR PRESIDENT.

The room was full. Crawford guessed there were five hundred people inside. There were a few curious students, not Robinson's normal constituency, but Crawford had insisted. It made him look more 'hip' and helped in his campaign to broaden his appeal to a younger audience. Crawford knew, too, that the governor was occasionally prone to phoning it in if the room was too friendly; it did him no harm at all to think that there was the possibility of awkward questions in the Q&A that would follow his speech. The rest of the audience were naturally right-leaning voters from the area, all of them given a little vim and vigour by the dozen or so backers that the campaign brought with them on the bus. They were doing their thing now, hooting and hollering as they watched a video of the governor's achievements as it played on the large screen that had been fixed to the wall.

The video ended, and Robinson walked through a storm of applause to the lectern.

'Thank you, Woodside. Thank you.'

Crawford looked around the room: five hundred avid faces hanging on every word.

'So what brought us here today? Why aren't we catching a game, the 49ers or the Raiders? I know, both teams stink, but it's better than coming here and listening to me for an hour, right?' He waited for the laughs to die down. 'What brought us together is a love of our country, isn't it? Because we can see that America is in trouble. She needs our help.'

Robinson stopped. He waited. One of the women in the audience called out, *'We're listening!'*

Robinson grinned and then gave the same speech that he'd given yesterday, and the day before that. He spoke of how many working-age men were out of work, how mortgages were being called in at a rate that hadn't been seen since the Great Depression, how divorce was through the roof. He raged against the current president and his policies, drew attention to the size of the national debt and the speed with which it was growing.

He went on in the same vein for another ten minutes. It was a bravura display, yet again. In his two years as Robinson's chief of staff, Crawford had probably heard him speak a thousand times, and that, right there, was another in a long line of brilliant speeches. He had the knack of making his audience feel as if he was one of them; the kind of fellow you could imagine having a beer with, shooting the breeze and setting the world to rights. It wasn't a conscious thing, a talent that he could calibrate and deploy with care and consideration; it was totally natural, so much so that he didn't even seem to realise what he was doing.

He stepped away from the lectern and made his way along the front row of the folding chairs, pumping offered hands, sometimes taking them in both of his and beaming that brilliant megawatt smile.

Crawford watched and smiled and shook his head in admiration.

No doubt about it: Joseph Jack Robinson was a natural.

He stayed with them for half an hour, listening to their stories, answering their questions and signing autographs, then they all followed him back downstairs and out to the campaign bus. Crawford and Catherine Williamson, the press manager, trailed the crowd.

Catherine looked at Crawford and raised her manicured eyebrow, an inverted tick of amusement that the governor had done it again. Crawford looked back at her and winked. J.J. did that, now and again; he surprised even the staffers who had been with him the longest. It seemed to be happening more often these days. As the speeches got more important, as the television crews that tailed them everywhere grew in number, as his polling numbers solidified and accrued, Robinson pulled the rabbit out of the hat again and again and again.

It was why they were all so excited.

This felt real.

It felt like they were backing a winner.

Crawford followed the governor up the steps and onto the bus.

'Great speech,' he told Robinson as he opened his brief-case and took out the papers he needed for the trip.

'You think?'

'Are you kidding? You had them eating out of your hand.'

Robinson shrugged and smiled. Crawford found that habit of his a little annoying, the *aw-shucks* modesty that was as false as the gleaming white veneers on his teeth. The governor knew he was good. Everything was done for a reason: every grin, every knowing wink, every handshake and backslap and beam of that radiant smile. Some of the rivals he had crushed on the way had been good, too, but not as good as him. They had a nagging sense of the ersatz that stuck with their audiences and curdled over time, seeds of doubt that grew into reasons why the voters chose Robinson instead of them when they finally got to the polling booths. The governor didn't suffer from that. He was a good man, completely trustwor-thy, honest to a fault, or, more relevantly, that was what they thought. The greatest expression of his genius was to make the whole performance look so effortlessly natural.

'Those questions on immigration . . .' Robinson began.

'Go vague on the numbers. We don't want to get caught out.'

'Not the numbers. The message. It's still holding up?'

'People seem to agree with you.'

'Damn straight they do. If I can't say it like it is, what's the point?'

'I know – and I agree.'

'These fucking *wetbacks*,' Robinson said with a dismissive flick of his wrist, 'taking jobs that belong to Americans; damn straight we should be sending them back.'

Crawford looked around, making sure they weren't overheard. 'Easy,' he advised.

'I know, I know. *Moderation*. I'm not an idiot, Arlen.' He dropped down into the seat opposite and unbuttoned the top button of his shirt. 'Where next?'

'Radio interview,' Catherine said. 'And we're an hour late already.'

Robinson was suddenly on the verge of anger. 'They know that?' he demanded.

'Know what?'

'That we're gonna be late.'

'Don't worry. I told them. They're cool.'

They were all used to his temper. He switched unpredictably, with even the smallest provocation, and then switched back again with equal speed. It was unnerving and disorientating for the newest members of the entourage, who had not had the opportunity to acclimate themselves to the vagaries of his character, but once you realised it was usually a case of bark over bite, it was just another vector to be weighed in the calculus of working for the man.

Catherine disappeared further up the bus.

'No need to snap at her,' Crawford said.

'You know I hate being late. My old man used to drill it into me—'

'You'd rather be thirty minutes early than a minute late. I know. You've told me about a million times. How's the head?'

'Still pretty sore. You should've told me it was time to go.'

'I did.'

'Not early enough. We should have left about an hour before we did. You didn't insist.'

'Next time, I will.'

'We probably shouldn't even have been there.'

'No,' he said, 'we should.'

The party had been a little more raucous than Crawford would have preferred, but it was full of donors and potential donors, and it would've been unseemly to have given it the bum's rush or to have left too early. The hour that they had been there had given the governor plenty of time to drink more than he should have, and Crawford had spent the evening at his side, a little anxious, trying to keep him on message and making sure he didn't do anything that would look bad if it was taken out of context. It had been a long night for him, too, and Crawford knew he would have to find the energy from somewhere to make it through to the end of the day.

'You get the Secret Service if you have to. Tell them to drag me out.' He paused theatrically. 'Do I have a detail yet?'

'Not yet,' Crawford said, playing along.

'You know what I'm looking forward to most? The code name. You know what they called Kennedy?'

'No, sir.'

'LANCER. And Reagan?'

'No, sir.'

'RAWHIDE. What do you reckon they'll call me?'

'You want me to answer that? Really?'

'No.' He grinned. 'Better not.'

8

Crawford settled back in his seat as the bus pulled out of the school car park, closed his eyes and allowed himself to reminisce. They had come a long way. He remembered the first time he had met J.J. God, he thought, it must have been at Georgetown almost twenty years ago. He had been involved in politics ever since he'd arrived on campus, standing for various posts and even getting elected to a couple of them. J.J. had been the same. They had both been in the same fraternities – Phi Beta Kappa and Kappa Kappa Psi – and they had served on the same committees.

Eventually, they stood against each other for president of the Students' Association. After a convivial two-week campaign, Robinson had defeated him. But *defeated* was too polite a word; it had been an *annihilation*. A good old-fashioned straight-up-and-down slobberknocker. Crawford knew the reason. J.J. had always been a handsome boy, something of a surfer dude back in those days, and the aura of charisma that clung to him seemed so dense as to be able to deflect all of Crawford's clever thrusts. It was like a suit of armour.

The campaign was civil enough so as to require them to temper their attacks, but the list of deficiencies in his opponent that Crawford had hoped to exploit – his vanity, his privileged background, the suspicion that he was doing this for his résumé rather than from a spirit of public service – were all neutralised the moment he switched on his smile and dazzled his audience with a serving of his West Coast charm. They had debated each other twice, and both times, even the most biased of observers would have had to admit that Crawford had destroyed J.J. on the issues at hand. It didn't seem to make the slightest scrap of difference; J.J.'s election victory was the largest landslide in college history.

It was a good lesson learnt: style trumped substance every single time. It was ever thus.

Crawford retired from student politics with good grace. He was better as the man in the background, the overseer with the long view to better plot strategy and tactics, and he was happy to cede the spotlight to characters like J.J. They had both become friendly during their jousting, despite the occasional low blow, and Crawford had agreed to work with on the Students' Association to make his term of office productive and useful. By and large, it was. They stayed in loose touch as they went their separate ways on graduation.

Crawford was always going to go into law. His father was an attorney, and he had known that he would follow in his footsteps since he was young. Crawford made a career for himself in property and taxation, esoteric subjects that were complicated enough to be remunerative for the few who could master them. His firm served the nascent technology industry in Silicon Valley, and his roster of clients included Microsoft and Apple. He did well. There was the big house in Palo Alto, the BMW in the driveway and a boat. The trophy wife who wouldn't have looked twice at him if they had met at college. Two healthy and happy kids. And it still wasn't enough. Law was never what he would have described as fun or even satisfying, even though he was good at it. Eventually, each month became a long and depressing slog that was made bearable only by the massive pay cheque at the end of it.

Stuck in a rut, Crawford stayed at the firm more than long enough for it to lose its lustre. Law had been the easy decision out of school, cashing in his degree for the easy money despite the nagging suspicion that he would have been better satisfied doing something else: academia, perhaps, or something where he could write. And then he turned forty, and he realised, with a blinding flash of self-awareness that was frightening in its certainty, that he was wasting his life. He quit the next day, called an old friend at Georgetown and asked him for a job.

The man had obliged. Crawford had been teaching the legislative process to keen young up-and-comers for three years when two very different offers came at the exact same time: the first was the offer of millions as a partner at a lobbying firm in Washington, and the second was J.J. Robinson inviting him out to dinner.

He had watched his old opponent's career with a strange mixture of jealousy and relief that it wasn't him. Robinson had run for the House of Representatives as a twenty-eight-year-old

Republican but had been handily defeated by the incumbent. Instead, he had switched his target to the Attorney General-ship, and after defeating a host of minor opponents, he had been elected at the age of thirty. Two years later, Robinson defeated the Democratic governor of Florida and finally took the high office that he had always craved. He had managed to hold onto his youthful appearance, a fact that gave his opponents some-thing to latch onto when they laid into him; he was routinely derided as the 'Boy Governor' and not to be taken seriously. He lost popularity over misjudged taxation and immigration poli-cies and was ousted by his Democratic challenger after just one term of office. He licked his wounds in a lobbying practice for a short while before winning the governorship again, this time serving for ten years.

Crawford had taken up his offer of dinner. He remembered the conversation. There had been some small talk, nothing consequential, until Robinson explained the reason for get-ting back in touch. He was forty-six now, a political veteran, and he was looking for a new challenge.

He was running for president.

And he wanted Crawford to be his chief of staff.

* * *

The bus pulled up outside the campaign office, and the entou-rage duly decamped. The office was the same as the others all across the country. It was entirely generic. It didn't seem to matter where they were, everything looked the same. There was some comfort to be had in that, Crawford thought. There was the usual clutch of pollsters working the phones, entering data into laptops, pecking at the platter of sandwiches from the deli around the corner, the cellophane wrapper still halfway across. Empty soda cans were stacked on desks. Some wore headphones, nodding their heads to the music that seeped out. Crawford knew some of them from the convention last year, but most were new recruits, drawn into the candidate's orbit by the tractor beam of his charisma, offering their time for free.

He saw Sidney Packard standing to one side, a half-eaten sandwich in one hand and his phone in the other. It was pressed to his ear, and he had an expression of deep concentration on his face. Packard was older, bald-headed and wrinkled, and when he moved, his limbs flowed with a lazy confidence. He had been in the police before, and before that, there was talk of the army. He was head of the security detail, and he had been working with the governor for the last ten years. It was an interesting job.

Crawford watched him speaking, and eventually, the other man noticed that he was looking at him and gave him a single, curt nod. Crawford interpreted that as good news, went to the nearest platter of sandwiches and loaded up a plate.

The radio crew had already set up their gear in the conference room, so Crawford went looking for the governor. He opened the door to the bathroom, and there he was; he was buttoning his shirt and fastening his belt. He recognised the young staffer, too. She was adjusting her clothes in the stall behind the governor.

'I'm sorry,' Crawford said.

The woman seemed confused. Robinson drew her out and put his arm around her. 'This is Karly Hammil,' he said. 'She's working for us now.'

'Yes,' Crawford replied. 'I know. I hired her. Hello, Karly.'

She seemed to brace herself against the washbasin and just about managed a shy smile, an attempt to maintain the appearance of propriety that was redundant in the circumstances. Robinson, on the other hand, did not appear to have the capability of being embarrassed. It was as if he had just come out of the stall after using the toilet. Nothing unusual. Nothing out of order. It was an act he had, no doubt, perfected over many years. My God, Crawford thought, there had been plenty of practice. He had seen that shit-eating grin many times since he had started working for him.

'Well, then,' Robinson said. 'We ready?'

'We are,' Crawford said.

Robinson winked at Crawford as he stepped outside and moved over towards the food.

Crawford followed behind him.

'You can't keep doing this,' he said, and the note of resignation he heard in his voice made him feel even more pathetic.

'Relax.'

'How many times do I have to tell you?'

'No lectures today, Arlen.'

'If just one of them tells their story, you do know what'll happen, right? You do understand?'

'Arlen—'

'I'm just checking, because I don't think you've thought about it.'

'No one's saying anything, are they?'

Crawford bit his lip. 'If they did, that'd be the end of it for you. End of the road. That kind of thing— J.J. I'm telling you, you need to listen to me. This isn't the 60s. You're not JFK.'

'Not yet.'

Crawford clenched his teeth; the man was infuriating. 'It's toxic,' he protested.

Robinson took Crawford's right hand in his and squeezed it tight. Depending on his mood and what was required, the governor had several ways of shaking hands. He might place his left hand by the elbow or up around the shoulder or take your hand in both of his. That meant that he was especially interested, underscoring a greeting and making the recipient feel as if they were the most important person in the room. Other times, he would squeeze the shoulder, or for those he really wanted to bring within the dazzling aura of his personality, he might loop the arm across the shoulders and pull them in for a hug. He did this now, releasing Crawford's hand, draping his arm around his shoulders and squeezing him tight.

'I'm keeping a lid on it,' he said. 'You need to stop worrying. You'll get an ulcer.'

Crawford felt like sighing at the sheer boring predictability of it and the frustration that, despite it all – despite increasingly doom-laden warnings of what would happen to the campaign if any of his indiscretions were to be aired in public – the governor just would not listen to him.

9

Milton drove back to Belvedere. It was a little after eight as he navigated the Explorer out of the city, heading north out of the Mission District until he picked up the 101 and then passed through Presidio. He paid more attention this time, orientating himself properly and memorising as much of the landscape as he could. Newly formed whitish fog filtered through the harp strings of the bridge and then puffed out its chest as though pleased with its dramatic entrance; its only applause was the regular blare of the two foghorns, the lapping of the waves as they disappeared under the silent mass and the constant hum of the traffic. He passed turn-offs for Kirby Cove Campground and the Presidio Yacht Club, continued on after Southview Park and Martin Luther King Jr Park, the big cemetery at Fernwood and then, as he turned east and then back south, Richardson Bay Wildlife Sanctuary and McKegney Field with the placid waters of Richardson Bay off to the west. The darkness and the fog – deep and thick – reduced visibility to a handful of yards. Milton drove carefully.

He turned off the coast road and continued to the gate.

The radio was on and tuned in to a talk radio channel; the presenter was speaking to one of the Republican candidates ahead of the presidential election. He sat for a moment, half-listening to the conversation: immigration, how big government was wrong, taxation. The man had a deep, mellifluous voice accented with a lazy drawl. Milton had heard of him before: the governor of Florida, seen as a front-runner in the race. Milton had little time for politicians, but this one was convincing enough.

He turned the dial to switch the radio off, lowered the window and entered the code that Madison had given him last night.

2-0-1-1.

The final digit elicited a buzz, and the gate remained closed.

The code had been changed.

Milton looked at the gate and the community beyond. Why had the code been changed? He tried the combination a second time, and as the keypad buzzed at him again, he noticed the dark black eye of a CCTV camera pointed at him from the gatehouse. He hadn't noticed that being there last night.

He put the car into reverse, and the camera jerked up and swivelled as it tracked him. He turned around and drove slowly back down the drive until he was around the corner and out of sight. He killed the lights and then the engine and reached into the back for the black denim jacket he had stuffed into the footwell. He had a pair of leather gloves in the glove compartment, and he put them into the pockets of the jacket along with a pair of paperclips he removed from old invoices. He took the S&W 9mm that he had confiscated from the guard outside the house and slipped it into the waistband of his jeans. He put the jacket on, opened the door and, keeping within the margin of the vegetation at the side of the road, made his way back towards the gate again.

About fifteen yards from the gate, a wooden pole carried the high-tension power cabling from the substation into the estate. Three large cylindrical transformers were rigged to the pole, twenty feet in the air, and the wire crossed over to a corresponding pole on the other side of the wall. From there, individual wires delivered the current to the houses.

Milton took out the S&W and racked a bullet into the chamber. There were better ways to disable a power supply – Mylar balloons filled with helium would have shorted it out very nicely – but he was working on short notice, and this would have to do. He took aim at the ceramic insulators that held the wire onto the pole. It was a difficult shot; the insulators were small targets at a reasonable distance, it was dark and the fog was dense. He fired once, but the shot missed. He resighted the target, braced his right wrist with his left hand and fired again. The insulator shattered, and the wire, sparks scattering into the gloom, swept down to earth in a graceful arc.

The light above the gate went out.

Milton cut into a dense copse of young firs that crowded close to the left of the road and, using it as cover, moved carefully to the wall. It was made of brick and topped with iron spikes. He reached up and dabbed a finger against the top, feeling for broken glass or anti-climb paint. All he could feel was the rough surface of the brick. Satisfied, he wrapped each gloved hand around a spike and, using them for leverage, hauled himself up, his feet scrabbling for purchase. He got his right foot onto the lip of the wall and boosted himself up until he was balancing atop it. The vantage point offered an excellent view of the community beyond. He could see half a dozen big houses in the immediate vicinity and, as the road turned away to the east, the glow of others. There was no one in sight. He stepped carefully over the spikes and lowered himself onto the ground.

The big house where the party had been held was quiet. All the windows were dark. Milton moved stealthily into the cover of a tree and, pressing himself against it, scoped out the road. It was empty in both directions. There was no one visible anywhere. He ran quickly across, vaulting the low fence and making his way through the large garden to the back of the house. He remembered the layout from the quick glimpse through the window last night: the T-shaped swimming pool with the underwater lamps; the series of terraces on different levels; trees and bushes planted with architectural precision; the firepit; the dark, fogged waters of the bay.

A redwood platform abutted the house here, a sheer drop down the cliff to the rocks below on the right-hand side. The surf boomed below, crashing against the cliff, and the air was damp with salty moisture.

Milton followed the platform.

He pressed himself against the back wall and risked a glance through the windows. The living room beyond was very different now from how it had been the previous night. It was empty. The furniture had been returned to more usual positions around the room. The DJ equipment was gone. The bar, which had been strewn with bottles and glasses, was pristine. The salvers of cocaine that had been so ostentatiously left on the tables had been removed. The room was cool and dark and quiet. The windows were still open a little at the tops, and the curtains shivered in and out on each breath of wind – the only movement that Milton could see.

It was as if the party had never even happened.

Milton flitted quickly across the window to a door that was set into a long extension that had been built across one side of the house. He tried the door. It was locked. Taking off his gloves, he took the paperclips from his pocket and bent them into shape. He slid one into the lower portion of the keyhole, used it to determine which way the cylinder turned, applied light tension and then slid the other clip into the upper part of the keyhole and felt for the pins. He pressed up and felt the individual pins with the tip of the clip, finding the stiffest one and pushing it up and out of the cylinder. He repeated the trick for the remaining four pins, adjusting the torque for each. He turned the cylinder all the way around, and the door unlocked.

Milton scrubbed the lock with the sleeve of his shirt, put the gloves back onto his hands and went inside. It was a utility room. He closed the door behind him, leaving it unlocked, and then paused for a moment, listening carefully. He could hear nothing. He was confident that the house was empty. He walked quickly into a huge kitchen with wide windows, then a hallway, then into the living room. It was gloomy, but there was just enough suffused moonlight from outside for him to see his way.

He checked the downstairs quickly and efficiently. There was another formal living room with a large, carved stone mantel. A secret doorway in the bookshelves led to a speakeasy-style wet bar. The dining room looked like it was being used as a conference room, with a speakerphone in the middle of the table and videoconferencing equipment at the other end. A spiral staircase led down to a wine cellar that had been built around crouching monk corbels that had been turned into light fittings; there were hundreds of bottles, thousands of dollars' worth of wine, but nothing of any obvious interest.

Milton found the stairs and climbed to the first floor. There were four bedrooms, all with en-suite bathrooms. He climbed again to the second floor: three more bedrooms, all enormous. He searched them all quickly and expertly. There were no clothes in the closets and no products in the bathrooms. No signs of habitation at all.

It looked as if the house was vacant.

Distantly, down the stairwell, two storeys below, Milton heard the sound of the front door opening.

He froze.

Footsteps clicked across the wooden floor.

'Power's out,' the voice said.

'The fuck?'

'Whole road, from the look of things.'

'Place like this, millions of dollars, and they lose the power?'

'Shit happens.'

'If you say so.'

'I do.'

'You got a flashlight?'

'Here.'

There was a quiet click.

'You know this is a waste of time.'

'It's gotta get done.'

'What we gotta do?'

'Just make sure everything looks the way it should.'

'Why wouldn't it? What we looking for?'

'Anything that looks like there was a crazy-ass party here.'

'Looks clean to me.'

'Had professionals in – everything you can do, they did.'

'So what are we doing here?'

'We're making sure, okay? Double-checking.'

Milton stepped further back, to another door. He moved stealthily. He could hear footsteps down below. He opened the door; it led to another bedroom. The footsteps downstairs were hard to make out. Was that somebody walking up the stairs to the floor below, the first floor? Or somebody walking through the foyer on the ground floor? He couldn't tell, but either way, he was stuck. If he crossed the landing there, he would have to go past the stairwell, and then he might be visible from below for a certain amount of time.

'You ever seen a place like this? Look at all this shit. This is where the real money's at.'

'Concentrate on what you're doing.'

They were definitely up on the first floor now.

'Go up there. Check it out.'

'Just gonna be more bedrooms.'

'And crazy-ass parties end up in the bedroom, so go up and check them all out.'

'What about you?'

'I'm calling the boss.'

Milton could hear scuffed footsteps coming up the stairs; it was the unenthusiastic, resentful one of the pair. That was probably fortunate.

He dropped to the floor and slid beneath the bed.

'It's me,' the other man was saying, his voice now muffled by the closed door. 'We're at the house. Yeah – looks good. Clean as a whistle. Power's out, though. Alarm was off. Whole neighbourhood. I don't think that's anything to bother us. One of those things.'

Milton held his breath as the door to the bedroom opened and heavy footsteps sounded against the boards. A torch swept the room. The bed was low down, the boards and the mattress snug against his back, and he couldn't see his feet; he thought they were beneath the valance, but he couldn't be completely sure. He felt horribly vulnerable and suddenly cursed himself for picking the bed over the walk-in cupboard he could have sheltered in. He could have pulled the gun in there, too. If the man saw him under here, there would be nothing he could do. It was a rookie mistake.

He was trapped.

He turned his head to the right and looked through a gap between the fabric and the floor. He saw the soles of a pair of boots: heavy treads, worn and scuffed leather uppers, lots of buckles.

The boots made their way from one end of the room to the other.

A door opened, creaking on rusty hinges, and then closed again.

The man downstairs was still on the phone. 'Up to you, obviously, but I say we check the garden, then get out of here. All right? All right. Sweet. We'll see you there.'

The torch swept across the floor, the light glowing through the thin cotton valance.

The boots came closer, shoes on polished wood. Milton saw them again, closer this time. He could have reached out and touched them.

The boots moved out of sight, away to the door; steps sounded, going away again.

'Nothing up here,' the man said.

'You sure? They want us to be absolutely sure.'

'Check yourself if you don't believe me.'

'If you say it's okay, it's okay. Take it easy.'

Milton slid carefully out from under the bed and stayed low, crouching, listening. He heard steps, a pause, more steps, a door opening downstairs, then closing, then another door, a heavier door and finally, silence.

He moved quickly but quietly out onto the landing, gently pulled the door closed and then descended, treading on the sides of the steps as he made his way down to minimise the risk of putting weight on a creaking board. He did the same on the next set of stairs. He was halfway down the final flight, facing the big front door and about to make the turn to head back along the long hall to the kitchen and the rear door, when he heard the sound of a key in the front door's lock.

He froze: too late to go back up, too late to keep going down.

The door didn't open.

He realised what it was: they had forgotten to lock it.

The fresh, cool evening air hit Milton's face as he opened the rear door and stepped out into the garden. He breathed it in deeply. He heard the sound of two powerful motorcycle engines grumbling and growling into life, the sound fading as they accelerated away.

He shut the door behind him and walked carefully and quickly to the road.

10

Milton made his way towards the house that Madison had run to last night, the one with the old man who had threatened to call the police. It was another big place, a sprawling building set within well-tended gardens and fronted by a stone wall topped with ornamental iron fencing. Milton buzzed the intercom set into the stone pillar to the right of the gates and waited. There was no answer. He tried again with the same result. He was about to leave when he saw the old man. He came out of a side door, moving slowly and with the exaggerated caution of advanced age. Behind him was a wide lawn sloping down to the shore. A collie trotted around the garden with aimless, happy abandon, shoving its muzzle into the flower beds in search of an interesting scent.

'Can I help you?'

'I hope so,' Milton said. 'Could I have a word?'

Milton assessed him as he approached. He was old; late eighties, he guessed. He was tall, but his frame had withered away with age so that his long arms and legs were spindly, sharply bony shoulders pointing through the fabric of the polo shirt that he was wearing.

'What can I do for you?'

'I was here last night.'

The man thought for a moment, the papery skin of his forehead crinkling. He remembered, and a scowl descended. 'This morning, you mean?'

'That's right.'

'She woke me up, all that racket – my wife, too. You with her?'

'No, sir. But I drove her out here.'

'So what are you? A cab driver?'

'That's right.'

'What's your name, son?'

'John Smith. And you?'

'Victor Leonard.'

'Sorry about all the noise, Mr Leonard. The disturbance.'

'What the hell was she so exercised about?'

'I was hoping you might be able to tell me – did she say anything?'

Milton watched through the bars of the gate as Leonard pursed his withered lips. 'Didn't make a whole heap of sense. She was in a terrible panic. Just asking for help. I've no idea what she wanted help for. She had her cell phone out and kept trying to make a call, but it didn't look like she was getting through. I could see she needed help, so I told her she could come in. Didn't help – she got a whole lot worse. Couldn't make any sense out of her. My wife called 911, told her the police were coming, but that seemed to panic her. She bolted.'

'And?'

'And nothing much. Police came around half an hour later. It was a single officer; he had a look around the place. Said he looked around the whole neighbourhood, but he couldn't find her anywhere. They asked me the same questions I guess they ask everyone: what did she look like, what was she wearing, what did she say, all that. I told them what I could remember.' He paused.

'Which was . . . ?'

'She was high. Big eyes – pupils practically as big as saucers. And she wasn't making any sense. If that's not someone under the influence of something or other, I don't know what is. You ask me, whatever she thought her problems were, they were in her mind – hallucinations or whatever you want to call them.'

'Did you see where she went?'

'Over the fence. Straight into Pete Waterfield's garden. She pounded on his door, but he's off on vacation with his grandkids, and when she didn't get an answer, she kept on going.'

'Where?'

'Over there,' he said, pointing.

'That leads down to the cliffs?'

'Sure does. You see the boat he's got parked down there? Behind the car?' Milton said that he did. 'She stopped there for a moment. I saw her try to make a call on her phone again, but I guess it didn't get anywhere, like the others, because she upped and made a run for it. And that's the last time I saw her.'

'Yes,' Milton said. 'Me too. The cliffs are fenced off there?'

'Around the house, sure they are. But not further down.'

'You think she might have gone over the edge?'

'I hope not. That's a fifty-foot drop right onto the rocks.' He paused. 'What's it got to do with you, anyway? She's just a customer, right?'

'I'm worried.'

'Ain't like no taxi drivers I know, get worried about the people they drive.'

'I think something bad has happened to her.'

'Nothing bad happens around here, Mr Smith.'

'I don't know about that.' Milton took a business card for his taxi business from his pocket. 'I appreciate you talking to me. Maybe I am worrying too much, but maybe I'm not. The police won't even treat this as a missing person enquiry until she's been gone a couple more days, and even then, it's not going to be very high up their list of priorities. I wonder, if you think of anything else, or if you hear anything, or if anyone says anything to you, could you give me a call?'

'Sure I can.'

Milton passed the card through the bars of the gate.

'One more thing,' he said. 'The house over there' – he pointed to the house he had just been inside – 'do you know who owns it?'

'The company place?'

'What do you mean?'

'It's owned by a company, one of the tech firms down in Palo Alto. Was on the market last year. Ten million dollars. What do you think of that?'

Milton made a show of being impressed.

'Good for the rest of us, too. They send executives – guys they've just hired – to stay there before they can find a place of their own. None of them ever make much of an effort round here with the rest of us. Not unreasonable, I suppose. Why would they? They're only stopping on the way to something else.'

'Know who's in there now?'

'Afraid not. It's empty, I think.'

'Apart from last night.'

'You can say that again.'

Milton thanked him, and the old man went back to his front door. Milton turned back to the big house again. The place was quiet, peaceful, but there was something in that stillness that he found disturbing. It was as if the place was haunted, harbouring a dark secret that could only mean bad things for Madison.

11

Milton pressed the buzzer on the intercom and then stepped back, waiting for it to be answered. It was early, just before nine, and the sun was struggling through thinning fog. The brownstone was in Nob Hill, a handsome building that had been divided into apartments over the course of its life. Rows of beech had been planted along both sides of the street twenty or thirty years ago, and the naked trees went some way to lending a little bucolic charm to what would otherwise have been a busy suburban street. The cars parked beneath the overhanging branches were middle-of-the-road saloons and SUVs. The houses looked well kept. Both were good indications that the area was populated by owner-occupiers with decent family incomes. Milton thought of Madison and her reticence to talk about the money she was making. It must have been pretty good to be able to live here.

'Hello?'

'It's John Smith.'

The lock buzzed. Milton opened the door and climbed the stairs to the second floor.

Trip was waiting for him inside the opened door.

'Morning, Mr Smith.'

'Anything?'

Trip shook his head.

Milton winced. 'Two days.'

'I know. I'm worried now.'

He led the way into the sitting room.

'You've spoken to the police?'

'About ten times.'

'What did they say?'

'Same – they won't declare her missing until this time tomorrow. Three days, apparently; that's how long it has to be. It's because of what she does, isn't it?'

'Probably.'

'If this was a secretary from Sacramento, they would've been out looking for her as soon as someone says she's not where she's supposed to be.'

Milton gestured to indicate the apartment. 'Do you mind if I have a look around? There might be something you've missed. The benefit of fresh eyes?'

'Yeah, that's fine. I get it.'

'Could you do me a favour?'

'Sure.'

'Get me a coffee? I'm dying for a drink.'

'Sure.'

That was better. Milton wanted him out of the way while he looked around the apartment. He would have preferred him to have left the place altogether, but if he worked quickly, he thought he would be able to do what needed to be done.

The place was comfortably sized: two bedrooms, one much smaller than the other, a bathroom, a kitchen-diner. It was nicely furnished. The furniture was from IKEA, but it was at the top end of their range; Milton knew that because he had visited the store to buy the things he needed for his own place. There was a sofa upholstered in electric blue, a large bookcase that was crammed with books, a coffee table with copies of *Vogue* and *Harper's Bazaar* and a crimson rug with a luxurious deep pile. A plasma screen stood on a small unit with a Play-Station plugged in beneath it and a selection of games and DVDs alongside. There was a healthy-looking spider plant standing in a pewter vase.

Milton went straight to the bedroom. It was a nice room, decorated in a feminine style, with lots of pastel colours and a pretty floral quilt cover. He opened the wardrobe and ran his fingers along the top shelf. He opened the chest of drawers and removed her underwear, placing it on the bed. The drawer was empty. He replaced the clothes and closed the drawer again. Finally, he took the books and magazines from the bed-side table. He opened the magazines and riffled their pages. Nothing. Once again, beyond the detritus of a busy life, there was nothing that provided him with any explanation of what might have happened to her in Pine Shore.

He went back into the sitting room. A MacBook sat open on the coffee table.

'Is this hers?'

'Yes.'

'Did you have any luck?'

'No. Couldn't get into it.'

Milton tapped a key to kill the screen saver, and the log-in screen appeared. He thought of the specialists back in London. Breaking the security would have been child's play for them, but his computer skills were rudimentary; he wouldn't even know where to start.

'The police will be able to do it if they have to.'

'You think that'll be necessary?'

'Maybe.'

Trip had left a cup of coffee next to the laptop. Milton thanked him and took a sip.

'So,' he said, 'I went back to Pine Shore last night.'

'And?'

'It was quiet. Peaceful. I had a look in the house—'

'You went in?'

'Just looked through the window,' he lied. 'It was clean and tidy, as if nothing had ever happened.'

'Who lives there?'

'One of the neighbours told me it belongs to a company.'

'Which one?'

'I don't know. It was sold last year. I looked it up online. It was bought by a trust. The ownership is hidden, but the deal was for ten million, so whichever company it was has plenty of cash.'

'A tech firm.'

Milton nodded. 'I think so.'

'You get anything else?'

'Another neighbour said she ran into his house. He said she was out of it, didn't make much sense. He called the police, and that was when she ran off again. He's not going to be able to help much beyond that.'

The boy slumped back. 'Where is she?'

Milton took a mouthful of coffee and placed the cup back on the table again. 'I don't know,' he said. 'But we'll find her.'

'Yeah,' he replied, but it was unconvincing.

'You know what – you should tell me about you both. Could be something that would be helpful.'

'What do you want to know?'

'Everything you can think of. Maybe there's something you've overlooked.'

Trip sparked up a cigarette and started with himself. He was born and raised in New York and had had a rough start. He was bad at school and there had been some petty crime, including a robbery for which he had been caught and given three years in a juvenile facility. He was twenty when he finally came out. He had relatives in San Francisco, moved west to get out of the way of temptation and enrolled at community college to try to round out a few qualifications so that he could fix himself up with a job. He found out that he had an aptitude for electronics and he took a course in electrical engineering. He parlayed that into an apprenticeship, and now he was employed fixing up the power lines.

He met Madison while he was out celebrating his first pay packet. She had been at the bar on her own, reading a book in the corner and nursing a vodka and Coke. He introduced himself and asked if he could buy her a drink. She said he could, and they had started to get to know each other. She was a big talker, always jawing, and he said how it was sometimes impossible to get a word in edgeways. (Milton said he had noticed that, too.) She was living out of town at the time, taking a bus to get into work. She said she was a secretary. Trip figured out the truth by the time they had been on their third date, and he had been surprised to find that it didn't bother him. If he didn't think about it, it was bearable. And, of course, the money was great, and it was only ever going to be temporary. He always tried to remember that. She had big plans, and she was just escorting until she had saved enough to do what she wanted to do.

'She wants to write,' Trip said. 'A journalist, most likely, but something to do with words. She's always been into reading. You wouldn't believe how much. All these' – he pointed at the books on the bookcase – 'all of them, they're all hers. I've never been into reading so much myself, but you won't find her without a book. She always took one when she went out nights.'

Milton looked at the bookcase, vaguely surprised to see so many books, always a clue to a personality. They were an odd mixture: books on astrology and make-up, novels by Suzanne Collins and Stephenie Meyer. Some books on fashion. The collected poems of Ralph Waldo Emerson. Milton pulled it out to look at the cover. Several pages had their corners turned down. Not what he would have expected to find. He slipped it back into its slot on the shelf.

'That's one of the things I love about her. She gets so passionate about books. She writes, too. Short stories. I've seen a couple of them, the ones she doesn't mind showing me. And I know I'm no expert and all that and I don't know what I'm talking about, but the way I see it, I reckon some of her stuff's pretty good.'

'What's she like as a person?'

'What do you mean?'

Milton searched for the right word. 'Is she stable?'

'She gets bad mood swings. She can be happy one minute and then the whole world is against her the next.'

'You know why?'

Trip screwed the cigarette in the ashtray and lit another. 'Family.'

He explained. Madison had two sisters and a brother; she was the oldest of the four. Her father had left the family when she was five or six. Her mother, Clare – a brassy woman full of attitude – told the children it was because he was a drunk, but Madison had always suspected that there was something else involved. She had no memories of her father at all, and whenever she thought of him, she would plunge into one of her darker moods. Clare moved a series of increasingly inappropriate men into the house, and it was after one of them started to smack her around that the police were called. The authorities got involved and the kids were moved into foster care. Clare got Madison's sisters and brother back after a year, once she was able to demonstrate that she could provide a stable environment for them, but she had left Madison with the family who had taken her in. She would run away to try to get back home and then be taken back into the foster system.

There was a series of different places, several well-meaning families, but she never settled with any of them.

'Have you spoken to her mother?'

'Last night. She hasn't seen her. Same goes for her sisters and brother.'

'Does she get on with them?'

'So-so. Depends when you ask, really.'

'Why didn't her mother take her back?'

'She never said. I think Madison was a little wild when she was younger, though. She was a tough kid to live with. She can still be a handful now.'

'How?'

'She has a temper on her. If she feels like she's being ignored or rejected, it all comes back again, and then, you know' – he made a popping noise – 'look out.'

'Could that be a reason for what's happened? Something's upset her?'

'No,' he said. 'She's been really good with her mom for the last couple of months. They've been speaking a lot. Now she's got money, she's been buying things for them – for her mom, her sisters, for her nieces and nephews, too. I've tried to tell her she shouldn't need to do that, but she likes it. They never had much money growing up, and now she has some, she likes to spread it around, I guess.'

'All right,' Milton said. 'Go on.'

He did. Around the time of seventh grade, Madison moved to live with her aunt in San Diego. The woman was young, and Madison felt that they had something in common. It was a better town, too, with better schools, and she was encouraged to work hard. That was where her love of reading and writing found expression, and she started to do well. For the first time in her life, he said, she felt wanted and useful, and she started to thrive.

'Have you spoken to her? The aunt?'

'No. I don't have her number.'

Milton's phone vibrated in his pocket. He scooped it up and looked at the display. He didn't recognise the number.

'John Smith,' he said.

'Mr Smith, it's Victor Leonard from Pine Shore. We spoke last night.'

'Mr Leonard – how are you?'

'I'm good, sir,' the old man said. 'There's something I think you should know – about the girl.'

'Yes, of course – what is it?'

'Look, I don't want to be a gossip, telling tales on people and nonsense like that, but there's a fellow who's been saying some weird things about what happened up here the other night. You want to know about it?'

Trip raised his eyebrows: who is it?

'Please,' Milton said.

12

Milton was getting used to the forty-minute drive to Pine Shore. Trip was in the passenger seat next to him, fidgeting anxiously. Milton would have preferred to go alone, but the boy had insisted that he come, too. He had been quiet during the drive, but the mood had been oppressive and foreboding; Milton had tried to lighten it with some music. He had thumbed through his phone for some Smiths but then, after a couple of melancholic minutes, realised that that hadn't been the best choice. He replaced it with the lo-fi, baggy funk of the Happy Mondays. Trip seemed bemused by his choice.

Milton drove to the address that Victor Leonard had given him and parked. It was eleven in the morning. Milton climbed up a set of steps that rose up beyond the level of the pavement and rapped the ornate iron knocker three times. There was a vertical panel set into the side of the door, and Milton gazed inside. He made out the shape of a telephone table, a flight of stairs leading up to the first floor, a jumble of shoes against the wall, coats draped off the banister. It looked messy.

A man turned out of a doorway to the left of the lobby and came towards the door; Milton stepped away from the window.

The door opened.

'Dr Brady?'

'Yes? Who are you?' Andrew Brady was very tall, with a plump face, greasy skin and a pendulous chin. His hair was chestnut streaked with grey, and his small eyes had retreated deep into their sockets. He was unshaven, and despite his height, he was overweight and bore his extra pounds in a well-rounded pot belly. He was wearing a fuchsia-coloured windbreaker, a mesh cap and a pair of wading boots that were slicked with dried mud up to just below his knees.

'My name is John Smith. This is Trip Macklemore.'

'I'm sorry, fellas,' he said. 'I was just going out. Fishing.' He indicated the waders and a fishing rod that was propped against the wall behind him.

'Could we speak to you? It would just take a moment.'

Brady glared out from the doorway at them with what Milton thought looked like an arrogant sneer. 'Depends on what about.'

'The commotion around here the other night.'

'What commotion?'

'There was a girl. You didn't hear?'

'The girl – oh, yes.'

'I understand you spoke to her?'

Brady's eyes narrowed suspiciously. 'Who told you that?'

Milton turned and angled his face towards the house diagonally opposite. 'Mr Leonard. I spoke to him earlier. Is it true?'

'No,' Brady said. 'It isn't.'

'Do you think we could have ten minutes of your time? It's important.'

'What do you both have to do with her?'

'I'm her boyfriend,' Trip explained.

'And you, Mr Smith?'

'I'm a taxi driver. I drove her up here the night she went missing. I'd like to see that she gets home safely again.'

'How honourable,' Brady said with a half-smile that could have been derisory or amused – it was difficult to tell. 'A knight of the road.' The bluster was dismissed abruptly, and Brady's face broke out into a welcoming smile. 'Of course, of course – come inside.'

Milton got the impression that this was a man who, if not exactly keen to help, liked people to think that he was. Perhaps it was a doctor's self-regard. He bent down to tug off his boots and left them against the wall amidst the pile of shoes. Milton guessed he was in his early fifties, but he might have been older; the greasy skin made it difficult to make an accurate guess.

Brady led them both into the living room. There was a kitchen in the far corner and a breakfast bar with bar stools arranged around it. There was a large television tuned to CNN, a shelf of medical textbooks and, on the wall, a picture of a younger Brady – perhaps ten years younger – posing in army uniform with a group of soldiers. The photograph was taken in a desert; it looked like Iraq. He cleared the sofa of the discarded remnants of a newspaper so that they could sit down.

'Could I get you something to drink?'

'No, thanks,' Trip said, struggling with his impatience.

Milton smiled encouragingly at the boy. 'No,' he repeated. 'That's all right. We're fine.'

Brady lowered himself to the sofa. 'So what did Victor have to say about me?'

'Just what he said that you've been saying.'

'Which was—'

'That she – the girl, Madison – was here. That she knocked on the door and you took her in. He says you used to specialise in getting kids off drugs and that you run a retreat here. Kids with problems come up here, and you help them get clean. That true?'

'Yes, that's true.'

'And Madison?'

'No, that isn't true. And I don't know why he'd say that.'

'It didn't happen?'

'I heard the clamour – my God, the noise she was making, it'd be impossible not to hear her. She must've clambered over the wall at the bottom of the garden and went straight across, screaming for help at the top of her lungs. I was up working.'

'At that hour?'

'I was an army doctor, Mr Smith. Served my country in the Gulf, both times.'

Milton tried to make a connection with him. 'I served, too,' he said.

'Iraq?'

'Yes.'

'Doing what?'

'Just a squaddie the first time I went out. Then Special Forces.'

'SAS?'

'That's right.'

'You boys are tough as hell. Came across a few of your colleagues.'

'You know what,' Milton said, smiling at him. 'I will have that coffee.'

Brady smiled. 'Not a problem. Young man?'

'No,' Trip said. 'I'm fine.'

Brady got up and went to the kitchen. There was a coffee machine on the countertop, and Brady made two cups of black coffee. 'You been to Afghanistan, too?' he asked.

'Several times,' Milton replied.

'What's it like?'

'It wouldn't be on my bucket list, put it like that.'

'Never been out there myself, but that's what I heard from the guys I know who have. Ragheads – you ask me, we leave them to get on with whatever it is they want to do to each other. One thing you can say about them, they know how to fight – right?'

Milton ignored his distaste for the man. 'They do.'

'Gave the Russians a bloody nose when they tried to bring them in line, didn't they?

Brady rambled on for a moment, his remarks scattered with casual racism. Milton nodded and made encouraging responses, but he was hardly listening; he took the opportunity to scan the room more carefully: the stack of unpaid bills on the countertop; the newspaper, yellow highlighter all over a story about the Republican primary for the presidential elections; a precarious stack of vinyl albums on the floor; the textbooks shoved haphazardly onto the shelves; framed photographs of two children and a woman Milton guessed must have been Brady's wife. Nothing stood out. Nothing out of the ordinary. Certainly nothing that was a reason for suspicion.

'Milk and sugar?'

'No, thanks. Black's fine.'

Brady passed him a mug of coffee and went back around to sit. 'So – the girl.'

Trip leant forwards. 'Madison.'

'Must be.'

'Did you speak to her?'

'Not really. I went to the door and called out, but she didn't even pause. Kept going straight on.'

'She didn't come in?'

'No, she didn't. Like I said, she ran off.'

'Why would Mr – Leonard tell me that you said she did come in?' Milton asked, sipping the hot coffee.

'You'll have to ask him that. Between us, Victor's an old man. His faculties . . . well, let's be charitable about it and say that they're not what they once were.'

'He's lying?'

'I'm not saying that. Perhaps he's just mistaken. It wouldn't be the first time.'

'Right.'

Brady spoke easily and credibly. If he was lying, he was good at it.

The doctor sipped his coffee and rested the mug on the arm of the chair. 'You've reported her missing?'

'Of course,' Trip said tersely.

'And?'

'They were useless.'

'She's not a kid, though, is she? Most likely reason must be that she's gone off somewhere on her own. I'm sure she'll come back when she feels like it.'

'She's *missing*,' Trip said, his temper up a little.

Milton felt the atmosphere in the room change; the boy was angry, and the doctor's air of self-importance would only inflame things. They had got all they were going to get from this visit. It was time to go.

He stood. 'Thanks for the coffee. I'm sorry we had to bother you.'

Brady stood, too. 'I'll tell you what,' he said, reaching into his pocket and fishing out a business card. 'This is my number. I'll be happy to help out if you need anything. I'm on the board of the community association here. If you want to speak to anyone else or if you want to put flyers out, that sort of thing, please do just give me a call. Anything I can do, just ask.'

Milton took the card. 'Thank you,' he said as they made their way back down the corridor. They shook hands at the door. Brady's hands were bigger than his, but they were soft, and his grip was flaccid and damp, unimpressive.

Milton thanked him again, and impelling Trip onwards with a hand on his shoulder, they made their way down the steps to the pavement. Milton turned back to the house and saw Brady watching them from a side window; the man waved at him as soon as he realised that he had been seen. Milton turned back to the car, went around and got inside.

'*Bullshit,*' Trip said. 'One of them is lying, right?'

'Yes,' Milton said. 'But I don't know who.'

13

Milton met Trip in Top Notch Burger at noon the next day. Julius bagged up Milton's cheeseburger and the 'original' with jalapeños that the boy had ordered, and they ate them on the way back to Pine Shore. Trip had printed a missing person poster overnight, and they had stopped at a Kinko's to run off two hundred copies. The poster was a simple affair, with a picture of Madison smiling into the camera with a paper birthday hat perched on her head. 'MISSING' was printed above the photograph in bold capitals, her name was below the photograph and then at the foot of the flyer were Trip's mobile number and his email address.

Milton parked outside Andrew Brady's house, and they split up and set to work. He had purchased a stapler and staples from the copy-shop, and he used them to fix flyers to telegraph poles and fences. He went door to door, knocking politely and then, if the residents were home, explaining what had happened and what he was doing. Reactions varied: indifference, concern, a couple of the residents showing mild hostility. He pressed a copy of the flyer into the hands of each and put one through the letterboxes of those who were not home. It took Milton an hour to cover the ground that he had volunteered to take.

He waited for Trip in the car and stared up at the plain wooden door to Andrew Brady's house. The doctor had been the subject of several conversations with the other residents as he made his way around the neighbourhood. Milton had visited the library that morning, and his research, together with the information he was able to glean, enabled him to build up a more comprehensive picture. Brady was an interesting character, that much was obvious, and the more Milton learnt about him, the more questions he had.

Brady had moved into Pine Shore in the mid-90s. There was the doctor himself; his French wife, Collette; and their two young children, Claude and Annabel. Brady was the son of an army general who had served with distinction in Korea. He had followed his father into the military and had apparently enjoyed a decent, if not spectacular, career. He had been pulled back from the frontline for unspecified reasons and moved into an administrative role. It had evidently been a disappointment after his previous experience. He gave an interview to the local press upon his appointment as chief of surgery at St Francis Memorial Hospital explaining that while he would always love the army and that his military career had made him the man he was, he was a man of action and not suited to 'riding a desk'. He wanted to do something tangible and 'make a difference in the community'.

The family appeared to be affluent. Their house was one of the more expensive in the neighbourhood, and there was a

Lexus and an Audi in the driveway. Milton had asked around. Some of the residents spoke with a guarded warmness about them. Andrew and Collette were gregarious to a fault, becoming friends with their immediate neighbours. Andrew had been elected to the board of the residents' association, and it appeared that most of the other members were on good terms with him. There was Kevin Heyman, the owner of a large printing business. There was Charles Murdoch, who ran a real estate brokerage with another neighbour, Curtis McMahon. Those families were close, and there was talk of barbeques on the Fourth of July and shared festivities in the winter.

The closeness wasn't shared with all, and for all those who described Brady as friendly and approachable, there were others who described him as the head of a closed and overbearing clique. While some spoke of his kindness, often visiting the sick to offer the benefit of his experience, others saw him as a loud-mouthed blowhard, looking down on his neighbours and pretending to be something that he was not.

Milton heard stories that called his honesty into question. The most troubling concerned his professional reputation. During his time at the hospital, there had been a serious road incident on the interstate outside of San Mateo. A truck loaded with diesel had jackknifed across the 101, slicking the tarmac with fuel so that a series of cars had ploughed into it. The resulting fireball had been hot enough to melt the metal guard rails that ran down the median. Brady had been forced to resign in the aftermath of the crash after local reporters suggested that he had talked up his role in the recovery effort. He had claimed that he had driven himself to the scene of the disaster and, badging his way past the first responders, he had made his way into the heart of the inferno and administered first aid to survivors as they were pulled from the wreckage of their vehicles. The fire service later denied that he had been present at all and stated that he would never have been allowed to get as close to the flames as he had claimed.

In another incident, Brady recounted the story of being on his boat in Richardson Bay when a yacht had capsized and started to sink. He boasted that he had swum to the stricken boat and pulled a man and his son to safety. It was subsequently found that there was no record of a boat getting into difficulty that day and no father and son ever came forward to corroborate the story. An anonymous source even suggested that Brady had not even been on the water.

He had not taken another job since his resignation, and the suggestion had been made that there had been a large pay-off to get rid of him. He had retreated to Pine Shore and made himself busy. He took it upon himself to act as the resident physician, attending neighbours and offering help that was sometimes not welcome. He had assisted locals with minor ailments and worked hard to help the kids with addiction issues, seemingly intent on gaining the trust and respect of the community. Despite that, he continually told tales that were simple enough to debunk, and when they were, they damaged the good that he had done. He suggested that he had worked with the police. He boasted that he was a qualified pilot. He spoke of having obtained a degree in law through distance learning while he was in the army.

It seemed to Milton that Brady was intent upon making himself the centre of the community. His role as the chair of the residents' association seemed particularly important to him, and there was grudging acceptance from many that he did good and important work to make Pine Shore a better place to live. But not everyone felt the same way. More than one person confided to Milton that there was bad blood when it came to the committee. The chairmanship was an elected post, and it had been contested when the previous incumbent had stood aside.

The other candidate in an election that was described as 'pointlessly vicious' was Victor Leonard.

Trip opened the passenger door and slid inside.

'How did it go?' Milton asked him.

'Got rid of all of them.'

'Learn anything?'

'That this place is full of crap. You?'

'The same.'

Milton told him what he had learnt about Brady.

'He told others that he worked in Washington after coming out of the army. Homeland Security. He's full of shit, Mr Smith. How can we trust anything he's told us?'

'I'm not sure we can,' Milton admitted.

'So where does that leave us? You ask me, Madison was in there.' He stabbed his finger angrily against the window three times, indicating Brady's house.

'I don't know. But we need to find out.'

14

One of the campaign boosters was a big wine grower, exporting his bottles all over the world for millions of dollars a year, and one of the benefits of that largesse was an executive box at Candlestick Park. Arlen Crawford could take it or leave it when it came to sports, but his boss was an avid fan. The 49ers were his team, too, so the prospect of taking in the game against Dallas was something that had kept him fired up. It wasn't all pleasure, Crawford reminded him as they walked through the busy stadium to the level that held the luxury suites. Plenty of potential donors had been invited, too, not all of them on board with the campaign yet. They needed to be impressed. Robinson needed to deploy that beguiling grin, and his charisma needed to be at its most magnetic.

They reached the door, and Robinson opened it and stepped through into the box beyond. There was a long table laden with cold cuts, beers and snacks and, beyond that, an outside seating area. The governor's smile was immediate and infectious; he set to work on the other guests, working his way through the room, reaching out to take hands, sometimes pressing them between both of his, rewarding those who were already on the team with jovial backslaps or, for the lucky few, a powerful hug. It took him fifteen minutes to reach the front of the box and the open French doors that allowed access to the outside seats.

Crawford stepped down to the front of the enclosure and allowed himself a moment to breathe.

The field was brilliant green, perfectly lush, the gridiron markings standing out in vivid white paint. The stadium PA picked up the intensity as the teams made their way out through an inflatable tunnel in the corner of the stadium. Fireworks shot into the air, flamethrowers breathed tendrils of fire that reached up to the upper decks, music thumped, cheerleaders shimmied in formation. The 49ers' offence was introduced by the hyperbolic announcer, each armoured player sprinting through a gauntlet fashioned by the defence, chest-bumping those that had made the procession before him.

Crawford turned away from the noise and the pageantry to watch the governor deep in conversation with the multimillionaire who owned cattle ranches all the way across the south. Two good old boys, Crawford thought to himself. Winning him over would be a slam dunk for Robinson. They would be drinking buddies by the end of the afternoon, and a cheque with a lot of zeroes would be on its way to them first thing in the morning.

Suddenly tired, Crawford slid down into a seat and closed his eyes. He thought about the sacrifices he had made to get them as far as this. Robinson was the main draw, the focus, but without Crawford and the work that he did for him, he would be just another talker, high on star power but low on substance and destined for the level he was at right now. If Robinson was the circus, Crawford was the ringmaster. You couldn't have one without the other. It just wouldn't work.

He opened his eyes as the home team kicked off, the kicker putting his foot through the ball and sending it high into the air, spinning it on its axis all the way to the back of the end zone. The return man fielded it and dropped to one knee. Touchback.

The others settled into their seats. Robinson saw Crawford, grinned and gave him a wink.

He hoped that all this effort was going to be worth it.

15

Tuesday night's A.A. meeting was Milton's favourite. He stopped at a 7-Eleven and bought two jars of instant coffee and three different types of cookies. Yet more mist had risen from the ocean and was beginning its slow drift across the town. It was a cloudy night, the moon hidden. The signage of a bar on the opposite side of the street from the church was buzzing, flicking on and off. Milton parked and left the engine idling for a moment, the golden beams of the headlights glowing and fading against the banked fog. He killed the engine, got out and locked the door and crossed the street. He took the key from his pocket, unlocked the door and descended into the basement of the church.

It was a tired room, with peeling beige paint and cracked half-windows that were set far up towards the ceiling, revealing the shoes and ankles of the pedestrians passing by. Milton filled the urn with water and set it to boil. He took the coffee from the cupboard and then arranged the biscuits that he had brought on a plate, a series of neat concentric circles. The mugs hadn't been washed from the last meeting that had used the room, so he filled the basin and attended to them, drying them with a dishcloth and stacking them on the table next to the urn.

Milton had been coming to meetings for more than three years. London, all the way through South America, then here. He still found the thought of it counter-intuitive, but then the complete honesty that the programme demanded would always be a difficult concept for a man who had worked in the shadows for most of his adult life. He did his best.

It had been more difficult at the start, in that church hall in West London. There was the Official Secrets Act, for a start, and what would happen to him if it came out that he had a problem. He had hidden at the back, near the door, and it had taken him a month to sit all the way through a meeting without turning tail and fleeing. He had gradually asked a regular with plenty of years of sobriety and a quiet attitude if he would be his first sponsor. He was called Dave Goulding, a musician in his late forties, a man who had been successful when he was younger and then drank his money and his talent away. Despite a life of bitter disappointment, he had managed to get his head screwed on straight, and with his guidance, Milton had started to make progress.

The first thing Dave insisted upon was that Milton attend ninety meetings in ninety days. He had given him a spiral-bound notebook and a pen and told him that if he wanted him to remain as his sponsor, he had to record every meeting he attended in that notebook. Milton did that. After that, a little trust between them developed, and they worked on his participation in the meetings. He wasn't ready to speak at that point – that wouldn't come for more than a year – but he had been persuaded to at least give the impression that he was engaged in what was going on. Dave called the back row at meetings the Denial Aisle and had drummed into him that sick people who wanted to get well sat in the front. Milton wasn't quite ready for that, either, but he had gradually moved forwards. Each month he moved forward again until he was in the middle of the action, stoic and thoughtful amidst the thicket of raised arms as the other alcoholics jostled to speak.

He had found this meeting on his first night in 'Frisco. It was a lucky find; there was something about it that made it special. The room, the regulars, the atmosphere; there was a little magic about it. Milton had volunteered to serve the drinks on the second night when the grizzled ex-army vet who had held the post before him had fallen off the wagon and been spotted unconscious in the parking lot of the 7-Eleven near Fisherman's Wharf. Milton always remembered Dave explaining that service was the keystone of A.A., and since taking care of the refreshments was something he could do without opening himself up to the others, it was an excellent way to make himself known while avoiding the conversations that he still found awkward.

He opened the storage cupboard, dragged out the stacked chairs and arranged them in four rows of five. The format of the meeting was the same as all of the others that Milton had attended. A table was arranged at the front of the room, and Milton covered it with a cloth with the A.A. logo embroidered on it in coloured thread. There were posters on the wall and books and pamphlets that could be purchased. Milton went back to the cupboard, took out a long cardboard tube and shook out the poster stored inside. It was made to look like a scroll; he hung it from its hook. The poster listed the Twelve Steps.

Milton was finishing up when the first man came down the stairs. His name was Smulders, he worked on the docks, he had been sober for a year, and he was the chairman of this meeting. Milton said hello, poured him a coffee and offered him a biscuit.

'Thanks,' Smulders said. 'How've you been?'

'I've had better days.'

'Want to talk about it?'

'Maybe later,' he said – the same thing he always said.

'You know what I'm going to say, right?'

'That I shouldn't brood.'

'Exactly. Get it off your chest.'

'In my own time.'

'Sure. Mmm-hmm. Good cookies – gimme another.'

Milton had already begun to feel a little better.

* * *

It was a normal meeting. The chair arranged for a speaker to share his or her story for the first half an hour and then they all shared back with their own experiences. Smulders had asked one of the regulars, a thirty-something docker that Milton knew called Richie Grimes, to tell his story. They sat down, worked through the preliminaries and then Smulders asked Richie to begin.

'My name is Richie,' he said, 'and I'm an alcoholic.'

Milton was dozing a little, but that woke him up. Richie was a nice guy.

'Hi, Richie,' the group responded.

'I'm pleased I've been asked to share tonight. I don't always talk as much as I know I ought to, but I really do need to share something. I've been holding onto it for the last six months, and unless I deal with it, I know I'll never be able to stay away from coke and the bottle.'

The group waited.

'I'm grandiose, like we all are, right, but not so much that I'd argue that mine is an original problem. You know what I'm talking about – *money*.' They all laughed. 'Yeah, right. Most alkies I know couldn't organise their finances if their lives depended on it, but if I'm not the worst in the room, then I'd be very fuckin' surprised, excuse my French. I lost my job a year ago for the usual reasons – attendance was shitty, and when I did turn up, I was either drunk or thinking about getting drunk – and instead of taking the hint, I decided it'd be a much better idea to get drunk every day for the next month. By the end of that little binge, the savings I had managed to keep were all gone, and the landlord started making threats about throwing me onto the street. I couldn't work; no one would even look at me, not least give me a job. If I got evicted, it was gonna get a hundred times worse, so I thought the only thing I could do was borrow some money from this dude that I had heard would give me credit. But he's not like the bank, you know? He's not on the level, not the kind of dude you'd want to be in hock to, but it wasn't like anyone legit was about to give me credit, and my folks are dead, so the way I saw it, I didn't have much of a choice. I went and saw him and took his money, and after I dropped a couple of Gs on a massive bender – the one that took me to rock bottom – then I found the Rooms, and I haven't drunk or drugged since.'

A round of warm applause was punctuated by whoops from the eager alkies in the front row.

'I know, it's good, best thing I've ever done, but despite it being his cash that allowed me to stay in my place, give me somewhere to anchor myself, the stability I need to try to do all this stuff, he don't necessarily share the sentiment. He's not into community outreach, know what I mean? So he sent a couple of guys around yesterday. They made it clear that I'm running out of rope. He wants his money back. With interest and "administration charges" and all that shit, I'm looking at the thick end of six grand.'

He laughed at this as if it was a particularly funny joke, then put his head in his hands and started to sob. His shoulders quivered, and Milton watched him awkwardly until one of the other guys shuffled across the seats and put his arm around him.

There was silence for a moment until Richie recovered himself. 'I got a job now, like you all know about, but even though it's the best thing that's happened to me for months, it still barely covers my rent and groceries, and if I can save twenty bucks a month, then I reckon I'm doing well. That don't even cover the interest on the loan, not even close. I don't expect any of you to have any clever ways for me to fix this. I just wanted to share it because, I gotta be honest, I've felt the urge to go and buy a bottle of vodka and just drink myself stupid so I can forget all about it. But I know that'd be a crazy idea, worst thing I could do, and now, especially after I've shared, I think maybe I can keep it behind me, at least for the time being. But I've got to get this sorted. The more it seems like a dead end, the more I want to get blasted so I can forget all about it.'

16

Milton was stacking the chairs at the end of the meeting, hauling them across the room to the walk-in cupboard, when he noticed that the woman he knew as Eva was waiting in the entrance hall. She was sitting against the edge of the table, her legs straight, with one ankle resting against the other, and a copy of the Big Book held open before her. Milton watched her for a moment, thinking, as he usually did, that she was a good-looking woman, before gripping the bottom of the stack of chairs, heaving it into the air and carrying it into the cupboard. He took the cloth cover from the table, tracing his fingers over the embroidered A.A. symbol, and put that in the cupboard, too. He shut the cupboard, locked it, then went through. Eva had stacked all the dirty cups in the kitchen sink.

'Hello,' she said, with a wide smile.

'Hello. You all right?'

'Oh, sure. I'm great. Just thought you could do with a hand.'

'Thanks.'

She stood and nodded down at the table. 'Where does that go?'

'Just over there,' Milton said. 'I've got it.' He lifted the table, pressed the legs back into place, picked it up and stacked it against the wall with the others. He was conscious that she was watching him and allowed her a smile as he came back to pick up the large vat, the water inside cooling now that the element had been switched off. She returned his smile, and he found himself thinking, again, that she was very attractive. She was slim and petite, with glossy dark hair and a Latino complexion. Her eyes were her best feature: the colour of rich chocolate, smouldering with intelligence and a sense of humour that was never far from the surface. Milton didn't know her surname, but she was a voluble sharer during the meetings, and he knew plenty about her from the things that she had said. She was a lawyer, used to work up in Century City in Los Angeles doing clearance work for the networks. Now she did medical liability work at St Francis Memorial. She was divorced with a young daughter, her husband had been an alcoholic too, and it had broken their relationship apart. She had found the Rooms; he hadn't. She shared about him sometimes. He was still out there.

'Enjoy it tonight?' she asked.

'*Enjoy* might not be the right word.'

'Okay – get anything from it?'

'I think so.'

'Which other meetings do you go to?'

'Just this one. You?'

'There's the place on Sacramento Street. Near Lafayette Park?'

Milton shook his head.

'I do a couple of meetings there. Mondays and Fridays. They're pretty good. You should— well, you know.'

He turned the urn upside down and rested it in the sink.

'How long is it for you?' she asked.

'Since I had a drink?' He smiled ruefully. 'One thousand and fifty days.'

'Not that you're counting.'

'Not that I'm counting.'

'Let's see.' She furrowed her brow with concentration. 'If you can manage to keep the plug in the jug for just a little while longer, you'll be three years sober.'

'There's something to celebrate,' he said with an ironic smile.

'Are you serious?' she said, suddenly intense. 'Of course it is. You want to go back to how it was before?'

He got quick flashbacks. 'Of course not.'

'Fucking right. Jesus, John! You have to come to a meeting and get your chip.'

Anniversaries were called birthdays in the Rooms. They handed out little embossed poker chips with the number of months or years written on them, all in different colours. Milton had checked out the chip for three years: it would be red. Birthdays were usually celebrated with cake, and then there would be a gathering afterwards, a meal or a cup of coffee.

He hadn't planned on making a fuss about it.

He felt a little uncomfortable with her focus on him. 'You've got more, don't you?'

'Five years. I had my last drink the day my daughter was born. That was what really drove it home for me – I'd just given birth, and my first thought was, God, I really need a gin. That kind of underlined that maybe, you know, maybe I had a bit of a problem with it. What about you? You've never said?'

He hesitated and felt his shoulders stiffen. He had to work hard to keep the frown from his brow. He remembered it very well, but it wasn't something that he would ever be able to share in a meeting.

'Difficult memory?'

'A bit raw.'

The flashback came back. It was clear and vivid, and thinking about it again, he could almost feel the hot sun on the top of his head. Croatia. Zagreb. There had been a cell there, laid up and well advanced with their plan to blow up a car loaded with a fertiliser bomb in the middle of the Ban Jelačić square. The spooks had intercepted their communications, and Milton had gone in to put an end to the problem. It had been a clean job – three shots, three quick eliminations – but something about one of them had stayed in his head. He was just a boy – the intel had said sixteen, but Milton had guessed younger, fourteen or fifteen at the outside – and he had gazed up at him and into his eyes as he levelled the gun and aimed it at his head and pulled the trigger. Milton was due to extract immediately after the job, but he had diverted to the nearest bar and had drunk himself stupidly, horribly, awfully, dangerously drunk. They had just about cashiered him for that. Thinking about it triggered the old memories, and for a moment, it felt as if he was teetering on the edge of a trapdoor that had suddenly dropped open beneath his feet.

He forced his thoughts away from it, that dark and blank pit that fell away beneath him, a conscious effort, and then realised that Eva was talking to him. He focused on her instead.

'Sorry,' she was saying, 'you don't have to say if you'd rather not, obviously.'

'It's not so bad.'

'No, forget I asked.'

A little brightness returned, and he felt the trapdoor close.

'It's fear, right?' she said.

'What do you mean? Fear of what?'

'No, F.E.A.R.' She spelt it out.

He shrugged his incomprehension.

'You haven't heard that one? It's the old A.A. saying: Fuck Everything And Run.'

'Ah,' Milton said, relaxing a little. 'Yes. That's exactly it.'

'I've been running for five years.'

'You still get bad days?'

'Sure I do. Everyone does.'

'Really? Out of everyone I've met since I've been coming to meetings, you seem like one of the most settled.'

'Don't believe it. It's a struggle just like everyone else. It's like a swan, you know: it looks graceful, but there's paddling like shit going on below the surface. It's a day-to-day thing. You take your eye off the ball and, bang, back in the gutter you go. I'm just the same as everyone.'

Milton was not surprised to hear that – it was a comment that he had heard many times, almost a refrain to ward off complacency – but it seemed especially inapposite from Eva. He had always found her to have a calming, peaceful manner. There were all sorts in the Rooms: some twitchy and avid, white-knuckling it, always one bad day from falling back into the arms of booze; others, like her, had an almost Zen-like aspect, an aura of meditative serenity that he found intoxicating. He looked at them jealously.

'What are you doing now?' she asked him impulsively.

'Nothing much.'

'Want to get dinner?'

'Sure,' he said.

'Anywhere you fancy?'

'Sure,' he said. 'I know a place.'

* * *

They were the only people in Top Notch. Julius took their order and set about it with a cheerful smile, and soon, the aroma of cooked meat filled the room. He brought the burgers over on paper plates and left them to get on with it, disappearing into the back. Milton smiled at his discretion; there would be wry comments when he came in tomorrow.

The food was as good as ever, and the conversation was good, too, moving away from A.A. to range across work and family and life in general. Milton quickly found himself relaxing.

'How are you finding the Steps?'

'Oh, you know . . .' he began awkwardly.

'Which one are you on?'

'Eight and Nine.'

'Can you recite them?'

He smiled a little ruefully. '"We made a list of all persons we had harmed and became willing to make amends to them all."'

'And?'

'"We made direct amends to such people wherever possible, except where to do so would injure them or others."'

'Perfect,' she said. 'My favourites.'

'I don't know. They're hard.'

'You want my advice? Do it in your own time. They're not easy, but you do feel better afterwards. And you want to be careful. Plenty of people will be prepared to take your amends for you—'

'—And they can, too, if they're prepared to *make* my amends.'

'You heard that one before?'

He smiled. 'A few times. Where are you? Finished them?'

'First time around. I'm going back to the start again now.'

'Step Ten: "We continued to take a personal inventory."'

'Exactly. It never stops. You keep doing it, it stays fresh.'

Eva was an easy talker, something she affably dismissed as one of her faults, but Milton didn't mind at all; he was happy to listen to her, her soft West Coast drawl smoothing the edges from her words and her self-deprecating sense of humour and easy laughter drawing him in until it was just the two of them in an empty restaurant with Julius turning the chairs upside down on the tables, a hint that he was ready to call it a night and close.

'That was really nice,' she said as they stood on the pavement outside.

'It was.'

'You wanna, you know – you wanna do it again next time?'

'I'd love to.'

'All right, then, John.' She took a step towards him, her hand on his shoulder as she raised herself onto tiptoes and placed a kiss on his cheek. She lingered there for a moment, her lips warm against his skin, and as she stepped back, she traced her fingertips across his shoulder and down his arm to the elbow. 'Take it easy, all right? I'll see you next week.'

Milton smiled, more easily and naturally than was normal for him, and watched her turn and walk back towards where she had parked her Porsche.

17

Peter Gleason was the park ranger for the Golden Gate National Recreation Area. He had held the job for twenty years, watching all the communal spaces, making sure the fishermen and water-sports enthusiasts observed the local regulations, keeping an eye on the wildlife. Peter loved his job; he was an outdoorsman at heart, and there couldn't be many places that were as beautiful as this. He liked to say that he had the best office in the world; his wife, Glenda, had heard that quip about a million times, but he still said it because it was true and it reminded him how lucky he was.

Peter had been a dog-lover all his adult life, and this was a great job to have a hound. It was practically a requirement. He had had four since he had been out here. They had all been Labradors. Good dogs, obedient and loyal; it was just like he always said, you couldn't go far wrong with a Lab. Jethro was his current dog. He was two years old and mongrel – part Labrador and part pointer. Peter had picked him out as a puppy and was training him up himself. He had the most even temperament out of all the dogs, and the best nose.

It was an early Tuesday morning when Peter stopped his truck in the wide, exposed and bleak square of ground that served visitors to Headlands Lookout. It was a remote area, served by a one-track road with the waters of Bonita Cove at the foot of a sheer drop on the left. He stepped carefully; yet another dense bank of fog had rolled in overnight and visibility was down to twenty yards. It was cold and damp, the curtain of solid grey muffling the sound. The western portion of San Francisco was just on the other side of the bay, usually providing a splendid vista, but it was invisible today. The only sign that it was there was the steady, eerie boom of the foghorns, one calling and the other answering.

There were only two other cars in the lot. Fishermen still visited with reels to try to catch the abundant fish, and as Peter checked, he noticed that a couple of them had followed the precarious path down the cliff face to get to the small beach. Oystermen came, too, even though the oyster beds, which had once been plentiful, had grown more scarce. Others came with binoculars to watch the birds and the seals. Kayakers, clad in neoprene wetsuits, cut across the waves.

The margins between the road and the cliff had grown too wild in places for a man to get through, but the dog was keen to explore today, and Peter watched as he forced himself into thickets of bramble. He walked on, following the headland around to the west. He watched the dog bound ahead, cutting a line through the poison oak and salt hay that was as straight as an arrow.

Peter lived on the other side of the bay, in Richmond, and he had always had a keen interest in the local flora and fauna. He found the rough natural world interesting, which was reason enough, but it was also professionally useful to have some knowledge of the area that you were working in. As he followed Jethro through the salt hay that morning, he found himself thinking that this part of the world would not have changed much in hundreds of years. Once you were down the slope a ways and the city was out of sight, the view would have been unchanged for millennia.

He stepped carefully through the bracken, navigating the thick clumps of vegetation before breaking into the open and tramping down the suddenly steep slope to the water's edge. All along the beach were stacks of rocks brought over from Tiburon. They had been piled into makeshift breakwaters to help combat the constant erosion, and the salty bite of the tide had caused them to crumble and crack.

The dog paused for a moment, frozen still, his nose twitching, and then as Peter watched with a mixture of curiosity and anticipation, he sprinted towards the deep fringe of the undergrowth. He got six feet in and stopped, digging furiously. Peter struggled across the soft, wet sand as the dog started to bark. When he got there, the dog had excavated the sand so that a flap of canvas sacking had been exposed. He called for Jethro to stay, but he was young and excited and knew he was onto something, so he kept digging, wet sand spraying out from between his hind legs.

By the time the ranger had fastened the lead to the dog's collar, he had unearthed a skull, a collarbone and the start of a ribcage.

PART II

MEG GABERT

Meg Gabert had always wanted to run track. She was a born athlete. She hadn't decided exactly what her talents best suited – long distance or sprints, she could do both – but there was no question about it in her mind: she was going to go to the Olympics and she was going to win gold. It wasn't in doubt.

When she was in seventh grade, she had started running at a local club. She decided that she was going to concentrate on long distance; she was tall and lithe, and, as she went farther and farther in her training, she found that she had plenty of endurance. She ran her first half-marathon when she was fifteen and then finished Boston the next year in a very competitive time. Her coach said that she had real talent, and she believed him. It was something she would never forget: the excitement she felt as she ran the final few hundred yards, the crowd hollering their encouragement, the older runners struggling to get over the line while she still felt she had more in the tank. If she had needed any confirmation about the course she had chosen for herself, this was it.

But things got harder as she got older. She wasn't great at school and left without any real qualifications. Running was expensive, and she knew that it would take time before she was able to support herself through athletics. Until that happened, she had paid her way with a little hooking. It had started with web-cams, but then she had realised there was more to be made by going further. She had posted an ad on the Fresno/Adult Services page of Craigslist a year after she graduated from high school. She had a killer photo that an ex-boyfriend had taken of her, and the replies had been instantaneous.

Eventually, she moved from Illinois to San Francisco. The johns there were of a different class; they had more money, and she found that she could clear five hundred a night with no problem. The cash got to be addictive, and, as she enjoyed buying herself new clothes and fancy holidays, she forgot all about her running. Her track shoes started to gather dust in the back of her closet.

* * *

Meg heard the Cadillac before she saw it. It backfired loudly from a couple of blocks away, the noise carrying down the street and around the corner to where she was waiting at Sixth and Irving. The engine sounded throaty and unhealthy, as if it was about to expire, and she was nonplussed as it pulled over to stop at the edge of the sidewalk opposite her. The man she had spoken to on the phone had said that he was an executive from a company that dealt in cattle all the way across the south-west. He certainly had the accent for it, a mild Southern burr that lent his voice a musical quality. She hadn't expected him to be driving a beat-up car like this, but as she crossed the sidewalk to the open window, she chided herself for jumping to conclusions.

A bum begging for change next to the entrance to the department store watched as the door was opened for her. He watched as she carefully slid into the car, her hands pressing down her skirt as she lowered herself into the seat. The man didn't think twice about it, and she hardly registered; he was hungry and more interested in adding to the couple of bucks in change that had been tossed into the cap on the sidewalk before his folded legs. If he had paid attention, perhaps he would have noticed the confusion on the girl's face as she looked, for the first time, at the man who had picked her up. He might have remembered more if he had known that he would be the last person to see the girl alive.

18

Milton leant back and traced his fingers against the rough vinyl surface of the table. It had been marked by years of graffiti: gang tags, racial epithets and unflattering remarks about the police, some of them quite imaginative. There was a dirty glass of water, an ashtray that hadn't been emptied for days and, set against the wall, a tape recorder.

He crossed his arms and looked up at the police officers who were sitting opposite him. The first was a middle-aged man with several days of growth on his chin, an aquiline face and a lazy left eye. The second was a little older, a little more senior, and from the way the two of them had behaved so far, Milton could see that he was going to keep quiet while his partner conducted the interview.

The younger of the two pressed a button on the tape recorder and it began to spool.

'Just to go through things like we mentioned to you, we're gonna do a taped interview with you.'

'That's fine,' Milton said.

'There's my ID. And there's my partner's.'

'Okay.'

'So I'm Inspector Richard Cotton. My colleague is Chief of Detectives Stewart Webster.'

'I can see that.'

'Now, first of all, can you please state your name for me?'

'John Smith.'

'And that's S-M-I-T-H.'

'Correct.'

'Your date of birth, sir?'

'Thirty-first of October, 1968.'

'That makes you forty-five, right?'

'It does.'

'And your address at home?'

'259 Sixth Street.'

'What's that?'

'A hotel.'

'An SRO?'

'That's right.'

'Which one?'

'The El Capitan.'

'How are you finding that? Bit of a dive, right?'

'It's all right.'

'If you say so. Phone number?'

He gave them the number of his mobile.

'Are you all right for water?'

'Yes.'

Cotton tossed a packet of cigarettes on the table. 'Feel free to light up. We know this can be stressful.'

Milton had to stifle a long sigh of impatience. 'It would be stressful if I had something to hide. But I don't, so I'll pass, but thanks anyway. Now, please – can we get started? There's already been too much waiting around. Ask me whatever you like. I want to help.'

Cotton squinted one eye, a little spooky. 'All right, then. John Smith – that's your real name, right?'

'It is.'

'And you're English, right?'

'That's right.'

'I've been to England. Holiday. Houses of Parliament, Buckingham Palace, all that history – one hell of a place.'

Milton rolled his eyes. Was he serious? 'Just ask me about Madison.'

'In a minute, John,' the man said with exaggerated patience. 'We just want to know a little bit about you first. So how come you ended up here?'

'I've been travelling. I was in South America for a while, and then I came north.'

'Through Mexico?'

'That's right.'

'How long you been here?'

'Six months. I was here once before, years ago. I liked it. I thought I'd come back and stay a while.'

'How have you been getting by?'

'I've been working.'

Cotton's good eye twitched. 'You got a visa for that?'

'Dual citizenship.'

'How's that?'

'My mother was American.' It was a lie, but it was what his passport said. Dual citizenship saved unnecessary nonsense that would have made it more difficult for him to work. Being able to claim some connection to the United States had also proven to be useful as he worked his way north up the continent.

'All right, John. Let's change the subject – you want to talk about Madison, let's talk about Madison. You know we've dug up two bodies now, right?'

'I've seen the news.'

'And you know neither of them are her?'

That was news to him. 'No. I didn't know that.'

'That's right – neither of them. See, Madison had a metal pin in her hip. Fell off her bike when she was a girl, messed it up pretty good. They had to put one in to fix it all together. The remains in the morgue are all whole, more or less, and neither of them have anything like that.'

Milton felt a moment of relief but immediately tempered it; it was still surely just a matter of time.

'That doesn't mean we won't find her,' Cotton went on. 'If you've been watching the news, you'll know that we're still searching the beach, and we're very concerned that we're gonna find more. So, with all that being said, let's get down to meat and potatoes, shall we?'

'Please.'

'Why'd you do it, John?'

Milton wasn't surprised. 'Seriously?'

'What did you do with her body?'

'You've got to be kidding.'

'I'm not kidding, John.'

'No, you've got to be. It's nothing to do with me.'

'Answer the question, please.'

He looked dead straight at the cop. 'I just answered it. I didn't do it. I have absolutely no idea where she is.'

'So you say. But on your own account a few months back, you were the last person to see her alive.'

He clenched his fists in sudden frustration. 'No – that's not what I said.'

'You got a temper, John?'

'I don't know that she's dead. I hope she isn't. I said that I was one of the last people to see her before she *disappeared*. That's different.'

'We know the two girls we've got in the morgue were both hookers. Madison was hooking when she disappeared. It's not hard to join the dots, is it?'

'No, it isn't. But it has nothing to do with me.'

'All right, then. Let's change tack.' Cotton took a cigarette from the packet and lit it, taking his time about it. He looked down at his notes. 'Okay. The night after she disappeared – this is the Sunday – we've got a statement from Victor Leonard that says you went back to Pine Shore. He said he saw you coming out of the garden of the house where the party was the night before. Is that right?'

'Yes.'

'We checked the security camera, Mr Smith. There's one on the gate. We looked, and there you are, climbing over the wall. Why'd you do something like that?'

Milton gritted his teeth. The camera must have run off rechargeable batteries that would cut in if the power went out. 'The gate was locked,' he said.

'Why didn't you buzz to get in?'

'Because someone had changed the code to the gate after Madison disappeared. Rather than wasting your time with me, I'd be asking why that was. A girl goes missing, and the next day the code to the gate is changed? Why would they want to keep people out? Don't you think that's a little suspicious?'

'We'll be sure to bear that in mind. What were you looking around for?'

'Anything that might give me an idea what caused Madison to be so upset that she'd run away.'

'You spoke to Mr Leonard?'

'Yes.'

'Why?'

'Madison went to his house. I wanted to know what she said to him.'

'He say anything useful?'

Milton thought of Brady. 'Not really.'

'And you don't think all this is something that the police ought to do?'

'Yes, I do, but Madison's boyfriend had already reported her missing and he got the cold shoulder. Most crimes are solved in the first few hours after they happen. I didn't think this could wait.'

Cotton chain-smoked the cigarette down to the tip. 'Know a lot about police work, do you, John?'

'Do you have a sensible question for me?'

'Got a smart mouth, too.'

'Sorry about that. Low tolerance level for idiots.'

'That's it, John. Keep giving me attitude. We're the only people here keeping you from a pair of cuffs and a nice warm cell.'

Milton ignored the threat.

Cotton looked down at his notes. 'You said she was frightened?'

'Out of her mind.'

'That's not what security at the party said.'

'What did they say?'

'Said you barged in and went after her.'

'I heard her screaming.'

'How'd you explain how one of them ended up with a concussion and a broken nose?'

'He got in my way.'

'So you broke his nose and knocked him out?'

'I hit him.'

'It raises the question of that temper of yours again.'

Milton repeated himself patiently. 'I heard Madison screaming.'

'So?'

'So I went in to see if she was all right.'

'And?'

'I told her I'd take her home.'

'And?'

'She got around me and ran.'

Cotton got up and started to circle the table. 'You mentioned Madison's boyfriend' – he consulted his notes – 'Trip Macklemore. We've spoken to him. He said you had Madison's bag in the back of your taxi.'

'I did. I gave it to him afterwards.'

'What was it doing in your car?'

'She left it there.'

'But you'd already taken her where she needed to go. Why would she have left it?'

'I said I'd wait for her.'

'You didn't have another job to go to?'

'She was nervous. I didn't think it was right to leave her there, on her own, with no way to get back to the city.'

'You were going to charge her for that?'

'I hadn't decided. Probably not.'

'A favour, then? Out of the goodness of your heart?'

'It was the right thing to do.'

'He's English,' the other man, Webster, offered. 'What is it you call it?'

'Chivalry?'

'That's right, *chivalry*.'

'Don't know about that, boss. Doesn't strike me as all that likely. Taxi drivers aren't known for their charity.'

'I try to do the right thing,' Milton said.

Cotton looked down at his notes. 'You work for Vassily Romanov, too, right? Mr Freeze – the ice guy?'

'Yes.'

'We spoke to him. He had to have words with you the afternoon after she went missing. That right?'

'I dropped an ice sculpture.'

'He says you were agitated.'

'Distracted. I knew something was wrong.'

'Tell me what happened.'

'I already have.'

Cotton slapped both hands on the table. '*Where* is she?'

Milton stared at him and spoke calmly and carefully. 'I don't know.'

He drummed the table. 'What did you do with her body?'

'It's got nothing to do with me.'

'Is she on the headland?'

'I don't know.'

'Let me share a secret with you, John. The D.A. thinks you did it. He thinks you've got a big "Guilty" sign around your neck. He wants to throw the book at you.'

'Knock yourself out.' Milton calmly looked from one man to the other. 'We can go around the houses on this all day if you want, but I'm telling you now, if anything has happened to Madison, it has absolutely *nothing* to do with me, and it doesn't matter how you phrase your questions, it doesn't matter if you shout and scream, and it doesn't matter if you threaten me – the answers will always be the same. *I didn't do it*. It has nothing to do with me. And I'm not a fool. You can say what you want, but I know you don't think that I did it.'

'Really? How would you know that, John?'

'Because you would have arrested me already and this interview would be under caution. Look, I understand. I know you need to eliminate me. I know that I'm going to be a suspect. It stands to reason. I'll do whatever you need me to do so that you can be happy that I'm not the man you want. The car I was driving that night is parked outside. Get forensics to have a look at it. You can do it without a warrant – you don't need one, you have my authorisation. If you want to search my room, you've just got to ask.' He reached into his pocket and deposited his keys on the table. 'There. Help yourself.'

'You're awfully confident, John.'

'Because I have nothing to hide.' Webster was fingering the cigarette packet. Milton turned to him. 'You're the ranking officer here, right? I'm not going to tell you your job, but you've got to put a lead on your friend here and get off this dead end – right now. You're wasting time you don't have. If Madison is still alive, every minute we're doing this makes it less likely she'll be alive when you find her.'

Webster cocked an eyebrow. 'You like telling us what we should be doing so much, Mr Smith – what would you be doing?'

'I'd be looking at the footage from that CCTV camera. Maybe you'll see what happened. And everyone who went to the party that night will have gone through the gate. You should start looking into them.'

'The footage has been wiped,' he said.

'What?'

'There's nothing from the Saturday night.'

'Who wiped it?'

'We don't know.'

'You need to talk to whoever did that, then. Right?'

Cotton took over. 'Let's put that aside for the moment. You got anything to tell us, John?'

Milton thought about the two men in the house after the party. He would have told the cops what had happened, what he had overheard, but how could he do that without telling them that he had broken in? Why would he have done something like that? It wasn't going to be possible. That was a lead that he would have to follow for himself.

'All right, officers. Is there anything else?'

They said nothing.

'I'm going to be on my way. You know where I am, and you've got my number. If you want me to stay, you're going to have to arrest me.'

He pushed the chair away and stood up from the table.

19

Milton needed a meeting. As he drove across town, he felt as if he needed one even more than usual. He wasn't overly worried – he knew he would be able to run rings around the police – but the interview had still left him angry and frustrated. He had known that the police would treat him as a suspect – he would have done the same, if the roles had been reversed – but they seemed fixated. The longer they wasted on him, the worse it would be for Madison. And also, for a man in his particularly precarious position, there was the overriding need to be careful. More than careful. An arrest, his fingerprints and mugshot taken, metadata passing between anonymous servers – he knew that was all the spooks at GCHQ or the NSA would need to pin him down, and then it would all kick off again. The firestorm that had blazed around him in Juárez would spark back to life. Worse this time. He knew the prudent thing to do would have been to jump town the moment that there had been even a sniff of trouble. The day after Madison had disappeared. Now, though, he couldn't. The city had closed around him like a fist. If he ran, the police would see it as a sign of guilt. They would have all the evidence they needed to push their suspicions about him up a notch. There would be a manhunt. His name would be in the papers. His picture on the internet.

He might as well telephone Control.

I'm in San Francisco.

Come and get me.

No, he thought, as he drove across town. He had to stay and see this through until the end.

He gripped the wheel tightly and concentrated on the pattern of his breathing. The Rooms had taught him that anger and frustration were two of his most delicate triggers. A good meeting was like meditation, and he knew that it would help him to put the lid back on his temper.

Eva was waiting for him, leaning against the wall by the door. She was wearing a woollen jumper, expensive, long enough to reach well down beyond her waist, a pair of jeans and chunky leather boots. She had a black felt beret on her head. She looked supremely cute.

'Hello, John.'

'You're early.'

She leant forward, pressing herself away from the wall. 'Thought maybe I'd give you a hand. That all right?'

'Course,' he said.

They worked quickly and quietly: preparing the room, setting up the table with the tea and coffee, washing the crockery. Milton's thoughts went back to the meeting with the police. He thought about everything he knew. Two escorts found dead on the same stretch of headland. Madison going missing just five miles from the same spot. It looked bad for her. Maybe there was another explanation for what had happened, but then again, maybe there wasn't. The most obvious explanation was often the right one.

'You all right?' Eva asked him.

'I'm fine,' he said.

'Looks like you're a thousand miles away.'

'Sorry,' he said. 'I've got some stuff on my mind.'

'A problem shared is a problem halved.'

'I know.'

The regulars started to arrive twenty minutes before the meeting was scheduled to begin. Milton went behind the table and made their coffees. The room was quickly busy. Eva was waylaid by a young actor who obviously had a thing for her. She rolled her eyes, and as he nudged her towards the room for the start of the meeting, she paused by the table.

'You want to get dinner?'

'I'm not sure I'll be the best company tonight.'

'I'll take the risk.' She looked straight at him and winked.

'Okay.' He smiled. 'That'd be great.'

The room emptied out as it got closer to the top of the hour, and Milton quickly poured himself a coffee.

Smulders hijacked him as he was about to go inside.

'About time you opened that mouth of yours in a meeting, John.'

'Do I get to say no?'

Smulders looked at him with an intense sincerity. 'Man, you need me to remind you? You need me to explain? You're *sick*. And the cure for your sickness, the best cure I ever found, is to get involved and *participate.*' He enunciated that last word carefully, each syllable pronounced slowly, and then pressed a pamphlet into his hands. The title on the pamphlet was THE TWELVE PROMISES. 'Here they are, Smith. Read them out when I tell you and think on them when you do. All right?'

'Fine.'

Milton sat down as Smulders brought the gavel down and opened proceedings. He had recruited a speaker from another meeting that he attended, a middle-aged woman with worry lines carved in deep grooves around her eyes and prematurely grey hair. She started to speak, her share focusing on the relationship with her ex-husband and how he had knocked her around. It was worthy, and she was a powerful speaker, but Milton found his thoughts turning back to the interview and the police. They had already wasted too much time, and now they threatened to waste even more.

Milton didn't know if Madison was still alive, but if she was, and if she was in danger, the longer they wasted with him made it less likely that they would be able to help her.

The speaker came to the end of her share, wiping away the tears that had fallen down her cheeks. Smulders thanked her, there was warm applause, and then the arms went up as men and women who had found similarities between the speaker's story and their own – that was what they were enjoined to look for, not differences – lined up to share their own feelings. Milton listened for ten minutes but couldn't help zoning out again.

Richie Grimes put his hand up. He had come into the room late, and Milton hadn't noticed him. He looked now and saw, with shock, that the man's face was badly bruised. His right eye was swollen and almost completely shut, a bruise that ran from black to deep purple all the way around it. There was a cut on his forehead that had been sutured shut and another beneath his chin. Milton watched as he lowered his arm again; he moved gingerly, pain flickering on his face. Broken ribs.

'My name is Richie, and I'm an alcoholic.'

'Hi, Richie,' they all said.

'Yeah,' he said. 'Look at the fucking state of me, right? It's like what I've been sharing about the past few months, you know, the trouble I'm in? I guess maybe I was hoping it was all bluster, that it'd go away, but I always knew that was just wishful thinking. So I was coming home from work last night, and – *boom* – that was it, I got jumped from behind by these two goons with baseball bats. Broken nose, two broken ribs. I got a week to pay back all the money that I owe or they're coming back. I'd tell the police, but there's nothing they can do – what are they gonna do, put a man on me twenty-four hours? Nah' – he shook his head – 'that ain't gonna happen. If I can't find the money, I'm gonna get more of the same, and now, with the ribs and everything, I'm not sure I can even work properly. I gotta tell you, I'm closer to a drink today than I have been for months. I've been to two other meetings today already. Kinda feel like I'm hanging on by my fingertips.'

The others nodded their understanding and agreement. The woman next to him rested her hand on his shoulder, and others used his story to bounce off similar experiences of their own. If Richie was looking for advice, he didn't get any – that was "grandiose" and not what you came to A.A. to find – but he got sympathy and empathy and examples that he could use as a bulwark against the temptation of getting drunk.

Milton listened to the simple tales that were told, his head down and his hands clasped tightly on his lap. The meeting drew towards a close, and Smulders looked over to him and nodded. It was time. Milton took the pamphlet that his fingers had been fretting with all meeting and cleared his throat.

"'If we are painstaking about this phase of our development, we will be amazed before we are halfway through. We are going to know a new freedom and a new happiness. We will not regret the past nor wish to shut the door on it.'" He cleared his throat awkwardly. "'We will comprehend the word serenity and we will know peace. No matter how far along scale we have gone, we will see how our experience can benefit others. The feeling of uselessness and self-pity will disappear. We will lose interest in selfish things and gain interest in our fellows. Self-seeking will slip away. Our whole attitude and outlook upon life will change. Fear of people and of economic insecurity will leave us. We will intuitively know how to handle situations which used to baffle us. We will suddenly realise that God is doing for us what we could not do for ourselves. Are these extravagant promises?'"

The group chimed back at him, 'We think not.'

"'They are being fulfilled among us – sometimes quickly, sometimes slowly. They will always materialise if we work for them.'"

Peace.

Serenity.

We will not regret the past nor wish to shut the door on it.

We will *not* regret?

Milton doubted that could ever possibly come to pass. Not for him. His transgressions were different to those of the others. He hadn't soiled himself in the office, slapped his wife or crashed his car. He had killed nearly one hundred and fifty men and women. He knew that he would always regret the past, every day for as long as he lived, and what was the point in even trying to shut the door on it? The room behind his door was stuffed full of bodies, stacked all the way up to the ceiling, one hundred and fifty corpses and gallons of blood, and the door wouldn't begin to close.

They said the Lord's Prayer and filed out. Milton put away the coffee and biscuits and started to clean up. The usual group of people were gathering in the lobby to go for their meal together, and Eva was with them, smoking a cigarette and waiting for him to finish up. Milton was turning the tea urn upside down in the sink when the door to the bathroom opened and Richie Grimes hobbled out.

Milton turned to Eva and mouthed that he would be five minutes. She nodded and went outside.

'You all right?' Milton asked Grimes.

'Yeah, man.'

Milton offered the plate that had held the biscuits; it was covered with crumbs and one solitary cookie. 'Want it? Last one.'

'Sure.' Richie reached across and took it. 'Thanks. It's John, right?'

'Right.'

'Don't think I've ever heard you share.'

'I'm more of a listener,' he said. 'How are you feeling?'

'Like I've been ten rounds with Tyson.'

'But it was good to get it off your chest?'

'Sure. Getting rid of the problem's another matter. I ain't barely got a cent to my name. How am I gonna find the money he wants?'

'There'll be a way.'

'I wish I shared your confidence. The only way I can think is to get another loan, but that's just putting it off.' He gave him an underwhelming smile. 'Time to run. See you next week?'

The man looked like a prisoner being led out to the gallows. Milton couldn't let him go like that.

'This guy you owe the money to – who is he?'

'What good's it gonna do, telling you that?'

'Try me. What's his name?'

'Martinez.'

'Works down in the Mission District?'

'That's right. You know him?'

Milton shrugged. 'Heard the name.'

'I should never have gotten involved with him.'

'If it were me, Richie, I'd make sure I stayed in my place apart from when I was at work or at meetings. I wouldn't put myself somewhere where I could get jumped again.'

'How am I gonna get the cash if I hide out at home?'

'Like I say,' Milton said, 'there'll be a way. That's what they tell us, right – we put our faith in a power greater than ourselves.'

'I've been praying for six months, John. If there's a power, it ain't been listening.'

'Keep praying.'

20

Arlen Crawford was nervous. The first debate was two weeks to the day before the primary. It was held in a converted hat factory that had been turned into a new media hub with start-ups suckling the teats of the angel investor who owned the building, offering space in exchange for a little equity. There was a large auditorium that had only recently been done out, still smelling of fresh paint. There was a live audience, card-carrying local party members packed into the cramped seating like sardines in a tin. There was a row at the front – fitted with much more comfortable seating – that was reserved for the heavy-hitters from Washington, who had made the trip west to see the candidates in action for the first time.

Crawford looked down from the back of the room and onto the temporary stage, bathed in the glare of the harsh television lights. Each candidate had a lectern with a name card placed along the top. Governor Robinson's was in the centre; that had been the prize following an hour's horse-trading with the other candidates. The prime position would be fought over for the remaining two debates. Other bargaining chips included the speaking order, whether or not there would be opening and closing remarks, and a host of other ephemera that might have appeared trivial to the unenlightened observer. Crawford did not see them that way at all; to the politicos who were guiding the campaigns of the candidates, they were almost worth dying for. You lose the little battles and you better get ready to lose the war.

Robinson moved among his rivals like a Mafia don, giving them his double-clasped handshake, clapping them on the shoulders, squeezing their biceps, all the while shining out his gleaming smile. He laughed at their jokes and made his own, the consummate professional.

Crawford didn't have that ease with people, and never had. It was an unctuousness that you had to possess if you were going to make it as a player on the national stage. That was fine. He was happy with his strengths, and he recognised his weaknesses. That kind of self-awareness, in itself, was something that was rare to find and valuable to possess.

Robinson had amazing talents, but his instincts were off. Crawford's instincts were feral, animal. He was a strategist, a street fighter, and you needed a whole different set of skills for that. Robinson was surface, but Crawford was detail. He devoured every tiny bit of public life. He hovered above things like a hawk, aware of the smallest nuances yet always conscious of the whole. He could see how one small change might affect things now or eleven moves down the line. It wasn't a calculation he was aware of making; it was something that he processed, understood on a fundamental level.

One of the local party big shots came into the room and announced that it was time. Robinson, who was talking to the senator for New Mexico, wished everyone good luck. Crawford waited at the back, absorbing the energy of the room and the confidence – or lack thereof – that he could see in the other candidates. The retinues filtered into the auditorium. He hooked a doughnut from the refreshment table and followed them.

* * *

The debate couldn't have started any better. Robinson was totally in control, delivering his opening position with statesmanlike charm, so much so that Crawford found himself substituting the drab surroundings of the auditorium for what he imagined the General Assembly of the United Nations might look like with his boss before the lectern, or with the heavy blue drapes of the Oval Office closed behind him during an address to the nation. He was, Crawford thought with satisfaction, presidential.

The first question was posed – something on healthcare reform – and Robinson stayed away from it. The others went back and forth, each of them losing something as they sought to deploy the best lines, the most effective soundbites.

'Next question,' the moderator said.

'Delores Orpenshaw.' A shrew in a green dress and white pearls. 'The way folk around here see it, this country is broken. My question for the candidates is simple: how would they fix it?'

'Governor Robinson?'

Crawford felt the momentary chill of electricity: nerves.

Robinson looked the questioner right in the eye. 'How would I fix it? Well, Delores, there are some pretty fundamental things that we need to do right away. We need to reverse the flood of Third World immigration. We need to stop the flow, and we need to send back the ones who are here illegally.'

Robinson went off on a prepared riff but, as usual, made it look spontaneous. He railed against liberal snowflakes, somehow managed to get onto climate change, jumped across to reviving the manufacturing industry and then bringing glory back to the country. It was a bravura performance; there was a smattering of applause that grew in intensity, triggering more applause and then more, and then, suddenly, it had become a wave as the audience – almost all of them – rose to their feet and anointed the governor with an ovation. The moderator struggled to make her voice heard as she asked the others for their views. None of them looked like they wanted any part of the follow-up.

It went on for another hour in the same vein. Robinson picked his spots and was rewarded volubly every time he finished speaking. Eventually, the moderator brought the debate to an end. They made their way to the spin room, where Crawford and the rest of his team split up and worked the room, buttonholing the hacks from the nationals, talking up the points that Robinson had made that had gone down well and quietly de-emphasising the points that hadn't found their marks. There was no need to spin things.

They had won, and it hadn't even been close.

21

Milton turned the key. The ignition fired, but the engine didn't start. He paused, cranked it again, but still there was nothing. He had serviced the car himself a month ago, and it had all looked all right, but this didn't sound good. He drummed his fingers against the wheel.

Eva paused at the door of her Porsche and looked over quizzically.

He put his fingers to the key and twisted it a final time. The ignition coughed, then spluttered, then choked off to a pitiful whine. The courtesy light dimmed as the battery drained from turning over the engine. He popped the hood, opened the door and went around to take a look.

'Not good?' Eva said, coming over as he bent over the engine.

'Plugs, I think. They need changing.'

Eva had insisted they come back to Top Notch. Julius had never let him down, and the meal had been predictably good. The unease that Milton had felt after reading the Promises had quickly been forgotten in her company. He almost forgot the interview with the police. They had talked about the others at the meeting, slandering Smulders in particular; they agreed that he was well meaning, if a little supercilious, and she had suggested that he had form for coming onto the new, vulnerable male members of the fellowship. She had cocked an eyebrow at him as she had said it. Milton couldn't help but laugh at the suggestion. His troubles were quickly subsumed beneath the barrage of her wit as she took apart the other members of the group. The gossip wasn't cruel, but nevertheless, he had wondered what she might say about him in private. He had said that to her, feigning concern, and she had put a finger to her lips and winked with unmistakeable salaciousness. By the end of the main course Milton knew that he was attracted to her, and he knew that the feeling was mutual.

She watched now as he let the hood drop back into place.

'What are you going to do?'

'Walk, I guess.'

'Where's your place?'

'Mission District.'

'That's miles.'

That much was true. He wouldn't be home much before midnight, and then he would have to come back out in the morning – via a garage – to change the plugs. He was a little concerned about his finances, too. He had been planning to go out and drive tonight. He needed the cash. That obviously wasn't going to happen.

'Come on – I'll give you a ride.'

'You don't have to do that.'

'You're not walking,' she said with a determined conviction.

Milton was going to demur, but he thought of the time and the chance to get some sleep to prime him for the day tomorrow, and he realised that would have been foolish. 'Thanks,' he conceded as he locked the Explorer and walked over to her Cayenne with her.

The car was new and smelt it. It wasn't much of a guess to say that her job paid well – her wardrobe was as good a giveaway as anything – but as Milton settled back in the leather bucket seat, he thought that perhaps he had underestimated how well off she really was.

She must have noticed his appraising look as he took in the cabin. 'I've got a thing for nice cars,' she said, a little apologetically.

'It's better than nice.'

'Nice cars and nice clothes. It used to be Cristal and coke. The way I see it, if you're going to have an addiction, it better be one that leaves you with something to show for it.'

She put on an old Jay-Z album as she drove him across town. Milton guided her into the Mission District, picking the quickest way to his apartment. The area was in poor condition; plenty of the buildings were boarded up, others blackened from fire or degraded by squatters with no interest in maintaining them. The cheap rents attracted artists and students, and there was a bohemian atmosphere that was, in its own way, quite attractive. But it felt even cheaper than usual tonight, and as Milton looked out of the window of the gleaming black Porsche, he felt inadequate. He and Eva shared a weakness for booze, but that was it; he started to worry that there was a distance between the way they lived their lives that would be difficult to bridge.

The El Capitan Hotel and Hostel was a three-storey building with eighty rooms. The frontage was decorated with an ornate pediment and a cinema-style awning that advertised 'OPEN 24 HOURS A DAY' and 'PUBLIC PARKING – OPEN 24 HOURS'. It was a dowdy street, full of tatty shops and restaurants. To the left of the hotel was the Arabian Nights restaurant and, to the right, Modern Hair Cuts. Queen's Shoes and Siegel's Fashion for Men and Boys were opposite. There were tall palm trees, and the overhead electricity lines buzzed and fizzed in the fog.

'This is me,' Milton said.

Eva pulled up outside the building.

She killed the engine. 'Thanks for dinner.'

'Yeah,' he said. 'That was fun.'

There was a moment's silence. 'So – um . . . ?' she said.

He looked at her with an uncertainty that he knew was ridiculous.

'You gonna invite me up?'

'You sure that's a good idea?'

She smiled. 'What do you mean? Two recovering addicts? What could possibly go wrong?'

'That's not what I meant.'

'Really?'

'Maybe it was.'

'So?'

He paused, couldn't find the words, and laughed at the futility of it. 'Come on, then. It's at the top of the building, so you're going to have to walk. And I'll warn you now, save the view, it's nothing to write home about. It's not five-star.'

'Not what I'm used to, you mean?' She grinned. 'Fuck you, too.'

She locked the Cayenne and followed him to the door of the building. The narrow heels of her shoes clacked against the pavement as she took his arm and held it tightly. He was aware of the powerful scent of her perfume and the occasional pressure of her breast against his arm. He opened up and accepted her hand as she pressed it into his.

The reception was incredibly bright; the fluorescent tubes did not flicker, shining down harshly. The night manager nodded at them from behind the glass enclosure. There were all manner of people here. For some, it was a permanent residence, and for others, a room for the night. Many of the residents had mental-health problems, and Milton had seen plenty of disturbances in the time he had been there. No one had ever bothered him – the cold lifelessness behind his eyes was warning enough – and the place had served him well.

They climbed the stairs together, and he gently disengaged as he reached into his pocket for the key to his door. Milton opened the door. Inside was simple and ascetic, but it was all he could afford. The owner was happy enough to take cash, which saved him from the necessity of opening a bank account, something he was very reluctant to do.

Milton's apartment was tiny, an eight-by-twelve room that was just big enough for a double bed with a chair next to it and a small table next to that. There wasn't much else. The bathroom and kitchen were shared with the other rooms on the floor. Milton had always travelled light, so storing clothes wasn't an issue; he had two of everything, and when one set was dirty, he took it down to the laundromat around the corner and washed it. He had no interest in a television, and his only entertainment was the radio and his books: several volumes of Dickens, Greene, Orwell, Joyce and Conan Doyle.

'What do you think?' he said, a slightly bashful expression on his usually composed face.

'It's . . . minimalist.'

'That's one way of describing it.'

'You don't have much . . . *stuff*, do you?'

'I've never been much of one for things,' he explained.

She cast a glance around again. 'No pictures.'

'I'm not married. No family.'

'Parents?'

'They died when I was a boy.'

'Sorry.'

'Don't be. It was years ago.'

'Siblings?'

'No. Just me.'

He had a small pair of charged speakers on the windowsill; he walked across and plugged these into his phone, opening the radio application and selecting the local talk radio channel. The presenter was discussing the Republican primary; the challengers had just debated each other for the first time. The candidates were trying to differentiate themselves from their rivals. J.J. Robinson, the governor of Florida, was in the lead, by all accounts. They were saying that the primary was his to lose. Milton killed the radio app and scrolled through to his music player. He selected *Rated R* by the Queens of the Stone Age and picked out the slow, drawled funk of 'Leg of Lamb'.

'Good choice,' she said.

'I thought so.'

The room was on the third floor, and the window offered a good view of the city. She stood and looked out as he went through the affectation of boiling the kettle for a pot of tea. It was a distraction; they both knew that neither would drink a drop.

Milton took the pot to the table and sat down on the edge of the bed; she sat on the chair next to him. She turned, maybe to say something, maybe not, and he leant across to press his lips gently to hers. He paused, almost wincing with the potential embarrassment that he had misjudged the situation even though he knew that he had not, and then she moved towards him and kissed harder. He closed his eyes and lost himself for a moment. He was only dimly aware of the physical sensations: her breath on his cheek, her arms snaked around his shoulders as her mouth held his, her fingers playing against the back of his neck. She pulled away and looked into his face. Her fingers reached up and traced their way along the scar that began at his cheek and ended below his nose. She kissed it tenderly.

'How'd you do that?'

'Bar fight.'

'Someone had a knife?'

Milton had no wish to discuss the events of that night – he had been drunk, and it had ended badly for the other guy – so he reached for her again, his hand cupping around her head and drawing her closer. Her perfume was pungent, redolent of fresh fruit, and he breathed it in deeply. He pulled off her sweater and eased her back onto the bed with him. They kissed hungrily. He cupped her neck again and pulled her face to his while her hands found their way inside his shirt and around, massaging his muscular shoulders. They explored their bodies hungrily, and Milton soon felt dizzy with desire. Her lips were soft and full; her legs wrapped around his waist and squeezed him tight; her underwear was expensively insubstantial, her breasts rising up and down as she gulped for air. He kissed her sweet-smelling neck and throat as she whispered out a moan of pleasure. He brushed aside the hair that framed her face. They kissed again.

His mobile buzzed.

She broke away and locked onto his eyes with her own.

Her eyes smiled.

'Don't worry. I'm not answering.'

The phone went silent.

He kissed her.

Ten seconds later, it rang again.

'Someone wants to speak to you.'

'Sorry.'

'Who is it? Another woman?'

He laughed. 'Hardly.'

'Go on – the sooner you answer, the sooner they'll shut up. You're all mine tonight.'

Milton took the call.

'Mr Smith?'

The boy's voice was wired with anxiety. 'Trip – is everything all right?'

'Did you see the police today?'

'Yes,' he said.

'They say you're a suspect?'

'Not in as many words, but that's the gist of it. I'm one of the last people to see her before she disappeared. It stands to reason.'

'They had me in, too. Three hours straight.'

'And?'

'I don't know. I think maybe they think I'm a suspect, too.'

'Don't worry about it. They're doing what they think they have to do. Standard procedure. Most murders are committed by— well, you know.'

'People who knew the victim? Yeah, I know.'

Milton disentangled himself from Eva and stood. 'You haven't done anything. They'll figure that out. This is all routine. Ticking boxes. The good thing is that they're taking it seriously.'

'Yeah, man – like, finally.'

Milton took out his cigarettes and shook one out of the box. He looked over at Eva. She was looking at him with a quizzical expression on her face. He held up the box, and she nodded. He tossed it across the room to her, pressed the cigarette between his lips and lit it. He threw her the lighter.

'There was another reason for calling.'

'Go on.'

'I had a call ten minutes ago. There's this guy, Aaron; he says he was the driver who usually drove Madison to her jobs. He was the guy who didn't show the night she went missing, so she called you. He heard about what's happened on the TV.'

'How did he get your number?'

'Called the landline. Madison must've given it to him.'

'You need to tell him to go to the police. They'll definitely want to talk to him.'

'He won't, Mr Smith. He's frightened.'

'Of what?'

'He knows the agency she was working for. He says they're not exactly on the level. If he rats them out, they'll come after him.'

'You need to tell the police, Trip.'

'I would, Mr Smith, but this guy, he says he'll only speak to me. He says he'll tell me everything.'

'When?'

'Tomorrow morning. I said I'd meet him at Dottie's. Nine.'

Milton knew it. Dottie's was a San Francisco institution, and conveniently enough, it was right at the top of Sixth Street, just a couple of minutes from the El Capitan. Milton yanked up the sash window and tossed the cigarette outside. 'I'll be there.'

The relief in Trip's thanks was unmistakeable.

'Don't worry. Try to sleep. We'll deal with this tomorrow.'

Milton ended the call.

'What was that?'

Milton hadn't told Eva anything about Madison, but he explained it all now: the night she disappeared, Trip and the days that he had helped him to look for her, the dead bodies that had turned up on the headland, the interview with the police.

'Did you have a lawyer there?' she said. There was indignation in her voice.

'I didn't think I needed one.'

'They spoke to you without one?'

'I haven't done anything.'

'Are you an idiot?' she said angrily. 'You don't speak to the police investigating a *murder* without a lawyer, John.'

'Really,' he said, smiling at her. 'It was fine. I know what I'm doing.'

'No,' she insisted, sitting up. 'You don't. Promise me, if they bring you in again, you tell them you're not speaking until I get there. All right?'

'Sure,' he replied. 'All right.'

'What did he want?'

Milton related what Trip had told him.

'All right, then. This is what we're going to do. I'm taking tomorrow morning off. I'll drive you so you can get your car fixed and then you can go and see him.'

'You don't have to do that.'

'You don't listen much, do you, John? This isn't a democracy. That's what we're doing. It's not open to debate.'

22

Eva drove Milton to the garage to pick up a new set of spark plugs and then they returned to Top Notch. She waited while he changed the plugs and until the engine was running again.

He went over to the Porsche. They hadn't said much during the ride across town to his car, and he felt a little uncomfortable. He had never been the best when it came to talking about his feelings. He had never been able to afford the luxury before, and it didn't come naturally to him.

'Thanks for the ride,' he said.

'Charming!'

He laughed, blushing. 'I didn't mean—'

'I know what you meant,' she said, the light dancing in her eyes. 'I'm joking.'

The words clattered into each other. 'Oh – never mind.'

'You're a funny guy, John,' she said. 'Relax, all right? I had a nice night.'

'*Nice?*'

'All right – better than nice. It was *so nice* that I'd like to do it again. You up for that?'

'Sure.'

'Be at the next meeting. My place for dinner afterwards. Now – come here.'

He leant down and rather awkwardly kissed her through the window.

'What's up?'

'I was wondering,' he said. 'Could you do me a favour?'

'Sure.'

He told her about Doctor Andrew Brady and his potential involvement on the night that Madison went missing. He explained that he had worked at St Francis, like she did, and asked if she could find out anything about him.

'You want me to pull someone's personnel file?' she asked with mock outrage. 'Someone's *confidential* personnel file?'

'Could you?'

'Sure,' she said. 'Can you make it worth my while?'

'I can try.'

'Give me a couple of days,' she said.

'See you,' he said.

'You will.'

* * *

Trip was waiting outside Dottie's, pacing nervously, catching frequent glances at his watch. He was wearing a woollen beanie, and he reached his fingers beneath it, scratching his scalp anxiously. His face cleared a little when he saw Milton.

'Sorry I'm late. Traffic. Is he here?'

'Think so. The guy at the back – at the counter.'

'All right. That's good.'

'How we gonna play this?'

'I want you to introduce yourself and then tell him who I am, but it might turn out best if I do the talking after that, okay? We'll play it by ear and see how we get on.'

'What are we going to do?'

'Just talk. Get his story.'

'And then the police?'

'Let's see what he's got to say first – then we decide what we do next.'

The café was reasonably large, with exposed beams running the length of the ceiling with a flat glass roof above. The brickwork was exposed along one side, there was a busy service area with a countertop around it, and the guests were seated at freestanding tables. Blackboards advertised breakfast and a selection of flavoured coffees. A counter held home-made cakes under clear plastic covers, and wooden shelving bore crockery and condiments. A single candelabra-style light fitting hung down from the ceiling, and there were black-and-white pictures of old Hollywood starlets on the walls. The room was full.

Milton assessed the man at the counter automatically: the clothes were expensive, the empty mug suggested that he was nervous, the Ray-Bans he still hadn't removed confirming it. He was sitting so that he could see the entrance, his head tilting left and right as he made constant wary assessments of the people around him. Milton paused so that Trip could advance a step ahead of him and then followed the boy across the room.

'Aaron?' Trip asked.

'Yeah, man. Trip, right?'

'Yes.'

He looked up, frowned and stabbed a finger at Milton. 'He with you?'

'Yes.'

'So who is he?'

'It's all right. He's a friend.'

'Ain't my friend, bro. I said just *you*. Just you and me.'

'He was driving Madison the night she went missing.'

That softened him a little. 'That right?'

'That's right,' Milton said.

'I don't like surprises, all right? You should've said.'

'Shall we get a table?'

A booth had emptied out. Aaron and Trip went first; Milton bought coffees and followed them.

'Thanks,' Aaron said as Milton put the drinks on the table. 'What's your name, man?'

'I'm Smith.'

'You a driver, then?'

'That's right.'

'Freelance or agency?'

'Mostly freelance, bit of agency.'

'Police been speaking to you?'

'All afternoon yesterday.'

The hardness in his face broke apart. 'I'm sorry about you being involved in all this shit. It's my fault. It should've been me that night, right? I mean, I'd been driving her for ages. The one night I didn't turn up, that one night, and . . . I can't help thinking if it had've been me, she'd still be here, you know?'

There was an unsaid accusation in that, too: if it were me, and not you, she would still be here. Milton let it pass. 'You were good friends?'

'Yeah,' he said with an awkward cough. 'She's a good person. Out of all the girls I've driven, she's the only one I could say I ever really had any kind of fun with.' He looked at Trip and, realising the implication of what he had just said, added, not persuasively, 'As a friend, you know – a good friend.'

Milton found himself wondering if that disclaimer was insincere – the way his eyes flicked away from Trip as he delivered it – and whether Aaron and Madison had been sleeping together. The boy was certainly all broken up about what had happened. Milton wondered whether Trip had started to arrive at the same conclusion. If he had, he was doing a good job of hiding it.

'What do the police think has happened to her?'

'They've got no idea,' Trip said. 'It took them finding the bodies on the headland for them to start taking it seriously. Up until then she was just a missing person, some girl who decided she didn't want to come home, nothing worth getting excited about.'

'Jesus.'

'Why didn't you call before?' Milton asked him.

'I don't know,' he said. 'I felt awkward about it, I guess, you being her boyfriend and all.'

'Why would that matter?' Trip said tersely.

189

'No, of course, it wouldn't—'

Milton nudged Trip beneath the table with his knee. 'You said you could tell us who Madison was working for.'

'Yeah,' Aaron said vaguely. 'Same agency I work for, right?'

'Has it got a name?'

'Fallen Angelz. It's this Italian guy, Salvatore something, don't know his second name. I was out of work, got fired from the bar I was working at; I had a friend of a friend who was driving for them. I had no idea what it was all about until he explained it to me. I had no job, no money, not even a car, but I had a clean licence, and I thought it sounded like an easy way to make a bit of cash, maybe meet some people, a bit of fun, you know? Turns out I was right about that.'

'How did it work?'

'Straightforward. The girls get a booking, some john all on his own or a frat party or something bigger – some rich dude from out of town wants company all night, willing to pay for a girl to come to his hotel room. Celebrities, lawyers, doctors – you would *not* believe some of the guys I drove girls to see. Each girl gets assigned a driver. If it's me, the dispatcher in the office calls me up on my cell and tells me where I have to go to pick her up. They gave me a sweet whip, a tricked-out Lexus, all the extras. So I head over there, drive her out to wherever the party's at, then hang around until the gig's finished and drive her back home again or to the next job, whatever's happening. It's a piece of cake; the more girls I drive, the more money I make.'

'You get a slice of their takings?'

'That's right. When you've got a girl charging a grand for an hour and she's out there for two, maybe three hours, well, man, you can imagine, you can see how it can be a pretty lucrative gig, right? I was getting more money in a night than I could earn in two weeks serving stiffs in a bar.'

'What about drugs?' Milton asked.

Trip shot a glance at him.

'What about them?' Aaron said.

'They ever involved?'

He shifted uncomfortably. 'Sure, man, what do you think? These girls ain't saints. The agency offered it to customers as an extra and I'd bring it along. Sometimes I'll get some to sell myself. I've lived here my whole life; it's not like I don't know the right guys to ask, you know what I'm saying?' He delivered that line with a blasé shrug of his shoulders, like it was no big thing, but Milton wasn't impressed and fixed him in a cold stare. 'I ain't *endorsing* it,' Aaron backtracked. 'Can't say I was ever totally comfortable with having shit in the car, but the money's too good to ignore. You can make the same on top as you do with the girls.'

'What about Madison?' Milton asked. 'Does she use at all?'

'Yeah, man, sure she does.'

'*Bullshit*,' Trip said.

Aaron looked at Trip with a pained expression. 'You don't know?'

'She doesn't.'

'It's the truth, dude, I swear. They use, all of them do.'

Trip flinched but held his tongue.

'What does she use?' Milton asked.

'Coke. Weed.'

'Anything hallucinogenic?'

He shook his head. 'Never seen that.'

'All right. Tell us about her.'

Aaron shifted uncomfortably. 'What do you want to know?'

'Everything.'

He shrugged again. 'I don't know, man. I'd driven her before, this one time, maybe a year ago. We hit it off right away. She's a great girl, a lot of fun – the only girl I ever drove who I looked forward to seeing. Most of them— well, most of them, let's just say they're not the best when it comes to conversation, all right? A little dead behind the eyes, some of them; not the smartest cookies. But she's different.'

'Go on.'

He looked over at Trip and then back to Milton. He looked pained. 'Is this really necessary?'

'Come on,' Trip insisted. 'Don't pussy out now.' He must have known where this was going, but he was tough, and he wasn't going to flinch.

Aaron sighed helplessly. 'All right, man. I guess this was seven, eight months ago, before she went missing. The dispatcher said it was her, and I was happy about it. I'd had the same girl for a week, and she was driving me crazy. I went over to Nob Hill and picked Madison up in the Lexus. She talked and talked, told me everything that was going on in her life. Turns out that they put us together for two shifts after that. That's like almost two whole days and nights. The third time out, it was quiet, just two or three gigs, and we talked more. The next night was the same. I found a place to park the car and we had a drink. I had a wrap of coke in the glove compartment, and we ended up doing bumps of that, too. She said things about the work that I hadn't heard from the other girls.'

Aaron cleared his throat and looked down at the table.

'Keep going,' Milton said, knowing what was coming next and hating himself for pressing, hating what it was going to do to Trip.

'Then – I guess it just sort of happened. We had sex.'

'And?'

'She said she liked it. I didn't really believe it, but then, the next time I was driving her, like a couple of days after that, it happened again.'

Trip stood abruptly. Without saying a word, he turned on his heel and stalked out of the café.

'I'm sorry, man,' Aaron said helplessly. 'I didn't want to say—'

Milton stared at him. 'Keep going.'

He frowned, his eyes on the table again. 'I had a girlfriend then, but I ended it. I couldn't stop thinking about Madison. I knew it wasn't right. My girl was cut up, and I knew Madison had a guy, but I couldn't help it – neither of us could help it. I was getting pretty deep into working for the agency then, and my girl had always been jealous about that, the girls I was driving, but Madison didn't have any of that. No jealousy, just totally cool about it all. She got me, totally, understood where I was coming from. Sometimes I drove her, and sometimes I didn't, but it didn't matter. We were both cool with how it was. When I drove her, we slept together between calls. Sometimes she'd pretend to be on call during the day, but she'd meet me, we'd check into a hotel and stay there all day.'

'What was she like?'

'How do you mean?'

'Ever think she was depressed?'

'She had her moments, like all the girls, but no – I don't think so. If you mean do I think she's run away or done something worse, then, no, I'd say there was no chance. That'd be completely out of character. You want my opinion, I'd say that something bad has happened. No way she stays out of touch this long. She says nothing to me, nothing to your friend – no, no way, I ain't buying that.'

'You know you have to tell the police, don't you?'

'About us?'

'Yes, and about the agency.'

His eyes flickered with fear. 'No way, man. Talk to the cops? You mad? Salvatore, he's connected, you know what I mean? *Connected.* It's not like I know everything about how it works, but my best guess, the things I heard from the girls and the other drivers, he's fronting it for the Lucianos. You know them, man? The fucking *Lucianos?* It's fucking Mafia, right? The *Mafia!* Ain't no way I'm getting myself in a position where they might think I was ratting them out to the cops. No way. You know what happens to guys they reckon are rats, right?'

'Your name doesn't have to come out.'

'Fuck that shit, man! What you been smoking? That kind of stuff don't ever stay under wraps. They got cops on the payroll; everyone knows it. My name would be on the street in minutes, and then they'll be coming over to talk to me about it, and that ain't something that I want to think about. Next thing, I'd be floating in the bay with my throat cut. Fish food, man.'

'All right,' Milton said, smiling in the hope that he might relax a little. 'It's okay. I understand.'

Aaron looked at him suspiciously. 'You're just a driver, right?'

'That's right.'

'So why you asking all the questions, then?'

He spoke with careful, exaggerated patience. 'Because I'm one of the last people to have seen Madison before she disappeared. That means I'm a suspect, and I'd rather that I wasn't. Trip is a suspect now, too, and it'll probably get worse for him when the police find out that you were sleeping with his woman. Jealousy, right? That's a good motive. The more information you can give us, maybe that'll make it easier for us to find out what happened to her, and then maybe the police will realise me and him had nothing to do with it. Understand?'

'You wait for her that night?'

'Yes.'

'Why didn't you help her, then? If it was me out there, I guarantee nothing would've happened.'

Milton looked at him dead straight, staring right into his eyes; the boy immediately looked down into the dregs of his coffee. 'She didn't give me a chance,' Milton said sternly. 'Something happened to her at that party, and there wasn't anything I could do about it. By the time I got to her, she was already in a mess.'

'So where is she?'

'She ran. That's all I know.'

Aaron gestured towards the door. 'That dude – you tell him I'm sorry, will you? I didn't want to say anything, and you know, muscling in on another guy's girl, that ain't the way I do things, that ain't my style at all, you know what I'm saying?'

'I'm sure it isn't,' Milton said.

'All right,' he said. 'I'm done.'

'The agency. How can I get in touch with them?'

'What are you gonna do?'

'I'm going to visit them.'

'And?'

'And get as much information as I can.'

'No way, man. I *can't*. That shit's gonna come back to me, right? They'll figure out I've been talking. I don't know. I don't know at all.'

Aaron got up quickly, the chair scraping loudly against the floor. He made to leave, but Milton reached out a hand, grabbed the boy around the bicep and squeezed.

'Shit, dude!' he exclaimed. 'That hurts.'

Milton relaxed his grip a little, but he didn't let go. 'Have a think about it,' he said, his voice quiet and even. 'Think about Madison. If you care about her at all, you give me a call and tell me how I can get in touch with the agency. Don't make me come and find you. Do we understand each other?'

'Shit, man, yeah – all right.'

Milton took a pen from his pocket, pulled a napkin from the chrome dispenser and wrote his number on it. 'This is me,' he said, putting it in the boy's hand. 'Take the rest of the day to think about it, and call me. Okay?'

The boy gulped down his fear and nodded.

Milton released his grip.

23

Milton drove them as near to Headlands Lookout as he could get. Trip was nervous, fidgeting next to him, almost as if he expected them to find something. The police had blocked the road a hundred yards from the car park, a broad cordon cutting from the rocky outcropping on the right all the way down to the edge of the cliff on the left. Half a dozen outside-broadcast trucks had been allowed down to the lot, and they were crammed in together, satellite dishes angled in the same direction and their various antennae bristling.

Milton slowed and pulled off the narrow road, cramming the Explorer up against the rock so that there was just enough space for cars to pass it to the left. The sky was a slate grey vault overhead, and rain was lashing against the windscreen, pummelling it on the back of a strong wind coming right off the Pacific. Visibility was decent despite the brutal weather, and as Milton disembarked, he gazed out to the south, all the way to the city on the other side of the bay.

They made their way through the cordon and down to the car park. There were several dozen people there already, arranged in an untidy scrum before a man who was standing on a raised slope where the cameras could all get a decent view of him. Milton recognised him. It was Commissioner William Reagan, the head of the local police. He was an old man, close to retirement, his careworn face chiselled by years of stress and disappointment. The wind tousled his short shock of white hair. He pulled his long cloak around him, the icy rain driven across the bleak scene. An officer was holding an umbrella for him, but it wasn't giving him much shelter; he wiped moisture from his face with the back of his hand.

'Ladies and gentlemen,' he said into the upheld microphones, 'before I get into my remarks, let me identify those who are here with me. I got Chief of Detectives Stewart Webster – everyone knows the chief – and I got Inspector Richard Cotton.' He cleared his throat and pulled out a sheet of paper. 'As you know, we've found two bodies along this stretch of the headland. I wish we hadn't, but that's the sad fact of it. It appears that they were taken down from the road into the foliage and hidden there so that they wouldn't be seen. We're assuming they were dumped here by the same person or persons.'

A brusque man from cable news shouted loudest as he paused for breath. 'You identified them yet?'

'No,' Reagan said. 'Not yet.'

'So you're saying you've got a serial killer dumping victims along this stretch of land?'

'It would be a big coincidence if it was two separate people.'

'You expect to find anyone else?'

'That's impossible to say. But we're looking.'

'So are you, or are you not, looking at it being the same guy?'

'Well, you know, I'm not gonna say that, but, certainly, we're looking at that.'

* * *

The press roadshow decamped and moved to Belvedere. A slow crawl of traffic worked sluggishly along the narrow road, with Milton and Trip caught in the middle of it. Their purpose in driving out of the city had been to go and speak to Brady, but Milton had not anticipated all this extra company. It made him nervous. The vehicles turned left and headed north, taking the right and doubling back to the south.

Milton gripped the wheel tightly and ran the morning's developments through his mind. It wasn't surprising that they had reached the conclusion that Madison's disappearance must have been connected. Why not? Two working girls turning up murdered just a few miles away, another working girl goes missing: it was hardly a stretch to think that she was dead, too, and dead at the hands of the same killer.

As they reached Pine Shore, it was obvious that the prospect of a community of potential suspects was just too tempting to ignore. The gates stood open – it looked as if they had been forced – and the cavalcade had spilled inside. Reporters and their cameramen had set up outside the two key properties: the house where the party had taken place and Dr Brady's cottage. Police cars were parked nearby, but the cops inside seemed content to let them get on with things.

Milton parked the Explorer and joined Trip at the front of the car. They watched as two reporters for national news channels delivered their assessments of the case so far – the discovery of the two bodies, the fact that a third girl had gone missing here – and suggested that the police were linking the investigations.

Milton looked at the cameras.

'We shouldn't be here,' he said, more to himself than to the boy.

'What are they doing outside his place?' Trip said, his eyes blazing angrily as he started up the street towards Brady's cottage.

'Trip – stop.'

'They think *he* did it, right? That must be it.'

Milton followed after him and took him by the shoulder. 'We need to get back in the car. They'll be all over us if they see us and figure out who we are.'

Trip shook his hand away. 'I don't care about that. I want to speak to him.'

He set off again.

Milton paused. He knew he should leave him, get back into the car and drive back to the city. He had been stupid to come up here. He should have guessed that it would be swarming with press. It stood to reason. He didn't know if they would be able to identify him, but if they did, if he was filmed and if the footage was broadcast? *That* would be very dangerous indeed.

Milton's phone vibrated in his pocket.

'Hello?'

'Mr Smith?'

'Speaking.'

'It's Aaron Pogue – from this morning.'

Milton put his hand over the microphone. 'Trip!'

He paused and turned. 'What?'

'It's Aaron.'

The boy came back towards him.

'You there?' said Aaron.

'Yes, I'm here. Hello, Aaron.'

'I've been thinking about what you said.'

'And?'

'And I'll tell you what you need. The agency, all that.'

'That's good, Aaron. Go on.'

'I don't have a number for the agency – the number they use when they call, it's always blocked, so there's nothing I can do to help you there. But Salvatore, the guy who runs it, I know he owns the pizza house in Fisherman's Wharf. That's just a cover – the agency is his main deal, that's his money gig; he runs it from the office out back. That's it.'

'Thank you.'

'You'll keep my name out of it?'

'I'll try.'

'I hope you find her.'

Milton ended the call.

'What did he say?'

'He told me where to find the agency.'

The thought of confronting Brady seemed to have left Trip's mind. 'Where?'

'It's in the city,' Milton said. 'Want to come?'

24

Milton parked the car on the junction of Jefferson and Taylor. He had explained his plan to Trip during the drive back into the city and persuaded him that it was better that he go in alone. Trip had objected at first, but Milton had insisted and, eventually, the boy had backed down. Milton didn't know what he was going to find, but if the agency was backed by the Mafia, what he had in mind was likely to be dangerous. He had no intention of exposing Trip to that.

'I won't be long,' he said as he opened the door. 'Wait here?'

'All right,' Trip said.

Milton stepped out and walked beneath the huge ship's wheel that marked the start of Fisherman's Wharf. He passed restaurants with their names marked on guano-stained awnings: Guardino's, The Crab Station, Sabella & LaTorre's Original Fisherman's Wharf Restaurant. Tourists gathered at windows, staring at the menus, debating the merits of one over another. A ship's bell clanged in the brisk wind that was coming off the ocean, the tang of salt was everywhere, and the clouds pressed down overhead. It was a festival of tacky nonsense, as inauthentic as it was possible to be. Milton continued down the road.

The Classic Italian Pizza and Pasta Co. was between Alioto's and The Fisherman's Grotto.

He climbed the stairs to the first floor and nodded to the maître d' as he passed him as if he were just rejoining friends at a table.

It was a decent place: a salad and pasta station, tended to by a man in a chef's tunic and a toque, was positioned beneath a large Italian tricolour; string bags full of garlic and sun-dried tomatoes hung from a rack in the area where food was prepared; a series of tables was arranged on either side of an aisle that led to the bar; the tables were covered with crisp white tablecloths, folded napkins and gleaming cutlery and glassware. Two sides of the restaurant were windowed, the view giving out onto the marina beyond on one side and the wharf on the other. It was busy. The smell of fresh pizza blew out of the big wood kiln that was the main feature of the room.

Milton went into the kitchen. A man in grimy whites was working on a bowl of crabmeat.

'I'm looking for Salvatore.'

The man shifted uncomfortably. 'Say what?'

'Salvatore. The boss. Where is he?'

'Ain't no one called Salvatore here.'

Milton was in no mood to waste time. He stalked by the man and headed for the door at the end of the kitchen. He opened the door. It was a large office. He surveyed it carefully, all eyes. First, he looked for an exit. There was one on the far wall, propped open with a fire extinguisher. There was a window, too, with a view of the wharf outside, but it was too small to be useful. There was a pool table in the middle of the room and a jukebox against the wall. There was a desk with a computer and a pile of papers. A man was sitting at the computer. He was middle-aged, burly, with heavy shoulders, biceps that strained against the sleeves of his T-shirt and meaty forearms covered in hair. Both arms were decorated with lurid tattooed sleeves, the markings running all the way down to the backs of his hands and onto his fingers.

The man spun around on his chair. 'The fuck you want?'

'Salvatore?'

He got up. 'Who are you?'

'My name is Smith.'

'And?'

'I want to talk to you.'

'You think you can just bust into my office?'

'We need to talk.'

'Then make an appointment.'

'It's about your other business.'

The man concealed the wary, nervous turn to his face behind a quick sneer. 'Yeah? What other business?'

Milton looked at him with dead eyes. He had always found that projecting a sense of perfect calm worked wonders in a situation like this. It wasn't even a question of confidence. He knew he could take Salvatore, provided there were no firearms involved to even the odds. Milton couldn't remember the last time he'd lost a fight against a single man. He couldn't remember the last time he'd lost a fight against two men, either, come to that.

'Your escort business, Salvatore.'

'Nah.'

'Fallen Angelz.'

'Never heard of it.'

'It would be better to be honest.'

'I don't know nothing about it, friend.'

Milton scanned for threats and opportunities. There were drawers in the desk that might easily contain a small pistol. No way of knowing that for sure, though, so he would just have to keep an eye on the man's hands. There was a stack of cardboard trays with beer bottles inside, still covered by cellophane wrap, but Milton wasn't worried about them. A bottle wouldn't be all that useful as a weapon, and, in any case, it would be necessary to tear through the cellophane wrap to get at them. No time for that. He glanced at the pool table. That would work. There were the balls, good for throwing or for using as blunt weapons in an open fist. There were the cues held in a vertical rack on the nearest wall. Any of those would make a decent weapon.

Milton watched the Italian carefully. He could see from the way that the veins were standing out in his neck and the clenching and unclenching of his fists that it would take very little for things to turn nasty.

'So – let's talk about it.'

'Don't you listen? I don't know what you're talking about.'

'So I wouldn't find anything in those papers if I were to have a look?'

'Reckon that'd be a pretty dumb thing to go and try to do.'

Salvatore reached down slowly and carefully pulled up the bottom of his T-shirt, exposing six inches of tattooed skin and the stippled grip of a Smith & Wesson Sigma. He rested the tips of his fingers against it, lightly curling them around the handle.

'This isn't the first time I've seen a gun.'

'Could be your last.'

Milton ignored that. 'Let me tell you some things I know, Salvatore. I know you run girls out of this office. I know you distribute drugs on the side. And I know you sent Madison Clarke to a party at the house in Pine Shore.'

'Yeah? What party was that?'

'The one where she went missing.'

He stared at him. A flicker of doubt. 'Madison Clarke? No. I don't know no one by that name.'

'I don't believe you.'

'You think I care what you believe?' He stood up now, his right hand curled more tightly around the grip of the handgun. He pointed to the telephone on the desk with his left hand. 'You know who I'm gonna call if you don't start making tracks?'

'I've no idea.'

'I'm gonna call an ambulance. I'm telling you, man, straight up, you don't get out of here right now, you won't be leaving in one piece. I'm gonna fucking shoot your ass.'

'I tell you what – you tell me all about the escorting business and maybe I won't break your arm. How's that sound?'

Salvatore slapped his hand against the gun. 'You miss this, man? Who the hell are you to tell me what to do?'

'Let's say I'm someone you don't want to annoy.'

'What's that supposed to mean?'

'I'm a concerned member of the public. And I don't like the business you're running.'

Milton assessed the distance between them – eight feet – and couldn't say for sure that he would be able to get all the way across the room before the man could draw and shoot. And if Salvatore could get the gun up in time and shoot, it would be point-blank and hard to miss.

That wasn't going to work.

Plan B.

Milton stepped quickly to the table, snatched up the eight-ball and flung it. His aim was good, and as Salvatore turned his head away to avoid it, the ball struck him on the cheekbone, shattering it.

Milton already had the pool cue, his fingers finding the thin end.

Salvatore fumbled hopelessly for the gun.

Milton swung the cue in a wide arc that terminated in the side of Salvatore's head. The wood crunched and splintered and blood splashed over the computer monitor. Salvatore slid off the chair and onto the floor. He stayed down.

Milton discarded the remains of the cue and started to look through the papers on the desk.

* * *

Trip was listening to the radio when Milton reached the Explorer again. He opened the door and slid inside, moving quickly. He started the engine and pulled away from the kerb.

'You get anything?'

'Nothing useful.'

'So it wasn't worth coming down here? We should've stayed in Belvedere?'

'I wouldn't say that. I made an impression. There'll be a follow-up.'

25

Milton heard the buzzer as he was cleaning his teeth. He wasn't expecting a delivery, and since very few people knew where he lived, he was about as sure as he could be that whoever it was who had come calling on him at eight in the morning wasn't there for the good of his health. He put the brush back in its holder and quietly opened the window just enough that he could look downwards. The window was directly above the entrance to the building, and he could see the three men who were arrayed around the door. There was a car on the corner with another man in the front. It was a big Lexus, blacked-out windows, very expensive.

Four men. An expensive car. He had a pretty good idea what this was.

Milton toggled the intercom. 'Yes?'

'Police.'

'Police?'

'That's right. Is that Mr Smith?'

'Yes.'

'Could we have a word?'

'What about?'

'Open the door, please, sir.'

'What do you want to talk to me about?'

'There was an incident yesterday. Fisherman's Wharf. Please, sir – we just need to have a word.'

'Fine. Just give me five minutes. I work nights. I was asleep. I just need to get changed.'

'Five minutes.'

He went back to the window and looked down at them again. There was no way on earth that these men were cops. They were dressed too well in expensive overcoats, and he saw the grey sunlight flickering across the caps of well-polished shoes. And then there was the car; the San Francisco Police Department drove Crown Vics, not eighty-thousand-dollar saloons.

He waited for the men to shift around a little and got a better look at them. Three of the men he had never seen before. The fourth, the guy waiting in the car, he recognised. Milton looked at him as he wound down the window and called out to the others. It was Salvatore. His face was partially obscured by a bandage that had been fixed over his shattered cheek. Milton waited a moment longer, watching as the men exchanged words, their postures tense and impatient. One of them stepped back, and the wind caught his open overcoat, flipping his suit coat back, too, revealing a metallic glint in a shoulder holster.

That settled it.

The three guys at his door were made guys; that much was for sure. So what to do? If he let them in, then the chances were they'd come up, subdue him and Salvatore would be called in to put the final bullet in his head. Or if he went down to meet them, maybe they would take him somewhere quiet, somewhere down by the docks, perhaps, and do it there. Milton had known exactly what he was doing when he beat Salvatore, and the way he saw it, he hadn't been given any other choice. There was always going to be consequences for what he'd done, and here they were, right on cue. An angry Mafioso bent on revenge could cause trouble. *Lots* of trouble.

So maybe discretion was the better part of valour this morning. Milton dropped his mobile in his jacket pocket and went through into the corridor. There was a window at the end; he yanked it up. The building's fire escape ran outside it. He wriggled out onto the sill, reached out with his right hand, grabbed the metal handrail and dropped down onto the platform.

He climbed down the stairs and walked around the block until he had a clear view onto the frontage of the El Capitan. The Lexus was still there, and the three hoodlums were still waiting by the door. One of them had his finger on the buzzer; it looked like he was pressing it non-stop.

Milton collected the Explorer. It was cold. He started the engine and then put the heater on max. He took out his phone and swiped his finger down, flipping through his contacts. He found the one he wanted, pressed call and waited for it to connect.

26

The sign in the window said 'BAXTER BAIL BONDS'. The three words were stacked on top of one another so that the three Bs, drawn so they were all interlocked, were the focus that caught the eye. The shop was in Escondido, north of San Diego, and Beau Baxter hardly ever visited it these days. He had started out here pretty much as soon as he had gotten out of the Border Patrol down south. He had put in a long stint, latterly patrolling the Reaper's Line between Tijuana, Mexicali, Nogales and, worst of them all, Juárez. Beau had run his business from the shop for eighteen months until he came to the realisation that it was going to take years to make any serious coin, and, seeing as he wasn't getting any younger, he figured he needed to do something to accelerate things. He had developed contacts with a certain Italian family with interests all the way across the continental United States, and he started to do work for them. It paid well, although their money was dirty and it needed to be laundered. That was where having a ready-made business, a business that often ran on cash and dealt in the provision of intangible services, sometimes anonymously, came in very handy indeed.

So Beau had kept the place on and had appointed an old friend from the B.P. to run it for him. Arthur 'Hank' Culpepper was a hoary old goat, a real wiseacre they used to call 'PR' back in the day because he was the least appropriate member of the crew to send to do anything that needed a diplomatic touch. He had always been vain, which was funny because he'd never been the prettiest to look at. That didn't stop him developing a high opinion of himself; Beau joked that he shaved in a cracked mirror every morning because he thought of himself as a real ladies' man. His airs and graces might have been lacking, but he had made up for that by being a shit-hot agent with an almost supernatural ability to nose out the bad guys.

He wasn't interested in the big game that Beau went after nowadays; there was a lot of travel involved in that, and there was the ever-present risk of catching a bullet in some bumble-fuck town where the quarry had gone to ground. Hank was quite content to stick around San Diego, posting bond for the local scumbags and then going after them whenever they were foolish enough to abscond. He had his favourite bar, his hound and his dear old wife (in that order), and anyways, he had a reputation that he liked to work on. Some people called him a local legend. He was known for bringing the runners back in with maximum prejudice, and stories of him roping redneck tweakers from out of the back of his battered old Jeep were well known among the Escondido bondsmen. It was, he said, just something that he enjoyed to do.

Beau pulled up and took a heavy black vinyl sports bag from the rear of his Cherokee. He slung it over his shoulder, blipped the lock on the car, crossed the pavement and stopped at the door. He unlocked it, pushed down the handle with his elbow and backed his way inside. The interior was simple. The front door opened into the office, with a desk, some potted plants, a standard lamp and a sofa that had been pushed back against the wall. There was a second door, opposite the street door, that led to a corridor that went all the way to the back of the building. There was a kitchenette, a bathroom and, at the end, a small cell that could be locked.

The safe was in the kitchen, the kettle and a couple of dirty mugs resting atop it. Beau spun the dial three times – four-nine-eight – and opened the heavy cast-iron door. He unzipped the bag and spread it open. It was full of paper money.

Fifteen big ones.

The smell of it wafted into the stuffy room. Beau loved that smell.

He took out the cash, stacked the fifties in neat piles and locked the safe.

He locked the front door, got back into his Cherokee and headed for the hospital.

*   *   *

Hank was sitting up in bed, his phone pressed between his head and shoulder while his right hand was occupied with tamping tobacco into the bowl of the pipe in his left hand. He was in his early sixties, same as Beau was, and lying there in bed like that, he looked it. Man, did he ever look *old*. The whole of his right side was swathed in bandages, and there was a drip running into a canula in the back of his hand. He hadn't shaved for a couple of days, and that added on a few extra years. He wasn't wearing anything above the waist, and his arms – Beau remembered them when they were thick with muscle – looked withered and old. The tattoo of the snake that he had had done in Saigon was wrinkled and creased where once it had been tightly curled around his bicep.

Old age, Beau thought. That was the real reaper. Coming for all of us. Still, he thought, I'd rather eat five pounds of cactus thorns and shit-sharp needles than look like *that*.

He raised a hand in greeting, and Hank reciprocated with a nod, mouthing that he would be two minutes, before speaking into the receiver again: 'I'm telling you, Maxine, the judge don't give a sweet fuck about that. What he's gonna get now ain't a pimple on a fat man's ass compared to what he's gonna get. If he don't make it for the hearing tomorrow, the judge'll make an example out of him. I'm telling you, no shit, he's looking at five years before he even gets a sniff of parole. *Five.* Is that what you want for him? No? Then you better tell me where he's at.'

Beau could hear the buzz of a female voice from the receiver.

There was a coffee machine in the hall, and Beau went outside for two brews in white Styrofoam cups. He searched the small wicker basket next to the machine for a packet of Coffee-mate, came up empty, went back through into the room and found a bowl of sugar instead. He spooned a couple into both cups, stirring the sludgy brown liquid until it looked a little more appealing.

'Fine. Where – Pounders? All right, then. I'm gonna send someone to go and get him.'

Beau sat down and stared at his old friend. He thought about the first time they had met – 1976. They'd graduated from the Border Patrol Academy and been posted up in Douglas at about the same time. Hank had been a uniformed cop near the border in El Centro, California, before coming on duty with the B.P.

'I'm serious, Maxine,' Hank was saying. 'If he comes back, you call me right away. He really doesn't want to rile me up right now. I'm not in the mood to go chasing him down all over the state, and if he makes me do that, I ain't promising he don't get brought back in cuffs and with a bloody nose. You hearing me straight, darling? I ain't messing. Don't you dare make me look like a fool, now.'

He ended the call.

'You ain't chasing anyone tonight, partner,' Beau said.

'She don't know that.'

'Who is it?'

'Fellow named George Bailey. Been stealing cars. This time, though, the dumb fuck had a pistol on him while he was doing it. "Possession of a concealed weapon" – he's looking at five, minimum, probably seven or eight depending on which judge he gets. He decided he'd take his chances on the road; I'm trying to persuade his lovely *girlfriend*' – that word was loaded with sarcasm – 'otherwise. He's out getting drunk, so I'm going to send George McCoy to go pick him up. Unless you wanna do it?'

'Uh-huh,' Beau said with a big smile, shaking his head. 'I'm not into that no more.'

'Only the big game for you now, partner?'

'That's right.'

'What was the last one?'

'Mexican.'

'And?'

'Not so bad.'

Beau had finished the job the night before. It had been an easy one by his usual standards. The Lucianos had interests in a couple of big casinos in Vegas, and one of their croupiers, this wiry beaner by the name of Eduardo del Rio, had entertained the thought that he could run south with fifty grand of their money. The Lucianos had sent Beau after him. He must have been the most dumbshit robber in the Mexican state of Sonora that night, and it had been a simple bust. He had run straight home to his wife, and Beau just had to wait there for him. He'd been a little punchy when Beau confronted him, but his attitude had adjusted just as soon as he started looking down the barrel of Beau's 12-gauge pump.

'Boy was as dumb as you like,' Beau said. 'Dumb as a box of rocks.' He sipped his coffee; it was foul. 'All right.' Beau crossed his legs, the hem of his right trouser leg riding up a little to show more of his snakeskin cowboy boot. 'Now then. You wanna tell me what in God's name has been going down round here?'

'Meaning what?'

'Meaning *what*? Which sumbitch shot you up, Hank?'

'Ever heard of Ordell Leonard?'

Beau shook his head. 'Can't say I have.'

'Big brother from 'Bama. Quiet fella until he gets on the drink, then you never know what you're gonna get. They had him for driving under the influence and resisting arrest. All he was looking at was a couple of months, but he reckons they're prejudiced against black men from the South round here, so he decides he's gonna take his chances and takes off. I ended up in Arkansas before I could catch him. Fucking Little Rock, can you believe that shit? Two thousand miles, man. It took me three days there and three days back, although, course, he was in the back coming home, so I had to listen to his goddamn problems the whole way. The whole experience made me think I ain't getting a good enough shake out of this here thing we got going on.'

He was grinning as he said it; Beau knew he was fooling around.

'And then?'

'And then I got lazy, I guess. We was right back up at the store when I let him out. I was going to put him in the cell until I could transfer him to the courthouse. He'd been on best behaviour for the whole trip, and I'd taken off his cuffs. Clean forgot. Dude cold-cocks me, knocks me down, then gets my shotgun from the front and fires off a load. I'm not sure how he missed, to be honest with you. Ended up catching me in the shoulder, but it could've been a helluva lot worse.'

'Know where he's headed?'

'Got a brother in Vallejo. I'd bet you a dime to a doughnut that's where he's gone.'

'All right, then. You can leave that one to me.'

'You sure? Not much money in it, Beau.'

Beau looked at Hank again. He was getting on. Couldn't have that many years left in him doing what they were doing. A shotgun at close range? He'd got lucky. Maybe it was time Beau suggested Hank took it easy. Maybe it was a message. 'Ain't about money all the time, partner. Dude shot you all up. I can't stand for that. Bad for our reputation.'

'Ah, shit – I'll be fine. I was gonna enjoy seeing him again.'

'How long they going to keep you in?'

'Couple more days.'

'By which time he'll be long gone. Nah, Hank, don't worry about it. Leave him to me.'

Hank sucked his teeth and, eventually, nodded his assent. 'Shit,' he said. 'I remembered something; you had a call back at the office. Jeanette took the details down and told me about it.'

Jeanette was the secretary who kept things ticking over. 'Who from?'

'She said he called himself Smith. Sounded like he was English, she said; he had that whole accent going on. She says you weren't around and could she take a message for you, and he says yes, she could, and he tells her that he wants you to call him pronto. He gave her a number – I've got it written down in my pants pocket.'

'He say what he wanted to speak to me about?'

'Nope,' Hank said, shaking his head, 'except it was urgent.'

27

Beau drove north. It took him eight hours on the I-5, a touch under five hundred miles. He could have flown or caught a northbound Amtrak from San Diego, but he liked the drive, and it gave him some time to listen to some music and think.

He spent a lot of time thinking about duties and obligations. He had always lived his life by a code. It wasn't a moral code because he couldn't claim to be a particularly moral man; that would be fatuous, given the profession he had latterly chosen for himself. It was more a set of rules that he tried to live his life by, and one of those rules insisted that he would always pay his debts. It was a matter of integrity. Beau's father had always said that was something you either had or you didn't have, and he prided himself that he did. Getting the Mexican journalist away to safety had been the right thing to do, but he couldn't in all honesty say that he thought it had completely squared the ledger between them. He figured the Englishman had done him two solids down in Mexico: he had saved him from *Santa Muerte* and then drew the fire of whoever it was who'd hit *El Patrón*'s mansion so that he and the girl could get away. Helping the girl had paid back only half of the debt. At the very least, he could drive up to San Francisco and hear what the Englishman had to say. If it wasn't something Beau could help him with, then he would book into a nice hotel for a couple of nights and enjoy the city. He really had nothing to lose.

And if nothing else, he could find out how on earth Smith had gotten out of Mexico. It hadn't looked so good for him when Beau and the girl had made tracks. That guy, though – he was something else.

Beau could mix in a spot of business, too. Ordell Leonard was up there, and there was no way on God's green earth Beau was going to let him have even an extra second of liberty. He would never have admitted it to another person, but seeing Hank in the hospital like that, old and shot up, had reminded him of his own advancing years. He had been thinking about his own mortality a lot recently. He was sixty-two years old. Every morning, he seemed to wake up with another ache. Everyone came to the end of the road eventually, that was the one shared inevitability, but Beau was determined that he wasn't there yet. The more he thought about it, the more he understood his own reaction: Ordell Leonard was a bad man, a dangerous man, and he would have been a challenge to collar ten years ago, when he and Hank were fitter and meaner than they were now. Bringing him in now would be his way of thumbing his nose at the notion that he was ready to retire.

Ordell would be the proof that Beau wasn't ready to hang it up just yet.

* * *

Beau booked a suite at the Drisco, and five minutes before the time that they had agreed to meet, he was waiting in the bar downstairs.

John Smith was right on time.

'Beau,' he said, sitting down opposite him.

'All right, English,' Beau said. 'Didn't think I'd ever be seeing you again.'

'I guess you never know what's around the corner.'

'I guess you don't.'

'What happened to the girl?' Smith asked.

'As far as I know, she's safe and sound.'

'As far as you know?'

'That's all I can say. The man who makes people disappear, this guy my employers use when they need to send someone out of harm's way, the arrangement is strictly between him and the client. No one else gets to know anything about it. She could be in Alaska for all I know. She could be back in Mexico, although I hope for her sake she ain't. But what I can say for sure is that I got her into the country like I said I would, and she was just fine and dandy when I dropped her off.'

Smith nodded at that. 'You get paid for the job?'

'Sure did,' Beau said.

He had delivered the body of Adolfo González to the Lucianos nine months ago. The job had been to bring him in dead or alive, yet there had been consternation that it was in the former condition that *Santa Muerte* was delivered. Beau had explained what had happened – that the girl journalist from Juárez had put a bullet in the Mexican's head while he

227

was outside their motel room getting ice – but his honesty had led to recriminations. The awkwardness had been underscored by the requirement, stipulated by Beau, that the girl was to be given a new identity and kept hidden from the cartels. There had been a moment when Beau had been unsure that they were going to let her leave in one piece, but he had stuck to his guns and, eventually, they had conceded. Beau didn't necessarily care about her either way – she wasn't his problem, after all – but he had promised Smith that he would get her out of Mexico and set up in the States, and Beau wasn't the sort of man who went back on his word. Doing the right thing had eventually lightened his payment by fifteen grand; the Italians docked ten from his bounty for spoiling the fun they had planned for González and the other five went to pay the fee of the professional who made people disappear.

Fifteen.

Beau hadn't been happy with that, not at all.

'I appreciate it,' Smith said.

'No sweat, English. Least I could do, circumstances like they were.' He paused and lit up a smoke. 'So – how'd you get out alive?'

'There was a lot of confusion. I took advantage of it.'

'Who were those dudes?'

'Best not to ask.'

'What about *El Patrón*?'

'What about him?'

'He got himself shot dead a couple of days later. That wouldn't have been anything to do with you, would it?'

'Me? No,' Smith said. 'Course not.'

Beau laughed and shook his head. The Englishman was something else. Quiet and unassuming for the most part, but when he got all riled up, there weren't many people who would have concerned Beau more. He remembered the way he had strode through *El Patrón*'s burning mansion, offing gangsters just like he was shooting fish in a barrel. He had been ruthlessly efficient. Not a single wasted shot and not a moment of hesitation. The man was private, too, and Beau knew that there was no point in pushing him to speak if he didn't want to.

'You said you needed a favour,' he said instead. 'What can I do for you?'

'The syndicate you've been working for – it's the Lucianos?'

Beau paused and frowned a little. He hadn't expected that. 'Could be. Why?'

'I have a problem – you might be able to help.'

'With them? What kind of problem?'

'I put one of their men in the hospital.'

'Why would you want to do a crazy-assed thing like that?'

'He pulled a gun on me. I didn't have much choice.'

'By "hospital" – what do you mean?'

'He's not dead, Beau. Broken nose, broken ribs. I worked him over with a pool cue.'

'Jesus, English.'

Smith shrugged.

'You wanna tell me why he was going to pull a gun on you?'

'They're running an escort business. This man fronted it for them. I had some questions about it, and he didn't like them.'

'What were they?'

'They sent a girl to a party. She hasn't been seen since, and I was one of the last people to see her. Apart from anything else, the police have got me down as a suspect.'

'For what?'

'You hear about those dead girls up north?'

'Sure.'

'The party was right around there. I'd say there's a good chance her body'll be the next body they find.'

'Murder, then.'

'I'm not concerned about me, I know I didn't do it, and I know they're just going through the motions.'

'Kicking the tyres.'

He nodded. 'Exactly. But I got talking to her before.'

'An escort?'

'I was driving her. I have a taxi.'

'Chef. Cab driver. You're full of surprises.'

Smith brushed over that. 'She's a nice girl. And her boyfriend's a good kid. When the police realise I don't have anything to do with it, they're going to go after him, and maybe he isn't quite as single-minded as me, maybe they need a conviction, and he looks like he could be their guy. Maybe they *make* him their guy. I'd like to get to the bottom of what happened, one way or another.'

Beau shook his head. 'You've got yourself in a mess over another woman? You got a habit for that. What is it with you, English?'

'I need to talk to them, Beau, but at the moment, I think they'd rather put a bullet between my eyes. I was hoping you might be able to straighten things out.'

'Put a good word in for you, you mean?'

'If you like.'

Beau couldn't help but chuckle. 'You're unbelievable. Really – you're something else.'

'Can you do it?'

'Can I ask them not to shoot you? Sure I can. Will they listen? I have absolutely no idea.'

'Just get me in a room with whoever it is I need to speak to. It might not look like it, but we both have a stake in this. If she's dead, I'm going to find out who killed her. It's in their best interests that I do. Because if I don't, there's going to be a whole lot of heat coming their way. You'd be doing them a favour.'

'Well,' Beau said, 'you put it like that, how can I possibly refuse?'

28

'I know you've got a temper,' Beau said to him as he reverse-parked his Jeep into a space next to the bowling alley, 'but you'll want to keep it under wraps today, all right? Apart from the fact that I vouched for you, which means it'll be me who gets his ass kicked if you start getting rambunctious, these aren't the kind of dudes you want to be annoying, if you catch my drift.' He paused. 'You *do* catch my drift, John, don't you?'

'Don't worry, Beau,' Milton said. 'I'm not an idiot.'

'One other thing, let me do the talking to start with. Introduce you and suchlike. Then you can take the conversation whichever way you want. If you get off on the wrong foot with them, you'll get nowhere – you might as well just pound sand up your ass. This has to be done right.'

The car park was half full, mostly with cheap cars with a few dings and dents in the bodywork, nothing too showy, the kind of first cars that kids new to the business of driving would buy with the money they had managed to scrape together. Beau had parked next to the most expensive car in the lot. It was a Mercedes sedan with darkened windows and gleaming paintwork. There was a driver behind the wheel. Milton could only just make him out through the smoked glass, but there he was; it looked like he was wearing a uniform, the cap of which he had taken off and rested against the dash. He had reclined the seat, and he was leaning back, taking a nap.

They got out of the car and Milton followed Beau inside.

He looked around. It was a scruffy dive, dirty around the edges and showing its age, staffed by kids in mismatched uniforms trying to make beer money. There were two exits. One was the door they had just come through; the other was at the end of a long, dark bathroom corridor all the way in back. An air-conditioning unit over the door was on its last legs, running so hard that it was trembling and rattling, but it wasn't making much difference to the humidity in the air. Seven bowling lanes had been fitted into what might once have been a large warehouse. It was a generous space, the roof sloping down towards the end of the lanes with dusty skylights at the other end. There was a bar at the back with ESPN playing on muted TVs, then some upholstered benches, then a cluster of free-standing tables and then the lanes. There were computerised scoring machines suspended from the roof. All sorts of bottled beers behind the bar. The place was loud. Music from a glowing jukebox was pumped through large speakers, but that was drowned out by the sound of balls being dropped onto wood, falling into the gully and smashing into the pins. The machinery rattled as it replaced the pins, and the balls rumbled as they rolled back to the players.

'What is this place?'

'What's it look like?'

'Looks like a bowling alley.'

'There you go.'

'The family owns it?'

'Sure they do. They own lots of things: pizza parlours, nail bars, couple of hotels.'

'All useful if you've got money you need to wash.'

'Your words, John,' he said, with a big smile that said it was all the way true.

Milton checked the clientele, counting people, scanning faces, watching body language. Kids, mostly, but there were a few others that caught his eye. At a table in a darkened corner away from the bar were two guys talking earnestly, their hands disappearing beneath the table, touching, then coming back up again. A dealer and his buyer. There were two guys further back in the room, sat around a table with a couple of bottles of beer. Big guys, gorillas in sharp suits. The first was a tall, wide man with collar-length hair and a black T-shirt under a black suit. The second was a little smaller, with a face that twitched as he watched the action on the nearest lane. They were a pair. Milton pegged them as bodyguards. Operators. Made men, most likely. He'd seen plenty of guys like that all around the world. They'd be decent, dangerous up to a point, but easy enough to take care of if you knew how to do it. There would be a point beyond which they were not willing to go. Milton had their advantage when it came to that; he didn't have a cut-off. The men were sitting apart from each other, but their twin gazes were now trained on the table in a private VIP area that was raised up on a small platform accessed by a flight of three steps and fenced off from the rest of the room.

A further pair of men were sitting there.

'Is that them?'

Beau nodded. 'Remember – I'll do the introductions, and for God's sake, show them a little respect. You're not on home territory here, and I don't care how tough you think you are, they won't give two shits about that. Wait here. I'll go and speak to them.'

Milton sat down at the bar. One of the televisions was tuned to CNN. They had a reporter out at Headlands Lookout, ghostly in the thick shroud of fog that alternated between absorbing and reflecting the lights for the camera. The man was explaining how the police had set out the large area that they would search, breaking it down into smaller areas that were then administered by several officers. The item cut to footage of the search. The narrow road he had previously driven down was marked with plastic signs pointing to where remains had been found. Marker flags had been driven into the scrub and sand on each of the sites. Officers were working in the bramble, using the flags as their reference points.

Beau came back across. 'All right,' he said. 'They'll see you. Remember, play nice.'

'I always do.'

Milton approached the two men. One was older, wrinkled around the eyes and nose. He had a full head of hair, pure black, the colour obviously out of a packet. There was a beauty spot on his right cheek, and his right eyelid seemed to be a little lazy, hooding the eye more than the other. He was wearing a shirt with a couple of buttons undone, no tie, with a jacket slung over the back of the chair. The second man was younger. He had a pronounced nose with flared nostrils, heavy eyebrows and beady eyes that never stayed still.

Beau sat down on one of the two empty seats.

Milton sat down, too.

'This is Mr Smith,' Beau said.

'How are you doing?' the older man said, nodding solemnly at him. 'My name is Tommy Luciano.'

He extended his hand across the table. Milton took it. His skin was soft, almost feminine, and his grip was loose. He could have crushed it.

'And my friend here is Carlo Lucchese.'

Lucchese did not show the same hospitality. He glowered at him across the table, and Milton recognised him; he was the one who had been on the intercom to him at the El Capitan, one of the four who had come to kill him.

He didn't let that faze him. 'Thank you for seeing me.'

'Beau said it was important. That wouldn't normally have been enough to interrupt my afternoon, but he told us that you were *very* helpful with a small problem we had over in Juárez.'

'That's good of him to say.'

'And so that's why we're sitting here. Normally, with what you've done, you'd be dead.'

Lucchese looked on venomously.

'Perhaps,' Milton said.

'You had an argument with one of my men.'

'I'm afraid I did.'

'Want to tell me why?'

'I have some questions that I need to have answered. I asked him, and they seemed to make him uncomfortable. He threatened me with a gun. Not very civil. I wasn't prepared to stand for that.'

'Self-defence on your part, then?'

'If you like.'

Beau put a hand down on the table and intervened: 'John's sorry, though – right, John?'

Milton didn't respond. He just kept his eye on the older man.

'He don't look sorry,' Lucchese said.

'Carlo . . .'

'This douche broke Salvatore's face. Messed him up real good. And we're *talking* to him? I don't know, Tommy, I don't, but what the goddamn fuck?'

'Take it easy,' the old man said, and Milton knew from the way that he said it that he was about to be judged. The next five minutes would determine what came after: he was either going to get the information he wanted, or he was going to get shot. 'These questions – you wanna tell me what they are?'

He didn't take his eyes away from the older man. 'There was a party in Pine Shore. I drove a girl up there.'

'You drove her?'

'I'm a taxi driver.'

Luciano laughed. 'This gets better and better.'

Milton held his eye. 'Something happened at the party, and she freaked out. She ran, and she's not been seen since.'

'Pine Shore?'

'That's right. Near where the two dead girls turned up.'

'I know it. And you think this girl is dead?'

'I think it's possible.'

'And what's any of it got to do with us?'

'Fallen Angelz. She was on the books.'

He looked at him with an amused turn to his mouth. 'Fallen Angelz? That supposed to mean anything to me?'

Milton didn't take his eyes away. 'You really want to waste my time like that?'

Beau stiffened to Milton's right, but he said nothing. The younger man flexed a little. Milton stared hard at Luciano, unblinkingly hard. The old man held his glare steadily, unfazed, and then smiled. 'You have a set of balls on you, my friend.'

'Aw, come on, Tommy – you can't be serious. You said—'

'Go and do something else, Carlo. I don't need you around for this.'

'Tommy—'

'It wasn't a suggestion. Go on – fuck off.'

Lucchese left the table, but he didn't go far. He stopped at the bar and ordered a beer.

Milton didn't relax, not even a little. He was very aware of the two bodyguards at the table across the room.

'All right,' Luciano said. 'So suppose I said I do know about this business. What do you want?'

'A name – the person who booked the girls that night.'

'Come on, Mr Smith, you know I can't give you that. That business only works if it's anonymous. We got some serious players on the books. Well-known people who would shit bricks if they knew I was letting people know they took advantage of the services we offer. They need to trust our discretion. I start spilling their names, there are plenty of other places who'll take their money.'

'You need to think bigger than that, Mr – Luciano. Telling me who booked her that night is the best chance you've got of keeping the business.'

'That so? How you figure that?'

'One of your drivers told me that the girl was sent by the agency. You could say he's had a crisis of conscience about it. He knows he ought to be telling the police. So far, that hasn't been strong enough to trump the fact that he's terrified that talking is going to bring him into the frame. That's his worst-case scenario.'

'No, Mr Smith. His worst-case scenario is that *I* find out who he is.'

'But you won't find out, not from me.'

'So what's his worry?'

'If he goes to the cops? That he gets charged with procuring prostitution.'

'So he's not saying anything.'

'Not yet. But you know the way that guilt is. It has a way of eating away at you. I'm betting that he's feeling worse and worse about what happened every single day, and the longer the police dig away without getting anywhere, the harder it's going to be for him to fight off going to them and telling them everything he knows. And if she turns up dead? I reckon he calls them right away. The first thing that's going to happen after that is that Salvatore gets a visit about the murders. The second thing is that he gets arrested and charged. The police need to be seen to be doing something. They'll go after the low-hanging fruit, and three dead prostitutes linked – rightly or wrongly – to an illegal agency like Fallen Angelz would be a perfect place to start. And, without wanting to cast asper-sions, Salvatore didn't strike me as the kind of fellow with the character to stand up to the prospect of doing time when there's a plea bargain on the table. I don't need to go on, do I?'

'You sure Salvatore would flip? Just like that?'

'Are you sure he won't?'

'You saying you can help me?'

'I've got a few days' head start on the police. Maybe that's enough time for me to find out what happened. Maybe my girl isn't linked to the other two. Maybe something else has happened to her. And maybe, if I can find some answers, the driver decides he doesn't have to say anything.'

'And if this girl is dead?'

'Provided it had nothing to do with you, maybe I can find a way that leaves you out. That agency's got to be valuable to you, right? It's got to be worth giving me the chance to sort things out. What have you got to lose?'

Luciano looked at him shrewdly. 'I could speak to the driver myself. Find out what he knows.'

'You don't know who he is.'

'*You* do. You could tell me.' He smiled thinly, suggestively.

'Forget it,' Milton said, smiling back. 'I'm not frightened of you.'

'What did you do before you drove cabs, Mr Smith?'

'I was a cook,' he said.

'A cook?'

'He was working in a restaurant when I met him,' Beau said.

'You think he's a cook, Beau?'

'No.'

Luciano sucked his teeth.

Milton clenched his fists beneath the table.

'All right – let's say, just for the sake of discussion, that I give you what you want. Why are you so interested? What does it have to do with you?'

'The police have me down as a suspect, and it's not in my interest for my name to come out. The sooner I can clear this up, the better.'

'Publicity is bad for you?'

'Very bad.'

Luciano shook his head, a small smile playing on his lips. 'You're a very interesting man, Mr Smith. That's all I need for now. I'll speak to Beau. You can wait outside.'

* * *

Milton made his way down from the raised area and across the wide room. As he passed the bar, he saw Carlo with another man. The newcomer held himself at an odd angle, his left arm clutched to his side as if he was in pain, and he had a huge, florid bruise on his cheek. There were purples and blues and greys in the bruise, and the centre was pure black and perfectly rounded, as if it had been caused by a forceful impact with something spherical. The nose was obscured by a splint.

Salvatore glared at Milton as he crossed in front of him, his eyes dripping with hate. Milton nodded once, a gesture he knew he probably shouldn't have made but one that he just couldn't resist. The injured man lost it, aggrieved at the beating that he had taken, aggrieved at seeing Milton walk out of the bowling alley with impunity, not a scratch on him, and he came in at an awkward charge, moving painfully and with difficulty, his right fist raised. Milton feinted one way and moved another. The Italian stumbled past, Milton tapped his ankles, and Salvatore tripped and fell. He grimaced as he pushed himself to his feet again, but by then Milton had backed off and turned around and was ready for the second go-around. Salvatore came at him again, his fist raised, lumbering like a wounded elephant. Milton ducked to one side and threw a crisp punch that landed square on his nose, crunching the bones again. Salvatore's legs went, and he ate carpet. He stayed down this time, huffing hard.

Milton raised his hands helplessly and looked over at the VIP area, wondering whether things were going to get heated. Beau looked anxious, but neither Tommy Luciano or Carlo Lucchese did anything. Milton turned to look at Luciano, then to Lucchese, then to Salvatore; then he pushed out of the door and went outside to wait for Beau in the cold, bright afternoon sun.

29

Milton had gone to a meeting that evening. It wasn't his usual, and Eva wasn't there. He had gone out for dinner afterwards with a couple of the guys, and by the time he returned to his flat, it was midnight. He was reasonably confident that there would be no more issues with the Lucianos – at least for the moment – but he couldn't completely rule out that Lucchese might ignore his boss and come at him again, so he had driven around the block twice before going inside. He saw nothing to make him anxious, and there was nothing in the blindingly bright lobby to suggest that his visitors had returned or that they intended to. He climbed to the third floor. He knew exactly where the light switch was, and it was with a single blur of motion that he opened the door, flicked it on – and stood in the threshold with the door open wide, scanning the room with practised eyes. Everything looked as if it was in order.

He stepped forward and locked himself inside, bending down to examine one of his own black hairs, which still lay undisturbed where he had left it before going out, placed carefully across the drawer of the coffee table. He had left a faint trace of talcum powder on the handle of the bedroom door and that, too, had not been disturbed. These were, he knew, extravagant measures to confirm his safety, but years in a business as dangerous as his had hardwired him with caution. Paying heed to that creed, and to his instincts, was the reason he was still alive. The precise application of a routine like this had saved his life on several occasions. The Mafia was a blunt instrument compared to the secret services of the countries that he had infiltrated – a cudgel as to a scalpel – but that was no reason to treat them with any less respect. A cudgel was still deadly.

Milton propped a chair beneath the door handle, locked the window that faced the fire escape and slept with his fingers wrapped around the butt of the Smith & Wesson 9mm that he kept under the pillow.

* * *

He rose early the next morning. There was a lot to do. First, though, he dressed in his running gear, pulled his battered trainers onto his feet and went downstairs. It was a crisp, bright day, the sun's cold rays piercing the mist that rose off the bay. Milton ran south on Mason Street, turned onto Montgomery Street and ran until he reached the Embarcadero, the piers, the bridge to Oakland and, beyond it, the greenish-blue of the ocean. He ran north, following the road as it curved to the west, listening to the rhythmic cadence of his feet and clearing his mind. This had always been his preferred way to think. It was his meditation before he found the sanctuary of the Rooms, a peaceful retreat where he had the time and the luxury to let his thoughts develop at their own speed, without even being conscious of them.

He ran onto Jefferson, turned left inside Aquatic Park and then followed Hyde to Broadway and then, finally, Mason Street and home.

He passed through the lobby and took the stairs at a jog.

There were two men waiting outside the door to his room.

He recognised them both.

'Inspector Cotton. Detective Webster.'

'Mr Smith.'

'How can I help you?'

'We're going to need to talk to you.'

'Again? Really?'

'A few more questions.'

'I answered them before. Is there anything else?'

'I'm afraid there is. We found another body this morning.'

PART III

MILEY VAN DYKEN

Miley Van Dyken had been having second thoughts about how she had chosen to live her life. She'd told friends about them, how she was thinking about getting out. She knew that turning tricks could be a dangerous business, but it seemed to her that there had been more stories of psychos preying on working girls recently. There had been all those poor girls down on the beach, for one, and the police still had no idea who was responsible for their deaths.

But still she carried on. There were plenty of benefits that came from doing what she did; the money, obviously, but the freedom of working to your own schedule was another that other girls often overlooked. That was true, but it had been getting to the stage that her doubts and fears were starting to get so bad that she couldn't ignore them.

Her latest john had hired a room in The Tuscan on North Point Street in North Beach, five minutes from Pier 39. Miley usually preferred to sort the room herself, charging a little extra as expenses so that she still cleared her two hundred per hour, but the guy had apologised that he couldn't very easily leave the hotel and, when he had sensed her reluctance, had offered to pay a further fifty bucks on top to 'make up for her inconvenience'. He sounded nice enough, kind, speaking with a lilting Southern accent that put her in mind of that guy Kevin Spacey played in the Netflix thing, and even though she had initially turned him down and hung up, she stewed on it for fifteen minutes and changed her mind. She didn't have another job booked, he had been polite on the phone, and most importantly, she needed the money.

She tried not to think about her fears as she rode the bus. The driver smiled at her as she disembarked outside the hotel.

He was the last person to see her alive.

It was a small hotel that catered to travelling business people. It was a two-storey building surrounded by a parking lot. It didn't appear to be very busy; the lot was almost empty, save for a couple of rentals and a beaten-up Cadillac Eldorado. She went around the car on the way to the lobby when the driver's-side door opened and a man got out. He was tall and skinny, dressed in a white T-shirt, jeans and a pair of cowboy boots. He said her name. She recognised his voice.

30

Cotton and Webster didn't sit, so neither did Milton. Webster wandered absently to the window and looked down onto the street below. Cotton took a book from the shelf – it was *The Unbearable Lightness of Being* – made a desultory show of flicking through the pages and then put it back again. He looked around, his face marked by a lazy sneer.

'Nice place you got here,' he said.

'It suits me very well.'

'I don't know, Mr Smith. We get called out to places like this all the time. Don't you find it a bit tawdry?'

'You didn't come here to critique my accommodation.'

'No.'

'And I have things to do. What do you want?'

The cop took out his phone and selected a picture. He slid it across the table. Milton looked at it; it was a picture of a woman, white, slender with a short-cropped elfin hairstyle. Very pretty. 'Recognise her?'

Milton looked at the picture. 'No.'

'You sure about that? Swipe right for the next one.'

Milton did as he was told. It was the same girl, this time in some sort of prom dress. She looked young. 'No,' he said. 'I've never seen her before. Who is she?'

'Her name is Miley Van Dyken.'

'I don't know her, detective.'

'Where were you three weeks ago last Wednesday?'

'I'd have to check.'

'Like I say, it's a Wednesday. Think.'

Milton sighed exasperatedly. 'I would've gone to work in the afternoon and driven my car at night.'

'We can check the afternoon. What about the night – can anyone prove you were driving?'

'If my calls were from the agency, then maybe. If they came straight through to me, then no, probably not.' He slid the phone back across the table to him. 'Who is she? Number three?'

'That's right, Mr Smith. We found her this morning. Same place as the other two.'

'There's only so many times I can say it – I've got nothing to do with this.'

'Can I ask you something else?'

'Please do.'

'You own any firearms?'

Milton felt his skin prickle. 'No.'

'So if we looked around, we wouldn't find anything?'

'Help yourself. I don't have anything to hide.'

'Reason I'm asking, that guard you put on the ground at the party, he said you took his gun from him. Smith & Wesson. Pro Series, 9mm – very nice gun.'

Milton concentrated on projecting a calm exterior. He had left the gun under the bed. It wasn't even well hidden, all they would need to do would be to duck down and look. 'No,' he said. 'I don't know anything about it. I don't own a gun. To be honest, I doubt I'd even know what to do with one.'

'All right, then.'

'Is that it?'

'No,' Webster said from the window. 'There is one more thing you can help us with.'

'Please.'

'When we spoke to you before, you said you came across the border from Mexico. Six months ago. February. That's right, isn't it?'

'Yes.'

'Where did you cross?'

Milton started to feel uncomfortable. 'Juárez into El Paso.'

'That's weird,' Webster said. 'You know, there are forty-six places where you can legally cross over from Mexico. We spoke with Immigration. We checked El Paso, Otay Mesa, Tecate, Nogales. Hell, we even tried Lukeville and Antelope Wells. We found a handful of John Smiths who came across the border around about then. That's no surprise, really, a common name like that, but the thing is – the thing I just can't get my head around is – that when we looked at their pictures, none of them looked anything like you.'

That, Milton thought, was hardly surprising. He had crossed the border illegally, trekking across country east of Juárez into the Chisos Mountains and then Big Bear National Park. The last thing he had wanted to do was leave a record that would show where he had entered the country. He had not been of a mind to give the agents pursuing him any clue at all as to his location.

'Mr Smith?' Webster and Cotton were eyeing him critically.

Milton shrugged. 'What do you want me to say to that?'

'Can you explain it?'

'I was working in Juárez. I crossed into El Paso. I can't explain why there's no record of it.'

'Do you mind if we take your passport for a couple of days?'

'Why?'

'We'd just like to have a look at it.'

Milton went over to the bedside table and took his passport from the drawer. He could see the dull glint of the brushed steel on the handgun, an inch from his toe. He handed the passport to Webster. 'There you are,' he said. 'I've got nothing to hide.'

'Thank you.'

'Anything else?'

'Nah,' Cotton said. 'We got nothing more for you now.'

'But don't leave town without telling us,' Webster advised. 'I'm pretty sure we'll want to talk to you again.'

31

Milton had a lock-up at Extra Space Storage at 1400 Folsom Street. He had hired it within a couple of days of arriving in San Francisco and deciding that it was the kind of town he could stay in for a few months. The lock-up was an anonymous place, a collection of industrial cargo crates that had been arranged in several rows. Each crate had been divided into two or four separate compartments, and each was secured with a thick metal door padlocked top and bottom.

It cost Milton twenty dollars a week, and it was easily worth that for the peace of mind that it bought. He knew, eventually, that Control would locate him again and send his agents to hunt him down. He didn't know how he would react to that when it happened – he had been ready to surrender in Mexico – but he wanted the ability to resist them if that was what he chose to do. More to the point, he knew that his assassination of *El Patrón* and the capture of his son would not be forgotten by La Frontera. There would be a successor to the old man's crown – a brother or another son – and then there would be vengeance. They would have put an enormous price on his head. If they managed to find him, he certainly did not want to be unprepared.

Milton took out his key and unfastened the locks. He checked again that he was alone in the facility and, satisfied that he was, opened the door. He had stocked the storage crate with everything he would need in an emergency. There was a change of clothes, a cap, a packet of hair dye and a pair of clear-lensed spectacles. There was a go-bag with three false passports and the money he had found at *El Patrón*'s super-lab before he had torched it. Five thousand dollars, various denominations, all used notes.

At the back of the crate, hidden beneath a blanket, was a Desert Eagle .50 Action Express with a picatinny rail. It had been *El Patrón*'s weapon, and like everything else in his comic-book life, it had been tricked out to clichéd excess. The gun was gold-plated with diamonds set into the butt. Milton had no idea how much it was worth – thousands, obviously – but he didn't really care about that. The semi-automatic was one of Milton's favourite weapons. It was gas-operated with a firing mechanism usually found in rifles as opposed to the more common short recoil or blowback designs. The mechanism allowed for far more powerful cartridges, and he had purchased a box of Speer 325-grain .50 AE ammunition for it the day after he had arrived in town. He tore back the cardboard and tipped the bullets onto the floor of the unit; they glittered in the light of the single naked bulb that had been fitted to the roof of the crate. Lethal little golden slugs.

Milton detached the magazine and thumbed seven into the slot.

He slid the Desert Eagle into his jeans, his belt pressing it against his skin. The golden barrel was icy cold, the frame flat against his coccyx. He filled his pockets with the rest of the bullets. He dropped the Smith & Wesson 9mm into the go-bag and slung it over his shoulder.

He shut and locked the crate.

He wouldn't be coming back again.

Things were already too hot for him in San Francisco. He hadn't been named in any of the newspaper reports that he had read about the missing girls, but that was probably just a matter of time. It was a little irrelevant, too; his name would have been recorded by the police, and Control would sniff that out soon enough. They could be here tomorrow or next week; there was no way of knowing when, except that they were coming. Under normal circumstances, he would have moved on already, but he didn't feel able to leave until he had tried a little harder to find Madison. Trip would have no chance without him, and besides, he had a lead now. He would find out what he could and then disappear beneath the surface again.

The Explorer was parked close to the entrance to the facility.

He nodded to the attendant and made his way out to his car.

* * *

A short detour first. Manny Martinez ran his operation out of a grocery shop in the Mission District, not far from Milton's place. Milton had called ahead to make an appointment, and when he arrived, he was ushered all the way to the back of the store. There was a small office with a desk and a computer. A clock on the wall. Martinez was a big man, wearing an old pair of cargo pants and a muscle top that showed off impressively muscled biceps and sleeves of tattoos on both arms. His head was shaved to a furze of rough hair, and he had a tattoo of a tear beneath his right eye. Prison ink. Milton checked the office; his eye fell on the cudgel with a leather strap that was hanging from a hook on the wall.

'You Smith?'

'That's right. Thank you for seeing me.'

'How much you want?'

'I don't want anything.'

'You said—'

'Yes, I know – and I'm sorry about that. It's something else.'

He sat up, flexing his big shoulders. 'That right?'

'One of your customers – Richie Grimes?'

'Yeah,' he said. 'I know Richie. Fucking reprobate. Drunk.'

'How much does he owe you?'

'What's it got to do with you?'

'I'd like to buy his debt.'

'Just like that?'

'Just like that.'

'What if I don't wanna sell?'

'Let me make you an offer – if you don't want to sell after that, that's fair enough.'

Martinez swivelled the chair so that he was facing the computer and clicked through a series of files until he found the one he wanted. 'He's in the hole for fifty-eight hundred. He wanted four, and the vig was ten per cent.'

'How'd you get to fifty-eight from there?'

'Compound interest, buddy. Interest on top of interest.'

'Hardly ethical.'

'*Ethical*? These are the streets, buddy. *Ethics* don't get much play here.'

'I'll give you five.'

Martinez shook his head. 'No.'

'Debt's only worth what someone'll pay for it.'

'What are you? An economist?'

'Five. That's a grand clear profit.'

'I can get seven.'

'Not from him.'

'Don't have to be from him, does it?'

The second hand on the clock swept around the dial. Milton opened his bag and reached for the stolen drug money inside. He would put it to good use. He took out the five bundles, each secured by an elastic band around twenty fifties, and put them on the desk.

'Five thousand. Come on, Mr Martinez – it's right there.'

Martinez looked up at him with an amused cast to his face. 'I said no.'

'What's the point in dragging this out? He's got nothing.'

'He told you that? Guy's an addict, like I said. You can't believe a thing they say.'

'I believe him,' Milton said. 'He can't pay.'

'Then he's got a problem.'

'Is that your final word?'

'That's right.'

Milton nodded. He picked up the money and put it back into his bag.

'Come back with seven, maybe we can talk.'

Milton looked at him, then the cudgel. He was a big man, but he was lounging back in his chair. He was relaxed. He didn't see Milton as a threat, but Milton could have killed him, right there and then. He could have done it before the second hand on the clock had skirted another semicircle between the nine and twelve. Fifteen seconds. He thought about it for a moment, but that wouldn't solve Richie's problem. The debts would be taken over by someone else, and that person might be worse. There would have to be another way.

'See you around,' Martinez said. A gold tooth in his mouth glittered as he grinned at him.

'You will,' Milton said.

* * *

Milton called Beau Baxter as he drove to the airport.

'Morning, English. What can I do for you?'

'Did you get a name for me?'

'I did. You got a pen and paper?'

'Go on.'

'You want to speak to Jarad Efron. You know who that is?'

'I've heard the name before.'

'Not surprising. He's a big noise on the tech scene.'

'Thanks. I'll find him.'

'Goes without saying that you need to leave the Italians out of this.'

'Of course. Thanks, Beau. I appreciate it.'

'Anything else?'

'There is, actually. One other thing.'

'Shoot.'

'Do our friends have an interest in the lending business?'

'They have interests in lots of things.'

'So I'll assume that they do. There's a loan shark in the Mission District. A friend of mine owes him money. I just made him a very generous offer to buy the debt.'

'And he turned you down?'

'Thinks he can get more.'

'And how could our friends help?'

'I get the impression that this guy's out there all on his own. A lone operator. I wondered, if that's something they're involved in, whether the competition is something they'd be happy about. You think you could look into it for me?'

'What's this dude's name?'

'Manny Martinez.'

'Never heard of him. I can ask around, see what gives. I'll let you know.'

Milton thanked him and said goodbye, ended the call and parked the Explorer. He took his go-bag and went into the terminal building. He found the Hertz desk and hired a Dodge Charger, using one of the false passports and paying the three hundred dollars in cash. He drove it into the long-stay car park, put the go-bag in the boot, locked it and then found his way back to the Explorer.

He felt better for the preparation. If he needed to get out of town on short notice, he could.

He put the car into gear and drove away.

There was someone he wanted to see.

32

The man was in his early forties, in decent shape, just a little under six foot tall and with the kind of naturally lean frame that has gone a little soft with the onset of middle age. He had dark hair with flecks of grey throughout it, and the expensive glasses he wore were borne a little uncomfortably. His clothes were neat and tidy – a crisp polo shirt, chinos and deck shoes – the whole ensemble marking him out as a little vain.

Milton had parked in the car park for thirty minutes, the angle good enough for him to see the place side on, and to see all the comings and goings. It was more like a campus than an office. It looked like a busy place. The car park was full, and there had been a steady stream of people going in to start their working day. He had been waiting for one man in particular, and now, here he was. Milton eyed him as he opened the passenger door of his red Ferrari Enzo and took out a rucksack.

Milton looked at the scrap of paper that he had stuck to the windscreen of the Explorer.

It was a picture.

The man in the Ferrari and the man in the picture were the same.

Jarad Efron.

Milton got out of his car, locked the door and followed the man as he exited the car park and started towards the office. The campus was in the hills outside Palo Alto, surrounded by a lush forest bisected by streams, hiking paths and mountain-bike trails. The wildness of the landscape had been transplanted here, too, with grasses and wildflowers allowed to grow naturally. Purple heather clustered around the paths, and coneflowers, evening primroses and asters sprouted from natural rock gardens. Milton quickened his pace so that he caught up with Efron and then overtook him. He gave him a quick sidelong glance: he had white iPhone earbuds pressed into his ears, something upbeat playing; his skin was tanned; his forehead was suspiciously plump and firm; and there was good muscle tone on his arms. He was gym fit.

Milton slowed a little and entered the lobby just behind him.

After he had spoken with Beau yesterday morning, he had spent the afternoon doing research. Three hours at the local library. They had free internet and cheap coffee there, and he had had plenty of things that he wanted to check.

Jarad Efron was familiar to him from the news, and a quick Google search filled in the details: the man was CEO of StrongBox, one of the survivors of the first dotcom bubble that had since staked a claim in the cloud storage market. He was a pioneer. The company owned a couple of massive data farms in South Carolina, acres of deserted farmland rammed full of servers that they rented out to consumers and, increasingly, to big tech companies who didn't want to build facilities of their own. They offered space to Netflix and Amazon, among others. The company was listed on the NASDAQ with a price of $54 per share. Another search revealed that Efron had recently divested himself of five per cent of the company, pocketing thirty million dollars. He still owned another two million shares.

A paper fortune of $108,000,000.

Milton looked around quickly, taking everything in. The lobby was furnished sparsely, minimally, but every piece of furniture – the leather sofas, the coffee table – looked exceedingly expensive. Two security guards wore light blue uniforms and well-shined shoes, big boys with a stiff posture. They both had holstered .45s hanging from their belts. The staff behind the reception desk looked like models from a high-end catalogue, with glossy, airbrushed skin and preternaturally bright eyes.

Milton knew he only had one opportunity at this, and straightening his back and squaring off his shoulders, he followed right alongside Efron as the man beamed a bright smile of greeting to the girls and headed for the lifts. One of the girls looked past him at Milton, a moment of confusion breaking across her immaculate face, but Milton anticipated it and shone out a smile that matched Efron's for brightness and confidence. Her concern faded, and even if it was with a little uncertainty, she smiled right back at him.

Milton dropped back again and let Efron summon a lift. There were six doors; one of the middle ones opened with a pleasant chime, and Efron went inside.

Milton stepped forwards sharply and entered the lift as the doors were starting to close.

'Which floor?' Efron asked him absently.

Milton looked: ten floors, and Efron had hit the button for the tenth.

'Five, please.'

Efron pressed the button and stood back against the wall, leaving plenty of space between them.

The doors closed quietly, and the lift began to ascend.

Milton waited until they were between the second and third floors and hit the emergency stop.

The lift shuddered and came to a halt.

'What are you doing?' Efron protested.

'I've got a few questions. Answer them honestly.'

'Who are you?'

Efron's arm came up and made a sudden stab towards the button for the intercom. Milton anticipated it, blocked his hand away with his right, and then, in the same circular motion, jackhammered his elbow backwards into Efron's gut. It was a direct hit, just at the right spot to punch out all the air in his lungs, and he staggered back against the wall of the lift with his hands clasped impotently to his sternum, gasping for breath. Milton grabbed the lapels of his jacket, knotted his fists into the fabric and heaved Efron backwards and up, slamming him into the wall so that his feet were momentarily off the ground. Then he dropped him.

'Hello?' said a voice through the intercom speakers.

Efron landed on his behind, gasping. Milton lowered himself to the same height, barred his forearm across the man's throat and pressed, gently.

'It's in your best interests to talk to me.'

'They'll call . . . the police.'

'Probably better for you if they didn't. The police are going to want to talk to you soon anyway, but you'll do better with a little time to prepare. If they show up now, they'll ask me what I was doing here. And I'm going to tell them all about the party you had in Pine Shore.'

'What party?'

'I was there, Mr Efron. I drove Madison Clarke. You remember – the missing girl? I went inside. I saw it all. The drugs. The people. I recognised some of them. I have an eye for detail, Mr Efron, and I have a very good memory. You want the police to know that? The press? I know a man like you, in your position, you definitely don't want this in the papers. Bad publicity. It'd be a scandal, wouldn't it? So we can speak to them if you want – go right ahead. I'll wait.'

Milton could see him working out the angles, a frown settling over his handsome face.

'Fuck,' he cursed angrily, but it was from frustration backed by resignation; there was no fight there.

'Better sort that out.' Milton indicated the intercom. 'You hit the button by mistake. Tell them it's all right.'

He stood aside.

Efron's breath was still a little ragged. He pushed the button to speak. 'It's Jarad,' he said. 'I pressed the wrong button. Sorry. Can you reset it, please?'

'Yes, sir,' the girl said.

The lift started to rise again.

It reached the fifth floor. The doors opened, no one got on, the doors closed and the lift continued upwards.

'Is your office on the tenth?'

'Yes.'

'We'll go inside and shut the door. Don't do anything stupid, and I'll be gone in five minutes.'

They reached the tenth floor, and the doors opened again. Efron stepped out first, and Milton followed. The floor must have been reserved for StrongBox's executive team. Milton looked around. The big lobby was bright, daylight streaming in through huge floor-to-ceiling windows. One of the windows was open, leading out to a terrace area. The room was airy and fresh, very clean, the furniture and décor obviously chosen with great care and a generous budget. Efron led the way to an office with a wide picture window that framed the gorgeous landscape beyond: the deep green of the vegetation, the brown flanks of the distant mountains, infinite blue sky and crisp white clouds. There was a leather sofa, and Milton indicated that Efron should sit. He did as he was told. Milton shut the office door and sat on the edge of the desk.

'Don't get too comfortable,' Efron said. 'You're not staying.'

'You better hope not. Tell me what I want to know, and I'll be on my way.'

'What's your name?'

'You can call me Smith.'

'So what do you want?'

'Just to find the girl.'

'What girl?'

'The girl who went missing after the party.'

'I really have no idea what you're talking about.'

'Playing dumb is just going to mean this takes longer, Mr Efron. And I'm not the most patient man in the world.'

'What's her name?'

'Madison Clarke.'

His shrug didn't quite mask a flicker of disquiet. 'I don't know anyone by that name.'

'But you own a house in Pine Shore.'

'No, I don't. The *company* owns it. We're expanding. Hiring a lot of new talent. Time to time, we have new executives stay there while they're looking for places of their own. It's not mine.'

'There was a party there.'

'Okay. So there was a party there. Your point?'

'Madison is a prostitute. She was hired to be there.'

'You're fucking crazy. We're gearing up for an IPO. Do you know how stupid it'd be to invite a hooker onto company property?'

'You weren't there?'

'I was in Boston.'

'That's strange.'

'Come on, man. Enough with this shit!'

'No, it's strange, Mr Efron, because you hired her.'

'What?'

Milton saw him swallow.

'I didn't!'

'You've never used Fallen Angelz?'

'No.'

'Yes, you have. You paid, in advance, with a credit card registered to your company.'

He was starting to panic. 'Someone used a StrongBox credit card?' he gasped. 'So? Maybe they did. Lots of people have a company card.'

'Including you?'

'Of course. I'm the CEO. But it wasn't me.'

'I thought you might say that, Mr Efron, so I did a little extra checking. The things you find out when you speak to the right people, know what I mean? Here's what I know: I know it's not the first time you've used that agency. I know you're a valued customer. One of the regulars. I know the girls speak highly of you. A good payer, they said. A nice guy.'

He swallowed again, harder.

It was a bluff. Milton looked at Efron, setting aside the bland mask and letting him see him as he really was: a seasoned, iron-willed operative. 'Now,' he said. 'Bearing that all in mind, you want to reconsider?'

'Okay.'

'Okay what?'

'Okay, yes. I hired her. All right?'

'Better. Keep going. And you were there.'

'Yes.'

'You saw her.'

'Only briefly. I was hosting.'

'What happened to make her so upset?'

'I didn't know she was – not until afterwards.'

'You know she hasn't been seen since the party?'

'Yes – but only because the police said.'

'Have they spoken to you?'

'Not to me, but to a couple of guys who work for me. We said it was their party, and that's how it needs to stay. The IPO is everything, man. I got three hundred people working here. Their jobs depend on getting it right. If I get involved in a scandal now, we'll have to pull it.'

'I don't care about that, Mr Efron. I just want to find out what happened to Madison.'

'And I told you I don't know.'

'Someone who was there does know.'

'Maybe it was nothing to do with the party at all.'

'Give me a list of the people who were there.'

'You're kidding?' He shook his head. 'No way.'

'Last chance. Don't make me ask you again.'

'I can't do that.'

Milton got up and walked straight at Efron. The man scrabbled backwards, into the chair, and held up his hands to ward him away. Milton swatted them aside, hauled him out of the chair and dragged him across the room to the terrace. He struggled, guessing what Milton had in mind, but his right arm was jacked up behind his back with the fingers splayed, almost pointing all the way up. The more he tried to free himself, the harder Milton pushed his palm, flattening it, each added ounce of pressure closer to breaking Efron's wrist and fingers.

'Last chance.'

'I can't tell you.'

'Your choice.'

Milton shoved him up against the wooden balustrades, the rail at waist height, then forced him over it until his feet were raised off the floor. He fixed his right hand in the waistband of Efron's trousers, locking his bicep to bear the weight, and used his left to press him down. Efron's head went almost vertical, looking straight into the ten-storey drop.

Milton kept his voice calm. 'Who was there?'

'Jesus!'

'Who was there, Jarad?'

'Shit, man, please! I'll tell you, *I'll fucking tell you!*'

* * *

Milton took the lift back down to the ground floor. He had a sheet of A4 paper that Efron had printed for him; he halved it, then quartered it and slipped it into his inside pocket. He waited patiently as the lift descended, the floors ticking off with the same pleasant chime as before. He reached the ground floor, and the doors parted. He wasn't particularly surprised to see the two security guards waiting for him.

'It's all right, boys,' he said. 'No need for any trouble. Your boss is fine, and I'm leaving.'

They each had their hands resting on the butts of their identical Colt .45s.

'Don't move,' the nearest one ordered. He was a big boy – bigger than Milton – and stood with the kind of lazy confidence that a guy gets from being young, a little stupid, six-three and two-ten. The other one had a similar stance: quarterback type, jock, used to getting whatever he wanted. At that age, Milton thought, they'd probably tried out for the police but been shit-canned because they weren't bright enough. They didn't fancy shipping out to the desert in the army, so private security was their best chance to wear a uniform – they probably thought they looked cute doing it – and to wield a little authority.

'You sure you want to do this?'

'Turn around.'

Milton shrugged, made it look like he was resigned to doing as they asked, but as he turned he flung out his right hand in a streaked blur of motion, his fingers held straight with his thumb supporting them beneath. The jab caught the first guard above the larynx, hard and sharp enough to dent his windpipe; he fell backwards, his mouth open in a wide 'O' of surprise, his hands flapping impotently, gasping for breath that wasn't getting into his lungs as easily as it had done before. The second man went for his holstered .45. Milton hit him high on the cheekbone with his right fist, rocking him back, fired in a left jab, then shoved the guy in the chest to bounce him off the wall, and as he came back toward him, he delivered a headbutt straight to his nose. He caught the man's wrist in his hand, yanked his arm around and pivoted so that all of his weight propelled him back into the lift. He bounced face-first off the wall of the lift and landed on his knees. Milton caught the second man by the belt and collar and boosted him into the lift after his friend, reaching around the corner and slapping the button for the tenth floor.

'Tell your boss if he does anything stupid like that again, I'll be back.'

He stepped back as the doors closed and the lift began to ascend.

Then he turned. The two receptionists and the handful of staff in the lobby were all gawping helplessly at him. Milton pulled at his jacket to straighten it out, squared his shoulders again, wished them all a good morning and then walked calmly and purposefully into the car park to his car.

33

Arlen Crawford sat at the desk in the hotel room with policy papers scattered around him. There was a stack on the desk, three distinct piles on the carpet by his feet, and a pile – ready to be read, digested and sorted – spread out across the bed. The speech at the Moscone Center that afternoon was starting to look a whole lot like a coronation, and he wanted to make sure that everything about it was perfect. He had *CNN* on the flat-screen TV that had been fixed to the wall inside a frame to make it look like a painting – it didn't work – and he was drinking from a glass of orange juice, staining a paper on fiscal prudence with wet, concentric circles.

He looked up at the TV. The newscaster was introducing a panel discussion on the San Francisco killings. A third girl had been found and the show featured three specialists who had been brought on to discuss the case. They discussed the findings so far, agreeing that the police didn't appear to have very much to go on. Eventually, and egged on by the host, they diverted to a discussion about the name that should be given to the killer. They looked back through history: BTK,

Zodiak, the Green River Killer, and settled on the Headlands Lookout Killer.

Crawford was roused from his distraction by a soft knocking at the door.

He got up, took a sip of the orange juice and padded across the room in his stockinged feet. It was just after breakfast, and he wasn't expecting anyone.

He opened the door. Karly Hammil, the young female staffer who had been with Robinson after the speech in Woodside, was on the other side.

'What is it, Karly?'

She was anxiously chewing her bottom lip. 'Could I have a word?'

'Yes, of course. Come in.'

He stood back, and she came into the room, closing the door behind her.

'What is it?'

'This is difficult, Mr Crawford.'

'Call me Arlen.' He felt a moment of apprehension. He pointed to the opened minibar. 'You want anything? Water?'

'No, I'm fine.'

'Want to sit?'

'I'd rather stand if that's all right.'

'Well, I'm going to sit.'

She stammered. 'I-I—'

She was nervous, and that made him nervous, too.

'You better tell me what it is.'

She drew a breath. 'There's no point sugar-coating this, I guess. All right, then. Okay.' Another breath. 'Okay. I guess you know some of this already. Five weeks ago, the governor made a sexual advance to me. I know he has a reputation, everyone knows that, but I couldn't believe it. And I resisted it at first; I told him to forget about it, it was a crazy idea, but then he tried again the day after that. I told him no again, but he was more persistent. You know what he can be like, so persuasive, that feeling you get when he fixes his attention on you, like you're the most important person in the world. Well, that's what he made me feel like, and he persuaded me that he really meant all those things he was telling me.'

Crawford felt himself deflate, the air running from his lungs.

'We've been sleeping together once or twice a week ever since.'

'You *have been* – this is past tense?'

'He's stopped it. I saw him last night after the speech. He said he couldn't do it anymore. Something about his wife. It's bullshit, obviously. I guess he's just had what he wanted. He doesn't need me anymore. He's probably already onto the next one.'

Crawford tried to marshal himself. He needed to deal with this. He needed to be diplomatic. He needed her to think that he was sympathetic and understanding. He had experience with this kind of motherfucking nonsense – *plenty* of experience – and he knew what he needed to do. 'I'm sure it isn't like that, Karly. You know what he's like.'

'He's unsafe for a woman to work around is what he is,' she said angrily.

'Why are you telling me? What do you want me to do?'

She looked at him as if he was stupid. '*Seriously?*'

'Tell me.'

'You need to look after me.'

'Of course you'll be looked after. I'll make sure you get an apology. And it'll never happen again.'

'Not like *that*.'

'Then like what?'

'Come on, Mr Crawford. You want me to spell it out?'

'Money?'

'Maybe I should sit tight, wait until he's better known. A story like this, what kind of book deal do you reckon I'd get if I waited until later? His inauguration, maybe? The day before the election?'

Crawford felt the familiar, cold knot of anger tightening in his gut. 'All right, I get it. I get it. How much do you want?'

'I don't know.'

'You have to give me a number.'

'Okay. Fifty thousand – that's what I would've earned this year.'

'Fifty.' He felt his temperature rising.

She hesitated uncertainly. 'What do we do now?'

'First time you've shaken somebody down?' he spat sarcastically.

Her eyes flashed. 'You're angry with *me*? Maybe you ought to think a little about him, Mr Crawford.'

He tried to defuse the tension. 'Arlen – call me Arlen, please.'

She ignored the attempt at conciliation. 'You don't know how close I was to putting this out there. A man like him, a weak man – how is that good for our country to have him in high office?'

Crawford forced himself to take a breath, to regain a little composure. 'No, you're right. Quite right. I'm sorry, Karly. It'll take me a little while to sort this out. It's not quite as straight-forward as you think, that much money. It needs to be done quietly. Is that all right?'

'Of course.'

She exhaled.

He had a moment of empathy; it had probably been one of the most difficult conversations she had ever had. She didn't deserve his anger. It wasn't her fault. Robinson, on the other hand, *did* deserve it. His behaviour kept putting him in intolerable situations. Robinson was irresponsible and child-ish, ignoring his clear instructions that he had to put this behind him and keep it zipped. Cleaning up the mess that he left in his wake was becoming a full-time job. An *expen-sive* full-time job.

Crawford told the girl that she just had to be patient, that he would sort it all out for her, and then he showed her to the door of his room. He switched channels on the television, lay back on his bed and stared at the ball game that was playing on repeat for five minutes, not paying any attention to it, running the situation around in his head and wondering if there was any other way it could be resolved.

He decided that there was not.

He picked up his phone from the bedside table and called the usual number.

34

Milton was headed to the Moscone Center when his mobile buzzed in its cradle. He glanced at the display; Trip Macklemore was calling. He pulled out of the traffic, parked and called him back.

'Have you heard?' Trip said as soon as he accepted the call.

'Heard what?'

'They've found another body – it's on the news.'

'It isn't Madison.'

'How do you know that?'

'The police turned up again.'

'You're kidding?'

'It's just routine. It's nothing.'

'It might not be her now, but it's just a matter of time, isn't it? You know that – she'll be next.'

'We don't know that.'

'*I* do.'

Milton thought he could hear traffic on the call. 'Where are you?'

'In a cab. I'm going up there.'

'What for?'

'To see Brady.'

'No, Trip—'

'Yes, Mr Smith. He did it. It's fucking obvious. It's *him*. We know he's been lying to us right from the start. What else has he been lying about? I'm gonna make him admit it.'

'How are you going to do that?'

'It's all right. I'll take it from here.'

Milton gripped the wheel. 'Don't,' he said. 'Turn around and come back. We just need to wait. Getting into an argument up there will make things worse.'

'I'm sick of waiting. Nothing's happening. They're not doing shit.'

Milton was about to tell him about Efron and what he had learnt, but the call went dead.

He redialled, but there was no answer.

Dammit.

The boy had sounded terrible, wired, his voice straining with stress, as if at his breaking point. Milton had to stop him before he did something stupid, something that would wreck his life. He put the Explorer into gear, pulled out into traffic and swung around.

He drove as fast as he dared. Trip was already on the way. Where was he? The traffic was mercifully light as he accelerated across the Golden Gate Bridge, and it stayed clear all the way to the turning onto Tiburon Boulevard. He swung to the south, still clear, and reached Pine Shore without seeing the boy.

He drove inside the gates. There was an outside-broadcast truck parked across the pavement and a reporter delivering a piece to a camera. Great, Milton thought. He was hoping the media would all have moved on by now, but the new body had juiced the story again, and with the police still floundering, they were going to focus on the place where the next presumed victim went missing. There was nothing else for them to go on.

An empty San Francisco cab was coming the other way.

Too late?

Milton parked outside Brady's cottage and hurried up the steps. The door was ajar, and he could hear raised voices from inside.

He made out two bellowed words: '*Tell me!*'

He pushed the door and quickly followed the corridor through into the living room. Brady was on one side of the room, next to the wide window with the view down to the bay. Trip was opposite him.

'I know she was in here!' Trip said, angrily stabbing a finger at the doctor.

'No, she wasn't.'

'Don't fucking lie to me!'

'Get out of my house!'

'I'm not going anywhere. What did you do to her?'

Milton was behind Trip, and it was Brady who noticed him first. 'Get this meathead out of here,' he ordered. 'You got ten seconds, or I'm calling the cops.'

'Go ahead and call them,' Trip thundered back at him. 'Maybe they'll finally ask *you* some questions.'

'I've told you – I had nothing to do with whatever it was that happened to your girlfriend. You know what? Maybe you want to stop harassing me and start thinking that maybe if you'd done something to stop her from going out hooking, then none of this would have happened.'

That really pushed Trip's buttons; he surged forward, knocking a chair out of the way. Brady's face registered stark fear as Trip raised his fist and drilled him in the mouth. The doctor stumbled backwards, overbalanced and slammed against the low wooden coffee table, the impact snapping one table leg and tipping a fruit bowl onto the floor.

'Where is she?' Trip yelled.

Brady shuffled away from him on the seat of his pants. 'I don't know,' he stammered, blood dribbling out of the corner of his mouth.

'Trip!' Milton said. 'Calm down.'

'Fuck that. What's that got us so far? Nothing. We need to *do* something.'

'We are doing something.'

'Yeah? What are you doing? I don't see anything happening. Doing things your way hasn't got us anywhere, has it? It's my turn now. I'm telling you, man, this piece of shit is going to tell me what happened to my girl.'

The boy reached down with his right hand, and Milton saw, just in time, the glint of silver that emerged from the darkness of his half-open jacket. He thrust his own arm out, his hand fastening around Trip's wrist.

'No,' the boy said, struggling, and he was young and strong, but Milton knew all kinds of things that the boy could only dream about, and he slid his index and forefinger around to the inside of his arm, down until it was two fingers up from the crease of his wrist, and squeezed. The pressure point was above the median nerve, and Milton applied just enough torque to buckle the boy's knees with the unexpected shock.

'Don't,' Milton said, looking at him with sudden, narrow-eyed aggression.

Trip gritted his teeth through the blare of pain. 'He did it.'

Milton kept the pressure on, impelling Trip back towards the hallway. 'No, he didn't.'

He looked at Milton in fuming, helpless entreaty. 'Then who did?'

'I have a better idea,' he said.

Confusion broke through the pain on the boy's face. 'Who?'

'You're going to go outside now,' Milton said in a firm voice that did not brook disobedience. 'There's a reporter out there, down the road, so you need to be calm, like nothing's going on – we don't want there to be a scene. Understand?'

'*Who* is it?'

'I'll tell you on the way back. But you have to tell me you understand. Do you understand?'

Trip's eyes were red-raw, scoured and agitated. He looked as if he had gone without sleep. 'Fine.'

Milton gave him the keys to the car. 'I'll be right after you.'

'What are you going to do?'

'Just go.'

Milton waited until he heard the squeak of the front door as Trip opened it.

He went across the room and offered a hand to Brady. The man took it, and Milton helped him back to his feet.

Brady went to the galley kitchen, picked up a dishcloth and mopped the blood from his face. 'If you think that's the end of this, you're out of your mind.'

'It *is* the end of it,' Milton said.

'You saw – he sucker-punched me!'

'I know, and he's sorry he did that. So am I. I know you've got nothing to do with what happened to Madison.'

'Damn straight I don't.'

'But I also know that it's better for you to forget that just happened and move on.'

'You reckon? I don't think so.'

'I do. A friend of mine works for St Francis. Legal department. You said you used to work down there, so I thought maybe it was worth getting her to have a look into your record, see if it stacked up like you said it did. And it turns out you have a pretty thick personnel file there.'

'How dare you—'

'Here's what I know: you didn't choose to leave, you were *asked* to go. Two sexual harassment cases. The first one was a nurse, right?'

Brady scowled at him, but said nothing.

'And the second one was a technician. She had to be persuaded from going to the police. You had to pay her a lot of money, didn't you?' Milton was next to the picture of Brady in the desert; he picked it up and made a show of examining it. 'It was an interesting read, Dr Brady. You want me to go on?'

'Get out,' Brady said.

* * *

Trip was waiting in the car. Milton leant across towards him and used his right hand to reach inside his coat. His fingers touched the butt of a small gun. He pulled it out. It was a .25 calibre semi-auto, a Saturday Night Special. Milton slipped the gun into his own pocket.

'You're an idiot,' Milton said. '*What* were you thinking?'

Trip stared out of the window. 'I had to do something,' he said with a surly inflection that made Milton think how young he really was. 'Someone had to do something.'

'And so you were going to threaten him with a gun?'

'You got a better plan?'

'You would've gone to prison.'

'I don't care.'

'Yes, you do. And so do I. And anyway, it would all have been for nothing; he didn't do it.'

The boy frowned, confused. 'How do you know that?'

'Brady is a talker. He likes to be the centre of attention. He has enemies in the neighbourhood, too, and maybe those enemies like other people to believe that he's up to no good. Victor Leonard and Brady hate each other. If you ask me, Leonard put us onto Brady because he wants to see him in trouble. But Brady's got nothing to do with this. If he's guilty of anything, it's being a fantasist and a braggart.'

'I don't buy that,' Trip said, although Milton could see that he was getting through to him.

'So are you going to let me drive you back into town?'

'You said you had something.'

'I do. I have a very good lead.'

'What do you mean?'

'I think I know what happened to Madison.'

35

Arlen Crawford drove around the block three times until he was sure that he was not being followed. It was an abundance of caution, perhaps, but Crawford was an operator, experienced enough to know all the tricks. He knew staffers who had been tailed before, heading to meet a friendly journalist to leak something explosive, only to find that their meeting was photographed and reported, and before they knew it, *they* were the story, not the leak. There was no way that he was going to let that happen to him. He was too good. And the consequences didn't bear thinking about.

Not for this.

The guys operated out of a warehouse in Potrero Hill. It was a low-slung building in the centre of a wide compound surrounded by a perimeter of ten-foot-high wire. Floodlights stood on pylons, and there were security cameras all over. The warehouse was owned by a company that distributed beer, and the compound housed three trucks. Empty kegs had been stacked against the wall of the warehouse, and next to that, four big motorcycles had been parked. An old Cadillac Eldorado had been slotted alongside the bikes.

Crawford drew up against the compound gate and sounded his horn. The single black eye of the security camera gleamed down at him, regarding him, and then there was the buzz of a motor and a rusty scrape as the gate slid aside. Crawford put the car into gear and edged inside. He parked next to the Caddy and went into the warehouse. The main room had been fitted with comfortable chairs, a large television and a sound system that was playing stoner rock. The place smelt powerfully of stale beer; it was strong enough that Crawford felt like gagging.

The four men were arranged around the room. Their leader was a tall, skinny man with prison tattoos visible on every inch of exposed skin. There was a swastika etched onto the nape of his neck, just below the line of his scalp. His name was Jack Kerrigan, but they all referred to him as Smokey. Crawford had been introduced to him by Sidney Packard, their head of security. He had recommended him and his boys as a solution for problems that could only be solved with the radical measures that they could implement. Strong-arm jobs, pressure that needed exerting to shut people up or to get them to do things that they naturally didn't want to do. The others were cut from the same cloth as Kerrigan: tattoos, lank hair worn long, a lot of greasy denim.

Kerrigan got up and stretched, leonine, before sauntering across to him.

'Mr Crawford,' he said, a low Southern drawl.

'Jack.'

The air was heady with dope smoke; Crawford noticed a large glass bong on the table.

'How's our boy doing?'

'He's doing good.'

'Good enough to get it done?'

'He'll win,' Crawford said. 'Provided we keep him on the right track.'

'That's all that matters.'

Crawford nodded at that, then scowled a little; he had forgotten the headache he had developed the last time they had dragged him out here. It was the dope, the droning music, the dull grind of the necessity of making sure the dumbfuck rednecks stayed on the right path.

'Wanna beer?'

'No, thanks.'

He nodded at the bong. 'Smoke?'

'What do you think?'

'Nah, not your scene. All business today, then. I can work with that. What's up?'

'We've got a problem.'

'If you mean the girls – I told you, you need to stop worrying.'

'That's easy for you to say.'

'I have a little update on that, something that'll make you feel better.' Kerrigan stooped to a fridge and took out a bottle of beer. He offered it to Crawford. 'You sure?'

'No,' he said impatiently. 'What update?'

Kerrigan popped the top with an opener fixed to his keychain and took a long swig.

'What is it, Jack?'

'Got someone who knows someone in the police. Friend of our persuasion, you know what I mean. Fellow soldier. This guy says that they have no clue. Those girls have been out there a long time – all that salty air, the animals, all that shit – there's barely anything left of them.'

'Clothes?'

'Sure, but there's nothing that would give them any idea who they were.'

'I wish I shared your confidence, Jack. What about the others?'

'You know, I can't rightly recall how many there were, and I ain't kidding about that.'

'*Four.*'

'It'll be the same. You might not believe it, but we were careful.'

'They're all in the same place.'

'Give or take.'

'You think that's careful?'

'The way I see it, the way we left them girls, all in that spot and all done up the same way, police are gonna put two and two together and say that there's one of them serial killers around and about, doing his business.'

'I heard that on the TV already,' one of the other men, Jesse, chimed in. 'They had experts on, pontificating types. They said they was sure. Serial killer. They was saying Zodiac's come back.'

'Son of Zodiac,' Kerrigan corrected.

Crawford sighed.

'They're gonna say it's some john from the city, someone the girls all knew.'

'The Headlands Lookout Killer. That's what they're saying.'

'Exactly,' Kerrigan said with evident satisfaction. 'And that's what we want them to think.' He took a cigarette from a pack on the table and lit it. 'It's unfortunate about our boy's habits, but if there's one thing we got lucky on, it's who they all were. What they did. In my experience, most hookers don't have anyone waiting for them at home to report them missing. They're in the shadows. Chances are, whoever those girls were, no one's even noticed that they're gone. How are the police going to identify people that they don't know is missing? They ain't. No way on earth. And if they can't identify them, how the hell they gonna tie 'em all back to our boy?'

'I don't know,' Crawford said impatiently.

'I do – I do know. They *ain't.*' Kerrigan said it with a sly leer. 'Make you feel any better?'

'Oh, yes,' Crawford replied, making no effort to hide his sarcasm. 'I can't tell you how relieved I am. I would've felt even better if you'd done what I asked you to and made them all *disappear.*'

'What happened to them, Mr Crawford, it's the same thing. They are disappeared. You've got to relax, man. You're gonna give yourself a coronary if you keep worrying about stuff that don't warrant no worrying about.'

'Someone has to.'

'Fine.' Kerrigan took another long pull of his beer. 'You worry about it as much as you want, but I'm telling you, there ain't no need for it.' He finished the beer and tossed it into an open bin. 'Now then – you didn't come here to bitch and moan at us. What can we do for you?'

'There's another problem.'

'Same kind of problem as before?'

'The exact same kind.'

Kerrigan shook his head. 'Seriously? Number five? You want to get our boy to keep his little man in his trousers.'

'You think I haven't tried? It's not as easy as you think.'

'Who is it? Another hooker?'

'No, not this time. Worse. She's on staff. He's been schtupping her for a month, and now she's trying to shake us down. We either pay up, or she goes public. One or the other. It couldn't be any more damaging.'

'And paying her wouldn't work?'

'What do you think?'

Kerrigan's greasy hair flicked as he shook his head. 'Nah – that ain't the best outcome. She might get a taste for it. You want her gone?'

There it was – the power of life and death in the palm of his hand. It still gave Crawford chills. And what choice did he have? Joseph Jack Robinson II, for all his faults, was still the medicine that America needed. He was the best chance of correcting the god-almighty mess that the country had become, and if that meant that they had to clean up his messes to keep him aimed in the right direction, then that was what they would have to do. It was distasteful, but it was for the greater good. The needs of the many against the needs of the few.

'Sort it,' he said.

'Same as before. No problem.'

'No, Jack. *Not* the same as before. Make it so she disappears. Properly disappears. This stuff on the news—'

'I'm telling you, that was just bad luck is what that was.'

'No, Jack, it's fucking amateur hour, *that's* what it was. I never want to hear about her again. Not next week. Not next month. Not when some mutt puts its snout into a bush on the beach next fucking year. You get me? *Never.*'

'Sure I do.' Kerrigan fixed him with gimlet eyes, and Crawford remembered what the man was capable of; the man was a snake – venomous, lethal – and like a snake, he needed careful handling. 'You got her details? We'll get looking into it right away.'

36

'Thank you so much. Thank you all very, very much. Thank you all. I can't tell you how wonderful that makes me feel.'

The crowd roared. Robinson took the applause, raising his arm above his head and waving broadly, shining his high-beam smile out over the adoring crowd. He walked across to the right-hand side of the stage, paused to bask in the acclaim – occasionally pointing out people in the crowd who he recognised, or those who he wanted to give the impression that he recognised – and then came back to the left, repeating the trick.

Milton was almost entirely apolitical, a personal choice he had made so that he was able to carry out his orders dispassionately and without regard to the colour of the government that he was serving, but even he could feel the electricity in the air. The woman next to him was glassy-eyed and a little unsteady on her feet. The man at her side was booming out the three syllables of Robinson's name with no regard to what the others around him might think (not that it mattered; they were just as fervent as he was). The air thrummed with excitement. It was close to mania.

Robinson came down the steps. A path had been arranged right down the centre of the hall, maintained on either side by metal railings that slotted together to form a barrier. There were photographers there, their cameras ready to take a thousand snaps of the governor in the midst of his people.

Milton knew he would only have one chance to get at him, and he had to move fast. He pushed his way to the front of the crowd, muscling through the throng until he was pressed up against the barrier. Robinson was ten feet away, the crowd swelling until Milton was squeezed even tighter against the metal. He thrust his elbow back to free his right arm and extended it out, over the guardrail, bending his usually inexpressive face into a smile. 'Great speech, Governor.'

'Thank you, sir.'

Robinson bathed him in that brilliant smile and took his hand, emphasising the gesture by placing his left on top of Milton's right. A nearby camera flashed, white streaks blasting across his eyes.

Milton maintained his own smile.

He tightened his grip.

He leant in even closer.

'I need to speak to you, Governor.'

A flicker of concern. 'I'm afraid I'm a little busy.'

Milton didn't release his hand.

'And you need to talk to me. It's very important.'

Robinson tried to pull his hand away, but Milton just tightened his grip, taking the strain easily.

Robinson took his left hand away and tugged again with his right. 'Let go.'

Milton did not. The governor's expression mutated; the fixed grin and the sparkle in his eyes were both washed away by a sudden flush of fear. The security man in the suit, less than five paces away, had noticed what was happening. He started to close in. Milton guessed he had a couple of seconds.

'I know about you and Madison Clarke.'

The fear in Robinson's eyes was subtly altered. It graduated from an immediate fear, a response to the physical threat of the smiling man with the cold eyes who wouldn't let go of his hand, to a deeper fear, more primal, more fundamental, one that required calculation to properly assess.

Milton could see him begin to make that calculation.

'Let go of the governor's hand,' the man in the suit said.

Milton held on.

His mouth was inches from Robinson's ear.

'I *know*, Governor. You need to talk to me. Your campaign is going to end tomorrow if you don't.'

37

Arlen Crawford followed the governor into the back of the building. He was worried. He had seen the man to whom Robinson had been speaking. It could only have been a short conversation, a handful of words, but whatever had been said had spooked Robinson badly. Normally, after a speech that had been as well received as that one had been, the governor would have been exhilarated, anxiously seeking the redundant confirmation from Crawford that it had gone as well as it had appeared. He would have soaked up the acclaim. This was different; his eyes were haunted, there was a sheen of light sweat across his brow, and the tic in his cheek that was only noticeable when he was nervous had started to twitch uncontrollably.

Crawford hurried to catch up. 'What did he say?'

'Something about me and Madison.'

'What about her?'

'That *he knows*, Arlen. He knows about me and her. He said I needed to talk to him, and if I don't, he'll end the campaign.'

Crawford's stomach immediately felt empty. 'Let me handle it.'

'No. Not this time.'

Robinson walked quickly through a service corridor. Crawford had trouble keeping up with him.

'He's a crank. We've had them before, and there'll be more and more of them the better we're doing. Please, sir – let *me* speak to him first. If it's anything we need to worry about, I'll let you know. You speaking to him now is just asking for trouble.'

'No, Arlen.'

'We don't even know who he is!'

'We'll do it in private, out back. I want to hear what he has to say. I don't want you reporting it back to me, pulling your punches – you do that all the time.'

Crawford trailed after him. 'I don't understand. Why are you so worried about him?'

'I told you before – I still don't know what happened with me and Madison.'

'It was nothing.'

'No, Arlen, it was. She just stopped taking my calls. One day, it was great; the next, nothing. It was out of character. I never got an explanation.'

'We spoke about that. It was for the best. If it came out . . . you and her . . . a prostitute . . . Jesus, J.J., that would sink us for good. There's no coming back from a story like that.'

Robinson stopped abruptly and turned to him. 'Do you know what happened to her?'

Crawford took a quick breath and covered his discomfort with a vigorous shake of his head. 'No, sir, I don't. But we've been lucky so far. No one has said anything about the two of you. I just don't see the point in pushing it.'

'Noted.'

'So you'll let me handle this?'

'No. I want to speak to him.'

Robinson pushed through wide double doors and into the kitchen that served the conference centre. The doors banged back against Crawford's shoulders as he followed in his wake. It was a large space, full of scratched and dented metallic work surfaces, large industrial ovens and burners, walk-in fridges and freezers, dinged pots and pans hanging down on racks suspended from the ceiling. Chefs in grubby white jackets were preparing the lunch that would be enjoyed by the governor's guests. The space was filled with noise, warm aromas and clouds of steam.

Robinson walked right into the middle of the busy chaos; the man to whom he had been speaking was waiting for them at the edge of the room, standing next to the two security guards who had brought him back here. Crawford hurried in his wake, straining for a better glimpse of his interlocutor.

He didn't recognise the man. He was a little over six feet tall and slender, at least when compared to the muscular security on either side of him. He had dark hair and a scar across his face. A cruel mouth. His eyes were blue, crystal blue, and they were cold and calm. There was something unsettling about him. He looked perfectly composed, a centre of calm in the frantic activity that clattered and whirled around him. He wasn't fazed by the guards. He wasn't fazed by the governor, either.

'What's your name, sir?' Robinson asked him.

'John Smith.'

'Let's get this over with as quickly as we can.'

'I think that would be best.'

'So – what is it you want to say?'

'Wouldn't you prefer this to be in private?'

Robinson told the security guards to stand aside.

'Who's this?' Smith asked, indicating Crawford.

'This is my chief of staff. I have no secrets from him. Now – please – what do you want to tell me?'

'I know that you were having an affair with her.'

'How do you know that?'

'There was a party in Pine Shore. A fundraiser for your campaign. Jarad Efron hosted it.'

He frowned. 'And? How is that relevant?'

'Madison Clarke was there. Obviously, you know she was an escort.'

'The governor doesn't know that,' Crawford interposed hurriedly. 'And he doesn't know who the girl is, either.'

'It would be better if we didn't waste time,' Smith said, looking straight at Robinson rather than Crawford. 'I spoke to Mr Efron. He said you were at the party. And he said that you and Madison were seeing each other. I understand that he introduced the two of you – he said that he was a client of hers and then you took a shine to her. I believe you had been seeing her for several weeks. He arranged for her to be there.'

Crawford felt a red-hot scorch of anger. Why had Efron said that? What was he thinking? And then, a flash of divination:

there was something about Smith. It was self-evident what had happened. There was a deadness in the man's eyes. It was unnerving, a little menacing. Crawford guessed that he could be very persuasive.

'You *were* seeing her, weren't you?'

'I was,' Robinson confirmed quietly. 'She's special. I'm very fond of her.'

'Did you see her at the party?'

'The governor wasn't at the party.'

'Arlen—'

'You know she went missing afterwards?'

Robinson looked at Crawford, then back at Smith. 'I had no idea.'

Crawford felt a shiver of anxiety. 'She hasn't been seen since.'

Crawford stepped forwards. 'What does this have to do with you, Mr Smith?'

'I drove her to the party.'

'So, what – you're her friend? Her agent?'

'I'm just a driver.'

'And so what's this about? What's it *really* about? You want money or you're going to the papers? They won't believe you, Mr Smith—'

'I don't want money,' he interrupted. 'I want to know what happened to her.'

'Arlen—'

Crawford ignored the governor. 'Let's say he did know her, just for the sake of argument. She was a *prostitute*, Mr Smith. You said so yourself. Maybe she had money problems? Maybe she's hiding from someone? Maybe she had an issue with drugs? There could be any number of reasons.'

'Arlen—'

Smith pressed ahead. 'Those things are all possible, but unlikely, considering the circumstances. I waited for her that night. I was going to drive her back into the city again. But then I heard her screaming.'

'It was *that* party?' Robinson said to Crawford. 'I remember. You dragged me away? She was there?'

Crawford clenched his teeth.

'I went into the house to get her out,' Smith said. 'She was in a terrible state – panicking, she said someone had threatened to kill her.'

'Arlen?'

'This is news to me.'

'She ran away and disappeared,' Smith said.

'So she's hiding somewhere,' Crawford said sharply. 'Report it to the police.'

'I did that. But now I think she might not be missing. I think she's been murdered. The bodies that have been turning up along the coast road—'

'How on earth is that relevant—'

'—Up on the headland?' Robinson interrupted.

'Yes,' Smith said. 'You know about that?'

'Only vaguely.'

'I think her disappearance might be connected.'

'You think the governor has something to do with that?' Crawford managed to splutter.

Smith shrugged. 'I didn't say that. But he might know something that could help find her, one way or another.'

Crawford felt like he was losing control of the conversation and, beyond that, his tenuous grip on the whole situation. 'That is all speculation,' he protested. 'Dangerous speculation with no basis in fact. And it has nothing to do with the governor.'

'Of course it does, Arlen! I was seeing her, and then she disappears. Maybe something has happened to her. Of course it's relevant. At the very least, I need to speak to the police. Maybe I can help.'

Smith pressed. 'You've no idea what happened?'

'Of course he doesn't know!'

Smith ignored him; he moved around slightly so that he was facing away from him, placing his shoulder between himself and Robinson so that Crawford was temporarily boxed out of the conversation. 'If there's anything you can tell me, sir, I would appreciate it.'

'I can't think of anything. Really – I can't.'

Crawford pressed himself back into the conversation. 'What are you going to do?' he asked Smith.

'That depends. You need to speak to the police. I think you should do it right away. I'm not an expert at these things – crisis management, I suppose you'd call it – but it would probably be best for you and your campaign if you're seen to be volunteering information. Maybe they can keep it confidential, I don't know. But you have to speak to them. I'll wait until tomorrow, and then I'll tell them what I know.'

'We'll tell them,' Robinson said. 'Right away. Thank you for speaking to me, Mr Smith. I really do appreciate it.'

The governor had a dazed look on his face. He shook the man's hand, an automatic reaction after these long months of campaigning, and made his way out of the kitchen. Crawford turned to follow, then paused, turning halfway back again, wanting to say something to the man, something that might make the problem go away, but he didn't look like the kind of person who could be intimidated or bought off or deflected from his course in any way whatsoever. His posture was loose and easy, and he returned Crawford's angry stare with implacable cool. It was unnerving.

Crawford turned back to the door again and hurried after the governor.

He was waiting for him in the service corridor.

'We need to think about this, sir.'

'What's there to think about? It's obvious what we have to do.'

'We mustn't act hastily. Everything is at stake.'

'I have to speak to the police.'

'That's a bad idea. A *terrible* idea.'

'No, Arlen. It's the right thing to do.'

'J.J. please – this doesn't have to be a threat. All he has is what Efron told him.'

'But it's *true*.'

'All he can say is that you were at the same party as she was.'

'And I was seeing her.'

'No one can prove that.'

'It doesn't matter if they can or they can't. She's missing. Those girls have turned up not five miles from there. Maybe this is connected. And maybe there is something that I can help the police with. Don't you think it's possible?'

'No, I don't. But if you're determined, then, all right, fine – but let me speak to them.'

'No,' he said. 'It has to be me.'

38

Milton got into his car and drove. He wasn't sure how to assess the meeting. Had he scared Robinson enough? He was confident that he had. The governor had received the message, but it was obvious that Crawford held significant influence over him. There was a base cunning there, Milton had seen it clearly, and he could see that he would try to limit the governor's exposure. How would he do that? Milton wasn't sure. Would Crawford be able to stop him from going to the police? Perhaps. All he had were guesses about what would happen next. Milton had meant what he said, though; he would give them until tomorrow to do the right thing. If they did not, he would take matters into his own hands and go to the police himself.

He checked his watch: six. He was late for his next appointment. He drove quickly across town to Pacific Heights and parked in a lot near to the Hotel Drisco. It was a boutique place, obviously expensive, everything understated and minimal. Milton climbed the steps to the smart lobby, all oak panelling and thick carpet, a little out of place in his scruffy jeans, dirty shirt and scuffed boots. The doorman gave him a disapproving look, but Milton stared him down, daring him to say anything, then walked past him and into the bar.

Beau was sitting at a table beneath an ornate light fixture, a copy of the *San Francisco Chronicle* spread out on the table before him. His glass was empty, so Milton diverted to the bar, paid for a beer and an orange juice and ferried them across.

'Evening,' Milton said, sitting down.

'Evening, English.'

Milton pushed the beer across the table.

Beau thanked him and drank down the first quarter of the glass. 'That name you got from the Lucianos – you do what you needed to do?'

'Yes.'

'And?'

'And thanks for your help.'

'I should know better than to ask what it was all for?'

'Probably best.'

'You're a secretive fella, ain't you?'

Beau folded the paper but not before Milton saw the news on the front page: an article on the bodies that had been dug up on the headland. He said nothing and watched as Beau drank off another measure of the beer. 'How long are you here for?' he asked him.

'Couple days. I've got some work to attend to.'

'Anything interesting?'

'Not particularly. I ever tell you about my other business?'

'I don't think we ever had the chance.'

Beau put the glass on the table. 'I'm a bail bondsman—well, least I used to be. You have them in England?'

'It doesn't work like that.'

'Guess the whole thing is a little Wild West. I got into it when I got out of the Border Patrol. Probably why I used to like it so much. I don't do so much of that no more, though, but it's still my good name above the door, still my reputation on the line. An old friend of mine who runs the show while I'm away got shot trying to bring a fellow back to San Diego to answer his obligations. This fellow's got family up here, and the word is that he's hiding out with them. Sure as the sun rises in the east and sets in the west, he's coming back down south with me. You calling was good timing – I was going to have to come up here anyways. Two birds with one stone. Now I'm going to have a look and see if I can find him.'

Milton sipped his orange juice. Time to change the subject. 'So – did you speak to the Italians?'

'About the other thing? The loan shark? I did.'

'And?'

'They did a little looking into it. Like you thought – your Mr Martinez has been running his operation without cutting them in. Strictly small-time, just a local neighbourhood kind of deal, but that ain't clever on his part. You want to play in that particular game, you got to pay your taxes, and he ain't been paying. They were unhappy about it.'

'Unhappy enough to do something about it?'

'Oh, sure.'

'What are they going to do?'

'Let's call it a hostile takeover. You just need to tell me where he's at, and I'll see that it gets sorted.'

'I can do that. What about my friend?'

'They'll wipe out the debt.'

'How much do they want for it?'

Beau held up his hands. 'No charge. They'll be taking over his book – that's worth plenty to them. His debt can be your finder's fee. They'll give it to you.'

Milton took his orange juice and touched it against the side of Beau's beer. 'Thanks, Beau,' he said. 'I owe you.'

'Yeah, well, about that. There's maybe something we can do to square that away. This fellow I've come to take back down to San Diego, there's no way he's going to play nice. Some of the runners we go after, they're real badass until it comes down to the nut-cutting, and then, when the moment of true balls comes around, most of them capitulate. This guy, though? There's always one asshole in the crowd who has to be different, and I'm not getting any younger. I was thinking maybe I could use a hand.'

'When?'

Beau finished his beer. 'You doing anything now?'

39

The place was in the hills outside Vallejo. It was a clear evening, and for once, there was a perfect view all the way down to the Golden Gate Bridge and the lights of the city beyond. Beau drove along Daniels Avenue until he found number 225. Hank had given him the address, and Beau had had it checked with an investigator they sometimes used when they had runners in Northern California. It was a small, two-storey house painted eggshell blue. There was a line of red-brick steps that led up from a carport to the first-floor entrance. The brick wall was topped with imitation lanterns on the corners, the garden was overgrown and scruffy, and the car in the driveway was up on bricks. It was down-at-heel, the worst house on the street, and tonight, it looked like it was hosting a party. A couple of men were smoking in the garden, and loud music was coming from inside.

'That the place?'

'It is.' Beau drove on and parked out of sight.

'A busy place, drink, maybe drugs? That'll make things more difficult.'

'I know.'

'Still want to do it?'

'I'm picking him up come hell or high water.'

'How do you want to play it?'

Beau looked at the house, assessing it. 'You got a preference?'

Milton looked at him with a smile. 'Old man like you?' he said. 'You go around the back, and get ready if he runs. I'll go in and flush him out.'

'All right,' he said. 'You know what he looks like?'

Smith had studied Beau's photograph on the drive north from San Francisco. 'Big. Nasty-looking. I'll recognise him.'

'Goes by the name of Ordell,' Beau reminded him.

'Don't worry. I got it.'

Beau held up the cosh. 'Want this?'

'Keep it. I'll give you ten minutes to get yourself around the back, and then I'll go in.'

* * *

Beau rolled the car around the block until he found an access road that ran between the back gardens of Daniels Avenue. It was a narrow street that climbed a hill with broken fencing on both sides, wooden garages that were barely standing and unkempt trees that spread their boughs overhead. A row of cars, covered over with tarps, was parked along one side of the road. He recognised Number 225 from the peeling blue paint and settled into place to wait behind the wing of a battered old Ford Taurus.

He had barely been there a minute when he heard the sound of raised voices and then crashing furniture.

He rose up quickly.

The back door exploded outwards, the limp body of a man tumbling through the splintered shards.

He took a step forward just in time to intercept the big, angry-looking man who was barrelling out of the shattered doorway. He looked madder than a wet hen. He held one hand to his nose, trying unsuccessfully to stem the flow of blood that was running down his lip, into his mouth and across his chin.

Beau stepped into his path.

'Oh, *shit*,' Ordell Leonard said.

Beau swung the cosh and caught him flush on the side of the head. He went jelly-legged and tripped, Beau snagging the lapels of his shirt as he went stumbling past him, heaving his unsupported weight and lowering him down to the road.

He was out cold before his chin hit the asphalt.

Smith came out of the house, shaking the sting out of his right fist.

'That was easy,' he said.

40

Arlen Crawford was working on the preparation for the next debate. They were in Oakland, another anonymous hotel that was the same as all the others. They were all high-end, all luxury. All the same, one after another, after another, a never-ending line of them. The sheets on the bed were always fine Egyptian cotton, the bathrooms were always Italian marble, the carpets were always luxuriously deep. They were all interchangeable. It was easy to forget where you were.

He put down his pen and leant back in his chair. He thought of John Smith and his threats. That certainly was a problem, and if it had been left to metastasise, it would have grown into something much, much worse. But Crawford had it under control. He had been with Robinson when he reported his connection to the girl to the police. They had done it yesterday evening. He had called in a whole series of favours to arrange for a friendly detective to take the statement. The detective had come to them to avoid any whiff of it getting to the press. There would be no shots of the governor on the steps of a police precinct house. The process of the interview looked official, just as it should, but the statement would never see the light of day. It would never be transcribed, and the tapes onto which it had been recorded had already been shredded.

The detective had reassured Robinson that there was little chance that his liaison with Madison had anything to do with her disappearance. He went further, just as Crawford had suggested, saying that there was no evidence to suggest she had anything to do with the dead girls. The governor's conscience was salved, and now they would be able to get back to the business of winning an election.

Some things were just too important to be derailed.

There was Smith himself, of course. He would need to be dealt with, but that was already in hand. The background checks had turned up very little. He wasn't registered to vote. He didn't appear to pay any taxes. A shitty place in an SRO in the Mission District. He worked nights as a cab driver and worked days hauling blocks of ice. He was a nobody. Practically a vagrant. They had two good men on his case now. Good men, solid tails, both with surveillance experience, the sort who could drift in and out of a crowd without being spotted. They had already got some good stuff. The man went to a meeting of Alcoholics Anonymous. That was useful to know. There was no family, but it looked like there was a girl.

That, too, might be helpful.

Leverage.

He turned his attention back to his work. Crawford had just been emailed the latest polling numbers, and the news was good. They were tracking nicely ahead of the pack, and the last debate ought to be enough to nail the lead down. They had blocked out the weekend for preparation. Crawford was going to be playing the role of Robinson's most likely rival, and he was putting together a list of questions that he knew would be difficult if they came up. Forewarned was forearmed, and all that. Fail to prepare, prepare to fail. Crawford knew all the questions and had drilled them into the rest of the team; drilled them into the governor. That was a difficult proposition given his propensity to shy away from preparation and rely upon his instinct. Crawford preferred a balance, but—

There was a fierce knocking on the door of his hotel room.

He put his pen down. 'What is it?' he called.

'Arlen!'

The banging resumed, louder.

He padded across the carpet and opened the door.

It was Robinson.

'Have you seen the news?'

He looked terrible; his face was deathly pale.

'No,' Crawford said. 'I've been working on the debate.'

'Put it on. *CNN*.'

Crawford rescued the remote from the debris on the desk and flipped channels to *CNN*. It was an outside broadcast. The presenter was standing on the margin of a road with scrub and trees. It was heavy with fog, a dense grey curtain that closed everything in. The ticker at the bottom of the screen announced that the police had finally identified all three sets of remains that had been found at Headlands Lookout.

'Turn it up,' Robinson demanded.

Crawford did as he was told.

'... the bodies of three women found near Headlands Lookout, just behind me here. The victims are twenty-one-year-old Tabitha Wilson of Palo Alto, twenty-five-year-old Megan Gabert of San Francisco and twenty-one-year-old Miley Van Dyken of Vallejo. A police official has revealed to me that there were substantial similarities in how the women died but declined to reveal their causes of death. The same source suggested that the police believe that the three women were killed at a different location, but then their bodies were dumped here. Lorraine Young, Tabitha's mother, has said that police forensic tests, including DNA, have confirmed that one of the bodies belonged to her daughter. The bodies were found within fifty feet of each other in this stretch of rocky grasslands, hidden by overgrown shrubbery and seagrass.'

Crawford felt his knees buckle, just a little.

'What the fuck, Arlen? What the *fuck*?'

Crawford muted the TV.

The muscles in his jaw bunched as he considered all the possible next moves.

None of them were any good.

'Arlen! Don't play dumb with me.' Robinson stabbed a finger at the screen. 'What the fuck!'

'Calm down, sir.'

'*Calm down*? Are you kidding? Seriously? Those girls – you know who they are. Jesus Christ, Arlen, you remember, I know you do.'

Yes, he thought bitterly, I do remember. There were no next moves now. Checkmate. End of the line. The situation was completely out of control, and it could only get worse before it got better. He had been managing it, carefully and diligently, nudging events in the best direction and very discreetly burying all of this so deep that it would never be disturbed. That, at least, had been his intention. The girls were never supposed to be seen again.

'I do remember,' he said.

And then came the recrimination. He should have seen to this himself rather than trusting others; that was his fault, and now he would have to live with it. He had been naïve to think that those dumbass rednecks could be expected to handle something so sensitive in the way it needed to be handled. The brakes were off now, and momentum was gathering. There was little to be done, and knowing that, Crawford almost felt able to relax. The sense of fatalism was strangely comforting. He had, he realised, been so intent on keeping a lid on events that he had neglected to notice the pressure that was building inside him. The stress and the constant worry. The campaign, twice-daily polling numbers, the places they were strong and the places they were weak, the governor's appeal across different demographics, how was he playing with the party, how would the Democrats go after him?

His erratic behaviour.

The suicidal appetite that he couldn't sate.

Time bombs.

Crawford had done his best for as long as he could, but it was too much for one man to handle.

And he didn't have to handle it anymore.

Maybe this had always been inevitable.

Robinson gaped as if the enormity of what he was discovering had struck him dumb. 'And – I—'

'Yes, Governor. That's right.'

'I—'

'You were seeing them all.'

'But—'

'That'll have to come out now, of course. There will be something that ties them to you, something we couldn't clean up: a text message, a diary entry – anything, really. Nothing we can do about that, not now. That ship has sailed.'

The governor put a hand down against the mattress to steady himself. He looked as if he was just about ready to swoon. 'What happened?'

'You don't recall?'

'What's going on, Arlen?'

'You had your way with them for as long as it suited you, and then you put them aside and moved on to whoever you wanted next. The same way you always do. They all came to me. They were hurt and angry, and they wanted revenge. They threatened to go to the press. They asked for money. The problem with that, though, is that you can't ever be sure that they won't come back for more. They get their snouts in the trough, they're going to think that it's always going to be there. It's not hard to see why they might think that, is it? I would. They still have the story to sell. We can't run a campaign with that hanging over us, let alone a presidency.'

'*You* did this?'

'I arranged for things to be sorted.'

'"*Sorted*?"'

'That's right.'

'You *murdered* them?' Robinson slumped.

'No, sir. *You* did.'

'Don't be—'

'I arranged for things to be sorted. What else could I have done?'

'And Madison?'

He shrugged. 'I shouldn't think it'll be long until she turns up.'

'Oh, Jesus . . .'

'It's a bit late for that.'

'Who did it?'

'Friends who share our cause. It doesn't matter who they are. There are some things that are more important than others, Governor. Country, for one. I love this country, sir. But I look at it, and I can see everything that's wrong: unchecked immigration; drugs everywhere; invasive government; standards through the floor; weak foreign policy; the Chinese and the Russians making us look like fools at every turn. That's not what this country was founded to be. We haven't fulfilled our potential for years. *Decades*. You were the best chance of making this country great again. You are . . . No' – he corrected himself, a bitter laugh – 'you *were* . . . very electable. We would have won, Governor. The nomination, the presidency and then whatever we wanted after that. We could've started the work that needs to be done.'

Robinson was hardly even listening to him. 'You *killed* them.'

There was no anger there, not yet, although that would come. He had been stunned into a stupor. The life had been sucked from him. It was a depressing thing to see; the sight of him on a stage, in full flow, railing against the state of the world and promising that he would make things right – that, Crawford thought, *that* was something special. Something to experience. But it was also a mirage. The man was a fraud. No sense in pretending otherwise. A snake-oil salesman. Joseph Jack Robinson II, the most inspirational politician that Arlen Crawford had ever seen, was just another man selling moonshine.

He went over to his suitcase and opened it.

'Why did you do it, Arlen?'

'What happened was necessary for the greater good, sir. It's regrettable, of course, but what were they? Four prostitutes and an intern. They were expendable.'

'An intern? What? What do you mean? *Karly?*'

'That's in hand.'

Robinson jackknifed over the edge of the bed and, suddenly and explosively, voided his guts. He straightened up, wiping the back of his hand across his mouth.

'It's all over now, sir. You had everything. The charisma, the way you command a room, the good sense to know when to listen and adopt the right ideas. You would have been perfect.

Perfect, Governor, if it wasn't for the fact that you're weak. No discipline. I should have realised that months ago. There was always only ever going to be so much that I could do for you, and now, after this' – he pointed to the TV – 'we've gone past the limit. The only thing we can do now is try to limit the damage.'

The smell of his vomit was strong, acrid and cloying.

Crawford took out a gun with a silencer and pointed it at Robinson.

'Arlen—'

'I'm sorry it's come to this, sir, but I don't see any other way.'

PART IV

KARLY HAMMIL

*Mr Crawford had said to meet her at a lookout point in Crissy
Field. He had arranged for her to take a temporary leave of absence
from the campaign, saying that she had contracted glandular fever
and would be out of action for at least a month. That, he said,
would be enough time for them to come up with something better,
but she knew that she would never be going back. In the meantime, he had promised that he would see to the money, and the
rendezvous was so that he could deliver the first instalment to her.
She had driven up to the park and sat in her car and watched as
the sun went down over the bay. It had been a bright day, and as
the sun slipped slowly beneath the horizon, the rusty red metal of
the bridge glowed brightly in its dying rays. The lights of Treasure
Island and, beyond that, Oakland began to flicker, twinkling in
the gloaming, growing brighter.*

*Karly wound down the window and let the air into the car.
She took a pack of cigarettes from the dashboard, held them to her
mouth and pulled one out with her lips. She lit it, sucking the
smoke into her lungs, closing her eyes and enjoying the hit of the
nicotine. The park was empty, save for a couple of joggers who
were descending the hill back towards the city. The night grew*

darker. The last ferry headed back to the mainland from Alcatraz. A jet laid down grey vapour trails as it cut through the star-sprinkled sky overhead. Gulls wheeled on lazy thermals. It was a spectacular view.

She saw the high beams of a car as it turned up the steep road that ended in the vantage point. Karly finished the cigarette and flicked the butt out the window. The car was an old Cadillac, and it was struggling with the incline. As it drew closer, she could see that it was dented on the front-right wing and the number plate was attached to the chassis with duct tape. It slowed and swung into the bay next to her. She squinted through the glare of the headlights, but they were bright and she couldn't make out anything about the driver or the passenger. The door opened, and the driver came over to her side of the car.

41

Julius had a small TV set on a shelf above the door, and he was flicking between channels; they were all running with the same story. Joseph Jack Robinson II, the presumptive candidate as Republican nomination for president, had been found dead in his hotel room. Details were still sketchy, but the early indications were that he had taken his own life. Suicide. There was unconfirmed speculation that he had been found on his bed next to a bottle of Scotch and empty bottles of prescription sleeping tablets. The anchors on all of the channels were reporting the news with the same breathless, stunned sense of disbelief. A major piece in the political life of the country had been swiped from the board. Friends and colleagues were interviewed, some of them fighting back tears. No one could believe that Robinson had killed himself. It didn't make sense, they said. He had been full of life. He had been determined to win the nomination, and now that he had almost achieved that, he was gearing up for election year. To do this, now, to end it all when he had so much to look forward to? It didn't make any sense at all.

There were four other customers in the place today. They were all watching the television.

'*Unbelievable*,' Julius said as he slid a spatula beneath a burger and deftly flipped it. 'Someone like that just topping himself? Don't make no sense.'

'Goes to show,' said one of the others. 'You never know what's in a man's head.'

The coverage switched to an outside broadcast. It was a hotel. Flashbulbs flashed as a figure emerged from the lobby of the hotel and descended until he was halfway down the steps, a thicket of microphones quickly thrust into his face.

'Turn it up, would you?' Milton said.

Julius punched the volume up.

Milton recognised the man. It was Robinson's chief of staff, Arlen Crawford.

'Mr Crawford,' a reporter shouted above the hubbub, 'can you tell us what you know?'

'The governor was found in his room this afternoon by a member of the election team. Paramedics were called, but it was too late – they say he had been dead for several hours. We have no idea why he would have done something like this. I saw him last night to talk about the excellent progress we were making with the campaign. I saw nothing to make me think that this could be possible. The governor was a loud, enthusiastic, colourful man. This is completely out of character.' He looked away for a moment, swallowing, and then passed a hand over his face. 'More than just being my boss, Joseph Jack Robinson was my friend. He's the reason I'm in politics. He's the godfather to my son. He was a good man. The best.' His voice quavered, almost broke. 'What happened this morning is a disaster for this country and a tragedy for everyone who knew him. Thank you. Good day.'

He turned back and made his way into the hotel.

'It might be a personal tragedy,' Julius opined, 'but a *national* one? Nah. Not for me. Boy had some pretty strident views on things, you know what I'm saying? He wouldn't have got my vote.'

Milton's phone rang.

It was Eva.

'Afternoon,' Milton said. 'Are you watching this?'

There was no reply.

Milton checked the phone's display; it was definitely her. 'Eva?'

'Mr Smith,' a male voice said. 'You've caused us a whole heap of trouble, you know that? And now you're gonna have to pay.'

'Who is this?'

'My name's not important.'

It was a Southern accent. A low and lazy drawl. A smoky rasp.

'Where's Eva?'

'She's with us.'

'If you hurt her—'

'You ain't in no position to make threats, Mr Smith.'

'What do you want?'

'To talk.'

'About?'

'You know what about. We need to be sure you won't mention' – there was a pause – 'recent events.'

'The governor.'

'That's right.'

'And if I persuade you that I won't say anything, you'll let her go?'

'Perhaps.'

'Right. I wasn't born yesterday.'

There was a rasping laugh. 'Perhaps and perhaps not, but if you don't play ball with us now, well then, it's a definite no for her, ain't it? How much does she know?'

'She doesn't know anything.'

'Gonna have to speak to her to make sure about that.'

Milton's voice was cold and hard. 'Listen to me – she doesn't know anything.'

'Then maybe we just need you.'

'Where are you?'

'Nah, partner, it ain't gonna happen like that. We know where you are. We'll come to you. You stay right there, all right? Finish your meal. We'll be along presently.'

42

Milton checked the joint out after he had finished speaking to the man on the phone and could guess which of the other four patrons had followed him inside: a scrawny weasel of a man with three days' worth of stubble and a face that had been badly scarred by acne. Milton stared at him, and the man eventually found the guts to make a sly nod, emboldened, no doubt, by the prospect of imminent reinforcements and his opinion that they had the advantage. That knowledge wasn't enough to stiffen his resolve completely, and as Milton stared at him, his confidence folded and he looked away. Milton wondered if there was some way he could use the man to even the odds, but he knew that there would not be. What could he have done? They had Eva, and that, he knew, eliminated almost all of his options.

They arrived in an old Cadillac Eldorado ten minutes after the call. Milton finished his burger, wiped his mouth, laid ten dollars on the counter and went to the car. He got into the back without complaint. There was no point in making things difficult for them.

That would come later.

There were four of them in the car, each of them wearing a biker's leather jacket and each, helpfully, following the biker habit of having a nickname badge sewn onto the left shoulder lapel. The man in the passenger seat was Smokey. It looked like he was in charge. He was tall and slender, all knees and elbows, and Milton saw a tattoo of a swastika on the back of his neck. The driver was bigger, wearing a denim jacket with cut-off sleeves that revealed heavy muscle. His badge identified him as Dog. The men flanking him both had long hair, like the others, and they smelled of stale sweat, pot and booze. There wasn't much space in the back, and they were pressed up against him. The one on his right was flabby, Milton's elbow pressing into the side of his doughy gut, with a full red beard and shoulder-length red hair. His badge identified him as Orangutan. The one on his left was different, solid slabs of muscle, hard and unyielding. If it came down to it, he would be the one to put down first. His nickname was Tiny.

They had a radio on; it was a news channel, and the show was dominated by talk of the governor's death. They discussed it with animation, and Milton quickly got the impression that they considered it a tragedy.

The four of them seemed pretty secure in themselves and their ability to keep Milton in line. He noticed that they didn't blindfold him or do anything to prevent him from seeing where he was being taken. Not a good sign. They didn't plan on him making a return trip, and so, they reckoned, it made no difference what he found out. They were right about one thing: Milton wasn't planning on going back to wherever it was they were going. There would be no need after he was through. He would be leaving, though, and he would be taking Eva with him. And if they thought he would be as pliant as this once they had him wherever they were taking him?

Well, if they thought that, then more fool them.

They drove out to Potrero Hill, the gritty industrial belt on the eastern boundary facing the bay and, on the other side of the water, Oakland. There were warehouses, some old, others cheaply and quickly assembled prefabs. They navigated the streets to the water's edge, prickling with jetties and piers, and then drew up to a gate in a tall mesh wire fence. The compound contained a warehouse, and Milton saw stacks of beer barrels and trucks with the logo of a local brewery that he thought he recognised.

There were four big motorcycles parked under cover next to the warehouse.

Dog hooted the horn, and the gates parted for them.

They took him into the warehouse through a side door. He paid everything careful attention: ways in and out of the building, the number of windows, the internal layout. The place smelt powerfully of hops and old beer, sweat and marijuana. He watched the four men, assessing and reassessing them, confirming again which were the most dangerous and which he could leave until last when it came time to take them out.

They followed a corridor to a door, opened it and pushed him inside.

It was empty, just a few bits and pieces. It looked like it was used as a basic kitchen and dining area. A trestle table with one broken leg. Rubbish strewn across the table. Three wooden chairs. Several trays with beer bottles stacked up against the wall. A dirty microwave oven on the floor next to a handful of ready meals. A metal bin overflowing with empty food packaging. Breeze-block walls painted white. A single naked light bulb overhead. A pin-up calendar from three years ago. No windows. No natural light. No other way in or out.

Eva was standing at the end of the room, as far away from the door as she could get. There was another woman with her.

The skinny guy stepped forwards and shoved Milton in the back so that he stumbled further into the room.

Eva stepped forwards.

'Are you all right?' Milton asked her.

'Yes,' she said.

He kept looking at her. 'They haven't hurt you?'

'No,' she said. She gestured to the other girl. 'This is Karly.'

'Hello, Karly,' Milton said. 'Are you okay?'

She nodded. There was no colour in her face. She was terrified.

'Don't worry,' Milton told her. 'We'll be leaving soon.'

'That right?' Smokey said from behind him, his words edged by a braying laugh.

Milton turned back to him.

'All right then, partner. We got a few questions for you.'

'You should let us leave.'

'You'll go when I say you can go.'

'It'll end badly for you otherwise.'

Smokey snorted. 'You're something, boy. You got some balls – but it's time for you to pay attention.'

'Don't worry. I am.'

'My questions, you gonna answer 'em, one way or another. No doubt you're gonna get slapped around some, don't really matter if you co-operate or not. Only issue is whether we do it the hard way or the *fucking* hard way. Your choice.'

Milton glanced over. The other three men were all inside the room. Smokey was just out of reach, but the big guy, Tiny, was close. The stack of beer bottles was waist high. The cellophane wrapper on the top tray had been torn away, some of the bottles had been removed, and the necks of those that remained were exposed.

'Who are you working for?' Milton asked.

'See, you say you're paying attention, but you ain't. I'm asking, you're answering.'

'Is it Crawford?'

Smokey spat at his feet. 'You gonna have to learn. Tiny – give him a little something to think about.'

Tiny – the big man – balled his right hand into a fist and balanced his weight to fire out a punch. Milton saw and moved faster, reaching out and wrapping his fingers around a bottle, feeling it nestle in his palm, pulling it out of the tray and swinging it, striking the guy on the side of the head, just above his ear. He staggered a little, more from shock than from anything else, and Milton struck the bottle against the wall and smashed it apart, beer splashing up his arm. He closed in and jabbed the jagged end of the bottle into the man's shoulder, then stabbed it into his cheek, twisting it, chewing up the flesh. He dropped the bloodied shards, grabbed Tiny by the shoulders and pulled him in close, driving his knee into his groin, then dropped him down onto the floor.

Three seconds, start to finish.

'The fucking hard way, I guess,' Milton said. He wasn't even breathing hard.

Smokey pulled a pistol from his waistband and brought it up. 'Get back. Over there. Against the wall.'

Milton knew he wouldn't be able to take them all out, but that wasn't what he had in mind. He just wanted a moment alone with Eva. He knew they wouldn't kill him, not yet. They needed some answers before they could think about that, and he wasn't minded to give them any. He did as he was told and stepped back. The man waved the pistol, and he kept going until he was at the rear of the room, next to Eva and Karly.

'Get him out of here,' Smokey said to Orangutan and Dog, pointing at the stricken Tiny. They helped him up, blood running freely from the grisly rent in his cheek, and half-dragged him out into the corridor beyond.

'Last chance,' Milton said.

'For what?' Smokey yelled at him.

'To let us out.'

'Or?'

'I'll make what just happened to him look like a love bite.'

His bravado seemed to confuse, and then amuse, the man. 'Are you out of your fucking mind? Look at you – look where you are. You're *fucked*, brother. You can have a couple of hours to think about that until a friend of ours gets here.'

'Mr Crawford?'

'That's right. Mr Crawford. He wants to speak to you. But then that'll be the end of it after that. You're done. *Finished.*'

43

Milton tried the door. It was locked. He paused for a moment, thinking. He could hear the deep, muffled boom of the foghorns from outside.

Eva came to him. 'Jesus, John,' she said. 'Look at you.' She pointed to a spot on his shirt. 'Is that yours?'

He looked down. A patch of blood. 'No. I'm fine. It's his.'

She turned to the front of the room and the splatter of blood across the bare concrete floor. Her face whitened as she took it in and what it meant. He could read her mind: the horror at what he was capable of doing, the ease and efficiency with which he had maimed the man. How did someone like him, so quiet and closed off, explode with such a terrifying eruption of violence? How did he even have it in him? Milton recognised the look that she was giving him. He had seen it before. He knew that it would presage a change in the way that she felt about him. She was going to have to see more of it, too, before the day was over. Worse things. It couldn't possibly be the same afterwards. Tenderness and intimacy would be the first casualties of what he was going to have to do to get them out.

'Don't worry,' he said. 'It's fine. I'm going to get us out.'

'Don't worry? John—?'

'Are you sure you're all right? They didn't hurt you?'

'No. They just threw me in here. They asked me a few questions about you, but that was it.'

'What kind of questions?'

'Who you are, what you do, how long I've known you.'

He took her by the shoulders. 'I'm very sorry,' he said, looking into her eyes. She flinched a little. 'You should never have been involved. I don't know how they found out about you. They must've been following me.'

'I don't understand why, though? Why would they follow you? What have you done?'

'Nothing.'

'What you did to that man – Jesus, John, you fucked him up – are you some sort of criminal?'

'No.'

'Then what?'

'It's to do with the girls they've found.'

'Which girls? The ones on the beach?'

'I know who did it.'

'Who?'

'Governor Robinson,' the other girl, Karly, answered. 'Right?'

'Do you know him?' Milton asked.

'I worked for him.'

'And you had a relationship with him?'

She nodded.

Milton asked her to explain what had happened and she did: how Robinson had discarded her, how she had gone to Crawford for help, and how the bikers had abducted her and brought her here.

'You know he's dead?'

'No,' Karly said, her mouth falling open.

'This morning. They found him in his hotel room. They're saying suicide, but I don't think it was that. Robinson was also seeing the three girls they've found up on Headlands Lookout. I'm guessing the same thing happened with them as happened to you, Karly.'

'He killed them?'

'I doubt he knew anything about it. Crawford found out about them, maybe they threatened to expose Robinson, and he covered everything up. I spoke to Robinson yesterday afternoon and told him I knew about him and Madison. I said that if he didn't go to the police and tell them that he was seeing her, then I'd do it for him. The names of the girls came out this morning. If I had to guess, I'd say he found out. It wouldn't have been difficult to work out what had happened to them after that. He went to Crawford and confronted him, and Crawford killed him.'

Eva listened, and as he explained more, her disbelief was replaced with incredulity. 'So who are these men?'

'They're working with Crawford.'

Eva's brow clenched angrily. 'None of this has anything to do with me.'

'I know it doesn't. They took you to get my attention. They've got it now, but they're going to wish they hadn't.'

'John – look around. We're stuck.'

'No, we're not. These boys aren't the smartest. There are plenty of things we can use in here.'

She picked up a utensil from the table. 'A plastic knife isn't going to be much use against a gun, and I doubt they'll let you come at them with a bottle again.'

He picked up a roll of duct tape from the table. 'I can do better than a plastic knife.'

* * *

He didn't know how long they had. Two hours, Smokey had said, but it might have been more or it might have been less, and he wasn't sure how much time had already passed. He had to make his move now. Milton went to the stack of beer, tore away the rest of the cellophane wrapper on the top tray and took out three bottles. He took the duct tape and wrapped each bottle, running the tape around it tightly until they were completely sealed. He needed to make sure the caps didn't pop off. A little resin would have been perfect, but that was asking for too much. This should work well enough. It was the best he could do.

He opened the microwave and stood the bottles neatly inside.

'What are you doing?' Eva asked him.

'Creating a diversion.' He closed the microwave door. 'I've seen four men. One of them won't be a problem, so that makes three. Have you seen any more?'

'No,' Eva said.

'Karly?'

'Four, I think.'

'Did you see any guns?'

'He had a gun.'

'I mean big guns – a shotgun, anything like that?'

Eva shook her head. 'I didn't see anything.'

'I think I saw one,' Karly said.

'Are you sure?'

'Pretty sure. Yes. I'm sure.'

A shotgun, and they would be wary now. It wasn't going to be easy.

'Both of you – get to the back of the room. In the corner. And when the time comes, look away.'

'What are you doing?'

'Trust me, okay? I'm getting us out.'

'"When the time comes"? What does that mean?'

'You'll know.'

Milton set the microwave's timer to fifteen minutes and hit the start button.

He hammered on the door.

Footsteps approached.

'What?'

'All right,' he called out.

'What you want?' It was the red-haired biker, Orangutan.

'I'll talk. Whatever you want.'

Footsteps going away.

There was a pause. Milton thought he could hear voices. They were muffled by the door.

Minutes passed.

The foghorns boomed out.

He watched the seconds tick down on the counter.

14.12.

13.33.

12.45.

Footsteps coming back again.

'Stand back,' Smokey called. 'Right up against the far wall. I'm coming in with a shotgun. Don't try to do anything stupid, or I'll empty both barrels into your face.'

Milton looked down at the microwave timer.

9.18.

9.16.

9.14.

It would be close. If they noticed it too quickly, it wouldn't work, and he didn't have a Plan B. If the man did have a shotgun, he would be hopelessly outmatched. Too late to worry about that. He stepped all the way back, putting himself between the microwave and the two women.

The door unlocked.

It opened.

Smokey did have a shotgun, a Remington. The room was narrow and not all that long. A spread couldn't really miss him from that range, and the man was careful now, wary, edging into the room, his eyes fixed on Milton.

Once bitten, twice shy. He knew Milton was dangerous. He would be careful now. No more mistakes.

That was what Milton wanted.

It was the reason for the demonstration earlier.

He wanted all of his attention on him.

'Change of heart?'

'What choice do I have?'

'That's right, buddy. You ain't got none.'

'What do you want to know?'

'The governor – you tell anyone what you know about him and the girls?'

'The dead ones?'

'Them, that one behind you, any others.'

'No,' he said.

'No police?'

'No police.'

'What about her?' he said, chin-nodding towards Eva. 'You tell her?'

'No,' he said. 'She doesn't know anything.'

'You tell anyone else?'

'I told you – no one knows but me.'

'All right, then. That's good. How'd you find out?'

'I had a chat with Jarad Efron.'

'"A chat"? What does that mean?'

'I dangled him off a balcony. He realised it'd be better to talk to me.'

'Think you're a tough guy?'

'I'm nothing special.'

'I ain't scared of you.'

'You shouldn't be. You've got a shotgun.'

'Damn straight I do.'

'So why would you be scared?'

Milton glanced down at the microwave.

7.17.

7.16.

7.15.

'You want to tell me what happened to the girls?' he asked.

'Obvious, ain't it?'

'They wanted money.'

'That's right.' He flicked the barrel of the shotgun in Karly's direction. '*She* wanted money.'

'And then you killed them?'

'They brought it on themselves.'

'Who told you to do it? Robinson?'

'Hell no. Robinson didn't know nothing about none of this shit. We took care of it on his behalf.'

'Crawford, then?'

'That's right. Crawford and us, we just been cleaning up the governor's mess is what we been doing. He had his problems, y'all can see that plain as day, but that there was one great man. Would've been damn good for this fucked-up country. What's happened to him is a tragedy. *Your* fault, the way I see it. What you've done – digging your nose into business that don't concern you, making trouble – well, old partner, that's something you're gonna have to account for, and the accounting's gonna be scrupulous.'

'What about Madison Clarke?'

'Who?'

'Another escort. The governor was seeing her.'

'This the girl you took up to the party in Pine Shore?'

'That's right. You all came out that night, didn't you?'

'That's right.'

'You find her?'

'You know what? We didn't. We don't know where she is.'

Milton glanced down at the microwave.

6.24.

6.23.

6.22.

Come on, come on, come on.

'We don't need to do this, right?' he said, trying to buy them just a little more time. 'I'm not going to say anything. You know where I live.'

Smokey laughed. 'Nah, that ain't gonna cut it. We don't never leave loose ends, and that's what y'all are.'

5.33.

5.32.

5.31.

Smokey noticed Milton looking down at the microwave.

'Fuck you doing with that?' he said.

'I was hungry. I thought—'

'Fuck *that*.'

He stepped towards it.

'Please,' Milton said.

The man reached out for the stop button.

He saw the beer bottles inside, turning around on the platter: incongruous.

Too late.

The liquid inside the bottles was evaporating into steam; several atmospheres of pressure were being generated; the duct tape was holding the caps in place; the pressure was running up against the capacity of the bottles. Just at that precise moment, there was no more space for it to go. It was fortunate; it couldn't have been better timing. The bottles exploded with the same force as a quarter-stick of dynamite. The microwave was obliterated from the inside out. The glass in the door was flung across the room in a shower of razored slivers, the frame of the door cartwheeled away, and the metal body was broken apart, rivets and screws popping out. Smokey was looking right at it, close, as it exploded; a parabola of debris enveloped his head, the barrage of tiny fragments slicing into his eyes and the skin of his face, his scalp, piercing his clothes and flesh.

Milton was further away, yet the blast from the explosion staggered him backwards, and instants later, the red-hot shower peppered his skin. His bare arms were crossed with a thin bloody lattice as he dropped his arm from his face and moved forwards.

He looked back quickly. 'You all right?'

Neither Eva nor Karly answered, but he didn't see any obvious damage.

He turned back. Smokey was on the floor, covered in blood. A large triangular shard from the microwave's metal case was halfway visible in his trachea. He was gurgling, and air whistled in and out of the tear in his throat. One leg twitched spastically. Milton didn't need to examine him to know that he only had a minute or two to live.

The Remington was abandoned at his side.

Milton took it and brought it up. He heard hurried footsteps and ragged breathing and saw a momentary reflection in the long, blank window that started in the corridor opposite the door. He aimed blind around the door and pulled one trigger, blowing buckshot into one of the other men from less than three feet away. Milton turned quickly into the corridor, the shotgun up and ready, and stepped over the second man's body. He was dead. Half his face was gone.

Three down.

One left.

He moved low and fast, the shotgun held out straight. The corridor led into a main room with sofas, a jukebox, empty bottles and dope paraphernalia.

The fourth man popped out of cover behind the sofa and fired.

Milton dropped flat, rolled three times to the right, opening the angle and negating the cover, and pulled the trigger. Half of the buckshot shredded the sofa while the other half perforated the man from head to toe. He dropped his pistol and hit the floor with a weighty thud.

Milton got up. Save the cuts and grazes from the explosion, he was unmarked.

He went back to the kitchen.

Smokey was dead on the floor.

Eva and Karly hadn't moved.

'It's over,' he told them.

Eva bit her lip. 'Are you all right?'

'I'm good. You?'

'Yes.'

'Both of you?'

'I'm fine,' Karly said.

He turned to Eva. 'You both need to get out of here. We're in Potrero Hill. I'll open the gates for you, and you need to get out. Find somewhere safe, somewhere with lots of people, and call the police. Do you understand?'

'What about you?'

'There's someone I have to see.'

44

Arlen Crawford waited impatiently for the hotel lift to bear him down to the parking garage. He had his suitcase in his right hand and his overcoat folded in the crook of his left arm. The car had stopped at every floor on the way down from the tenth, but it was empty now, just Crawford and the numb terror that events had clattered hopelessly out of control. He took his phone from his pocket and tried to call Jack Kerrigan again. There had been no reply the first and second time that he had tried, but this time, the call was answered.

'Smokey,' he said. 'What the fuck's going on?'

'Smokey's dead, Mr Crawford. His friends are dead, too.'

'Who is this?'

'You know who this is.'

The elevator reached the basement, and the doors opened.

'Mr Smith?'

'That's right.'

'What do you want, Smith? Money?'

'No.'

'Then what?'

'Justice would be a good place to start.'

'It wasn't me. Jack killed the girls.'

'Come on, Mr Crawford. Don't insult my intelligence. I know what happened.'

He aimed the fob across the parking lot and thumbed the button. The car doors unlocked and the lights flashed.

'I didn't have anything to do with it. There's no proof.'

'Maybe not. But that would only be a problem if I was going to go to the police. I'm not going to go to the police, Mr Crawford.'

'What are you going to do?'

No answer.

'What are you going to do?'

Silence.

Crawford reached the car and opened the driver's door. He tossed the phone across the car onto the passenger seat. He went around and put the suitcase in the trunk. He got inside the car, took a moment to gather his breath, stepped on the clutch and pressed the ignition.

He felt a small, cold point of metal pressing against the back of his head.

He looked up into the rear-view mirror.

It was dark in the basement, with just the glow of the sconced lights on the wall. The modest brightness fell across one half of the face of the man who was holding the gun. The other half was obscured by shadow. He recognised him: the impassive and serious face, the cruel mouth, the scar running horizontally across his face.

'Drive.'

PART V

45

The meeting on the third anniversary of Milton's sobriety was a Big Book meeting. They were peaceful weekly gatherings, the format more relaxed than usual, and Milton usually enjoyed them. They placed tea lights around the room, and someone had lit a joss stick (that had been the subject of a heated argument; a couple of the regulars had opined that it was a little too intoxicating for a roomful of recovering alkies and druggies). Every week, they each opened a copy of the book of advice that Bill Wilson, the founder of the programme, had written, read five or six pages out loud and then discussed what it meant to them all. After a year, they would have worked their way through it and then they would turn back to the start and begin again. Milton had initially thought the book was an embarrassingly twee self-help screed, and it was certainly true that it was packed full of platitudes, but the more he grew familiar with it, the easier it was to ignore the homilies and clichés and concentrate on the advice on how to live a worthwhile, sober life. Now he often read a paragraph or two before he went to sleep at night. It was good meditation.

The reading took fifteen minutes and then the discussion another thirty. The final fifteen minutes were dedicated to those who felt that they needed to share.

Richie Grimes raised his hand.

'Hey,' he said. 'My name's Richie, and I'm an alcoholic.'

'Hi, Richie,' they said together.

'You know about my problem – I've gone on about it enough. But I'm here today to give thanks.' He paused and looked behind him; he was looking for Milton. 'I don't rightly know what happened, but the man I owed money to has sold his book, and the guys who bought it off him don't look like they're going to come after me for what I owe. I might be setting myself up for a fall, but it's starting to look to me like someone paid that debt off for me.' He shook his head. 'You know, I was talking to a friend here after I did my share last week. I won't say who he was – anonymity, all that – but he told me to trust my higher power. If I didn't know any better, I'd say he was right. My higher power has intervened, like we say it will if we ask for help, because if it wasn't that, then I don't know what the hell it was.'

There was a moment of silence and then loud applause.

'Thank you for sharing,' Smulders said when it had died down. 'Anyone else?'

Milton raised his own hand.

Smulders cocked an eyebrow in surprise. 'John?'

'My name is John, and I'm an alcoholic,' Milton said.

'Hello, John.'

'There's something I need to share, too. If I don't get it off my chest, I know I'll be back on the booze eventually. I thought I could keep it in, but . . . I know that I can't.'

He paused.

Richie turned and looked at him expectantly.

The group waited for him to go on.

Eva reached across, took his hand and gave it a squeeze.

Milton thought of the other people in the room and how they were living the programme, bravely accepting 'honesty in all our affairs', and he knew, then, with absolute conviction, that he would never be able to go as far down the road as they had. If it was a choice between telling a roomful of strangers about the blood that he had on his hands and taking a drink, then he was going to take a drink. Every time. He thought of what he had almost been prepared to say, and he felt the heat gathering in his face at the foolish audacity of it.

'John?' Smulders prompted.

Eva squeezed his hand again.

No, he thought. Some things had to stay unsaid.

'I just wanted to say how valuable I've found this meeting. Most of you know me by now, even if it's just as the guy with the coffee and the biscuits. You probably wondered why I don't say much. You probably think I'm pretty bad at all this, and maybe I am, but I'm doing my best. One day at a time, like we always say. I can do better, I know I can, but I just wanted to say that it's my third year without a drink today, and that's as good a reason for celebrating as I've ever really had before. So' – he cleared his throat, constricted by sudden emotion – 'you know, I just wanted to say thanks. I wouldn't be able to do it on my own.'

There was warm applause, and the case of birthday chips was extracted from the cupboard marked PROPERTY OF A.A. They usually started with the newest members, those celebrating a day or a week or a month, and those were always the ones that were marked with the loudest cheers, the most high-fives and the strongest hugs. There were no others celebrating tonight, and when Smulders called out for those celebrating three years to come forward, Milton stood up and, smiling shyly, went up to the front. Smudlers shook his hand warmly and handed him his chip. It was red, made from cheap plastic and looked like a chocolate coin, the edge raised and stippled, the A.A. symbol embossed on one side and a single 3 on the other. Milton self-consciously raised it up in his fist, and the applause started again. He felt a little dazed as he went back to his seat. Eva took his hand again and tugged him down.

'Well done,' she whispered into his ear.

46

It was time. He had already stayed longer than was safe. He had thought about skipping the meeting altogether, and he had gone so far as getting to the airport and the long-stay car park, but he had been unable to go through with it. He needed the meeting, and more than that, he needed to see his friends there: Smulders, Grimes and the other alcoholics who drank his coffee and ate his biscuits and asked him how he was and how he was doing.

And Eva.

He had needed to see her.

She stayed to help him clear away.

'You hear what happened to the governor's aide?'

'Yeah,' Milton said vaguely. 'They found him in his car up in the Headlands.'

'He'd killed himself, too.'

'Yes.'

'Put a hose on the exhaust and put it in through the window.'

'Guilt?' Milton suggested.

She bit her lip.

'You're sure he had something to do with those men? Those girls?'

'He did.'

Milton looked at her, and for a moment, he allowed himself the thought: could he stay here? Could he stay with her? He entertained the thought longer than was healthy or sensible, until he caught himself and dismissed it. Of course he couldn't. How could he? It was ridiculous, dangerous thinking. He had made so much noise over the last few days. The spooks back home would be able to find him without too much bother now. Photographs, references in police reports, all manner of digital crumbs that, if followed, would lead them straight to him. The arrival of the Group would be the first that he knew of it. They would be more careful this time. A sedative injected into his neck from behind; a hood over his head before being muscled into a waiting car; a shot in the head from a sniper a city block away. He'd be dead or out of the country before he could do anything about it.

Thinking about staying was selfish, too. He knew what Control would order. Anyone who had spent time with him would be a threat.

A loose end.

The guys at the meeting?

Maybe.

Trip?

Probably.

Eva?

Definitely.

'What are you doing now?'

It startled him. 'What?'

She smiled at him. 'Now – you wanna get dinner?'

He wanted it badly, but he shook his head. 'I can't. I've got— I promised a friend I'd catch up with him.'

If she was disappointed, she hid it well. 'All right, then. How about tomorrow?'

'Can I give you a call?'

'Sure,' she said.

She came over to him, rested her hand on his shoulder and tiptoed so that she was tall enough to kiss him on the cheek. Her lips were warm, and she smelled of cinnamon. Milton felt a lump in his throat as she lowered herself down to her height.

'It was good to hear you speak. I know you're carrying a burden, John. You should share it. No one will judge you, and it'll be easier to carry.'

He smiled at her. His throat felt thick, and he didn't trust himself to speak.

'See you around,' she said, rubbing her hand up and down his right arm. 'Don't be a stranger, all right?'

* * *

Milton drove back to the El Capitan for the last time. He recognised Trip Macklemore as he slotted the Explorer into the kerb outside the entrance to the building. He scanned his surroundings quickly, a little fretfully, but there was no sign of anything out of the ordinary. The Group were good, though.

If an agent was using the boy and didn't want to be seen, he would be invisible. Milton felt an itching sensation in the dead centre of his chest. He looked down, almost expecting to see the red crosshatch of a laser sight, but there was nothing there. He turned the key to switch off the engine and stepped outside.

'Hello, Trip.'

'Mr Smith.'

'Are you all right?'

'I'm fine.'

'What can I do for you?'

'There's someone you need to talk to.'

Milton noticed that there was someone else waiting at the entrance to the building.

She smiled nervously at him.

Milton couldn't hide his surprise. '*Madison?*'

'Hello, John.'

'Where have you been?'

'Is this your place?' she said, rubbing her arms to ward off the chill. 'Can we maybe go in? Get a coffee? I'll tell you.'

47

She explained. To begin with, she edged around some of the details for fear of upsetting Trip, but when he realised what she was doing, he told her – a little unconvincingly – that he was fine with it and that she should lay it all out, so that's what she did.

It had started in April when Jarad Efron booked her through Fallen Angelz for the first time. She had no idea who he was other than that he was rich and generous and fun to be around. They had had a good time together, and he booked her again a week or two afterwards, then several times after that. The eighth or ninth booking was different. Rather than the plush hotel room to which they usually retreated, this was a private dinner party. Some sort of fundraiser. He had bought her a thousand-dollar dress and paraded her as his girlfriend. It was a charade, and it must have been easy to see through it, but there were other escorts at the party, a harem of young girls with rich older men. Madison recognised some of them, but it didn't seem like any of it was a big deal.

One of the other guests came over to speak to Efron. She guessed within minutes that the conversation was an excuse;

he was more interested in finding out about her. She hadn't recognised him at first; he was just another middle-aged john with plenty of cash, charming and charismatic with it. He didn't explain who he was, and when she asked what he did for a living, all he said was that he worked for the state government. They had exchanged numbers, and he had called the next morning to set up a meeting the same night. She reserved a room at the Marriott; they had room service and went to bed together.

He booked her two more times until, one day, she was idly watching the TV in a bar where she was waiting for Trip and she had seen him on the news. The bartender had made some quip about how they were watching the next president of the United States. She googled him on her phone and nearly fell off her stool. He booked her again the day after her discovery, and she had told him, when they were lying on the bed together afterwards, that she knew who he was. He asked if that bothered her, and she said that it didn't. He asked if she could keep a secret, and she had said that she could. He had said that he was pleased because he thought that she could be special – 'different from all the others' – and he wanted to see her more often. Mentioning that there were 'others' didn't make her feel all that special, but she told herself that he was with her, and that she *was* special; she would make him see that, and then, maybe, eventually, it would just be the two of them.

Robinson had been good to his word, and they saw each other at least once a week for a month or so. She had persuaded herself that he really did see her as more than just another working girl and that, maybe, something might come of it. She dreamt that he would take her away from hooking and give her a better life: money, a car, a nice place to live. He had made promises like that, and she had bought all of them. She read about him online and watched him on the news. The fact that a man like him, with so much to lose, had started a relationship with her and trusted her to keep it secret? Man, that was totally *crazy*. The proximity to power was intoxicating, too, and she admitted that she had let it get to her head. He told her that his wife was a bitch, and he would be leaving her as soon as the election was over. She started to believe his spin that, if she was patient, they could be together. At no point did she question how any of that could ever be possible for a working girl. She loved him.

'And then he dropped me,' she said. 'No warning. Just like that. He called me and said he couldn't see me again. I asked why, and he said it was one of those things – we'd had a good run, he said, we'd both had fun, but all good things have to come to an end. No hard feelings, goodbye, and that was it. Just like that.'

She moped for a week, wondering whether there was any way she could put things back the way they had been before. She blamed herself: she had pushed him too fast, talking about the future and the things they could do together once they were a couple. That, she saw then, had been childishly naïve. She had scared him off. She called the number he had given her, but the line had been disconnected. She saw that he was speaking at a rally in Palo Alto and had hitched down there in the vain hope that she might be able to speak to him, but that, too, had been a failure. She had found a space near the front, but he had been absorbed in his speech, and even as he beamed his brilliant smile into the crowd, his eyes passing right across her, she knew that he hadn't even noticed that she was there.

Two days later, Efron called.

'He was having a party,' she explained. 'A fundraising thing for the campaign. He was inviting people that he knew, CEOs and shit, these guys from the Valley, and Robinson was going to be there, too. He asked if I could come. I couldn't understand it at first – I mean, why would he want me to be there after what had happened between me and J.J., but then I realised, there was no way he could've known how involved we'd been and what had happened since. All he knew was that Robinson had taken a shine to me, so he thought he'd get me to be there too because he thought that'd make him happy.' She laughed bitterly. 'That's a laugh, right? I mean, he couldn't possibly have been much more wrong about that.'

'What happened?'

'You drove me to the house. It was fine at first. Robinson wasn't there. Jarad was sweet, looking after me – the place was jammed with rich guys, totally flush, and there was as much booze as you could drink.'

Madison said that Joseph Jack Robinson and Arlen Crawford arrived at a little after midnight. Milton remembered the town car that had pulled into the driveway and the two guys who had stepped out; he hadn't recognised them – it had been dark and foggy – but it must have been them.

Crawford had been aghast to see her. He sent Robinson into another room and came over to deal with her. He had been kind, she explained, taking her to one side and having a quiet drink with her. He explained that the governor couldn't see her that night, that there were people at the party who couldn't be trusted and that it would be damaging to the campaign if anything leaked out, but as she protested, he told her that the governor was missing her and that he would call her the next day. She had been overwhelmed with relief, and as Crawford refilled her glass, and keen to ingratiate herself more fully with him, she had accepted his offer to do a pill with him. He said it was ecstasy, and although she rarely did it these days, she had swallowed it, washing it down with a slug of Cristal. She realised afterwards that he had not taken his pill and then, after that, that it wasn't ecstasy but something that was making her feel woozy and out of it.

'I asked him what it was that I'd taken, and he said not to worry, it was just MDMA, and then when I told him I was feeling worse, he said it was just a bad trip and that he'd get me a car and take me home. He was on his cell, making a call, and he had this weird expression of concern and irritation on his face. Mostly irritation, like I was this big inconvenience for him, this big problem he was going to have to deal with. I knew then that Jack never wanted to see me again and that Crawford was getting rid of me. I told him that. He snapped at me, said I was a fucking embarrassment and a mistake and a liability and why couldn't I have stayed away? I shouted back at him. I went totally nuts, so he lost his cool too, and when I tried to get away, he grabbed me and told me I had to stay until they could drive me back, and that's when I screamed.'

'Do you remember me being there?' Milton asked.

She shrugged. 'Sort of.'

'Why didn't you let me help you?'

'Because I was out of my head and terrified. I didn't believe Crawford, not then, not for an instant, and I knew I was in trouble. Whatever it was he'd given me was seriously messing me up. I didn't even know where I was. I just felt like I was underwater, and I kept trying to swim up, I was really trying, but it felt like I was going to fall asleep. I remember an argument, men shouting at each other, and then I knew I had to get out of there, right that instant, before it got worse and I couldn't move, and so I took off.' She paused, frowning as she tried to remember what had happened next. 'I know I went to a house over the road. There are bits after that that are a complete blank. The pill, whatever it was, totally wiped me out. I woke up in the woods behind the houses. Five, six in the morning. Freezing cold. There was no way I was going back there, so I just kept going through the trees until I hit a road, and then I followed that until I got onto the 131. I hitched a ride back to San Francisco.'

'After that?'

'I've got a girlfriend in L.A., so I got on the first Greyhound the next morning – this is like at seven – and went straight there. I didn't want to stick around. I didn't think it was safe. I just kept my head down. Stayed in the apartment most of the time.'

'Why didn't you call?'

'I heard about what had happened to them . . . those other girls.'

'No one knew that they were connected to Robinson.'

'Yeah,' she said. 'But it freaked me out. It just felt a little close to home. And then when they said who they were, like last week? I was about ready to get out of the state.'

'Did you know them?'

'Megan – I met her once. This one time, at the start, before I was seeing Jack properly, there were two of us. Me and her. She was a sweet girl. Pretty. She was kind of on the outs then, but I liked her. I remember her face, and then, when they put pictures up on the news and said she was one of the girls they'd found, and then I thought what had nearly happened to me, I realised what was going on. I mean, it was obvious, right? Robinson likes to have his fun, and then, when it's all said and done and over, if they think the girl is gonna cause trouble, they get rid of her.'

'You could've called the police,' Trip said.

'Seriously? He is – *was* – the governor of Florida. How do you think that's going to sound – I call and say I've been with him, and they ask how, and I say it was because I was a hooker, and then I say I think he wants to kill me? Come on, Trip. Get real, baby. They'd just laugh.'

'You could've called me,' he said sadly.

'Yeah,' she said, looking away for a moment. 'I know.'

'You have to go to the police now, Madison,' Milton said. 'It's pretty much wrapped up, but you have to tell them.'

'I know I do. Trip's going to take me tomorrow.'

They finished their drinks quietly. Milton had packed his few possessions into a large bag. The apartment looked bare and lonely, and for a moment, the atmosphere was heavy and depressing.

'I'm gonna go and wait outside,' Madison said eventually. They all rose, and she came across the room, slid her arms around his neck and pulled him down a little so that she could kiss him on the cheek. 'Probably wasn't what you were expecting when you picked me up, right?'

'Not exactly.'

'Thank you, John.'

She disengaged from him and made her way across the room. Milton watched as she opened the door and passed into the hallway, out of sight.

He looked over at Trip. He was staring vaguely at the open doorway.

'You all right?'

He sighed. 'I guess,' he said quietly. 'Things aren't what they always seem to be, are they, Mr Smith?'

'No,' Milton said. 'Not always.'

Trip gestured at his bulging travel bag. 'You going away?'

'I'm leaving town.'

'For real?'

Milton shrugged. 'I like to keep moving around.'

'Where?'

'Don't know yet. Wherever seems most interesting. East, I think.'

'Like a tourist?'

'Something like that.'

'What about your jobs?'

'They're just jobs. I can get another.'

'Isn't that a bit weird?'

'Isn't what?'

'Just moving on.'

'Maybe it is, but it suits me.'

'I mean – I thought you were settled?'

'I've been here too long. I've got itchy feet. It's time to go.'

He walked across to the bag and heaved it over his shoulder. Trip followed the unsaid cue and led the way to the door. Milton took a final look around – thinking of the evenings he had spent reading on the sofa, smoking cigarettes out of the open window, staring out into the swirling pools of fog, and above all, the single night he had spent with Eva – and then he pulled the door closed, shutting off that brief interlude in his life. It was time. He had taken too many chances already, and if he had avoided detection, it had been the most outrageous luck. There was no sense in tempting fate.

Quit while you're ahead.

He locked the door.

* * *

They walked down the stairs together.

'What are you going to do now?' he asked the boy as they crossed into the harsh artificial brightness of the lobby. 'With Madison, I mean?'

'I don't know. We're right back to the start, I guess – that's the best we can hope for. And I'm not stupid, Mr Smith. Maybe we're through. I can kinda get Robinson, how it might be flattering to have someone like that chasing after you. Efron, too, all that money and influence. But there's the other guy – the driver. I thought he was kinda dumb if I'm honest. I don't get that so much. All of it – I don't know what I mean to her anymore. So, yeah – I don't know. I've got a lot of thinking to do.'

'You do.'

'What would you do? If you were me?'

Milton laughed at that. 'You're asking *me* for relationship advice? Look at me, Trip. I've got pretty much everything I own in a bag. Do I look like I'm the kind of man with anything useful to say?'

They stopped on the street. The fog had settled down again, cold and damp.

Milton took out the keys to the Explorer. 'Here,' he said, tossing them across the pavement at the boy. He caught them deftly but then looked up in confusion. 'It's not much to look at, but it runs okay, most of the time.'

'What?'

'Go on.'

'You're giving it to me?'

'I don't have any need for it.'

He paused self-consciously. 'I don't have any money.'

'That's all right. I don't want anything for it.'

'Are you sure?' he said awkwardly.

'It's fine.'

'God, I mean, thanks. Do you want – I mean – can I drop you anyplace?'

'No,' he said. 'I'll get the bus.'

'Thanks, man. Not just for this – for everything. For helping me. I don't know what I would've done if you hadn't been here.'

'Don't worry about it,' Milton said. 'I'm glad I could help.'

The corners of the books in his bag were digging into his shoulder; he heaved it around a little until it was comfortable and then stuck out his hand. Trip shook it firmly, and Milton thought he could see a new resolution in the boy's face.

'Look after yourself,' Milton told him.

'I will.'

'You'll do just fine.'

He gave his hand one final squeeze, turned his back on him and walked away. As the boy watched, he merged into the fog like a haggard ghost, melting into the long, bleak street with its shopfronts and palm trees shrouded in fog and whiteness. He didn't look back. The foghorn boomed as a single shaft of wintry moonlight pierced the mist for a moment.

Milton had disappeared.

EPILOGUE

The two newcomers came into the bar with trouble on their minds. They were both big men, with broad shoulders and thick arms. The bar was full of riggers from the oil fields, and these two fitted right in. Milton had ordered a plate of barbeque chicken wings and fries and a Coke and was watching the Cowboys' game on the large flat-screen TV that was hanging from the wall. The food was average, but the game was close, and Milton had been enjoying it. The bar was busy. There were a dozen men drinking and watching the game. Three young girls were drinking next to the pool table. He watched the two men as they made their way across the room. They ordered beers with whisky chasers, knocked back the latter and set about the beers. They were already drunk, and it looked like they were fixing to work on that a little more.

Milton had been in Victoria, Texas, for twelve hours. He had dropped his rented Dodge back at the Hertz office and was just wondering what to do next. He still had four thousand dollars in his go-bag, enough for him to just drift idly along the coast with no need to get a job just yet. He thought that maybe he'd get a Greyhound ticket and head east from Texas into Louisiana and then across to Florida, and then, maybe, he would turn north up towards New York and find a job. That was his rough plan, but he was taking it as it came. No sense in setting anything in stone. He had taken a room in a cheap hotel across the street from the bar, and rather than spend another night alone with just his paperbacks for company, he had decided to get out, get something to eat and watch the game.

Milton took a bite out of one of the chicken wings.

'Good?' said the man sitting on the stool to his right.

Milton looked at him: mid-twenties, slender, acne scars scattered across his nose and cheeks.

'Very good.'

'All in the sauce. Hot, right?'

'I'll say.'

'That's old Bill's original recipe. Used to call it "Suicide" 'til folks thought he ought to tone it down a bit. Calls it "Supercharger" now.'

'So I see,' Milton said, pointing to the menu on the blackboard above his head. 'It packs a punch.'

'Say – where you from?'

'Here and there.'

'Nah, man – that accent, what is it? English, right?'

'That's right,' Milton said. He had no real interest in talking, and eventually, after he made a series of non-committal responses to the man's comments on the Cowboys' chances this year, he got the message and quietened down.

The two newcomers were loud. Milton examined them a little more carefully. One of them must have been six-five and eighteen stone, built like one of the offensive linemen on the TV. He had a fat, pendulous face, a severe crew cut and small nuggety eyes deeply set within flabby sockets; he had the cruel look of a school bully, a small boy transported into the body of a fully grown man. His friend was smaller but still heavyset and thick with muscle. His head was shaved bald, and he had dead, expressionless eyes. The other men in the bar ignored them. It was a rough place, the kind of place where the threat of a brawl was never far from the surface, but the way the others kept their distance from these two suggested that they were known and, probably, that they had reputations.

The bald man saw Milton looking and stared at him.

Milton turned back to the screen.

'*All right!*' the man at the bar exclaimed as the full back plunged over the goal line for a Cowboys' touchdown.

The two men sauntered over to the table where the girls were sitting. They started to talk to them; it was obvious that they were not welcome. The big man sat down, preventing one of the girls from leaving. Milton sipped on his Coke and watched as the girl pressed herself against the wall, trying to put distance between him and her. He reached across and slipped an arm around her shoulders; she tried to shrug it away, but he was persistent. The bald man went around to the other side of the table and grabbed the arm of the nearest girl. He hauled her up, encircled her waist with his arm and pulled her up against his body. She cursed him loudly and struggled, but he was much too strong.

Milton folded his napkin, carefully wiped his mouth with it and then stood.

He walked to the table.

'Leave them alone,' he said.

'Say what?'

'They're not interested.'

'Says who?'

'I do. There's no need for trouble, is there?'

'I don't know – you tell me.'

'I don't think so.'

'Maybe I *do* think so.'

Milton watched as he sank the rest of his beer. He knew what would come next, so he altered his balance a little, spreading his weight evenly between his feet so that he could move quickly in either direction.

The bald man got up. 'You ought to mind your own business.'

'Last chance, friend,' Milton said.

'I ain't your friend.'

The bald man cracked the glass against the edge of the table and rushed him, jabbing the sharp edges towards his face. Milton took a half-pace to the left and let the man hurry past, missing him completely with his drunken swipe. He reached out with his right hand and snagged the man's right wrist, pivoting on his right foot and using his momentum to swing him around and down, crashing his head into the bar. He bounced backwards and ended up, unmoving and face down, on the floor.

The big man reached out for a pool cue from the table. He swung it, but Milton stepped inside the arc of the swing, took the abbreviated impact against his shoulder and then jabbed his fingers into the man's larynx. He dropped the cue; Milton took a double handful of the man's shirt, yanked him down a little, butted him in the nose and then dumped him back on his behind.

The bald man was out cold, and the big man had blood all over his face from his broken nose.

'You had enough?' Milton said.

'All right, mister! Get your hands up!'

Milton turned.

'Come on,' he groaned. 'Seriously?'

The man he had been talking to earlier had pulled a pistol and was aiming it at him.

'Put your hands up now!'

'What – you're police?'

'That's right. Get them up!'

'All right. Take it easy.'

'On your head.'

'You want me to put them up or on my head?' He sighed. 'Fine – here.' He turned away and put his arms behind his back. 'Go on. Here we go. Cuff me. Just relax. I'm not going to resist.'

The young cop approached him warily, moved his hands behind his back – and fixed handcuffs around his wrists.

'What's your name?'

'John Smith.'

'All right then, buddy. You have the right to remain silent. Anything you say can and will be used against you in a court of law. You have the right to an attorney.'

'Come on.'

The big man wiped the blood from his face and started to laugh.

'If you cannot afford an attorney, one will be provided for you. Do you understand the rights I have just read to you?'

'Of course.'

'With these rights in mind, do you wish to speak to me?'

'Not particularly.'

'John Smith – you're under arrest.'

Turn the page for a preview of

GHOSTS

the next book in the John Milton series

PART I

LONDON – 8 YEARS AGO

1

The van was parked at the side of the road. It was a white Renault and it had been prepared to look just like one of the maintenance vehicles that Virgin Media used. It was parked at the junction of Upper Ground and Rennie Street. The spot had been chosen carefully; it allowed an excellent view of the entrance to the Oxo Tower brasserie on London's South Bank.

The interior of the van had been prepared carefully, too. A console had been installed along the right-hand side of the vehicle, with monitors displaying the feed from the low-light colour camera that was fitted to the roof. There was a 360-degree periscope that could be raised and lowered as appropriate, various recording devices, a dual-band radio antenna and a microwave receiver.

It was a little cramped in the back for the two men inside. The intelligence officer using the equipment had quickly become oblivious to any discomfort. He reached across to the console and selected a different video feed; they had installed a piggyback into the embassy's security system two weeks ago and now he had access to all those separate feeds, as well as to an array of exterior cameras they had also hijacked. The monitor flickered and then displayed the footage from the security camera that monitored the building. He could see the big Mercedes S280 that the chauffeur had parked there, but, apart from that, there was nothing.

The second man was sitting just to the side of the technician, watching the action over his shoulder. This man was anxious, and he knew that it was radiating from him.

'Change views,' he said tensely. 'Back inside.'

The technician did as he was told and discarded the view for another one from inside the restaurant. The targets were still in the main room, finishing their desserts. The first target was facing away from the camera but she was still recognisable. The second target was toying with an unlit cigarette, turning it between his fingers. The second man looked at the footage. It looked as if the meal was finally coming to an end. The two targets would be leaving soon.

'Group,' the second man said into the headset microphone. 'This is Control. Comms check.'

'Copy that Control, this is One. Strength ten.'

'Eight, also strength ten.'

'Twelve, copy that.'

'Ten, strength ten.'

'Eleven, same here. Strength ten.'

'Five. Ditto for me.'

'Eleven, what can you see?'

The agent code-named Eleven was standing at the bar, enjoying a drink as he waited for a table. His name was Duffy and he had latterly been in the Special Boat Service. Control could see him in the footage from the camera and watched as he angled himself away from the couple and put his hand up to his mouth.

'They're finishing,' he said, his voice clipped and quiet as he spoke into the discreet microphone slipped beneath the strap of his watch. 'The waiter just asked if they wanted coffees and they didn't. Won't be long.'

Satisfied, Control sat back and watched. Very few people knew his given name. He was dressed well, as was his habit, in a pale blue shirt and tastefully spotted braces. He held his glasses in his right hand, absently tapping one of the arms against his lips. He had been in day-to-day command of Group Fifteen for several months but this was the first operation that he had overseen from the field. He was a desk man by nature. He preferred to pull the strings, the dark hand in the shadows. The puppet master. But this operation was personal and he wanted to be closer to the action. He would have preferred to smell the gun smoke, if that had been possible. He would have preferred to pull the trigger.

Watching would be an acceptable substitute.

It was an expensive and exclusive restaurant. The wall facing the river was one huge expanse of glass, with doors leading out onto a terrace. The views were outstanding and Control knew, from several meals there himself, that the food was just as good.

The bright sunlight refracted against the watch that the first target wore on her wrist and the diamond earrings that must have cost her a small fortune. Control watched and felt his temper slowly curdle. He had been introduced to her by a mutual Iranian friend. The name she had given him was

Alexandra Kyznetsov. He knew now that that was not her name. Her real name was Anastasia Ivanovna Semenko and, instead of being a businesswoman with interests in the chemical industry, she was an agent in the pay of the Russian Federal Security Service. She was in her early forties but she had invested heavily in cosmetic surgery and, as a result, she could have passed for a woman fifteen years younger. Control had found her attractive and he had enjoyed her flirtatious manner on the occasions that they had met.

Now, though, that just made her betrayal *worse*.

Control stared at the screen and contemplated the frantic action of the last three days. That was how long he had had to plan the operation. Three days. It was hopelessly insufficient, especially for something as delicate as this, but the role that Semenko played cast her as something of a globetrotter and it was difficult to find a reliable itinerary for her; she tended to change it on a whim. She had only just returned from business in Saudi Arabia. Control had only green-lit the operation when it was confirmed that she was stopping in London before returning to Moscow. The team had then been assembled and briefed. Control had considered the precise detail of the plan and, by and large, he was satisfied with it. It was as good as he would be able to manage in the limited time that he had available.

The second target laughed at something that Semenko said. Control switched his attention to him. He had introduced himself as Andrei Dragunov, but, again, that was a lie. His real name was Pascha Shcherbatov. He, too, was

Russian. He was in his early middle-age and he was a long-time KGB agent, an intelligence man to the quick; since the fall of the Wall, he had amassed considerable influence in the SVR, the successor to his notorious previous employer, and was now considered to be something of an operator. A worthy opponent, certainly.

Semenko clasped the hand of the maître d', her face beaming. They both got up, leaving money on the table, and made for the archway that opened into the lobby.

'Dollar and Snow are on the move,' Control reported. 'Stand ready.'

Shcherbatov's phone rang and he stopped, putting it to his ear. Semenko paused, waiting for him. Control stared at the pirated feed, willing himself to read Shcherbatov's lips, but it was hopeless: the angle was wrong and the quality of the image was too poor. He watched, frowning hard. Shcherbatov smiled broadly, replaced the phone and spoke with Semenko. Control hoped that their plans had not changed. That would throw things into confusion.

'Control to One and Twelve,' Control said into the mike. 'They are on the move.'

'*One, Control. Copy that.*'

Control watched as Semenko and Shcherbatov headed towards the exit. The pair stepped beneath the camera and out of shot. 'Keep on them,' Control said, and the technician tapped out a command and switched views to a new camera. This one was in the lift and, as Control watched, the doors opened and the two of them stepped inside. Shcherbatov pressed the button for the ground floor. The camera juddered as the lift began to descend.

'Targets are in the lift,' Control reported. 'One and Twelve, stand ready.'

'One, Control. Copy that.'

The technician swung around on his chair and brought up another feed on the second monitor. It offered a wide-angle view of the street outside the restaurant. Control could see Semenko's chauffeur. He was a large man, powerfully built, with a balding head. They knew he had a background in the Spetsnaz and would certainly be armed. He wore a pair of frameless glasses and was dressed in a dark suit and open-necked shirt. Control watched as he stepped out of the shadows, tossing a cigarette to the floor and stomping it out.

The lift came to a stop and the door opened.

Semenko emerged into the wide shot first, walking with a confident bounce across the space to the Mercedes. Shcherbatov followed, his phone pressed to his ear again. The chauffeur opened the rear door for his passengers and, as they slipped inside, he opened the front door and got in himself.

He started the engine. Control could see the fumes rising from the exhaust.

The Mercedes reversed and turned and then pulled away, moving quickly.

'Targets are in play,' Control reported.

2

Beatrix Rose was sitting astride a Kawasaki motorcycle on Rennie Street. The visor of her helmet was up and the cool air was fresh against her face. The usual buzz of adrenaline had kicked in as the operation moved into its final phase. She was a professional with years of experience behind her; too professional to let excitement render her less useful than she would need to be.

She listened to the comms chatter in the receiver that was pressed into her ear, the detailed commentary as the Mercedes passed from the back of the restaurant and onto Upper Ground. She had memorised this part of London, at first with the aid of a map and then, over the course of the morning, three hours of careful reconnaissance that had fixed the local geography in her mind. She was confident that she was as prepared as she could be.

'*They're turning east towards the Bridge,*' intoned Control.

There was another motorcycle next to her. The agent sitting astride it was nervous, despite the time he had spent in the army and then the SAS. He had a glittering résumé, with one mission behind the lines during the second Iraq War a particular standout, but it was one thing to go into battle during a war, when the rules of engagement were clear, and quite another to conduct a clandestine extrajudicial operation like this, with no backup or recognition, and the likelihood of incarceration, or worse, if things went wrong. The man had his visor open, like she did, but where she was clear-eyed and focused, he looked ashen.

'Milton,' she called across to him.

He didn't respond.

'*Milton.*'

He turned to face her. 'You all right?'

'Fine,' he called back.

'You look like you're going to be sick.'

'I'm fine.'

'Remember your training. You've done more difficult things than this.'

He nodded.

Beatrix Rose was Number One, the most senior agent in the Group. The man on the second bike was John Milton. He was Number Twelve. The Group was a small and highly select team. Twelve members. Milton was its most junior member and his presence in it was at least partly because of her influence.

Number Four, a cantankerous Irishman who had served with the Special Boat Service before being transferred to the group, had been killed in a firefight with al-Qaeda sympathisers in the Yemen six months earlier. Control had identified ten potential replacements to fill his spot on the team and had deputed the job of selecting the most promising soldier to her. She had interviewed all of them and then personally oversaw the selection weekend when their number had gradually been whittled down, one at a time, until Milton had been the last man standing.

Beatrix had known before the weekend started that it was going to end up that way. His commanding officers described him as a brilliant soldier who was brave and selfless. They also spoke of a steely determination and a relentless focus on the goal at hand. He did not allow anything to stand in his way. He had demonstrated all of that. He was the most promising recruit that she had ever worked with and, in all the time that she had been Number One, she had tutored two men and two women who had replaced fallen team members. There had been more than three hundred possible recruits for those four spots and Milton was better than all of them.

'Here they come,' she called out.

The Mercedes turned the corner and headed in their direction. Beatrix flipped her visor down and gave the engine a twist of revs. Milton did the same, gunning the engine and then, as the Mercedes moved past them, closing his visor and pulling out into the empty road.

'One, Control,' Beatrix said.

'*Go ahead, One.*'

'We're in pursuit.'

3

'Control, One. Roger that.'

Control had placed his agents carefully: One and Twelve east of the restaurant on Rennie Street; Five and Eight in a second van, currently idling in Southwark Street; Ten on a third bike, waiting on Stamford Street in the event that they went west instead of east; Eleven inside the restaurant. He was confident that they had all eventualities covered.

The driver of the surveillance van started the engine and they pulled out into the traffic and headed north. The Mercedes was out of sight, but One was providing a commentary on its movements and it was a simple thing to follow.

Control twisted the wedding ring on his left hand. Despite his satisfaction with their preparation, he was still nervous. This had to be perfect. The operation was totally off the book; usually, the files with the details of their targets were passed down to him by either MI5 or MI6, but that wasn't the case this time. Neither agency had sanctioned this operation and he would have even less cover than he usually did if anything went wrong. It wasn't just that this was unofficial business – all of the work they did was unofficial – it was personal.

None of his agents knew that. He had deceived them. 'Control, One. Report.'

'Target is waiting at the junction at Blackfriars Bridge.'

Control knew their itinerary for the rest of the day. Semenko and Shcherbatov were going to a meeting. As far as they knew, the meeting was with him.

It was an appointment that Control had no intention of keeping.

4

The Mercedes picked up speed as it turned onto Blackfriars Bridge. It found a small gap in the traffic. Beatrix opened the throttle in response, keeping the Mercedes a few car lengths ahead of them. Their intelligence suggested that the woman she knew as Dollar had an appointment with a contact on Victoria Embankment; it looked as if the intelligence would prove to be accurate.

Beatrix stayed between fifty and a hundred yards behind the car; Milton was another twenty yards behind her. She kept up a running commentary as they gradually worked their way south-east, towards the river. 'North end of the bridge, turning off . . . onto the Embankment, heading west . . . passing Blackfriars Pier . . . coming up to Waterloo Bridge, following the river to the south.'

The traffic started to queue as they reached Victoria Embankment Gardens. Beatrix bled away almost all the speed, ducking in behind a bus that was idling opposite Cleopatra's Needle. She could see the Mercedes through the windows of the bus and, beyond it, the Houses of Parliament.

'One, Control. Waiting at the lights at Embankment Pier.'

'*Acknowledged,*' said Control. '*They'll continue south.*'

'Copy that.' The lights changed, the traffic started to move, the last pedestrians broke into self-conscious trots as they hurried out of the way. 'He's accelerating towards Hungerford Bridge.'

She gunned the engine and sped forwards, not about to get stuck should the lights turn against her.

Control's voice crackled again. '*Control, Group. This is as good a spot as any. Five?*'

'*In position,*' reported Number Five. '*Eight, One and Twelve. Get ready. Here we come.*'

Beatrix watched: a white van, not dissimilar to the one in which Control was watching, had been running parallel to them on Whitehall. Now though, it jerked out into the traffic from Richmond Terrace and blocked the road in front of the Mercedes. Number Eight – Oliver Spenser – was at the wheel. Number Five – Lydia Chisolm – was alongside him. Both agents were armed with SA-80 machine guns but the plan did not anticipate that they would need to use them.

Beatrix braked to thirty and then twenty. 'One, Control. They're stopping.'

'*Control, One and Twelve. You have authorisation. Take them out.*'

Beatrix rolled the bike carefully between the waiting cars: a red Peugeot, a dirty grey Volvo, an open double-decker bus that had been fitted out for guided tours. The Mercedes was ahead of the bus, blocked in between it and the delivery van in front. Beatrix reached the car, coming to a halt and bracing the heavy weight of the bike with her right leg. Milton rolled up behind her. Neither of them spoke; they didn't need to, they were operating purely on instinct by this stage, implementing the plan. Beatrix quickly scoped the immediate location: the inside lane was temporarily clear to the left of the Mercedes, the pavement beyond that was empty and then it was the wide open stretch of the Thames. No need to concern themselves with catching civilians in the crossfire.

Beatrix released her grip on the handlebars and unzipped her leather jacket. She was wearing a strap around her shoulder and a Heckler & Koch UMP was attached to it. She raised the machine pistol, steadied it with her left hand around the foregrip, aimed at the Mercedes and squeezed the trigger.

The window shattered, shards spilling out onto the road like handfuls of diamonds.

Milton was supposed to be doing the same but he had stopped.

Beatrix noticed but didn't have time to direct him. She was completely professional. Even as the machine pistol jerked and spat in her hand, her aim was such that every round passed into the cabin of the car. The gun chewed through all thirty rounds in the detachable magazine, spraying lead through the window.

The driver somehow managed to get the Mercedes into gear and it jerked forwards. He must have been hit because he couldn't control the car, slaloming it against the delivery van, bouncing across the road, slicing through the inside lane and then fishtailing. It slid through one hundred and eighty degrees and then wedged itself between a tree and a street lamp. The horn sounded, a long and uninterrupted note. The car had only travelled twenty feet but Beatrix couldn't see into it any longer.

'Milton!'

She was fresh out of ammunition and he was the nearest.

'Milton! Move!'

He was still on the bike, frozen.

The passenger side door opened and Snow fell out. The car's wild manoeuvre meant that the body of the car was now between Beatrix and him; he ducked down beneath the wing, out of sight.

'Milton! Snow is running.'

'I've got it,' Milton said, but she could hear the uncertainty in his voice.

He was corpsing; Beatrix had not anticipated that.

She ejected the dry magazine and slapped in another, watching through the corner of her eye as he got off the Kawasaki and drew his own UMP.

Beatrix put the kickstand down. There was a terrific clamour all about: the Mercedes horn was still sounding, tourists on the bus – with a clear view of what had just happened – were screaming in fright as they clambered to the back of the deck, and, in the distance, there came the ululation of a siren.

Too soon, surely? Perhaps, but it was a timely reminder; the plan only allowed them a few seconds before they needed to effect their escapes.

She approached the car, her gun extended and unwavering.

It was carnage. The driver was slumped forwards, blood splashed against the jagged shards of windscreen that were still held within the frame. The full weight of his chest was pressed up against the wheel, sounding the horn. Dollar was leaning against the side of the car, a track of entry wounds stitching up from her shoulder into her neck and then into the side of her head. Her hair was matted with blood and brain.

Beatrix strode up to the car and fired two short bursts: one for the driver and one for Dollar. She kept moving forward, the machine pistol smoking as she held it ahead of her, zoning out the noise behind her but acutely aware of the timer counting down in her head. The man and the woman were unmoving. She looked through the driver's-side window and saw a briefcase on the passenger seat. They were not tasked with recovering intelligence but it was hardwired into her from a hundred similar missions and so she quickly ran around to the passenger door, opened it and collected it.

'*Control, One,*' came the barked voice in her earpiece. '*Report.*'

'The driver and Dollar are down.'

'*What about Snow?*'

'He's running.'

There was panic in his reply: '*What?*'

'I repeat, Snow is on foot. Twelve is pursuing.'

5

Milton left the bike behind him and sprinted. Snow was already fifty feet ahead, adjacent to the Battle of Britain memorial. The great wheel of the London Eye was on the other side of the river and, ahead, a line of touring coaches had been slotted into the bays next to the pavement.

The man dodged through the line of stalled traffic; nothing was able to move with the shot-up Mercedes blocking the road ahead. He turned his head, stumbling a little as he did, saw Milton in pursuit and sprinted harder. He was older than Milton, but he had obviously kept himself in good shape; he maintained a steady pace, driven on by fear. Milton's motorcycle leathers were not made for running and the helmet he was wearing – he dared not remove it for fear of identifying himself – limited his field of vision.

He took out his Sig and fired a shot. It was wild, high and wide and shattered the windscreen of one of the big parked coaches. It inspired Snow to find another burst of pace, cutting between two of the parked buses. Milton lost sight of him. He ran between a truck and the car in front of it, passed between the two buses behind the ones that his quarry had used and saw him again. A second shot was prevented by a red telephone box and then a tall ash tree.

Milton heard the up-and-down wail of a police siren. It sounded as if it was on the Embankment, behind him, closing the distance.

Milton stopped, dropped to one knee and brought up the Sig. He breathed in and out, trying to steady his aim, and, for a moment, he had a clear shot. He used his left hand to swipe up his visor, breathed again, deep and easy, and started to squeeze the trigger.

Snow ploughed into the middle of a group of tourists.

Shit.

Milton dropped his arm; there was no shot. He closed the visor and ran onwards, just as he saw the man again: he had clambered onto the wall that separated the pavement from the river and, with a final defiant look back in his direction, he leapt into space and plunged into the water. Milton zig-zagged through the panicking tourists until he was at the wall and looked down into the greeny-black waters. There was nothing for a moment and then, already thirty feet distant, he saw Snow bob to the surface. The currents were notoriously strong at this part of the river. The rip tides were powerful enough to swallow even the strongest swimmer, but Snow was not fighting and the water swept him away, quickly out of range.

The siren was louder now, and, as Milton turned to face it, he saw that the patrol car was less than a hundred feet away, working its way around the stalled queue.

Milton paused, caught between running and standing still. He froze. He didn't know what to do.

'*Milton,*' came Number One's voice in his ear.

He turned to his left.

Beatrix was on the pavement, between the river and the row of buses, gunning her Kawasaki hard. Milton pushed the Sig back into its holster and zipped up his jacket. Beatrix braked, the rear wheel bouncing up a few inches, then slamming back down again. Milton got onto the back; Beatrix had a slight figure and he looped his left arm around her waist and fixed his right hand to grip the rear of the pillion seat. Milton was six foot tall and heavy with muscle, but the bike had a 998cc four-cylinder engine and his extra weight was as nothing.

It jerked forward hungrily as Beatrix revved it and released her grip on the brakes.

6

Beatrix looked out of the window of Control's office. It was the evening, two hours after the operation. It was a habit to debrief as soon as possible after the work had been done and, usually, those were not difficult meetings. Normally, the operations passed off exactly as they were planned. They were not botched like this one had been botched.

Control was busying himself with the tray that his assistant, Captain Tanner, had brought in; it held a teapot, two cups, a jug of milk and a bowl of sugar cubes. He poured out two cups. Beatrix could see that he was angry. His face was drawn and pale, the muscles in his cheeks twitching. He had said very little to her, but she knew him well enough to know that the recriminations were coming. The crockery chimed as he rattled the spoon against it, stirring in his sugar. He brought the cups across the room, depositing one on her side of his desk and taking the other one around to sip at it as he stood at the window.

'So?' he began.

'Sir?'

'What happened?'

Beatrix had known, of course, that the question was coming. The mission had been an unmitigated failure. The watchword of the Group was discretion, and the shooting had been the first item on all of yesterday's news broadcasts and websites were leading with a variation of the same picture: Milton, in black leathers and a helmet with a mirrored visor, his arm extended as he aimed at the fleeing Snow, his abandoned motorcycle in the background. The headline on *the Times* website was typical: MURDER ON THE STREETS OF LONDON.

'It was just bad luck,' she said.

'Luck? We plan so that luck isn't a factor, Number One. Luck has *nothing* to do with it.'

'The driver managed to get the car away from us. That was just bad luck.'

'It was Twelve's responsibility to neutralise the driver. Are you saying it was his fault?'

She had given thought to what she should say. The honest thing to do would be to throw Milton under the bus. This had been his first examination and he had flunked it. He had frozen at the critical moment. They had the targets cold, helpless, and it had been his corpsing that had given Snow the opportunity to make a run for it. And even then, she knew Milton was a good enough shot to have taken him down.

She could have said all of that and it would have been true. She could have burned him but it wouldn't have been the right thing to do.

She had some empathy. She remembered her own introduction to the Group. The operation when she had lost her
own cherry had been a fuck-up, too; not quite like this, but
then she had been in Iraq and not on the streets of London,
far from prying eyes and the possibility of your mistakes being
amplified by a media that couldn't get enough of something so
audacious and dramatic. Her own wobble had been between
her, the female agent who had been Number Six in those days
and her victim, an Iraqi official who was passing information
to the insurgency; she had paused at the moment of truth and
that meant that the man she had just stabbed in the gut had
been able to punch her in the face, freeing himself for long
enough to hobble into the busy street outside. Number Six
had pursued him outside and fired two shots into his head
and then, keeping bystanders away with the threat of the gun,
she had hijacked a car and driven them both away. Beatrix
remembered how Control had asked her how it had gone. Six
had covered for her, telling him that the operation had passed
off without incident and that it had all been straightforward.
Beatrix would have been cashiered without hesitation if Six
had told Control the truth. So she understood what had happened to Milton. It did not diminish her opinion of him. It
did not make her question her decision to recommend him.

'It wasn't his fault,' she told Control, looking him straight
in the eye. 'He did his job, just as we planned it.'

'So you say. But he went in pursuit of Snow?'

'Yes.'

'And?'

'He never had a clear shot, not one he could take without a significant risk that he would hit a bystander. The rules of engagement were clear. This had to be at no risk.'

'I know what the bloody rules of engagement were, Number One,' he said sharply. 'I wrote them.'

'If you want to blame anyone, blame me.'

Control flustered and, for a moment, Beatrix was convinced that he was going to blame her. That would have been all right. She had been a member of the Group for six years and that was already pushing at the top end of an agent's average life expectancy. It wasn't an assignment that you kept if you had something to lose. Beatrix had a daughter and a husband and a family life that she enjoyed more than she had ever expected. She had done her time and she had done it well, but all things had to come to an end eventually. She wouldn't have resisted if he blamed her and busted her out of the Group. There would be something else for her, something safer, something where getting shot at was not something she would come to expect.

But he didn't blame her.

'It's a bloody mess,' he said instead, sighing with impatience. 'A bloody, *bloody* mess. The police have been told it's an underworld thing. They'll buy that, if only because the prospect of their own government sanctioning a hit is too bloody ludicrous to credit.'

'The only thing we left was Milton's bike, and that's clean. There's no way back to us from that.'

'You're sure?'

'Absolutely sure.'

Control took his saucer and cup to his desk and sat down. He exhaled deeply. 'What a mess,' he said again. He was frustrated, and that was to be expected, but the immediate threat of the explosion of his temper had passed. 'Where is Milton now?'

'Training,' she told him.

That was true. He hadn't left the quarters where the Group's logistics were based since the operation. He was firing a target pistol over and over until the targets were torn to shreds, then loading another target and pushing it further out and doing it all again.

'Are you still sure about him?'

'He'll be fine,' she said. 'When have I ever been wrong about a recruit?'

'I know,' Control said, leaning back. 'Never.'

He exhaled again and sipped at his tea. Beatrix looked beyond him, beyond the plush interior of his office where so many death warrants were signed, and out into the darkness. London was going about its business, just as usual. Beatrix's eyes narrowed their focus until she noticed the image in the glass: the back of Control's head and, facing him, her own reflection. She stood at a crossroads, with a choice of how to proceed: she could say nothing, and go back to her family, or she could do what she had decided she had to do and begin a conversation that could very easily become difficult.

'There was one more thing,' she said.

'What?'

'I pulled some evidence out of the car.'

Control sat forward. 'That wasn't in the plan.'

'I know. Force of habit, I suppose. It was there, I took it.'

'And?'

'And you should probably take a look.'

She had travelled to the office on her own motorbike and had stowed the case in a rucksack. She opened the drawstring, took it out and laid it on Control's desk. It had been locked and she had unscrewed the hinges to get it open; it was held together by one of her husband's belts at the moment. She unhooked it and removed the top half of the case. There was a clear plastic bag with six flash drives and, beneath that, a manilla envelope. Inside the envelope was a thick sheaf of photographs. They were printed on glossy five-by-eight paper and had been taken by someone from a high vantage point, using a powerful telephoto lens. It was a series, with two people in shot. The first person was a man. He was wearing a heavy overcoat and a woollen hat had been pulled down over his ears. The picture had been taken in a park during the winter; the trees in the foreground were bare and a pile of slush, perhaps from a melted snowman, was visible fifty feet away. The man was bent down, standing over a park bench. There was a woman on the bench.

Despite the distance and the angle that the picture had been taken, it was still obvious that the standing man was Control.

'What is this?' he asked brusquely.

'It was in the case ...'

'Yes,' he snapped. 'You said. I have no idea why.'

'That's you, sir, isn't it?'

'If you say so.'

The atmosphere had become uncomfortable, but Beatrix couldn't draw back.

'The woman on the bench . . .'

Control made a show of examining the photograph more closely.

'It's Dollar.'

He said nothing.

'I don't understand, sir . . .'

'Your job is not to understand, Number One. Your job is to follow the orders that I give you.'

He paused; Beatrix thought he was hesitating, searching for the words to say what he wanted to say, but he didn't say anything else. He just stared at her instead.

'Sir?'

He indicated the flash drives with a dismissive downward brush of his hand. 'Have you looked at these?'

'No, sir,' she said, although that was a lie.

'Very good.' He shuffled in his chair, straightening his shoulders. 'I want you to keep a close eye on Milton. It might be that we were wrong about him – and we can't afford passengers. If we were wrong, we'll need to reassign him. Understood?' She nodded that she did. 'That will be all for now. You're dismissed, Number One.'

She stood, still uncomfortable and confused, and then turned for the door.

She was halfway across the room before Control cleared his throat.

'Look, Number One ... Beatrix. Please, sit down again.' She turned back and did so. He had come around the desk and now he was standing by the mantelpiece. 'You're right. I did meet her. A couple of times. Looks like she decided she'd like some pictures to mark the occasion. I can't tell you why we met and I can't tell you what we spoke about, save to say that it was connected to the operation. The details are classified. All you need to know, Beatrix, is that you were given a file with her name on it. And you know what that means.'

'I do, sir. Termination.'

'That's right. Is there anything else you want to ask me?'

She looked at him: a little portly, a little soft, his frame belying his years of service in MI6, including, she knew, years behind the Iron Curtain during the Cold War and a distinguished campaign in the Falklands. He was looking at her with an expression that looked like concern but, beneath that, she saw a foundation of suspicion and caution. Beatrix was a professional assassin, Number One amidst a collection of twelve of the most dangerous men and women in the employ of Her Majesty. She was responsible for the deaths of over eighty people all around the world. Bad people who had done bad things. She was not afraid of very much. But Control was not the sort of man you would ever want to cross. She looked at him again, regarding her with shrewlike curiosity, and she was frightened.

The thought began to form that she had just made a very, very bad mistake.

MARK DAWSON is the bestselling author of the
Beatrix Rose, Isabella Rose and John Milton series
and has sold over four million books. He lives in
Wiltshire with his family and can be reached
at www.markjdawson.com

www.facebook.com/markdawsonauthor
www.twitter.com/pbackwriter
www.instagram.com.markjdawson

A Message from Mark

Building a relationship with my readers is the very best thing about writing. Join my VIP Reader Club for information on new books and deals, plus a free ebook telling the story of Milton's battle with the Mafia and an assassin called Tarantula.

Just visit www.markjdawson.com/Milton.

WELBECK

PUBLISHING GROUP

Love books? Join the club.

Sign up and choose your preferred genres to receive tailored news, deals, extracts, author interviews and more about your next favourite read.

From heart-racing thrillers to award-winning historical fiction, through to must-read music tomes, beautiful picture books and delightful gift ideas, Welbeck is proud to publish titles that suit every taste.

bit.ly/welbeckpublishing

WELBECK

ANDRE DEUTSCH

MORTIMER

MORTIMER

WELBECK

THE WAVES
ARE FREE

THE WAVES ARE FREE

ARE FREE

**Shetland/Norway Links
1940 to 1945**

"If there is anyone who still wonders why this war is being fought, let him look
to Norway. If there is anyone who has any delusions that this war could have
been avoided, let him look to Norway. And if there is anyone who doubts of the
democratic will to win, again I say, let him look to Norway."

Franklin D. Roosevelt

JAMES W. IRVINE

The Shetland Publishing Company
Lerwick
1990

First published by Shetland Publishing Company 1988
Paperback edition 1990

© James W. Irvine, 1988
Line drawings © Peter McLeod, 1988

ISBN 0 906736 12 9

The Publishers wish to acknowledge the financial assistance received
from Lerwick Community Council

Published by Shetland Publishing Company,
4 Midgarth Crescent, Lerwick.

Printed by Shetland Litho,
Prince Alfred Street, Lerwick.

Contents

List of Illustrations

I am indebted to the following for providing the illustrations used in this book:

Mrs Lenore Brown	55, 56
Mrs A. Davidson	11, 26, 38
Mrs H. Duncan	22
Frank Garriock	3
J. J. (Ian) Fraser	29
Mrs Ingrid Hamre	30
Admiral B. Helle	40
Alan Irvine	4, 12, 13, 14, 15, 16, 17, 18, 19, 33, 36, 39, 44, 45, 46, 47, 48, 49, 50, 51, 52, 53, 54, 60
Asbjørn Lie	59
Shetland Museum	1, 2, 5 to 10, 23, 25, 34, 35, 57, 58, 62, 63
Alf Terje Myklebust	42, 43
Anna Smith	41
Sverre Syversen	24, 31, 32, 37
Mrs Bjarnhild Tulloch	61
Tommy Watt	20, 21, 27, 28

Foreword

This book would probably never have been written but for Lerwick Community Council. It was the Council which, in 1987, asked me to go over to Norway and interview as many as possible of the "Shetland/Norway" war veterans, so that a permanent record of the period could be collected and collated before it was too late. After all it is now forty-three years since the young Norwegians who had escaped west over sea to the islands went back to their homeland at war's end, and the march of time means, inevitably, that their numbers are steadily decreasing.

I duly carried out the Council's request, and found the task to be both fascinating and absorbing. On my return I transcribed the contents of the interviews which I had recorded, and these transcripts and the tapes themselves are now in the safe custody of the Council. But because I had found it all so absorbing, I felt that, given ready access to it, a much wider public would find it just as interesting as I had done. The logical answer was to write a book, and this I have tried to do with the encouragement and support of the Community Council. In its pages I have told a little of the wartime years in both Norway and in Shetland. There is something, too, of the dangerous and daring escapes west to the islands made by hundreds and hundreds of Norwegians in craft of every shape and size, and often in atrocious weather conditions. There is something of the subsequent contribution to the fight for freedom made by the men of the "Shetland Bus", of the Motor Torpedo Boats, of the submarines and of the Sunderlands and Catalinas based at Sullom Voe. There is something of the Commandos' story, of the secret agents landed back again in Norway from fishing boats, MTBs, submarines and from the air, and something of the "export groups" who helped so many to escape the Gestapo. There is even a little of the ultimate degradation — the concentration camps. Through it all runs the bright thread of human courage, endeavour, suffering and endurance, and most importantly, the ever-strengthening bonds of friendship and comradeship between Norwegians and Shetlanders, bonds which have stood the test of time.

I would like to thank all those people in Norway whom I interviewed and asked for help, and who were so patient and so tolerant of all my questions. Most of them will find their names somewhere in the book. The Norwegian veterans now settled in Shetland have been most helpful, with Asbjørn Lie of great assistance with translation of much material, a field in which Elizabeth Morewood and Reidar Vetvik also provided considerable expertise. Frank Garriock kindly put wartime records at my disposal, and so did Lerwick Harbour Trust. Jack Moore of Scalloway, so well known to the men of the "Shetland Bus", gave me much first-hand information, as did Mrs Davidson of Breiwick Road with whom a number of Norwegians lodged during the war years. Wibby Leask's memories of wartime events have been of great assistance. In the Shetland Museum Tommy Watt, as always, has given willing and most valuable help with many of the illustrations, and I am obliged to Liv and Anders Schei for keeping me right in the chapter on Norwegian history between 1814 and 1940. To all of them, and to Lerwick Community Council, I extend my sincere thanks.

I hope the reader will find at least something of interest in what I have written. Possibly it will be seen as a history book, and I will be happy if that is so. For the book is about people — about their endurance, their determination, their bravery, their suffering and their sharing when human freedom was at stake, and surely these are important ingredients in real history.

James W. Irvine

Lerwick.
June, 1988.

Introduction

The bonds of deep friendship which linked the people of Shetland and the refugees from Norway during the dark days of the German occupation of that country were strong and enduring. When the *Leda,* in May, 1967, more than twenty years on, landed 300 veterans in Lerwick on a nostalgic return visit, they were received with open arms. Many a veteran, who had faced the worst dangers of war, had a tear in his eye when he met once again the Shetland friends he had known. Many of them said, with a kind of awed wonder in their voices, "It's just like coming home again!" A further twenty years on and the famous sub-chaser *Hitra,* lovingly rebuilt by the Norwegians, tied up once again in the Scalloway she knew so well. She had many of her old crew with her, and the greetings exchanged between them and the Scalloway people were warm, sincere and extremely moving. The get-together in the Scalloway Hall on the following evening was an occasion of such deeply-felt, genuine friendship that the memory will linger long in the minds of those privileged to be there.

Historians and students of the period have commented on this remarkable relationship, and are at a loss to explain how and why it should have grown so spontaneously and so naturally. Perhaps a glance at history would have helped them to a readier understanding.

The year 1469 saw the transfer of Shetland to the Scottish crown, and the Norse era in Shetland, which had lasted for over five centuries, officially came to an end. The changeover didn't happen with dramatic suddenness. After all, a people who had been Norse one day were hardly likely to become Scottish overnight. But the new Scottish influence gained increasing ascendancy as the flow of Scots northwards gathered momentum, until Norse customs, speech, laws and general way of life were relegated to the past. However, not a little of what was left has stood the test of time, and there is no lack of reminders of these days even in the Shetland of today. We still have our own dialect, for instance, and there you will find plenty of evidence of our Norse connection. Many of our words have an almost exact counterpart in Norwegian, many more clearly show their Norse origin. Where in the world, except in Norway, would people understand us when we use words like kline, nev, slokk, slushet, sturken? But in Norway they would have no difficulty, for their words are almost identical both in spelling and in meaning. Kline — Nor. *kline* — is to spread (butter); nev — Nor. *neve,* is fist; slokk — Nor. *sløkke,* is to extinguish; slushet — Nor. *slusket,* is slovenly; sturken — Nor. *størkne,* is coagulate. There are dozens more.

Our place-names, too, bear the distinctive Norse imprint. To take just one or two examples — the Norse *vik* — a small open bay — shows up in names like Maywick, Troswick, Levenwick, and so on. Many names include the Norwegian *seter* — a farm — though nowadays often in a shortened form, e.g. Baxter (Bakkasetter), Geoster (Geosetter) and Dalster (Dalsetter). Indeed the old influence is so strong in our place-names that over half of them can be shown to be of Norse origin. The streets of Lerwick, bearing names like King Harald, King Haakon, King Erik, St Magnus, St Olaf, St Sunniva, Ronald, Thorfinn, Sandveien, Nedersund, Nederdale, etc., are constant reminders of our past. And the unique Up-Helly-Aa Fire Festival, famous world-wide, although Shetlandic in conception, draws heavily for its trappings on Norse legend.

While the Norse came to Shetland primarily to settle and raise crops and animals, the sea was their natural element, and today in Dunrossness, at Shetland's southern tip, there is a six-oared boat called a "Ness yoal", which is virtually unchanged from the boats which our ancestors brought across from Norway, and used for fishing in the racing tidal waters around Sumburgh Head. For a long time after the Norse era in the islands ended Shetlanders continued to receive the boats from Norway in "pre-fab" kits. Then import difficulties forced the Dunrossness men to start building the boats themselves to the age-old pattern, and today it has the unique distinction of being the oldest surviving craft around the shores of Britain. Shetlanders and Norwegians would be in complete accord when talking about the boat's parts such as tilfers, kabes and humlibaands.

After Shetland became part of Scotland, the islands' interchange with Norway gradually declined. Bergen, so long the channel for trade and communication, was replaced by Aberdeen, and contact with Norway, in the absence of any kind of scheduled service, became virtually non-existent, even though Bergen was only 180 miles distant. But as the twentieth century dawned, Norway was rapidly reaching the status of the most important fishing nation in Europe, and the waters round Shetland, so rich in fish, saw much of Norwegian boats and Norwegian crews. Not surprisingly these same boats were often in Lerwick harbour, and many fishermen from Norway's west coast knew Shetland and Shetlanders well. It was fishing and fishermen which provided the main Shetland/Norway contacts during the first forty years of the present century.

When the Germans invaded Norway on 9th April, 1940, there was an immediate revulsion against the incomers, and many Norwegians were soon thinking of trying to get away so that they could make a more positive contribution to the struggle against the common enemy. And for people who lived by the sea, on the sea and from the sea, what more natural than that they should look to the sea as their means of escape. Almost immediately the traffic westwards began and continued to such good effect that during the years of occupation something like 5000 people got away by sea. Not surprisingly Shetland was the haven for most of them. In the main they were young people, fearlessly making the crossing, often in very rough weather and often in open boats. Not a few failed to reach a safe harbour and the sea was their grave. Invariably they left without telling their loved ones that they were going — to tell anything could be fatal, both to the escaper and to his parents. Families heard no more from them till war's end — not even whether they had survived the North Sea crossing. Sadly for many families the news they got in 1945 was of sons who would never return.

The refugees were well received in Shetland. Apart from the fact that the islanders saw them as fellow-fighters in the desperate struggle in which all were engaged, there was also a vague feeling of kinship in many hearts. That feeling was a survival from the distant past — perhaps just sentiment to begin with, but a feeling which grew in substance with the passing of the months.

Almost invariably the refugees were sent to London for thorough screening. It was not unknown for a Norwegian nazi to have infiltrated a boat-load of escapers. They were allocated to the various branches of the Norwegian forces, and were trained for the role they were destined to play. A good deal of that training was carried out in the Scottish Highlands. Having completed their training a considerable number were returned to Shetland. There they served with the Shetland Bus, the motor torpedo boats, the submarines, the Sunderlands and Catalinas at Sullom Voe, the Commandos — or were landed as secret agents in Norway itself. All of them were exposed to continuous risk, and all of them at war's end had remarkable stories they could have told. Some of these would have outdone the most imaginative of thriller writers. As they led their dangerous lives they were making friends with the Shetland people, friends who, though knowing something of the exciting missions on which they were engaged, never breathed a word to anyone about what they knew. It was in Scalloway above all where the bonds between natives and Norwegians were at their strongest. Here the Norwegians lived, laughed, loved and even married, and here they were treated by the people as if they were Shetlanders.

This book cannot hope to tell the stories of all these men. But it will attempt to tell a little about a few, and also a little about the land whence they came. Perhaps its pages will stand as a tiny tribute to those thousands of kinsfolk from the past who, in daring to escape and lay their lives on the line, not once but time and time again in the struggle for freedom, by their deeds wrote many illustrious pages to add to the story of their land. Perhaps the book will also help to show how proud Shetland is to have had the opportunity to extend the hand of friendship to those courageous men and women so far from home, and to have had a worth-while role to play in support of their daring exploits.

Chapter One

The Years to 1940

There are still quite a few people alive today who lived through both world wars. But those who played an active role in the 14/18 conflict are now pitifully thin on the ground. Yet surely their memories linger on, for it was the kind of war which produced experiences which must have been stamped indelibly on their minds. For those years saw the senseless slaughter by hidebound generals of hundreds of thousands of virile, eager young men. Thousands of their mangled, torn bodies sank to unmarked graves in the bottomless mud and slime which was the Western Front. On the seafloors of the world's oceans lay the bodies of thousands more, sent to their watery graves by the every-lurking, deadly U-boats. The old men can remember how, while the blood ran in an endless flood, the politicians in Britain continued to mouth their empty platitudes. "A war to end wars," they said. "You're making the World safe for Democracy," and "We'll build Homes fit for Heroes to live in," they said. Sadly for so many of those heroes the years that followed failed to match the specious promises. A temporary boom was followed by slump and depression, and many a hero was forced to eke out a miserable existence by begging in the streets. Depressed areas, unemployment and wide-spread poverty were the background to the lives of the mass of the ordinary people of Britain. And Britain had been one of the victors in the "war to end wars".

In Germany, as the war ended, the army claimed with some justification that they had never been beaten. German surrender was political, said the soldiers. But no amount of words could prevent the immediate post-war years being a nightmare for the people of Germany. The reparations demanded by the victors were swingeing, the conditions imposed severe, the country's economy was in chaos and the people were starving. Many historians claim that, though they won the war, the victors lost the peace. Be that as it may, conditions in Germany were ripe for the rise of a so far insignificant man, Adolf Hitler. His first "putsch" in 1923 failed, but, profiting from his mistakes, he now approached the really big men in Germany such as the steel barons Thyssen and Krupp, and others of their kind, with a proposition. He would smash communism and socialism in Germany if they would come up with the cash to further his plans. They agreed. They saw him as the ideal instrument to prevent the "rise of the masses", and at that stage they were not too concerned about the methods he might use. Of one thing they were sure and that was that their wealth and power depended on the "masses" being kept under strict control. By 1933 Hitler was Chancellor of Germany, and the League of Nations, which had promised so much, was already tottering.

For those who listened Hitler's aim was crystal clear almost from the beginning. He saw Germany as the home of a great totalitarian complex of military and economic power, with the rest of Europe as vassal states, built on the German model with so-called governments of their own, but of course all subservient to Germany. To inspire extra confidence he posed as the defender of Europe against the menace of Bolshevism. The economic collapse of the thirties was tailor-made for his ambitions, and sadly there were people in every country, including Britain, prepared to say that Hitler was a great man. The events of the thirties had a sort of inevitability about them. There was the rise of Mussolini, Italy's caricature of Hitler. There was the Spanish Civil War which provided a testing ground for German arms and the new German philosophy. There was the invasion of Austria, the feebleness of Munich, the dismemberment of Czechoslovakia and the invasion of Poland. But enough was enough, and when Chamberlain's quavering voice announced over the radio at 11 am on Sunday, 3rd September, 1939, that we were at war with Germany, it came as no surprise. Probably to many it brought a feeling of relief that at last the waiting and the uncertainty were over. It had been clear to most thinking people for a long time that sooner or later we would have to make up our minds whether we were prepared to fight to defend our personal freedom or simply acquiesce in becoming mindless cogs in the machine of an all-controlling foreign power. Our fathers and mothers in the First War had been naive enough to swallow the politicians' guff. Not so this time. Now it was the people, despite their poverty-stricken state, who could see clearly for themselves that personal liberty was at stake. It was the politicians, for reasons best known to themselves, who had continued to drag their feet, and left us woefully unprepared when the chips were finally down. But on 3rd September the die was cast, the dithering at last was over, and the years that followed would fill many pages of future history books.

The coming of war is a traumatic experience, and that applied in Shetland as much as elsewhere in Britain. It was only twenty years since the First War had ended, and fathers who had been at sea or in the trenches remembered only too vividly the horrors of the Western Front and the never-ceasing fear of the deadly torpedo wherever they sailed on the oceans of the world. Now they looked at their sons, wondering if they were soon to face similar or even more horrible dangers, and whether they would ever return. The sons attempted to present an unruffled acceptance of the fact that they would soon be in uniform. But there were few of them without some dread mixed with the thrill of the unknown. They had read in books about the glorious deeds of the First War, but they had heard from their fathers, who had been there, of the bloody reality. Now they were going to find out for themselves whether they would be equal to the demands that would be made on them — whether they would behave as men when they were really up against it. The mothers, as mothers do, worried about their children, and wondered, as always, why there had to be wars. Above all everyone wondered whether air power would prove to be the new and unspeakable horror that most people feared.

The War Comes to Shetland

Of course life in Shetland changed after 3rd September, but to begin with the change was slow. The Territorials and the Naval Reservists were the first to be called, but most of the rest waited for the conscription net to pull them in, for this time conscription came into force immediately. No pointing finger this time with the slogan, "Your Country Needs You". No more mealy-mouthed catch-phrases from the politicians. Shortly before war's outbreak, on 21st August, the *Earl of Zetland* had departed, having completed sixty-two years of service to the North Isles. She was soon to be back, while the new *Earl* went off to the busier Pentland Firth. The North of Scotland Shipping Company's "Saints" were all still on the go — *Sunniva, Magnus, Rognvald, Ninian, Clair* and *Clement*. But on 1st September the Admiralty requisitioned the *Sunniva, Magnus* and *Ninian*. In October a JU 88 swept past the *Clair* off Sumburgh Head with nothing more offensive than a wave of the hand from the pilot. Norwegian fishing boats were still calling. The *Sjøgutten* and the *Brattholm* for instance were both in harbour. No one could possibly have guessed under what conditions their next visit would take place. In fact, no one was giving much thought to Norway in those days. If people thought about her at all it was probably with envy that she had once again managed to avoid being embroiled in war.

The signs of war gathered momentum. On 17th September the Admiralty signalled its presence by taking over several of the offices in the Fish Market, and on 8th October a Swedish steamer was sunk by gunfire from a U-boat about 45 miles south of Flugga. One boat's crew landed at Norwick in Unst, but the captain's boat, with eight men on board, was presumed lost. In the same week an RAF pinnace made harbour after having been four days at sea in very rough weather. Two drifters and the lifeboat had searched for the small craft for many hours and had finally given her up as lost. Ten days later the British ship *Sea Venture* was sunk by a U-boat off Unst. Lerwick lifeboat fetched the crew to Lerwick from Skaw, where they had managed to get ashore. The crew had seen the lifeboat's lights when she was searching for them, but in the darkness they had feared it was the submarine back to finish them off, and they had not responded.

Soon the Rechabite Hall was taken over as a temporary billet for naval ratings, and at the end of October 80 German prisoners from sunk German ships were landed for onward transmission to PoW camps in the south. On the day they left the first German plane appeared in the sky over Lerwick. In November the first bombs were dropped, and a famous supposed casualty was the rabbit which gave rise to the popular war-time song, "Run, rabbit, run". The harbour was slow to reach the hectic state of activity which was to come later, but among the new callers were the big "Northern" trawlers, and over the months they included — all prefixed with *Northern* — *Sun, Princess, Sky, Dawn, Gem, Spray, Pride, Wave, Foam, Gift, Isles* and *Chief*. On 18th November the North Ness was taken over by the navy and the RAF.

Four days later came the first real attack by German planes, and the unknown, which had been a source of dread to many, became a reality. It had been a very rough morning with gale force wind and a heavy sea running. As so often happens in Shetland when a depression's centre moves over, the wind fell away and the sky remained dull and grey — but there was the almost eerie silence which comes with such calm. Suddenly six Heinkel bombers were overhead, flying at an extremely low altitude, with the air-raid siren failing to sound until the planes were actually over the town. Their very low altitude, and the suddenness of their appearance, with no indication of just where they would strike, was disconcerting to say

1. Raid on Lerwick — November 1940.

2. Sunderland flying-boat. 330 Nor. Squadron at Sullom Voe was equipped with these planes in 1943. (*See chapter 21*)

the least. After circling the town the planes dropped eight bombs on a flying-boat moored in the north harbour. Some of the sinister fear which the planes' black crosses had inspired was dispelled when it was observed that the "master race" were human after all — all the bombs missed their target. However, one of the planes came in machine-gunning the flying-boat until it caught fire. The crew all succeeded in jumping overboard, and six of them were quickly and skilfully rescued by the haddock-boats *Olive* and *Nellie,* skippered respectively by John T. Watt and Joseph Watt. The seventh man swam ashore to one of the herring jetties. Officers and a doctor from the RAF appeared on the scene, and a Lerwick man who was present noted that the crowd which had gathered to watch the crew being helped ashore were somewhat loudly hostile to the RAF "brass" for their failure to have brought dry clothing or stimulants for the soaked and half-frozen men. One forthright individual compared the conduct of the officers with that of the crew members in terms that were, to say the least, unfavourable to the officers. The town had had its first air-raid experience, and happily no lives had been lost. It might have been very different if the bombs had been directed at three trawlers lying at the Market — the *Northern Foam, Northern Isles* and *Northern Princess.* All three had large quantities of depth charges on board. Lerwick Harbour Trust recorded the incident concisely. "Six German Heinkel bombers flew very low over the town, dropping bombs in the north harbour, and machine-gunning a flying-boat which was ultimately set on fire. All the crew were rescued by two haddock boats." During that same week German planes were over the town on nine separate occasions.

On 28th November the survivors from the crew of the Swedish tanker *Gustav E. Reuter* were landed at the breakwater by Lerwick lifeboat. The tanker had struck a mine south-east of Shetland. The Admiralty tug *St Mellons* took her in tow in very bad weather, but gave up the task as hopeless when 25 miles south-east of Bressay light. Early units for the Shetland Garrison were arriving, initially 210 officers and men on the *St Clair,* drawn from the Black Watch, the Argyll and Sutherland Highlanders and the Gordons. The TA Hall housed them while hutted accommodation was being constructed.

Certainly the first seven months of the war in Shetland were not without incident, but they failed to produce the kind of intense activity and shattering events which many people had feared. The enemy was no nearer than he had been at the beginning, still hundreds of miles away. The unknown, in the shape of aerial attack, had been experienced, and people had come to terms with it. But there was the uneasy feeling that this was the calm before the storm. The papers labelled it the "phony war". The calm was shattered with a vengeance on 9th April, 1940. That was the day that four destroyers, the famous *Cossack,* along with the *Kashmir, Kelvin* and *Zulu* came into harbour, one of them listing badly and clearly having been in action. It was a portent of what was to come, because the BBC informed its listeners that day that the Germans had invaded Norway. Suddenly the enemy was only 180 miles away, with nothing but open water between him and the islands. Norway's 126 years of freedom from conflict were over. Now she was in it too. The calm was over, the storm had come, and though people still didn't realise it as they struggled to grasp the harsh realities of the situation, the fortunes of Norway and Shetland were to be closely intertwined during the days, months and years which lay ahead.

Chapter Two

Norway 1814 – 1940

When the quirks of fate threw Norway and Shetland together in 1940, it was surprising how little was known in the islands about Norway's history from the time of Shetland's handover, right on to the present century. But because the latter part of the period does have a bearing on the conduct of Norway's people during the years of occupation, and also on the country's reaction to Hitler's plans, it is worth looking briefly at the main events and issues.

From 1400 to 1814 Norway had been governed by officials appointed by the Danish king. But in 1814 King Frederik VI of Denmark, in the Treaty of Kiel, handed Norway over to the Swedish crown. The Swedish king at the time was Karl II, though his son, Karl Johan, adopted in 1810, acted as the effective ruler of Sweden until he became king in his own right on the death of his adoptive father in 1818. The Norwegians saw the Treaty as an opportunity. The country's first national parliament met at Eidsvold — the Eidsvold Assembly — and on 17th May, 1814, the terms of a brand new Constitution were promulgated, and the crown of Norway was offered to Prince Christian Frederik, who had been the Danish king's representative in Norway. The Prince accepted the offer, having first been required solemnly to promise to uphold the Constitution. The Norwegians saw a king as being of the people and responsible to the people, and who would stand inside and not outside the framework of the Constitution. It hardly mattered where he came from. He was a man of their own choosing, who swore to uphold the concept of "the land shall be built on law". (Cf Shetland Islands Council's "Með lögum skal land byggja".)

As was to be expected, Sweden didn't regard Norway's actions with favour, and fighting between the two nations began along the south-eastern border. The Norwegians fought bravely, but Christian turned out to be sadly devoid of military skill. However, with the big European powers, notably Great Britain, exerting pressure, Karl Johan broke off military action and undertook negotiation. The upshot was that Norway was to retain her new Constitution, which would give her self-governing status, but the Swedish king would also be king of Norway. Almost immediately there was friction. Karl Johan's interference in Norwegian affairs was seen as clear breaches of the Constitution, and there was furious reaction from the Norwegian people. The king climbed down but the enforced relationship between the two countries became increasingly irksome to Norwegians.

But Constitution Day, 17th May, was to become Norway's most important day. In the early years celebrations to mark the day were more or less confined to the Trondheim area, but from 1824 onwards such activities became more general. Henrik Wergeland, with his speeches and poems, enriched the day with something of his own character, and when Bjørnson's initiative in 1870 led to the first children's processions on the 17th, the Day was even more strongly established, in both town and country, as Norway's most important annual date.

Communications in Norway were always difficult, and the saying "the land divides, the sea unites" was self-evidently true. Mountains in the old days were an impenetrable barrier. The sea for Norwegians was the highway — and also the source of food. At least one male from virtually every family along the west coast was at sea. The country lacked coal, but towards the end of last century hydro-power more than compensated, the first electricity works being established in 1885, and electricity became a key factor in Norway's industrial development. In 1891 Hammerfest, in Norway's far north, became the first town in the world to be wholly lit by electricity.

In 1905 the reluctant union with Sweden was finally dissolved, and Norway at last was fully independent. Again the people chose a Dane to be king — Haakon VII. At this time Norway's was probably the most classless society in Europe. All titles had disappeared under the new Constitution, and as the country moved into the new century the Labour Party grew in strength. Yet between 1880 and 1907 Norwegians were emigrating to the U.S.A. at the rate of from 10,000 to 30,000 per year. It was claimed that from 1836 the total had reached 750,000.

The years between the wars saw notable advances in health and education. There were state schools for all children between the ages of seven and fourteen, and after that there was equal opportunity for all. In public health the country had one hospital bed for every 115 people — in Britain the ratio was one for 150. News was purveyed by no less than 200 daily papers, and there were also 900 periodicals; all that for a population under 3,000,000. The fishing industry had come on by leaps and bounds, and by 1930 it was the biggest in Europe, with boat ownership, as in Shetland, mostly in the hands of the crews. With the growth of the fishing fleet came the parallel growth of a huge merchant navy. Though a non-combatant in the First War, Norway had had nearly half her merchant ships sunk. Despite world depression, she rebuilt her fleet between the wars, and when 1940 came, half her ships were less than ten years old, and many of them were tankers. In total tonnage she ranked fourth in the world, coming just after Japan, and greatly exceeded by only Great Britain and the U.S.A. Her small population, behind her staggering 12,000 miles of coastline (including the fjords), had learned to work together in a multiplicity of voluntary organisations, where each supported the other, but at the same time they simply would not tolerate being bossed. The retention of that strong, rugged individuality was a great source of strength when the testing time came. They had come a long way along the road to true democracy since 1814. They had ensured that "the land was built on law". They had created a way of life which they believed in. Above all, they believed in themselves.

Events Leading to the German Occupation

As we have seen, Norway again chose a Danish king in 1905, and he was to prove, in peace and in war, a stauch upholder of the Constitution. Now Norway made neutrality the keystone of her foreign policy. She quite simply wanted nothing more than to be left alone. She had managed to preserve her neutrality during the First War, and between the wars she was a loyal member of the League of Nations. She also secretly had a great belief in the power of the British navy, and saw that power as a sure shield against a possible attack on her coastline. So secure did she feel in her neutral state that she maintained only a minimum of armed forces. However, a factor in the Second War which was accorded great importance by both the Germans and the British was Swedish iron-ore. The ore was mined in northern Sweden, and transported by train either to Lulea, a Swedish port on the Baltic, or to Narvik, a port on Norway's northern west coast. Lulea was ice-bound for six months of the year, so Narvik, ice-free all year round, was of great importance. By 1940 the German armaments industry was getting virtually all its iron from Sweden, so Germany desperately needed it. It was equally important for Britain to deprive her of it. Churchill frequently had Norway in mind, and strongly advocated mining the southern approaches to Narvik. This would have forced the German freighters to go outside Norway's neutral territorial waters, and would have allowed the British navy to get at them. He also mooted the possibility of landing an expeditionary force somewhere in northern Norway to establish a bridgehead. This plan had been sufficiently well received to have persuaded France and Britain to earmark upwards of 150,000 troops for its execution. But the settling of details dragged on, and in the end the plan fell through.

Hitler was well aware that Britain would be considering action in Norway. Indeed, his intelligence services had told him so. He was considering similar action. And from the German point of view occupation of Norway would bring several benefits. It would enable him to break the Bergen/Scapa blockade line which had proved so effective in the First War, and was already doing its job in the Second. It would provide access to ports which would make ideal submarine bases. It would secure the iron-ore supply, and, if carried out promptly, would forestall any projected British action. But perhaps what made such a step most attractive to Hitler was the fact that Norway was the prime example of a Nordic country, with Nordic people, the nearest in Europe to the true "herrenvolk" of Germany itself. Norway would be the ideal place for him to spread the ideology which he had imposed on Germany. He saw Norway as a showpiece in the "Great Germanic Union". If he could conquer Norway both politically and ideologically, it would be proof to the world that Nazism had really taken root outside the borders of the Reich. It would be the first real step in establishing the "New Order" in Europe.

Vidkun Quisling

Because his name became a word in the language of many countries, it is necessary here to look for a moment at the story of Vidkun Quisling. Theodor Broch, Mayor of Narvik at the time, refers to a visit to Narvik by the "mad Major Quisling". At the time he had given up military service — he had been a major — in order to devote his energies to his political studies, and the Narvik visit was for the purpose of giving a lecture. The Mayor commented, "A rather large group attended. It had been a long time since a circus had been in town." That comment reflected the general Norwegian attitude to Quisling in the pre-war years. He had been Norwegian military attaché in Russia after the First War, and had accompanied the legendary Nansen on his travels through the hungry districts of the Soviets. For a time thereafter he was a great admirer of communism, but as there wasn't much sale for that in Norway, he offered his services to the Labour Party. Getting a cold reception there, too, he turned to the far right, and mounted bitter attacks on Labour. Giving his support for a time to the Agrarian Party, he briefly reached the high-spot of his pre-war career as Minister of Defence, but the Agrarian government was short-lived. He then created his own Nasjonal Samling — National Unity Party — but it gained no real popularity. Narvik's mayor said, "We paid sixpence to listen to his talk. It was certainly not worth more." He noted that Quisling showed absolutely no sense of humour, and he reckoned that not a single person in the hall at Narvik agreed with the views Quisling expressed. At the time he was publishing a weekly paper in Oslo, and the Mayor dismissed his followers as "superannuated crackpots and discontented young unemployed" — which was probably a somewhat jaundiced view. The N.S. gained about 1% of the votes cast at two general elections, i.e. about 25,000. Such was the man destined to become an infamous household word.

Though the N.S. Party was modelled faithfully on the Nazi pattern, it was not until 1939 that Quisling managed to get German attention. He did so by means of a somewhat spectacular offer. After forming a new government in Norway, he said, he would invite a German landing, and would prepare the way for them. He actually twice had audience with Hitler, who approved the idea of Quisling taking over power in Norway by a coup d'état, but he would then use Quisling as his puppet. However, by March 1940, Hitler's plan for the occupation of Norway was complete, and Quisling had no place in it. Hitler's immediate stated aims were to forestall British action, secure the iron-ore supplies, and establish submarine bases. Quisling was given no inkling of the plans, though as late as 3rd April the Germans summoned him to meet them in Copenhagen where he was closely quizzed about Norway's defences. At the time Hitler's much more ambitious plans for the conquest of western Europe were also going ahead.

While Hitler pursued his inflexible path, and the British and French governments continued their dithering during the last month or two before the real war began, the "Altmark incident" hit the world's headlines. The *Altmark,* a German cargo ship, had accompanied the *Graf Spee* in the South Atlantic as a supply vessel until the *Spee* scuttled herself outside Montevideo harbour rather than face the cruisers of the British navy which had driven her into the port in the first place. Now she was returning home, using Norwegian territorial waters, and escorted by Norwegian MTBs. Units of the British navy also entered Norwegian waters, and the destroyer *Cossack,* commanded by Captain Vian, followed the *Altmark* into Jøssing fjord, ran alongside and boarded her. There was a hand-to-hand fight, and seven members of the German crew were killed, but 300 British seamen, prisoners on board, were freed. They had been members of crews of ships sunk by the *Graf Spee.* Norway protested strongly at this violation of her waters. Germany warned darkly of possible consequences of the action.

On 8th April the British navy at last laid a minefield in the southern approaches to Narvik. Again the Norwegian government were affronted by the violation of their territorial rights, and during the afternoon of the 8th they were occupied drafting the strongest possible protest to Britain. They were blissfully unaware that it would be a matter of hours only until the lives of all of them would be in mortal danger.

The Invasion of Norway

The first German troops for the Norwegian operation left Germany in both naval and merchant ships as early as 3rd April, with the actual landings timed for 4.15 am on the morning of 9th April. These landings were to take place at seven key points — Oslo, Arendal, Kristiansand and Egersund in the south, Bergen and Trondheim farther north, and, of course, Narvik, farther north still. A nation which had successfully preserved neutrality for 126 years was totally unprepared. The forces available to meet the onslaught were pitifully small, and completely lacking in active military experience. And yet there had been portents which might have given some warning. On Monday, 8th April, the wreckage of a German transport, the *Rio de Janeiro,* had drifted ashore on the coast of southern Norway. With the wreckage were dead horses and drowned soldiers. The soldiers were all young men. Nobody seemed to attach much importance to the incident. The same day the Danes reported from Copenhagen that a large force of foreign warships had passed on a northerly heading. But still the government wrestled with the terms of the protest to Britain.

The prime German target was, of course, Oslo. The intention was to land airborne troops at Oslo's Fornebu airport, and seaborne troops in Oslo harbour. The city would be taken in a pincer movement, and hopefully king and government would be captured. It didn't quite work that way. The first exchanges of fire between Norwegian minesweepers and German cruisers were taking place soon after midnight, thus alerting the shore batteries at the ancient Oskarsburg fortress, so that when the German navy steamed up the fjord the Norwegian gunners were ready. The destroyer *Brummer* and the battle-cruiser *Blücher* were sunk, and this was such a severe blow to the Germans that they drew back and landed their troops at various points along the fjord shore, so that it took them some considerable time to reach the capital. The delay gave sufficient breathing space for the king and his government to get away, though from then on, until they finally left Norway, they were ceaselessly hounded by the Luftwaffe.

The German landings came as a complete surprise to the Norwegian people. They were not to know that at 4 a.m. that morning the German ambassador had presented himself at the palace and demanded Norway's surrender, to be met with the king's point-blank refusal. Later in the morning the radio announced, "At dawn this morning without any declaration of war Germany launched an invasion of Norway at targets all along the coast." But before that the king and his ministers had gone, their destination initially Hamar. In Oslo the Germans were soon very much in evidence. A large column of soldiers, preceded by a military band, marched up Karl Johan's Gate to the palace, where the Norwegian flag was hauled down and the swastika hoisted. More and more swastikas appeared on public buildings, an intimation to all that these buildings were now German, and the rhythmic thud of marching jackboots was heard all over the city. The people stood on the pavements, watching it all, helpless to do anything, and many of them in tears.

That same evening Quisling managed to get access to Oslo radio, although the Germans of course now controlled it. He announced to the listening Norwegian people that, in the absence of king and government, he was taking over as Prime Minister, and he named his new Cabinet. Very few of the men he named had even been approached. He ordered all resistance to cease. His announcements created complete confusion until Haakon and his government, from their retreat at Hamar, announced their refusal to capitulate and also ordered general mobilisation. After a couple of days Falkenhorst, the overall German military commander, pushed Quisling aside as an irrelevancy. His job was to get on with the conquest of Norway.

On 15th April British troops were landed at a number of places including Namsos, Trondheim and Andalsnes, but they were inadequately trained and ill-equipped for the countryside in which they had to fight. In addition, the Norwegian resistance in the south was uncoordinated, and on 25th April these British troops in southern Norway were withdrawn. Farther north, particularly at Narvik, the picture was completely different, but Narvik deserves attention in its own right. On 7th June the king and his ministers sailed from Tromsø on the British cruiser *Dorsetshire,* and Allied forces in the north were also withdrawn. On 10th June Norway capitulated. Her fight had lasted for 62 days, and was reputed to have cost the Germans 60,000 casualties and one third of her total naval strength. But the story had been overtaken by events. On 10th May German tanks had rumbled into Holland and Belgium, and now western Europe was locked in desperate conflict with the Germans. British forces were badly needed at home.

The Fighting at Narvik

In the 1890s Narvik was a small trading post, with a population seldom reaching 300. Then a British company started buying up land in the area with a view to exploiting the Swedish iron-ore deposits. The plan was to build a railway through the mountains, across the narrowest part of Norway, down to the bay below Fagernes mountain, where flat land extends right to the shore at Ofotfjord. A great deal of work was carried out in the mountains preparing the way for the railway line, and streets were laid out where the city was to rise. It would be called Victoria Harbour. Then the company went bankrupt. However, the Norwegian government saw much merit in the idea, and they completed the scheme from the mountains down to the harbour. The city that was built was called Narvik, and its population was to reach 10,000 by 1940. The railway tracks fanned out down to the fjord, and between them in great cone-shaped mounds lay the iron-ore. The roar as it streamed into the holds of ships went on during the twenty-four hours of every day.

In these northern latitudes summer is short, but good while it lasts — basically first July to mid-August. Many German tourists came on holiday to Norway. Kaiser Bill had been a great admirer of the Norwegian countryside. In 1939 it was noticeable that German tourists had subtly changed. Now they travelled first-class, and all carried cameras and binoculars. And they were nearly all keen, when the opportunity arose, to laud the wonders of the new Germany. After war broke out in 1939 British and German ships continued to use Narvik harbour, and the swastika and the Union

Jack flew side by side. On the evening of 8th April, 1940, twenty-five iron-ore boats were in the harbour, as were two Norwegian navy boats.

A loud explosion, followed by several more, announced the Germans' arrival in Narvik on the morning of the 9th, and when the citizens emerged to look at their town they found that the German troops were already ashore, the swastika was flying at many points, and the two coast defence warships *Norge* and *Eidsvold* had been sunk with the loss of 300 lives. The Colonel in charge of the Norwegian army forces in Narvik (Colonel Sundlo) had surrendered without offering any resistance, and, apart from Quisling, this was probably the worst act of treason during the German invasion.

The German commandant was already ashore. He addressed the civic dignitaries. "I want to make it clear from the start that we have come as friends, to protect your country against any further British breaks of your neutrality. The German Wehrmacht has taken over the protection of Oslo, Bergen and Trondheim. We have encountered no armed resistance anywhere." "But our navy boats in the harbour?" someone asked him. "Sad, isn't it?" he replied. Without delay the Germans announced an 8 p.m. curfew. They also immediately produced their own Norwegian currency, printed in Germany. When asked who would redeem this currency the Narvik mayor was told the British would be forced to pay once they had been defeated. The people noted the irony of the German statements. They had come to protect Norway against all attacks — the Norwegians would be shot as traitors if they did the same. That was the 9th. On the 10th heavy gunfire was heard in the outer fjord. It came from five British destroyers led by Captain Warburton-Lee in the *Hardy*. They did much damage, but were forced to withdraw, Warburton-Lee receiving a posthumous Victoria Cross. Three days later heavy gunfire was again heard in the outer fjord. This time it was the battleship *Warspite* accompanied by nine destroyers including the famous *Cossack*. The Germans still had seven destroyers left, and this attack put paid to all of them. It was an overwhelming victory for the British navy, and the Germans ashore suffered a severe loss of morale. Some of them were already on their way to the Swedish frontier, and when the Norwegians ribbed some of them that their number was up they smiled sheepishly and muttered "Kamerad". By this time the harbour was a veritable graveyard of ships. Each day considerable numbers of the inhabitants evacuated the town in the hope of finding sanctuary elsewhere. As the days went by Allied forces began to close in on

Narvik from the landward side, and the RAF now had the use of an airfield south of Tromsø. Daily the Germans carried out systematic destruction of harbour installations, and even blew up the heavy locomotives. It was clear to everyone, including the Germans, that there was going to be an attempt to recapture Narvik. Fortunately there was only a handful of people left in the town — including the mayor.

On the evening of the 27th May the British fleet came steaming up the fjord in close formation and at high speed, enjoying the rare luxury of some air cover. To the people left in the town the night seemed to be one continuous explosion, and gradually all the German guns were silenced. Troops were landed in small landing craft, and others came in overland, including Norwegians, French Foreign Legion troops and a few Poles. In four hours of fighting Narvik was retaken for the loss of 150 men. Now the town suffered from daily German air attacks. The harbour was cluttered with the wrecks of over 30 ships, and the piers and shore installations were a complete shambles.

But it was all to no avail. On 6th June came the news that Narvik was to be given up. The town by this time was almost completely empty of Norwegians. On 7th June the king, ministers and Allied forces were all evacuated, and the overall Norwegian capitulation followed on 10th June. The German threat to Britain was now so menacing that it would have been foolhardy to try and maintain the operation in Norway. And yet here at Narvik the German land forces had suffered their first significant defeat of the war. It had been a considerable feat of arms by both the British navy and the Allied forces on land. In different circumstances a Narvik in Allied hands might have been very important indeed. But if it did nothing else it did show that the master race was not invincible.

Theodor Broch, mayor of Narvik, remained in the town till the last moment. He got away to Harstad, north of Narvik, where the Germans arrested him as a British spy. He was taken to the German H.Q. in a hotel, but, while his guard's attention was distracted, he managed to get out of the building and out of the immediate danger area in a taxi. He made his way in a fishing boat to the Lofotens, and from there by a roundabout route to the Swedish border. All the time the Germans were broadcasting his name as being wanted as a British spy. From Stockholm he made his way via Riga, Moscow and the Siberian Express to Vladivostock, then on a freighter to Japan. From Tokyo to Yokohama he went, and, after three weeks there, he finally reached Los Angeles on a Norwegian cargo boat.

It was 1941 before his wife and child, after several attempts, managed to escape to Sweden, and from there they, too, finally reached the United States. The family were reunited in Chicago. Theodor joined the Norwegian forces and went to Britain, again on a freighter. Like so many others he received much of his military training at Norwegian centres in Scotland. In 1943 he wrote of his experiences as Narvik's mayor, both in peacetime and under the Germans, in a book entitled "The Mountains Wait".

PMᶜLeod

Chapter Three

The Islands Wait

The news of Germany's occupation of Norway on 9th April, 1940, certainly came as a shock to the people of Shetland. But to begin with sympathy for these new victims of German aggression was the strongest feeling in most minds. It took a few days for the realisation to seep through that the Germans in Bergen were now only as far away as Aberdeen, i.e. twelve hours or so by sea, one hour by air. Did Shetland figure in Hitler's future plans? Would Shetland — and Orkney — be used as stepping stones to the invasion of Britain? How were the Norwegians faring under the German jackboot? There was plenty of rumour and plenty of scare stories, but the hard facts as purveyed by the BBC, scanty though they were, were certainly not reassuring. An early radio announcement had been, "Reuter reports that the Norwegian government has left Oslo and is going to Hamar in central Norway, and Oslo radio announces that general mobilisation has been ordered in Norway." Lord Haw-Haw, though nobody really believed that unctuous voice, poured out reports which, even if they had only a grain of truth in them, were disturbing, to say the least. Everyone wondered just what Britain and France were doing to help Norway. It was said that sixteen French transport ships had put into Sullom Voe. The BBC reported troops being landed in Norway, and there seemed to be heavy naval action at Narvik. Everyone seemed to know that both the *Sunniva* and the *Magnus* were in the thick of events on the other side. But an air of uncertainty hung over it all.

It wasn't long before harsh reality dispelled a lot of the uncertainty. On 15th April came news of a boat coming ashore at Haroldswick in Unst with twelve living men on board and seven dead. They were from the crew of a British freighter torpedoed north-west of Shetland. Two days later the tug *St Mellons,* escorted by three destroyers, one of which was the *Fury,* came in sight towing a fourth badly damaged destroyer. This was the *Eclipse* which had been severely damaged on the Norwegian coast during an air attack, her scars including a hole 6 ft by 4 ft in her flank, plus a great deal of damage from machine-gun fire. Over the next few days Lerwick harbour filled with cargo ships flying an assortment of flags — 1 Dane, 1 Norwegian, 2 Swedes, 1 Latvian, 1 Italian and 3 British. On the 24th what appeared to be four destroyers and a tug entered Breiwick Bay, one of the destroyers, F43, apparently badly damaged at the stern. This craft was, in fact, the *Pelican,* which was later towed into harbour by the tug *Fleetwood.* The *Pelican,* a sloop of the type used as fishery cruisers before the war, had been just off Molde, it was said, when she had been attacked. Pier-head reporters soon had the story that her depth-charges had exploded during the attack, and the explosion had literally rolled up her stern. There had been considerable loss of life among the crew and Shetland's own *St Sunniva* had appeared on the scene and taken off some of the men. When the *Eclipse* berthed at the Fish Market the full extent of the terrible damage she had sustained could be clearly seen. Apart from the gaping evidence aft, she was marked and holed all over. On the following day two men from her crew who had succumbed to their wounds were buried in Lerwick cemetery. Harbour security at this time had not yet become nearly so strict as it would be later, and large numbers of people were able to see the horrific results of war on the *Eclipse* and the *Pelican.* Now everyone began to realise that the fighting was no longer remote — it was literally on their own doorsteps. And much more harsh reality was just round the corner.

On 26th April the small Norwegian destroyer *Sleipner* entered the harbour at speed, the end of a long chase by the German cruiser *Nürnberg.* She was the last of the Norwegian naval vessels to get away. The *Sleipner* had put into Molde for oil, ammunition and a refit. But she had been almost continuously in action since 9th April. She had undergone attacks from at least ten aircraft, and over thirty bombs had been dropped on her, none scoring a direct hit though there had been plenty of near misses. But she survived, and in the process claimed at least one Heinkel bomber shot down. In Britain she was modernised, stationed at Rosyth, and carried out convoy escort duties up and down Britain's east coast, being frequently under attack by German aircraft. In all she escorted 156 convoys, and was finally decommissioned in March, 1944.

Now more boats from Norway began to come into Lerwick harbour. The small steamer *Borgund* from Ålesund had her own special interest, for she had a number of German prisoners on board — forty-two, it was said. They were landed at the Fish Market, and marched away under armed guard. Once again the people of Lerwick looked on, and this was their first opportunity to see at close quarters some of these "herrenvolk" who were terrorising Europe. Not a few of the onlookers recognised a familiar face among the prisoners. He was Karl Veidt, who had been a summer visitor to Shetland with the German herring firm Deufrika, and had been an enthusiastic photographer — as had been so many of the German "tourists" in Norway in the summer of 1939. A harbour official, watching the prisoners being marched away, commented in a tone of quiet satisfaction, "They've got you now, Karl."

The *Borgund's* arrival heralded the beginning of a stream of boats from the other side. The books of Lerwick Harbour Trust faithfully record their arrivals, and provide a valuable source of information. But over in Norway a man called Ragnar Ulstein in 1965 published Part 1 of a book called "Englandsfarten — Alarm i Ålesund", and followed it up in 1967 with Part II — "Englandsfarten — Søkelys mot Bergen". His two books contain the names of virtually all the boats which escaped from Norway's west coast between 1940 and 1945, and also in many cases list the names of those who were in the boats. Along with the Harbour Trust records and the records kept by James and Frank Garriock, they provide a marvellous wealth of information for anyone researching the Norwegian/Shetland link during the war years.

Shetlanders as we have seen were far from unfamiliar with Norwegian deep-sea fishing boats. There were few voes in the islands which had not heard the familiar "tonk-tonk-tonk" which was almost their trademark, produced by the two-stroke, hot bulb, 40-60 hp semi-diesel engines, often of Wichmann make. To the casual observer the boats all looked very much alike. They were all built of wood, mostly fir, they all had two masts, a high prow and a large wheelhouse aft. Their whole construction was held together by wooden pegs, and the hulls were normally not painted, but treated with linseed oil, with a band just below the gunwales painted white all the way round. To the eye of the connoisseur there were marked differences, as David Howarth points out in his book "The Shetland Bus". Those built in the south, he says, had a curved stem, a canoe stern and an external rudder. Farther north the Hardanger cutters had a straight stem with a high sheer, very low freeboard amidships, and a long fine counter. Further north still was the Møre cutter, a very compact craft, with a wheelhouse of more elaborate construction. Howarth unhesitatingly places the Møre cutter at the top of the Norwegian fishing boat list.

Because these boats have a considerable later role to play in

3. James Garriock and his son, Frank. James was Hon. Nor. Vice-Consul from 1922 – 1943. Frank from 1943 – 1969, and full Consul 1969 – 1983.

4. The Shetland Bus boat *Heland* now part of Ålesund Museum.

5. The German herring firm of Deufrika was well-known in Lerwick before the war. Karl Veidt, landed as PoW from *Borgund,* was an employee.

6. A minesweeper, equipped for acoustic and magnetic sweeping, lying at the Market.

7. Air raid shelters in girls' playground, Central School.

our story they are worth a little more attention. They were extremely seaworthy, and could stand up to just about the worst the North Sea had to offer. They had a maximum speed of nine knots, though they usually cruised at rather less, they had a range of up to 1000 miles, and they were generally about 60 ft in length, with a beam of 18 ft and a draught of 8 ft. They could carry ten tons of fish or other cargo, and were able to accommodate up to ten men, who could be fed from the galley which was part of every boat's accommodation. These were the best of the boats which now began the hazardous journeys across the North Sea to freedom, but there were many others much less seaworthy. Some were simply open boats perhaps little more than twenty feet in length, comparable to the Ness yoals mentioned earlier, and one or two were no more than about fifteen feet long. Escape attempts were made even in kayaks.

Lerwick Harbour records show the *Bergholm* as a caller on the same day the *Borgund* arrived. The *Bergholm* was later to be an important part of the Shetland Bus story, but she apparently first went back to Norway where she served as a guard vessel till the fighting ended. She then sailed to Iceland where she was later taken over by the navy. Now the stream really got going. The *Jåbaek* and the *Bomma* arrived on 4th May, the *Bomma* a Fred Olsen boat which had discharged 3000 sacks of flour at Molde before leaving Norway. Both boats had refugees and servicemen on board. The guard-boat *Bjerk* came in on the 5th, and among her contingent was a doctor and two medical students, plus five young Danish volunteers for the Norwegian army. The *Bjerk* was rebuilt as a minesweeper in Britain, and was stationed at Rosyth. During the next few days boats seemed to be constantly arriving; the *Veststein* on the 6th, the *Vailet, Porat* and *Sjøgutten* on the 9th, the *Vita, Havørn, Sandvikhorn, Vestern* and *Nyo* on the 10th, the *Leiv* on the 12th, the *Reidar* on the 13th and the *Vest* on the 18th. From then till the end of the month the flow eased somewhat, the arrivals in that period being the *Snål, Vega, Flink, Livlig* and *Vågsfjord*. The *Breisund* left Ålesund on 26th May, and reached Shetland, only to be wrecked on the Unst coast near Haroldswick. Her passengers, six Norwegians and five British soldiers, were all saved. Although all the boats coming to Shetland eventually reached Lerwick, many of them made their first landfall in Unst, Yell, Fetlar or Skerries. The *Leiv* had fourteen British soldiers as well as four Norwegians on board, and they were lucky indeed to reach Unst, as their boat was in very poor condition.

June saw a few more arrivals — *Roald, Nyken, Skarv,*

Slotterøy, Nordkynn and *Gneist.* The *Skarv* was a 21 ft open boat. In July the *Sjøglimt* came in. Among Ragnar Ulstein's interesting notes on these early arrivals was the fact, for instance, that the *Nyken* was skippered by her owner, Peder Paulsen, who had under-taken to lead four men westwards where they were to find a boat waiting for them. They went on and on but no boat materialised, and finally he agreed to take them over himself. They were unprepared for the trip, lacking both food and water, but harbour records show their safe arrival on 2nd June. The *Vågsfjord,* coming out from Fosnavåg with six Norwegians and nine British soldiers on board, passed a small open boat with two men rowing, setting out for Shetland. The 60 ft *Vågsfjord* took them on board and gave them a much safer and easier crossing. The *Veststein's* skipper was Hans Feie, who later carried agents over to Norway, before becoming a pilot on the Shetland-based MTBs. The *Gneist's* story was rather different. She left Jasfjorden on 10th June with a group of saboteurs who had come in from Shetland about 1st June. Her skipper was Oskar Leirvåg, who had taken 7 refugees, including a British diplomat from Oslo, over to Shetland on the *Snål* on 20th May. He took his wife and three children with him on the *Gneist.*

Shetlanders noted that the Norwegian boats all had distinctive registration numbers, which started with one or two letters, followed by a number and ending with one or two more letters. This was a little confusing in the islands where virtually every boat was registered LK with a number. Common among the early Nor-wegian arrivals were the prefix letters M or SF, with the occasional H, B, V and R. There seemed to be a great variety of end letters, but it wasn't long before the registration markings had meaning for the observers. SF, for instance, at the beginning of the registration, indicated that the boat's home area was Sogn and Fjordane, and within that area were places such as Selje, North and South Vågsøy (including Måløy), Bremanger, Florø, Askvoll, Solund, etc. Boats from these areas all had SF followed by a number, followed by S for Selje, NV for Nord Vågsøy, B for Bremanger, and so on. M, another common prefix letter, was for the general area of Møre and Romsdal, with the suffix letters again indicating places within that area, e.g. Å for Ålesund, V for Vigra, and so on. Seldom seen were boats with F for Finnmark, T for Troms, N for Nordland or ST for Sør Trondelag. The fact that there was such a tremendous variety of registrations emphasised the Norwegian west coast's plethora of fishing boats, and, of course, of fishermen. There were few households along the coast which didn't include either a fisherman or a merchant navy man. Of the first thirty arrivals in Shetland in those early days, eleven came from Ålesund, five from little Måløy, and four more from nearby Florø and Selje. Bergen, Sotra and Stavanger provided seven, with three from Bømlo and Karmøy. The *Porat* came from Telavåg on Sotra, a village whose tragic story will be told later.

Although Shetland was always the main destination for the Norwegian boats, a number also reached Faroe, mainly from the area around Ålesund. A total of ten had arrived in Torshavn and Klaksvik by the end of 1940. They had carried 140 refugees and twelve British soldiers. Ragnar Ulstein notes that 80-year-old Ole Solbjørg owned three seine-net boats. He took the first one, the *Utvaer* over to Faroe, then returned to Norway in a dory to fetch the other two — the *Eldøy* and the *Gå På*. A few of the biggest boats went to Iceland, including the *Bergholm, Brattholm, Sandøy* and *Andholmen,* all of which were to figure prominently in the Shetland Bus service.

The thirty or so boats which arrived in Shetland during 1940 brought over 200 refugees, including several women and children. They also brought more than 100 British servicemen, who came in dribs and drabs, at least twelve of the boats having some on board. This was some indication of the disorganisation which had accompanied the evacuation of British forces from southern Norway. There was also a number of Norwegian service personnel among the arrivals. Lieutenant Peter Juliebø had been on the *Borgund,* and he was put in charge of these men, drilling them daily until departing for the south with them on 23rd May. It was he who led the parade in Lerwick on Norway's Constitution day, 17th May, with all the Norwegians then in the town taking part, their first celebration of the National Day in exile.

A small number of the early boats made landfall much farther south. For instance the *Pluggen* came to Peterhead in July, and the *Viking,* a 21 ft open boat, to Aberdeen in August. She had a young man called Starheim on board and we shall hear more of him. But surely the real saga was the story of the *Haabet*. She was an 18 ft open boat, with a part-deck fo'r'ard. With two young men from Oslo on board she left Oslo Fjord on 2nd September, 1940, but was held by German harbour police in Drøbak for three days. Then they were allowed to go and set out westwards, but a German destroyer boarded them and towed them back to land. After interrogation they were again released, and again steered west, calling in at Mandal where they added a third man to their crew. On 14th September they were finally off on the big adventure, their start point Farsund, west of Mandal. The wind was strengthening rapidly and the sea was rising, but after four days and nights they found themselves under the Scottish coast. They signalled to a passing British plane that they wanted to be taken into port, but the wind, which had fallen away, again increased in force very rapidly, this time from the west, and they were driven back across the North Sea. Time and again their boat filled with water, and more than once one or other of them was washed overboard. When a really big sea overwhelmed them — which happened several times — they baled desperately. For eight days they endured a full gale, and by that time they were in a pitiable condition. One of them had taken a bad knock on the head, and had also swallowed a lot of seawater, another's hands were in a fearful state as a result of his desperate efforts to pump and bale. When they saw land they knew it was the Danish coast.

Now the wind veered to the north and eased a little, and with the last remaining dregs of strength they steered a south-westerly course. Finally they saw British planes overhead and signalled. Then a British destroyer came up and told them they were twenty miles from the mouth of the Thames. A second destroyer, the *Bedouin,* arrived and picked them up, and also hoisted their boat in the davits. Sadly, a heavy sea damaged her severely, and swept away much of her hull. From the moment they had started on their voyage she had leaked badly, and they knew her bottom was rotten. Her condition had deteriorated steadily as the voyage went on, but somehow she and they had survived fourteen days of the worst the North Sea could throw at them, and had endured extremes of exposure which would have finished many men. *Haabet* (Hope) was a suitable name for their boat.

The two young men from Oslo were Kåre Moe and Oluf Reed Olsen, while the young man from Mandal was Rolf Gabrielsen. Kåre and Oluf had been heavily involved in underground work almost from the moment the Germans arrived, and had been finally captured when removing some secret equipment from a crashed Heinkel at Fornebu airport. They were roughly treated by the Germans, but turned the tables when being transported in a lorry by attacking their guards and escaping. All of which might seem to be just another of the many heroic escapes from Norway. But Oluf Reed Olsen, as some readers may have realised, was to be the author of the best-selling book, "Two Eggs on my Plate". In it he tells how he and Kåre trained for the Air Force in Canada, where Kåre was killed in a flying accident. He himself served with 330 (Nor) Squadron in Iceland and in Shetland, but became a secret agent, and made his first jump into Norway in April, 1943, landing in a tree and dislocating his knee. That was merely the continuation of the story of heroism and hair-raising escapades which had started away back in April, 1940. Two eggs on your plate was the last special treat you were given before going on a specially dangerous mission. It was a treat Oluf came to be offered more than once.

The situation in Lerwick caused by the sudden influx of refugees from Norway was completely unexpected and unprepared for. Who could have foreseen, as April came in, that there would be a steady stream of people arriving, all needing accommodation, food, help and, not least, sympathy? The man in the hot seat was James Garriock of Hay and Company, who had been Norwegian Vice-Consul in Lerwick for many years. On him now fell the onus of looking after the incomers, housing them, feeding them and often clothing them, before sending them on, usually in the *Rognvald* or the *Magnus* to Aberdeen, and thence, in the early days, to Hamilton or Dumfries. The Norwegian vessel *Iris* helped out by taking a party down to Aberdeen on 2nd June. Fortunately James Garriock's son Francis (Frank), who was a territorial officer in the 5/7 Battalion Gordon Highlanders, was on leave in May, 1940, and was able to give his father much assistance. He had been associated with the firm of Hay and Company since 1924, and became a Director of the Company in 1938. In 1931 he arranged to have private tuition in Norwegian, and became a fluent speaker of the language, so that he was ideally suited to help in the sudden emergency. Later in 1940 he was given a release from the army to help in the work. Soon a refugee camp was established for the escaping Norwegians. It was organised at James Sutherland's herring station, on the left at the foot of Brown's Road, and the herring girls' huts served as emergency housing to begin with. Other buildings were erected, and Mr and Mrs James Adie were put in charge. The Adies were very much liked and highly respected by the Norwegians, not merely for their help and sympathy, but also because Mrs Adie, herself a Norwegian, could communicate with them in their own language. Many of the incomers didn't have a word of English, and Mrs Adie's presence must have meant a great deal to these people who had given up everything to escape to a foreign land. Perhaps not surprisingly the Norwegian government, in a letter written on 30th May, 1944, commented ". . . the exceptional reception which has been given them (the refugees) at Shetland has been indicated by every newcomer who has passed through Shetland. They have been met with kindness and understanding by everyone they have been in contact with, and for which we are very grateful.''

In the eyes of the military authorities Shetland was now in a completely new situation. Suddenly there was the very real possibility that the islands might prove a vulnerable back-door for Hitler's entry into Britain. That had to be prevented at all costs. Troops began to pour in on board the regular steamers, and also on the *Lochnagar,* the *Ben My Chree* and the *Lady of Mann,* with the *Amsterdam* joining them in 1941. So quickly did the troops arrive that tents had to absorb many of them for a time, but hutted camps sprang up, not merely in and around Lerwick, but also in many other locations, notably at Sumburgh and Sullom Voe, and in Scalloway. Sandbags by the thousand were filled and laid to afford protection from blast to some of the important buildings. Big six-inch guns were positioned at the Ness of Sound, the Knab and the Greenhead to protect the harbour approaches, and the boom barriers were strengthened. Ack-ack guns appeared at Sound, Montfield, Bressay, Sumburgh, Sullom, etc. Sand-bagged machine-gun posts sprouted everywhere. The approaches to Lerwick were mined, and concrete tank traps lined all the likely landing beaches. Old tar barrels filled with stones or rubble were scattered over level areas which might provide a landing space for aircraft. At Sumburgh work on the airport runways was intense, and by the end of the year three tarmacadamed runways were complete. At Scatsta a single runway was completed by September, 1940, but the really big developments there were to come in 1941, when the Scatsta airfield proper was constructed. The six Gloster Gladiators which had been the islands' first line of air defence were replaced by faster and deadlier Spitfires and Hurricanes, and soon there was a rumour that a Hurricane had shot down a Heinkel near Fair Isle. Most news was rumour in those days, as the stories the local newspapers would have liked to tell were strictly censored. However, when they carried a story which referred vaguely to a ''northern town'', it was usually a safe bet that they were referring to Lerwick. Almost alongside the Scatsta airstrip the Sullom Voe flying-boat base was established, and we will be returning there later. At Baltasound a slipway for smaller flying-boats was constructed, and at Sullom Voe the *Coventry* had suffered a near miss from a bomb dropped by a Dornier on 1st January, 1940.

To help the regular troops the Shetland Defence Company of First War veterans was set up, followed by the Local Defence Volunteers who were to become the Home Guard. They performed

8. The troopship *Lochnagar* at Lerwick.

9. A familiar wartime scene — Black's bakery queue.

10. A pre-war view of Lunna. (*page 37*)

11. Mrs Ingvald Johannessen and Mindur Berge (*pps 40 and 96*)

useful guard duties at the pier, the docks, the Knab, etc. Before 1940 was out Shetland was a veritable armed camp. The number of troops in the islands grew until they reached a figure of over 20,000 — more than the total civilian population. And now Shetland was a restricted area, and no one got in or out without the necessary official pass. Rolls of barbed wire sealed off the town's harbour front.

In May, just about the time the incoming Norwegian stream was at its peak, the flitboat *Lilybank,* loading high octane petrol for Sumburgh airport at the Anglo-Scottish, caught fire. She was machine-gunned along the waterline in an attempt to get her to sink and so extinguish the flames, but she refused to go down. Then a sailor, displaying great heroism, swam to her and affixed a tow-line, and the harbour drifter *Harmattan* towed her off. She was cast loose and drifted across the harbour, still in flames, until she sank near the Holm of Cruister. Her cargo of petrol had been urgently needed at Sumburgh, and her demise led to every truck in Lerwick being requisitioned to transport the precious fuel to the airport.

A cable had been laid from Scotland to Sound, and was purely for service use. The Earl of Cork and Orrery was appointed Commander of the Orkney and Shetland forces, swiftly gaining the nick-name of "Ginger Boyle". Invergordon had become the staging-post for troops proceeding in or out of Shetland. The *Highlander* became the toast of the islands when, on 1st August, 1940, she shot down two attacking German aircraft, and came into Leith with the wreckage of one of them on her foredeck. The episode attracted a great deal of publicity, and the *Highlander's* crew rightly feared that the Germans would have it in for them. On 14th November, just as she emerged from Aberdeen to join a north-bound convoy, two German seaplanes were waiting for her. Half an hour after sailing she was sunk by a torpedo, with the loss of thirteen crew members and one passenger. Twelve other crew members and four passengers were saved. There was considerable suspicion at the time that the Germans had had pre-notification of her sailing time, but nothing was ever proved.

Islanders quickly became accustomed to a new way of life. The Institute was taken over as a naval hospital, its pupils moved to the Central, and the Central pupils were farmed out to various halls, etc. The Bruce Hostel became HQ for the Earl of Cork, and the Janet Courtney was taken over by the RAF. St Clement's housed gas decontamination. Gas masks in cardboard cartons were carried by everyone, and school pupils, etc., reluctantly carried out the gas drills. Blackouts were strictly enforced, sticky tape criss-crossed window panes. Queues became a way of life, for strict rationing had been in force almost from the beginning, and by 1940 your ration card entitled you, each week, to: 2 oz of tea, 4 oz of bacon or ham, 12 oz of sugar and 1/10 (9p) worth of meat. Powdered egg had replaced eggs, fruit was rarely seen. Sweets were rationed, with milk chocolate a thing of the past. Bread was reasonably adequate, and there was no real shortage of potatoes, while townspeople who had relations or friends in country districts — and most people did — were occasionally the recipients of a bit of lamb or mutton, despite the export in the North boats, during 1940, of 186 horses, 350 pigs, 18,228 sheep and lambs, and 2012 cattle. There was always fish, and though belts were tightened, there was no real starvation. Shetland women were soon knitting garments for wives, sweethearts or mothers of the Shetland-based servicemen, and Shetland homes quickly began to offer a haven to which these lonely men, so far from home, could escape from the cold boredom of the ubiquitous Nissen huts to find warmth and friendship.

Chapter Four

Inside Norway 1940

We have seen that, even before the final capitulation in Norway, the little boats were streaming westwards from Norway's fjords and islands, each with its quota of escapers determined not to live in a country occupied by the Germans. But to the bulk of Norwegians the issue was not nearly so clear-cut in the summer months of 1940. When northern Norway finally surrendered on 10th June, and resistance came to an end, Norwegians had come through sixty-two days of war, but they had also suffered invasion, treason and defeat — and all after 126 years of peaceful neutrality. The people and their leaders had been caught both physically and mentally unprepared. Now, with their chosen king and their elected government no longer in Norway, and with the traitor Quisling setting himself up as the new Prime Minister, there was a period of terrible hopelessness and despair. So strong was that feeling that many were inclined to accept that the whole situation was simply part of the much larger struggle for power between Germany and Great Britain, in which Norway had no part. Why not, they suggested, accept what had happened and make the best of it?

The Germans were all-powerful. Hitler's personal representative in Norway was Reichskommissar Josef Terboven, an arrogant, cold-blooded Nazi, who had been a gauleiter in the Ruhr, and whose simple aim was to ensure that Norway made the maximum possible contribution to the German war effort. Everywhere the Norwegian flag, of which the people were so proud, was hauled down, and the swastika hoisted in its place. Aggressive, jack-booted Germans strutted the streets, often accompanied by the blare of German brass. Rationing was introduced immediately, the 800 Jews having a large J stamped on their ration cards. Public gatherings were forbidden, nor could you stop to chat to your friends in the street. No one was to listen to the BBC, the newspapers were rigorously censored, and travelling was severely restricted without an official pass. The traditional Constitution

Day holiday on 17th May, the most important date in the Norwegian calendar, was cancelled. The coastal steamers were all under German control, and the occupation troops were going through the shops buying up everything with Norwegian currency printed in Germany. It seemed as if all hope had gone.

But the Germans themselves were in something of a quandary. They had assumed that they would capture the king and his government in Oslo, and they would be able to deal with them as the people's elected representatives, in whom the people had complete confidence, gradually moulding them, under duress of course, to their wishes and gradually infiltrating their numbers from time to time with German nominees. Instead king and government, thanks to the guns at Oskarsborg fortress, had escaped, and the Germans had only Quisling — and he had no one's confidence or trust. The early summer was a period of disillusion and despair in Norway, with the mass media, now all controlled by the Germans, churning out ceaseless German propaganda. Pressure by Terboven was so strong that the remaining parliamentarians in Oslo in late June wrote to Haakon and his government in London, urging them to resign, and to hand over the functions of government to a "National Council" in Oslo. King Haakon's reply, broadcast to the people of Norway by the BBC, was as much a statement to his people as a response to the Oslo letter. "I came to Norway in 1905 at the call of the Norwegian people, and during the years that have passed since then I have endeavoured, to the best of my ability, to fulfil the duties that were thereby laid upon me." He went on to point out that what he was being asked to do was really "at the behest of foreign military occupation forces", and added that to agree would mean approving an arrangement which "conflicts with the Constitution of Norway, and which it is sought to impose by force upon the Norwegian people. By doing so I should abandon the principle which has guided my actions throughout my reign, namely to keep myself strictly within the Constitution." The final paragraph of his reply was particularly telling. "The liberty and independence of the Norwegian people are to me the first commandment of the Constitution, and I consider I am obeying this commandment, and watching over the interests of the Norwegian people best by adhering to the position and the task which a free people gave me in 1905."

This reply was heard by people listening to their radios all over Norway. It was distributed by all sorts of clandestine means, until everyone was acquainted with the king's words. For the people it was as if a beam of light had suddenly shone through the fog of propaganda which had been poured out by the Germans since 9th April. The mood of despair and defeatism was suddenly turned upside down. Everywhere people discussed the king's words. Suddenly it was realised that it was the Germans, through the men in Oslo, who were trying to destroy the Constitution and depose their king. The men in Oslo had to be told what was expected of them — and they were told by many voices. Terboven, of course, increased his pressure on them. He pointed to the great air onslaught under which Britain was reeling at that very moment. She, too, would soon be brought to her knees, and to whom could Norway turn then? But there was backbone in some of the Oslo men, and they refused to bend, so that the Germans failed to get a majority agreement to their plans. Their scheme had backfired. It was the end of the velvet glove era. Now Terboven showed the iron fist. He went on the radio and announced the new decrees he had formulated. There were no ifs or buts about them. The decrees included the immediate abolition of all political parties except the Nasjonal Samling (Quisling's). Of thirteen State Councillors whose appointment he announced, ten were Quisling nazis, the other three were pro-German. He banished the king and his government from Norway for all time to come, and any activity on their behalf was forbidden. Quisling himself, though given no real power, was accorded the title of Nasjonal Samling Führer, and Terboven declared that the only road to freedom and independence for the Norwegian people led through the Quisling nazis.

Nothing could have been more effective than the combination of the king's speech and Terboven's decrees in enabling Norwegians to make up their minds about the issues at stake. Now it was clear that the choice was glaringly simple, viz. (a) throw in your lot with Quisling's nazis and enjoy German favours or (b) follow the king and his government in their fight to support the Constitution, and thereby be labelled an enemy of the Germans. The waverers wavered no longer, the mood of despair and hopelessness vanished. This was Norway's future and Norway's freedom which was at stake, and almost overnight the people made their decisions. For every single individual who found the Quisling option attractive, over ninety came down firmly on the side of king and Constitution. But it had been a critical period. The likelihood that Hitler would see one of his dearest ambitions realised, in that Norway, his favourite Aryan nation, would tread the same path as the German Nazis had, for a time, been very real. But once the king brought the basic issues so sharply into focus there was never any doubt. From the first moments of the German invasion on 9th

April the Germans had handed out leaflets saying they came as friends of the Norwegian people, and that assurance had been reiterated repeatedly on radio and in the papers. Norwegians had given it little credence, but now it was seen even more clearly as the sham it really was. The will to resist strengthened daily — the silent cry for freedom was in every heart.

It wasn't long after Terboven's announcement of the "new era" in Norway that the Germans began to bring various aspects of Norwegian life into line with German wishes. No occupied country could be allowed any of their old freedoms; everything had to conform, in one way or another, to the German plan. In Norway the Germans soon found that aspiring to this aim was one thing. Achieving it was another. The first difficulty they encountered was in the legal profession. The Norwegian Justices of the Supreme Court of Norway still held their old posts. But some of the decrees Terboven came up with were clearly in direct contravention of the Constitution. The Judges refused to accept them, and resigned. The news of their resignation spread quickly, and was another clear sign to the people that the Germans were attempting to violate their beloved Constitution. It was another factor in firming their will to resist. Then came the Pastoral Letter which the Bishops and ministers proposed to read to their congregations. The letter itself was an indictment of German actions in Norway. Terboven forbade its reading. The ministers ignored the ban, and not merely read it in their churches but distributed many copies of the letter among the people. Coming from a highly respected source — the church — the ministers' action, allied to the content of the Letter had a tremendous impact. There was still no organised underground resistance in the country, but in these first months of occupation the king's letter, Terboven's dictats, the Judges' resignation and the Church's Pastoral Letter had a deep influence in polarising people's thinking. Probably the resistance movement which grew in strength in the days ahead had its roots in these very events.

As time went on the clashes between the Germans and various sections of the Norwegian community became ever more numerous and more bitter, until the propaganda weapon became unproductive and was finally abandoned. Inevitably the final German weapon was brought into play — terror. But we will come back to that later. Meanwhile the BBC broadcasts commencing with "Dette er London" followed by a burst of rousing music provided considerable uplift to Norwegian morale, especially when the RAF's achievements in the Battle of Britain became known.

During 1941 the number of little boats escaping west over sea to Shetland increased dramatically. Sweden to begin with was very careful to take no chances with violations of her neutrality, and so her border in the early days was no easy escape route for Norwegians. But some were getting over, and as time went on and Swedish fear of offending the Germans decreased, the numbers escaping via Sweden increased. More and more escapers were getting the opportunity to join Norwegian forces in Britain, and were thus making their personal contribution to the fight for freedom.

In spite of her defeat Norway didn't come empty-handed to the Allied table. Indeed, at all times, she more than paid her way. The gold reserves of the Bank of Norway had been successfully transferred to Britain, but, more importantly, her merchant fleet ensured her solvency. Not a single merchant navy captain at sea obeyed Quisling's instruction to take his ship into a Norwegian port. That meant that the Germans gained control of not more than one sixth of the total Norwegian merchant fleet, leaving nearly 4,000,000 tons to be added to the Allied total. A new company called Notraship was set up to manage this huge fleet. It was the biggest company in the world, and at war's end it was still the biggest, though nearly half the ships under its control had been sunk. So her merchant ships, as well as being a tremendous bonus to the Allied cause, also provided enough revenue to cover the costs of the various naval, army and air force units which were soon being operated by Norwegian personnel, under the Norwegian flag. And soon Shetland was acting as the base for the first — and probably the best-known — of the operations mounted against the Germans from the islands — the Shetland Bus.

Chapter Five

The Bus is Running

The flow of refugees from Norway's west coast which had dwindled to a trickle in the later months of 1940, showed little increase in early 1941. There was a flurry of activity in March, but April, May and June had only a few arrivals. July saw a marked upturn, and August, September and October averaged over a boat a day. By the end of 1941, according to figures produced by the Norwegian consulate in Lerwick, a total of 1881 refugees had passed through the port during the year. They included 155 women and 24 children, and the three months of August, September and October had seen the arrival of 1191 of them. In all 120 boats had carried them over to the islands. By this time it was standard procedure to send the refugees down to London, where they were accommodated to begin with in the Victoria Patriotic School. This was a former girls' boarding school, with large dormitories and walled grounds, and provided preliminary accommodation for the incomers of various nationalities while a thorough screening was carried out. Many Norwegians recall it under the nickname it acquired — "Sing-Sing". After screening, the refugees were given more normal accommodation in hotels such as the Shaftesbury and the County before being allocated to the various branches of the Norwegian armed forces, the merchant navy and so on.

As we saw earlier, several of the boats which escaped in the summer of 1940 carried out return trips to the Norwegian coast, all without mishap. Those successful missions had not escaped notice, and in November, 1940, a British army officer, Major L. H. Mitchell, was sent up to Shetland. His task was to organise this haphazard operation. Behind his presence lay the intention that those trips to the Norwegian coast should lead on to a traffic in messengers, saboteurs, intructors, radio operators and trained leaders for the underground resistance movement. Radio transmitters, explosives, weapons and ammunition would also be sent.

Mitchell got on with the job almost immediately, and just

before Christmas, 1940, the *Vita* was sent over to Nordhordland under skipper Hilmar Langøen, returning to Shetland on Christmas Day. Langøen had skippered the *Traust* on several of the trips she had made earlier in the year. He had been a member of a group known as the Arstad/Brun "Export" group in Bergen. A number of these groups came into being and were very active in late 1940 and '41, organising escape parties and helping them on their way — in other words "exporting" them. Another member of this same group was Birger Larssen, who came over on the *Smart* on 12th August, 1942. By that time his activities had made him a prime Gestapo target. Skippering the *Smart* was Nils Robertstad of the Bømlo/Bremnes group. Nils was to become a very effective secret agent, and we shall look at his story later. Still another member of the Arstad/Brun group was Harald Hundvin. He came over on 2nd August, 1941, on the *Soløy* along with another 26 refugees, six of whom were women. Harald revisted Shetland in the summer of 1987, but sadly died in November of the same year.

In the first four months of 1941 a number of trips were made using the *Vita, Mars, Igland* and *Blia*. Among the skippers were August Naerøy, a young fisherman, Ole Grotle, who had come over from Bremanger on the *Igland* on 23rd December, 1940, Ingvald Johannessen, and Petter Salen, who had been a mate on a merchant ship, and was to prove an outstanding skipper. The *Igland* it may be noted had four Grotles on board, another of whom, Bård, was her skipper on her crossing to Shetland. He was later to skipper the *Erkna* and the *Aksel*, and David Howarth speaks of him with deep admiration. Sadly he was lost with the *Aksel*. The *Erkna*, his first Bus command, deserves a note. She was a big boat, and had been used to carry fish from ports in north Norway to Trondheim. She set out for Shetland on 17th November, 1941, with 60 people on board, the largest group to seek freedom across the North Sea in one craft. By afternoon on the 19th they were north of Skerries when they saw a small steamer coming towards them. It was the old *Earl*. When the vessels were a few hundred yards apart the *Erkna's* engine stopped, and almost simultaneously a floating mine was spotted within a few boats' lengths of the Norwegian vessel. Fortunately the mine was disposed of by rifle fire from the *Earl*, which took the *Erkna* in tow to Symbister. Mrs Davidson of Breiwick Road, a passenger on the *Earl* on that trip, remembers looking towards the *Erkna* and being struck by the absolute forest of heads there seemed to be on her deck! The *Earl* on her North Isles' trips frequently took refugees on board, and a Norwegian security officer travelled regularly with

her. On this occasion he went on board the *Erkna* at Symbister to
carry out a preliminary screening, but recommended against the
Earl taking so many people on board. The *Erkna* was accordingly
towed to Lerwick. August Naerøy skippered the *Mars,* a boat
which he and his friends had "acquired" for their escape. Among
them was Mindur Berge, who, as we shall see later, was to meet his
death on land at the hands of the Germans. The *Mars* was
subsequently blown up by an enemy patrol boat, and Naerøy was
the only one of the crew still surviving at the end of the war.

Some of these early trips were organised from Lerwick, but
soon Catfirth was being used as the base. It was far from
satisfactory. There was too little depth of water at the pier. There
was no accommodation ashore for the crews. There were no repair
facilities. But it served. And when Sub-Lieutenant David Howarth
came north in May, 1941, to act as assistant to Mitchell, there were
six boats available for operations, and under Mitchell's
organisation thirteen trips had been made to the other side, with
destinations from as far north as Trondelag and as far south as
Bømlo. These trips had taught them a lot. Firstly, it was clear that
operations would have to be carried out during the winter months,
in darkness, and consequently when the weather was at its worst.
Secondly, German aircraft made frequent patrols along the coast,
up to about fifty miles off land. So the drill had to be to reach the
50-mile distance as darkness fell, and get into a credible fishing
position before daylight came in. Preferably that would be among
or near a group of Norwegian-based boats, which were, of course,
exactly similar in appearance to their own boats. Then they would
pretend to fish all day, and come into the coast in darkness.

The crews used on these trips were all civilians, and mostly
fishermen, though there was a sprinkling of merchant navy men.
They were all first class seamen, and a lot of them had been to
navigation school. A necessity for each boat was a good engineer,
all the more necessary as spare parts were unobtainable in Shetland
— or, indeed, in Britain. Fortunately it wasn't very long before that
difficulty was overcome, and in the most barefaced manner. The
factory making Wichmann engines was situated at Rubbestadneset
on the island of Bømlo, some way south of Bergen, and when a
part was needed arrangements were made for it to be picked up by
the next boat over, at some convenient spot. It was all done under
the very noses of the Germans. Surely it was one of the most bizarre
situations of the war — parts of engines with which to fight the
Germans being supplied by a factory under their control and in a
German-occupied country. As civilians the crews were well paid,

receiving to begin with £4 per week and £10 per trip, though this became £4 a week and £4 for their keep per week later. As civilians they could not be subjected to military discipline. But the answer was simple. If a man stepped out of line he was sent away. None of them wanted that.

So by the time Sub-Lieutenant David Howarth arrived to lend his weight to the organisation of this Shetland/Norway traffic, the foundation had already been laid and was ready to be built on. The Shetland Bus was running. Its story was to provide the material for David Howarth's best-selling book "The Shetland Bus", and also for Fritjof Saelen's "Sjetlands Larsen" in Norwegian. It was also to employ many brave men, one of whom, Leif Larsen, was to be awarded the Conspicuous Gallantry Medal, the Distinguished Service Medal and Bar, the Distinguished Service Cross and the Distinguished Service Order, along with other Norwegian decorations. No doubt he would also have received the Victoria Cross, but that supreme accolade is not awarded to foreigners. Nevertheless the medals bestowed on him by the British government made him unique — no other non-Briton has ever received as many British medals as were awarded to Larsen.

But Catfirth's shortcomings were critical, and somewhere another base had to be found. The long summer days of 1941, when there was little or no darkness either in Shetland or on the Norwegian coast, saw a break in the fishing boat operations, and gave Howarth and Mitchell time to look around for a place more suited to their requirements. Mitchell had taken over as his HQ the farmhouse known as Flemington in the Weisdale valley. Howarth uses the word "sinister" in describing the house. Maybe it was, for Flemington was the house built by a Scots farmer, Charles Fleming, who had come into Weisdale valley at the time of the eviction of the crofters by incoming landowner Black. Flemington was erected where the little croft cottages of Northouse used to stand, and perhaps the ghosts of the past haunted the new house. Probably the activities of the saboteurs who used it as their billet, and practised their trade in the surrounding countryside, would also have added to the sinister feel of the place. After looking at a variety of locations, the final choice fell on Lunna. Lunna was remote. No one lived there, apart from one farmer and the minister. There was a large, old mansion house, which could serve as HQ and provide accommodation for the men. There was plenty of water in the little bay, even at the small pier where Shetland fishermen used to land their fish from the sixerns. Apart from the big house, the farm and the manse, the only other building was a little, very old church. The coming and going of the boats would be completely hidden from the public. As Leif Larsen was to say in a broadcast after the war, "As the place was very remote, no people came in contact with us directly there. They couldn't see what we did, they couldn't see when we sailed, and they didn't know when we came back, so we weren't scared of anyone talking about us."

There were children at the farmhouse and children are notoriously inquisitive, but their mother, Mrs Johnson, said in the same broadcast, "Oh, they saw a little bit of what was going on, but they were warned not to tell, or to take any notice. But they knew what was going on. They couldn't miss it." She went on, "We just turned our back on it. But we were always glad when we saw the boats coming back." Her husband added, "The Norwegians were always very helpful people, and we got on very well with them. We knew what they were doing, but we were put on our guard not to say anything." And they never did.

Howarth was very satisfied with his little harbour, sheltered from all wind directions. The big, old house was also ideal, for into it could be crammed all fifty men who now made up the "Shetlandsgjengen". By the end of July, 1941, Lunna was ready, and the five fishing boats which made up the outfit at that time "tonk-tonked" into their new home bay and dropped anchor. The first trip from Lunna was organised for the end of August, and the *Aksel* was the boat chosen. She had come over on 5th May from Giske, close by Ålesund. She was one of Howarth's favourite Møre cutters, 65 ft long, and for her first trip she was under the command of August Naerøy, her destination Solund, at the mouth of Sognefjord. Also in her crew were Bård Grotle, Mindur Berge as engineer, and Andrew Gjertsen, a second mate from the merchant navy, who would later figure in the escape from Norway after the loss of the *Nordsjøen*. The *Aksel* returned on 5th September, having completed her mission successfully. But she had been away six days, and Howarth had expected her back after four. He had soon discovered how difficult it was to wait helplessly in Lunna and worry about his men who were now beginning to mean so much to him. Much as he would have liked to, he was forbidden to go on a trip himself. "Inevitably we knew too much of the organisation in Norway. That was one reason. We couldn't have stood up to the interrogation. (He meant the standard Gestapo torture inter-rogation.) Also we spoke Norwegian, but with a very strong British accent. We'd have been a hindrance to a crew if they had had to go ashore and travel overland." So David stayed at Lunna, and worried, and planned. But he was appreciated by the Norwegians.

Said Larsen later, "David Howarth was a very good man for us in Shetland. He worked very hard, and always tried to see we had the best of means to do things."

Howarth had to get used to worrying about his boys at sea in rough weather, and on an enemy coast. But his description of a really rough Shetland night has an almost poetic quality about it. "When they were overdue, or the wind rose, then it was hard to concentrate on other things. It was hard to sleep in a comfortable bed when I knew what the men at sea were facing. I used to lie awake, listening to the swelling of the storm: first the familiar moaning in the chimney and the spattering of hail on the windows, stray gusts which died to a sigh, and then to silence, so that one could hear the sea stirring; then, as the speed of the wind increased, an ever shriller note which rose to a scream and a hollow roar so deep that it was felt as well as heard; and at the height of the storm, the 'flans' which Shetlanders fear more than a steady blast — gusts or whirlwinds which one could hear far off as they roared in the hills like an approaching train, louder and louder till they struck the house with an impact which made its solid stone walls shudder and slates rattle like a million metallic footsteps rushing from end to end of the roof." Today when one visits Lunna and is permitted to see the room which Howarth used as his bedroom cum office, it is not difficult to realise just how much this sensitive, caring, human man suffered as he listened sleepless to the ferocity of a Shetland storm, knowing that his fearless Norwegians were in mortal danger — and he had sent them. But it was war, and they got on with it, with only three boats lost in the 41/42 winter.

As the winter months passed additional boats had been acquired, including *Siglaos, Nordsjøen, Arthur, Erkna, Heland, Olaf* and *Jakk*. New skippers included Leif Larsen, Gunnar Gundersen, Per Blystad and Peder Godøy. Something like forty trips were made, and from the autumn of 1941 the men were all provided with Norwegian naval uniforms. It was thought that, if captured, they would stand a better chance if they were in uniform. Later tragic events were to show the fallacy of this belief. It was still very much a "private" navy, so, as David Howarth relates, "We issued petty officers' rig to all the skippers and some of the engineers, and dressed the rest as seamen." But they still remained volunteers and were paid civilian rates. And each man was allowed the right to decide whether or not he would sail on any given operation.

One feature of the Bus operations in 41/42 was the excellent intelligence service which they enjoyed. For, as well as the information they themselves accumulated on their many trips across, the endless stream of refugees was coming from all along the west coast, and these people furnished them with a constantly up-dated picture of German naval and army dispositions, and the position of strong points, watch posts and patrols in great detail. Howarth claims in the "Shetland Bus" that one lad at Lunna knew every German N.C.O. in charge of a coastal watch post by his Christian name.

The first boat to be lost, in September 41, was the *Vita,* skippered at the time by Ingvald Johannessen. She had been only 24 hours in port when she was off again. Johannessen had earlier committed an absolutely forbidden act. When ashore in Norway he had posted a letter to his girl friend. But that wasn't all. In the letter he had told her where to meet him next time he was over. It was a terrible breach of security and might have had horrific consequences, but she duly met him, he took her to Shetland, and they were married. He suffered no dire consequences of a disciplinary nature for his act. On this trip, however, the Germans seized the *Vita* and her crew, and later in the war that would automatically have meant their deaths. But they fared rather better. After four years in a German prison camp they all survived and returned to their families.

The *Nordsjøen* was the next to go, in October. She had been fitted out as a minelayer, with Gjersten as skipper, and Leif Larsen as one of the crew. The mines were to be laid north of Trondheim. The job was successfully carried out, but in getting away they encountered extremely heavy seas and gale force wind. Their desperate need to put distance between themselves and the Norwegian coast compelled them to keep driving the *Nordsjøen* into sea and wind until she started coming apart at the seams. They were forced to turn back to the coast, but, after making Gripholen, their boat sank. The crew reached land, and after a number of close shaves, finally stole a boat called the *Arthur* in which five of them reached Lunna. The other two crew men also later returned safely.

The next boat to go was the *Blia,* skippered by Ingvald Lerøy. She had made three trips to Norway in early 1941, and sailed again on 9th November for Bremnes. There they learned that an export group on Stord had nearly 40 people they wanted to get to Shetland, many of them being on the Gestapo list. *Blia* sailed with forty-two people on board, and ran into a ferocious storm almost immediately. Neither she nor any of the people on board were ever seen or heard from again. It was the biggest loss of life in the history of the west over sea traffic.

The storm which sank the *Blia* blew with vicious intensity in Shetland as well. Instructions had come from on high that many of the larger boats escaping from Norway were to be retained in Shetland. Obeying that order had meant finding suitable anchorages, and that had not been easy. In the end a number were anchored in Catfirth, and a few in other voes. In the wild weather of November, 1941, a number of these boats dragged their anchors and drove ashore. Even in sheltered Lunna three boats at anchor suffered the same fate, though they were all undamaged.

As well as the *Blia,* the Lunna boys had another boat at sea during this period. This was the *Arthur,* for the first time under command of her new skipper, Leif Larsen, elected to the position by the crew. David Howarth has told the story of this trip by the *Arthur,* but a member of the crew, Kåre Iverson, still remembers it very vividly, for he lived through every moment of it. Kåre was typical of many of the young Norwegians escaping to Shetland in 1941. He was living just outside Namsos when Norway was invaded. There was a watch station manned by four men near Namsos, but they went on unofficial "leave" on 9th April, 1940, and never retured. Kåre was one of the volunteers who took over the manning of the post. Still there was no sign of any Germans in their little area, until at the end of May a boat came in bringing eight Germans who promptly took over the pilot station, etc. Kåre remembers them as fairly good fellows on the whole, apart from two of them who were Hitler Jugend products. The whole party used to come to Kåre's house to listen to the German news, then, when the Norwegian news from London came on, the men were all ordered out, and only the officer stayed to listen. Kåre obtained work on a Trondheim/Hammerfest coaster, their cargo being mainly blackjack. His father had a 42 ft boat, the *Villa II,* and Kåre put up the money for a third share in her. Keeping his plans to himself, he had her slipped and made ready for sea. The local merchant guessed what was in the wind, and promised him all the fuel he would need to take him to Shetland. When two likely fellow-passengers appeared on the scene, he went to get the promised fuel, but found only the merchant's wife and daughter at home. The wife was a little surprised and dubious when she heard the large amount he wanted, but the daughter clearly understood what was at stake, as she told her mother, "He's going on a long journey, mother!"

They left on 20th May, 1941, there being three men on board in addition to Kåre, one of them a police sergeant and one a Swede. When about 60 miles west over, a German plane attacked them.

They sustained a number of hits, one breaking the wheelhouse window, one hitting the bunk on which one of the men was lying, and one just missing the engine. But they survived and went on, Kåre remaining in the wheelhouse for the whole journey. They made landfall in Fetlar, anchored, and went ashore and up to a house. There they had a good wash, but a Home Guard sergeant and a private appeared on the scene and came back on board with them; they were now officially prisoners and would remain so until the screening process was complete. However Kåre reckoned their guards were not very strict — when he turned in he found a lump in his bunk. It was one of the guard's rifles, and when they went to sleep their guards did likewise. They lay at Fetlar for a day or two, then the duty boat came north and towed them to Lerwick. Many Shetlanders will remember that boat. It was the old *Research*. In Lerwick they went through the usual routine of a lengthy interrogation, but they had a bottle of Advocaat with them, and they and the Customs official drank it during the questioning.

A night in the refugee camp which had now been established, then down to Buckie in company with the *Klippen* and the *Solveig*. The *Klippen* had had 13 people on board and the *Solveig* 19, including six women and two children. One of the girls, Elisabeth Holvik from Måløy, we shall meet again later. From Buckie it was down to London, where they found themselves objects of suspicion at the Patriotic School. The Swede they had carried over with them in good faith had arrived in London before them, and during his screening had blackened their names in advance of their arrival. After lengthy interrogation they got things straightened out, but later they learned that the Swede had been well-known to the Norwegian underground; they had given him the ultimatum to get out or they would kill him. All of which simply illustrated how necessary thorough screening really was.

Now they were recommended to go and see a man whom we have not yet encountered — Lieutenant Martin Linge. He told them to take 24 hours to make up their minds, but they joined him on the spot after listening to what he had to say. He had that effect on men. That night, when Kåre left his hotel, a man came up to him asking a lot of questions. He got rid of him, but later a second man came up. He shook him off, too, but when he got back to his billet he found the first one again waiting for him and wanting to come in for a drink. Going upstairs, he found that the other two boys had had almost identical experiences. Next morning, when they reported to Linge, he smiled broadly, and said, "You did very well last night, boys." It had been Linge's way of testing out the newcomers — the men had been his men. The boys had passed that test. Now they were given a spell of rigorous military training in British army uniforms. After that back to London, where khaki was changed to navy blue, then up to Aberdeen with a party of nine men. Though they probably didn't realise it at that stage, they were now part of the SOE set-up. From Aberdeen to Lerwick on the *Magnus,* and from there to Lunna on the back of a lorry. To begin with it was all far from exciting. Making a road from the pier up to Lunna House and helping with the peats at Flemington were certainly not what the boys had expected to be doing.

But it was now that Larsen took over the *Arthur.* "I want someone who knows the engine," he said. Kåre commented that he didn't think the engine would present any difficulty. "I went down and started her, and when he saw that I knew what I was doing he took me on as his engineer." They left Lunna on 8th November, made the Norwegian coast without incident, landed two agents at one spot, and a load of the usual weapons and supplies at another. When they sailed for Shetland again the weather looked extremely threatening. By midnight the seas were mountainous, and *Arthur's* bulwarks were damaged. The wind steadily increased to hurricane force. They had to reduce speed — no boat could have withstood the pounding. They were aiming for the north end of Unst, and after what seemed an endless time they calculated they must be getting near. At this time the mizzen sail was still set, and crewman Sangolt volunteered to go out on deck and take it down. Just as he left the wheelhouse they were hit by a mountainous sea, which flooded the engine-room and stopped the engine. They were now in dire straits, completely at the mercy of wind and sea. And although they didn't realise it until later, they had lost Sangolt. He had been washed overboard. With the boat out of control they continued to ship water.

But those men had been trained in a hard school. They set to work pumping by hand, and baling with buckets, and the level of water was gradually lowered. They had taken all the blankets, tied them to a rope, and thrown the makeshift bundle over the side to act as a sea anchor. Though they lost them after a bit, it did seem to steady the *Arthur* a little as they struggled to save her. Finally the water was low enough in the engine-room for Kåre to coax the engine back to life, and, running it at half speed, managed to keep the boat's head into the south-east storm. Below decks everything was a shambles, and uninhabitable. Everyone crammed into the wheelhouse. Finally they managed to cut a hole from the engine-room into the after cabin. Of course the galley, too, was in the most awful mess, and everything eatable was ruined. But they had taken a roast with them when they left Shetland. Now it was lying soaking in seawater. They rinsed it off with fresh water and ate it with the utmost relish.

The storm raged unabated for four days. At one point a German plane appeared overhead and fired a burst at them. They hardly noticed, and afterwards wondered if it had really happened. Bullet marks found later convinced them that it had. By the evening of the fourth day after shipping the huge sea, the wind moderated a little. With Kåre nursing the engine, Larsen steered a southerly course at perhaps four knots. At dawn they saw land. It was Fetlar, and they duly reached Lunna. The fuel tanks were dry. They had been away nine days, and they had survived the worst storm Shetland had seen for many a year. In the "Shetland Bus" Howarth describes the *Arthur's* return. "The mizzen mast was lying on the stern in a tangle of rigging. The bulwarks were smashed, and the gun mountings swept off her decks. Down below was a chaos of broken crockery, spilt food and broken lockers. But she was a fine ship. She had not leaked at all or suffered structural damage." It was common practice to paint a false registration number on a boat going over to the other side. Kåre recalls that it was on this trip, while on the Norwegian coast, they suddenly realised that the number they had painted on one side was different from the number on the other.

Though we are jumping ahead we can trace a litle more of Kåre's story, of which this trip on the *Arthur* was just the beginning. He was to make several more trips with her, and several on the *Feie,* with one on the *Siglaos,* before joining August Naerøy on the *Heland.* He made his last trip from Lunna in the late winter of 41/42, and then moved to Scalloway with the rest of the Shet-landsgjengen. The winter of 42/43 was a bad one for losses, but that's another story. He made one trip on MTB 626, before the arrival of the sub-chasers. He was mainly on the *Hessa,* but he made trips on all three of them. He married a Shetland girl, and when the war ended he had fifty-seven trips to the Norwegian coast to his credit.

The terrible first trip on the *Arthur* did nothing to discourage Larsen. He had come over to Lerwick on the *Motig* on 9th February, 1941, and included among his passengers was a Jew from Bergen. Larsen had seen action in the Finnish war, and, when that ended, he wasted no time in getting over to Shetland. As he later said quietly, "At the beginning of the occupation we had the Germans walking the streets in my home town. I didn't very much like it, so I decided to get into the forces." In the days to come this calm, dependable, single-minded man, who displayed the same qualities when in action or in extreme danger, was to illuminate the story of the Shetland Bus. Howarth, who probably knew him as well as anybody, thought very highly of him as a man, describing him as a humble, gentle, peaceful person. "He was always the same. I was often in his company with people of every rank from the Commander-in-Chief Home Fleet and the Crown Prince of Norway to the cook of his own crew, the British army privates of our shore staff, or the humblest of Shetlanders. He remained himself with them all, never raising his soft, gentle voice with his juniors, and never being obsequious or over-awed with his seniors; so of course both seniors and juniors liked him." When the time comes — hopefully still far distant — what a beautiful epitaph that would be for this remarkable man. Captain Arthur Sclater, Royal Marines, who came to Shetland in October, 1941, to join the Bus team, and who went under the name of Rogers at that time because he had many relations living in Norway, said of Larsen, "He was the man other men would instinctively follow." Jack Moore saw another side. "I always thought he had respect neither for himself nor his ship. But then he always got through. We liked him, we all liked him. One of the women used to knit socks for him. He was often in our house. We always made him welcome."

On 25th October the *Siglaos,* with Gunnar Gundersen in charge, went over to Bømlo. All went well, and two young men from the district where the boat tied up were able to go ashore and visit their families. One of them was Nils Nesse. When she finally sailed on her return journey she had two men, two women and three children on board as passengers. She was only about fifty miles from the coast when they were attacked by a German plane. Although the boat received considerable damage, only one man was hit — Nils Nesse. He died shortly afterwards. They kept going westwards, and at length came up with Sumburgh Head. They continued north to Lunna, where young Nils was buried in the churchyard beside the ancient little church, in the presence of every man at the base. His was the second Norwegian grave in the churchyard. The first had been a seaman, possibly from the Norwegian freighter *Hop* which had been lost with all hands on her way from Bergen to the Tyne, departing from Bergen on 3rd February, 1940. She had fifteen of a crew, and six or seven bodies came ashore in Fetlar and Unst shortly after that date. That unkown seaman was buried at Lunna on 15th February, 1940. The third burial was on 9th June, 1942. It was a body found by farmer John Johnson of Lunna when off fishing. Assumed to be a Norwegian, the body in this grave was known only to God. In 1948 the body of Nils Nesse was exhumed and taken home to Norway for reburial. In 1985 Nils' brother and his wife came to Shetland to see for themselves the spot where Nils had lain. Today three simple crosses still mark the graves, and the Shetland/Norwegian Friendship Society has erected a plaque on the churchyard wall in memory of these three young men who died so tragically. In Mid Yell church-yard is a memorial erected by relations from Haugesund in memory of the people on board the *Kantonella* which left Haugesund on 19th February, 1941, and was wrecked on Yell with the loss of all on board.

Sevrin Roald had made more than one trip over from Vigra in his boat the *Heland,* but the Germans were getting close to him, and with 23 people on board, including his wife, he finally came to stay. How close the Germans had been was only too clear when they arrested fifty people shortly after the *Heland's* departure. Many of the twenty-three people on board had been on the Gestapo list, much of the information about them having been provided by just about the worst Norwegian in Norway, the traitor Henry Rinnan. After screening in London Sevrin came back to Shetland to become chief shipwright for the Shetland Bus boats.

By this time the boats had all been armed to the point where they could put up a reasonable show if attacked from the air. At stem or stern were ·5 Colt machine-guns on low mountings, which, though not invisible, were not eye-catching. But the most ingenious idea came from David Howarth himself. It consisted of twin Lewis machine-guns mounted on a telescopic stand inside an ordinary forty-gallon steel barrel. The top of the barrel was sawn off, and replaced on top when the guns were out of sight down the barrel. It only needed a sharp pull on the lid to bring the guns, ready loaded, springing up into the firing position. Inside the barrel was a lining of concrete, which gave some protection against enemy machine-gun fire. The work of making these unusual but very useful gun mountings was carried out at both Moore's yard and at the Makakoff.

Chapter Six

Shetland and Norway 1941

Before continuing our look at the Shetland Bus story we can pause briefly to see what was happening in Shetland and Norway during 1941. While Shetlanders were well aware that fleeing Norwegians were arriving in large numbers, most of them knew only vaguely about the Shetland Bus activities. They had their own war to get on with, and 1941 was a year which saw German air activity increased, and produced a brand new danger in the shape of drifting mines. Two Burra men were killed in February when working with a cone mine, and three children were injured. In the same month another mine damaged a house at Quarff, while in March three more came in at the Waari Geo. Allan Laurenson, a well-known and popular young Lerwick man, was a naval lieutenant stationed in Shetland. He was a mine expert, and in February he was up in Whalsay disposing of one. Sadly he met his death later in the year from another mine which came in at the Knab below the new cemetery. Two naval ratings assisting him were also killed. The year started with the ack-ack guns around Lerwick in action on 4th January, and the 16th brought the news that two Hurricanes from Sumburgh had shot down a Heinkel which had crashed in Fair Isle. An RAF launch was sent to the Isle to bring out the survivors, but ran aground and later became a total wreck. In the end the lifeboat brought the men to Lerwick, and in 1987 they revisited Fair Isle. In February a German plane dropped five bombs on the town and harbour, with very little damage, and on the morning of 2nd March a Heinkel bomber made a bold, low-flying attack on shipping in the harbour, missing his main target with the two bombs dropped. Just after noon there was a second attack. Harbour Trust records say, "A further and more determined attack on shipping was made by three Dornier bombers whose six bombs narrowly missed their target. There was slight damage to property." Later in March it was learned that a ME110 had been downed by ack-ack fire at Sullom.

In April the *Magnus* was bombed and machine-gunned but survived, and in October it was the *Earl's* turn at the hands of a JU88. The plane dropped bombs, one or two of which were near misses, but every rivet in the old boat took the strain, and bullet-holes in the funnels were her only scars. Other air attacks in 1941 included machine-gunning at Gutcher and at Whiteness where schoolchildren were the target. But there were many air raid warnings when German planes came over without attacking and obviously on reconnaissance, reflecting Germany's growing interest in our islands. A sad note was struck during War Weapons Week at the end of October when two Blenheims, putting on an aerial display, collided in mid-air. One crashed at the Knab, killing all three of the crew, the other force-landed in Bressay. So with blackouts, strict rationing, shortages of everything, and the ever-increasing danger both from air and sea, Shetlanders saw out 1941, most of them more concerned about the welfare of loved ones in the armed forces than about their own safety.

In Norway

In Norway there was no lightening of the gloom, as the Germans were still there, making their presence increasingly felt. We have seen the judges, bishops and ministers had already made their stand. The sporting organisations were the next to be put under pressure. The Nazis set up a new Central Association for sport, and the immediate result was that every one of the 300,000 members of sporting organisations in Norway boycotted anything which was organised by the new Association. The farmers were next in the firing line — they refused to join a corporation run on fascist lines which would replace their own Association. Then their own Association's office-bearers were removed from office, and Quisling nazis appointed in their place. But the majority of the farmers remained loyal, and their Association virtually ceased to function. The fishermen were not forgotten. An attempt was made to remodel the Fishermen's Association on Nazi lines. The fishermen rejected the whole idea. The doctors lodged very strong protests about the appointment of unsuitable and unqualified people within their profession, and also about the forcible abduction of one of their colleagues. Although there was a lot of bluster, the Germans climbed down. The civil servants were asked to sign a circular pledging loyalty to Quisling's leadership. Nearly everyone refused. There was an attempt to use actors for the dissemination of Nazi propaganda. The result was a theatre strike lasting for several weeks.

But the most important event of this period was what became known as "The Letter of the Forty-Three". The letter was addressed to Terboven, and on behalf of forty-three organisations demanded that German or Quisling interference in the work of officials carrying out their duties under the terms of the Norwegian Constitution should cease. This letter was a highlight in the German/Norwegian relationships at the time. And it was given special importance in that it had the support of the unions. One of the men mainly responsible for bringing unity to the unions was Viggo Hansteen, who had followed the king and government north while the fighting lasted, and who had been in Narvik during the desperate days there. Now back in Oslo he was fully engaged in organising union resistance. And now the unions tabled a demand for wage increases to meet the higher cost of living, and at the same time they protested about Nazi interference in the internal conduct of the unions.

By this time it had become very clear to Terboven that, no matter how much Hitler might like to see a peacefully Nazified Norway lining up alongside the Greater Germany, all efforts to that end were coming to naught. Propaganda, infiltration and the velvet glove had all failed. Now it was time for recourse to the weapon which he, as a Nazi gauleiter, understood so well — terror. After an initial show of false clemency to the unions, his next step was to go on the radio to announce that Hitler had given him the powers to declare a state of emergency whenever he thought it was necessary. Norwegians waited in a state of tension for the next step — but nothing more was done. Then suddenly three Norwegians were executed, and an order was issued for the confiscation of all wireless sets in the coastal regions of Norway, soon to be followed by similar orders for the whole of Norway. Before the year was out he made his next announcement — there would be no wage increases. Then one morning when the workers came into the factories they were told that there would be no more work-place milk rations. With rations already at rock-bottom this seemed the last straw. The workers downed tools, and almost immediately 60,000 of them were on strike.

On 10th September Viggo Hansteen was asked to step over to Gestapo HQ in Victoria Terrasse in Oslo. A few hours later he was dead, shot along with a little-known trade unionist, a young shop steward. Now Terboven declared his threatened State of

Emergency. 1000 people were arrested, many of them trade union officials. They were nearly all sentenced to long terms of hard labour, or to the concentration camps. As if that was not enough to establish the rule of terror, the full military might of the German machine was displayed in the streets of Oslo, by jack-booted parades, the ostentatious setting-up of machine-gun posts in the streets, and a non-stop outpouring of decrees, threats and punishments, on the radio and in the papers. The unions' funds were all confiscated, and all the officials now appointed were Quisling nazis. Along with the subjugation of the unions went the elimination of many of the voluntary organisations. In six days Terboven probably felt that he had brought Norway — or at least Oslo — to heel. What he and his kind didn't understand — or if they did they ignored it — was that his brutal handling of the situation, while apparently having the immediate desired results, was in reality kindling a new fire of resistance. The killing of Hansteen was seen as a foul crime. It welded the ordinary people together as probably nothing else could have done. From now on German propaganda would fall on deaf ears. Quisling, elevated by the Germans on 1st February, 1942, to the position of "Minister-President of Norway", immediately assumed powers similar to the king's. Everyone clearly saw that this was a flagrant breach of the Constitution. Quisling's importance was still largely in his own head. The people would always see him as an unimportant but evil crank. To the Germans he was no more than a puppet.

The withdrawal of the milk ration in the factories, which precipitated union action, might not seem of tremendous importance to the reader of today. But the fact was that the official food ration for Norwegians had sunk very low. The German occupation forces, at this time somewhere between 300,000 and 400,000 men, represented an increase of more than 10% in the population. But that 10% appropriated very much more than 10% of the food available. All meat, for instance, disappeared from the shops. Fish, when available, had to provide the main course at a meal. Cream was a thing of the past. Black bread took the place of white. The weekly ration of all fats was 7 oz, of sugar 6 oz, and of coffee substitute or tea 1 oz. More often than not even these meagre amounts could not be met in full.

SOE and Martin Linge

The resistance put up by teachers came in 1942, and we shall return to that. What has been said about 1941 clearly indicates the stiffening of resistance at group level. But the underground or secret resistance was also slowly beginning to find its feet, and the fact that the Shetland Bus landed forty-three agents during 1941 was an indication that sources in Great Britain were keenly interested in lending aid to the movement. Those sources are best summarised under the title of SOE — Special Operations Executive. SOE had been set up in London with its early aim to keep in touch with patriotic elements in countries overrun by the Nazis. It would also concern itself with guerrilla warfare, raids on enemy-occupied territory, sabotage and so on. The proposals for an organisation of this nature were very much frowned on by many of the old-school, regular, army officers. But Churchill had no qualms. He saw it as something that would "set Europe ablaze". In it there was a section devoted to Norwegian activities. Its chief was Commander Frank Stagg, Royal Navy. He spoke Norwegian well, and was familiar with Norse history. One of his liaison officers was Lieutenant Boughton-Leigh, who was reputed to know the Shetland Islands well. But the man in the Norwegian section who really mattered was Lieutenant Martin Linge, soon to be promoted to Captain.

Even today Martin Linge's name is well-known in Norway. In the little town of Måløy stands his statue, raised by a grateful people, and graced with the royal presence at its unveiling. For it was here, just after Christmas, 1941, that Linge fell, fighting for his country's freedom. Near the statue is the little town's main hotel — the Kaptein Linge Hotel. Who was this man who became a folk hero?

Before the war Linge had been an actor. Jon Leirfall, possibly Norway's most prolific writer, met him more than once in those far-off days. Says Jon, "He was a light-hearted, happy man, but quiet and gentle. I did not think that he would become so serious about the war." Martin had been to a military school when younger, and when the Germans came he immediately reported for duty, making his way north to Andelsnes, where he heard the British were landing. There he became a liaison officer, and served with the British until the evacuation at the end of the first week in June. He was wounded in the foot, and was taken to Britain along with the British forces, finishing up in London. When the SOE was set up the British officers who had fought with Linge in Norway urged his appointment to the Norwegian section. He was immediately a key figure, and in the short time that fate allowed him, he proved how right his superiors had been to choose him. One of his functions was recruitment. He wanted the kind of man who would carry the fight to the Germans inside Norway itself —

as agents, saboteurs, raiders, or in any other way that the planners could dream up. We have already seen how he recruited Kåre Iversen. There were many like Kåre. In August, 1940, three young men arrived in Aberdeen in a 21 ft open boat, the *Viking,* after a hair-raising journey from southern Norway. Their leader was Odd Kjell Starheim, and the other two were Alf Lindeberg and Fritjof Pedersen. Their story is told in "Mannen som Stjal Galtesund" by Eiliv O. Hauge. The three friends were held in Aberdeen prison for four days while being interrogated. On the fourth day a young Norwegian officer came to see them. (*Probably their lengthy custody in Aberdeen had been to await the young officer's arrival.*) He leaned on a stick when he stepped forward to greet them, and he absorbed their attention. "Tall, with a quick, penetrating eye, he was erect, but not stiffly military, energetic in his movements, with dark hair and the pale, sensitive features of an artist. He wore the grey-green uniform of the pre-war Norwegian army." The boys looked with respect at the stick — the wound in his foot was still troubling him — and at the first Norwegian officer they had met who had actually smelt gunpowder and had actually fought the invader. They learned his name was Martin Linge. And as he took them down to London by train they learned more of what the Norwegians who had reached Britain were trying to do, and without hesitation they offered Linge their services, to use in whatever way he thought best. Starheim must have impressed Linge. He was taken to meet King Haakon, and he also got to know Linge's fiancée. The boys' reaction to Linge was a measure of the man's honesty, charisma and leadership qualities.

Joachim Rønneberg, whose story deserves a place in any book about Norway, came over on the *Sigurd* on 10th March, 1941. He met Linge soon after his arrival in London. Says Joachim, "He was an impressive man. He was a personality with a very, very human touch and completely informal. He made friends with everyone, and everyone felt happy in his company. Though an officer he invited privates out for lunch, for instance, and to say the least that was unusual in Britain." One can imagine how some blimpish eyebrows in 1940 would have elevated in horror at the very idea. "When he recruited people he left them in no doubt that it was for special service. As he said, 'We will help you along as best we can, but you will have to rely primarily on yourself. We don't look on you as an officer or a private. You are simply here to be trained — then it's up to you. You will be on your own.' For the kind of people who were needed he was the ideal recruiter. He was a very, very, fine man." Two of the men on the first Linge training course were Joachim Rønneberg and Leif Larsen. Arne Nipen, another of his recruits, says, "Linge was a fine man. He was a very clever man."

While the main thrust of Norwegian SOE operations was operated from London and from Lunna, there was also a small secret SOE section in Stockholm. In charge there was Major Malcolm Munthe, who had been wounded in the fighting in Norway and who had escaped from the Germans. It was he who translated "Mannen som Stjal Galtesund" into English under the title "Salt Water Thief", and he was of course a friend of both Linge and Starheim. Linge realised that in young Starheim and his friends he had young men who were eager and willing to return to Norway to help confound the Germans — men like himself, in fact. He had warned them that the whole SOE set-up had to be kept secret. After all, even in Britain, there were many who strongly disapproved of the whole idea. If they were sent back to Norway they would be better to use false names, and in fact Starheim used the name Ole Svendsen when the time came.

Linge had indeed chosen well in the three young men. Soon Alf and Fritjof were off up to Shetland to be taken back to Norway by one of the fishing boats (probably the *Siglaos*) and landed on the coast. They had with them a wireless transmitter in a suitcase, and a small quantity of arms. This was to become a typical operation for "Linge boys". No word came back from them, but at the end of 1940 Starheim himself went over by submarine. He, too, carried a heavy suitcase. It, too, contained a wireless transmitter. He was committed to the task of setting up an underground network in southern Norway which would operate under the code-name "Cheese". He was informed soon after landing that both his friends had been picked up by the Gestapo. Both were later shot.

Starheim himself proceeded single-mindedly to such good effect that he soon had a transmitter operating, and contacts in Kristiansand, Stavanger, Flekkefjord and Oslo. His operator, known familiarly as Young Tom, was a printer's typesetter and an amateur wireless fiend. He lived in a farmhouse away up the valley. Soffie Rorvig, who worked in the local milk depot, at the lower end of the valley, was his messenger and helper. For added effect Tom joined Quisling's NS party, which gave him extra cover and made him privy to much of what was going on on the other side, but it also meant that he was looked on with the utmost suspicion and dislike by all "good" Norwegians. He considered this a necessary price to pay. From Oslo Starheim went into Sweden via one of the escape routes established by Korsvig Rasmussen, and made contact with the SOE man in Stockholm. From there he was flown back to Scotland. The first intelligence network for southern Norway had been established. Soon Tom's transmitter was sending the position of an early German radar station to London. The RAF bombed and destroyed it. And it was his transmitter which sent the first information about the *Bismark* entering the North Sea.

PMcLeod

Chapter Seven

Raids on Norway

During 1941 three separate raids on Norway's west coast were carried out. In addition the evacuation of both Norwegians and Russians from Spitzbergen (Svalbard), jointly held by both countries at that time, was successfully accomplished in the spring. Albert Eilertsen, a Norwegian veteran who now lives in Shetland, was on board a salvage vessel lying in the fjord outside Narvik when the Germans came on 9th April, 1940. German destroyers steamed up the fjord, shepherding all the merchant ships in their path into Narvik harbour. Somehow they missed Albert's grey-painted ship where it lay close to the shore on the far side of the fjord. It got away to the Lofotens and thereafter there was no lack of salvage work to keep them busy so long as the naval engagements at Narvik continued. When that finished they were ordered to Svolvaer in the Lofotens, where they were all paid off.

In the end of 1941 he got a job on an ice-breaker which was to go up to Svalbard, and which sailed with no German control on board. While up there British ships appeared on the scene, among them the liner *Empress of Canada*. They proceeded to evacuate both the Norwegians and the Russians from Svalbard, landing the Russians at a Russian port. Instead of returning to Norway, Albert's ice-breaker now headed for Iceland, and that was how he escaped from the Germans. As he says, "It was good to get away from German occupied Norway. By the time I left they had been there for a year, and already things were really bad. You daren't say aloud what you really felt, you couldn't complain about anything, and everyone felt completely powerless. Unless you have experienced your country's occupation by people like the Germans, you cannot conceive what it was like." We will meet Albert again later. According to Ragnar Ulstein's "Englandsfarten" 767 Norwegians were evacuated from Svalbard.

An official account says that on 4th March, 1941, British troops and light naval forces, aided by Norwegian marines, carried out a raid on the Lofoten Islands, near Narvik. They destroyed the fish-oil production plant, sank eleven enemy ships, took a number of prisoners, brought off about 300 Norwegian patriots, and left supplies for the local population. Little opposition was encountered, and no casualties suffered. Other sources say the actual number of Norwegians brought back was 285, and it is also suggested that by no means all of them were patriots. Opposition seems to have been almost entirely lacking. Apparently Martin Linge went on this raid, which was organised by Commander Frank Stagg, chief of the Norwegian section of SOE. It was probably seen as valuable experience.

It was at the end of 1941 that the biggest effort took place. It was to be a two-pronged raid, one half code-named "Anklet" on the Lofotens, the other half code-named "Archery" on the island of Vågsøy. The raid was planned for 26th December, and "Anklet" was duly carried out on that day. The Lofotens' objective was the little village of Reine, and originally it had probably been the intention to occupy and hold a beach-head there, which conceivably could have posed a serious threat to German communications on the Norwegian coast. But if that had been the plan, the Japanese attack at Pearl Harbour probably caused a rethink. So the raid was really a hit and run affair. The Lunna boys of the Shetlandsgjengen were involved, for they had been asked to prepare, man and despatch seven fishing boats then lying at Invergordon to the Norwegian coast, their task to extinguish all the navigation lights in the inner channels for some distance south of the Lofotens. The complete darkness would have been a considerable hardship to German vessels which might steam north to counter-attack. Howarth got the order only a week before Christmas. He went down to Invergordon, and found the boats in a terrible state of unseaworthiness. He hadn't even been told the precise task for which the boats were required. Eventually a makeshift assortment was assembled at Lerwick and shortly they sailed in the teeth of rapidly deteriorating weather. Soon three returned to Lerwick. Three more went into Lunna. Of the Lunna three, two set out again, and after various misadventures, reached their objective, only to find that the British forces had been and gone. Only one boat, the *Havørn,* returned and she made a friendly landfall at Stornoway instead of Shetland. The fishing boats' involvement was extremely ill-conceived, and Howarth had been given neither time nor means to make anything of the project.

Vågsøy is the island on which stands the town of Måløy, which has been Lerwick's friendship town for many years. Indeed

proposals are presently under consideration to expand the friendship link to cover the whole of the Vågsøy Commune and the whole
of Shetland. Apart from the contact which Måløy fishermen had
always had with Lerwick, a new connection was forged in 1931. In
that year a ship called the *Venus* was wrecked on the south-west
corner of Vågsøy. She was a "rum-runner", and on board were
nine men from Lerwick. They had taken berths on the ship at a
time when unemployment was very severe in Shetland, and the
chance of work of any kind was welcome to men with families to
support. All the Lerwick men lost their lives in the wreck, but the
bodies of only four of them were ever recovered. One, John
Corkish, is buried in the churchyard beside Måløy's church. Three,
William Davidson, Magnus Edwardson and Charles O'Neil are
buried in Vågsvåg cemetery, not very far from where the *Venus*
went down. Today a corner of the cemetery is known as the
"Shetland corner", and a huge rock brought from the scene of the
wreck by the Vågsøy Council, bears a plaque provided by Lerwick
Community Council, with a suitable inscription.

When the Germans came in 1940 Måløy was a little, young
town, just beginning to grow. Its population was probably in the
region of 2000, and most of the houses were near the shore in the
streets called Gate 1 and Gate 2. There was no bridge then linking it
to the mainland — access was by ferry only. Today the Gates are
numbered up to 7 and No. 8 is now being started. No longer do the
people rely on a ferry, as a beautiful bridge links the island to the
mainland. From the beginning the people resented the Germans'
presence. Five boats came over to Shetland in the months
immediately following the invasion, and there were about ten more
during 1941. A lot more people from the district came over in boats
which had start points in other areas. One young girl of twenty who
realised she would have to get away was Elisabeth Holvik. She was
a waitress in a cafe in the little town, and from the first moment she
saw them she hated the Germans. On more than one occason she
couldn't prevent herself showing her feelings in the presence of the
German soldiers. She was frequently rude to them, on one occasion
even damaging their radio. Her friend overheard Germans in the
Hagens Hotel discussing her, and concluding that she was a girl
who needed an eye kept on her. In due course it became clear that
they were both watching and listening, as she was taken in front of
them to be "examined", i.e. interrogated.

Clearly she was in danger, and when she learned of a boat
being organised by Sverre Brosvik for a Shetland run she asked if
she could go. The boat was the *Solveig,* and Brosvik, a man of

thirty-six at the time, skippered it. They reached Lerwick on 25th August, 1941, the nineteen passengers including six women, two of them schoolteachers. As was the usual practice, it was first Buckie then London for Elisabeth. After a considerable period in Britain, when she worked both in London and up in Scotland, she met her future husband, and Ruth, her first child, was born at Dingwall. Today Ruth, her husband and two children live in Måløy and are the very dear friends of the writer and his family.

Otto Hoddevik was under twenty when the Germans came to Måløy, and their presence soon became intolerable to him. At the end of May, 1941, along with twenty-three others he reached Skerries in the *Nordhav,* their departure point Ålesund. Otto was to do varied and often exciting service over the next few years, much of it from Shetland, and we will come back to his story. One man who remained very much part of the scene right up to the time of the Vågsøy raid was Johannes Nessen, who lives today in Bergen. Part of his story is told in Arfinn Haga's book "Natt på Norskekystene", and Johannes confirms the accuracy of Haga's account.

Before the war he was a fisherman in Solund and was briefly in the merchant navy. In 1939 he had been in Danzig, not a happy place at that time, and while there he had got the feel of the danger which the Nazis represented. When the Germans arrived in Norway he was working for Johannes Mathieson of Solund, a man who was later to be involved in the "export" business to Shetland. Then he got a chance on lifeboats and found himself on the *Namsos* stationed at Måløy. The lifeboat radio was sealed but it could be manipulated so that they could hear the Norwegian news from London. They so used it, and as a result it developed a serious fault. They were ordered to Bergen, and Johannes feared the game was up. But there they were told the lifeboats would now be regarded as neutral, and their radios could henceforth be "open".

One day, in the post office in Måløy, one of the staff whispered to him. Would he listen to the radio on the *Namsos* on a certain wavelength at a certain time, when at sea? He was to write down what he heard and pass it to the man in the post office. Twice he did this. Then some time before Christmas he was asked if he would go to the Hagens Hotel on Christmas Eve. It was known that on that evening virtually all the Germans in the area were to gather in the hotel for a meal. He was to check their units and their total. In his best suit he duly sat at a corner table, and did just that, passing the information to his post office friend the same evening. His calculations showed that there were approximately 250 soldiers and 25 marines in the area, with an additional 25 men who had come to spend Christmas on the island. Of course he had no idea that the information was being collected to help in the impending raid on Vågsøy.

On the other side of the North Sea the final touches were being put to organising a flotilla of ships at Scapa Flow in Orkney. The flotilla was made up of the cruiser *Kenya*, the destroyers *Oribi, Offa, Onslow* and *Chidwell*, the troop transports *Prince Charles* and *Prince Leopold*, the last two doubling as assault ships, and the submarine *Tuna*. Rear-Admiral Burrough was in command of the flotilla and flew his flag on the *Kenya*. The little fleet sailed out of Scapa Flow on the evening of 24th December. They were to be the force which would attack Vågsøy island, while at the same time a second force raided the Lofotens.

As the ships sailed out of Scapa people were just going to a Christmas Eve party in the Masonic Hall, Lerwick. The party had been organised by Norwegian Consul Wendelbø. The Norwegians had set up a separate consular office to ease the burden on the Garriocks. The guests were mostly Norwegian, though a sprinkling of local people had also been invited. Some of them still remember that party. In particular they remember a young captain who was the life and soul of the evening, and who won a doll in a raffle. That young captain was Martin Linge who had done so much in London to recruit the kind of men he wanted, and who was now leading a troop of these men to land and face the Germans on the soil of their homeland. This was only half his total force — the other half was committed to the Lofoten raid. The party went on into the early hours of the morning and no one enjoyed himself more than Martin. Who could have guessed that he had a date with destiny within a matter of hours?

Prior to sailing from Scapa all the troops had been well briefed on the operation they were about to undertake, with a liberal use of maps and models. No doubt the information collected by Johannes Nessen, and passed on by his contact in the Måløy post office proved very useful. Certainly there was very full information about the German forces — their numbers and even the fact that they had one tank on the island. (*In the event it turned out to be an armoured car.*) There were two coastal defence batteries guarding the main anchorage, and the little islet in the sound, usually referred to as Måløy islet, housed a battery of four Belgian 75s, captured by the Germans in 1940. The northern entry to the sound had 105 mm guns, and air cover for the area was available from Herala, Stavanger and Trondheim. About forty Messerschmidts used these bases. It was stated that fighters from Wick and Sumburgh would provide air cover for the flotilla for part of the way, but there would be a bomber force accompanying the operation. The Commando units were under the overall command of Brigidier J. C. Haydon. Other officers were Lt. Col. John Durnford-Slater, Commander of No. 3 Commando, Major Churchill (Mad Jack), who commanded Troops 5 and 6, and Captain Peter Young. Slater was to receive the DSO, Young the MC for their parts in the raid. Churchill had won the MC at Dunkirk. The total force numbered five hundred and twenty-five non-commissioned officers and men, with fifty-one officers. The Norwegian section numbered twenty-seven NCOs and men, with seven officers.

As the flotilla came north from Scapa Flow on Christmas Eve they were pounded by a Force 8 westerly gale, and the two troop carriers, with their landing craft providing ungainly top weight, rolled in the most astonishing fashion and also sustained some damage. It was a miserable trip for the troops on board, most of whom suffered badly from seasickness. The damage sustained by the troopers caused a delay of twenty-four hours, while they lay in Sullom Voe to effect repairs, but by 4 pm on the 26th they were again ready to sail, and they set out on the final leg of 300 miles to Vågsøy. By this time the wind had moderated, and they were picking up signals from the submarine *Tuna* which was already in the sound between Vågsøy and the mainland, and was acting as the perfect direction indicator. The Lofoten raid, also planned for the 26th, was taking place as they sailed.

The approaches to Vågsøy sound had look-out posts at Vågsvåg and at Husevåg to give warning of an enemy approach. Sure enough the man on duty at Husevåg saw the ships approaching — he could hardly fail to notice them, even though it was still early on a dark, snowy, December morning. He tried to get through on the telephone to the battery on Måløy islet, but the battery commander's batman was busy polishing his master's boots, and didn't even bother to pick up the receiver. The look-out man then tried the harbour-master's office at South Vågsøy. This time a clerk answered, and he told him that there were seven blacked-out destroyers entering the fjord. Of course it was still only 27th December, and the clerk kindly suggested that it was all in the look-out man's imagination, probably due to rather too much imbibing in the Christmas celebrations. In sheer frustration the watchman finally managed to pass his message by lamp signals to a sailor at the signal station on Måløy island. At last he had got someone to believe him, but the sailor, instead of urgently alerting the battery on the island, proceeded to the Hagens Hotel to report to the naval officer in charge. A lot of valuable time had slipped past, and by the time German gunners were alerted the British force was already in action.

If the Germans were surprised the townspeople were even more so. Their first awareness that something was afoot was the sound of gunfire. Some of it, they reckoned, was ack-ack. Some of it was certainly of a heavier calibre. There were planes overhead — clearly British. They waited in considerable trepidation for what would happen next. Actually three landing craft were already in the water, one going in at Holvik, round the corner from Måløy, the other two going along the sound to Måløy itself. Almost simultaneously the *Kenya* had opened fire on the guns on Måløy island, and in nine minutes she pumped 400 six inch shells on to the target. The German guns were wiped out, having got off just one round. *Onslow* and *Oribi* were adding their fire, but, with the Germans putting up a heavy fire from the shore against the landing craft, Hampden aircraft were called in to drop smoke bombs on the landing sites. Sadly one bomber, apparently hit by ack-ack fire from the German trawler *Föhn,* dropped a large phosphorous smoke bomb which fell into one of the landing craft, burning and killing half the troop.

But a landing was successfully effected, and was followed by a period of intense street fighting, especially along the front, and the British reserve troop was committed. Numerous casualties were suffered on both sides. Farther north on Vågsøy Troop No. 5 had been landed, and, having blown up the road to cut off any possible German reinforcement, they moved south to Måløy. By mid-day German resistance was virtually over. Some demolition work was carried out by the British, and by 1 pm the order to re-embark had been given.

So much for a synopsis of the action. For the people of Måløy the whole thing was a traumatic experience. They saw the British soldiers landing, they heard the thunder of the naval guns, planes both British and German were overhead, machine-guns clattered, hand grenades were being thrown by both sides, a number of houses were already on fire. The intense fighting, added to the cacophony of sound convinced them that this was something big. It had to be the beginning of invasion — this had to be the day freedom was coming to Norway.

Meanwhile the *Namsos,* preparing for sea when the first British bomber flew over, stayed where she was. Johannes Nessen observed the action with a great deal of interest. He noted that the German guns at the south end of the entrance put up a good fight before being silenced, but he was more interested in the landing craft coming in and the fact that there were some Norwegians among the assault troops. The German naval captain drove up in a car, jumped out, and ran to shelter behind some bales of hay. His second-in-command went up the stairs of a sea-front shop. He met a British bullet, and a Commando dragged him into the shop. A British soldier in the street was wounded by a German bullet. "It's very cold," he said, and Nessen went to get him a blanket from the shop. As he opened the door the wounded German lying in the passage looked up. "Es ist sehr kalt," he said. Nessen indicated the captain's car to the Commandos, and they used it to ferry wounded to the landing craft. He picked up a British rifle dropped by a casualty, and soon met a Måløy man carrying a machine-gun. Sniper fire was still coming from the hillside. Near where the boats had come in he met a journalist friend, who asked him if he was going over. Looking at the rifle in his hands Nessen commented, "I reckon it won't be too good for me to stay here now."

Another man in Måløy that day was Birger Igland from Bremanger. He had escaped to Shetland on board the *Stanley* on 28th September, 1941, along with thirty-two other people. They had made landfall in Baltasound, and he had gone on to become a Linge man. On the Måløy raid he had been given a special job — to arrest a Norwegian nazi. There weren't all that many of them in the area, but Birger knew this one in Måløy well. He was the manager of the canning factory. Birger had found him. Of course he denied that he was the man Birger was after. But Birger was having none of it. "For sure you are," he said. "It's only a month or two since I spoke to you." He took his prisoner and hid in a cellar until things quietened down, then took him to the boats. The writer had hoped to call on Birger in 1987, but sadly he had died earlier in the year.

The whole action had been fraught with danger for the Måløy people. Jon and Ingeborg Osmundsvaag were living at that time in a house on the hillside, at the edge of the trees, and directly above the tiny island in the sound with its German batteries. Today the house still stands where it did, virtually unchanged. Jon had lived there all his life. On that distant morning, with seasonal snow on the ground — "the third day of Christmas", Jon calls it — they were suddenly aware of the action starting up quite near to where they lived. The Commandos who appeared on the scene at the back of their house had landed at Holvik, a little farther south, had neutralised the German position there, and were now approaching

12. The Shetland corner in Vågsvåg cemetery.

13. Måløy foreshore, with bridge supports resting on the islet in the sound.

14. Måløy monument to the Allied fallen in the 1941 raid.

15. The Osmundsvaags' house in Måløy as it is today.

through the cover of the trees to assist their comrades in the main thrust on the German positions in Måløy itself. Approaching from that direction the Osmundsvaag's house was the first one they came to, and some of them came in. The *Kenya* had shattered the gun positions on Måløy island, and the surviving Germans from there were trying to escape up the hillside directly below the house. More landing craft were coming in, and the navy's fire had now switched to the German guns on the mainland at Deknepollen. This was probably the most intense phase of the fighting, and the Germans trying to escape up the hillside were coming under fire from the Commandos among the trees and also from those in the house. Two of the latter were Linge men from Linge's small troop. Many of the houses in this area were on fire, although Jon's house and the church remained surprisingly undamaged.

A British captain had been severely wounded in the arm by a German-thrown hand grenade, the soldier having come up from the German HQ in the Ulvesund Hotel. The Commandos promptly shot the German, and the captain was taken into Jon's house, where his sister-in-law and his fiancée bound up his wounds. Jon then carried the captain on his back all the way to the landing craft. By the time he delivered his load German prisoners were beginning to be brought down. The Måløy people in Jon's area were in a high state of excitement, and the children added to the chaos. It was difficult to achieve any kind of order, and many of the people were fleeing to the greater safety of the trees.

Ingeborg still remembers it all quite clearly. "It all happened very quickly," she says. "The first thing I remember were brown khaki legs going over a fence. Some friends and neighbours came in and we all went down to the cellar." Her pride in her husband's behaviour is very plain. He had kept coming and going regardless of the gunfire, trying to calm things down, and his action in carrying the wounded captain back to the landing craft had called for great courage. "Jon was a brave man that day." The Commandos had used their house because it commanded such a good field of fire. "Those who were trying to escape from the island came up past our house, but of course the Commandos were firing at them. When we finally left the house to seek shelter among the trees, we had to step over the body of a dead German just outside our door. But the Commandos had casualties too, in the open ground just below our house. They seemed to expose themselves unnecessarily. Jon's sister-in-law was a nurse, and she and I bandaged up the British captain. I could speak English and was acting as interpreter. He gave me a cigarette."

When the fighting ended and the British had gone she went away for the night to stay with friends. Jon's brother-in-law was a doctor, and Jon remained in Måløy to help carry away the wounded and the dead. Many were German, but they tended to them all, regardless of nationality. The Commandos who were in the house didn't leave entirely empty-handed. They took with them some little items, no doubt as souvenirs, just to show as proof they had actually been ashore in Norway. Ingebord didn't mind, but she says with a smile, "The things they took weren't Norwegian — they were items I had bought in England!"

The women-folk returned the day after the raid. They were not a little afraid of German reaction, but there were no immediate repercussions. Nevertheless she and Jon went up to the farm she came from at the head of Nordfjord. After all they had both been helping the British, and she spoke English as well! After a few days they came back. They were left in peace. In Jon's brother's house the Germans found some bits and pieces of a radio. He was arrested, but after interrogation he was released, though the Germans requisitioned the house. Certainly the people were on tenterhooks for some time after the raid, but the reprisals which everyone had dreaded did not materialise to any great extent. The greatest disappointment was that the raid had been so short — and apparently so pointless. As they said, "Still we wondered. What was the purpose of the raid?"

Over in Britain the answer to that question was possibly clearly evident. As an operation the raid was brilliantly successful. 16,000 tons of German shipping had been sent to the bottom. An important fish factory had been destroyed. The German forces in Vågsøy had been almost entirely wiped out or taken prisoner — there were only about forty left. The big German guns had all been silenced. Seventy-nine Norwegians went back to Britain with the raiders. ("Some of them we could well do without," was the perhaps unkind comment of one Måløy resident.) And the price? Fifty-two Allied officers and men lost their lives — forty-five British, two Australian, two Canadian, two New Zealanders, and one Norwegian. But in Måløy the people hardly saw it like that. They had been sure the landings were the beginning of the liberation of Norway. They were all highly excited and expectant. And then the let-down, when the British simply sailed away, leaving behind a little town with many houses badly damaged, and a number still burning. The damage to industrial buildings meant that a number of jobs had gone, and the people were now open to German reprisals in a way even worse than before. But there were no complaints.

What of Johannes Nessen? He got away on a Dutch boat. Some injured and dead were brought on board, and his journalist friend also came with him. He was asked to take command, and they were soon putting up ack-ack fire at two German aircraft which both sheered off. At midnight they stopped and committed their dead to the deep, and without further incident they arrived at Scapa Flow. Nessen joined Kompani Linge and trained with them until Petter Salen came looking for men for the Shetland Bus. And so he came to Shetland, and later skippered the *Andholmen,* one of the four big Arctic whalers which had escaped to Iceland, and all of which became important parts of the Shetland Bus. Nine times he took her to the Norwegian coast, and well remembers the trip they made to the Lofotens on 11th December, 1942. They were away for thirteen days. When the sub-chasers arrived he joined the *Hessa* with Petter Salen as commander.

The raiding force, as they withdrew through Vågsfjord about 2.30 pm, shot up several watch-posts as they passed, and by 4 pm next day, the 28th, they were back in Scapa Flow. And what of Martin Linge, whose memory lives on in the hearts of the men of the "Lingeklubben"? He had landed with his troop, and had been in the heart of the fighting along the front. They had come to the Ulvesund Hotel, the German HQ, and Martin had approached the entrance and shouted that all inside should come out at once and surrender. The German answer was a burst from a machine-gun, and he fell, mortally wounded. His "Linge boys" immediately threw in hand grenades which practically destroyed the building and accounted for the Germans inside.

There were many German bodies to be buried after the raid. There were also a number of the Allied fallen whom the raiders had had to leave behind. To the Germans' credit they carried out the Allied burials on 31st December with full military honours, and a German guard of honour fired a volley over the graves. In 1945 all the bodies were exhumed and sent to be buried in their homeland or in other military cemeteries. Some accounts say that Linge was buried at sea, but the more likely account is that his body was not discovered until a day or two after the raid, and he was buried in the same grave as a British sailor found in a wrecked landing craft.

The numerous journalists who accompanied the raiders brought back both the story and many pictures. It was given considerable prominence in British papers and periodicals, and provided a tremendous boost to British morale at a time when any kind of good news was hard to come by. In Måløy, where some of the fiercest final fighting took place in and around the dentist's house, bullet holes in the woodwork are still mute testimony to the events of that memorable day. Martin Linge's statue, where it stands beside the Kaptein Linge Hotel, keeps his memory fresh, and the Kompani Linge, which grew from his early beginnings, will always occupy an honoured place in Norwegian history.

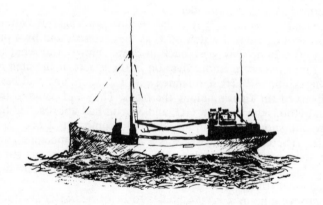

Chapter Eight

Some Bus Men

Already we have met a few of the young men who manned the boats of the Shetland Bus in its early stages. But more were needed and more kept coming. Two qualities nearly all of them had in common — they hated the Germans and they wanted action. Action, they had been led to believe, was something that could be found in Shetland.

But it wasn't as simple as that. There was first of all the big decision — whether to go or to stay. To go meant leaving family and friends, and quite possibly leaving them in danger. To stay meant an intolerable way of life under the Germans. If the decision was to go, then there was the problem of a boat in which to reach Shetland. Having found a boat, or a place on a boat, there was the very real danger inherent in any attempt to cross the North Sea in wartime. To reach Shetland successfully was a big achievement, but that was followed by a long trip to London, lengthy interrogation, mostly with no knowledge of English, and then a period of rigorous training. Only then did you get the chance to return to Shetland, and then only if you were considered suitable. The Shetland Bus needed a very special breed of men.

War historians tend to concentrate on the deeds of men and women in action, and this book will do that too. But each of these Shetland Bus men had a considerable story to tell before ever they made their first trip on a Bus boat. Sadly many of them have gone, but happily quite a few remain. They are not easily persuaded to say very much about these far off days. There are no heroics, no boasting. Everything is very matter-of-fact. Most of them are now in their late sixties or early seventies, but with many of them one can still recognise the carefree, adventurous, fearless spirit that drove them to leave home, family and country, and journey to a foreign land to join the fight for freedom. Let us look at the early stories of just a few.

We saw how Kåre Iversen made fifty-seven trips to the

Norwegian coast. Arne Melkevik was another such man. Arne belonged to the village of Telavåg, later to suffer so tragically at the hands of the Germans, and when he left Norway he took the name Arne Nipen to lessen the chances of the Germans taking reprisals on his family. Today he and his Shetland wife Baba live at Klokkarvik just across the island of Sotra from Telavåg. Arne was a fisherman, and his boat was just coming in from the fishing on the morning when the Germans steamed up the fjord to occupy Bergen. There wasn't much he could do about it, so he kept on fishing through the summer and the winter of 1940/41.

One day he heard that the *Blia* was going to Shetland. He wanted to go with her, but his skipper's reaction, though sparing in words, was definite enough. "You're not going anywhere." We may note in passing that the *Blia* crossed successfully on this occasion. It was eight months later that she was lost with all forty-two people on board. Arne was still determined to get to Shetland, and on 21st July, 1941, the chance came. With three friends he stole the *Ingeborg,* the same boat on which he went to the fishing, and they set off for Shetland. That looks simple enough on paper, but the whole thing involved considerable preparation. He was living at the time with his brother, just south of Bergen, and the Germans had a strong-point nearby. Among the German soldiers there was a group of Hitler Jugend products, who were ready to throw their weight around on any pretext. Arne was certain that it was only a matter of time before he would be involved in trouble with them. It was time to go.

His brother and his family rowed across the sound to Sotra with him. As they rowed a dogfight developed in the sky above them between two planes, one German, one British, The women-folk were frightened as the machine-guns clattered. With the twinkle in his eye which tells the listener that in his youth Arne must have been quite a lad, he says, "My brother and I had some home-made ale in the boat. We thought this was a good moment to sample it." In Telavåg he met his friends and arranged to leave on the following evening, having first stolen the *Ingeborg*. Perhaps his skipper's earlier refusal to let him go influenced his decision to take this particular boat!

The following evening came, but no friends. Arne heard there was a dance going on, on the other side of the island. He went over, and there were the boys, dancing away in great style, and with a good dram on board. "Aren't you coming?" "Yes, of course," but they wanted to take their girls with them, and the girls were quite willing to go. "No, no women," said skipper Arne with all the authority of his twenty-one years. "We're better off without them." The rest of the gear they needed had been acquired in the same way as the *Ingeborg*, i.e. without payment, and on a fine summer's evening they set off. They didn't know much about navigation, but his brother-in-law had taught Arne to read the compass, and had told him the course to steer. What more did they need? Later in the night a British plane passed over flying west, but on a slightly more southerly course than the *Ingeborg*. Skipper Arne changed course accordingly, and 24 hours after leaving Telavåg they were outside Lerwick. The first man they saw on the quay when they tied up was a young naval lieutenant who spoke Norwegian. His name was David Howarth, and he was a great help because none of the four boys spoke a word of English.

The boys were taken ashore, guarded and interrogated. Arne had his accordion with him. They also had a bottle of aquavit. The guards liked both the accordion music and the aquavit, and a very pleasant night of "interrogation" was spent by all. Next morning it was down to Buckie, where all the accommodation was full up. They were eventually found sleeping space in the waiting room of the maternity hospital. Sometime during the night a nurse had come in to make a phone call, and she put down a small baby she was carrying while she made the call. Arne came awake to find the baby lying beside him.

The journey to London had its own amusing interest. They had a policeman with them as escort. He assured them he couldn't speak a word of Norwegian, but the boys had a strong suspicion that he could. However, no ruse they tried could make him give any indication that he knew a word of the language. "Then we began to tell each other dirty stories, and finally he burst out laughing. That was a dead giveaway." The Norwegian-speaking policeman was simply one of the ways by which the authorities tried to make sure of the bona fides of the incomers. Not infrequently they unmasked a nazi infiltrator.

In London it was the Patriotic School, and there Arne sold his accordion. "It was too heavy to carry around." Then on to the County Hotel, a medical examination, and a query as to what branch of service he wanted. He indicated he wasn't fussy, and was given a slip of paper with the name "Martin Linge" on it. "I went and saw him. We spoke about all sorts of things. Then he gave me a piece of paper, and told me to read what was on it. If I liked it I could sign it. I read it, and I signed it. I was a Linge boy." After that it was Commando training. He and Per Blystad, with whom he had become friendly, finished their training up in Scotland, and then seven of them were sent down to London. "At the Bailey Hotel us seven Norwegians and some high-ranking officers were the only ones allowed into one of the rooms. There were guards at the door. Then we were told what it was all about. We were going back to Shetland." So it was up to Lerwick on the *Magnus,* and from there to Lunna, passing Catfirth where the *Olaf* lay at anchor. The first stage was over — the big adventure was about to begin.

Otto Hoddevik was still a youth of under twenty when the Germans came. They didn't appear in his home town of Måløy immediately, and the people had time to form a Home Guard which even took some prisoners. It was well into May before the first of the enemy appeared, and their arrival was fairly low-key. They had their HQ down near the harbour, and they had watchmen on the quays. Young fellows like Otto wandered about, frequently shouting rude remarks at the Germans. Some of the soldiers very much resented this, and Otto was taken aside and told there must be no more of it. He realised that he and the Germans could never get on — it was time to get away. The opportunity to do so came through the "export" organisation up in Ålesund. Leader of that group was Sverre Nielsen, a friend of Thoralf Walle, whose story we will come to.

The boat in which Otto was to escape was the *Lill,* but she was in such poor condition that, when only a few miles off the coast, the engine packed in. They had two young men from the ship-building yard among the twenty-six people on board, but they couldn't get it to go. A makeshift sail took them to a trawler which was fishing not far away, and they asked the skipper for a tow. There was nothing doing until he finished fishing, and in the meantime they had no option but to lie by, never allowing more than 3/4 people on deck at any one time. They finally told the trawler skipper what was on the go, but he was still willing to tow them into Vigra, where they anchored.

Now two men were sent into Ålesund to try and raise another boat, and at this point two of the party decided that they'd had enough, and also went ashore. "About mid-day a German plane came over, and landed quite near to us. We were sure it was us he was after. But after about twenty minutes — it was a heck of a long twenty minutes — he took off again." They lay still where they were till about 5 pm when the two boys they'd sent out returned with another boat, the *Nordhav,* which belonged to the uncle of one of the boys on board. This time they had a good ship with a good engine, and though the first night was very rough, with a strong head wind, they made Out Skerries in forty-nine hours.

They had discovered shortly after they left that there was no fresh water on board — had they overshot Shetland they would have been in dire straits. "The Skerries people were good to us. We ate white bread for the first time in many months."

From Lerwick they took several of the Norwegian fishing boats which had collected there down to Buckie. Then it was on to Aberdeen, and a night or two in the Douglas Hotel, while they gave the British authorities as much information as they could about German dispositions on the Norwegian coast. There was the usual progression through the Patriotic School, then up to Skegness for training. One day the CO told them they were going to Aberdeen. He followed them out, then spat in the Norwegian gesture for good luck. They asked why the spitting. "Where you're going you'll need all the luck you can get." Their destination was Peterhead, where several Norwegian fishing boats were lying. Their first job was to take one of them, the *Harald,* over to Norway and land two agents, of whom one was called Dagfinn Ulricksen. He had skippered the *Notbas* to Shetland on 4th May, 1941, with eight people on board. He was twenty-six, the second agent, Atle Svandal, twenty-four. The *Harald* went in to land in darkness. "The sister of our pilot was to be our contact. She came down to meet us, and said it wasn't a very good time for us to come. When we asked her why, she said the Gestapo had come just a fortnight before and had taken away her two brothers. But she invited us ashore, and gave the two agents some bread she had baked. They set up their radio in a small hut on what was little more than a rock, about two miles from her house. There they sat for something like two months, reporting regularly to London."

On this first trip they were attacked by a German plane on the way back. Otto was alone in the wheelhouse when he saw the plane in the distance. As it came nearer he could suddenly make out its black crosses, and called the crew on deck. The plane, after seeming to be going away, turned and came back and bombed them. The man on the machine-gun behind the wheel-house opened fire, and Otto kept trying to steer the *Harald* round to keep head on to the plane. He suddenly realised that, because of this manoeuvre, the machine-gunner's fire was passing uncomfortably close to the wheelhouse. However, the plane had had enough. It made off and soon after exploded in mid-air. Apparently the pilot hadn't called for help, as they reached Lerwick without further incident. "We thought it was all a piece of cake. We didn't know any better. We were all still so green." And so young.

Hoddevik did a number of trips with the *Harald*. They landed a number of agents and picked up a number. One who failed to appear at the rendezvous was presumed lost. But one day he appeared again in Peterhead, large as life, having stolen a pilot boat in which he escaped. It was now that the engine in the *Harald* packed in, and they had to take over the *Streif* as replacement. This was Øivind Steinsvåg's boat. And now followed what was surely one of the most bizarre stories of the war. Otto had to go into hospital with suspected diphtheria, leaving the *Streif* short of a navigator. All he could do was to give the crew the course to steer, and such other advice as he could think of.

Off they went, and duly landed their agent as planned. On the way back the engine gave up on them. They had just got it going again when a British plane came over, and they flashed it an SOS. When it flew off it headed east, which made them think that they were out to the west of Shetland, so they steered south. Eventually they saw a long, low shoreline, and soon they ran ashore on a sandbank. They jumped over the side and waded ashore. The first men they saw were German soldiers! They were ashore on the Dutch coast. They waded and swam back on board, dumped all their arms and equipment over the side, and prominently displayed the fishing gear they still had on board. In the morning when the Germans boarded them to take them ashore, they had their story ready. They had been taken by the British, they said, and forced to fish for them. But they had managed to escape and had made their way to Holland. To the Germans their story was apparently credible, for they were put in an ordinary prison camp, and survived the war. Had their true function become known their fate would have been far different. Otto's suspected diptheria turned out to be a false alarm, and he now joined the motor torpedo boats, where we will meet him again later.

Øivind Steinsvåg was only fourteen when the Germans arrived in 1940. He was living in Bømlo at the time, and young as he was had already started going to the fishing. His father was still living, but his mother had died, and Øivind was a very self-reliant boy. He knew that a lot of young fellows were going over to Shetland, and he yearned to go too.

His chance came on 27th August, 1941. He and two others stole a 57 ft boat called the *Streif*. Of the three boys Jakob Steinsvåg, at twenty-one, was the oldest, Øivind, at fifteen, the youngest, but acting as engineer. On 29th August they made landfall at Noss, their navigation clearly having been first class. After the usual 24 hours in Lerwick, the *Streif* and two other boats were ordered down to Buckie, meeting a fourth boat, just arriving from Norway, on the way down. All four went into Buckie, and we have already followed the *Streif's* continuing story, until she ended up in Holland. Øivind says that for years after the war the Dutch were still writing with queries about her engine. The Patriotic School was of course the next stage of their journey. Øivind had always dreamed of joining the Air Force and becoming a pilot. He did go for preliminary training, but he was still only fifteen, and things didn't show much progress. He made contact with naval HQ, and that resulted in him being sent to Shetland — still only a boy of fifteen. "I admitted my real age — that gave me the right to change my mind at any time if I wanted to." Not surprisingly there was no immediate place for him on any of the boats, and he came in for quite a bit of boring chores. But then came a shortage of crews, and Øivind was given his chance on the *Siglaos,* with Petter Salen as skipper. Of Salen Øivind says, "He was absolutely the best," and Øivind does not bestow praise lightly. He made four or five trips on the *Siglaos,* now at the ripe old age of sixteen, then a couple of trips on an MTB, before joining Salen on the sub-chaser *Hessa.*

Jacob Roald was a young man of twenty-one in Ålesund when the Germans came. Strangely, they seemed to ignore Ålesund to begin with. Molde, not far away, was bombed, but Ålesund was almost untouched and free of the enemy. People wondered why. Was it because Kaiser Wilhelm had always liked Ålesund for his holidays? Was it because a lot of German money had helped in rebuilding the town after the great fire? No one knew, but it was away into June before the Germans arrived in force. Long before they came boats were slipping away, west over to Shetland, with young men on board. Of course the Germans soon got to know, and the Norwegians were warned. Some of those organising escapes took the hint and escaped themselves. Commenting on how resistence began to stiffen, and how the fight put up by the teachers was a great boost to morale, Jacob also remembers the Norwegians who were willing to co-operate with the enemy, and were given uniforms, in which they were soon marching round the streets, working at the airport, and so on. Then came the German move to arrest the parents of those who escaped — but that had no effect.

Jacob was working for a building firm which did business with the Germans, and one day, when his boss was away, a man came into the office, and said that some of the Norwegian collaborators were going to start work with the firm. Jacob was only a clerk, but he immediately said no. He was arrested, interrogated for a whole day, then released. Next day the collaborators started work. He was only too well aware that, from now on, he was a marked man. The time had come to get away.

He had to wait, but at last he got a place on one of the boats leaving for Shetland. "Just as I came up in a rowboat in the darkness of Ålesund harbour, a taxi came along and I was told it was no go for me, for so many people had come from Oslo with a desperate need to get away, as they were all on the Gestapo wanted list. They all duly got away in a boat which had been stolen." But on 27th October, 1941, his turn came again. A boat had been organised, and thirty-nine refugees were to be on board. They came from all over, and as usual many of them were wanted by the Gestapo. The boat was the *Haugen*. The shipyard boys had over-hauled the engine and they came along too. Though it was a big boat there was a large crowd of people, so most people lay on the floor of the hold. They had some engine trouble, but the boys from the shipyard soon had it going again. The man who was to have been skipper had disappeared. His father had refused to let him go! A man from Oslo took his place, but became seasick almost as soon as they left, disappeared below and was not seen on deck again. Jacob and some of his friends had a little sea knowledge, so they pooled what they had and set course. At least they had a compass and they knew how to steer by it.

They encountered severe gale conditions which continued for nearly two days. Huge seas had flooded the deck, but hadn't swamped the engine, though the passengers had a terrible time lying in the hold. By the time the wind fell away the deckhouse had gone, and the boys in the wheelhouse had had an unbroken stint of forty-eight hours on duty. By the Sunday evening they thought they were seeing land, but nothing was visible on Monday morning. They headed south and lay-to on Monday night. On Tuesday they saw land again, and went ashore in the small boat. From Jacob's description it appears to have been Bressay. At the first house they reached a couple of British soldiers came out and told them it was a prohibited area. "We said we were Norwegians. They asked us when and how we had come — they hadn't seen the *Haugen*. A vessel came and escorted us into Lerwick, and in due course our boat was handed over to the navy."

Standing on the quay in Lerwick, Jacob saw a rowboat which he recognised. It was from his father's ship which the Germans had requisitioned. He had seen the boat in Ålesund the previous week. It turned out that seven boys from the High School in Ålesund had come over in a motor-boat, and they had taken the rowboat along with them. The *Haugen's* passengers were kept in Shetland for seven days while they answered many questions. After all, there was a large number of them, and they all had bits of information which might prove useful. Jacob and his friends had had their suspicions about one of the men in the party. He was a Norwegian army lieutenant, whom Jacob had seen staying in the Scandinavie Hotel in Ålesund. They had been afraid of him, though another man had told them that he was OK. When the *Haugen* had left Norway it had gone along the coast for some distance in full view of any watchers, but no boat or plane had approached them, although the Germans by that time must have been aware of their departure in a stolen boat. All of that merely increased their suspicions; they had no proof. They were all sent down to London, and the lieutenant was still with them. After the war Jacob received a query about this same man. Again all he had to go on were suspicions. However, other testimony was forthcoming, and the lieutenant was brought to trial. It was established that he had been a German under-cover agent, and had gone the whole war without detection. He got eight years imprisonment.

Louis Rasmussen was a lorry-driver in Oslo when the Germans arrived. He heard on the radio what was going on, then went down to the front to see for himself. "Immediately," he says, "there was hate in my heart for the Germans. This was my country — they were taking it over — they were the enemy." His home was in Ålesund, and, a fit young man of twenty-one, he wanted to do his bit. It was no use in the south but the fighting was still going on in the north. He had just reached Ålesund when Norway capitulated. He went and joined his uncle on his farm near Ålesund, but he was constantly on the alert for a chance to get over to Shetland. Everyone knew a lot of young people were going, but there was always a waiting list. Finally the chance came. The boat was the big 76 ft *Haugen* — the same boat on which we have just seen Jacob Roald crossing. Louis also comments on the fact that the people on board came from all over Norway, and that the Walle group had had a hand in organising it. We'll meet the Walles later. Strangely, while Jacob had his suspicions about the naval lieutenant, Louis was wary of one of the young women who wanted to be put ashore shortly after they left. These suspicions mentioned by both Jacob and Louis vividly illustrate the fear of betrayal under which "good" Norwegians spent their days. Says Louis, "It was a good feeling to get into Lerwick. We were free, and we met some of our countrymen already in uniform."

In London Louis became a Linge boy very quickly, and under-

went the usual rigorous training, first outside London, then up in
Scotland, where they remained for some time seeing no action. But
that wasn't what they had come over for. A lot of the Norwegian
escapers had the feeling that Shetland was the place if you wanted
action, so he and a friend without further ado volunteered for
Shetland. They were sent north, and Louis was allocated to the Bus
boats. His stay in Shetland was interrupted when he was sent down
to Burghead, which was being used in a small way for trips to the
Norwegian coast. He was posted to the *Feie* whose skipper was Ole
Grotle, then for one trip on the *Harald*. Back in Shetland with a
name like Rasmussen it was inevitable that he should become
known as "Rasmie". He made seven trips on the *Harald,* their
calling points anywhere from Ålesund to Bømlo. She was skippered
firstly by Petter Salen and later by Olai Hillesøy. Later he served
with Leif Larsen on the *Vigra,* but in between he made one trip on
MTB 618, with Lieutenant Danielsen as commander. Their
destination was Trondheimfjord, and the two big whalers, *Risør*
and *Horten,* towed them over for part of the way, for this was a
long trip. As they closed the coast they topped up the fuel tanks,
then threw what was left of the extra fuel overboard. Cans of high
octane fuel on the deck of an MTB in action were a risky business.
Louis was manning a machine-gun, and suddenly a torpedo leapt
from one of the MTB's tubes. He thought he must have
accidentally touched the trigger. However, when he looked, he saw
that the torpedo was heading straight for a German ship, which
records show was the *Anke.* She sank.

Harald Angeltveit was chief engineer on the coast boat
Haugland in the early days of the Germans in Norway. They had
been in at Rubbestadneset one day — where the Wichmann engine
factory was situated — when the yard boat came out and took the
skipper ashore, leaving the mate in charge. They knew something
was up and they got confirmation at their next port of call, when
they were told that they were to take the boat and go to Shetland.
Harald dashed home to get his wife, a Faroese lady, and his
10-year-old daughter. His wife wanted to come but his daughter
refused point-blank, so he had to leave them both behind. They set
out with the *Haugland* on the evening of 27th November, 1941, and
by 1.30 am, on the 28th they were well out into the North Sea. By
this time a very heavy swell was running, and the forty-one
passengers, who included fourteen women and four children, were
suffering badly from seasickness. Among them were about thirty

people who were on the Gestapo wanted list, and the Germans had been getting dangerously close. Hence the episode with the captain, and the *Haugland's* hurried departure.

At one stage on the way over they found themselves in the midst of a minefield, and stopped for a time, but at last got underway again and in due course they sighted Fair Isle. They altered course to take them north to Sumburgh Head, and on that evening the sweeping flash, so familiar to the folk of the Laich Ness, was switched on and was very helpful to them. They came to Lerwick and lay outside until a patrol boat came and took them in. They were kept in Nissen huts in Lerwick for nearly a week. "I would almost call it a prison," said Harald. Then it was down to Invergordon on the trooper, and thence of course to the Patriotic School in London. In due course Harald was picked for the Shetlandsgjengen, and his first destination was Lunna. Shortly he was moved to Scalloway, and he and three others stayed with a lady whose name he cannot now remember. Her house was quite near the Royal Hotel where Arne Nipen and Per Blystad were staying, and they had some of their meals there. Harald became chief engineer for the Bus boats, and was shore-based. He reckons that the shore-based boys had the easiest job. In off-duty hours they went fishing, caught lobsters and shot cormorants. On one occasion when the roads were blocked with snow, Harald and two or three of the men from Norway House were asked to take one of the boats and transport mails and supplies to a number of points around Shetland. They loaded nearly a full cargo at Blacksness, and men from the Department of Supply and the Post Office came with them. They spent a full day on their round, and it was long dark by the time they got back to Blacksness.

Harald stayed on in Scalloway until July, 1945, and his memories of Shetland are warm and nostalgic. "We worked in unison with the Shetland people in every way," he says. "They are the best. They were very fine people to mix with in every way. Those of us who lived in Scalloway came to know a lot of people, among them many fishermen. We became friendly with a lot of people in Lerwick, too, where they liked us to come and visit." Mrs Davidson in Breiwick Road remembers Harald well, when he came to call on the Norwegian boys who stayed with her.

Kåre Mørk was on a merchant ship going north to Kirkenes on the day the Germans invaded. His home was in Trondelag, north of Trondheim. When the raids on Måløy and the Lofotens took place at Christmas, 1941, Kåre was at Svolvaer in the Lofotens, a member of the crew of the coastal steamer *Kong*

Harald, operating under German control. Kåre was among the escapers who came over with the ships of the raiding parties, and they were taken to Thurso, where they were put on a special train to London. They were all in civilian clothing. The usual screening took place, and he took it for granted that he would go to the merchant navy. But the grapevine had it that there was a chance of immediate action, so he joined the Kompani Linge, now sadly bereft of the man who had given it its name. He spent several weeks in a private house in London, which seemed to be run by the Secret Service, and there he began to learn English. Next it was a Commando course, run by British officers, just outside London, and from there up to Scotland for final training. The next step was up to Shetland, and to a place on his first Bus boat, the *Andholmen,* skippered by Johannes Nessen.

Edvard Pettersen's attempts at getting away from Norway and joining the fight for freedom were beset by many frustrations. At the time the Germans came he was in Lofoten waters at the fishing. A big plane went over — the biggest they had ever seen — and it had black crosses on its wings. They could also see the dim loom of a very large vessel appearing and disappearing as the snow showers came and went. They didn't know what it all meant, and they didn't hear, until many hours later when they came in to land their catch, that Norway had been invaded. It didn't take Edvard and his friends long to decide that they wanted nothing to do with the Germans, and they made for the Swedish border. But when they crossed the Swedes apprehended them and sent them back under escort. They came back on a Swedish train which was stopped at the border and rigorously searched by the Germans. Everyone without satisfactory papers was put off, and Edvard was one of those. Held prisoner for some time he was eventually sent back to Narvik by train. One of the railway bridges had been badly damaged in the fighting at Narvik, and was still not properly repaired, so only half the train was allowed to cross. The other half was uncoupled and left in a siding all day. Edvard was in that half.

Having arrived back at Narvik he was ordered out of the train, escorted on to the fjord boat, and left. He stayed at home in Tysfjorden util the autumn of 1941. Then, with forced labour for young men looming, he and four friends once more headed for the Swedish border. After plodding on for two and a half days they reached the frontier and crossed. This time they were not sent back, but after lengthy interrogation they were sent to work in the forests. Edvard was very discontented. Then one day a Norwegian inspector came round, and Edvard appealed to him to get him away. Four days later he was asked if he was willing to go on. "Anywhere, as long as it's out of this forest," he said. Soon he was taken to Stockholm, and there was interviewed by a British officer, who eventually divulged their main concern. The Shetlandsgjengen had been losing boats and needed men urgently. Was he willing? "I didn't leave Norway to cut wood," he replied.

In due course he was on a plane to Scotland, and then to the Patriotic School, where his interrogation was devoted in the main to establishing the best points at which to cross the Swedish frontier. Special training in the Highlands of Scotland was followed by a posting to Burghead, where the *Harald* and the *Andholmen* were temporarily stationed, and then it was on to Scalloway. The sub-chasers arrived shortly afterwards, and he was made an engineer on the *Hitra,* but unfortunately an infection hospitalised him. When he came out he was sent to Aberdeen on the *Andholmen*. Eidsheim wanted him back on *Hitra,* but Nessen in the *Andholmen* held on to him.

Torleif Fagertun was in Kristiansand in south Norway when the Germans invaded. They left harbour almost immediately, and when they came outside they saw, floating in the water, the bodies of German soldiers from a sunk German ship. (*This may have been the 'Rio de Janeiro' sunk on the previous day.*) They went up as far as Austevoll, which is not far from Bergen, but his home was in north Norway. He knew that fighting was still going on there, so he and two friends were determined to get in on it. All three of them were under twenty, and they now took a rowing-boat, and set out on a marathon row of over three hundred miles to their homes. The boat was very much on the lines of a Ness yoal, and they each rowed a pair of oars. The enormity of the journey they had undertaken didn't daunt them. "We were young and strong," says Torleif.

On the way north a German patrol started firing at them from a mountainside, but fortunately their aim was poor and there were no hits. The boys decided that they would row into the shore and face the Germans. They were met with bullying questions, but of course they couldn't speak German, so a German/Norwegian phrase-book was produced. "You seamen?" "Yes," and more in the same vein. Clearly the Germans didn't know what to do with them, so after a lot more bullying bluster they were allowed to go on. It took them a fortnight to row north to Helgeland, but they reached home on 2nd June. A week later Norway capitulated, so that was that.

Torleif endured the Germans until 1942, by which time the

pressure on young men to work for the enemy was getting much
more intense. He had no intention of doing any such thing, so he
knew it was time to get away. His way was over the mountains, and
across the Swedish border. In Sweden he was kept working as a
forester for a couple of months. Then it was down to Stockholm,
and final escape to Scotland by air, in a small plane carrying only
five passengers. He remembers the Patriotic School by this time
was generally known as "Sing-Sing", and after his screening there
he underwent a course of military training at Skegness, a five
weeks' gunnery course at Dumbarton, and then to Burghead,
where he was to spend several months doing Commando training.
It was 1943 before he was sent to Shetland, where almost at once he
found himself on the sub-chasers, making six trips with the *Vigra*
and thirty-four on the *Hessa*.

Hans Bakkland probably had a harder road than anyone to
tread before he got to Shetland. He was living away up in north
Norway at the time of the invasion, about a hundred miles from the
little town of Kirkenes. The Germans didn't appear in the far north
immediately — probably the fighting at Narvik engaged their full
attention for a time. While they waited the people in the north
actually raised a battalion to go south and help in the fight. When
the Germans did come Hans went to Kirkenes to work, and was
very soon involved with the underground. The nearest escape point
was Russia, and he planned to hijack the pilot-boat to make a
getaway. But hardly anyone else was prepared to take the risk. So
he set off for Russia single-handed in a small sailing-boat, but he
was stopped and sent back. Next he went down to Tromsø to stay
with relatives, but he had no ration card, etc., and he was keen to
try again. He and a friend successfully crossed the border into
Sweden, and the two of them were given work on a farm near
Stockholm. But that was far too tame a life for Hans at a time
when the hated Germans were lording it in his homeland. Soon he
managed to become a Linge boy through the SOE contacts at the
British Legation, and for a time he led a dangerous, cloak-and-
dagger existence, acting as guide, courier and adviser to groups
trying to cross the border from Norway into Sweden. He changed
his name to Kristoffersen, and time and again he made the
dangerous crossing, carrying a gun when on the Norwegian side,
and leaving it secretly hidden when coming into Sweden, its
location known only to himself and his Swedish contact. The
conditions under which he worked, and the risks he repeatedly ran
would have graced the pages of any fictional spy thriller. On one
occasion one of the women escapers, while still on the Norwegian

side, started to scream uncontrollably through sheer tension and fear. Hans took her in his arms, talked quietly to her, reminded her of what would happen to them all if she didn't control herself, and gradually her screaming subsided, and they went on to make a safe crossing.

That should have been a life sufficiently exciting for anyone. But Hans had set out originally to make his way to Britain, and he had never abandoned that aim. Once more he was off, this time down to southern Sweden, his single-minded determination as strong as ever. With two friends he set sail in a small boat from near Göteborg. A Swedish guard boat picked them up, and this time they were held under guard. But Hans was resilient. A woman working nearby took a message from him to the Norwegian consulate. The message was effective — after all he was a Linge boy — and soon he was at the British Embassy. It was now 1943, and arrangements were made to fly him to Scotland. But the RAF plane on which he was supposed to fly was full up, and he couldn't get on. The next plane was also full, but one passenger got off, and Hans got the vacant place. It was all very fortunate for him — the first plane was shot down but the plane in which he travelled reached Scotland safely. Clearly a number of Norwegians were crossing the North Sea by air at this stage of the war, and Hans concurs in this supposition, believing that the numbers crossing were considerably higher than most people have thought.

As usual it was the Patriotic School, then Commando training up in Scotland. He was now classed as a Kompani Linge marine Commando. Next he had a period of wireless operator training, so clearly he was earmarked for agent's work in Norway. But he had heard vague stories about the Shetlandsgjengen, and if any of it was true, then it sounded just the sort of thing he wanted. So he volunteered. He was sent to Buckie, and from there came north on the *Siglaos*. The sub-chasers were to arrive soon afterwards, but before they came he made a couple of trips on MTB 618, the same one Louis Rasmussen went on. He was then posted to the *Vigra,* and made every one of her forty-two trips. He made many friends in Shetland, and has always retained a strong liking for the islands. As late as 1987 he made a visit to friends in Burra Isle.

The events which led to Rolf Nordhus becoming part of the Shetland Bus were a little out of the ordinary. He had been living on Stord, not far from Leirvik, when the Germans came, at the time aged seventeen-and-a-half. He was already a fisherman on a big herring boat, filling in when not at the fishing with forestry work. His first act of defiance against the Germans was just after they invaded. He and his brother saw a Dornier seaplane coming over, and they dashed inside for the family shotgun and started firing at it. Some of the neighbours were highly disapproving of their actions — they thought it was asking for trouble. The boys hated the Germans, but to begin with there was very little they could do to give expression to that hatred.

After a time Rolf came to Bergen, where some of his mother's women friends were already involved in underground work, and he became their only male assistant. When the women heard of someone in danger and desperately trying to evade the Gestapo, Rolf was called on to act as guide in getting the fugitive to a place of safety. "I was just a young country boy, and in German eyes that made me a little simple. They took very little notice of me, so I was able to do the job for some time without attracting attention."

But in 1943 an informer gave the Gestapo his name. He had to get away. "Along with the last man we helped to escape the Gestapo I set off for Shetland on board the *Start*. She was quite a big boat, 62 ft of keel." (*Another 'Start', a 25 ft open boat, reached the Fair Isle in 1944 with two boys on board. Their crossing had been extremely dangerous.*) When Rolf's *Start* was in the middle of the North Sea the engine packed in. To make matters worse a severe gale had blown up. They had a makeshift sail on board, but they didn't dare to hoist it in case it was whipped away by the wind. They drifted helplessly for five days until they were almost back at the Norwegian coast.

Now the wind was a little easier and they hoisted the sail. When they came in past the Utvaer lighthouse they knew where they were, but they didn't go right in because they knew they would encounter Germans. They cruised up and down until daylight, when they were just off Husøy. The approach was extremely rocky and dangerous, but they went in, Rolf standing in the bows watching the rocks and shouting directions to the helmsman. They made it, and got into the fjord just in time to see the German guard boat passing outside. They holed up in a sort of cove with a north-west entrance. When a sea was running nothing could get in. They lay there for fourteen days. A German plane came over, and a German boat appeared at the entrance to the cove, but the heavy sea prevented her getting in. The danger they were in had become very pressing, and they decided to get away. They left on foot, and not a moment too soon as the Germans arrived overland at the cove next morning looking for them.

They had two Englishmen with them, Basil Morris and Jimmy Holmes, who, Rolf says, had been involved with midget submarines in Bergen harbour. Perhaps it was their presence which now caused London to arrange for an MTB to come over and pick them up, the date, according to MTB records, being 7th October, 1943. Rolf was of course sent down to London for screening, then a short period of training at Skegness, before being sent straight to Scalloway. By this time it was 1944, and the sub-chasers had arrived. His first billet was Norway House, and an immediate posting to the *Hitra,* with skipper Ingvald Eidsheim. Rolf's experiences in Scalloway were both exciting and amusing, and we shall come to him again.

Note: Rolf's comments about two Englishmen involved with midget submarines in Bergen harbour are interesting, because in 1944 two highly successful attacks were made in that harbour by the same midget submarine X24. On the first occasion the midget was towed over by the submarine *Sceptre* to within 35 miles of the Norwegian coast. Departure point was Burrafirth in the north of Unst, and the target was the German floating dock at Laksevåg in Bergen harour. The attack was made successfully except for one snag. The midget sank a large merchant ship instead of the dock. Nothing daunted, a second attempt was made in September, using the same midget. This time departure was from Baltasound, on 7th September, but they met with atrocious weather on the way over and one of the midget's crew was lost. However they pressed on into Bergen and this time the dock was well and truly sunk, and the little submarine made a clean getaway.

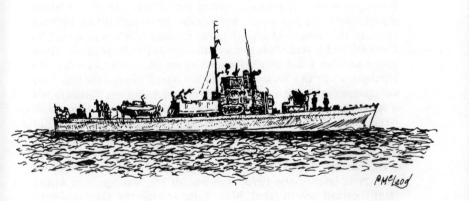

Chapter Nine

The *Olaf*

The boys of the Shetland bus were well accustomed to danger. It came in various guises. The enemy was bad enough — they ran the risk of a face-to-face confrontation with Germans on every trip they made. But bad as that danger was, they considered the sea to be even worse. Every voyage was made in the darkness of winter when the roaring winds frequently whipped the North Sea to a cauldron. And they had to come in on a rocky coast in pitch blackness, without a glim of light to help. Their lives depended on quick reactions and steely courage. But they also depended on their boats and their engines. If either was less than first class their chances were slim.

There was nothing special about the *Olaf*. Indeed, though a typical fishing boat from Norway's west coast, she was smaller than most of the boats used for the Shetland Bus. She had reached Lerwick on 30th September, 1941, from Vigra, with seventeen people on board, the escape having been organised by the Walle group. She had been stolen, but in that she was no different from many of the others. After arriving in Shetland she lay at anchor in Catfirth, and it was while she was there that Per Blystad and Arne Nipen saw her when they were passing on their way to Lunna. To Howarth's surprise Blystad fancied her, small though she was, and volunteered to fit her out and make her ready for the "Bus trade" if he could go as her skipper. Howarth agreed. Arne Nipen and Arne Lerøy were the men charged with taking the *Olaf* down to Lerwick. Her engine was out of order and they had to tow her with the *Fernanda,* a Telavåg boat which had brought thirty-six people across on 21st September, among them Knut Svendsen whom we shall meet later. Arne Lerøy was one of the two brothers whose family owned the ill-fated *Blia*. After towing the *Olaf* down to Lerwick the boys had to take the *Fernanda* back to Catfirth, then retrace every inch of the way to Lerwick on foot. They got a room for the night, but it had been a long day. Says Nipen, "We were tired and fed up. During the night a severe storm sprang up, and the complete window in our room blew in. I slept through the lot.''

After a few necessary repairs at the Malakoff, Per and Nipen took the *Olaf* round the Heads to Scalloway. ''It was an awful trip. Everything stood on end. The engine was far from 100%, and there were only the two of us on board.'' They anchored in Scalloway, but on the very first night another storm raged, and despite putting out extra borrowed hawsers, the boat sustained some damage. But to them belonged the honour of being the first Norwegians to take up residence in Scalloway, and they got accommodation with Mrs Blance at the Royal Hotel. Arne didn't have a word of English and relied entirely on Per to do his translating for him. Per was an able man, fluent in several languages including English. He had a habit of becoming completely absorbed in any task on which he was engaged, and was capable of working perhaps thirty-six hours virtually non-stop, perhaps in pouring rain, and then turn in to sleep in the same sodden state. Mrs Moore used to invite him up for a meal, and Jack Moore remembers him well. ''If you had had a regiment of Per Blystads,'' comments Jack, ''they would have gone through anything.''

The two friends worked away at the *Olaf,* and when Per was on a working jag Arne would go up to the hotel, primed by Per with the English words he had to say, and repeating them to himself all the way up. Then like a parrot he would tell Mrs Blance, ''My friend come at eight o'clock.'' They complemented each other well — Arne's love of mischief contrasting with Per's more serious outlook. And as they worked they got to know many of the Scalloway people, and vice versa. Says Arne, ''As the days went by I got to know every stone in the road along the front. Even though I still couldn't speak English I was making friends. I found it quite easy to communicate with the girls, even though I couldn't speak their language.'' (*He certainly manged to communicate with lovely, 18-year-old Baba Christie, for she married him on 27th January, 1944.*) Jack Moore, in his ususal practical way, reckons that the girls were the best aid to the Norwegians learning English. ''The girls were long-haired dictionaries,'' he says.

With Per as skipper and Arne as engineer, they made a preliminary trip on the *Siglaos* in December, 1941, and then it was back to putting the finishing touches to the *Olaf.* She was finally ready for sea. Her engine had been reconditioned at Moores' shipyard, even though the yard had only limited experience of the Norwegian semi-diesels. But apart from Jack Moore the yard did have a remarkable engineer — James Thomson. Arne says of him,

"Jeemsie was very good. He was the best engineer I have ever known. He could do anything with an engine. Anything you weren't sure about you just asked Jeemsie. He would help. He could make anything."

The *Olaf's* first trip was to Telavåg, Arne's home village, where she landed supplies and agent Tor Gulbrandsen. On her second trip fate attempted to throw her and young Starheim together. Linge's death at Måløy had been a sad blow to his friends, particularly young Starheim, who grieved at the memory of how he and Martin's fiancée had seen him off on his ill-fated trip. His death left a huge gap in the Norwegian section of SOE. But new plans were made and Starheim was eager to be part of them. He was dropped back into Norway by parachute, his task to arrange for a new transmitter to be established near Oslo, and also for the reception of a load of arms. The operator was to be Frederik Aaros, arms instructor to be Thor Hugo van der Hagen, and these two would come over on the *Olaf,* along with the consignment of arms. Both the boys had been on the Lofoten raid, and the *Olaf* was to await Starheim's signal to come. Starheim had found the organisation he had established on his previous mission to be in good heart, and he went on to visit his contact in Oslo, Korsvig Rasmussen. While there the Gestapo burst in to arrest Korsvig, and, though Starheim was caught up in the confusion, he managed to escape through the bathroom, and got away with the help of a "good" Norwegian lorry driver. Korsvig underwent severe Gestapo torture, but he managed to hang himself before he could be forced to give anything away. When you fell into the hands of the Gestapo death was nearly always more welcome than life. Free again, Starheim sent his message for the *Olaf* to come.

Arne remembers the trip, though of course he didn't know the background. They had both the Linge boys and the arms on board, and they made land at Utsira lighthouse off Karmøy, which they knew was much too far north. Their destination was near Egersund, and they accordingly headed south. It was mid-February, and the early weeks of 1942 had brought very severe wintry conditions to Norway's west and south coasts. There was a great deal of pack ice in the area near Egersund, and try as they might they could not find a clear lead by which they could get into their scheduled landing place. Finally they had to abandon the attempt. They turned and went out, and set course for Shetland. It was 8.30 am, a bad time to be leaving an enemy occupied coast, but they had no option. Sure enough, a Messerschmidt 109 appeared overhead about 11.30 am, and started machine-gunning them. Says

Arne, "I had just come on deck from the engine room, and I saw the plane coming up from behind. I ran forward and shouted to the crew — there were two in the wheelhouse, the rest below. Arne Albertsen in the wheelhouse grabbed the Bren, and started firing almonst immediately, before the rest of the crew could bring anything to bear. He shot the b------ down. He came down in the sea about a hundred yards in front of us."

An hour after the first plane had been shot down a Heinkel 111 appeared on the scene and bombed them, but this time they were all ready and opened fire with Bren, Lewis and everything they'd got. They damaged him, and he made off towards the land which he only just managed to reach as they heard later. The hard work put in by Per and Arne in Scalloway making the *Olaf* ready for just such a trip paid off. They had filled the gap between the inner and outer skins of the wheelhouse with concrete, and had made a kind of loophole for the Bren on each side. Forard and aft a half-inch steel sheet had been fastened on the inside of the bulwarks. Though the *Olaf* sustained considerable damage during these attacks, there were no casualties — at least no human ones. But down in the hold, where two gallon jars of rum had been lying on top of the arms, a bullet had smashed one, and the contents were lost. Everyone now felt that after the morning's experiences a stimulant was both necessary and in perfect order. "So we took the remaining jar of rum and poured out a generous tot for each man, then filled the jar up again with water. We didn't half feel small when we tied up at the little pier at Lunna, and the first man down to us was Sergeant Sherwood with a bottle of rum in his hand for us." (*Sherwood was one of Howarth's NCOs.*)

But what of Starheim, who had been anxiously awaiting the *Olaf's* arrival? He had heard of her difficulties in the pack ice, and that she would neither be able to land agents and arms, nor pick him up and take him back to Shetland. He also had the problem of getting Einar Skinnerland over to Britain, because he was carrying, in a brief case, a great deal of information about the factory at Vemork near Rjukan in Telemark. We know now that this was the heavy-water plant, but at the time little was known either about the factory or its purpose. All Skinnerland knew was that he was in possession of information of the utmost importance, which was clearly also top secret. With the *Olaf* unable to land, Starheim was not a man to sit back and do nothing. He decided they would take over one of the coast steamers, and sail her to Aberdeen. That sort of bold, fearless concept was typical of the short life of this remarkable young man. The steamers he considered included *Kong*

Harald, Vestri, Austri, Tromøsund and *Galtesund.* It was an audacious plan, even more so when one considers he intended using only six men. Skinnerland was to be one of them, but before they could put the plan into action Skinnerland badly damaged a knee. It required an operation, which had to be carried out in secret. At the young man's insistence it was done without the use of anaesthetic, and never for a moment, even while on the operating table, did he relinquish hold of the precious case. Instinctively he knew that what he was carrying had momentous implications.

The *Galtesund,* a ship of 620 tons, was the one finally chosen for this daring venture. The hijacking party consisted of six men who included the crippled Skinnerland. Though in great pain he played his part. Apart from the crew, who numbered seventeen seamen, two pilots and two stewardesses, there was only one passenger on board. To cut a long story short (it is told in full in "Mannen som Stjal Galtesund" or "Salt Water Thief"), Starheim was successful in getting the crew's and pilots' acquiescence when it became clear that they had no option. On land his friend Tom radioed London at an agreed time saying the *Galtesund* was on her way, hijacked, and asked the British to provide an escort. They soon had a Catalina flying with them, and later two fighters arrived to add to their air cover. It was a triumphant entry into Aberdeen, and not surprisingly Starheim received the highest British decoration for which he was eligible — the DSO. It was a deed of great courage, organisation and determination, and history has perhaps given it less attention than it deserves. But we will meet Starheim again. Tor-Hugo, unable to land from the *Olaf,* was parachuted into Norway.

In March the *Olaf* went up to Silda, not far from Måløy, to pick up Thoralf and Lilly Walle, the heads of an "export" group on the run from the Gestapo. We will look at that story in another chapter. Then on 17th April, 1942, she made another trip to Telavåg. There she landed two Linge boys, Arne Vaerum and Emil Hvaal. Vaerum was to go to Stavanger, Hvaal to Oslo. The boat crews never asked any questions of the agents they carried. It was tacitly recognised that the less anyone knew, the better — just in case. Of these two Arne Nipen says, "They were fine fellows. One of them was an excellent cook and made us some smashing soup. It was the only trip I ever remember making to the Norwegian coast from Shetland when the sea was so smooth. I could sit on the hatch cover with a plate of soup on my knee and not spill a drop." When Arne points to the little fjord at Telavåg where the *Olaf* came in more than once to land men and supplies, it seems incredible that they could have taken the risks they did. He matter-of-factly recalls going ashore in Telavåg on one trip, and was walking along just past the bridge over the little fjord when he met his sister-in-law. They both recognised each other as they passed, but neither gave the slightest sign of recognition, and no word passed between them. One could never be sure who was watching or listening. Vaerum and Hvaal now went to stay with Laurits and Marthe Telle, and the arms landed from the *Olaf* were also stored in the village. Arne sadly left his native village, and the *Olaf* went farther north and picked up eight refugees to take back to Shetland with them. They had no foreboding of the events which were about to follow in Telavåg.

Telavåg

Perhaps the fact that something like 10% of the Telavåg population had already escaped west over to Shetland, and that so far the village had had little attention from the Germans, although they must have known what was going on, had engendered a sort of complacency among people like Laurits Telle, who was helping both escapers and Linge boys. But almost certainly whispers which had gone out from the village, possibly naming names, had reached the ears of the Gestapo. Hindsight can tell us that for Vaerum and Hvaal to stay almost openly with the Telles was asking for trouble. After all they had everything with them they would have needed to live rough for a few days, with a minimum of risk to anyone else. But at the time there was no thought of danger.

It was now that two state policemen came to Telavåg, one posing as a bookseller, the other as a would-be Shetland escaper. They were nazi under-cover men, and it is now clear that they knew something. The pretended escaper, Per Hansen, made his way to the Telles' house, and asked Laurits if he could arrange a passage to Shetland for him. Laurits was unsuspecting. He told him there was no boat going at present. Marthe and Elisabeth, Laurits' wife and daughter, were not so trusting. A simple phone call was enough to tell them that the address Hansen had given them as his home was false. However by that time it was probably too late to have altered the course of events. Hansen had already jubilantly told his fellow-nazi all that he had learned, and the Gestapo in Bergen were immediately informed.

Next day was Sunday. Early in the morning German troops came ashore from the Customs' launch and more from a mine-sweeper. It was a big show of force; the plan was to go directly to the Telles' house. Hansen led the way, with Behrens, a top Gestapo man, just behind him. Behrens was very important indeed, being a personal friend of Terboven's. Beside Behrens was his second-in-command, Bertram, and immediately behind him the much-hated Gestapo man, Klötscher. This remarkable array of top-level Gestapo brass indicated the great importance the Germans attached to getting their hands on members of the Shetlandsgjengen.

The Telle family were already up. Suddenly daughter Elisabeth cried out — grey shadows were coming from the darkness near the house. They were carrying pistols and guns, and before anyone could warn the Linge boys upstairs, they had burst in, rushing from room to room and then upstairs. Clearly this was a moment to be savoured by the Germans, and Behrens, Bertram and Klötscher led the way. Vaerum and Hvaal were ordered out of bed and told to get dressed. Four Gestapo men stood watching with pistols at the ready. Vaerum bent down to pick up his trousers, and as he straightened knocked Behrens to the floor and almost in the same movement grabbed his pistol and shot him through the head, rapidly getting off a second shot at Klötscher, who fell, wounded. The two remaining Germans fired at Vaerum, and killed him. Meanwhile Hvaal had also grabbed a German pistol and shot Bertram, but fell, wounded by a bullet from the fourth German. Young Åge Telle, who had been sleeping in the room with the Linge boys, dashed for the door and the stairs, a bullet just missing him as he went. Of the six men in the room a few moments before, two high-ranking German officers were dead and a third wounded, one Linge boy was dead, and the other badly wounded. Leaving aside for a moment the tragic events which were to follow, this was an heroic performance by the Linge boys, and a tremendous vindication of the rigorous training they all underwent in Britain. But what they had done was a searing blow to German pride. Revenge was inevitable.

In the evening the Telles were dragged off to prison, as were other supposed ringleaders, such as Joseph Øvretveit and Karl Nipen — and of course poor Hvaal. Vaerum's body was stuck in a sack and thrown in the sea. But nobody thought for a moment that was the end of German action. Terboven would never allow the death of his friend and the affront to his dignity to pass without suitable reprisals. He hadn't been a gauleiter in the Ruhr for nothing. He had told the Norwegian people, "We have tried to win you over with kindness without result. If you won't learn to love us, we will make sure that you fear us." He came to Telavåg to supervise the punishment in person. The seventy-six men between

16. The little fjord in Telavåg where the *Olaf* landed agents and supplies.

17. Arne and Baba Nipen at home in Klokkarvik, Sotra, 1987.

18. The Roll of Honour on the memorial in Telavåg.

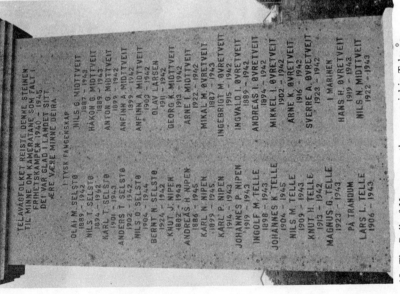

19. A German woman's apology beside the memorial in Telavåg.

16 and 60, having first been told that they would all be blown up, were assembled to watch while the Telle house and those of other suspected ringleaders were blown up. Then, having seen the prescribed action duly commenced, he went back to Bergen to attend the grandiose funerals of Behrens and Bertram. On the same day the seventy-six men were brought to Bergen, en route to concentration camps in Germany.

On 1st May the Germans collected all the women, children and old people. The oldest woman was ninety-three, and had to be carried. The youngest were ten babies. They also had to be carried. They were all sent to a special prison. In all 268 human beings were uprooted and sent away. Every animal was driven away — sheep, cattle, dogs, cats — every living thing. Then every building was set on fire and razed to the ground. The fires smouldered for days, but the village of Telavåg was no more. It had been wiped off the face of the earth. Of the seventy-six men sent to the concentration camps thirty-one failed to survive. And the Germans gained sufficient information from their prey to lead them to several other underground organisations in Stavanger, Bulandet and Oslo.

Today the village of Telavåg has been rebuilt. A new house stands on the site of the building which was once Arne Nipen's home. When he came back at the end of the war all that remained to remind him of home were bits of a sewing machine among the rubble of stones. Nearby stands a beautiful memorial bearing the names of Telavåg people who died through German brutality. Quite close is another stone, erected apparently by a German woman, expressing regret at the terrible treatment meted out to the villagers. Arne's new home is only a mile or two away. It was some time after the tragedy before he got the news. "It's all a long time ago. Nursing bitterness does no one any good." That trip to Telavåg was the last made by the *Olaf* during the 41/42 winter season. It was during the summer that her skipper, Per Blystad, went over with the little *Sjø* and was captured. He was never heard from again, and almost certainly the Germans shot him.

Chapter Ten

The Bus Comes to Scalloway

The 1941/42 winter had gone well from the Shetland Bus point of view. The boats had carried out a large number of successful trips — over forty in fact. Forty-three agents had been landed and nine picked up. 130 tons of arms and equipment had been put ashore, and 45 refugees brought back to Shetland. The Germans were now well aware of the existence of the Shetlandsgjengen, and very conscious of the potential danger they posed. Norwegians everywhere talked about the Shetland Bus, and many had already had cause to bless it. But with the lighter spring nights bringing a cessation of Shetland/Norway traffic, it was time to rethink the situation.

Lunna had been attractive because of its very remoteness. But that sometimes had inherent drawbacks. First and foremost was the question of repairs and maintenance. Very little could be done at Lunna, and the Malakoff yard, which had been doing most of the work they required, was becoming increasingly swamped by Admiralty work. Secondly, it was clear that Shetlanders did not pose a security risk. They knew when to keep their mouths shut. Thirdly, and perhaps even more importantly, was the problem of occupying the men's time when ashore. There was nothing for them to do at Lunna. And yet they were lively, virile, young men, with a great deal of steam and surplus energy to be found an outlet. This was especially so when they returned from a lengthy trip to the Norwegian coast, their lives having been in almost constant danger from the moment they left home base in Lunna. Relief of the tension which had built up was a necessity. Lerwick was the nearest place for anything like a "night out", but it was many miles away over roads that left a lot to be desired. And the base's transport was, in the main, a truck and a shooting-brake. That they made their way to Lerwick whenever possible goes without saying. That their behaviour was reasonably restrained, even with pockets better lined than those of British servicemen or Shetland civilians, was a considerable tribute to these young men.

The time for a move had come. The question was — where? To Lerwick — or to Scalloway? The answer was quickly arrived at — it was Scalloway. David Howarth was later to say, "We went to Scalloway entirely because of Jack Moore's workshop." A number of aspects of the Scalloway situation obviously influenced him, but there is no doubt that Jack's workshop, containing as it did every conceivable item that men might need when messing about with boats, held a great fascination for him. Of Jack he said, "Jack himself was the hardest worker I've ever met in my life. He never knocked off till midnight, and was always back on the job at seven o'clock."

The firm of William Moore and Sons in Scalloway was a family business, and in 1942 Jack was the driving force, with his brother Bob working as fitter and James Thomson as turner and engineer. Jack's father, though an old man, was still doing some blacksmith work. The bulk of the firm's work before the war had been among fishing boats, and that included quite a few Norwegians. Since the Shetland Bus had started up they had also done a number of jobs for the Bus boats, both at Lunna and at Lerwick. But with the decision to base the Bus at Scalloway the firm was freed from Admiralty work, and they devoted their full-time efforts to servicing the Norwegian boats. Inherent in the arrangement was the agreement to allow Norwegian tradesmen to work with Shetlanders in the yard, and soon the workforce contained eight Shetlanders and six Norwegians. The two leading Norwegians we have already met — Harald Angeltveit, chief engineer, and Sevrin Roald from Vigra, chief shipwright. Sevrin had his wife with him, and she lived with Mrs Young in Houl Road.

Jack had been involved in work for the British services since the outbreak of war. He had done a number of jobs for them, and in 1940 he was in Fair Isle, connecting water and sanitation facilities in a camp being prepared for a party of soldiers who were to be billeted in the Isle. While there he got an SOS to come with his portable welding plant to Sumburgh. Moores' possessed the only such plant in Shetland. Arriving at Sumburgh he found that the work required had to do with the radar set. Radar was still in its infancy — even the word was a novelty — and it was very highly secret. At this stage the Germans didn't even know that Britain had it. But an experimental set had been sent up to Sumburgh airport, and the whole thing was sited on the top of Sumburgh Head. It had an aerial which was controlled by a man sitting on a contraption like a pushbike. When he pedalled the aerial turned. The thing had already given trouble, and Jack, a master of improvisation, had made it much stronger by adapting a Ford Ten back end drawn from the voluminous stock of bits and pieces in his workshop. This time a gale had caused the aerial to lean drunkenly right over the edge of Sumburgh Head. Needless to say Jack succeeded in effecting the necessary repairs, and then he stood in the control room watching while the operator tried it out. He saw a spot on the screen, but he made no comment. He knew he shouldn't really be in the control room at all. As he came out he asked an officer the time. On being told he realised that the spot on the screen was almost certainly Highland Airway's Rapide which was due in at Sumburgh in about ten minutes' time. The radar had shown it probably twenty or thirty miles to the south. Jack must surely have been the first Shetlander to see radar actually in operation.

His first work in connection with the Shetland Bus was when he was asked to come to Sullom Voe — again with his welding plant. There on the beach lay a vessel about 25 ft long. Its tow hook had broken off, and Jack's job was to weld a new one. A simple job, he thought, until he was told the craft's cargo was TNT, and only a small space fo'r'ard had been cleared behind the hook to allow him to work. He did the job in small stages — he didn't think it was wise to generate too much heat! From then onwards he began making trips to Lunna for repair jobs. But the whole thing came nearer home when the firm was asked to put down moorings in Scalloway harbour for a number of Norwegian boats — and Moores had to find the anchors. They actually put down seven or eight, and Jack confirms that our old friend the *Olaf* with Per and Arne on board, was the first to arrive and "take up residence".

There had been troops in Scalloway for some time. The RAF who manned the two air-sea rescue launches were at Castle Camp, the Artillery at Berry Camp, and the public hall was a 100-bed hospital, with the RAMC in Nissen huts beside the hall. The Norwegians added another seventy or eighty men, later rising to over 100, so that in all, in this little village of 1000 people, there were probably more servicemen than villagers. The First War produced a barbed-wire mentality among military brass, and when this highly secret operation was moved to Scalloway, the powers that be immediately said the village would have to be ringed with rolls of barbed wire. To the villagers it seemed that doubts were being cast on their discretion. And they didn't like the idea of living in a prison camp, sealed off from the outside world by barbed wire.

20. Prince Olaf slipway, Scalloway.

21. Norway House — to become a garage after the war.

22. Moores' slipway staff, with sub-chaser as background, early 1945. David Howarth in centre holds the base's plaque with "Alt for Norge" inscription. Shetlanders in back row, on right, are Loll Anderson, Hugh Hughson and John Williamson; centre row, right, Anna Smith and Helen Smith; front row, right, James Thomson, Jack Moore and Cecil Duncan; third left, front row, Bob Moore. Chief Nor. shipwright Sevrin Roald is next to Anna, and chief Nor. engineer, Harald Angeltveit, is on Howarth's right in back row.

However, wiser counsels prevailed, and no wire was ever used. And no Scallowegian ever breathed a word which might have endangered the boys of the Bus.

A slipway for the new operation was an absolute priority. There was only one slipway in Shetland, and that was at the Malakoff. Howarth was allocated £750 with which to build a slipway. It wasn't much and everything had to be done on the cheap. He bought some second-hand rails in Aberdeen, and brought them north "They were very second-hand," says Jack. "We had to straighten most of them." The winch was brought from the top of a hill in Fair Isle. The engine came from a wrecked boat, and the highly necessary fairlead was dug out of the concrete at Broonie's Taing. The Taing trustees were not overly pleased — after all they hadn't been consulted! The concrete ramp was run 170 feet below low water level, and when the sub-chasers arrived it was extended to take boats up to 110 feet. All that was followed by the building of a pier, and in October, 1942, Prince Olaf came north and was delighted to have the slipway given his name. The Commemorative plaque is still on the wall close by Main Street.

Now the boats began to arrive and they included the *Heland, Aksel, Feie, Arthur, Andholmen, Sandøy, Harald, Bergholm, Siglaos* and *Feiøy*. The *Bergholm, Brattholm, Andholmen* and *Sandøy* were all big 75 ft whaling vessels which had been released from their duties up in Iceland. Accommodation for the crews when ashore was provided in the old net store, now rechristened "Norway House", and in Nissen huts at the back. The men slept in the loft where conditions were hardly luxurious and far from warm. Some of the boys remember waking in the morning, their blankets covered with a dusting of snow which had silted in through roof weak spots. Other office and store accommodation was taken over along Main Street, and the house called 'Dinapore' became the HQ. Patrick Stewart could hardly have guessed that one day his castle would house explosives and ammunition to be used against a German enemy.

During 1941 the Shetlandsgjengen had got a great deal of their up-to-the-minute information about the disposal of German forces on Norway's west coast from the ceaseless flow of refugees who came west over to Shetland. But during the summer of 1942 the flow had slowed to a trickle. Up-to-date information was dangerously lacking. Per Blystad volunteered to put it right. He would go during the summer months in a small open boat exactly similar to hundreds of others on the Norwegian coast, and gather the necessary details. We have already seen Per's activities with the

Olaf, and have seen something of the make-up of this remarkable man. But to add to his hatred of the Germans it appears that some woman near to him had formed a liaison with a German officer. At the back of Norway House stood a cut-out figure of Hitler. Whenever Per saw it he would draw his revolver and aim a round or two at it. The boat he chose for his dangerous mission — and to go in the long, light days of summer made it doubly dangerous — was the 26 ft open *Sjø,* in every way appearing to be the same as so many others in Norway. His companion on the trip was Mindur Berge, and they duly made the Norwegian coast, and proceeded at least as far north as Vågsøy without mishap. On the way south they apparently ran into an unexpected German control, were taken prisoner, and held for some time in Bergen. They were taken away from there and at that point their story ends. There can be no doubt they were executed by the Germans. The Nazis kept few records of such deeds.

So the Norwegians came down from Lunna and quickly felt at home. They were invited into people's homes, and were treated with great kindness, which they returned in full measure. There is little doubt the opposite sex found them attractive, perhaps more so than the boys of the RAF, the RA, the infantry or the RAMC. One young lady possibly summed it up when she said, "I got to know the Norwegian boys quite well. I thought they were so much like our own Shetland boys." And with so many of our own Shetland boys away in the merchant navy and elsewhere, boys just like them taking their place were understandably welcome. One Bus boy, Rolf Nordhus, speaking many years later, said, "We had so many friends there. We could walk around, go anywhere we liked, be friends with the children and the grownups, without ever being asked where we had been or where we were going. It was the most security-minded situation one could imagine. No one spoke about what we were doing. The Shetlanders and the Norwegians were friends. Even though it was wartime we had a wonderful time in Scalloway. I remember one occasion when there was going to be a dance, and it was organised mainly by the villagers and the Norwegians. Servicemen from other units came to the dance and the Shetlanders warned us that there was going to be trouble. And there was. But the Shetlanders and the Norwegians joined forces and we cleared the hall."

The Bus boys were well paid — much better than British servicemen — and Rolf was probably quite unaware that jealousy was the moving force prompting the British servicemen's actions. Farther south the well-loaded Yanks had the same effect on the underpaid lads in British uniform. But watching the twinkling feet of this still young but elderly man on the dance floor of the *St Clair* in Bergen, and also in the Scalloway Hall in the summer of 1987, and noting the lively twinkle still in his eyes, one can imagine the mischief that he and more like him must have brought to the quiet village even in the midst of war. Would he, perhaps, have been among the party who went into the church one night, where one of them started playing the organ? And did one of them have a captive chicken or hen with him? It was a pity the fowl got loose and left numerous feathers strewn over the pews, though it has to be said it was finally recaptured. And was it accidentally that someone started ringing the church bell as they were leaving? After all, that was the warning of invasion! The police came. Explanations were given. No arrests were made, no charges preferred. But then the policeman was Archie Nicolson, a man of great good common sense, who steered an equitable and much appreciated path among a populaton which had doubled with the coming of war — in short, a real community policeman.

Kåre Mørk, another of the Bus boys, has been back in Shetland within the last few years, and of course he made a pilgrimage to Scalloway. As he wandered the familiar roads he once knew so well he heard a shout, "Hi! Mørk!" He didn't know the man, but obviously the man knew him. Of course he had been only a boy when Kåre left Scalloway. But the grown-up stranger turned out to be a son of Archie Nicolson's.

While the winter of 42/43 has left many happy memories for the boys of the Shetland Bus who survived, it was also a period of extreme tragedy, for the losses, though heroic, were indeed grievous. No fewer than six boats failed to return, with the loss of over forty men. That was more than half the total number manning the base when the winter began. David Howarth has told the story of these losses, some of them in detail, but they deserve mention here as well. We have seen how the little *Sjø* was lost. The *Arthur* was the next to go. She was the boat Larsen had stolen for his getaway after the sinking of the *Nordsjøen,* and was his first command, for he had been only a crew member on the *Nordsjøen*. The *Arthur* had been the boat chosen to take the two-man "Chariots" to Trondheimfjord, in an effort to torpedo the *Tirpitz*. It came so near to succeeding. They were only five miles from the great ship when the "Chariots" broke adrift, but success would have had such far-reaching effects on Britain's whole naval strategy.

The operation itself had been meticulously planned, and Larsen had shown remarkable skill and iron nerves in arriving so near to the target. It was the worst possible luck that they should have run into such rough weather so far up the fjord as to cause the "Chariots" to break loose. But the men's conduct during the long trek to the Swedish border after scuttling the *Arthur* was of the highest order. Only one man failed to return. He was A. B. Evans who had been wounded in a gunfight with the Germans and captured. The Germans nursed him back to health, then shot him. The final stage of the crew's escape was a flight back to Britain from Sweden, and it was now that Larsen was awarded the Conspicuous Gallantry Medal.

The *Aksel,* skippered by Bård Grotle, went down some 200 miles north of Shetland. The crew managed to get into their dinghy and a rubber float, but though a Catalina could report sighting them it was too rough for the plane to land, and the whole crew perished before a rescue ship could get to the spot. The *Sandøy,* one of the big whalers, was sunk by German aircraft off the coast of northern Norway, while the *Feiøy* was lost with all hands off Sunnhordland in January, 1943. (David Howarth shows the *Feie* as being lost, but Norwegian records show the *Feie* going back to Norway in 1945, and being renamed the *Kines,* before being sold abroad in 1978. Registration number of the *Feie* was H 145 AM and of the *Feiøy* H 10 AM.)

The *Bergholm,* with Leif Larsen as skipper, had landed three agents and four tons of cargo at Traena, and on the way back to Shetland was attacked by two twin-engined German planes. His crew consisted of Johann Kalve, who had been with him on the *Arthur,* engineers Faerøy and Vika, deckhands and gunners Klausen, Enoksen and Noreiger, and radio operator Hansen. Jack Moore remembers working one day on a submarine in Lerwick. He was doing a welding job near the fuel tanks, and he was being helped by a young Norwegian from the Scalloway base. Suddenly a wad of oily waste caught fire, and two of the submarine crew who had been keeping a close eye on the welding, immediately turned foam extinguishers on the area. Though the danger was immediately snuffed out, Jack and the young Norwegian came on deck smothered in foam. Waiting on the quay was a land-rover from the Scalloway base which had come to pick up the young man. His boat was on the point of sailing and he was urgently needed. The young man's name was Vika, his boat was the *Bergholm,* and she was about to sail on her last voyage.

The German planes which attacked the *Bergholm* were damaged by fire from the vessel, but they pressed home their attack and left her in a sinking condition. Larsen knew they would have to abandon her, and they hastily patched up bullet holes on the badly damaged small boat with bits of tin cut from bully-beef cans. Five out of the eight men were wounded, and it was a difficult task to get them all into the small boat. They were 75 miles from the nearest point on the Norwegian coast, 350 miles from Shetland. Shetland was out. Larsen reasoned that the Germans would expect them to make for the nearest point on the Norwegian coast. So they should avoid going there. They had friends in the Ålesund area, but that was 150 miles away. And they had only three men who were fit to row. But no one who knew Larsen would have been surprised to learn that he decided, without hesitation, to make Ålesund their destination. Once underway two men rowed at the time, while the third tended to the wounded. Sadly Vika, the young man who had had to hurry from Lerwick to be in time to catch the *Bergholm*, was severely wounded, and he died from his wounds a few hours later. They buried him at sea.

In 1987 an exhibition of Larsen memorabilia was mounted in the library in Fyllingsdalen in Bergen. (Hopefully it will come to Shetland one day.) Among the items on show was the small boat from the *Bergholm*. It was small, 16 ft long, clumsy, and would clearly have been extremely heavy to row with two oars and the weight of seven men on board. And yet, somehow, after four days they were approaching the land they had aimed for. Unfortunately they encountered a fleet of fishing boats on the way in, and spoke to the crew of one of them. That skipper duly reported their presence to the Germans when he returned to land. The Germans mounted a massive search for them and they had to lie very low for a time, helped and hidden by "good" Norwegians. Eventually a man came for them with a small boat. That man was Sverre Roald from Vigra. He still lives in Vigra today, a quiet, strong, able man, whose many cool and daring deeds, which foiled the Germans time and time again, have never been fully told. He got them safely to Vigra, where he transferred them to a larger, decked boat. But bad weather came on, and for five days they lay at anchor, less than 100 yards from the big radio station on Vigra which was manned and heavily guarded by the Germans. Sverre came to them every day. Finally, when the weather moderated, he took them down to Skorpen and left them there. And to Skorpen on 11th April, 1943, came MTB 626, commanded by Lieut. Bogeberg. He took the seven survivors on board, and carried them back to Shetland.

We have already noted the numerous decorations bestowed on Leif Larsen by an admiring and grateful British government. We have seen him coming back from Norway with the *Arthur,* stolen for a getaway; escaping over the border into Sweden after failing by a whisker to pull off one of the greatest feats of the war in the same *Arthur;* we have followed his incredible voyage in a tiny boat with six companions, four of them wounded. Ahead of him still lay two more years of war, and more fearless ventures in this beloved sub-chaser *Vigra.* No wonder he collected decorations. How characteristic was his comment describing their departure from Norway on MTB 626 after many days of extreme danger: "We were glad to be on our way."

The *Brattholm* was the third of the big whalers to go. With a crew of eight, four agents and a great deal of arms and explosives on board, she had gone north to the Tromsø area, the intention being to land the agents who would establish a well-supplied underground organisation. Things went wrong. The Germans were informed of their presence, and suddenly an enemy warship appeared in the mouth of the little fjord where they lay. They managed to blow up the *Brattholm,* but one man was killed and several wounded. The Germans, after barbaric treatment of the ten men they took prisoner, shot them. One man, Jan Baalsrud, escaped. After a nightmare journey, which lasted two months, and during which he shot two Germans pursuing him, he reached Sweden. He lost all the toes on one foot, and most of those on the other. The story of his escape is told in full by David Howarth in "Escape Alone". Jan got back to Shetland, and once again landed in Norway as an agent. He was there when the German capitulation came.

The loss of the *Brattholm* had a particular poignancy for one house in Scalloway. That was the house of Mrs Laura Malcolmson in New Road, whose two sons were in the merchant navy. Her house had the kind of atmosphere in which young Norwegian seamen felt at home, and a number of them called frequently to be regaled with cups of tea and to listen to the gramophone. A special friendship grew up between Mrs Malcolmson's daughter Tamar and young Fritjof Haugland, who was on board the *Brattholm* on her ill-fated trip. Losses among the boats had been heavy, and from the outset it was recognised that the *Brattholm's* operation carried particular danger. Perhaps both Fritjof and Tamar had a presentiment that this particular trip was one which should have been avoided — but no one avoided a trip, no matter how dangerous it might seem.

Another boat of which neither Howarth nor Saelen makes mention is the 70 ft *Frøya.* This boat came over on 16th March, 1942, from Giske, near Ålesund, with five men on board, one of whom was the Linge man Knut Aarsaether. Ragnar Ulstein records that this boat joined the Shetlandsgjengen and was sunk in the same year. It is believed the following story came from the grandchild of one of the crew, almost certainly a man by the name of Alfred Leonard Langøy — or possibly Langøen. Alfred had come over in August, 1941, on the 24 ft *Loyal*. His escape was a spur of the moment decision, because he was out in a rowing boat when the *Loyal* came past. When he heard where she was going he hopped on board. On the way over they ran out of fuel, and they made a sail using a fishing line, a needle and four blankets. They ran into a gale and continued to steer approximately south-west. Finally the wind eased, and they were reduced to drifting. At night they saw a number of lights and suddenly realised they were in the midst of a convoy. One of the escort ships picked them up and landed them in Leith.

Alfred became an established member of the Shetland Bus, and in April, 1942, the *Frøya,* loaded with supplies for the resistance, set out for Tromsø. She had a nine-man crew, including Alfred. It was a long trip to Tromsø, and when three days out a German aircraft bombed them, forcing them to abandon ship. The lifeboat was very small, and could hold only five men. They constructed a make-shift raft of oil barrels tightly lashed together for the other four. Whether the small boat should stay with the raft or go to seek help was a heart-wrenching decision to have to make. But it was made — they set off to seek help. They headed east with a makeshift sail hoisted, but making best progress rowing. Very heavy seas were running, and what little food and water they had was washed overboard during the first night. The pangs of hunger and thirst soon began to be felt. They huddled down as best they could when a German plane came over, probably looking for them, and the plane failed to spot them. Then one of the men, making his first trip, drank seawater, and shortly became completely demented. He had to be tied up. On the following day they saw the Norwegian mountains with their snowy tops, and that cheered them up until they realised they were coming in to a part of the coast where the heavy seas made a landing impossible. With the wind beginning to go easterly, they decided to try and make Shetland.

But thirst was now becoming acute. Two of the boys began to have fantasies, and soon three out of the five on board were for very little use. Alfred and a man called Bergsvik rowed on. Alfred had thrown all the guns overboard except Bergsvik's, but he had removed the magazine from that one as well. Suddenly, as they rowed, Bergsvik pulled out his pistol, pointed it at Alfred, and pulled the trigger. Happily there was no bullet, but clearly Bergsvik was now no longer in control of his actions. Alfred swung his oar and hit him on the head. Now he was rowing on his own. However, when Bergsvik regained consciousness he was back to normal, and they went on rowing an oar each. Once again they rowed all night, and they began to hear imaginary voices now and again. Then it hailed, and they greedily sucked the large hailstones. With daylight they were sure it was Muckle Flugga they were seeing, but they were now so weak they were making little progress. Happily a Norwegian destroyer and a tanker appeared on the scene, and they were taken on board, being landed at Lerwick that night. They had each been given a glass of whisky when taken on board the destroyer, and the spirit on an empty stomach made them uproariously merry. On landing in Lerwick two were taken to hospital, and three to the Norwegian refugee camp where a Norwegian lady married to a Shetlander (Mrs Adie) gave them civilian clothes. Alfred had sustained a leg wound, which had had no attention and was causing him a lot of pain. Boats had been sent out to look for the raft with the four men on it, but had been attacked by German planes north of Unst and had been forced to return.

In response to much pleading, the *Olaf* was now sent out, with both Alfred and Bergsvik on board. It was perhaps not surprising that German planes were lying in wait for just such an attempt, and attacked them. The *Olaf* put up spirited resistance, but she sustained a lot of damage. Alfred was badly wounded in his lower legs and had one thigh crushed. After patching up the wounded the best they could, they steamed towards land, and finally got into Baltasound. One of the fishing boats came for them, but some of the wounded were in such a poor way that an "aeroplane boat" (probably a Walrus) was sent for them, and got them quickly to hospital. Several died, including one of those who had been in the little lifeboat, Johannessen. Alfred was sent down to the Norwegian hospital in Edinburgh, where "Professor Holst and Captain Worsleff operated on Grandad and patched him together again".

After their ordeal in the small boat, it was remarkable that the three men who were reasonably fit after that nightmare journey should insist on going immediately to sea again on the *Olaf* to look for their friends. It was almost certainly a suicidal mission they embarked on, because it was a foregone conclusion that the

Germans would be expecting them to come out — and they were waiting for them. In wartime, when the lives of friends are at stake, men's actions often run far beyond cold common sense.

By the end of March, 1943, it was clear that the Germans were now so much on the alert for the coming of the Shetland Bus boats that losses had reached the point where they were no longer tolerable. As Jack Moore puts it, "You would be working alongside a man one day, and the next he was gone, never to return." What was to be done?

Chapter Eleven

Shetland and Norway, 1942

Shetland

There was little in the events of 1942 to raise anyone's spirits in Shetland. Certainly the invasion of Britain, which had seemed so likely after Dunkirk, had not taken place, nor had the Germans so far crossed the North Sea to plant their oppressive boots on Shetland soil. But the Shetland boys at sea, or facing the Germans in North Africa or the Japanese in the Far East, were constantly at risk, and families at home, as in the First War, dreaded the arrival of a War Office telegram with news of tragedy.

A German air presence over Shetland seemed almost continuous, for by May, 1942, there had been 151 alerts in Lerwick since the beginning of the war. History shows that a large number of these aerial visits were purely for reconnaissance purposes, but on occasion they also meant casualties and damage. In the Fair Isle, towards the end of 1941, the buildings at the north lighthouse had been badly damaged by bombs, and at the end of the year the south lighthouse had been machine-gunned and a keeper's wife and daughter were killed, as was a soldier on a nearby gunpost. The lighthouse buildings were demolished. On 18th January the Skerries light was bombed, and Mrs Anderson was buried under collapsed masonry. She succumbed to her injuries before she could be brought to hospital. The stream of refugee boats crossing the North Sea, which had been such a feature of the summer and autumn months of 1941, had dried to a trickle, and only about a dozen boats arrived during the whole of 1942.

Across the North Sea the great German battleship *Tirpitz* moved from the Baltic to Trondheimsfjorden in January, 1942. Even if that fact had been known to Shetlanders at the time it probably wouldn't have aroused much interest. But the event was of major concern to the Admiralty, and, indeed, to the British government. For the *Tirpitz* was someting special. She carried eight

15 in guns, each throwing a shell weighing nearly a ton. Our biggest ships, the *King George V* and the *Prince of Wales,* for instance, had ten 14 in guns, firing shells 3 cwt lighter than the German's. Add to that the fact the *Tirpitz* was at least three knots faster, and was protected by much superior armour, and one can understand why Churchill reckoned it would take two of our biggest battleships to be a match for the German champion. She clearly posed a tremendous threat to British shipping, all the more so because the convoys carrying vital supplies to the north Russian port of Murmansk had now commenced. The need to sink her was the constant preoccupation of both British naval and air power.

There was to be no early success in that direction. The worst British fears were realised in March. The *Tirpitz* put to sea, her prey convoy PQ12 on its way to Murmansk. Fortunately she failed to make contact, and retreated safely to her anchorage, despite an attack by British torpedo bombers. This was to be her only real sortie during the whole of the two years and ten months she spent in Norwegian waters. Her only other outing — an unimpressive one — was to Spitzbergen, where she fired a few practice rounds from her big guns.

As the months went by the mortal danger which the big ship represented didn't diminish in any way, and there were numerous desperate efforts by both the RAF and the navy to neutralise that danger. None of them met with any success for a long time. We have seen how near Larsen and the "Chariots" came to achieving the seemingly impossible, but it was not until the *Tirpitz* was lying away up north in Altafjorden that midget submarines in 1943 carried out one of the most difficult and successful operations of the whole war. Six of the bigger submarines, *Thrasher, Truculent, Stubborn, Sea Nymph, Syrtis* and *Sceptre,* all of them familiar sights in Lerwick harbour, towed six of the midget submarines or X-craft, across the North Sea up to Altafjorden where the *Tirpitz* lay at the head of a narrow fjord, sixty miles from the open sea. It was an eight days' tow, a distance of 1500 miles. It was not to be expected that an operation so difficult would be trouble free, and it wasn't. Broken tows and other mishaps meant that in the end only two of the midgets reached their goal, i.e. underneath the *Tirpitz.* There they dropped their eggs — four two-ton amatol charges. All of them exploded more or less simultaneously, and the damage sustained by the big ship was enough to ensure that she would be out of action for at least a number of months. The Commanders of the small craft, Lieuts Place and Cameron, were awarded Victoria Crosses, an indication of the importance attached to their successful mission. One of the midgets which, because of mechanical trouble, failed to reach the target by the appointed time, was being towed back to Shetland by the *Stubborn,* when a message was received that a severe storm was imminent, and the midget was to be scuttled. On arrival in Lerwick the crew were transferred to the waiting *Truculent,* which took them to Rothesay.

Jumping ahead a little, we can note that the end came for the *Tirpitz* in November, 1944. Twenty-eight Lancaster bombers, each carrying 12,000 lb "blockbuster" bombs, took off from Lossiemouth. They unexpectedly achieved almost complete surprise, and dropped their bombs with great effect, scoring a number of hits, and the great vessel finally turned turtle, and ended up with her mast and superstructure resting on the bottom. All the Lancasters returned safely, but 1000 members of the crew of the *Tirpitz* perished. Thirty men who had survived in an air pocket inside the ship were successfully rescued by cutting a hole in the vast hull. During her stay in Norwegian waters she had been subjected to seventeen air attacks, and over 700 sorties had been flown against her by planes of the RAF and the Fleet Air Arm. With a minimum of effort, and without ever really being in action, this one ship had occupied the attention of a sizeable part of the British navy for nearly three years.

Shetlanders were very conscious that British planes were carrying out raids on Norway, because repeatedly the bombers passed overhead both going and coming back. For example, one night in February, 1942, many planes passed over during the night, and again just before dawn. At the end of April fifty bombers passed over Unst about 10 pm, crossing Lerwick on their return about 3-4 am. For some time this kind of spasmodic air traffic continued, with Sumburgh airport being frequently used for refuelling purposes, and not infrequently used for emergency landings by aircraft returning in a damaged condition. The BBC cautiously revealed that some of the raids were directed at the Trondheim area, where it is now known the *Tirpitz* was lying at anchor. And of course Shetland saw some of the results of aerial action. In January, 1942, a Catalina crashed in Yell. Seven of the crew were killed, three survived, with the least injured, the wireless operator, receiving a decoration. In February a twin-engined Blenheim crashed at Skerries, on the south end of Grunay. Some of the *Earl's* crew tried to help, but it was no use — there were no survivors. Another plane returning from a *Tirpitz* raid crashed at Dale, with three men killed, and a damaged Beaufort crash-landed at Sumburgh. The wreck of a Halifax bomber was discovered at the back of Fitful Head in April, with all the crew dead. Also in April a Whitley bomber force-landed in Foula, and a Beaufighter came down in the sea beside Lady's Holm off Scatness, with the crew being rescued by boat. And, of course, there were others.

Meanwhile, Lerwick harbour saw the coming and going of the *Earl,* the *Magnus* and the *Rognvald,* as well as the troopers *Amsterdam, Lady of Mann* and *Prague,* along with a wide variety of naval craft and merchant ships. But a new type of vessel was becoming increasingly prominent in the harbour — submarines. They had started using the harbour extensively towards the end of 1941, with the Dutch P14, which came in on 9th August, being one of the forerunners of the dozens which were to follow. A regular caller in 1942 was the big *Trident.* After a successful early career, she had been sent with the *Tigris* to northern Russia in August, 1941, and had there operated to great effect against German shipping. In February, 1942, she was back in the North Sea, using Lerwick as a secondary base, and in the same month she torpedoed the German cruiser *Prinz Eugen* near Trondheim. About this time a submarine "mother" ship arrived in the harbour. Among the many other submarines seen often in Lerwick during 1942 was the Norwegian *Uredd,* to be followed early in 1943 by the *Ula,* and later still the *Utsira.* We shall look more closely at them in another chapter.

On 10th November, 1942, there were important newcomers on the harbour scene. These were the Norwegian motor torpedo boats. At the time they were the 30 MTB Flotilla, but they were to become the 54 Flotilla from 1st August, 1943. They were known officially only by numbers, which were, to begin with, 618, 619, 620, 623, 625, 626, 627 and 631, and they were to write an illustrious page in Norwegian history. We will look more closely at their story later.

For the people of Shetland it was the vagaries of wind and sea that carried the greatest danger. From the beginning of 1942 there were frequent reports of mines drifting here and there around the coast, and on the night of Friday, 23rd January, sheer disaster hit the town of Lerwick. It happened that the strong south-east wind and heavy seas drove a mine in towards the Waarie Geo. It exploded and left a considerable part of the south seaward side of the town looking as if it had just suffered a severe air raid. The houses in Breiwick Road, particularly those numbered in the sixties, suffered very badly, with many windows blown in and not a few blown out. Slates and ridging were stripped from roofs and chimney pots blown down. People were just getting over the shock of this violent explosion when another one went off, almost at the same spot, at 8 pm. This time the electricity wires came down, and considerably more damage was caused to houses. All that was bad enough, but more was to come. About 1 am on Saturday morning a third mine went off, this time at the Slates, followed an hour later by a fourth. These two did tremendous damage to the new houses round Slates Road, and also those at the foot of Breiwick Road and King Harald Street. Windows, roofs, interior plaster and even doors were all badly damaged, and here and there rocks had been hurled through the air, some of them crashing through the roofs of houses. The cold light of a winter morning showed a scene of complete desolation from about Ronald Street to the Slates. There wasn't a whole window in the fronts of any of the houses, and very few in the backs. It was only now that most people heard that Walter Jamieson, the warden, had been killed. He had been helping to repair a neighbour's window when the second mine went off. He was hit in the stomach and died in hospital.

The south-east gale continued to blow strongly, and there were heavy snow showers. With their houses standing open to the weather people had no option but to evacuate. Forty families left their homes. Some went to relatives, some found make-shift accommodation in the Wesleyan schoolroom. Even the Gilbert Bain hospital had to be evacuated. The empty houses created the possibility of looting, and the police kept a watchful eye. On the Saturday morning two more mines appeared in Breiwick Bay. Mine disposal men arrived and started firing at them, and then three more appeared. Of the five, three were sunk, one exploded and one sank and exploded on the bottom.

During Sunday night two more mines went off, but this time not near enough to do damage. By Sunday evening the wind had fallen away, and people were beginning to try and make some order out of the chaos. Boarding up windows was the only way of making homes reasonably weatherproof, but for those with holes in the roofs repairs were much more extensive. It was clear now that damage was not confined to the Slates/Breiwick area. Windows in King Harald Street and St Olaf Street had gone, and even the big stair window in the County Buildings. Down at Commercial Street a number of business premises had lost a lot of glass, while a length of mine mooring chain was found at Freefield and a piece of mine casing at the door of the old Workmen's Club. With the wind dropping a hard frost set in, water pipes froze, and householders had this added drawback to contend with.

Now people were saying that the mines had been spotted in Breiwick Bay as early as Friday afternoon and had been reported to the authorities who had failed to take any action. Feelings ran high about that. On Wednesday the final act in this sad war-time drama was played out when the funeral of warden Walter Jamieson, killed in the performance of his duty, took place. Not surprisingly there was a large turnout. Many of the townspeople were there, as well as strong contingents from all the local uniformed organisations. The night of the mines had brought the harsh reality of war right into people's homes. It had also brought a strong new feeling of togetherness.

Norway

As we have seen, pressure was applied to a number of groups and organisations in Norway during 1941, pressure which culminated in the terror tactics employed in trying to cow the trade unions. But up to that time the educational field had been left virtually untouched. Indeed a number of teachers had been associated with the famous "Letter of the forty-three". However the Germans were well aware that the minds of young people formed the most fertile ground in which to sow the seeds of Nazi ideology. Regulations had already been announced which made German rather than English the first foreign language to be taught in the schools; all classes were to receive instruction in the history and doctrines of the Nasjonal Samling (*Quisling's party*); and Quisling's portrait was to hang in every classroom. Teachers had consistently ignored these instructions. But the Germans never lost sight of their primary aim — the controlling of the minds of the young people. That meant also controlling the conduct of the teachers, and that, they felt, should not be too difficult. After all the state paid their wages.

On 1st February, 1942, the Germans gave Quisling the grandiose title of "Minister President of Norway". On 5th February he dissolved all the teachers' organisations, and established a Teachers' Corporation (Laerersamband), which all teachers had to join. On the following day he decreed that all young people between the ages of ten and eighteen would henceforth be automatically members of the NS Youth Movement. They would be called up for compulsory physical training, ideological training and labour service. This would give him control of 400,000 young people, and would be near enough a replica of the Hitler Jugend organisation in Germany. There was an immediate outcry. 200,000 parents lodged protests on behalf of their children. 11,000 out of the total 14,000 teachers wrote to say that they could not, and would not, be part of Quisling's plans. The church gave the teachers their emphatic support. Faced with so much opposition Quisling played for time. He closed all schools for a month, on the pretext that there was a shortage of fuel. But he felt he still had the whip-hand. He controlled their wages. So he played his trump card. Only those teachers who signed the following would receive any pay: "I hereby declare that I am a member of the Teachers' Corporation." Unhappily for Quisling, it didn't prove to be a trump card at all. 95% of the teachers gave him a point-blank refusal. He resorted to intimidation. On 10th March 100 or more teachers were rounded up, and thirty of them were sent to work at the German airport at Oerlandet. This action had absolutely no effect on the teachers. Up to this point the Germans had merely watched the proceedings, but now they saw that Quisling was failing them once more, and they intervened. They could not allow a situation to develop where the teachers were actually posing a threat to German power.

The position as they saw it was that 12,000 teachers were effectively on strike. One remedy was to shoot a lot of them — that was always a popular Nazi remedy. But it was decided that a more effective lesson would be to crush their spirit — and they had found that that could always be achieved by extremes of harsh treatment. 1200 teachers, selected from lists supplied by Quisling informers, were arrested, and 700 of them were sent to the notorious Grini concentration camp near Oslo. Here they were in the hands of hard-bitten camp staff, many of them sadists, who from the start behaved towards the teachers with excessive brutality. After several days of the "treatment" they were paraded before the Camp Commandant, and given until 8.30 the following morning to sign. Five out of the 700 gave in, mainly through sheer physical weakness. Now the rest were taken on a nightmare journey to a camp at Jøerstadmoen, near Lillehammer, where for fourteen days they were subjected to the worst treatment the Germans could devise. Again they were given the ultimatum — sign, or else. Twenty had been broken — they signed — they were phyically ruined men.

150 or so were sent back to the terrible Grini. Over 500 were sent on another nightmare journey. For eighteen hours they travelled in locked, unheated, cattle trucks, with no food and the temperature below zero, and finally arrived in Trondheim. There they were crammed into the little steamer *Skjerstad,* an old boat built to carry perhaps 200 people. After fourteen days of incredible hardship, the old steamer round North Cape, and finally came to

the little town of Kirkenes, which today is very near the Russian border. Here they were housed in filthy sheds, clad in prison garb, given the poorest of food, and worked for twelve hour shifts in the bitter sub-zero temperatures unloading ships. Then the 150 from Grini were sent north to join them, so that they were again all together in their own private hell. Four of those from Grini were so weak that they got no farther than Trondheim, while one of the those already at Kirkenes was dead.

Support for the teachers at this time from both adults and children was intense. When the first arrests had taken place, parents had turned out to march behind the teachers to the railway stations, and children ran up and gave them gifts of fruit and flowers. Even on the journey to Trondheim in the locked cattle trucks, people got to know about it, and gathered at every station on the way to sing the national anthem as the train passed. Efforts to smuggle food to the teachers at the stops were brutally frustrated by the guards. Those teachers who were left in the schools when they reopened read a declaration to their pupils, explaining the reasons for the teachers' struggle, and concluding with these words, "I will never ask you to do anything that I consider to be wrong, nor will I teach you anything which in my opinion is not in accordance with the truth." Even as they spoke their friends in Kirkenes were undergoing extreme suffering to support that very principle. One of them said afterwards, "It was highly dangerous work down in the holds of the ships, with boxes, bombs, guns and all sorts of things swinging from side to side on the crane hooks. Out on the refrigerator ship we were working in a temperature fifteen degrees below zero. Here a teacher form Narvik fell down and was killed. A teacher from Oslo ate raw meat and became very ill. He had eaten pieces he tore from a carcase as he was carrying it to the lifting platform. We received very bad food. For about three weeks we were given soup made from rotten fish. When it was brought in the smell spread right through the huts, and made us vomit. Many could not swallow it — but some were able to eat their own ration and more."

After about six months the Germans began to realise that their favourite weapon — terror — wasn't working. In dribs and drabs they began to release their prisoners. It could only be construed as a victory for the teachers. Quisling was livid. "You teachers are spoiling my game. You are preventing me concluding peace with Germany. It will be your fault if Norway does not regain her freedom." Quisling had never had any standing in the eyes of the Norwegian people, and now the Germans had had enough of always having to come to his aid. For all his big plans and impressive words he had so terribly little actual achievement to show his masters. Membership of his party never rose beyond the 30,000-40,000 level — little more than in the days before the occupation, despite all the perks which NS membership now carried. The Norwegian Legion to serve on the Eastern Front was launched with a fanfare. It probably never reached the 2000 mark, and its losses in the east were heavy. Something like 5000 Norwegians in all did war service for Germany, and of these over 1000 died in German uniform. But if it was a bad time for Quisling, there was little joy for the Germans in the news from the battle-fronts. The disaster at Stalingrad, the retreat in North Africa — it was disturbing news. It was all very hard to swallow by people who believed in the complete invincibility of Hitler and the great German Reich. To add to the unhappy picture was the realisation that Norway would never be a Nazi puppet state. The events of the occupation years were simply strengthening the belief in real democracy.

Of all the resistance offered to the Germans in 1941 and 42 by the collective efforts of groups and organisations, the fight put up by the teachers fired the feelings of everyone and had the greatest effect in bolstering morale. The Germans were amazed that the teachers should have shown the strength of body and of spirit that they did. It had been felt that intellectuals, as they considered the teachers, would have been much more easily bent. But it was not only with the teachers that the Germans had miscalculated. They had misjudged the whole Norwegian people. Resistance had not been confined to a particular class, calling or category. It had spread over the whole spectrum of Norwegian life. The occupants of Grini were living proof of that fact: professors, teachers, ship-owners, doctors, lawyers, farm labourers, shipwrights, nurses, housewives, road workers, students, railway workers, bank clerks — and many more.

So far the main struggle had been fought on the issues of the rule of law, freedom of the individual and democracy, and it had been an "open" struggle, i.e. waged openly by groups and organisations. The results achieved were two-fold. The Germans had been made finally to realise that their ideas of what they could achieve with Norwegians were completely wrong. Secondly, the Norwegians themselves had had their resolve tremendously stregthened, and that resolve was never to have any truck with the Germans. A letter arrived in Britain in 1942, by some clandestine route, from a Norwegian in Oslo. "We know now what we shall have to face," it said. "We are ready to go through to the end. Even if the Allies should lose the war we will never give in."

Though it is true to say that the 1941/42 resistance had been mainly "open", there had nevertheless been considerable underground activity, and Milorg, the military branch of the underground, had been recognised by the government in exile as early as the end of 1941. In the autumn of 1942 the underground suffered a severe blow when 200 men of the Stein organisation were arrested, and that of course led to unfortunate repercussions for many more. One important aspect of resistance activity, virtually from the beginning of the occupation, had been the underground press. As time went on some of the underground papers appeared with impressive regularity, and featured the Norwegian broadcasts from London. This was certainly a very important factor in maintaining morale. The Germans were more and more conscious of unwanted activity, and responded by increasing the number of occupation troops. The Linge boys, i.e. members of Kompani Linge, were the SOE operatives, and they were responsible for establishing most of the early transmitters which passed information to London. By 1942 there were something like thirty transmitters operating. Among those countering underground activity was the "worst man in Norway", Henry Rinnan and his gang. He was responsible for betraying a considerable number of Norwegians, including the "export" group headed by Thoralf and Lilly Walle, and all the people on board the boat *Viggo*. We'll look at that later.

Up north, from the end of 1941 to the middle of 1942, a considerable amount of arms and ammunition had been landed in the area between Trondheim and Bodø. Much of it had come over in the boats of the Shetland Bus, and along with the arms had come a number of Linge boys. It seems there was still in existence a British plan to establish a bridge-head in this part of Norway — indeed it had the codename "Jupiter" — and the build-up of arms had created the impression among Norwegians in the area that a British invasion could not be long delayed. The Germans were sensitive to what was going on, with Henry Rinnan feeding them inside information. A radio operator was arrested, and was being forced to show the Germans the location of an arms dump in the Majavatn area, when his comrades opened fire, killing two Germans. Shortly afterwards there were sabotage attempts on a power-plant and the iron-ore mines, and Terboven reacted by declaring a state of emergency from Majavatn to Trondheim. Many people were arrested, houses were razed to the ground, and in all it is said that thirty-four people suffered the death penalty. Over all it was a bad year for the resistance, and particularly for Milorg, with an estimated total of fifty lives lost. But from now on the "overt" resistance which had characterised 1941 and 1942 would cease, and the real effort of resisting the Germans would henceforth be underground, with the numbers involved, as we shall see, growing at an impressive rate.

Chapter Twelve

The Motor Torpedo Boats

Lerwick Harbour Trust's records show six motor torpedo boats arriving in Lerwick Harbour on 10th November, 1942. These were Nos. 618, 619, 620, 623, 625 and 631. The official Norwegian "Marinens Fartøyer" shows slightly later operational dates for 626 and 627, so they would have been the last to arrive to make up the eight MTBs of 30 MTB Flotilla. They were to become 54 MTB Flotilla on 1st August, 1943.

Though this was the first Shetland had seen of Norwegian MTBs, the story had started back in 1939, when Norway had ordered eight MTBs from Britain. War came before they could be delivered, and the British navy took over six of them. But even while fighting was still going on in Norway, the first Norwegian MTB unit was established at Portsmouth, equipped with the two MTBs from the 1939 order not requisitioned by the British navy. Throughout the war the Norwegian MTBs would be known by numbers only, and these first two were numbers 5 and 6. The history of No. 6 was short; she sprang a leak and was abandoned. No. 5 survived until an explosion in her engine room put her permanently out of action.

In July, 1941, the Norwegians took delivery of six new boats. They were numbered 50, 51, 52, 54, 56 and 71, and were again based at Portsmouth. They were powered by Thorneycroft engines. In October 56 carried out the first operation by an MTB in Norwegian waters. The old destroyer *Draug,* with Sverre Syversen as a member of her crew, towed 56 across. (*'Draug' had escaped the Germans in April, 1940, and had arrived in Britain with 67 German prisoners on board, captured from the German transport 'Main'. Since that time she had carried out a variety of duties, including service at Dunkirk. She even appeared in Lerwick harbour in March, 1942.*) No. 56 lay hidden all day and then, in the evening, she successfully torpedoed and sank a 3000 ton German merchant ship at the south end of Sotra. This was the *Borgny,* and 56 was commanded by Lieut. Danielsen. It was his second success; the first had been a 5000 ton merchant ship sunk in the Channel. The *Draug* again appeared on the scene to tow 56 back. The Norwegians very much wanted to centre their MTB operations in Norwegian waters, but it was soon clear that the boats they were using were far from sturdy enough to face up to crossings of the North Sea in all weathers.

The next move was to secure eight Fairmile D Class MTBs. They had double-skinned hulls, 115 ft long, and were driven by four Packard engines each of 1250 hp, which gave them a speed of thirty knots, and their normal crew numbered twenty-six men. They were armed with two torpedo tubes, twin Oerlikons, twin ·5 Colts, ·303 machine-guns, pom-poms and, later, 6-pounder guns. Wooden channels on deck acted as chutes for dropping defence mines, and they carried two depth charges in cradles. These were simply dropped over the side when required. They carried almost 5000 gallons of high octane fuel, which gave them a range of over 600 miles at their most economical cruising speed of 18 knots.

Lieut. R. Tamber, commanding 619 when the flotilla arrived in Lerwick, was made Commanding Officer, and Lieut. Herlofson took over 619. The other skippers were Lieut. A. H. Andresen in 618, Lieut. Prebensen in 620, Lieut. Haavik in 623, Lieut. Hjellestad in 625, Lieut Bøgeberg in 626, Lieut. Henriksen in 627 and Lieut. Matland in 631. The boats soon became familiar sights in Lerwick. They made the south end of the Fish Market frontage their own for loading torpedoes, ammunition and supplies, and they set up their own crane there for the purpose. The same crane was used for lifting out the big Packard engines whenever an overhaul was needed. Their fuel dump was over on the Bressay shore, and the mines were stored up at Lunna. Also over on the Bressay side, at Heogan, they were to have their own floating dock, and they did a lot of their slipping there. They also had their own camp, canteen and workshop at the Anglo-Scottish, and their own blacksmith at the Malakoff. Lerwick had already seen a huge influx of British troops, sent north to garrison the islands. Now eight small but dangerous-looking craft had arrived with twenty-six men on each, plus a number of shore staff and replacement crew-men. The people of Lerwick took it all in their stride, and it wasn't long before the newcomers were being welcomed into local homes, and warm and lasting friendships were developing.

The new MTBs had done some training at Gosport, and then they had come to Scapa Flow, where they had engaged in intensive target practice, firing at targets both on the sea and in the air. By the time they arrived in Shetland they were fully operational, and they soon showed that they meant business. They had arrived on 10th November; on the 22nd 619, 626 and 631 were on their way across the North Sea to the Norwegian coast, destination Stord and Bømlo. No target presented itself that night, and next day the Germans spotted them in Bømmelfjord. Discretion advised a return to Shetland. No mention was made in their report that they had passed at speed through the channel which forms Haugesund harbour. The three boats' massive wash had left the small boats moored in the channel dancing like corks in their wake.

They had completed the first trip — the ice was broken. The distance had been relatively short, and the contents of their tanks had provided all the fuel they needed. But on most trips they would carry additional fuel in two gallon tin cans, two cans to a carton, and all on deck. The extra fuel was necessary, of course, on long trips, but on all trips it was useful for topping up the tanks at intervals to reduce the amount of highly volatile gas in each tank, for it was high octane fuel they were using. Indeed crews were soon complaining of nausea and headache caused by the fumes. Each tank had a good covering of insulating material which was self-sealing if pierced by a bullet. The second operation was mounted just four days after the first. This time the destination was Askvoll, a little way south of Florø, and 620 and 623 were the boats involved. It was an exciting and fruitful trip, for 620 torpedoed the German *Harvestehude,* and 623 the *Hertha,* both ships lying at anchor when the small boats attacked. Thus early the MTBs had proved how effective they could be, and in the next two and a half years this flotilla was to make 161 sorties. Every trip was exciting; every trip was extremely dangerous; some were costly to the Germans, a few brought tragedy to the Norwegians. What sort of men were they who manned these dashing, dangerous craft? Let us look at a few.

Asbjørn Lie was an engineer on 619 when she came to Lerwick. When the Germans invaded Norway he had been on a Norwegian oil tanker bound for Santos, and they had been ordered to go to the nearest neutral port, which for them was Cape Town. "We heard about the invasion when we were at sea. I was eighteen at the time. My father and mother were still alive, and there were four of us brothers, all of us in the merchant navy. Our home was in Kongsberg." Asbjørn remained on the tanker until 1942, his ship like all the Norwegian merchant ships under the control of Notraship, now the biggest shipping company in the world. She was a ship of 12,000 tons, which was quite big for a tanker in those days. They landed cargoes at many ports world-wide, including Swansea, Southampton and Manchester. Each of these three ports had either just undergone, or were undergoing, bombing attacks when they were there.

On one voyage they had left Halifax in a convoy of thirty-two tankers. They had proceeded some distance into the Atlantic when they were joined by an escort of corvettes and destroyers, which would accompany them to Scotland. As they sailed on the great mass of the battleship *Hood* passed the convoy, and all the escort ships, apart from one corvette, left them to accompany the *Hood*. They didn't know it, but the *Bismarck* was out in the North Atlantic. The convoy was now virtually without protection. About midnight a raft with a light on it was seen in the middle of the convoy. No one could figure out its meaning, but almost from that moment the sinkings started. The whole ocean, as far as the eye could see, appeared to be on fire, with here and there the bow or the stern of a sinking ship silhouetted against the flames. There was the tragic sight of crews trying to get away from their blazing, sinking ships, but no vessel was allowed to stop to pick up survivors. The men in the surviving ships sailed on with heavy hearts — surely nothing can equal the pathos of leaving good men to die without being able to do anything to help.

Orders were given for the remnants of the convoy to scatter, and at their normal speed of twelve knots they finally reached Scotland. Fifteen tankers from that convoy alone had been sunk. Apart from the terrible loss of life the loss of the cargoes was a severe blow to the British war effort. And to make matters worse they heard when they tied up that the battleship *Hood* had been sunk — the information coming first in a broadcast by the infamous "Lord Haw-Haw".

After three years in the merchant navy Asbjørn joined the fighting navy, in Halifax. He was sent to a small town called "Camp Norway", and there he was posted as chief engineer to Shackleton's old ship *Quest*. She had been down in the tropics on charter, and she was so dried out she was leaking like a sieve, and that was how she started her first wartime voyage as a naval vessel across the Atlantic. Although she was a small ship, Asbjørn was most impressed with her seagoing qualities — she seemed totally unaffected by rough seas. None of her officers had any knowledge of British naval signalling, and every night there was an exchange of signals between the Commodore and the ships in the convoy, when changes of course, etc., were notified and acknowledged. One night a destroyer dashed up to the *Quest*, and demanded to know where were all the torpedoes? It turned out that the *Quest's* supposedly innocent acknowledgement of the Commodore's signal had in reality been a message saying that the *Quest* had forty-two torpedoes in her hold! After the ships arrived in Glasgow the destroyer's officers came on board and told them with great relish and much amusement the real meaning of some of the signals the *Quest* had sent. But now Asbjørn's real navy experiences started — he joined MTB 619 at Gosport.

Sverre Syversen came to Lerwick on MTB 623, but that was far from the first of his naval service. His home was just outside Frederikstad, and he was one of a family of three sisters and two brothers. He was twenty, and had done four years deep sea sailing before he was called up in January, 1940, for his national service, during which he did several months on an old battleship at Horten. He was classed as a stoker, and there were twenty-five of them on the old battleship. They were all posted to different ships on completion of training, Sverre's posting being to a small passenger ship which had been converted into a warship. The remaining twenty-four were posted to naval vessels which were sunk by the Germans at Narvik, and Sverre became the only survivor from the twenty-five who had trained together.

It was the job of Sverre's ship to patrol the coast north and south of Bergen, and they saw plenty of German ships. Some seemed to stay more or less in the same positions, moving only short distances north or south at slow speed. They were not to know that these ships were part of the German invasion fleet. Numbers of them appeared to be cargo boats, but in reality they had perhaps six feet of coal or coke on top, and down below large numbers of German troops. The Norwegian sailors' suspicions were of course aroused, but there was nothing they could do. On 8th April Sverre's ship was in port, but just after midnight on the 9th they were ordered to sea. As they went out of Bergen harbour they met the first German warship coming in. The shore batteries opened fire without result, and the first Germans landed in Bergen between four and five am.

A converted passenger boat can never be a formidable fighting force, but as they went up the fjord that didn't occur to them. They saw smoke approaching, and it turned out to be an armed German trawler. They promptly sank her with their four inch gun. She had 200 German troops on board. Sverre was down in the engine-room when the next action developed. This time it was a German destroyer which opened fire on them, with their four inch defiantly replying. "I was alone in the engine-room, and each time we fired the door fell off the boiler! Suddenly I got the impression that we had greatly stepped up our rate of fire. I went on deck to find that we were aground, and the German shells were hitting the rocky face behind us, which was the reason for my feeling that we had increased our rate of fire. The destroyer fired a torpedo at us, but it missed. So far they hadn't scored a direct hit. It suddenly dawned on me that I was the only man on board — the crew had abandoned ship by going ashore. They had forgotten all about me down in the engine-room. I decided that I'd better go ashore too!''

They sheltered in a tunnel at Stanghelle for 3/4 hours, then walked out at the other end. Sverre and the cook went down and borrowed a Shetland model type boat from a crofter, and rowed along the fjord until they had their own ship between them and the Germans. They climbed on board and Sverre started up the engine. The ship had drifted off the rocks, and was heading up the fjord. He opened the throttles to their widest, and "we belted up the fjord", the Germans not risking pursuit in such narrow and unknown waters. Finally they tied up. They were high-spirited young men who had been through a nerve-racking experience, and they were still tense, but there was a strong feeling of jubilation at outwitting the Germans. They knew there was a case of whisky in the skipper's cabin, a gift from one of the Fred Olsen boats — the *Black Prince* or the *Black Watch*. They went below and opened a bottle. They had good reason for a toast or two, and when the skipper finally returned on board they were feeling no pain!

There was still a little more they could do. They could get into Dale at high tide, and there the Germans were already ensconced in a large, white house. They blew it to bits. They went as far up the fjord as Mo, and there they tied up and put the gun and engine out of action. They were in the Nordfjord area when southern Norway capitulated, and they were told they could go home. But home in sailor's uniform meant being made prisoner by the Germans. So they hung around for a day or two, then discovered there was a 3000-ton Danish cargo boat, the *Flydenberg,* lying at Raudeberg. She had been bombed, had sustained a number of casualties, but, while most of her deck structures had been blown away, she was still basically sound, and the engine worked. Their party now numbered seven, and they decided to sail the ship to Britain. Before doing so they went to Nordfjordeid, where the Norwegians were holding a number of German air-crew prisoners. They picked out several who, by their uniform markings, seemed to be of the highest ranks, and took them on board. They now numbered seven Norwegians, ten Danes and nine German officer prisoners. Only emergency toilet arrangements were possible on board because of bomb damage, and the sanitary facility was simply a hole in the deck. It was a considerable come-down for Germany's élite officer class to have to squat over a hole in the deck under the pistol of a supposedly subjugated Norwegian. But everything went well, and they sailed their steamer into Kirkwall harbour. There the Germans disembarked, and later ended up in Canada as PoW. The Norwegians were sent to Scapa and posted to the destroyer *Draug,* and from there it was down to Swansea. There they earned the harbour-master's comment, "Never before have I seen a navy boat failing to sail on the tide because the stokers were drunk." Sverre had plenty of excitement on the old *Draug,* but in 1942 he was posted to the MTBs. He was on 623 when she made her first trip to the Norwegian coast, and it was on that trip that they torpedoed the German *Hertha.*

Roy A. Nielsen was one of the crew of MTB 688, which was not one of the first to come north. He had been at navigation school, aged twenty, when the Germans invaded. By the time he finished his course he was twenty-one, and almost immediately he was involved in escape attempts. The first boat acquired for taking a party over was rotten, and unfit for sea. But their activities had been sufficient to rouse German suspicions, and he was actually already on their wanted list. The second boat they acquired was a small rowing boat with a 3 hp engine, and a sail made from flour bags. They had got to within twenty miles of Aberdeen with this one, when bad weather forced them to put about and return to Norway. They had been six days at sea by the time they regained the Norwegian coast, and now of course they had to be extra careful, for the Germans badly wanted to get their hands on them. A friend hid Roy, near Mandal.

His terrible experience in the earlier attempt did not discourage him, and once more a boat was obtained. This time it was twenty feet long, and had a 5 hp engine. With three other young men, all of them little more than schoolboys, they set out again. Again they had to contend with violent storms, and to make matters worse the boat leaked. But six days after leaving, on 17th September, 1941, they arrived at Blyth, a journey of 340 miles across the North Sea in a boat little other than a Ness yoal. If she had a name it is not known, but her registration number was VA 77 HH.

Roy had American papers, because he had been born in Brooklyn. "They wanted to send me to the States, but I didn't want to go there and maybe find myself serving in the Pacific. I wanted to be in the fight nearer to Norway. The people down in London were very suspicious of us. I was the oldest and I was only twenty-one. They said a bunch of boys could not possibly have carried out the trip we said we'd done, not in the kind of weather which prevailed at the time.'' Finally he was sent for training, and his first posting was to a big whaling boat being used as a submarine hunter and operating out of Halifax, Londonderry and other ports. This was one of the big whalers which had been in South Africa when the Germans invaded.

Eventually he was posted to the MTBs in Lerwick, his first billet being a Nissen hut in Knab camp. Before he could make his maiden trip to the Norwegian coast, he dropped a depth charge on his foot and had to go to hospital. But in due course he joined 688, commanded by Lieut. Sveen. For a short time 688 operated out of Aberdeen, when targets were mainly in south Norway, but it was in Lerwick that he felt at home, for there he had met a Lerwick girl who became a very dear friend, and soon they were engaged. He was made very much at home by his fiancée's family, and indeed became very good friends with a wide circle of Lerwick people. When his fiancée fell ill and died the loss for him was extremely poignant. It took him a long time to recover from this terrible personal tragedy, and even today he speaks with pathos of the happy days they had together. The war had ended and he was back in Norway before he was able to make a beginning at putting his life together once again.

Albert Eilertsen has already appeared in these pages when he escaped to Iceland after Spitzbergen was evacuated. In Iceland he volunteered for ''Special Service'', and after thorough training he arrived in Scapa Flow, posted to the old *Iron Duke*. That wasn't at all to his taste, so he volunteered for the Shetlandsgjengen. Though they wore navy uniforms, their connection with the regular Norwegian navy was very slim. They trained for the whole of the 1942 summer at Scapa Flow, practising laying mines, action groups, landings from the sea, physical fitness — everything required to make them proficient in landing and thereafter dealing silently and effectively with the enemy. ''Never leave any behind alive!'' was the maxim. That way ensured a better chance of a safe return.

From Scapa they came to Shetland, taking with them the *Gullborg, Sjølivet* and *Lygrefjord,* and anchored at Catfirth. Albert was on the *Lygrefjord,* and they went over to the Norwegian coast to lay mines. They also took over and hid emergency fuel supplies for the MTBs. Then, in the spring of 1943, he transferred to MTB 618, but not before he had had a particularly dicey trip on

23. Asbjørn Lie outside North Star cinema.

24. Karl Johanessen and Sverre Syversen on MTB 711.

25. Albert Eilertsen at foot of Harbour Street.

26. Top MTB pilot Terje Teige.

27. The bell from MTB 618.

28. 618's steering wheel in Town Hall, Lerwick.

29. 618, only surviving Nor. wartime MTB, now a houseboat in Shoreham, on the English south coast.

the *Lygrefjord,* when they were caught in a very severe storm, and took 14 days to reach Lerwick, with the *Lygrefjord* leaking like a sieve. His period on the MTBs provided plenty of excitement and danger, which Albert categorises as "routine", then later in 1943 he married his Shetland girl-friend, and got a generous period of leave for his honeymoon. Perhaps it was this new status of husband that prompted him to apply for a transfer to shore duties, and he became the chef at the Commando camp in Lerwick at Grantfield.

Terje Teige was the sort of man who was of tremendous value to the whole MTB operation in Shetland. For he was one of the pilots, quite possibly the best. Terje had been arrested in Ålesund by the Gestapo in 1942, because he was under suspicion for having provided boats for refugees. An informer had given him away, and it was generally accepted that the culprit was a woman who had been known to feed the Germans with information. However on this occasion the Germans finally decided that they had no firm evidence against him, and he was allowed to go. He was well aware that, though he was free, he was now a marked man. He had to get away. There is no mention of his name among the passengers listed as having escaped on fishing boats, so we can probably assume he found passage on one of the Shetland Bus boats.

Terje sadly died of cancer in 1985, and in post-war years he told little of his wartime exploits with the MTBs. But his daughter Trudi, who obviously loved and admired her father greatly, recalls very clearly the bits and pieces he did tell her. She remembers that the MTB men used to say of him that he knew the coast so well that, when they came in to land in darkness, he would ask them to stop the engines, and then, after listening to the sound of the waves breaking on the shore, he would tell them exactly where they were.

One episode he did mention concerned taking two brothers from Fosnavåg in to the coast to allow them to land and set up a radio transmitter. The MTB took them in past Skorpa, through very dangerous channels, and with a considerable German presence around them. Terje piloted the MTB in, then went with the small boat to land the boys on the other side of the fjord. They stayed in a cave up the mountain for some months, until shortly before the war ended a message came for them to be picked up. Again Terje piloted the MTB in, and again he went with the small boat to fetch the two boys. On the way back the engine in the small boat conked out, and they had to row. The MTB had to be away before full daylight came in, and her engines were already running, and she was on the point of leaving when Terje and his charges came in sight. The MTB picked them up, but by that time they were under fire from the Germans. They got away. Terje kept a leather sheepskin-lined jacket hanging in a cupboard at home. Trudi recalls that he always maintained it was this same jacket which had saved his life. In the shoulder was a hole where a bullet had penetrated, and had wounded him slightly, but the jacket had absorbed the force of the bullet. When ashore in Lerwick he used to stay in Breiwick Road with Mrs Davidson, who still remembers him with affection and respect. She remembers the hole in the jacket — and she still has the misshapen bullet which made the hole.

Another episode Trudi learned at secondhand was when she was working in Bergen, and a doctor told her he owed his life to her father. The occasion had been when in Lerwick in November, 1943, a British MTB lying alongside a Norwegian MTB caught fire. The high octane fuel exploded, and burning blobs of petrol were flying through the air. Some fell on the doctor, and his clothing immediately caught fire. Terje was standing beside him, and immediately whipped off his thick jacket and wrapped it round the flaming man, quickly smothering the flames. After the war Terje continued as a fisherman in his well-known "Teigenes" boats, with a great deal of success. Typical of the man was the fact that he bore no ill-will to the person who had betrayed him. "This is no time for revenge," he said. "This is a time for rebuilding."

Chapter Thirteen

An MTB Family

On 14th August, 1941, Oskar Hovden, the oldest son of the Hovden family, went across to Shetland on the *Valder* from Batalden. There were five people on board, but the name of only one other of them is known — Sigurd Ulriksen. Oskar left behind on the island of Hovden, from which the family took its name, his father, mother Marthe, wife Margit, three brothers already at the fishing with their father, young brother Lars, and young sister Ingrid. Lars and Ingrid were both too young to be working. Oskar saw service on a Norwegian destroyer, and had been in action in the English Channel, when a German shell had exploded in the control room where he was standing. The man beside him was killed, while he escaped with minor injuries. Subsequently he had joined the MTBs and was a quartermaster on 618 commanded by Lieut. Alv Andresen when the boats arrived in Shetland.

Otto Hoddevik we met when he was with the *Harald*, operating out of Peterhead. Subsequently he joined the MTBs, and served to begin with in the small boats, then on the Thorneycroft-engined boats operating out of Portsmouth, Dover and other Channel ports. When the Fairmile boats were acquired he came up to Lerwick as second-in-command of 623. As we have seen Otto's home was in Måløy, on the island of Vågsøy, not very far north of the island of Hovden. The paths of Oskar and Otto came together on 20th January, 1943.

MTBs 618 and 623, the former commanded by Andresen, the latter by Prebensen, in the absence of the unfit Haavik, had crossed to Norway and gone in past Batalden, before tying up and camouflaging the boats. It was a fine winter's night, and Oskar Hovden on board 618 felt quite at home — for this was his island. He suggested to his commander that, since he was so near, he might go ashore and call at his home. Andresen agreed, and Sub-Lieut. Hoddevik was sent in the small boat with him. "We had had reports that there were Germans in the Kvanhovden lighthouse," says Otto, "so as we rowed away in the small boat we had a machine-gun with us. The plan was for Oskar to go up to the Hovden house, while I lay on watch outside till he got in and saw if the coast was clear. It was a very cold night, with the temperature below freezing point. I was lying behind a big rock, extremely cold, and I knew that he had gone in. But he never came out! I lay there, getting number and number with the cold, until I began to think that I was seeing Germans all over the place. But I shouldn't have been surprised. Oskar had found his wife — he'd forgotten all about me! Finally he came out and told me to come in, assuring me that there were no Germans about. But it was some time after I came into the house that I realised that I still had a knife in one hand and a revolver in the other."

Ingrid was just a young girl on that never-to-be-forgotten night. "I knew something was happening that night," she says. "I heard a knocking at the window. Mother and Margit went to the door. I was not allowed to get up, but I knew — I just knew — that it was my brother Oskar who had come." Marthe assured Ingrid that it was two strangers who had come. The less children knew in those days the better. It would have been so easy for a child to let slip some dangerous bit of information without realising that it was important.

Fru Hovden made a good meal for Otto and Oskar, and they finally left on the understanding that a decision would be made as to whether or not the family were going to Shetland when father and the boys returned from the fishing. Ingrid recalls that she got up in the morning and the two callers had gone. She was surprised when she was told that she was not to go to school that day. "I protested that I wasn't ill, but still mother wouldn't let me go." Says Lars, "Mother didn't tell me anything either." When father and the other three boys — Inge, Jon and Arne — came home in the morning they were told the news. They had the chance to go to Shetland. What was it to be? A family council was held. Did it take long to reach a decision? Says Ingrid, "I don't know. I was never asked for an opinion!" But Lars says everyone was asked for an opinion except Ingrid and himself, and the decision was "Shetland!"

During the day preparations were made. Father Hovden insisted on going back to Kalvåg to collect the money he was owed for fish. A special dinner was prepared — there was no point hoarding food now — and it was their last meal on Norwegian soil. The two young ones knew something was going to happen, but they still hadn't been told just what. All day they showed themselves as

30. MTB boys all — the Hovden family. Top, Oskar and Lars; bottom, Jon and Arne; centre, Inge.

31. Afternoon tea-dance in North Road hall. Centre, far side, Nan Robertson, Isobel Herculeson and Syverre Syversen.

32. A group of MTB men in their mess hall. Violet Mundie is in centre.

little as possible, but in late afternoon they embarked on two small rowing-boats, taking very little with them beyond a few clothes. Their cover story if stopped was that they were going to visit an uncle who lived quite near to where the MTBs were lying, south-east of the island. They had a row of about three kilometres. Otto says there had been quite a few local people about during the day, so a number of people knew of their presence. They had given away the bulk of their rations to these people. When the Hovdens came up in the two small boats they were divided between the two MTBs, with the two women and the two children in one, the father and the three boys in the other. Then they were off.

One memory remains with Ingrid. "They set off a torpedo — the boat was shivering." The torpedo had been fired at a coastal steamer which Hovden senior told them often carried German troops. It was in fact the *Kong Harald,* but the torpedo missed. A Måløy man told Otto after the war that he had been on board the steamer that night, and he was glad the torpedo didn't hit! Before they set course for Shetland they shot up a German watch-post and barracks. Down below the women and children heard the explosion when the torpedo hit the land, and the noise of the guns above their heads when the Germans were under fire was a new and frightening experience for them. But once they were really under way it took them only about eight hours to reach Lerwick. On landing Ingrid was given a doll and some chocolate — Lars doesn't remember getting anything!

It was down south to the Patriotic School for screening for all of them. Oskar, of course, remained with his MTB, and father was very quickly back in Shetland as he was badly needed as a pilot for the MTBs. Jon, Arne and Inge went to Skegness for training, and Ingrid went to school in the south. When Oskar was on leave he came to see her, and, realising how desperately lonely she was, he took her to Aberdeen, and put her on the boat to Shetland to rejoin her mother who had already gone north. Jon, Arne and Inge were all posted to the MTBs. So now the whole family was in Shetland, the four boys and the father on the MTBs, mother working in the officers' mess in the Burgh Road, Ingrid at school, and Lars still not fifteen, but old enough to have left school and desperate to get in on the action. He was finally accepted, young as he was, as a sort of trainee engineer. Their home was in Hope Villa in St Olaf Street.

Lars was the first to suffer. Two MTBs were lying at the Anglo-Scottish. 625, on which Oskar was now a crew member, had come in the night before with engine trouble. Lars, along with an engineer, went on board to carry out repairs. "We were early. The cook said we were to come and get some coffee before we started work," says Lars. "When we came below the crew were just finishing breakfast. There were no clean cups, so I washed some, and we sat down to wait for the coffee. By this time the crew had all gone on deck and there were just the three of us in the cabin."

Up on deck there was a mine with a faulty detonator. It should have been landed as faulty, and should have been destroyed, but the crewman whose job it was to arm the mines decided to try to fix it. He was working immediately above the cabin where Lars was sitting, and the rest of the crew were up in the bows. Oskar was ashore. Suddenly the mine exploded. The crewman was killed instantly, and Lars and the two men in the cabin were severely injured. Lars was taken to the hospital up in the Institute, where he lay for five weeks before being taken down to the Norwegian hospital at Craiglockhart in Edinburgh, where he remained for a further two to three weeks before being sent home. It was a time of great worry, with everyone trying to hide from Ingrid just how serious Lars' injuries really were.

And of course all the time the MTBs were coming and going on their dangerous missions to the Norwegian coast. One son already badly injured, the other four and her husband risking their lives almost daily — it must have been a time of terrible strain for Fru Hovden. Lars himself, still just fifteen, still too young to be taken as a crew-man, was back at his engineering work the moment he was fit enough. He saw his brothers coming and going and longed to be with them. He saw Oskar coming back with a head wound from a shell splinter. Inge and Arne say little about their war-time experiences, but Inge does cautiously admit, "We did have one bad trip on 716. It was our last trip. We had some casualties." Records show that that trip was probably carried out in March, 1945, when a German patrol boat was set on fire during a fight at close range. On the same trip there had been an exchange of fire with the Germans on Slåtterøy.

At the end of the war the whole family, except Oskar who was regular navy, gradually made their way back to Hovden. Says Ingrid, indignation still in her voice, "The Germans had been living in our house, eight of them, I think. They had left the house in a terrible mess. I remember they had all carved their names on the kitchen table. The whole house had been very badly treated." They all stayed in Hovden until 1949, when Inge bought a farm near Selje, and mother and father followed him there. Ingrid got married at nineteen. Today Ingrid, Inge, Lars and Arne all still live in the Selje area, and Fru Hovden also still survives. They have many grandchildren — for instance Lars has fifteen, Ingrid fourteen. They have many memories of the wartime years and the time they lived among us. Their welcome for Shetland visitors is friendly and warm, and one is made instantly at home.

Chapter Fourteen

MTBs in Action

The Norwegian MTB operation based in Lerwick was both successful and important, and warrants a leading place in the story of the Norwegian navy's activities during the war. The Fairmile boats which formed 30 Flotilla, and later 54 Flotilla, were much sturdier and more powerful than the earlier MTBs, and they proved that they could stand up to all but the very worst of North Sea weather. Their speed and manoeuvrabililty made them ideally suited for work among the holms and skerries of Norway's west coast, and when covered with their camouflage nets they could lie undetected from all but the closest scrutiny. From the moment they started operating, they became a serious irritant to the Germans, who were forced to strengthen coast defences to meet the new threat. Enemy coastal shipping, too, became increasingly nervous of the new danger, and not without cause, as the boats by war's end had sunk a total of forty-two ships and damaged many others. To go in on an enemy-occupied coast is always dangerous, so every trip the MTBs made carried real danger. Often the log of the trip showed little in the way of action, but there were countless occasions when fire was exchanged with shore guard posts, patrol boats, and so on, all of which was taken so much for granted that it seemed hardly worthy of mention.

Sometimes they went right in and landed agents. On other occasions they picked up agents or people who were on the run from the Gestapo. Sometimes they carried a "cigar" or "chariot", slung on each side of the boat — "chariots" were one or two-man human torpedoes, as used in the abortive raid on the *Tirpitz*. Sometimes they lay under their camouflage nets, waiting for a suitable target to appear. On some of these occasions they holed up so near to a German post that they could watch the enemy all day with their binoculars, unseen under their nets. Any man showing himself outside the nets was liable to a pay deduction. Frequently a local fisherman would row past within hailing distance, blissfully unaware of the hidden eyes watching him from the decks of the deadly little craft. Occasionally they would land a man who would climb to a vantage point on a nearby hillside, and watch for the appearance of a suitable target. Sometimes they carried parties of perhaps a dozen Commandos, who would be landed if there was an appropriate shore target to be attacked. The MTB boys felt sorry for the Commandos on these trips. Life on an MTB driving at speed in heavy seas is anything but pleasant, and needs a lot of getting used to. The Commandos had had no experience of such conditions, and by the time the boats reached the Norwegian coast on a rough day the Commandos were far from the peak condition which was necessary if they were soon to be face to face with the enemy.

In December, 1942, only a few weeks after they commenced operations, there was the spell of very rough weather conditions which we have already noted. On 27th December, 619 and two other boats were out in a very severe storm, and although they had to turn back before reaching their objective, they survived, and prompted the following British report: "That all the boats returned safe and sound on 27th December says a lot for the boats and their commanders. It is now certain that these hulls are seaworthy enough, which lends weight to the argument that it was wise to strengthen them, even if it meant the loss of a little speed."

On 21st January, 1943, the MTBs carried out what was probably their most effective operation of the whole war. All the MTBs, with the exception of 619, which was out of action undergoing repair, took part in the raid, and the whole thing was a classic of good planning, meticulous execution and sheer bravery. Two men who now live in Shetland, Asbjørn Lie and Sverre Syversen, both took part in the raid, and both remember it very clearly. What follows is a condensed account of the operation, although a much fuller and detailed version is contained in "Klar til Kamp" by H. Storm-Bjerke.

The whole operation, which was given the code-name "Cartoon", was meticulously planned. The objective was the destruction of the ore mine at Litlabø on Stord, and up-to-date information on German dispositions in the area was essential. It was duly obtained by sending two boats, the *Gullborg* and the *Sjølivet*, to land men who would fill the role of fishermen on local boats while gathering details of German numbers, strong-points and other defences in a wide area around the target. Readers will recall that the two boats had come up from Scapa Flow along with the *Lygrefjord,* but before that the *Gullborg* and the *Sjølivet* had both arrived in Lerwick from Norway on 23rd September, 1941, the former with 17 people on board, the latter with 26. A German plane had circled the *Sjølivet* shortly after leaving Norway, but had not attacked. On the following day they passed the wreckage of the *Odd,* which had almost certainly been the German's target. Perhaps the fact that she had two Germans on board as well as three Norwegians had something to do with her being regarded as a priority target. It would seem the Germans may well have been deserters.

Having received the up-to-date information brought back by the two boats, the HQ staff in Lerwick formulated the scheme of action, and then called in the MTB commanders for briefing. Saturday, 23rd January, 1943, was departure day. Lerwegians were accustomed to the coming and going of the MTBs by this time, without knowing a great deal of what they were up to, but in the darkness of this early Saturday morning a large party of Commandos was seen going quietly down to the quay and boarding the MTBs. There were fifty in all in the Commando party, most Norwegians but with a sprinkling of Scots, and with Major Fynn commanding. After they were all aboard and below decks, their equipment was loaded, and we know now that that equipment was mostly explosives, and other gear needed for the sabotage of the Stord mine. A Lerwick man has noted that the Commandos had been in town since Thursday, living at the Norwegian camp at the Anglo-Scottish.

People living near Lerwick harbour were accustomed to the wide variety of harbour noises, but on this particular Saturday morning the thunderous roar of 1250 hp Packard engines on seven MTBs must have ensured that everyone was awake. As the sky began to lighten in the east they passed through the south entrance boom defence in single file, with 626, commanded by Lieut. Bøgeberg and with the flotilla CO Lieut. Tamber on board, leading the way. 627, 620, 631, 625, 618 and 623 followed in that order, their commanders, in the same order, being Lieuts. Henriksen, Prebensen, Matland, Hjellestad, Andresen and Herlofson. 619 was the only member of the flotilla missing, and that was because she was undergoing repairs. However, a number of her crew had been drafted on to other boats — Asbjørn Lie to 623, for instance — and most of the remainder were on board one or other of the boats, lacking official permission to be there, and so behaving as unobtrusively as possible.

German aircraft spotted and shadowed them almost from the Shetland coast, and Tamber ordered a more southerly course to fool the watchers. It fooled Major Fynn as well — he thought they were going back! The small port of Sagvåg on the south-west coast of Stord had been chosen for the landing, as it was not far from their target — the mine. Two MTBs, 626 and 627, were to carry out the attack on the port, and land the Commandos. The others were to take care of possible German interference or reinforcement, with 618 and 623 covering the northern flank and 620, 625 and 631 taking care of the south and east. As the flotilla drove south from Marstein where they had first made land, 618 and 623 broke away to take up their alloted station. When off Sagvåg 626 and 627 went into action, 626 firing two torpedoes which blew up the quay in the harbour and the German heavy guns with it. Both 626 and 627 followed up this success by plastering the target with fire from every available weapon. At midnight they went in, 626 landing her Commandos at the remnants of the quay, 627 landing her quota, led by Major Fynn, at the small jetty on the other side of the harbour. As they all disappeared into the darkness the occasional glint of an eye in the moonlight was all that showed in the blackened faces. But they were still under fire and a corporal was killed as he stepped ashore, his death being the signal for combined fire from both MTBs to wipe out the remnants of German resistance. A blazing house joined the moonlight in providing a lurid illumination of the battle scene. Now all the two small boats could do was wait. They had no way of knowing whether their colleagues in the other boats would be successful in preventing the Germans mounting a counter-attack by bringing in reinforcements.

Meanwhile 620, 625 and 631 were having their own adventures to the south and east. They deliberately invited German attention and came under fire from a number of strong points. 620 and 631 went right into Leirvik harbour looking for a target, and 625 went up the east side of Stord and laid mines. 620 launched her torpedoes at a German ship coming south, and both passed underneath her and exploded on the far shore. The German immediately opened fire, but 620 replied with energy and accuracy, and the *Ilse M. Russ* was soon on fire, out of control and running aground. 620 had to take some punishment as well. Their return journey was punctuated by intense German fire from different shore locations, and they sustained some damage, but they had reason to believe their return fire had also been effective, as at least one of the shore positions was silenced. Now all three came up and lay just outside Sagvåg.

On shore the Commandos' operation had been carried out both successfully and entirely according to plan. The mine equipment and fittings had been blown up, and the mine very effectively put out of production for a considerable time to come. The MTBs had wiped out the German force in Sagvåg and destroyed their guns. Seven of 626's crew had been wounded, and the Commandos had one man killed and two wounded; they brought back three German prisoners with them. It had been a copy-book operation, but now it was time to go, and, after leaving delayed action charges to complete the destructon at Sagvåg the two small boats and their passengers pulled away from the harbour.

In the morning a plane appeared overhead, which was presumably the one which was to rendezvous with them at nine am. When it twice failed to respond to an Aldis-lamp challenge, it became clear that it was no friend but a German Junkers 88. It came in fast with guns blazing at 625, the bullets whipping the sea to a froth alongside the MTB. But the little boats were ready and they answered the plane's fire to such good effect that it suddenly exploded in mid-air. One German, thrown from the wreckage, floated down on a parachute and disappeared beneath the waves, to be seen no more. The weather had become very rough and it was late afternoon before they tied up in Lerwick. The dead, wounded and prisoners were taken ashore, the prisoners glad to be on land, even if it was Shetland, for they had been violently seasick all the way across, without eliciting any marked sympathy from their captors.

What of 618 and 623 who were guarding the north flank? They had come up to Store Kalsøy and had been heavily engaged by the guns from the nearby heavily fortified German strongpoint. It was fast and furious for a time, with both the MTBs and the Germans scoring hits. Asbjørn Lie and Sverre Syversen were both on 623, and this is an action they well remember. Some of her guns were put out of action, and an ammunition locker on 618 was set on fire. A deckhand opened the locker and threw the burning magazine overboard. When they finally pulled away they knew they had scored quite a few hits, but they had suffered too. They had had three men wounded, and 618 had two holes above the waterline and another two below, and both boats had many bullet holes. Lerwick people watched them come in, and it was clear that they had been in heavy action, but there was an air of jubilation about all the crews. And it wasn't long before a few of the men working around the harbour had got hold of bits of the story. They were a little confused when the German radio report said there had been a raid on Larvik, because they well knew the boats had not been away long enough to have been there. The BBC said the raid had been successful, but didn't say where. But within a day or two the pierhead stories were sufficiently accurate to have a number of the details, although the location of the raid was still not common knowledge. One or two people knowledgeable about Norway put two and two together, and concluded that the German report had probably said Larvik through ignorance, when Leirvik was what they should have said.

Not surprisingly the MTB crews were highly delighted with the operation. They'd all been in it together, and they'd all shared in the pleasure of giving the Germans bloody noses. The celebrations on the evening of the return were light-hearted and understandably a little noisy. There was singing, the most popular song one they had composed themselves, their own "MTB Song". In the song Tamber and Alv Andresen, who was later to die at German hands, come in for special mention. A day or two later a German broadcast from Oslo caused some amusement. It ran as follows: "Oslo Radio, 25th January, 1943. Seven fast-moving British MTBs tried on the night of Sunday to push forward into Leirvik on Stord, and put ashore saboteur troops there. The German coastal defence, in co-operation with German guard-boats, forced the enemy MTBs to turn. Because of poor visibility one could not at first ascertain the result of the German defence, but just after the Observer Corps reported that five MTBs had run back. One can reckon the other two were lost." The MTB boys knew better. In addition to all the damage at the mine and at Sagvåg, a 2500-ton ship had been sunk and a plane shot down, as well as another ship which had been blown up by one of the mines laid by 625.

One unhappy note was the loss of the boat *Dagny,* which had been taken to the Norwegian coast by Gjertsen, who had commanded the *Gullborg* on her earlier trip. His purpose was to act as a direction indicator to the MTBs but he failed to make contact. He was short of fuel, so went back to the coast to obtain sufficient from friends to take him back to Shetland. He set out again for the islands, but nothing more was ever heard from him.

The British navy took a little time to evaluate the raid. Finally, at the end of June, 1943, the chief of the British Home Fleet, Admiral Fraser, sent a belated congratulatory message, via Vice-Admiral Wells. "I was very interested in your report to the British Admiralty regarding Operation Cartoon. I would be very grateful if you would convey my warm congratulations to all the officers and crew concerned in the operation."

Although the radio announcement from Oslo gave a completely false account of Operation Cartoon, Hitler had apparently not been kept completely in the dark, for very soon after the raid this order was forthcoming from his HQ. "The enemy's lucky MTB attack on the Norwegian coast recently, when a coast fort was surprised and taken, a cannon destroyed, and fourteen out of nineteen men either killed, wounded or taken prisoner, showed they were quite unprepared and lacked readiness." The area commander was placed under open arrest, and Hitler's displeasure was undoubtedly felt by even the humblest private. In the services — whether German or British — when someone at the top gets a rocket, those at the bottom feel it worst.

At the end of February 619 and 631 lay camouflaged for eight days and nights waiting for a target, but none appeared, so they laid mines and returned. They had, however, gained a great deal of information from the ceaseless watch they kept on enemy movements from underneath their nets, and they brought back a Linge agent. On 12th March the same two boats set out again, this time with Herlofson in command of 619, and Matland on 631. Their departure had been observed by Lerwick people, and on the evening of 14th March it was observed that the Bressay lighthouse was lit, and a searchlight was pointing skywards at the Ness of Sound. Clearly it was feared that someone was in trouble, and for those who watched these things it was known that 619 and 631 had not returned. But nothing appeared to happen that night. Next day, however, two MTBs came into harbour, their decks crowded with men. People wondered. One was 619, the other had left the harbour in haste some hours previously. Of 631 there was no sign. Then the BBC announced that light forces had attacked Germany's searoutes successfully. Two boats had gone into Florø Fjord, and had torpedoed two ships. One had caught fire — the other blew up. One MTB had been hit and sunk, her crew being taken on board her companion. There was as usual a great deal of local rumour about what had happened, but once again Asbjørn Lie was on the raid, on board 619, and the real story can be told from his recollections, and also from the account in "Klar til Kamp" by Storm-Bjerke.

The two MTBs had made landfall at Skorpen with 619 leading the way, because they had an excellent pilot (*possibly Terje Teige.*) Soon after midnight they were tied up and camouflaged and in the morning Herlofson and Matland paddled ashore and selected a lookout point from which all traffic in and out of Florø could be observed, and a watchman was posted there. Nothing much happened that day. Then on the 14th the wind fell and the sky cleared, and the watchman came down to report that several ships were now anchored in Florø harbour. This was what they had been waiting for. The skippers went up and checked the situation through binoculars, and made a simple plan of attack. Just as they were getting under way the radio operator brought the latest weather report from Scapa Flow: the wind would strengthen to strong gale force during the next twenty-four hours.

As they went up the channel towards Florø they dropped their small defence mines in their wake, and finally passed through a channel so narrow they could almost touch the shore on either side. This entry was never used by shipping, and the Germans ignored it. But the Norwegians knew all about it. Herlofson in 619 was in overall command. He went first. He could see a large, dark shadow — a big ship at anchor. This was a new arrival since they had checked. At a distance of 400 yards he fired two torpedoes, and then reversed at full power. He was very close to his target and there was little room to play with. 631 pushed ahead looking for the next target, and suddenly the two torpedoes hit and exploded, one amidships and one in the engine-room. The ship broke in two and sank like a stone. On 631 the water came down in a deluge, but a target had been spotted and Matland launched his torpedoes. One hit the ship amidships, and she erupted into flames. She was to sink soon afterwards. The second torpedo was heard exploding somewhere on the shore. It was time to go.

619 led the way out of the harbour, 631 following. Asbjørn believes what happened was that the wash 619 was making hid from 631 a skerry which lay just a little off the course they were following. Whatever the cause, 631 suddenly seemed to lift in the air and list to port. It took a moment for the crew to realise they were well and truly aground — high on a Norwegian skerry. 619 had disappeared on ahead, but frantic lamp signals brought her back. Matland was preparing for the worst, destroying all papers and dumping the confidential box overboard. 619 made several attempts to tow 631 off, but all to no avail. It was decided to abandon ship, but first they would set her on fire. Matland fired his signal pistol at a fuel tank. No result, so he tried again. Still no use. They left her and boarded 631, which now riddled the doomed boat from stem to stern with machine-gun fire. Says Asbjørn, with memories of blazing tankers still fresh in his mind, "Never have I seen a ship so unwilling to burn." But they had wasted enough time — the Germans would be on the scene at any moment. They couldn't go the short way out, because they had laid mines, so they had to go the long way round.

Herlofson set course at full speed, and they were soon at

Batalden. It was just after midnight. South of them they could see the silhouette of a German destroyer, but they slipped past and they thought they were clear away. But the destroyer took up the chase, and for hour after hour it continued in heavy seas, until finally the German gave up. They had driven 619 as hard as they could to get away, and she had gradually begun to succumb to the rough treatment, until, as Asbjørn says, "She was like a concertina." By the time they had shaken off pursuit they were away out into the Atlantic. They could still transmit, though they couldn't receive, and their fuel was very low. They put out a sea anchor, lay by, and waited. Conditions were extremely bad, and the boat was terribly overcrowded. Beside the two crews there were over twenty Commandos on board, because both boats had been carrying about a dozen Commandos in case a suitable opportunity arose to use them on the operation. One can imagine how men unused to the sea and to MTBs must have felt during the long chase in very heavy seas, with the MTB doing everything but stand on its head. On the following day a plane came over and indicated a course for Shetland. On arrival it was on to the Malakoff slipway immediately, and after temporary repairs 619 was sent down south, encountering rough weather in the Pentland Firth which undid all the Malakoff work. So that was the story behind what the Lerwick people had seen — the Bressay light, the searchlight, the crowds of men on the two MTBs when they came into harbour. The second MTB had been sent to 619's assistance as soon as her position was known.

Unlike Operation Cartoon, this raid aroused a great deal of interest. Naval HQ in London were enthusiastic, and the British Admiralty reacted almost at once. "Bring to officers, crews and base personnel of 54 Flotilla their Lordships' congratulations on the recently carried out operation in the Norwegian fjords." 54 Flotilla was the first to receive such recognition. Once again the Germans had been caught with their pants down. When they realised what was going on they had manned the guns at the harbour, but before they could get off a round Matland's second torpedo hit, and practically lifted the whole quay, guns and all, into the air. Items from the cargoes of both sunk ships began to float ashore next day, and among them were items of food, salvaged by the Norwegians with much appreciation. But the Germans soon put a stop to that — the food was much too good for Norwegian stomachs.

631 lay on the skerry. Several days later, when convinced that no delayed action bomb awaited them, the Germans refloated her

33. The narrow channel on Bømlo through which two MTBs passed.

34. The Norwegian floating dock in Bressay Sound.

35. An early Shetland/Norwegian marriage — Helen Isbister and Gunder Vinje, with baby Caroline in pram.

and took her to Bergen, where she was put on the slip, and received much attention from the German authorities. A gunner was carrying out an inspection of the little ship's armament, and was handling the twin machine-guns, when they suddenly started firing. Recoil and shock almost threw him out of the gunner's seat. But by December, 1943, she had been changed to S631, and was under the orders of the German Admiral commanding Norway's west coast. In Florø the German garrison was stepped up to 700 men, several more craft were stationed there, and additional gun emplacements were constructed. It had been a productive raid by 619 and 631.

On 11th/12th April MTB 626 with Bøgeberg commanding, went over to pick up Leif Larsen and the crew of the *Bergholm* — that story is told elsewhere. On 11th April 620, 625, 627 and 653 proceeded on Operation Carry. 653 had come north to replace 631. The little boats had 85 Commandos on board, and the object was to land the Commandos who would destroy the German battery on Rugsundøy, at the mouth of Nordfjord. Tamber had himself gone on this operation, and when he found very unsuitable conditions at the place where they were supposed to lie up, he simply ordered a return to Shetland. His action incurred criticism from ACOS — Tamber had abandoned the plan's original objective; not merely that, but he had suggested alternatives which he felt had a better chance of success. For the British navy steeped in tradition that was a bit much — and from a mere lieutenant! The Commandos had been brought to Shetland for this operation, and two days later they left for the south again on the trooper. The German radio reported that a Commando raid "had been driven off".

Regular operations continued, some of them not achieving anything very spectacular, but all of them adding to the unease of German coastal defences, and causing a gradual build-up in the number of troops being absorbed into the Norway occupation forces. On 29th April, 1943, MTB 626 towed a coble across the North Sea, and, when five miles off Geitungen, at the south end of the island of Karmøy, put Lieut. Godwin and six men aboard, dropped the tow and returned to Lerwick. The coble was an engined open boat, similar in size to a big Shetland sixern, and in it were two kayak-type canoes, limpet mines and other equipment. The intention was to make land in the coble and use it as a sort of moving base, while the kayak crews would carry out sorties to attach the limpet mines to German ships which, hopefully, would be found in Karmsund or in the little town of Kopervik on Karmøy. An MTB would come back on 9th May, rendezvous with the Godwin party at Urter island, and take them back to Shetland.

On 9th May the weather was extremely foggy, and the MTB had to return without finding the island. 16th May was the next scheduled date, and this time the island was duly reached, but there was no sign of life, though a party was landed and a thorough search made. Over succeeding days, four more trips were made by the MTBs, all without discovering any trace of Godwin's party, and attempts at his rescue were finally abandoned. His fate, and that of the men with him, was a mystery.

Thanks to a book by Kenneth Macksey published in 1987, and titled "Godwin's Saga", we now know virtually all that happened to the party. To begin with the coble developed engine trouble almost as soon as it left the MTB, and a successful landfall at the south end of Vestre Bokn was only achieved by using the canoe paddles. For part of the way they were in full view of a German gun-post. Already the plan was going wrong, but, leaving the coble behind, the two canoes were paddled as far as Kopervik, where the only target was a minesweeper, to which mines were successfully affixed.

Meanwhile the three men left with the coble, desparing of the canoeists' return, moved the boat to a different hide, then finally abandoned it, having left an explosive charge on board to ensure its destruction. They set off on the long trek to the Swedish frontier. By the time they were well underway the Germans had mounted an intensive search. The sinking of the minesweeper had alerted them. Then the coble had been found, undamaged, and in it tell-tale charts, etc. Soon, with assistance from a Norwegian informer, the three men were captured. When the canoe men finally returned and found no trace of the coble, they proceeded to paddle the considerable distance to the rendezvous island, which they duly reached. The 9th having passed without the hoped-for pick-up because of the fog, they awaited the 16th, but in the meantime they had been spotted, the Germans arrived in force, and they were made prisoner.

All seven were taken first to Haugesund, then to Stavanger and from there to the Grini concentration camp near Oslo. From Grini they were taken to Sachsenhausen, where to begin with they were in with the Norwegian prisoners. In November, 1943, they were put in with men undergoing "special" treatment, and in their case the treatment was marching thirty miles a day, on a figure of eight track, testing boots. They were marched for 420 days, and covered 12,600 miles.

The end came on 2nd February, 1945. A large party, including five of the British party, among whom was Lieut. Godwin, were taken out to be shot. It is believed that the British and some others staged a last desperate attack on the way to execution, and probably managed to inflict a number of casualties on the Germans before meeting their deaths. Two of the party, one of whom had been in the camp hospital, escaped the execution, and were soon afterwards taken to the notorious Belsen camp. There one of them was shot, and the other died only four days before Belsen was liberated by the British. (*The stories of Svein Salhus and Knut Henriksen in Chapter 20, "Arbeit Macht Frei", throw an interesting sidelight on the Godwin saga.*)

On 15th April, 1943, a mine exploded on 625 in Lerwick, when Lars Hovden was injured, and in June 626 torpedoed and sank the German ship *Altenfels*. Then, along with 620, they engaged in a gunfight with the German escort, M468, and also came under fire from shore batteries. Two men were killed on 620, and Tamber, who had been on 626, and Prebensen were both wounded. Lerwegians noted that the two MTBs came back with several wounded on board, and two died in hospital. They were big men, it was said, both over six feet tall. It was known that the Commanding Officer had been wounded, and a number of the men were walking about wearing bandages, and some with arms in slings. But again ACOS came up with warm praise for the operation. The light days and nights of summer were very unfavourable for MTB operations, but they still continued to go across, and in August the German *Verma* struck a mine laid by 623, and sank.

Now they were carrying more agents and saboteurs and landing them in Norway, and they were continually laying mines. In the autumn Captain Horve replaced Tamber as CO, and one or two younger men were being drafted in to take command of MTBs. On longer trips two of the big whalers, usually the *Horten* and the *Risør,* were used to tow the MTBs for part of the way across, and this had happened when 618 and 627 torpedoed the *Anke* in Trondheimfjord in September. Two British MTBs, 686 and 699, came north and joined the flotilla, and later another two, 675 and 684. On 17th September the *Risør* and the *Horten* were again towing three MTBs across, but the British 686 had engine trouble, and *Risør* had to tow her back.

As the trips went on through the autumn they were being spotted more frequently, and on several occasions they were engaged by enemy destroyers and patrol craft. On 22nd October, 688, 699, 653 and 686 (699 and 686 were British) went over and sank the German *Kilstraum* at Bessakerholmen, away to the north of Trondheim, with gunfire. They were seen by a German patrol boat, but they laid smoke and headed out for sea. Three fighter planes attacked them, and 688 suffered one killed and five wounded. The planes came in a second time, and the British 699 was set on fire, the crew being taken off by 688. Later 688 was again attacked, but she survived, and in the face of a severe storm and heavy sea, was finally escorted back to Lerwick. 653 and 686 had been on a different course and did not make contact.

In September, 1943, four "chariots" — human torpedoes — had arrived in Shetland, and one or two MTBs had been fitted with davits to carry two of the strange craft, one on each side. The idea was that an agent would be landed in a small boat, with a short-range transmitter. He would keep watch, while the MTB would lie under camouflage. When a suitable target was sighted he would radio the MTB and the chariots would be dropped, ready to go into the attack. The idea was good, but there is little record of success being achieved by the "chariots". On occasion they could cause trouble, as Otto Hoddevik recalls. They had been carrying two of the "chariots", which had not been used, and on the way back, in heavy seas, one of them broke partly loose, and began to endanger the safety of the MTB. As the boat rolled heavily, Otto cut the last securing wire with an axe, and the "chariot" disappeared over the side.

On 22nd November there was an explosion on the British 686 where it lay at the Anglo-Scottish quay, tied up alongside 626. Both boats blazed fiercely, and four Britons and one Norwegian were killed, with a number of British and six more Norwegians wounded. The death roll later mounted to eight in all. Both MTBs had to be sunk by gunfire. As the winter progressed the MTB activity never wavered, and a number of casualties were sustained in actions on the Norwegian coast. In February, 1944, 619 for instance had her commander Christiansen and two men wounded. At the same time 625 returned full of water, having sprung a leak. She was considered unfit for further service. A week later 627 and 653 were towed over by the *Molde,* another of the big whalers, and attacked a German convoy at about 1000 metres range. 627 sank the *Irma,* while 653 accounted for the *Henry.* Both ships had both German and Norwegian passengers, and the Quisling propaganda machine tried to make capital out of this episode. A Quisling marine officer said, "Norwegian seamen, the luck is with the Englishmen plundering among the Norwegian skerries. A new cowardly deed has been carried out. Did you recognise this cynical Enlishman, Norwegian seamen?" The men of the little boats had an appropriate answer.

In March 712 with Herlofson and 709 with Matland were sent to Larne in Northern Ireland for a time, while the remainder of the flotilla — 618, 623, 627, 653, 688 and 715 — were stationed in Great Yarmouth in the months before D-Day. Their field of operations was mainly over on the Dutch coast. In one skirmish 715 was hit and had four wounded. With complete Allied supremacy in the Channel their presence was no longer required, and they returned to Lerwick in September, when Lieut. Herlofson took over as Flotilla Commander. In October 722 with Bøgeberg commanding set the *Freikoll* on fire in Frøysjøen, saved the crew, and took the skipper and four volunteers back to Shetland. Also in October 618 was so badly damaged in heavy seas that she was condemned.

Late autumn and early winter 1944 saw frequent skirmishes on the Norwegian coast. At the beginning of November 712 and 709 sank two patrol boats, and later in the month 717 sank the *Wilhelm* at Askvoll. On 6th December, 653 with Martinsen and 717 with Olsen went over and lay camouflaged. About midnight both MTBs attacked the 3000-ton German ship *Ditmar Koel* in Korsfjorden. During the attack 653 grounded at the bow, but firing both torpedoes lightened her sufficiently to allow her to float free. 717 also attacked with torpedoes, and the German sank after three explosions. On the way back 653 was taking water badly, and the crew bailed desperately with buckets, and then the engines stopped. 717 took her in tow, and later the *Molde* came out and assisted in getting her back to Lerwick. The sinkings continued, and between late December 44 and the end of March 45 a further nine ships had been accounted for. In early April a U-boat was torpedoed in Hjeltefjorden and believed sunk, but this was never proved.

Certainly there was no doubt about the fate of U-637 which underwent an attack from 711 at Karmøy, on the last MTB sortie of the war on 26th April. 723 was also on the operation, and a British staff officer later commented that this action was all the more brave and daring in that it took place in broad daylight, and because U-boats had not previously been regarded as suitable targets for MTBs. The two boats lay waiting all night, he said, and when the sun came over the mountain tops they decided to return to Shetland. Suddenly a U-boat, on the way in from a trip, broke surface. Both boats turned towards it and fired torpedoes, but the U-boat changed course and was not hit. The boats opened fire with their six pounders and heavy machine-guns, and a running battle at speed now developed, while the boats manoeuvred to get into position to actually drop depth charges on top of the U-boat. The submarine was returning their fire with interest, but they pressed in close, firing all the time, and the U-boat was taking a lot of punishment. Suddenly flames shot up round the conning tower and there was a heavy explosion below. The MTBs now came in even closer, and dropped four depth charges on top of the U-boat, these exploding between the conning tower and the stern. Now the German was completely out of control and drove towards the shore. It keeled over and began to go down by the stern in a mass of flames. It was now in a sinking condition, and unable to offer any further resistance, so the MTBs pulled away. 711 had some damage, with one man killed and two wounded.

The dead man was a policeman from Bergen, who had made a late escape from Norway, via Sweden. He came along 711 one day, and asked if he could make a trip with them to the Norwegian coast, as he hoped soon to be an MTB man himself. The coxswain agreed to take him, and as the hours went by he thought the trip was very unexciting. After 711's two torpedoes missed, and MTB and U-boat started firing at each other, the only Norwegian casualty was the man from Bergen, killed instantly. Sverre Syversen was on 711 for this last operation of the war, and he still remembers it vividly. He had been on 623 for the very first sinking by the Lerwick-based boats in November 1942.

Shortly before the war ended the British Admiralty made it clear that they appreciated the role the MTBs had played. The attacks by the little boats had been designed to unsettle the Germans. "The enemy has obviously never known when he could expect the next visit. Many of his ships have been sunk or damaged, and he has been compelled to increase the number of convoy escort vessels and patrol ships. In addition the Germans on the Norwegian coast are clearly keyed up to a nervous pitch which in no small way is credited to the total MTB force which has been concentrated against them." Paying tribute to the offensive spirit shown by the MTB crews, the report finishes by commenting on how few mechanical failures there had been on the boats, and said, "The engine room crews deserve the highest recognition." Of the crews, six were killed in explosions, one fell in an air attack, six were killed in battle, six Norwegians and one Briton were executed by the Germans and a total of forty-seven were wounded. Of the MTBs themselves, 631 was lost at Florø, 345 was captured, 626 was burnt in Lerwick harbour, 625 suffered severe sea-damage and went out of service as did 618. 712 ran aground, and though she was put into dock, never returned to service.

37. Luftwaffe tender from airfield near Trondheim surrendered to MTB 711 north of Unst a few days before war's end, and brought to Lerwick by 711 crew members, including Sverre Syversen.

ALV HALDOR ANDRESEN
* 20.3.1920 ~ SANDEFJORD

BERNHARD KLEPPE
* 27.9.1919 ~ BERGEN

JENS KLIPPER
* 8.11.1919 ~ DRONTHEIM?

AGNAR INGOLF BIGSETH
* 10.11.1911 ~ BERGEN

HANS THORVALD BEREVAHR HANSEN
* 22.9.1922 ~ BERGEN

KJELL ØYSTEIN HALS
* 31.10.1921 ~ BERGEN

RENNIE HULL
* 5.10.1921 ~ BLACKPOOL, ENGLAND

36. On left, monument at Ulven to the murdered crew of MTB 345.

38. Three Norwegian and two British MTBs at Fosnavåg on 18th May, 1945. On 19th 709 and 715 were wrecked by heavy explosion.

39. An easily recognised landmark on Bømlo.

MTB 345

The story of MTB 345 will live long in Norwegian history. We have already come across Lieut. Alv Andresen, skipper of MTB 618 when the small boats first came north to Shetland. Before that he had commanded both 71 and 54 in the Channel, and in Portsmouth he had seen two or three very unusual MTBs. They were small and they were very fast, and he believed they could be used with great effect on the Norwegian coast. The fact that they needed a crew of only seven men was an added inducement. He managed to sell his idea to the authorities, and in due course he was sent to Portsmouth, with the men who would be his crew, to pick up one of the little craft. She was MTB 345, and they put her on a railway goods-wagon, covered her with tarpaulins and took her north by rail to Inverness. The whole operation was kept a close secret. In Inverness she was transferred from railway station to harbour, and soon was on her way north to Shetland in lovely, sunny weather. It was May, 1943.

The little boat attracted a great deal of harbour-front attention in Lerwick. She was 55 feet long, driven by two Thorneycroft engines, and capable of reaching a speed of over forty knots. She had two torpedo tubes, and was also armed with twin ·303 Lewis machine-guns and two depth charges. Apparently only one picture was ever taken of this little craft, and it shows her lying at the south end of the old Lerwick Fish Market. Frank Garriock remembers her in Hay's Dock, which was probably after completing her first trip to Norway. It hadn't been long after her arrival before she made her first trip — Alv was not a man to sit idly in harbour. She could not do a return journey on the fuel contained in her own tanks, so a second MTB had to accompany her to refuel her on the other side. 653 was given the task of accompanying her on her first mission, and they set out on 9th June. They ran into thick fog, and it was very difficult for 345 to follow in the wake of 653. After a time, sure enough, the wake was lost and the two boats were separated. Andresen decided to continue on to the Norwegian coast, and in the early hours of the morning he spotted Utvaer lighthouse, and continued in among the holms and skerries. They tied up about 3.30 am, and covered the boat with the camouflage nets. He now had far too little fuel to take him back to Shetland, and he had no idea where 653 was.

653 had come up along the coast, but saw no sign of 345, and as the summer morning came in Matland knew it was asking for trouble to stay on the coast. He returned to Lerwick, arriving in the

early afternoon, 345's cartons of petrol still on his deck. At midnight on the 11th Andresen cast off, and made for the bay which had been agreed as a rendezvous point. 653 wasn't there, so they settled down to wait, and in the very early hours of the 12th she arrived. Now the fuel was transferred to 345, and then 653 was off again. There was no night at this time of year, and the Germans only had to look to see them. 345 was OK now, and for the next twelve days she stayed on the coast, while Andresen compiled a large dossier about German military dispositions over a wide area, which he duly delivered to Lerwick.

This kind of operation was clearly dangerous in summer, so Andresen waited impatiently for longer nights to come. By 24th July he could wait no longer. This time 620 with Prebensen in command was the accompanying MTB, and by midnight they could see Utvaer lighthouse to the north-east. Both boats steered into the lee of some holms to carry out the transfer of petrol cans from 620 to 345. They were pretty sure the Germans were aware of their presence, because earlier they had been spotted twice, and now a signal flare was in the sky. It didn't take long to transfer a lot of the cartons of cans, but before they had finished a three-engined Bloehm and Voss seaplane was seen coming towards them, and 620 opened fire. Hits were scored, and the plane turned towards the land trailing smoke. Prebensen went back alongside 345, for there was still a lot of petrol to be transferred, but Andresen was the senior skipper and ordered him back to Shetland. The situation was now very dangerous, and Prebensen obeyed by heading for Shetland at full speed, rendezvousing with 618 on the way as arranged. German patrol planes spotted them, and almost certainly assumed that they were the two boats the German seaplane had been going to attack.

345 meantime, using only her silent auxiliary engines, glided in towards the little opening of Olderøy. She had not got sufficent fuel for her needs from 620, but Andresen knew a cache of petrol had been hidden by one of the boats on a previous trip, and all he needed was the contact man to show him where it was hidden. What happened next is according to the story as told by the contact man, and quoted in "Klar til Kamp". Andresen met this man, whose brother said the petrol was hidden in Aspøy, but Andresen and the two Norwegians, despite a thorough search, were unable to find it. But another man was traced who had more accurate information of the hiding place, and it was finally discovered lying at the bottom of the sea right beside where 345 was tied up under her camouflage nets. It was quickly brought to the surface, but to

Andresen's great disappointment the engineer reported that the fuel was the wrong octane. (*Some MTB men have expressed surprise at this. They feel that any petrol taken over from Shetland and hidden by an MTB would assuredly have been 100 octane.*) After discussing the situation with his crew, it was agreed that they might have just about enough fuel to get them back to Shetland, but certainly not enough to carry out their planned operations along the coast. A small open boat passed about 50 yards from 345, but the occupants gave no sign of having seen them. About 2 am the three Norwegians, who had remained with them while the search for the petrol was going on, left, and that is the last first-hand account which exists of the actual events involving 345. One is tempted to wonder why, if it had been decided to return to Shetland, they didn't get underway at once. But Andresen was a man who never liked giving up on anything, and he may still have been hoping that fuel from Shetland would be forthcoming.

The following morning was a fine, quiet, summer morning. They had posted a watchman on a good vantage point, and it wasn't long till he saw three German planes approaching. That was not unusual, as the Germans often sent out morning patrols. But these planes began circling over the spot where 345 lay hidden. There could now be no doubt that the Germans knew where they were. Almost immediately small German naval boats appeared on the scene and surrounded the hiding place. A mine with a timing device was activated on board 345, then the men took up positions to make a fight of it. The Germans opened fire from two sides, and the seven men responded, but it was a very unequal struggle, even though the MTB boys were well-trained and knew how to use their weapons. They were, of course, finally overpowered, with one of them seriously wounded and two slightly. It is said that sixteen Germans lay dead, but this is possibly an exaggeration. One of the crew during the fight managed to start a fire on 345, but sadly the Germans not merely put out the fire, but also threw out the mine before it could explode.

Andresen and his men were considered dangerous prisoners, and they were taken to Bergen and put under close guard. To begin with their treatment, though harsh, was correct by German military standards. Their first interrogation was carried out by a German Lieutenant — Fanger was his name — and his report on the prisoners has been preserved. On 28th July, he said (*this was the evening of the day of capture*), "I received seven men, a lieutenant, a second-in-command, a radio operator and four others. Apart from the radio operator who was English, the rest were Norwegian. (*It was common practice for the Norwegian boats to carry British radio operators.*) They wore uniforms — brown battle-dress tunics and gumboots. The uniforms were marked as for the Norwegian navy. The crew had their pay-books with them. Two men who were slightly wounded were seen by a doctor, a third, Hansen, lay on a stretcher. The prisoners were brought in to me one after another. First I spoke to the skipper, then to the second-in-command, then to the wireless operator, and finally to the four other men. The questions I put to them were concerning the MTB flotilla's operations on the Norwegian coast, the type of craft, their armament, equipment and technical instruments for locating U-boats. Further I asked for information about the Norwegian and British fleets, and sought information about Great Britain in the same way. The prisoners were tired, worn-out and downcast, but on the whole their bearing as soldiers was good. The results of the interrogation, which concluded at 03.30 on 29th July were therefore of little value."

But the whole thing had already assumed much greater importance than the young German army lieutenant realised. Our old friend Reichskommissar Terboven had already sent a telegram to Hitler's HQ in Berlin. "Commander of army police in Bergen reported to have taken prisoner seven Commandos who had come ashore from a British MTB. I suggest that these men should not be treated as ordinary prisoners of war, but as saboteurs, and that the matter be handled by the Secret Police." Terboven had immediately changed the men's status from MTB crew — as accepted by the army lieutenant — to saboteurs. Having worded the telegram in the way he did Terboven well knew that Hitler's answer was a foregone conclusion. "Führer agrees with your suggestion. Further orders concerning this matter are being sent to Army HQ in Norway. Keitel." Action quickly followed. The seven men were delivered to the head of the Secret Police in Bergen, Wilhelm Blomberg, in the afternoon of the 29th. The pretence that this was correct procedure was based on a directive which Hitler had issued in October, 1942. That directive indicated how sensitive Hitler had become to British activity, particularly on the Norwegian coast. He maintained that the underground were carrying out acts of violence contrary to the Geneva Convention, and that the conduct of so-called Commandos was particularly brutal as a result of the training they received. They gave no mercy and they asked for none. The Commandos were really saboteurs, as far as Hitler was concerned, and would get the same treatment. "German troops will finish them off wherever they are found," he said. "Whether they are in Europe or in Africa, in uniform or not, pretending to be soldiers, death will come to them either in the fight or later. It will make no difference if they come from ship or plane, or if they drop as parachutists from the sky — even if they surrender, no mercy will be given. Any such men falling into the hands of the army must immediately be handed over to the Secret Police. It is forbidden to hold them, even for a short time, in ordinary military charge, as for example in ordinary PoW camps or the like. Officers failing to follow these instructions will be treated as having refused to obey an order, and will be subject to military discipline." From the moment Terboven, in his telegram, referred to Alv and his crew as saboteurs, their fate, as he well knew, was sealed.

Blomberg stalled for time. He called Oslo to ask for clarification. The reply was that the MTB crew should be treated as "pirates", and shot at six o'clock in the morning. Blomberg still stalled. Possibly even he had a conscience. He wanted written instructions. But the military chief in Oslo refused to give them. He was well aware of the terrible nature of what they were doing. At 8 am the seven men were taken to Ulven prison camp, south of Bergen. They were taken there each in a separate car, and placed each in a separate cell. Before their arrival all other prisoners were confined to their cells, and all windows were covered and all doors locked. Anyone trying to see what was going on would be immediately shot. Guards round the camp perimeter were strengthened, and to the other prisoners it was clear that something particularly evil was about to happen. It is said that what did happen was observed by one of the prisoners — Haakon Kvanne — who later passed on his story.

By this time the crew must have been uneasy, though up to this point they had been given no reason to think that they would be treated other than as PoW. In fact Andresen scratched on the wall of his cell, "Taken as PoW 28th July, 1943." But they soon had reason for fear. The Gestapo men took them one by one for interrogation, using the usual infamous Gestapo methods. Poor, wounded Hansen was particularly vulnerable to their treatment. They were each taken to and from the interrogation room a number of times, but the Gestapo gained little from their brutal questioning. Blomberg was now under severe pressure from Oslo to carry out his instructions, but he still demanded the order in writing, and finally in the evening of the same day a telegram arrived. "Concerning the proposal from Terboven, the Führer has decided that the crew of British MTB 345, taken by the German authorities, should not be treated as ordinary prisoners of war. Their handing over to the Gestapo in Bergen has been arranged. Report when execution has taken place. Fehlis.''

Blomberg now had no option. He gave orders for the executions to take place not later than daylight next morning. At 4 am on the morning of 30th July the firing squad of six men took up their positions at the firing range near Ulven camp. The MTB men were brought in a Gestapo car, and one by one were led out, blindfolded and shot. It was cold-blooded murder. Even the final telegram to Blomberg had referred to them as the crew of an MTB and not as saboteurs, so it was clear that even the pretence that they were covered by the terms of Hitler's infamous decree had been dropped. Blomberg had obviously given instructions that there should be no traces left of the execution. Four of the bodies were put in coffins, the other three sewn up in sailcloth and fastened to stretchers. All were placed in an open lorry, and covered with branches and other greenery. That evening the lorry took the bodies to Gravdal, and they were loaded on a small German craft. This boat immediately put to sea, and stopped two hours later in Korsfjorden. The coffins were opened and filled with stones, iron bars were fastened to the stretchers, then one by one they were dumped overboard. The Germans hoped that by so doing they would obliterate all trace of yet another of the atrocities which so besmirched their wartime history.

It is said that the prisoner Kvanne was ordered to wash the seven pairs of white sea-boot socks the crew had been wearing. On one pair was the name-tab "Hull". He was the British radio-operator, and this name-tab was to prove important after the war when evidence about the crime was being collected. At the war criminals' trials in Oslo in 1945, much of the story which has just been told came out in the evidence concerning the case. The tribunal established that the Germans had got no information of any value from the seven men who, even in death, behaved with quietness and dignity, in accordance with the best naval traditions, and reflecting their behaviour in their previous actions against the enemy. It was concluded that it was impossible to say what had brought the Germans to 345's hiding place. The action with the seaplane had undoubtedly alerted the Germans to the fact that MTBs were in the area, but Andresen is reported to have said before he was shot that he was sure it was a Norwegian "good time girl" who had betrayed them to her German boy-friend. It was confirmed at the enquiry that two Norwegians had been in contact with the crew for over twenty-four hours, and four German planes had been seen circling the hiding place on the morning of the fatal day. There is a theory that the circling planes had been attracted by something they saw. 345 had used a length of brand-new, light coloured, hemp rope for mooring, and this of course protruded from underneath the camouflage nets. This is what the planes saw, it is suggested. It seems an unlikely theory.

Today at Ulven, on the site of the wartime prison camp, there are still some German hutments, and the firing range is also still there. But more importantly there is now a memorial to the seven-man crew of MTB 345. On the back of the memorial is a note in Norwegian, "In the forest area about 300 metres behind you the crime was carried out." On the front the inscription reads, "This monument was raised in memory of the crew of MTB 345 who, during the fight, were taken as prisoners, and without trial or judgement, were executed by German war criminals here in Ulven, 30th July, 1943." The crew list which follows reads, "Alv Haldor Andresen, Bernhard Kleppe, Jans Klipper, Agnar Ingolf Bigseth, Hans Thorvald Baerevahr Hansen, Kjell Øystein Hals, Rennie Hull." Andresen was of course in the Norwegian navy when the Germans invaded. Agnar Bigseth was an engineer who had escaped from Ålesund on 13th May, 1941, on the *Signal,* with eleven other refugees on board. The *Signal* developed engine trouble half-way to Shetland, but had the great good fortune to have the *Vita* come to her rescue. The *Vita* had originally escaped from Bremnes on 8th May, 1940, and was already engaged on trips to the Norwegian coast from Shetland, on this occasion having landed a load of supplies for the underground. Another man on baord the *Signal* was Ragnvald Myklebust. He and Bigseth both served on the MTBs in the Channel. Bigseth's fate we know. Myklebust became one of the crew of Larsen's *Vigra.* As for 345, she was salvaged by the Germans and put into service as SA7. A little over a month later she went up in flames off Shetland, and was lost. Perhaps there was a little poetic justice in her fate.

Author's Note. Most of the MTB men to whom I spoke could tell me the story of MTB 345, but they all appeared to rely heavily for detail on the account by H. Storm-Bjerke in his book "Klar Til Kamp". In the foregoing story of the little boat, I, too, have drawn widely on "Klar Til Kamp" for many of the details concerning the crew's capture and their subsequent barbarous execution.

Chapter Fifteen

"Just Routine"

The winter of 1942/43 was a tragic period for the Shetland Bus boys. The *Aksel, Sandøy* and *Feiøy* had been lost with all hands, the *Brattholm* had gone with only one survivor, half of the *Frøya's* men had perished, the *Arthur* had been scuttled, and the *Bergholm* had been sunk — though happily with the loss of only one man. Over half the little fleet of boats normally available had gone, and the lives of about half the total strength of the unit had been lost. The need for a complete reappraisal of the situation was clearly urgent. There were no complaints from the crews — they were quite prepared to continue their trips to the Norwegian coast, even though their chances of survival were now no better than one in two. But the men in charge realised that they could no longer continue on the same basis. The losses were unacceptable, and the operation as a whole was no longer so successful as it had been. The German defences on the west coast were being continually and systematically strengthened. And perhaps the most telling factor of all — fuel oil was now so scarce in Norway that the bigger boats had had to give up fishing. The Shetland Bus boats, particularly the big ones of the *Bergholm/Andholmen* class, stuck out like sore thumbs. No longer could they blend in with the general run of Norwegian boats still actively fishing. The day of the fishing boat as the core of the Shetland Bus operations was over. Something faster, stronger, and very seaworthy was needed. But where to find it?

The problem was given a great deal of thought but without a solution appearing. By this time the Norwegian MTBs were operating very successfully out of Lerwick, and their losses were minimal compared with the Bus boats. Not a few envious glances were cast at the MTBs by the Scalloway boys, but everyone realised that they did not completely fill the bill. They were fast and very manoeuvrable, but they had their limitations when the weather was really rough. The navy had nothing suitable to offer them, and, despite the great store of experience, expertise and contacts they had amassed, it did seem as if the end of the Shetland Bus had come. It was at this point that the American navy came to the rescue, in the person, to begin with, of Admiral Nimitz, Commander-in-Chief of the American naval forces in Europe. The Americans had a boat called a sub-chaser which they reckoned would just about suit what the Bus boys needed. Nimitz ordered three to be sent over to Britain, and with characteristic American get-up-and-go, they arrived within three weeks.

When Howarth first saw them he commented, "They looked like young destroyers." Their vital statistics were quite impressive for men who had been living in fishing boats. They were 110 feet long, 125 tons in weight when fitted out, and were powered by two 1200 hp diesel engines. They had a cruising speed of about 17 knots, which could be raised to 22 when required. They had a range of up to 2500 miles when driven at reduced speed. And being American they were, by fishermen's standards, luxurious. Everything was electric — in all there were 42 different electric motors in each boat. They had central heating, refrigerators, oil-fired galleys, hot and cold showers, etc., etc. Each boat, said Howarth, had two generators, one of which would have been sufficient to light the village of Scalloway. Their normal crews were twenty-four men. Not surprisingly Howarth and his colleagues had some misgivings. The engines, for instance, were a completely new type of diesels, of which none of their engineers had any experience. And compared to the fishing boats, the sub-chasers were extremely sophisticated and complicated craft. But the offer was too good to miss, and arrangements were quickly made to take them over.

Seventy to eighty men from the Scalloway base were selected to go south and take over the new boats. They were to have as skippers Leif Larsen and Petter Salen, now both promoted to sub-lieutenants, and Ingvald Eidsheim, who had come to Scalloway as second-in-command. This large party of Norwegians went south to Aberdeen on the *Magnus*. Louis Rasmussen recalls they had some time to wait in Aberdeen before their train to Glasgow was due to leave. "Guess where we all went!" he says. "I would love to have film of that trip. It was very funny!" Eighty young Norwegians loose in Aberdeen soon generated a party atmosphere, and when they boarded the train they were feeling no pain. On arrival in Glasgow they were taken to be billeted in an American camp, and for many of them, when they woke next morning, it was a great surprise to find themselves where they were. Their memories of the journey south and their arrival in the camp were, to say the least, somewhat hazy. For quite a few there were no memories at all!

The boats were, very appropriately, given the names of islands off Norway's west coast — *Hessa, Hitra* and *Vigra*. They were so very new and so very different — more than a little overpowering to begin with. But the American crews were very helpful, and confidence began to grow almost immediately. The engine-room staffs had the biggest problems to overcome, but with help from the Americans, and frequent recourse to the voluminous instruction books, they were soon reasonably familiar with their new charges. The boats' first trip was over to Londonderry to have the anti-submarine gear removed from the decks. While everything went according to plan, it was discovered that Irish whiskey was just as potent as the Scottish variety. A big electrician from the *Hitra* just happened to fall in the sea. He was rescued, but the Irish police got to hear of the incident, and came on board making enquiries. Someone overboard? No, nobody knew anything about that. The police must have got hold of the wrong story. In the midst of these innocent assurances the picture was more than a little spoiled by the subject of the enquiries appearing somewhat groggily on deck, well swathed in blankets. The police looked at him, shook their heads, and went ashore.

The three boats came north, home to Scalloway, and their crews were soon underway taking them to the Norwegian coast as if they had been using them for years. Eidsheim skippered the *Hitra,* Salen the *Hessa* and Larsen the *Vigra*. It was remarkable how quickly the men reacted to a completely new environment. It was perhaps even more remarkable how entirely suitable the boats were for the role they were being called upon to play. They proved almost immediately that they were splendid sea boats, and the men's confidence in them took root right away, and never had cause to falter. A number of the men had made one or two trips earlier with the MTBs, possibly with the idea of acclimatising them to whatever new craft might be forthcoming. But few of them liked these trips very much — the sub-chasers were very much more to their taste.

The first trip by the vessels was made in November, 1943, and the *Hitra* was the boat to do it. According to Arne Nipen the *Hitra* actually grounded on this trip, and ammunition, etc., had to be moved aft before she could be persuaded to float off again. Arne made every trip with the *Hitra* except one. That absence was due to a pressing engagement — his own wedding. That was on 27th January, 1944, and his bride was lovely 18-year-old Barbara (Baba)

40. Sub-chaser *Hitra*, commander Ingvald Eidsheim.

41. Anna Smith, wartime member of Moores' staff, greets veterans Andreas Faerøy and Harald Angeltveit during *Hitra*'s visit in 1987.

42. Kåre Iversen greets *Hitra* veteran Eidsheim in Scalloway, 1987. Other veterans from left are Rolf Nordhus, Øivind Steinsvåg, Johannes Økland and Håkon Bjorge.

43. Jack Moore greets two old Norwegian friends.

44. Author and Øivind Steinsvåg at his home on Bømlo.

45. The *Bergholm's* small boat, rowed for over 150 miles by three men (*page 99*)

Christie. Arne's first landlady when he came to stay in Scalloway was Mrs Blance at the Royal Hotel, and she was Baba's aunt. The minister (many older Shetlanders will remember Rev Parke Jones) married him in his real name of Arne Melkevik. Nearly all the congregation were sure the minister was making a mistake, because they all knew him as Arne Nipen. Hardly anyone apart from Baba knew that his real name was Melkevik. Arne still remembers the agents they carried across to Norway. "They were a lot of good blokes. They were well trained. We never asked them anything and they never volunteered anything." He was very saddened by the Telavåg tragedy. However, his father had been away working at the time, so the Germans didn't get him, but his sister, stepmother and the children were all imprisoned.

Kåre Mørk was very impressed with the sub-chasers when they arrived. He recalls the many refugees they carried across to Shetland, on one occasion having twenty-eight or nine on board. Though they made some trips up north the bulk of the refugees they carried were picked up in the Stord, Bømlo and Karmøy areas. They didn't go ashore much in Norway, seldom staying for more than an hour or so. They always depended on the darkness to cover their activities. He remembers one trip, for instance, on the *Vigra,* when they were approaching Bømlo, but still in more or less full daylight, and Larsen took her back out to sea, and cruised aimlessly until full darkness had come down. Kåre mentions a fact which others noted, that the sub-chasers in outline looked quite a lot like German E-boats, and this may frequently have confused the German coast lookouts.

Øivind Steinsvåg was with Salen on the *Hessa.* On one occasion she was depth-charged on her way back from Norway. The attacker was a British or a Canadian plane, and the pilot's report was to the effect that they had depth-charged a submarine. When his report was queried, he said that he had been sure it was a submarine, because no surface vessel the size of the one he saw below him could possibly have been out in the sea and weather conditions prevailing at the time. The *Hessa* sustained a good deal of damage, and required twenty-two planks in her bows replaced. The repair was done down south, but the wood used was much inferior to the Oregon pine used in the boat's initial construction, and during the first gale in which the *Hessa* was at sea after the repair the planks failed to hold. Øivind made every trip with the *Hessa* and says the men began to look on the missions as "just routine". On one occasion they evacuated all the inhabitants of a small fishing community who had been trying to escape, but their boat had broken down. Kåre Iversen was also on the *Hessa,* though he made trips as chief engineer on the other two boats as well.

Torleif Fagertun and Louis Rasmussen both remember a trip to north Norway on the *Hitra,* when a local man invited them ashore to his house for a drink. When they came to the house they went in, and found the living-room to be nice and warm, thanks to a good fire burning in the stove. Beside the fire stood a box containing what they assumed to be coal. It was only when the man put some more fuel on the fire that they realised it was neither coal nor peat. When they enquired what it was, he calmly told them that it was the stuff he'd taken from the inside of a mine which had drifted ashore on the coast. There had been several mines, and he had discovered that this stuff from their insides made excellent fuel. Both Torleif and Louis recall that they didn't wait for their drink — they suddenly remembered that they were in danger of being left behind if they didn't hurry back to the *Hitra!* They also remember hearing about the savage treatment by the Germans of the people in the Majavatn area, and believe Shetland Bus activities may have had some connection with that.

Hans Bakkland made forty-two trips on the *Vigra.* He remembers picking up the crew of a U-boat. There had been seventeen of them, but one had died. He was amazed by the British authorities' concern that the prisoners should be accorded absolutely proper and correct treatment, and on their way in they received frequent messages and questions concerning the surviving prisoners' welfare. They took them into Scapa Flow. The U-boat had shot down the Catalina attacking it but the submarine had also been sunk. (*See Hornell story, Ch. 21.*)

Rolf Nordhus was one of the crew of the *Hitra.* On one occasion they went into a place near Namsos where they were to land three agents. To get in they had first to pass a German fort, but they had been assured by intelligence that it was no longer fully manned. When they were landing the agents and supplies two contacts came down to the boat to see the agents on their way. One of the agents commented on how luckly they had been coming in as, if the guard post had been fully manned, they would probably have had a rough passage. Whereupon one of the Norwegians informed them that during the previous day or two the Germans had been reinforcing the troops there, bringing it up to full strength. "So we went out again with all the guns fully manned. We passed so near to the post that we could hear someone playing an accordion. Maybe the sound of the music drowned out the sound of our engines but we passed undetected."

46. The veterans' beautiful club building in Bergen.

47. A group of veterans at the club. From back, left to right, 1st row, Leif Skår, Knut Henriksen, Leif Lossius; 2nd row, Axel Madsen, Ingebrigt Tonning, Karsten Danielsen, Rolf Nordhus; 3rd row, Kåre Mørk, Knut Svendsen; 4th row, Trond Torp, Odd Mjelde; at front, Finn Olsen.

On another occasion they closed the coast in extremely dense fog. They couldn't risk going in without visual recognition of the coast where they were, so they radioed for instructions. They were told to hold off and wait for twenty-four hours. Next night was clear, and they went in and met their contact. He told them that he had heard engine noises on the previous night, but couldn't be sure what kind of craft were making them. A man was posted at the shore to keep watch, and before long he was able to see that the engine noises were coming from three German R-boats and two E-boats. The fog had been kind to the boys from Scalloway.

These boys of 1943/44 are now elderly men, and they talk lightly of how the trips on the sub-chasers became just routine, but that is very much understating what continued to be a dangerous operation. Bad as the Germans were, the greatest danger to the Bus boys remained always the sea and the weather. The sub-chasers could face virtually anything the North Sea could throw at them, but they didn't always go unscathed. Sometimes violent seas swept the decks clean of everything that could be torn away. There was the classic case of Larsen returning from a mission where the *Vigra* had encountered extremely severe weather, and her deck had been swept clean, with considerable damage to deck fittings. But Larsen had got wind of another mission he wanted to undertake immediately. Howarth remonstrated with him — the *Vigra* was in no condition to go out again without attention. Larsen looked down from the bridge, and in his usual quiet voice remarked, "What the sea has taken we do not need." He went off again.

The boats were fast, very well armed and absolutely excellent sea boats. In the first winter, 1943/44, they made thirty-four trips, landed forty-one agents, picked up thirteen, and gave passage to a considerable number of refugees. In the second winter, 44/45, they landed ninety-four agents, picked up thirty-three and also 235 refugees. And of course they landed a great deal of arms, ammunition, etc. All the time they remained virtually an independent force, with a minimum of interference from naval authorities, and yet enjoying excellent co-operation when called for. Officially there were known as the Norwegian Naval Independent Unit (NNIU).

It is difficult to assess just how far-reaching was the success of the Shetland Bus. In cold statistics it transported over four hundred tons of arms and ammunition to Norway, and much of these supplies were used by the underground or the Home Army as they were later known. By the end of the war sixty secret radio operators were at work, and nearly two hundred agents had been landed.

Over three hundred refugees had been picked up from all along Norway's west coast and brought to safety in Shetland. The early use of fishing boats had been both successful and important to the Norwegian people in that they knew there was always a way out west over sea. In 42/43 the losses had been tragically high, but with the coming of the sub-chasers the service which the fishing boats had started was greatly enlarged and improved. And there can be no doubt that German awareness of the dangers posed by the Shetland Bus, the MTBs and the Linge agents tied down large numbers of German troops which were badly needed elsewhere the longer the war went on.

Chapter Sixteen

Norway and Shetland 1943/44

By the end of 1942 almost every section of the Norwegian population had collectively shown their resistance to Nazism, and had demonstrated a burning ambition to defend their beloved Constitution and the rule of law. The teachers' courageous stand and the support they received from the people showed a deep determination to protect the minds of the young from infection by the Nazi disease. Even the Germans were realising that they had failed completely in their attempt to infiltrate people's minds. Their propaganda was having absolutely no effect. The Norwegian land is wild and rugged, and does not lend itself easily to conquest by man. The people who live in it must themselves be strong, rugged and independent if they are to survive. It was that virile individualism that stood the Norwegians in good stead when the need to resist was desperate. To a large extent they did not need leaders to tell them what to do — each man was ready and able to make up his own mind.

In 1943 and 1944 the Germans' main target was the mobilisation of Norwegian manpower to help Germany's war effort. In 1943 it was a big, new labour force that was wanted, which would be employed largely on strengthening the German defences along Norway's long west coast. This force would be controlled by the Todt organisation, which had already carried out much similar work along the coasts of France, Belgium and Holland. The target set for the new Norwegian labour force was 35,000 rising to 75,000 men. Quisling was once again the stooge, and his decree to put all this into action was called the "Law for General National Labour Service". The Norwegians responded by filling up the registration forms with false names, and besieging the registration offices with a multitude of unnecessary queries about how to fill up the forms, etc. The Germans realised what was going on, and suddenly demanded that 10,000 men should report immediately. But for once Teutonic efficiency was markedly lacking. When some of the men reported, they found that nobody knew anything about them — the call-up officials had forgotten to inform the labour organisation of what they were doing. The men were allowed to go home, and in the end only about 1400 were dragged in. On 20th April Oslo Central Labour Exchange was burned down, and the registration cards for the whole of Oslo were destroyed. In the end the great plan for producing up to 75,000 workers brought in less than 5000. Once again the Germans realised that it was a whole people defying them.

1944 saw a new attempt at mobilisation. This time it was introduced by a Quisling order for the special registration of all males between the ages of eighteen and twenty-five. In reality the order was camouflage for conscription into the German armed forces, and again the target was 75,000 men. German defeats at Stalingrad and in North Africa, with the loss of large numbers of men, allied to the growing strength of Britain, the USA and Russia, was creating a crucial German need for manpower. Nobody can live without food. So Quisling had another brilliant idea. An issue of new ration cards was due, but no man in the 18 – 25 age group would receive a ration card unless he could produce his calling-up papers. But by this time the Home Front was becoming well organised. They had got hold of the plan in advance. They called in the help of broadcasts from London to give details of the scheme, and these broadcasts were transcribed by the dozens of secret newsheets operating, and distributed far and wide throughout Norway. A lorry load of ration cards was highjacked, so no one needed to go short of a card. But in addition the young men at risk went into hiding, many of them finding work with farmers and small-holders in remote areas. Then the Germans again tried a sudden move. Men were given 24 hours only in which to report. But the Home Front had been busy. Thousands of record cards had been stolen from the record offices. These combined measures resulted in the latest mobilisation plans turning into a complete fiasco, and it was doubtful if even 1000 were recruited.

But Germans didn't react kindly to frustration, and by the autumn of 1944 the iron fist had never been tighter in Norway. Executions in the courtyard of Akershus Castle became more and more frequent. In late 1943 a fire in the University Hall in Oslo led to the arrest of over 1000 students, with 700 of them sent to a special camp in Germany. The university was closed down. In August of 1943 1100 Norwegian officers had been arrested, and sent to Germany, and of 470 policemen arrested, 271 were sent to concentration camps. There were virtual riots in the streets of Oslo.

By the New Year 1944, weariness, according to one writer, "lay like a cloud over the capital, dragging at the faces of the people".

Food was becoming steadily scarcer. In a restaurant you had to hand over a raw potato before you would be served with a cooked one. A few animals were being kept up in the mountains the whole year round, the summer barns being used to house them in winter. However, there were one or two bright spots. The news of the successful raid by the MTBs and the Commandos on Stord quickly spread, to the great delight of everyone. Even more exciting was the attack on the heavy-water plant at Rjukan by six Norwegian saboteurs trained in Britain. And all the time, in the background, the Home Forces were gathering their strength, improving their organisation, and increasing their activities. They were helped in no small measure by the MTBs and the Shetland Bus vessels based in Shetland, and also by drops from the air. There were 213 of these in 1944. In the summer of 1944 Crown Prince Olaf assumed command of all Norwegian armed forces, including those of the resistance. Gradually the forces controlled by Milorg grew until by the end of 1944 they numbered 40,000 men. Over in Sweden strict neutrality had been relaxed to the point where 12,000 Norwegian "police" troops were undergoing training there. Up in Majavatn it was known that a certain man had given the Germans information which had led to the arrest and execution of ten of his neighbours, all workmen and crofters. One day he received a parcel in the post. When he opened it the parcel exploded and he was killed. He had been executed for his treachery.

As 1944 went on sabotage was on the increase, with fuel stores a prime target. At Horten naval yard, in Oslo harbour and at Kongsberg, much damage was done. The underground's activities helped to create a severe fuel shortage, and then they turned their attention to the railway lines. Those connecting central and north Norway were effectively put out of action, and then the saboteurs turned to the lines which converged on Oslo and served southern Norway. They systematically put the whole network out of action. Perhaps the most audacious act of defiance was the sailing of eleven tugboats and a salvage ship from Frederikstad to the safety of a port in Sweden. The railways had been rendered unusable, road transport was severely limited through fuel shortage, and now the tugs necessary for handling sea transport had gone. At a time when troops from Norway were desperately needed to bolster both eastern and western fronts, the Germans' inability to move them was a big handicap to their war effort.

On 25th October, 1944, Russian troops crossed the Norwegian

frontier in northern Norway, in pursuit of German forces retreating from the Finnish front. The Germans were putting up very little resistence, but they operated what became known as the "scorched earth" policy — in other words they destroyed everything as they retreated. This is a bit of the last war which has received very little attention from historians, having been submerged in the more eye-catching headlines from the other fronts at the time. That didn't make it any less horrendous. The Germans quite deliberately uprooted 55,000 people from their homes and deported them, destroying their homes as they retreated. Most of them suffered terribly. In the town of Kirkenes only 28 houses and the hospital were left standing. Little fishing villages were wiped out. The whole of Norse Finnmark was made a huge no-man's-land, and even Hammerfest, the first town in the world to be lit by electricity, was plunged once again into the dark ages. Here and there people managed to evade the mass deportation, and continued to cling to life somehow or other in the devastated areas, living mostly in caves and enduring the extreme cold, lack of food and other hardships until the war ended, and rebuilding could at last begin. But in a country reduced to the depths of poverty by the Germans, that couldn't happen immediately.

The Norwegian government in London had wanted Norwegian troops to take part in the liberation of this northern part of Norway, and the Russians agreed to a token force being sent. Truls Håskjold was one of the men in that force, and his story makes interesting reading.

He was a Bergen boy, and he was just eighteen when the Germans arrived. He and his brother had sufficient presence of mind to get out of Bergen immediately, and they made for Voss where they joined the Norwegian army. But their service was short-lived — less than a fortnight, and then the Norwegians in southern Norway capitulated, and they were demobilised. They heard that a lot of arms had been hidden in the Voss area, and Truls one day happened to make a comment about it. A man who had overheard him came to him again, seeking more information, and Truls immediately sensed he was an informer. He dropped a hint about him to the Norwegian police, and clearly the man heard about this, as he came to Truls again threatening him. It was an early experience for the young man of a "bad" Norwegian.

Truls and five friends were soon planning escape. They knew that people were getting away and going west over sea, and their own departure was finally set for November, 1941, but they failed to get places on the boat, the *Blia*. (*Fortunately for them, as that was the trip when the 'Blia' was lost with all on board.*) It was 10th February, 1942, before they got away on the *Rupee* from Bremnes. She was a decked boat, about forty feet long, but they had forty-one people on board. Their point of departure was a little place called Vendanes, and the trip had been organised by the Bremnes group and the Stein organisation, many of whose members were wanted by the Gestapo. There were five or six women and children in the party. Most of them lay down in the hold, and, after some engine trouble shortly after they left, they duly made land in Fetlar, where they spent their first night ashore. They went through the usual screening process, first in Lerwick, then at the Patriotic School in London, before being sent to the different arms of the services for training.

Truls was sent up to Scotland, and received his training at Dumfries, Dornoch, Tain and Nigg. Training completed, he joined the Second Independent Mountain Company, at that time attached to the 52nd Scottish Division. After a period of fairly routine soldiering, his Company in 1944 was sent up to Scalloway in Shetland. There the Company, numbering 260 men, were embarked on a ship to join a convoy for Murmansk, under the escort of the cruiser *Berwick*. On arrival in Murmansk their greeting consisted of the Russians interning them for six days. The Russians had already advanced through northern Finland, and now the Norwegians were put on a train for Petsamo, not very far from Kirkenes. "We crossed the border into Norway at 6 am on 11th November, 1944. There were no houses. The Germans had burned everything. Shortly the Russians withdrew, but we were on our own Norwegian soil, and we went forward. We were poorly equipped, both for the weather and for the ground we had to cover, and we were very short of food. Six of us were attacked by forty Germans and some Norwegian nazis, and we were taken prisoner. We had wounded two Germans, and we had to carry them for thirty kilometres." The Germans took all their own gear away from them, and forced them to carry equipment and supplies as well as the two wounded. There was deep snow on the ground, and it was on foot all the way, without the benefit of snow-shoes or skis. "It was a terrible experience."

Finally the Germans allowed them to board a small fishing boat which took them down the coast as far as Narvik where they were landed. There they were transferred to a large troop transport, the Norwegians, of course, being accommodated in the very bowels of the ship, and were taken farther down the coast to Trondheim. They were then loaded into cattle trucks and taken by rail, just as the teachers had been, but this time in the opposite direction, until reaching the prison camp near Lillehammer, which was almost certainly the one which had housed the teachers. Now it was a concentration camp for Russians. "From there we were taken to a prison camp in Oslo, and held there until the end of the war."

Even as the retreating Germans were laying waste northern Norway, and forcing many thousands of Norwegians to evacuate their homes, the convoys loaded with vital war materials continued to make their danger-fraught voyages to the Russian port of Murmansk, undergoing repeated attacks from both U-boats and German bomber planes as they neared their destination. In the early days of these convoys they had often been inadequately escorted, and frequently their losses had been tragically severe. And if they escaped the human enemy, there was always the other enemy, the weather, to contend with. The winter seas and wind in the Arctic Ocean were only too often vicious in their intensity.

Among the last of the convoys to sail from the Clyde was JW64 which left on 3rd February, 1945. Though subjected to repeated attacks, it managed to reach Murmansk with relatively small losses. RA64 was the returning convoy, and it was made up of 34 ships. Just before the convoy sailed, intelligence reported that the inhabitants of the island of Sørøya, at the mouth of Altafjord, were suffering badly at German hands. Four destroyers went immediately to the island and evacuated all the inhabitants, men, women and children, amounting in all to 478. Subsequently the evacuees were distributed among the ships of the convoy.

On the way back the convoy ran into a gale of ferocious severity which scattered the ships. When it eased most of them regained station, but three days later an even worse storm blew up, and once again the ships were scattered. As the wind eased the whole convoy once more got together, with the exception of the American *Henry Bacon*, which had developed engine trouble. A straggler invited attack, and twenty German torpedo bombers came at her. For an hour she defied them, but was finally hit, and her magazine blew up. There was no option but to abandon ship and take to the boats. Sadly the boats couldn't hold everyone, for there were 35 of the refugees from Sørøya on board. The crew relinquished their places in the boats to these people, a very selfless act of heroism on their part. The boats were all picked up by destoyers, but twenty-two of the *Henry Bacon's* crew perished.

Shetland 1943/44

By 1943 events were beginning to take on a slightly rosier hue for the Allies. The Russians had stemmed the German flood, and the Nazis were already realising they had bitten off more than they could chew. The Shetland garrison had reached its peak, and from now on its numbers would decrease. Sumburgh and Sullom Voe both had important roles in the overall air picture. At Sullom there were now approximately 1200 RAF and 600 Norwegian personnel. It was during the construction of the Scatsta runway, perimeter tracks and so on that workmen discovered the great depth of peat which would later be such an obstacle to the oil men. When the war ended the airmen were to leave behind the runways, huts, etc., and in post-war years the officers' mess became useful as Sullom Voe Hotel, the pier built at Sella Ness served local fishermen well, and the airport was easy to renovate for the oilmen.

In addition to Norwegian aircrew there were now also Polish and Czech pilots and airmen in Shetland. In addition Lerwick harbour had become a veritable haven for submarines, and they carried even more nationalities than the aircraft. Apart from Norwegians and British there were also French, Dutch, Poles, Russians and Americans, with a couple of captured U-boats for good measure. Lerwick provided the chief centre for off-duty hours, and, even allowing for all its past mixed history, this must surely have been the most cosmopolitan period in the little town's story. Constant visitors were the Norwegian ships *Risør, Horten, Narvik* and *Molde*. As well as being frequently used to tow MTBs across the North Sea when going on their more distant missions, they also carried out minesweeping duties. The *Narvik* was also involved in rescuing the submarine *Stubborn* when she was in severe difficulty after an exceptionally successful trip in February, 1944. It was also the *Narvik* which was in attendance when the midget submarines used Unst as their start point when setting out on their attacks on the floating dock in Bergen harbour. Though the first attack in April, 1944, resulted in the wrong target being sunk — a big merchant ship instead of the floating dock — the second attack in September, 1944, was entirely successful, and in both cases the attackers made successful getaways, using the same midget, X-24, on each occasion.

The disastrous fire and explosions on the two MTBs in November, 1943, led to the temporary evacuation of many families in the Commercial Road, North Ness and Freefield areas. Eight lives were lost, and many houses lost their windows. Like the mines at the Waari Geo and the Slates, it was an experience which was to be long remembered. The fighters at Sumburgh were meeting with increasing success, and reports said that they had downed four German planes in a 17-day period. One Spitfire had to make a forced landing in Yell near Basta Voe, and it was entirely in keeping with the picture in most people's minds of our fighter pilots that he was said to have attended a dance in Mid Yell on the same evening. After the Battle of Britain our fighter pilots had seemed rather special to everyone. Perhaps what said more clearly than anything else that maybe better times lay ahead was the removal of barbed wire from the Esplanade and the harbour front at the beginning of 1944. Nothing could have indicated more clearly that, in official minds, a German invasion from Norway was no longer considered a serious possibility.

By late summer, 1943, British and Amercian forces stood ready to invade Italy via the island of Sicily. At the time Vivian Owers was serving on Motor Launch 445 of the 21st ML Flotilla. These anti-submarine launches were based at Longhope, but 445 had been detached for a week's service at Baltasound, following which it was to go to Lerwick. Instead it was ordered to Sullom Voe. On arrival there the crew were surprised to see seven other MLs from their own flotilla, along with upwards of twenty trawlers and the brand new destroyer *Savage*. On the following day *Savage*, followed by the trawlers with the MLs as escorts, left Sullom Voe and set course for Norway. It was all very mysterious, and the mystery deepened when the MLs and trawlers spotted two cruisers and an aircraft carrier with destroyer escort joining their fleet. It was only when they returned to Sullom Voe, and a debriefing was held aboard *Savage*, that it became clear that the whole thing had been an elaborate ruse.

The plan had been to give the appearance of a convoy in strength heading for the Norwegian coast — the clear intention, to an observer, being to put ashore troops in considerable strength somewhere on Norway's west coast. Hitler had always believed the British would invade Norway, and with evidence such as this he wouldn't be hard to convince that it was finally about to happen. The regular timetable of German weather reconnaissance planes was well-known to the British. One duly appeared and was allowed to have a good look at the large British fleet, and no doubt radioed back the disturbing news in some haste. The plane was then shot down by an aircraft from the carrier. A second German plane came out to check, and it received exactly the same treatment. By this time the brief summer night was coming down, rendering further air reconnaissance by the Germans impossible. But they had enough information to convince them that a landing in force was about to take place. The fleet now turned and steamed westwards, the small craft back to Sullom Voe, the big fellows back to their beat in the Denmark Strait, where the convoys to Russia were now a primary concern. The Germans reacted to the ruse by withdrawing troops from southern Italy to bolster the Norwegian occupation forces, and that was precisely the result the British had hoped to achieve. It made the landings in Sicily that much easier.

Not much was known of what was going on in Scalloway. Scalloway people didn't gossip about things that mattered. But when the sub-chasers started to come into Lerwick to land refugees, it was soon realised that these were the new Shetland Bus boats. Captain Bjarne Berkeland had arrived in Shetland in December, 1940, as naval vice consul, and had operated a separate consular office from that of James and Frank Garriock, as the stream of refugees was reaching such proportions that the work was far too much to be handled on a part-time voluntary basis. He was succeeded by Captain Per Wendelbø, who was in turn followed by Consul Thingvold, who closed the office down in May, 1943. From then on all the Norwegian activity was back in the hands of the Garriocks. In 1942 the Order of St Olaf, First Class, had been bestowed on James Garriock, but as the months passed his health deteriorated, and in April, 1943, he asked to be relieved of his duties. The Norwegian Ambassador accepted his resignation, and asked James' son Frank to take over. Although the stream of refugee boats had dried up, the coming of the MTBs, and more particularly the sub-chasers, created a tremendous upsurge in the number of refugees reaching Shetland, and Frank Garriock had his hands full again. The sub-chasers were the main carriers, sometimes bringing in as many as thirty people on one trip. But the records kept at the time were carefully worded so as not to give away the identity of the ship which brought them over. Instead of "29 refugees landed by *Hitra* from Norway", the record would read "29 refugees landed by special vessel". This traffic continued and, indeed, increased through 1944 and into 45. The reason in the main was simply that resistance was increasing in Norway on a big scale, and informers and Norwegian nazis were putting the Gestapo on to more people.

In the air there was much success, but also the occasional tragedy. A Catalina crashed at Sullom Voe, and earlier four Catalinas sank at their moorings in very rough seas, the mooring eyes on the fuselages having been torn out, and the planes then filling with water. The salvage of these aircraft was carried out by Robertsons (Lerwick) Ltd. We will look at the story of Norwegian aircraft at Sullom Voe in greater detail later, but no reference to war-time Sullom Voe would be complete without mention of Flying Officer John Alexander Cruickshank, VC, of 210 Squadron Royal Air Force. 210 was equipped with Catalinas, and Cruickshank was the pilot of one of them. His official citation says he went in to attack a U-boat, but his depth-charge mechanism failed to function, and the charges didn't drop. The submarine was putting up fierce ack-ack fire, but again he manoeuvred into position, and came into the attack a second time. The aircraft suffered repeated hits. The navigator/bomb aimer was killed, and the second pilot and two crew members were wounded. Cruickshank was hit in no fewer than seventy-two places, two of the wounds in his chest being serious, while ten more in his legs made them virtually useless. The Catalina was badly damaged, and the interior was a shambles. He pressed home the attack, and himself released the depth charges, this time successfully. The U-boat was sunk. He collapsed, and the second pilot took over the controls. However, Cruickshank regained consciousness, and again took over command, until he was sure the aircraft was on course for Sullom Voe. During the five and half hours' trip he drifted in and out of consciousness. On arrival at base he insisted on being carried forward and propped up in the second pilot's seat. He remained conscious while they landed, and then taxied in until they grounded. He was now so weak that he needed a blood transfusion before he could be removed to hospital. He was awarded the VC.

By the time 1944 came in there was a different spirit in the air. Ultimate victory could now be seen as a distinct possibility, and there was increasing talk of a "Second Front". In May "Salute the Soldier Week" in Lerwick saw an impressive military parade, with local people commenting particularly on the Norwegian Commandos. They were wearing the special Commando combat boots with rubber soles, and they marched silently, which struck onlookers as being in sharp contrast to the normal noisy rhythm of marching soldiers wearing the traditional army "ammunition" boots. A new-type air-sea rescue launch had appeared on the scene, this one with a range of 1000 miles. She was soon to prove her worth by going almost to Faroe to pick up the crew of a Catalina which had been shot down while successfully attacking a U-boat. Their dinghy had been nearly twenty hours in the water, and two of the crew had died. This was the occasion when Dave Hornell was awarded a posthumous VC. (*See Chapter 21.*)

In October a small Dutch cargo boat came into Lerwick harbour. The rumour this time was that the crew had overpowered the Germans on board, and, escorted by an MTB, had sailed the ship to Lerwick, where she moored out in mid-channel. Onlookers noted that a well-dressed man was brought ashore from the vessel, blindfolded, and apparently the possessor of three suitcases of luggage. Who was he? A few days later another MTB came in with a prize, this time a wooden Norwegian cargo boat. This vessel was probably the *Oksøy*. In November an air-sea Warwick rescue plane passed over the town, but developed engine trouble, and came down in the sea near Sumburgh. The lifeboat, the *Molde* and an air-sea rescue launch were sent from Lerwick on receipt of the news, but in the meantime another naval plane came over and dropped a lifeboat. The survivors drifted ashore at the back of Scatness, but one died in hospital. In December a crashed plane and its dead crew were found at Cunningsburgh.

Across the North Sea as 1944 ended the Norwegian people were also beginning to hope. But a constant worry was whether the Germans, from the fastnesses of the Norwegian mountains, might continue to hold out even after the Germans in the rest of Europe had surrendered.

Chapter Seventeen

Export Agents

The boys and grils who slipped away from Norway's west coast to make their way to Shetland and freedom well knew the risks they were running. They knew the dangers of the sea — that was something with which they were familiar. But they also knew there was the very real possibility of discovery by the Germans. That meant a sudden end by bombs or machine-gun bullets from the air, or, what was perhaps even worse, capture by the Germans with all that that implied. But they accepted the risks lightly. Anything was better than life under the Germans, and if they survived long enough to get fifty miles or so from the coast they knew their chances got better by the hour. Many of them would never have got away without help from the people of Norway. They were grateful to them, but once they were safely away they probably gave them little more thought. Who were these people?

As we have already seen the great stream of refugee boats had started in 1940 and increased greatly in 1941. It was during that period that groups of Norwegians got together and provided help for hundreds of refugees. They organised them into parties, found them boats and provisions, and very often had to provide sanctuary for them while a boat was being acquired, for only too frequently the Gestapo were close on the heels of those needing to get away. These groups are often referred to as "export" groups, and the very nature of their activities meant that they lived permanently on the knife-edge of danger.

Many of the refugees left from out-of-the-way spots in the Haugesund, Bømlo and Bergen areas, and a number of groups came into being in these places. They included the Årstad/Brun group, the Stein group and the Bømlo/Bremnes group. Farther north, in the Ålesund and Nordfjord districts there were others, including the Torsvik and Walle groups. Some of those people who risked their lives time and time again in helping others to get away are happily still with us. Two such are Thoralf and Lilly Walle.

Thoralf is a retired Captain of police, and when one looks at this big, calm, unruffled man, now in advancing years, it is still easy to picture him pitting his wits with confidence against the Gestapo. His wife Lilly was always at his side. Still a vivacious lady, she was, as her picture shows, a very beautiful girl of just twenty-one at the time, with her friend Gerd Gjørtz another active member of the group. They were at their busiest in the second half of 1941 and in early 1942. It is a privilege to hear them tell their story. They speak of these bygone days so matter-of-factly. There is no bitterness, no heroics. But it is a story which is full of raw courage, fearless daring and a very great deal of determined endurance.

When the Germans invaded Norway, and resistance in the south collapsed, Thoralf, as a soldier, was taken prisoner, but after about a fortnight was released. He went back to his job as a policeman in Ålesund, where he had been living since 1937. As it happened there were still no Germans in Ålesund when he returned, their main centre in that part of Norway to begin with being Trondheim. It was some time later before Ålesund was occupied in force. On one thing Thoralf and Lilly were immediately in complete agreement — they hated the Germans from the moment they arrived in Ålesund.

As we have noted there was no shortage of boats in this part of Norway, and there was no lack of people wanting to escape, so the traffic started immediately. Thoralf found himself involved in anti-German activity almost as soon as he returned. He had a good bunch of colleagues in the police force, and he thought very highly of them. They were good men, he says, and he always knew he could trust them. By early 1941 he had become very deeply involved in the escape activity, and he was conscious that he was rapidly reaching an undesirable state — he knew too much. "No one could be sure when the Gestapo might pounce, and no one knew just how much he would give away under torture." He and his friends were well aware that should they fall into the hands of the Gestapo torture was inevitable.

Many of the escapers simply stole the boats in which they got away, but the boats organised by the Walle group had all been purchased. Early on Thoralf made it a rule that they would help only people who were on the run, and were in deadly danger from the Gestapo. By making that rule they knew full well that they were automatically putting themselves at maximum risk — the Gestapo would exact terrible vengeance if they got their hands on people who were deliberately thwarting them. People came from as far afield as Oslo and eastern Norway seeking the group's help. But there had to be precautions. No one who came to the Walles' door was listened to unless the conversation started with the question, "Er Heidi heime?" (Is Heidi at home?) Soon the traffic became two-way, for some of the agents landed from Shetland — the "Linge" boys — had Thoralf's name as their contact in the area. The group had upwards of ten members, but none of them was in possession of as much information as Thoralf; it was not surprising that he was worried he knew too much.

Lilly says she only did what Thoralf told her to do. But there is no doubt she was his very able lieutenant. Beautiful and fearless, she did a tremendous amount of work acting as courier, accompanying escapers to safe houses and later to boats, and generally acting as her husband's second-in-command. "You were running terrible risks, Lilly?" "Yes, but I was young. And when you took a risk and got away with it, you soon forgot about it." They both lived one day at a time. They were always conscious that one or both might be taken at any moment, and they had a mutual agreement. If the Germans took one of them the other would assert that he or she had strongly disapproved of what the other was doing, and was very much against it. They think that in total they helped upwards of 150 Norwegians.

Almost inevitably the day came when they were all in mortal danger. The danger, as is so often the case, crept up on them unawares. A young fellow from Ålesund had gone to Trondheim to stay for a short time, and he made a habit of visiting a certain cafe, more or less every day, where he had a chance to chat with other customers whom he got to know. One day one of these customers said to him, "You are from Ålesund? I know there are a lot of good men in Ålesund, and I want to get away to Shetland. Can you help me?" The boy was taking no chances and denied any knowledge of such people in Ålesund. But the man was persistent, and continued to make the same approaches, and seemed desperately anxious to get away. The boy was finally convinced that he was genuine and contacted Kåre Viken in Ålesund. Kåre was a friend of Thoralf's, and was a leading member of a separate export group, while also sometimes acting as contact man for the Shetlandsgjengen. Kåre was a gymnast, and had represented Norway in the 1936 Olympic Games in Germany. Sometimes he would ask the Walle group for help. He told Thoralf about the man from Trondheim who was so anxious to get to Shetland, and who was coming to see him.

Ominously Henry Rinnan now came to Ålesund. Rinnan was a Norwegian nazi informer, and he headed a large gang who all pursued the same aims. "Henry Rinnan was the worst man in

Norway," says Lilly. After the war his crimes were exposed and he paid the penalty. But now he booked in at the Hotel Scandinavie, and he had a girl from Oslo with him. He also sent for two more of his gang from Trondheim to come down and join him. It is clear in retrospect that it was one of his men who had hoodwinked the boy in Trondheim, and now he was scenting his prey. When Kåre came to the rendezvous with the supposed escaper from Trondheim he was watched by the girl from Oslo, who duly reported the meeting to Rinnan. The net was closing.

The *Viggo* was the boat scheduled to be the next departure for Shetland, and the party to board her was being assembled. The Walles had five boys waiting in Spjelkavik, two of them very probably in the secret room in Perry Ørstenvik's house. (*That room is still there today. It really is a secret room, and defied all attempts by the author to locate it.*) As was the usual practice it was Lilly's job to take them by taxi into Ålesund, and there hand them over to a contact who would take them down to the boat. On this night the meeting with the contact was scheduled for 11 pm. As she drove up in the taxi she saw the contact waiting, but at the same moment a German car drove up. She recognised it as German immediately, because only the Germans were permitted to drive with full headlights. She could see three men in the car, one of whom, she says, she recognised as Rinnan. Another source has said that a second man in the car was the Gestaop chief in Ålesund. Lilly's young charges were all from eastern Norway, and had a very strong eastern Norway accent, which would have been an immediate giveaway to a Norwegian like Rinnan. "As the Gestapo man approached the taxi I hurriedly told the boys not to say a word — to let me do the talking. He demanded to know who I was, then demanded our papers. I told him we had been to Spjelkavik to a dance." Her contact was sitting on a wall nearby. He was also questioned. What was he doing so far out of Ålesund? He had come to meet a girl, he said, but she had never turned up. He was going back into town. As he spoke he had one hand in his pocket. In it was a pistol, which he was ready to produce in a flash if the need arose. Finally Rinnan himself came over to the taxi. "Where are you going now?" "We're going to a party in Ålesund," Lilly told him. The three muttered among themselves, then, with a last searching look at the five boys the taxi door was slammed and they were told they could go.

Lilly was certain now that Rinnan and the Germans were on to something, and she herself was very likely in extreme danger. They were probably just waiting for her to take the one step that would give her away. She stopped the taxi, took the boys up the hillside near the church, laying dire warnings on them to respond to no one but her. She went back home, and arrived to hear the phone ringing. Thoralf had the house key, so she had to break a pane of glass to get in. It was Thoralf on the phone. "Where have you been?" he asked. Lilly realised that in all probability, with the Germans suspicious of them, their phone call was being monitored by the enemy. So she answered Thoralf angrily, loosing a tirade at him for being drunk at the party and disgracing her before their friends, and so on. Thoralf sensed immediately that something was very wrong, and he played along. He abjectly assured her that he was sorry, and that he would be a good boy from now on. This he promised, if only she would let him come home again.

Neither Lilly's presence of mind nor her courage deserted her. She got hold of another taxi, went and picked the boys up again, and in the absence of her contact man, sent them down to the embarkation point without accompanying them. Thoralf meantime had been busy arranging the despatch of other refugees, and among them, though he did not know it, was a Rinnan man. Now he and Lilly made their separate ways back home. It was between one and two o'clock in the morning.

Of course neither of them could know that there were Rinnan informers among the *Viggo's* passengers. But they were heavy with a vague uneasiness. Lilly looked at Thoralf. "Thoralf," she said, "now it's finally over." Thoralf agreed. "It's over, Lilly." They got out a bottle of liqueur, and each had a substantial helping. While they sat silently sipping it, Kåre Viken came to the door, calling to see if everything had gone OK. They sat and chatted for a while, then Kåre went back home, to find the Gestapo waiting for him. He was immediately arrested, and his first thought was that the Germans would now go directly to the Walles. They didn't, but he had no way of warning his friends. However, at 6 am the Walles' phone rang. It was Kåre's closest friend. His message was brief. "Kåre has been taken." Apparently the Gestapo file on the Walles was not yet complete, but it could only be a matter of time — maybe minutes, maybe hours — before their qestioning of their prisoners would yield them all the information they needed.

Typically there was no panic on Thoralf's part. His first thought was for Kåre's mother, and he went off to break the sad news to her. Lilly, again on her own, considered her position. She had been supposed to go to Oslo that day as a courier, but clearly that would be asking for trouble. As she deliberated, the young man who had been her contact on the previous evening came to the

48. The house in Spjelkavik with the secret room.

49. The cupboard which hides the entrance.

51. Alan Irvine, using coat hanger in roof, swings feet first through opening.

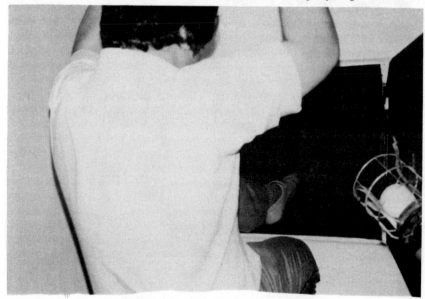

50. The cupboard swung back, the outer door open, and the shelves normally filling the wall space removed.

52. Inside, room for two.

53. Thoralf and Lilly Walle, fearless leaders of an "export" group. Thoralf was in the Norwegian police force, and later became the police captain in Ålesund.

54. Hotel Scandinavie and the end tower of police station in Ålesund.

door and told her that it was now clear that something was seriously wrong, but he hadn't got the details. Lilly went to the house of her good friend, Gerd Gjørtz, one of the group. She stayed there all night, and in the morning went down to the nearby cafe to see if she could glean any information. While there her young contact came in, signalled to her with his eyes, then went out again. She followed him out, and in a quiet corner he told her the worst. The *Viggo* had been taken, and the Germans were probably already in possession of all the details about everyone who had been involved, as two informers among the passengers had betrayed the refugees to the Germans. Kåre Viken had been the first victim among the organisers. Lilly realised that their cover had been completely blown, and she was now in deadly danger. She went back up to Gerd, and almost as she arrived the phone rang. It was Thoralf. He, too, knew the score, but he said he would see her soon. A Linge boy who had come over from Shetland was with him. Even as they spoke the Gestapo came to the door. Gerd answered, and they asked for Fru Walle. Gerd told them Lilly had been here, but had gone away. They had a well-known Norwegian informer with them, he too in uniform. Surprisingly the Gestapo accepted Gerd's story without coming in to search the house, and they left. Lilly was rolled in a blanket, and laid on a shelf in a small storeroom where she remained all day till 11 pm.

Late that evening three young men left the Gjørtz house. Two of them were Gerd's brothers, the third one, in the middle, with a cigarette dangling from his lips, was Lilly. They had an address to go to, but it was useless. They were directed to another house, but again it was no good — there were too many unreliable people about, said the man. Then she remembered a "good" Norwegian who lived not far away. But he waved her away. "I have a son in Shetland. I may be arrested at any moment. You wouldn't be safe here," he said. (*The Germans had now started arresting the fathers of boys who escaped.*) They had walked a long way, she was tired, and the night was spending. Then she thought of another man she knew. He lived in a little cottage, and there were Germans all around, but he took her in. It was a small house, and there were six people in it, with the wife still quite unwell after the recent birth of a child, but William Bye gave her food, treated her well, and kept watch till morning. The Gjørtz boys had seen her safe and then gone home.

Next day Thoralf managed to speak to her on the phone, and Konrad Korsnes took her on the next stage on his bike. But when she saw something going on up ahead, she left him and went to the home of Oscar Bigseth, another member of their group. She hid in his potato cellar all day, then, changed into women's clothes and with Oscar pushing a pram, they set out on the next stage. They came to the church, and it was at this point that Thoralf rejoined her. They hid her behind a gravestone, but Lilly says indignantly, "They were going to put me in a grave for safety." Thoralf had the Linge boy, Tor Stenersen, with him. Because of the dangerous situation in Ålesund, and without Thoralf to help him, he had decided to try and get back to Shetland with the Walles.

The next part of their escape was long and very exhausting. They went as far east as Hellesylt on Geiranger Fjord, before working their way west again by Nordfjord, finally to Selje and then by boat to Silda. When they had come to the Geiranger area they had gone to a house whose address they had been given and knocked on the door. The door was shut in their faces — the man thought they were quislings. Thoralf pulled out his revolver and ordered the man to open up, and when they had established their identity they were made warmly welcome, and indeed this man organised the next stage of their journey for them, although they were there for nearly two weeks before setting off. "The Linge boy was tough," says Lilly. But it was all new to him, and in some respects the Walles had greater strength than he did. He was frequently dependent on them. But Lilly says quite seriously, "His work was much more important than us."

The journey westwards, through deep snow, sapped Lilly's strength, and finally she was forced to say, "I can go no farther." The Linge boy took charge. "Now is the time for the pill." (*They all carried two pills — one for suicide, one to give a quick burst of energy.*) She took the pill. "Luckily it was the right one," she says, "and I went on again for a while like a new woman. But when we came down to Åheim I was finished." (*Åheim was not far from Selje*). When they at last reached Silda they stayed with Mons Silden, the postmaster. He was very good to them. He even went to Måløy and got Lilly some clothes — and a lipstick! They stayed with him for a fortnight. At last they were feeling safe again, and it was a happy little time. Then one night they heard the familiar "tonk-tonk-tonk", and in came the *Olaf*. Per Blystad was as usual the skipper, and he came ashore in his naval uniform, came into the house, looked at them and said, "Are these the married couple Walle?" Mindur Berge had come ashore with him. The *Olaf* had a load of weapons and equipment to discharge, and Thoralf went along to help. The plan was that, having discharged her load, and picked up the Walles and the Linge agent, Per would take her down to Rubbestadneset to collect some engine spares. But now he discovered that a blade of the *Olaf's* propeller was broken, so a direct return to Shetland was decided on. Mons had a family of four children, and he had been very, very good to the Walles. It couldn't have been easy to find food for three extra mouths in wartime Norway, but they had nothing they could give him. Thoralf hinted gently to Per, and that generous man immediately gave Mons all the spare cash he had, as well as all the rations they could spare.

They called in at one or two places before setting course for Shetland, and, though seasick, she enjoyed the "lovely white bread and butter from Shetland", when they were tied up. The trip to Shetland ended at last, but they were kept below for a time. There was no telling who might be on the pier. When the security officer came on board Thoralf's first request was for a jar of rum! He was given a sailor's uniform to wear, and they went up to Commercial Street. There an officer stopped Thoralf, and haughtily demanded to be told why Thoralf hadn't saluted him. "I was waiting for you to salute me," Thoralf replied. Perhaps not surprisingly Lilly's memory is of Per taking her up to Commercial Street and buying her some clothes.

They have many memories of these far-off days. Lilly remembers a man from Sweden coming to the door. He had the right password, "Is Heidi at home?" Lilly said she was, and the man then asked if Lilly was the maid. She took him in, and when Thoralf came home the man slit a seam in his coat and pulled out a crepe-de-chine package in the form of a letter. 'You must open this only if you are in desperate need," he told them — and that need came when they were on the run from the Gestapo. At one point during their escape a man came up to Thoralf. "You know me, Walle," he said. "I was in your jail last year." Their organisation was, of course, broken up after the *Viggo* betrayal, for their cover was completely blown, but not all the members of the group paid the penalty. Kåre Viken, perhaps surprisingly, was one of the survivors. In his prison camp a German officer discovered that they had been at the 1936 Olympics together, and the immediate result was that his life was spared. Not only that, but he was made a sort of "trusty" in the camp. Lilly's mother was taken by the Gestapo, but she survived. Thoralf recalls that when his undercover work was at its height, a German came into the police station in Ålesund every day to check on the station's activities. He was a pleasant fellow, and never seemed to have the slightest suspicion of what was going on. But when the Walles were sprung he was sent to the

Eastern Front as punishment for having failed to spot what was happening, and there he was killed.

Thoralf had bought the *Viggo* from its owners, in this case three men being the shareholders. He heard afterwards that one of the men had not been in complete agreement with the sale, and had removed a part of the engine. He doesn't know if there was any truth in this, but the *Viggo's* capture was certainly the result of the two informers on board, and the machinations of that evil man, Henry Rinnan. One of the passengers, Colonel Lars Dannevig, was shot in uncertain circumstances shortly after his arrest and interrogation in Trondheim. Eighteen more of the *Viggo's* passengers were shot on 30th April, 1942, that criminal act apparently being part of the reprisals connected with the death of the two Gestapo men in Telavåg.

While the Walles were busy with their export group up in Ålesund, another young man was occupied with the same kind of work much further south in the Stord/Bømlo area. That young man was Nils Robertstad. He was twenty-nine when the Germans came, living in Haugesund. His first thought was to join the Norwegian army, but resistance in the south was so short-lived that it wasn't worth while. He had come home in 1939 from his job as an officer in the merchant navy to get married, and he had still not gone back to sea in April, 1940. Now he moved farther east to where his wife had a house. It wasn't long before he found himself involved in the work of helping people wanted by the Gestapo to escape. In this he was ably assisted by his brother Peter who was a minister, a priest as they say in Norway, and soon a whole group of people were involved in the "export" work — the Bømlo/Bremnes group as Ragnar Ulstein calls them. Down here, as farther north, when escapes were being planned it was always Shetland that was seen as the destination to aim for, and of course from the very beginning of the occupation the escapes started. It was a good coastline for escapes — there were many small islands to make ideal jumping-off spots, and there was no shortage of boats. The minister knew everyone in the Bømlo area, and the grapevine on the west coast was very good. Few Norwegians were unaware that many of their young people were escaping, and by late 1940 there were instances of boats coming back from Shetland for a second load of refugees — this before the Shetland Bus was officially underway.

But as in so many other cases Nils' involvement finally led to German suspicion, and he knew he would have to get away. His decision was translated into action when a man wanted by the

Gestapo came to him, and asked him if he would take him to Shetland. "I said I would," says Nils. "I bought a small boat called the *Smart*. It was about 38 feet." He took his wife Ingerd with him, and there were three other men on board, plus the girl-friend of one of them. Most wanted man among them was Birger Larssen, one of the Bergen group, whom we last saw organising the *Rupee* in which Truls Håskjold among others escaped. They left on 10th August, 1942, and it was a wrench for Ingerd to leave her mother alone in the house. And she didn't much fancy crossing the North Sea in such a small boat. To begin with they had a gale from the south-east, which was followed by a quiet spell and then they ran into fog. They were pretty sure they were near land, and they did a lot of banging in lieu of a foghorn. Finally a boat came alongside, and told them they were only twenty minutes from Lerwick. Nils had been on the wheel for thirty-six hours without a break.

After the usual screening in Lerwick and then in "Sing-Sing", Nils joined the Norwegian navy, was sent on an officers' course, and was promoted to sub-lieutenant. After a spell at gunnery school as an instructor, he was asked if he would be willing to undertake trips to Norway. "I said I would, though I had no real idea of what was involved." He was summoned to Norwegian HQ in London, and was then sent to Shetland by air. He landed at Sumburgh from one of the little Rapides, having made the journey sitting among the mail-bags. His immediate task was to go to Norway and encourage more young Norwegians to come over to Shetland with their boats. As we saw earlier Shetland Bus losses in the winter of 42/43 had been extremely severe. So now for the first time he was landed as an agent. He was in full uniform battledress, and he was on his own. He had adequate food with him, and he carried a Colt ·45 revolver. He stayed for a week, contacting his brother Peter, and a few people he knew he could trust implicitly. Laurits Klubben had been a friend in the Bømlo/Bremnes export group, and Nils regarded him very highly. (*He was still alive in 1987 at the ripe age of ninety-one.*) At the end of the week it was either the *Harald* or the *Olaf* which came over and picked him up.

So now his career as an agent had begun, and in January, 1943, he was landed again, this time in company with another agent who was going to Bergen, and this time he had a transmitter with him. Again he made contact with his brother, who came in a small boat to meet him. Nils had no qualms about landing in Norway. He knew that he would get no mercy from the Germans if caught, but, he says, "We felt we were just as good as the Gestapo." In all he made six trips as an agent, the last seeing him ashore in Norway from November, 1944 until February, 1945.

On one of his trips, in March, 1944, he and two Linge boys had kayaks with them. They had been landed from the *Hessa,* and their objective was to get into Sagvåg on Stord *(readers will remember the Comomando/MTB raid there)* and attach limpet mines to German ships. They had been landed on the west side of Bømlo, and they carried the kayaks over to the east side, where they were immediately opposite Sagvåg. Nils led them across the Sound, but there was no shipping in the harbour. By the time a suitable target came along it was May, and there was far too little darkness. They made several abortive attempts, with fog disrupting their final effort. Ingerd had work in Dumbarton, and remained there throughout the war. She knew Nils was frequently away somewhere, but she never had any clear idea of what he was up to. As Nils explains, agents were people apart. They had to be, for the very essence of their continued existence was secrecy. They couldn't afford to make friends. When in Shetland he sometimes stayed in the officers' quarters at Scalloway, but frequently he was with Major Sclater at Flemington. He found the atmosphere at Scalloway extremely pleasant, with the Norwegians there seeming to be almost Shetlanders.

He doesn't often think about the old days, but "Now and again I dream, and in my dreams I always win," he says with a smile. He needs a lot of persuasion to say very much about the risks he took, and the escapes he had. Clearly, however, he hadn't been active as an agent very long when the Germans began to know quite a lot about him. They knew his name, and what he looked like, and the Gestapo snooped around asking questions about him. On a trip in 1944 he got word that the Gestapo were on to him, and were pretty sure of where he was and were heading his way. A man came for him with a small boat, but lost his nerve, ran off, jumped in the boat, and started rowing away. Nils knew his life was at stake, so he pointed his gun at him and "I told him I would shoot him dead if he didn't come back. The boat was the only chance I had to get away. I kept the gun on him, and he cried for me not to shoot. I didn't shoot him!" The daughter and grand-daughter of his old friend Laurits Klubben helped him, but for eight or nine days he was on the run living rough on the mountainside. He managed to make contact with a radio operator belonging to Arquebus — a branch of the underground — and he in turn contacted London. Result — Larsen arrived with the *Vigra* to pick him up, and that was a welcome sight for he and Larsen were good friends. But that trip was to prove the nearest he came to capture. Laurits Klubben was the main contact in the area, not merely for the Linge boys and other agents, but for the Shetlandsgjengen and the MTBs as well.

In 1943 Nils' brother Peter, the minister, was arrested by the Gestapo, along with some of the other men who had been active in the area. With Martin Stavland and Nils Bjerkelid, also from Bømlo, they suffered greatly at Gestapo hands, and were sent to a concentration camp. Nils himself arrived in Shetland on 8th May, 1945, and went down to the boats in Scalloway where celebrations at the war's ending were already in full swing. Everyone had a great day. His wife was still down in Scotland, and he was unable to take her back to Norway with him. Then on 23rd June he contacted some people he knew down in London, and found out that the *Vigra* would shortly be leaving Aberdeen for Norway. He telephoned his wife, telling her to make for Aberdeen, and to get hold of Larsen and tell him she wanted to come over with him. "But I don't know Larsen," she protested. "How will I recognise him?" "You can't miss him," Nils told her. "Just look for the man with the most medal ribbons!"

Chapter Eighteen

Heavy Water

The Second War produced much material for books and films, and many of the films which tell the story of wartime episodes provide excellent and exciting entertainment. Surely none more so than "Heroes of Telemark", which many Shetlanders have seen either on cinema screens or on television. The film tells the story of the destruction of the heavy water plant near Rjukan in Telemark in southern Norway. "Heavy water" had no meaning for the ordinary individual in the war years, but we have already had it mentioned in this book when we followed the story of Starheim's daring hijacking of the *Galtesund*. The determination of his friend, Einar Skinnerland, to get his case of information about the heavy water to Britain showed that he at least knew that it was highly important. Probably the information that he carried with him on the *Galtesund* was largely responsible for British intelligence realising just how dangerous for the Allies was the work on which the Germans were engaged near Rjukan. Clearly there was an urgent need to disrupt the work, and it was that urgency that led to the sending of two Halifax bombers, each towing a glider filled with twenty Commandos, whose task it would be to sabotage the German plant. Sadly the operation ended in complete disaster. One glider broke loose from its towing plane, and plunged to the ground. The other plane, along with its glider, crashed into a mountainside. The few survivors were captured by the Germans, and the probability is that they were shot by the Germans while held as prisoners in Stavanger.

This disaster in no way lessened the need for action to neutralise the plant, and the next measure decided on was to send over a small party of Norwegians who would be dropped by parachute, and would attack on foot. It was at that point that a man called Joachim Rønneberg appeared on the scene. Joachim's name is probably almost unknown in Shetland, but in Norway it is known to all, for Joachim is Norway's most decorated man. But even if his name is unfamiliar to us, his achievements are familiar enough, for he was the man who fearlessly led his five brave comrades on their successful raid on the German heavy water plant. Today he still lives in Ålesund, fit and active, and both physically and mentally capable of passing for a man twenty years his junior. A thoughtful, intelligent man, a conversation with him is extremely stimulating.

He was twenty-one when the Germans arrived in 1940. He hadn't still done his military service, so he was little use as a soldier. But when the fighting was over it didn't take long for Norwegians to realise that life had changed completely. Says Joachim, "There was the blackout. Germans were strutting about everywhere, and they were singing in the streets. And there were the orders — you were told what you could do and what you could not do, and frequently you were threatened with penalties if you did things the Germans didn't like. To escape from Norway — to get out of the country — was a crime, and, if caught trying it, you were sentenced to death. But that didn't stop young people trying to get away to join the Free Norwegian forces. Then, in the summer of 1941, the Germans thought they'd found the key to stopping the whole thing. They would arrest and imprison the parents of escapers. They thought that would put an end to it. But of course it never would. On the same day that a hundred parents were sent to a concentration camp in east Norway, two boat loads of escapers left for Shetland. Norwegians were not easily frightened."

Møre og Romsdal was an area much used by escapers in 1941. It was the first county north of the line to the south of which you needed a special identity card and a special pass if you wanted to travel. So most of the refugee traffic from eastern Norway came through this area. There were plenty of boats, many of them the famous Møre cutters. And of course the fishermen knew the road to Shetland well — it was like a "home road" to them. They were proud of their boats, and knew exactly how to handle them, and it is not surprising that many of them became Shetland Bus men.

"I was driven to conclude that Norway during German occupation was no place for a man to live. I wanted to join the Free Norwegian forces, so I contacted a man who was organising a boat, and on 10th March, 1941, we left on board the *Sigurd*. We had some engine trouble just outside Ålesund, but we knew the Germans were on our heels, so we managed to keep going all night, but finally we had to turn back and came in on the coast again just west of Måløy. We got the engine going, and this time when we set off we took just twenty-four hours to reach Baltasound." (*Kåre*

Viken seems to have been involved with the 'Sigurd's'escape. She carried seven people, and returned in the following month to pick up more refugees.)

Joachim says they had heard so many stories about landing in Shetland, but at Unst there was no sign of the military. They blew their siren and flashed their searchlight, and after some time they were taken into Baltasound, and lay there all night. "The soldiers stayed with us. They tramped up and down the deck above us, and we couldn't get any sleep. We finally asked them to do their tramping on the pier." They went through the usual security measures, including a thorough screening at the Patriotic School down in London. An absence of seasickness on the way across the North Sea made him think the navy was perhaps the place for him, but as we saw earlier it was now that he met Martin Linge. Joachim calls him an impressive man, and clearly he had great liking and respect for him. The two men had much in common, and developed an excellent relationship with each other. Joachim saw Martin as the ideal recruiter of men for Special Operations activities, and pays him the highest tribute by describing him as a "very, very fine man".

Joachim was sent to a variety of training schemes, aimed in the first place at finding out if the men recruited were of the right calibre, and then, if they were, graduating to the real thing, where they were given an inkling of what was expected of them. They had parachute training at Ringway, and then it was up to Scotland for the first Linge course, which was very rigorous indeed, and where another course member was Leif Larsen. There they were taught everything and prepared for everything, not a little of the instruction being highly suitable for anyone with a career as an agent or a spy ahead of them. Half of the group went to Shetland on completion of training, and were later to suffer heavy losses. Joachim was kept down south, to begin with as liaison man between the new volunteers and the training schools. Later he was made Norwegian Training Officer in Scotland, and had responsibility for a great deal of the instruction, with Aviemore as their main centre. The Cairngorms provided terrain very similar to Norway, and he says, "I was an extremely fit young man". He received advanced training in demolition and sabotage, and was recommended for further promotion, but he was not really interested, and in any case the Aviemore people protested that he was essential to them. Out of the blue, towards the end of 1942, he was sent for by the CO, and was soon on his way to Norwegian HQ in London.

"I was asked if I would pick five men to take on a certain job. That was how it started. After my long spell of instruction I was now to go on active service. I was keen to go. I wanted to be in action. I had privately been planning a scheme to take a trip to the mountains near Ålesund with the idea of infiltrating and disrupting communication links between eastern and western Norway, and the plan had been accepted in principle by the higher authorities. But we didn't know if it would ever come off. I knew everyone in the training groups, and it was not difficult for me to pick five men of the kind I wanted. We started intensive training. Then I was summoned back to HQ in London, and was told for the first time the nature of the operation. It was to sabotage the heavy water plant in Telemark, and I was to lead the expedition. I knew I would have very good men with me."

They were already well-trained and very fit, but they now had just a fortnight in which to obtain all the equipment they would need, and to make all the last-minute preparations. Their weapons they got mostly from the Norwegian army workshops in Dumfries, and also a good deal of their protective clothing, windshields, snow goloshes, toboggans, etc. The rest of the necessary items were not easy to find in wartime Britain. Joachim went on the search for sleeping bags, and finally called at a bedding firm in London, where the manager simply shook his head. "So I asked him if they had a factory in London. They did, down near the docks, and I went there. I showed the man in charge what we wanted, and asked if he could do it. He said he would try, and produced a sample on the following day, which, with very little alteration, was ideal. Similar sleeping bags became standard equipment for the Special Service boys." (*It was about this time that Jack Moore was asked to make several steel jemmies in a hurry. He completed the job from the many bits and pieces which were part and parcel of his workshop, and later heard they had been required for the Telemark raid.*)

By mid-December they were ready, but it was the full-moon period, and they had to wait. Then they had a flight over the plant at Vemork, but failed to make contact with the reception committee. (*This committee was largely the result of planning by Starheim.*) Next time over they decided not to bother with trying to contact the people on the ground, but asked to be dropped at a certain spot on the Hardangervidda, from where they would map-read their way to the target. The drop duly took place in clear weather from a Halifax stripped of all weapons except for the rear-gunner's twin ·303 machine-guns. Though a good target for the Germans in the clear sky they made the drop safely.

Assuming they were at the right spot, they set out for the target area, knowing that a lake lay almost immediately in front of them. In the bitter winter temperatures it would, of course, be frozen over. "But after a bit I saw some branches sticking out of the snow, and I thought it very strange to see branches growing out of a lake. The trees had to be rooted in good Norwegian soil, so clearly we were in the wrong place. We didn't know where we were. We retraced our steps and finally found the spot where we'd landed. Then it took us a whole day to establish our real position. We were about twenty-five kilometres from the point where we should have come down. You need a bit of luck in such ventures." Such a bad start might have upset lesser men. For these six it was merely a hiccup.

Having established their position they set out again, and successfully carried out one of the outstanding feats of the Second War — the blowing up of the German heavy water plant near Rjukan. The feat was accomplished without a single shot being fired, and the film "Heroes of Telemark" has paid tribute to their deed. A second film in which Joachim played himself added to that tribute. But he says little about the operation, although he does admit, "We felt we had done a good job. Indeed, we knew we had done a good job almost as soon as we were outside the door of the factory, for the bangs came almost immediately. We had been supposed to use two-minute fuses, but we used 30-second ones to be quite sure that we would know the job had been properly done. It was a happy feeling anyway — you had the blast in your back and it gave you an added lift." The next sentence is a classic of understatement, "After we blew up the plant we crossed the border into Sweden." No mention of hardships or dangers, no mention of the fact that it was probably something like 300 miles to the Swedish frontier, many of them over mountains. No mention of the hazardous approach to the factory in the first place, and the deadly danger they were in all the time they were placing their explosive charges. These were very brave and able men.

"We were actually the first men sent into Europe in British army uniforms to carry out a sabotage operation. Probably the British uniforms were used in the hope they would prevent reprisals against the Norwegian people. When we crossed into Sweden we had to present ourselves as refugees, and to some extent we had to hoodwink the Swedes. We established contact with the British in Stockholm, and we were finally given permission to emigrate to Britain! The Swedes were glad to be presented with such an easy solution to a difficult problem." Stockholm was very useful to

55. The heavy water plant near Rjukan in Telemark.

56. The bridge over the gorge near the plant.

them. The shops there had so much that was unobtainable in Britain, and, with an eye to the future, they obtained numerous articles which would be put to use on their next expedition. They were already thinking of the next one! "When we landed in Scotland it was a very happy moment. We had come home again! A cup of tea and a bun were immediately forthcoming. I don't think I am the only one who felt this, but when we were in Britain we were always talking about getting home to Norway, but when we landed in Norway we immediately started talking about going home again — and home meant Britain. It was as if we had two homelands, and we were very much at home in both of them."

The average individual, after an expedition such as the Telemark affair, would have been content to rest on his oars. Not so Joachim. The mountains of Romsdal still drew him. They made one flight over the area in October, 1943, but the pilot was unable to find the dropping spot. They tried again in February, 1944. Again failure, and the pilot came back to where they were sitting in the blacked-out fuselage to explain his failure to them. It was, of course, unknown country to the pilot, but it was home to Joachim, and when he pulled the blinds open he knew exactly where they were. They were now on their homeward journey, and from that point he guided the pilot on a course which avoided German defence points — and all without a map. Safely out at sea, the pilot demanded, "Why the hell weren't you up front with me all the way? You know this countryside like the back of your hand." "Put that in your report when we get back," said Joachim, and apparently he did, for next time Joachim was up front with the pilot all the way. He guided the plane to the dropping zone without mishap, only to have the crew throw out their equipment containers before they had jumped themselves. They hurried to follow, and "the sky was full of parachutes". As they came down he recognised the church, and that pinpointed exactly where they were, which was useful as the maps they were carrying were far from accurate.

Joachim and his two friends now spent twelve months up the mountainside, living in a tiny hut, half hidden by rocks and invisible to all but the closest scrutiny. The Germans knew someone was transmitting in the area, but they were never able to pinpoint the location of the transmitter. Their contact with London remained clear and unbroken, and Joachim still has pictures of the little hut where their existence centred on their workbench and their beds. They were good comrades, and lived in complete harmony. Inevitably there were times when tension imposed a severe strain, and on such occasions, as they had agreed before leaving Britain, the sufferer would go for a long trudge on the mountain, and return with mind again at ease.

Twelve months had gone by when Joachim developed severe stomach pains. When London was contacted they diagnosed appendicitis. "I was advised to go to Ålesund for an operation. We well understood the implications of such an action. We radioed London that the sick man was still alive, that he would see the nearest doctor, and that if an operation was deemed necessary we would request evacuation." London took the hint, and a spate of messages went backwards and forwards — from the mountain to London, from London to Ålesund, from Ålesund to the mountan, and perhaps most importantly, from London to Shetland. What then happened was that Joachim was taken down from the mountain to the island of Vigra, and from Vigra to Rimøy, from where he was taken to Shetland by Larsen in the *Vigra*. The man responsible for this difficult operation was Sverre Roald of Vigra, who not merely managed to get Joachim down from the mountain, but followed that up by taking him to the embarkation point and then accompanied his patient over to Shetland on the *Vigra*. This remarkable man, who still lives on Vigra, made a tremendous contribution to the underground fight against the hated Germans by helping many of those sought by the Gestapo to escape to safety in Shetland. He had a good relationship with the Walle and Viken export groups, but he lived on the island, and was therefore largely on his own. In all he himself found eight or nine boats for escapers, and when asked if he had to buy all these boats, his quiet answer was, "They were all freewill boats!"

There were no "bad" Norwegians on Vigra, says Sverre, and something like 80 of their young men had made their way to Shetland. Sverre was actively opposing the Germans during the whole of the occupation, but it is very difficult to get him to say anything about his exploits. It was a long time ago, he says, and he doesn't remember a lot of it. We have already seen how he helped Larsen and his boys to get away after the sinking of the *Bergholm,* but he says nothing of that. He doesn't even mention the fact that he was taken by the Gestapo towards the end of the war, and inevitably was tortured. Though suffering terrible pain he managed to hoodwink the Gestapo sufficiently to prevent them getting hold of Larsen and the *Vigra,* which would have been a tremendous coup for them. War's end came in time to save his life, though it didn't save his suffering. He is a quietly impressive man, whose exploits have received far too little attention, and now it is unlikely that we will ever be able to learn the full range of his activities.

Joachim is also a man of few words when it comes to describing situations fraught with danger, and this particular episode in his life is described thus: "Roald came up and got me down from the mountain, and Shetland's Larsen came over with the *Vigra* and picked me up and took me once again to Shetland."

Once more in Britain, now minus his appendix, Joachim was soon back at work, this time training officers who had been recruited to go over and reinforce the officer corps of the Home Front in Norway. In the event these men reached Norway only a few days before the German surrender. He returned to Norway at war's end, but the country was in a bad way, and he spent some months back in Britain working in one of the Norwegian offices, before finally going home in 1946. Much of his life since then has been spent with Norwegian broadcasting. "I have enjoyed it," he says. He has been over to Britain several times, and had his honeymoon there in 1949. He is still close friends with Arthur Sclater of Shetland Bus fame, and a few years ago was over at a special showing of the film "Heroes of Telemark", on which occasion the Queen Mother stayed with them for an hour and a half. His tremendous collection of medals has come from a number of countries — "I would look like a Christmas tree if I wore them all," — but medal presentations in wartime to a man like him was a ticklish business. Their operations were so secret that no one was supposed to know anything about them. One decoration ceremony was carried out in Baker Street, with both British and Norwegian royalty present, as a Buckingam Palace ceremony for secret heroes was forbidden. The Germans referred to Baker Street as "Gangster Street".

At war's end they were still young men, but old in experience. They had learned to live together, to share and to understand. The war years had had so much to offer in terms of friendship, communal effort and comradship. Says Joachim, "I don't think we will every again have such 'giving' days as we had during the war." He now accepts that what he and others like him did is part of history, and that two-thirds of the present Norwegian population were not born when it happened. He has come to feel that young people should know something about the occupation. "They need to know so that they can have the right attitude to their country and its defence. The only alternative to defence is occupation. In 1940 we didn't understand what the alternative was. But we learned what freedom means. Freedom is something you have to fight for. Freedom is everything. We had to fight for it when we were growing up — we need to tell our young people the story."

Chapter Nineteen

Commandos

Mention has already been made on several occasions of the participation of Commando troops in operations from Shetland. Mostly these references have included mention of MTBs, not surprisingly, perhaps, as on many occasions MTBs and Commandos shared operations. And as it happens both Commandos and MTBs arrived in Shetland almost together in November, 1942, the MTBs to make their base in Lerwick, the small initial Commando unit of twelve men under Lieut Harald Risnes to establish themselves at Baltasound in Unst. The unit came under the overall command of Major Fynn who led the British Commando unit from No. 12 Commando. This small group of Norwegians was earmarked quite appropriately for operations on the Norwegian coast.

Though few in numbers they were soon involved in action, and two or three of them were actually on board the three MTBs which made the flotilla's first trip to the Norwegian coast on 22nd November, 1942. A week later Risnes and two of his men were over again, and this time went across from Bømlo to Stord in a small motor-boat, to scout for suitable enemy shipping targets for limpet mines or for MTB attacks. They came to Stord at a time when the Germans were mounting a considerable land and sea search for British paratroopers. Though the local people had no knowledge of the cause, this was probably the follow-up to the two Commando-loaded gliders crashing when on their way to attack the heavy-water plant.

By January, 1943, the Commando squad at Baltasound had risen to about eighty men, many of the newcomers being from No. 5 Commando Troop. From them was to be formed the Special Boat Section for the Special Service Brigade, and their primary purpose would be to carry out sabotage against enemy shipping, and to assist in the landing and uplifting of agents. They were made up of both Norwegian and British personnel, and among their officers was Peter Scott, son of Captain Scott of Antarctic fame. Also included was a group of Norwegians who trained in kayaks and canoes, which, it was hoped, would provide the means for attaching limpet mines to enemy ships. Though the British officers were very keen on this idea, at least one of the Norwegian officers sounded a cautionary note. He felt that the sight of Eskimo kayaks in Norwegian fjords would almost certainly arouse speculation and rumour which would quickly reach German ears. However the training went ahead in very rigorous conditions, the only consolation being that the kayak men were now treated as naval ratings and got their daily rum ration. But the training was completed on the Scottish west coast, Unst winter waters proving just a little too boisterous.

The Commando involvement with the MTBs continued, and parties went across on numerous occasions, although often having little to show for their efforts. That was certainly not the case with Operation Cartoon on 21st January, 1943, when the Commando force, led by the Major Fynn mentioned earlier, executed the copy-book attack on the Stord mine, the story of that operation being fully described in the MTB section. On 22nd February there were Commandos on board 619 and 631 when they went over, picked up an agent, and then lay camouflaged waiting for a target. None came, and the weather deteriorated badly, so that neither a planned Commando attack on a German strong-point, nor a torpedo attack on German shipping proved possible. By the time they finally arrived back in Shetland they had been away for nine days, and had been presumed lost. Worst of all they had exhausted their food supplies! There were also about a dozen men on board both 619 and 631 when the two little craft went into Florø and torpedoed two German ships. The loss of 631 when she ran on a skerry and couldn't be refloated ment that 619 had to carry both the MTB crews plus over twenty Commandos, which created extremely overcrowded conditions. She then had to be driven at maximum speed in very heavy seas to get away from a pursuing German destroyer. Thorough as Commando training was, it did not include provision to meet this kind of situation, and the Commando boys probably remembered that experience for a very long time.

On 11th April, 1943, four MTBs carried 85 Commandos over to Skorpa on Operation Carry, the objective being the destruction of the German battery on Rugsundøy. Tamber himself was in charge of the operation, and when he found the lie-up place which had been selected for the MTBs to be unsuitable, he returned to Lerwick without landing the Commandos. On his return he even suggested an alternative plan to British HQ. It is said that ACOS was not too happy with Lieut. Tamber on this occasion.

One Commando story which has received little attention from historians has to do with a man we have already noted, Odd Starheim. When he had been waiting in Flekkefjord to carry out his daring hijacking of the *Galtesund,* he had noted that German convoys frequently anchored overnight in the sound between the island of Hidra and the mainland, at the entrance to the fjord leading up to the town of Flekkefjord. For a man who had the nerve to hijack a steamer, it was only a step further to conceive the idea of hijacking a convoy, and the idea was stored away in his mind. After he made his triumphant entry into Aberdeen with the *Galtesund,* his feat was seen by the authorities as something pretty important. He was awarded the highest Norwegian decoration as well as the British DSO. But he found that things had changed considerably in London since the early Linge days. There were far more people milling about, and to his horror he was set at a table to work with paper. It was no sort of life for his restless spirit.

Now he brought forward his plan to hijack the German convoy. The scheme, to take over up to five German ships, was approved, given the codename Carhampton, and was allocated 30 Commandos and 10 Norwegian navy men, mainly engineers, for its execution. The party immediately embarked on a period of strenuous training. Among the thirty Commandos was a man called Reidar Nilsen. Reidar was still at school in Ålesund when the Germans came. When he finished school he got work in an office, but all the time he was aware that many young people were getting away to Shetland, and going to do their bit for their country. He very much wanted to do something as well. He got a job with the local radio and was given a pistol, and he and his friends haunted the streets looking for a chance against the enemy. But now the longing to get away to Shetland became very strong, and, hoping that somehow it might give him a better chance, he went to work in his uncle's fishcuring business. Daily he saw the boats coming and going, and one evening, out of the blue, he got the word. "A boat is going. There's a place for you." The boat was the *Havtor,* and she was lying at a pier on the outskirts of Ålesund. On 7th March they were on their way, and shortly came to the *Blaegg* lying with her engine stopped. She had been on her way to Shetland. The *Havtor* took her refugees on board, bringing the total to twenty-eight, including two girls and numerous boys in their teens. Reidar himself was just nineteen.

They made landfall at Uyeasound on 9th March, and there one

of the boys sold his camera to raise a little cash. There was no military presence, says Reidar, but a small boat directed them to Lerwick, and there they were housed under guard in the Mission. Then it was down to Buckie, where they were taken to the Maternity Hospital for food, baths and a night's accommodation. There was a lack of pyjamas, but plenty of nightdresses! As usual the next step was the Patriotic School in London, and from there to the County Hotel, where he met his cousin, just leaving for Canada to train as a pilot.

He was offered office work, but he assured them he had not come over to be a clerk. So he was sent up to Scotland for training and went through the usual routine. His first army posting was to Fraserburgh, and on the night the Germans bombed Aberdeen they fired at the planes with their rifles. At the end of 1941 he joined the Linge Company, too late to meet Linge himself. Now he underwent intensive training similar to that described by Joachim Rønneberg, and on completion of that he was selected for an operation to the south of Norway. There were thirty men from the Linge Company in the party, and ten from the Norwegian navy. Their objective was explained to them. It was to go over to south Norway, land, and take over five ships from a German convoy which would be lying at anchor near the mouth of the fjord leading up to Flekkefjord. Six Linge boys and two navy men would be allocated to each ship, the Linge boys to provide the muscle, the navy lads the mechanical and navigational know-how.

On 14th November, 1942, the party assembled in Aberdeen and embarked on the *Bodø,* a slow-moving, but very sea-worthy ex-whaler. She set out, met extremely heavy weather, and returned to Aberdeen. The following night she sailed again, and came close up to the Norwegian coast, but was challenged by Germans on the shore, and again returned to Aberdeen. Thereafter there was a wait until the next moon period, and on 31st December the *Bodø* was ready once more. There was a last-minute snag — the British radio operator had sought permission to go ashore for a message, and he just didn't return. They sailed without him.

The *Bodø* reached the coast off Eigerøy on 2nd January, and though there was no sign of the looked-for reception party the forty men landed and the *Bodø* set off back to Aberdeen. When nearing the port on the way back she struck a mine, and went down with all thirty-three men on board. The Commandos after landing made an empty farmhouse their billet. "Below us the body of a dead German washed in and out with the tide," says Reidar. The Norwegian sheriff had heard about the dead German and had ordered the two owners of the farm to go and weight it with stones and sink it before the German authorities got to hear about it. The two arrived in a motor-boat, and Starheim promptly put them under guard and appropriated their boat. After a three-day wait the convoy appeared, and the attack commenced as planned. Flekkefjord was some distance along the coast, and the hijacked boat was employed to take the main party there, while a few went by road. There was almost immediate trouble with the boat's engine, and when they did get it going they encountered heavy seas and a head wind which delayed them. The road party had meantime cut the power and telephone lines, but by the time they were all in position the night was too far spent and they had to abandon the attempt and return to the farmhouse.

Ten more days they waited until another convoy came along, this time three merchant ships with a heavily armed escort. A second attack was now put in motion, more or less following the pattern of the first. Perhaps it should have been expected that the cutting of the telephone and power lines on the first attempt would have alerted the Germans to the fact that something was going on. But the Commandos didn't know that they had taken any action to meet a possible threat. Says Reidar, "We had planned to take the sentry down by the shore in silence, and we did just that, but unknown to us the Germans had doubled the sentries, and the second one saw us and started shooting. We had to open fire too, and kill him and the rest of the men in the guard hut. The German guard boat with the convoy now opened fire, as well as other Germans on shore, and we could see no hope of success. We had to withdraw." By this time the whole area was in chaos. The big guns on Hidra, which had been brought to Norway from the Maginot Line, started firing at an imaginary target out at sea, flares were going up and there was a hail of fire from all directions.

The Norwegian party withdrew very quickly over the hill to Abelnes, and down to the harbour. There they seized two rowing boats and rowed across the fjord to the opposite shore where they filled the boats with stones and sank them. A 900-ft precipice stared them in the face, and many of them were shod only in plimsolls. They had put them on to secure a quiet approach to the German position, and had been carrying their boots slung around their necks. In the hurried escape a lot of the boots had been lost. Says Reidar, "We climbed up the mountain, but we were not equipped for the mountain, especially our feet which were covered only with very light rubber shoes. We had no food. We climbed and trudged through the deep snow for ninety-six hours." They came to a derelict building with part of the roof missing, but it had a hearth, and on it there was a big kettle. "We got a fire going, and stripped some bark off the trees which we tried to boil. Two men we had sent out on a reconnaissance came back with a little sugar and a few carrots, which we boiled, then drank the sweetened water."

One or two of the party belonged to this particular area, and they made contact with the people at the farmhouse of Rudfjord, who sent all the food they could collect to the starving Commandos. Then transport was organised to take them right up to the head of the valley at Eiken, and the coach duly arrived at 3 am, with the local doctor in his own car acting as guide, and with another volunteer following with horse and sledge, obliterating their tracks. At Eiken food was waiting for them, and also a modicum of first-aid for the frostbite and exposure from which many of them were suffering. Next day they withdrew a further twenty kilometres into the mountains. All the time the Germans were trying to get a lead on them, and during daylight hours planes were overhead almost continuously.

They managed to get a new battery for the transmitter and established contact with London, asking for a parachute drop of boots, etc. A plane duly arrived, but, sadly, flew straight inland to their position from the coast and was spotted by the Germans who put two and two together, and followed its course inland in their search. Even worse the drop was poor and many of the bundles went astray. However some were salvaged, and enough boots were acquired to fit out almost all the men. But clearly the situation was getting more and more dangerous, so they went down to the farm at Rudfjord, where the farmer gave them shelter in his barn and found them food and even civilian clothing. "He was a good man," says Reidar. "The Germans were up the mountain looking for us, but despite the widespread watch they were keeping he put us on a bus which took us three miles down the valley, and there we stayed for some time — still forty of us."

Now the MTBs were called in, and the pick-up was to be on 26th February. But Starheim couldn't face the prospect of returning with nothing accomplished, so it was decided they would blow up the titanium mine at Ana Sira before they embarked. They went down in small groups all carrying suitcases or bundles, dressed in civilian clothes, and holed up in the woods about twelve miles from the mine. But again things went wrong — the weather prevented the MTB pick-up as planned. (Otto Hoddevik recalls MTB 623 being ordered to go south to Flekkefjord to pick up some Commandos. All they knew was that a party of Commandos had been landed to capture a convoy, and things had gone wrong. As they approached land there was a thick fog, and they couldn't pinpoint their position. Dagfinn Ulriksen, who had previously been over as an agent, rowed ashore with the small boat to see where they were. He duly reported and then the fog cleared and they could all see for themselves — they were right underneath the German strong-point on the island of Eigerøy! The MTB pressed on farther south. Sverre Syversen was, as usual, one of the crew of 623, and he remembers it was a beautiful, quiet night, but there was so much ice that their wooden-hulled boat simply couldn't force its way into the shore at the rendezvous point. Says Otto, "We were supposed to meet destroyers in the morning, who would escort us over to Scapa Flow. I was standing on the open bridge when a strong red light suddenly shone in my eyes. It was a destroyer — I hadn't seen him come up. He ordered us to go to Scapa. We resisted the suggestion — after all we had nothing to go to Scapa for. He tried to insist, but we went back to Lerwick." This was probably the farthest south that any of the Lerwick flotilla operated.)

Now Starheim, probably with memories of the *Galtesund* strong in his mind, radioed London for permission to take over another of the coastal boats, the *Tromøsund,* and London agreed. It was decided half the party — twenty men — would be used for this mission. It went well to begin with. The party went unobtrusively down to the quay, boarded the vessel, took control of crew, civilian passengers and also the Germans on board, then proceeded past the German controls and out to sea. London was alerted and aircraft from Coastal Command were sent out. They were with the *Tromøsund* for some time, but ran out of fuel and had to return. Destroyers were sent out at dawn on 1st March, but by the time they reached her expected location the ship had been sunk by German aircraft. The German controlled papers in Norway made quiet a paen of triumph out of this episode. After all the Commando party had tied up large numbers of German troops for two months. Sadly Starheim went down with the ship. He had meant to come ashore once the ship had been taken and rejoin the second half of the party, but circumstances had forced him to stay with the ship.

The Germans apparently knew that not all the Commoandos had gone down with the ship, and their search continued, so that, as Reider says, "We were forced to retreat again to the mountains. We went to a hut where we intended staying for two days, and that night we heard someone whistling. We whistled back, but no one appeared. Next day we heard the Germans had been out on a night exercise. We had been exchanging whistles with the Germans! But somehow we had to try to get back to Britain, and we moved down to Flekkefjord again, in little groups of two or three. As we came into the town we met a troop of Germans marching towards us on the other side of the road. The Germans wolf-whistled at two girls walking on our side, and they turned away. We tried to approach them. They turned away from us as well. We probably looked a bit disreputable in our borrowed clothing, carrying paper bags. Had they but known our paper bags contained ·45 Colt revolvers and 200 marks of German money. We went right down, into the railway station, bought tickets for Moi and sat down at a little table in the waiting room. While we sat waiting for our train two German officers came in, looked hard at us, then went out again without saying anything and without making a move to search us. We boarded the train among the Norwegian civilians and the German troops, our hands never far from the pistols in our paper bags, and got off at Moi, where we met up with the rest of the party who had come by bus.'' Outside the station in Moi an old farmer with a horse and cart looked at them. "You could just as well have been carrying your rifles,'' he said. Clearly they weren't fooling him.

They moved from place to place, and one night, when travelling by taxi over a long bridge, they were stopped by some Germans on horseback. They sat in the taxi, gripping their pistols, hidden in their laps, and looking at the Germans' booted legs in the stirrups just outside the taxi's windows. As they waited on tenterhooks, ready for instant action, the Germans told the driver to dim his headlights, then rode off. Finally they managed to get in touch with a man in Egersund who had a boat. He agreed to take them over, and they went on board, where they lay all day at a quay while the boatowner tried to obtain the necessary papers to allow him to pass the harbour control points. Their party now numbered eighteen, the radio operator and another man staying behind.

"The owner and his two younger brothers came on board and we cast off. There were three German control points to negotiate, and on each occasion the German guards stood on the deck above our heads. Had we been discovered we would have put up a good fight, but we would never have got away. As we left the harbour a British plane came over and dropped bombs. When well out at sea we developed engine trouble in the form of a broken fuel pipe, and we drifted for two or three days. Finally we got going again, and steered west hoping to make Aberdeen. At long last we closed a shore and saw a big factory, but we had no idea where we were. We launched a small boat and two men rowed ashore, read the name of the factory, and came back to say it was in France. Actually it was Redcar, in Yorkshire, and a boat came out and took us to West Hartlepool. No wonder we had steered an erratic course. We all had pistols and we had piled them all together near the compass after we got away from the Norwegian coast. We were regarded with some suspicion in West Hartlepool and were kept under guard and interrogated frequently. But we kept repeating a London telephone number which we wanted to be contacted. After a while they phoned that number, and almost immediately whisky, money, etc., was forthcoming and next day we went back to our own camp."

Though Reidar doesn't say much about it, the men were in a poor condition when they got back to Britain. For three months they had been hunted men, living in a continual state of danger, underfed and frequently suffering from exposure and frostbite. Less fit men would never have withstood the ordeal, but there is little doubt that the intense training which they had been given before they set out was an important factor in their survival. But though their bodies quickly recovered there could have been few of them without mental scars. There were ten men from Ålesund in the party, and four of them still survive. Little has been written about this operation apart from what is contained in the Starheim story "Mannen som stjal Galtesund". The Linge story records that it was the hardest job in the Linge Company's history, but gives little detail. Reidar feels, possibly rightly, that it failed to get attention because it was a failure. Failure it may have been in that the objective was not attained. There was certainly no failure in the men's morale, courage, determination, endurance and will to survive. The two lads left behind in Norway were surprised by the Germans in August, 1943. Fred Aaros, the wireless operator, was captured, but cut his own throat on the way to the prison to make sure he gave nothing away. His friend shot his way out, and escaped by standing for some time under a waterfall. The doctor who drove ahead of the bus, leading the way up the valley, was arrested by the Germans in the spring of 1944 and shot. Happily Tom, Starheim's first wireless operator, survived and married Soffie, his messenger girl at the foot of the valley.

The *Galtesund* book provides the postscript to Starheim's story. His body had drifted ashore on a small island near Göteborg in April, 1943. There was no means of identification apart from a small carved wooden spoon in a pocket. The spoon was kept after he was buried. Starheim's friend came to hear about the spoon, and he identified it as one he had himself carved, which had been in the pocket of a jacket he had given Starheim just before he went on board the *Tromøsund*. In the autumn of 1945 the body of this remarkable young man was brought home to Farsund and buried in the presence of a huge crowd, many of them from Britain.

Reidar's war was far from over. He was now posted up to Shetland, and became one of the crew of Larsen's *Vigra,* on which he did thirty-nine trips. On a number of the trips the *Vigra* as Reidar recalls acted as a sort of rescue ship. She picked up the sixteen survivors and one dead man from the crew of a sunken U-boat and took them into Scapa Flow. (*Hans Bakkland also mentions this.*) Another rescue boat picked up the crew of the Catalina which had sunk the submarine, but which had itself been shot down. On another occasion they went into Haugesund to collect the crew of a Canadian plane which had been shot down and whose crew had been hiding in the mountains for two or three weeks. Reidar was on board when they went into Rimøy to fetch Joachim Rønneberg. Rimøy was a place they called at fairly frequently — they even had a reserve fuel dump there — and of course Sverre Roald was their contact man. "There were some nice girls there. They used to come on board with newspapers, milk and things like that."

He remembers one trip very clearly. They had landed some agents in a fjord fairly far north, and they had some reserve fuel with them which they put in the tanks. But almost immediately after setting out on the long trip back to Shetland they ran into severe head winds and heavy seas, which steadily got worse. They had their spare fuel at Rimøy, but decided to chance carrying on with what they had on board. The deteriorating weather used up the contents of the tanks at an alarming rate, and it came to the point when the engineer was shutting off the fuel supply when the *Vigra* was going down into the huge troughs of the waves, then switching on again to come up the other side. They finally made Baltasound with tanks all but dry, and had to have fuel sent up from Lerwick before they could complete their journey back to Scalloway. Only two little tatters remained of a brand-new Norwegian flag they had hoisted just before they left Scalloway — the wind had whipped away the rest.

Reidar has been in Norwegian Customs for thirty-five years. His memories of Scalloway are still vivid, and like all the rest he remembers Jack Moore best. But they had a lot of fun, with parties and invitations out to tea, and they made many good friends among the Scalloway people. The good memories, he says, far outweigh the bad. There are still four or five of the Linge boys surviving in Ålesund and another three or four in Vigra. They meet often in Ålesund's North Sea Club.

Another Commando who had perhaps an even closer associ- ation with Shetland was Ludvik Smaaskjaer, for he was fortunate enough to find a Shetland girl-friend whom he later married. Ludvik lived in Svolvaer in the Lofoten Islands, and like so many young Norwegians, he hated the Germans. He and his friends soon made up their minds that they would escape at the first opportunity, and the chance came perhaps sooner than they expected. When the first British raid on the Lofotens took place in April, 1941, 285 people left the islands on board the raiding ships and escaped to Britain. Ludvik, along with several of his young friends, was among them. Sadly his father was the victim of a new German law, which was that parents would be arrested and imprisoned as punishment for the escape of their sons. He was sent to one of the worst prison camps in Norway, where treatment of prisoners was vile and degrading. It was only when he became very ill and the Germans believed he was dying of TB that they released him. He had nothing, of course, when he came out of the camp, and the underground helped to get him back to the Lofotens, where he survived, a broken man, until 1961.

Ludvik, having landed in Aberdeen, was drafted into the Norwegian army, and in due course became a Commando in No. 5 Troop of the No. 10 Inter-Allied Commando. No. 5 was the Norwegian Troop, and the other troops in the Commando included two French, one Dutch, three Belgian, one Polish, one Jugo-Slav and one of mixed personnel. Ludvik was among the men posted to Baltasound in Shetland, and made several trips to the Norwegian coast with the MTBs, on one occasion being ashore for three days with some Linge boys. With the main body of the Norwegian Commandos he went south to complete intensive training in the period leading up to D-Day. In the final campaign it fell to No. 5 Troop to play a prominent role in the fighting in Walcheren in Holland, where the Germans had flooded the countryside. Here some of the toughest and dirtiest fighting of the war took place, with the Commandos living more or less continuously in water for three weeks. There is little doubt that some of them received health damage which would leave its mark for the rest of their lives, and Ludvik may well have been one of those.

Helen Gray was the girl he had fallen in love with up in Shetland, and she heard nothing from him for a long time after he went away. It was not until the fighting in Walcheren was over that she got a telegram saying he was coming on leave. At war's end he went back home on his own to begin with. For a time he was a guard at a German PoW camp outside Bodø, but now of course he had to decide what to do with his life. Like so many other young Norwegians he had left home before his education was complete, still only a boy. Now he was a man, with a wealth of wartime experience behind him, but really knowing nothing except army life. And that in a country which had been reduced to dire straits by the occupying enemy. He decided to try and make the army his career. So he went to school with the army's permission and on army sergeant's pay, that being the rank in which he had finished the war. He slogged away with his books, and in 1947 Helen went across to join him. Like nearly all the Shetland wartime brides of Norwegians she travelled by the only means available — a fishing boat. It belonged to Fosnavåg, and was crewed by a father and his two sons who were very good to her, landing her at Ålesund. From there she went down the coast to Bergen, where she joined the steamer for Svolvaer in the Lofotens. One of the sons on the Fosnavåg boat later married a Scottish girl, and in 1958 brought his family to live in Buckie, where Helen visited him in 1980.

Her story has so much in common with so many more of the girls who went across that it can serve as an example of what they had to face. Norway was in a bad way — life in fact was grim, because the Germans had picked it bare. There was a terrible shortage of housing. Rationing continued to be severe for years after the war, with meat almost unobtainable right on to 1950 and beyond. Any meat available was usually whale meat. The winter climate in most of the country was harsh, and the hours of darkness the farther north you went became oppressive. Economically the country was at rock-bottom, and industry had to be virtually rebuilt. In the far north the Germans' scorched earth policy had left a huge problem of reconstruction from south of Hammerfest and northwards. This was the country to which many starry-eyed young brides now made their way. There were a number from Shetland, but many more from Scotland and some from England. For many of them, knowing nothing but life in an urban British environment, the harsh reality of the immediate post-war Norway proved too much of a shock, and quite a number were soon on their way back home.

For Shetland girls the conditions perhaps didn't come as quite so much of a shock. Helen herself was a north-east of England girl who had readily adapted to Shetland life. Now she adapted equally readily to life in Norway. To begin with, and most importantly, she liked the country and she liked the people. She had survived the North Sea crossing by fishing-boat without complaint. Now she found that communications in Norway were also far from easy. Having gone down to Bergen from Ålesund, she boarded the *Kong Haakon* for the trip to Svolvaer in the Lofotens, which was to take four days and four nights. The ship was packed with passengers, and there wasn't a hope of a berth. But, she says, "There was music, laughter and happiness." Everyone knew that things were going to be bad for some time, but they were not complaining. Anything was better than life under the Germans. The greatest miss had clearly been free speech, never knowing when the person next to you might be an informer. Their newly-recovered freedom was something one felt could almost be touched.

Arrived in Svolvaer she felt immediately at home with her in-laws, who were extremely good to her. Life was hard, and, as in Shetland, geared to the fishing. Opposite the town was an island, and on the island a "gut-factory" — just like Lerwick and Bressay. There were few of the modern luxuries of life. For instance, to do your washing you first broke the ice with a hammer. She wondered for a time why people sometimes seemed to get up very early in the morning — she discovered it was in order to do their washing when the tide was out! Apart from the shortage of everything material, there was also a shortage of professional people. Svolvaer, a town the size of Lerwick, had only one doctor.

But they continued living in Svolvaer even after Ludvik was commissioned and had to work full-time in army HQ in Narvik. Finally they were allocated a house in Narvik, and the whole family moved there. In 1957 Ludvik spent a year as an instructor at the Military Academy in Oslo, one of the students at the time being Crown Prince Harald. Sadly he died at the early age of thirty-five, his death quite possibly accelerated by his harsh wartime experiences. It was an army house the family occupied, and Helen and her children had to vacate it. She took the only course she felt was open to her for the sake of her children — she came back to Shetland. Her Norwegian story has this tragic ending, but she has no bitter memories. She is still frequently in touch with Ludvik's family, and she still loves her adopted country. Even now she sometimes finds herself "thinking in Norwegian".

Chapter Twenty

Arbeit Macht Frei

As we have seen various groups, including judges, churchmen, trade unions and teachers, openly expressed early Norwegian resistance to the German occupation. But all the time underground activity was slowly building up, and by the spring of 1941 three quite strong groups organised on a military footing had come into being in Bergen and the adjacent islands. One group was led by Major Kjeld Bugge, another by Captain Mons Haukeland, and the third by Kristian Stein, a mail clerk. The Stein organisation became relatively big, at one time numbering, it is said, something like 2000 members. Svein Salhus was one of the Stein boys.

Svein was living in Bergen when the Germans came. He was twenty-six years old, and was working in an iron-smelting business, where he continued after Norway was occupied. But he hated the Germans, and by the summer of 1941 he was very much involved with the Stein organisation. Their large membership was recruited mainly in Bergen, and they undertook military training, much of it carried out in the very heart of Bergen under the noses of the Germans. They were armed, their weapons having come from stores hidden at the time of the capitulation, or from supplies brought over by the Shetland Bus boats. At that time a British invasion of Norway was still seen as a very real possibility, and their role would have been to act as guerilas behind the lines when the British landed. Even at that stage they had established regular contacts with London, and were kept informed of what was happening.

With such a big organisation it was not surprising that one or two members had been picked up by the Gestapo, fortunately without very much real information being divulged. Then, says Svein, an informer infiltrated the group in the autumn of 1941, and passed much vital information to the Germans. Svein doesn't name him, but he was a man very much in the Henry Rinnan mould, and his name was Marino Nilsson. His method of gaining entry was the same as that used by so many informers — he pretended to be sorely in need of help. He had come down to Bergen from Ålesund at the beginning of July, 1941, and had approached Kristian Stein pretending to be in dire straits and asking for help. Stein accepted him at face value, and from that moment on the organisation was in danger.

Nilsson obviously passed a large amount of information to the enemy, because when the Gestapo swooped in October they arrested 200 men, and Svein was one of them. They were taken first to the old prison in Bergen, which is no longer there, and then to Gestapo HQ where, needless to say, they underwent the Germans' own special brand of interrogation. Svein says he was lucky, as he escaped the worst of the torture, just being badly beaten up a number of times. It was those who were suspected of being the leaders who came in for the most brutal treatment, and it continued for two months. But that was far from enough to satisfy the Gestapo, and they were then taken to the prison camp at Ulven, south of Bergen, where they remained for a further six months' special treatment. (*Readers will recall Ulven as being the camp to which the crew of MTB 345 were later taken before being shot.*)

The next stage in the prisoners' sad story came in May, 1942, when they were loaded on the ship *Oldenborg* at Oslo, and taken to Kiel, where, for over a year, they suffered in Kiel's jail. The Germans were always very sensitive to the danger of secret agents or subversive movements in the lands they occupied, and the Stein organisation was regarded as extremely dangerous. As prisoners they were kept isolated and closely guarded. At long last, in autumn 1943, they were taken to Rendsburg to be "tried". Their "interrogation" had lasted nearly two years. The charge against them was "being sympathetic to, and aiding and abetting the enemy". They were charged and tried one at a time, the ones considered most dangerous being tried by a "People's Court". The "trials" lasted only a minute or two, and in each case the sentence was death. The remainder faced a lower court, but again each travesty of a trial lasted only a minute or so, and here the sentences were from three to eight years' hard labour in a "special" camp — and in wartime Germany a "special" camp meant something really brutal.

From Rendsburg their next destination — for those who hadn't been shot — was Sonnenberg in the heart of Germany, some way south-west of Leipzig. They came there in early winter, 1943, and were there into the spring and summer of 1944. The prison building was an old monastery with massively thick stone walls and it was desperately cold. The Norwegians were housed in the attic, and slept on the floor which had a thin covering of straw. Each man was allocated 40 cm — less than 16 inches — of sleeping space, and it is not hard to imagine how grossly overcrowded the floor was when men tried to sleep. They were clad only in thin, washed-out prison garb, and they were each issued with one threadbare blanket. Of course they suffered badly from the cold which they tried to alleviate by lying in groups of six with all six blankets spread over the group.

Reveillé was at 5.30 am, and they worked two twelve-hour shifts. The work was making boxes for engine parts, and also tins for holding ball-bearings. They were driven extremely hard at work, with a beating for the slightest relaxation. There was no break during the whole twelve-hour shift. They were very badly fed, with most of what they got being sauerkraut (pickled cabbage). There were no dishes or cutlery, and they tried to scrounge empty tins to eat from. Conditions were degradingly insanitary, but then degradation was part of the German treatment aimed at breaking a man's spirit. Svein says quietly, "On an average one man died on every shift." Gazing into the distance he adds dispassionately, "It wasn't living — it was living hell." The old monastery housed twelve hundred prisoners, with sixty-six Norwegians among them to begin with. There were French, Dutch and Belgians as well, but no Russians. The Norwegians, branded as saboteurs, were regarded as non-people — they had no rights as human beings. Svein remembers the Germans had planted turnips in the yard, and of course prisoners would manage to combine bending down to fasten a shoe string with purloining a turnip, and they were at the stage where a turnip was regarded as the greatest delicacy. The unfortunate individual caught trying to work this dodge was immediately the subject of a very severe beating.

As was fairly common in German labour camps of this type the Commandant was the worst German of them all. He was a Gestapo captain, and the mere sight of him brought terror. He was a real sadist, and when it was known that he was approaching the prisoners had various ways of passing code messages to tell the others to "Look out!" As sometimes happened there was one older guard who was more human than the others. He had been a petty officer in the German navy and had avoided nazi indoctrination. Clearly he secretly listened to the BBC, and he passed on to the prisoners snippets of news he had listened to. But the thorough Germans were aware that this kind of situation could develop, and guards were never allowed to remain on the same duty for very long. One day he was no longer there, and their last link with humanity disappeared. But they were to see him again.

Their monastery doesn't appear in the list of ultra-evil places like, for instance, Belsen or Auschwitz. And yet its whole philosophy was equally bad, its treatment of its inmates equally barbarous. Then, in October, 1944, they were on the move again. This time their destination was the infamous Sachsenhausen concentration camp. This move was probably the result of the Russian advance, and their likely approach to the vicinity of Sonnenberg, for the prisoners had been hearing the distant thunder of the guns in the east for some days. Their new billet was about sixty miles north-east of Berlin, and the prisoners began to put two and two together. Because they had heard the guns in the east, and because they had been moved away, maybe it was a sign that the war was coming to an end. For men who had been so long without hope it seemed incredible that there was perhaps still a chance. But first they had to survive Sachsenhausen — and if they managed that, would they be allowed to live if the Germans were finally defeated?

On arrival at the camp they were checked out, then had their hair closely shorn. As they queued for their so-called haircuts they saw the guard who had shown them kindness at the monastery. Now he was a concentration camp inmate, having his hair shorn just like them, so clearly he had paid a heavy price for allowing himself to show just a little humanity. Round the centre camp at Sachsenhausen were a number of smaller camps, so the whole thing was a vast complex housing anything up to 50,000 prisoners. They were not segregated by nationality, but were all mixed up together. Their barrack chief was a vicious sadist. He had been a German criminal prisoner, and he was a really bad man. The only way to escape suffering at his hands was to do something that would result in being sent to the punishment block. That was actually better than being at the mercy of this monster, and Svein in desperation applied to be transferred to the punishment block. Strangely enough, this request was granted.

For the first few weeks in the camp there was a sorting and classifying of the new arrivals before they were allocated to work parties, and during that time they marched eighteen miles a day within the camp precincts, going nowhere. They were still the lowest of the low — they didn't officially exist — they received no letters — they got no Red Cross parcels. However the upper categories of prisoners did receive the occasional Red Cross parcel even in Sachsenhausen, and when one of those prisoners died his

friends kept his parcel, and tried to smuggle bits and pieces from it
to the lowest category, but that always involved having to bribe the
barrack chief with a large share of the smuggled items. The sad fact
was that the only hope of a morsel extra lay in someone's death.

When the Germans made their massive sweep in 1941 and
arrested 200 men from the Stein organisation, they inevitably
included some individuals who were completely innocent. After
two years of interrogation and degradation, even the Germans
admitted that a few of them were innocent, and acquitted them at
the trial in Rendsburg. But that didn't mean they were set free.
They were kept in prison camps in Germany, where they languished
till the end of the war, most of them making their way home via
Switzerland in 1945. It was cynical treatment for men who had been
acquitted. All the rest of the Stein men, apart from those who had
been shot — and there seems to have been nearly twenty who
received the death sentence — ended up in Sachsenhausen. They
never rose above the lowest category, and the slightest infringement
meant instant transfer to the punishment block. It is a terrible
commentary on the barrack chief that Svein found life more
tolerable in the punishment block than at the mercy of this
sadistically evil man.

When their work class had been determined after the first few
weeks they were sent to the smaller camps for specific trades —
Svein's work was now iron-moulding. Reveillé was at 5 am, outside
for roll-call, back in for what passed as breakfast, at work by 6 am.
"Arbeit Macht Frei" said the great notice above the camp's main
gate, and they certainly got plenty of work, but not much freedom.
Here, as in the monastery, it was a twelve-hour shift. Svein was
making parts for machines, and he feels the parts they were making
were desperately needed by the Germans at this stage of the war
when time was beginning to run out for the master race. As a result
there was the tiniest relaxation in their treatment. The odd Red
Cross parcel was now allowed, but of course the Russians, who by
this time were their fellow prisoners, received nothing. They were
starving, so the Norwegians, now slightly better off, tried to share
with them. They had all been sentenced to specific periods of hard
labour, but if, by any chance, someone survived long enough to
complete his term, it made no difference — they were simply kept
on under the same conditions.

They never had their prison numbers tattooed on their wrists.
That seemed to be a measure reserved for the Jews, gipsies and
some political prisoners, but they were well aware that, bad as was
their treatment, the Jews and the gipsies were considered even

lower than them. No inmate of Sachsenhausen could be unaware of the gas chambers — as Svein quietly comments, "We could see the mass of bodies being produced."

He recalls ten British prisoners being brought into the camp. They were in uniform, but were being treated as saboteurs, and he was led to believe they were part of the Commando force which had been sent over in two gliders to attack the heavy water plant near Rjukan. As we know the gliders had crashed and the Germans had captured the survivors. There was a captain among them, and he was kept separate from his men. Svein says they were clearly recognisable as soldiers, because they were in full battle-dress. They were, of course, being treated as saboteurs under the same decree that led to the death of the crew of MTB 345, the men of the *Brattholm* and numerous others. One morning Svein and his friends sensed that something special was on the go. The Germans came to take the British prisoners away. They didn't get to know what actually happened to them. Did the Commandos try to overpower their guards, and were they shot in the process? Or were they simply shot? One of them had previously been taken to the camp hospital — did he share the fate of the others? (*See note at end of chapter.*)

At the end of March, 1945, the white Swedish Red Cross buses arrived at Sachsenhausen, and took them to another camp. Only Norwegians and Danes were allowed to go, but the Germans were clearly aware that the war was nearing its end. Perhaps they thought that this slight act of clemency might generate a little goodwill in the days that lay ahead. They were told that they were bing taken to Belsen. They were not to know that Belsen at that time was in a considerably worse state even than Sachsenhausen. But word came that there was an outbreak of typhoid at Belsen, and the Scandinavians were taken to another camp, whose name Svein has forgotten. Its condition was clearly very similar to what the British found when Belsen was liberated. There were many, many dead bodies still lying in their bunks, and these had to be disposed of before the newcomers could come in. The living had kept the dead as long as possible so that they could continue to draw their meagre ration allowance. From there Svein and his party were transferred to a slightly better camp, but, although strictly speaking they were now free, it was the end of May before they got back to Norway.

Svein recalls that, as far back as the prison camp at Ulven, he learned that to be a tailor provided perks. So he learned how to sew, and when they came to Kiel he gave tailoring as his trade. This resulted in him being given the job of examining the clothes handed in by prisoners, and sometimes he found a little money in them. That enabled him to buy trifles of food from the trusties, which made a considerable difference to the semi-starvation routine under which they existed. In Sachsenhausen tailoring no longer had any advantage, so he reverted to his real trade of iron machinist.

Svein underwent a long period of suffering and degradation such as no human being should be obliged to endure. No physical marks remain visible, though mental scars there must be. Clearly he doesn't enjoy talking about his experiences, but he responds to questions simply, briefly and without embellishment, and his story is one we must never forget. Maybe he can feel just a little fortunate in the fact that he managed to survive. Out of the 200 men arrested, at least ten were shot and fifty-one more died in German hands.

When the Stein organisation was blown and so many were arrested, many more of its members realised the extreme danger they were in, and there was a sudden and considerable demand for places on boats escaping to Shetland. In September, thirty-nine boats in all came over, in October seventeen and in November six. Not a few of them left from the Bergen — Stord — Bømlo areas, and a number of them carried people on the Gestapo wanted list. The saddest was the *Blia*. She left Bremnes on 11th November, 1941, with forty-two people on board. There was a number of the Stein people among them, including Billy Fortun, who had been one of its leading members. As we have already noted the *Blia* and everyone on board was lost, a victim of the excessively severe storm conditions prevailing at the time.

Another Norwegian who was in Sachsenhausen was Knut Henriksen, who now lives in Bergen. The Germans wanted to test some new boots, and what better way to do so than by having men wear them. So a large number of Sachsenhausen inmates were ordered to put them on, among them being Knut. Day after day they marched the specified thirty miles round the figure of eight track, on a starvation diet. Among Knut's fellow sufferers were Lieut Godwin and his six Commando colleagues. Knut thinks he marched for an unbroken period of 178 days, which would have represented a distance of 5340 miles. When they were able they tried to sing to keep up their faltering spirits, and he still remembers the words of one such song. Quite possibly it originated with the small British party, but its words run as follows:

There's a Land of Begin Again

There's a land of begin again,
On the other side of the hill,
Where we start to love and live again,
When the world is quiet and still.

There's a land of begin again,
There's not a cloud in the sky,
And we never have to leave again,
And we never say good-bye.

There ain't any soldiers to guide you,
You don't need permission to stay,
But I know there is something inside you,
Showing you the way.

There's a land of begin again,
On the other side of the hill,
Where we start to love and live again,
When the world is quiet and still.

Author's note. As far as I can ascertain there were only five survivors from the gliders which crashed on the way to attack the heavy water plant at Rjukan. They were taken to Stavanger for Gestapo interrogation, and it seems likely they were shot there. It is therefore possible that the Commandos Svein Salhus remembers being brought to Sachsenhausen were in fact Lieut Godwin's party. As we noted earlier one of them was in the camp hospital when the Germans came to take them away for execution.

Chapter Twenty-One

In the Air

Although Lerwegians were familiar with the wartime presence of the MTBs, and Scalloway people were well aware of the comings and goings of the Shetland Bus fishing boats and, later, the sub-chasers, little was known of the activities of Norwegian flying men in Shetland. This was largely because the flying-boats in which they operated were based at Sullom Voe, and the wartime Sullom Voe area was both remote and sparsely populated, so that aerial activities impinged very little on Shetland civilian life. And yet their contribution to the overall war effort was considerable.

As early as 24th February, 1941, 330 (Norwegian) Squadron was formed at Reykjavik in Iceland, equipped in its early days with Northrop float planes produced in America. In August, 1942, the Squadron was partially re-equipped with twin-engined Catalina flying-boats, but retained Iceland as its operational base, before moving to Oban at the beginning of 1943. There the Squadron was converted to Sunderlands, and moved to Sullom Voe where it remained until after the end of the war.

One man who was up in Iceland in the early days of 330 Squadron was Olaf Rye Sjursen. He had been living in Laksevåg (Bergen) when the planes came over on 9th April, 1940, and it was only when he and his wife saw the black crosses on the wings that they realised that they were German. After a few days he and a friend heard that the Norwegian armed forces in southern Norway were at Voss in some strength, and they set out on bicycles to join them. Approaching Voss they found fighting going on in one of the many tunnels on the railway line, but when they finally managed to make contact with the Norwegian forces they soon realised that things were pretty disorganised, and it was clear that resistance wouldn't last much longer. They made their way north, where they heard the fighting was going better, and remained with the forces at Andalsnes until they, too, capitulated. The boys escaped down the coast to Bergen, then heard that Narvik was still holding out, and set off north again, but in Ålesund found that the last boat for Narvik had left the night before. So it was back to Bergen once more. Olaf was twenty-four at the time.

The months slipped by until March, 1941. Olaf was in a cafe in Bergen when a friend came over and said, "You must come now. We're just leaving." "I had a friend with me," says Olaf. "I just said to him as I got up, 'Good wishes to all at home,' but he didn't understand what I meant." He went to a place called Lerøy where, with his friend Anders Merkesdal, they went aboard a boat called the *Blia*. The *Blia,* which we have previously encountered, belonged to Jan Lerøy & Co. of Sund, and the two Lerøy brothers, Arne and Ingvald, were among the twenty people on board. This was the *Blia's* first crossing, and they had fine weather all the way. Fourteen of the twenty passengers were in their early twenties, and the oldest man on board was thirty.

There was a hitch at the start. "We were all below when we heard the crackle of machine-gun fire. The boat stopped, and we heard footsteps and German voices on deck. We thought it was all up with us, but after a bit it went quiet. The Lerøy brothers had both remained on deck and the Germans had ordered them to stop, but they had replied that they had got to get around the headland before the fog got thicker — luckily the fog was closing down. The Germans were finally convinced, and they let the boys go without searching the boat. But it was a close shave."

When they arrived off Lerwick they tried to signal the shore, but got no response. They feared there might be mines, and for some reason the Lerøy boys decided to go south, finally coming to Fair Isle. They steamed around the island, then went into a narrow opening with high cliffs, and hoisted the Norwegian flag. "A man came down a steep path, and came off to us in a small boat. He had a rabbit he had killed with him, in case the people on the boat were starving, because he understood there wasn't much food in Norway under the Germans." The Lerøy brothers managed to get in touch with Lerwick, and the following day a trawler arrived and escorted them to the town. As usual, after a day or two it was down to Aberdeen for all of them, then to the Patriotic School in London. Their first posting was to the old ship *Lyra* belonging to the Bergen Line, and then they found themselves in Reykjavik in Iceland, at the so-called Norwegian Naval Air Base. But nothing so exciting as flying came their way. They remained earthbound, their job being to help in the construction of the air base.

For nearly two years they laboured at Keflavik, then they came down to Scotland, to either Oban or Dundee, but probably

Dundee, as Olaf says there were Sunderland flying-boats there. Their next stop was rather unexpectedly at Sullom Voe in Shetland. There they were ground crew for the Sunderland flying-boats of 330 (Norwegian) Squadron. They soon found that not a great deal happened at Sullom Voe apart from flying-boats going out and coming back. But Olaf met and made friends with a few Shetlanders, and in an interview he pays them a spontaneous tribute. "This I can tell — the people on that island (Shetland) were very kind. They were that the first week we came from Norway. There was no end to it. We were always welcome. I should have been across to visit them and to thank them — but so far there has never been a chance."

Olaf was far from satisfied with his role as ground crew, and he applied for a transfer. But nothing had happened by the time he was again posted down south. This time, after a somewhat stormy interview with his CO, he was told he was being sent to Shetland again to join the MTBs. He was delighted. "It could not have been better. It was like being in a family again." Like all MTB men he saw some exciting action, but probably the trip which gave him greatest satisfaction was when MTBs 715 and 719 (Olaf's boat) went over and lay in wait for a U-boat which intelligence had told them was going on her maiden voyage. She duly appeared with an escort, and 715 fired two torpedoes, one of which hit in front and one behind the conning tower. Smoke rose from the enemy and the submarine disappeared below the waves. No one on the MTBs had any doubts that a U-boat had been sunk, and the official report said, "After four operations without result in Hjeltefjorden, it is with satisfaction that we are able to report with almost certainty that a U-boat was sunk on the 5th operation." But no U-boat sunk on that day appears in the end-of-war list of sinkings. "Almost certainty" was not enough; it needed "utter certainty" before a boat would be credited with a sinking.

Young Norwegians were never wholly clear about what it was that actually drove them to sail dangerously west over sea to Shetland. Olaf had one thing in common with all the rest. "I could almost not suffer the sight of the Germans." As he says, that feeling became stronger and stronger. "Then people talk about something called patriotism — maybe there's something in that. For instance, in Iceland we had a tender which carried fuel to the flying-boats. It caught fire, but three of us volunteered to go aboard. There was an explosion, but we managed to put the fire out. If you ask me why we did it, I think it was simply because we realised that the planes wouldn't be able to fly without the fuel. In the explosion I received a severe blow on the head, and it has troubled me ever since, but not enough to be a real handicap. I don't like talking about it much." Only when pressed does Olaf add, "We got a medal for it. It's nice to look back to."

Olaf's Shetland memories are still strong and warm. "Yes, well, when we speak about the people there — well, where would we have been if Shetland hadn't been there? That's something that often comes to my mind, and God knows they were the finest people in the world. They received us with sympathy and with friendship, and they did everything they could to help. There were nights when they arranged entertainment for us — I can't remember it all now, but it was very fine. I would like to send a thank you message to them all. We thought it was an isle in the ocean — a small fishing community — but how wrong we were! I am forever grateful for the time we had there."

One young man who finished up flying for Norway was Karsten Danielsen, who, when the Germans arrived in 1940, was still at school, aged only fourteen. He was going to the Junior High School on the east side of the island of Askøy, just opposite the town of Bergen. He was in lodgings, staying with a family from whom he rented a room. Gunfire awakened him early on the morning of 9th April, and he dismissed it from his mind as being simply Norwegian naval vessels practising. But at 6 am he got up and looked out of the window and saw German planes overhead. A little later the radio carried the story of the German invasion. He left school and went home. The school closed for two or three weeks, then reopened, and Karsten went back and stayed until the spring of 1941. By that time he was nearly fifteen, and, having finished school, he got work in the office of a sardine factory near where he lived.

Soon Karsten and some of his friends started planning to get away. He was fifteen now, and felt much older. Says Karsten, "In Norway in those days young people wanted to be doing something, and there was little opportunity in Norway itself. We all knew that young people were getting away west over to Shetland, so why not us? We were itching to get the Germans out, we wanted to help, and the best way to do that was by becoming part of the Norwegian fighting forces. At that time I don't think any of us felt that the war would last more than perhaps another year. Our parents' feelings if we left didn't come into our consideration — at that age you don't think of things like that. And of course the spirit of adventure is something that's very important to young people." Karsten's comments on life under the Germans are clear and vivid, and emphasise how strongly anti-German feeling had grown. "They had taken away our radios, and that was a bad blow for which we really hated them. They had made travelling almost impossible. You had to have a pass to go from the island of Askøy to Bergen, and that's only a mile or two. If you wanted to go anywhere you had to put in application for a pass to allow you to travel. Even to buy a pair of shoes or a suit you had to fill in an application form, and even if you got the permit the suit or the shoes would probably not be available. If you said anything the Germans considered in any way out of place you were arrested. We felt that we were tied, unable to do anything freely, and as long as we were home and working we were working more for the Germans than for our own people. The Germans imposed rationing almost immediately, and then they started going around buying things, using money they had printed themselves, with nothing to back it, and cleaned out our shops. Of course there were shortages of everything, particularly food, and people tried to hoard little bits and pieces."

"Living in an occupied country must have been terrible, Karsten?"

"Oh, yes — I don't know what to compare it to — it was like having gangsters in your house ordering you around at the point of a gun. We had simply no say."

Karsten at fifteen was the youngest of his group of six young men. One was twenty-two, three were nineteen and one eighteen. They had their eyes on a boat which they intended to steal, but the owner was wary, and when they went to take it an engine part was missing. But they enlisted the help of a navigator from Askøy, and their next choice of boat was a 56-footer which had been used for fire-fighting, a good sturdy vessel called the *Gullborg,* which we have already encountered earlier in this book.

Karsten's departure from Norway had much in common with many of the other escapes. There were the last-minute details to be seen to. The evening before departure day he was at a dance with his best friend. "I asked him whether he would want to come with me to Shetland if we could get a boat, and his immediate reply was that he would come the moment we got a chance." He came. The only doctor on Askøy had been helping two British airmen who had baled out when their plane was shot down, and he had asked if they could come too. However he managed to get them away on another boat before the boys were ready. A fuel supply and food were procured, they put their small boat on the *Gullborg,* someone cut the mooring ropes, and they were off, calling at two more places to pick up passengers. Just before they left three youngsters rode up on pushbikes, and asked if they could come — two girls had told them a boat was leaving for Shetland. They left their bikes and came. By the time they finally set course it was midnight, and they had twenty-seven people on board. They came from various walks of life — fishermen, office workers, students, etc. A German plane passed overhead on the following day, but did not attack.

About midnight on 24th September they saw land, and in the morning went into what they discovered was Baltasound. Two "veteran" soldiers escorted them down to Lerwick, where they anchored in the north harbour until a Norwegian petty officer came out and came on board. "When we came ashore all the tins in our food store were punctured as a check for possible contraband of any kind. We arrived at a time when refugees were pouring in. That day there were 50 – 60, and the following day saw the arrival of a similar number, among the stream being many who were on the run from the Gestapo. We hadn't really had a bad trip over, but some of the passengers were very sick. I remember one coming rushing on deck, dashing into the wheelhouse, pulling the steam whistle lanyard, then disappearing below again, where he remained. One who was very seasick lay in oilskins, unmoving, as if dead, and remained like that for the entire trip."

He recalls the wrench when young men left their families. If young and single, you were leaving father, mother, sisters and brothers, and usually you left without saying a word — you daren't say anything. Karsten was the oldest in his family of five children, the others being mostly much younger. Milk had become very scarce, but they got a little from a neighbouring farm, and one of the children went daily with a little pail to fetch it. On the night they left Karsten took the pail and went outside, one of his sisters going with him. "I set down the pail at the door, and told her I would be back later. But I never returned to fetch the milk." One of the sad things about such departures was that parents seldom knew whether or not their sons had got safely across the North Sea. Much later Karsten came to New York, and got in touch with relatives he had there. An aunt sent a telegram to Norway, via the Red Cross, saying Karsten was there and safe. It took a couple of months for the telegram to reach his family, and when it arrived his father said, "Yes, OK, Karsten was all right two months ago. But we don't know what's happened since then." Worry about his missing son affected his father's health.

Karsten's area had more than its fair share of "bad" Norwegians, i.e informers. A friend of his with some others had planned a Shetland escape, but they were no sooner aboard their boat than they were taken by the Germans, and sent to concentration camps in Germany. That was the work of an informer who had wormed his way in as a fellow-escaper and knew their plans. Karsten was lucky — they had no serious problems until they were ashore in Lerwick, and after a couple of nights they were off on the *St Magnus,* where Karsten's strongest memory is of the food they were given — hard-tack biscuits. Few British soldiers were unfamiliar with hard-tack — they will sympathise with Karsten and his aching jaws.

Karsten, of course, was still only fifteen, and London was exciting. The Underground provided a great attraction for him and his friends and they would take a trip, get off at random, and see if they could find their way back to their billet in the blackout. They spoke virtually no English. London to them was vast, and it was all so new and overpowering. Then came the chance to go to Halifax with about 100 other Norwegians to join Norwegian merchant ships. His first trip across the Atlantic was in one of Salvesen's ex-whalers, and it took three weeks, with the ever-present and overpowering smell of her previous occupation. He was signed on as a crew member, and was paid on arrival, immediately buying a new suit for twenty-five dollars.

At this time he reached his sixteenth birthday, and his first official sea-going post was as mess steward on an old tanker lying at Sydney, Nova Scotia. She was in a poor state, and her galley had no running water. Washing-up was done in a bucket, an early misadventure occurring when he was dumping the bucket of dirty water over the side. He had overlooked the fact that the mess cutlery was still in the bucket, as well as some cups. For the remainder of the trip someone was always short of a knife or a fork or a cup, and Karsten was the recipient of some bloodthirsty comments. "I tried to make sure they all had fair turns at going without!" He was soon on the first convoy to Murmansk, still only sixteen years old. Eventually, though still too young, he was accepted by the Air Force. He spent two years in Canada, but, at the ripe old age of nineteen, he finished the war with the Air Force near Exeter, and spent VE Day in Barnstaple.

Their return to Norway was on Sunderlands from Calshot, landing at Stavanger. When Karsten came to go they had been in the air for an hour when an engine stopped. They returned to Southampton, but fog had closed in, so they had to turn and go on to Stavanger after all. From Stavanger he took the night boat up to Bergen, and, "As I sat on a bench, waiting, I saw my uncle coming along the quay. He had a young girl with him. She looked at me and said, 'Don't you know me?' She was my sister, and when I met the rest of my family I didn't recognise any of them to begin with. I myself was just about the same size as when I left home.'' The same size he may have been, but he was over four years older, and, at the age of nineteen, he already had a lifetime of experience behind him.

A man who knew Sullom Voe well was Knut Svendsen. In 1940 he was just about to join the Artillery to do his national service, his call-up date being 2nd May. He was to have served with the ack-ack, but the Germans forestalled him by arriving on 9th April. His home was in Bergen, where he lived with his parents, two brothers and three sisters, a brother being the oldest and Knut the second in age. He was twenty-one at the time. The Germans duly arrived and for most it was a complete surprise. But it shouldn't have been, opines Knut, if they had been watching events in the rest of Europe. Bergen, of course, was a prime German target, and they had it in their power in a matter of hours. And to begin with their presence wasn't too obtrusive. ''I continued to work in the early weeks as did everyone else. But the German grip was tightened more and more, and the gravity of the occupation began to be understood ever more clearly by the people of Norway. Life became very hard. We had no freedom any more. We couldn't say what we wanted, we couldn't read what we wanted, we could hardly even think what we wanted.'' (*As Knut spoke one's eyes couldn't help straying to a notice on the wall of the room in the veterans' club in Bergen. It was a German notice dated September, 1940. Even that early in the occupation the hours of curfew were laid down as from 8 pm to 5 am, and these hours were rigorously enforced.*) In August, 1940, two Bergen men were sentenced to death, and shot, and now the character of the occupation was clear for all to see. ''Now we could understand how true were the terrible stories we had heard about the Germans in the other occupied countries of Europe. But we had to go on. All radios were confiscated. We had to bring them in to various schools and halls and hand them over. But some people had two sets, and a good few of these were retained for illegal listening to the news from London. Of course, anyone caught listening faced the death penalty.''

Knut remembers the broadcasts from London beginning, and telling the people that the fight would go on. Illegal newsheets began to proliferate, and groups of young people got together to plot and to plan and to distribute newsheets. And now the exodus to Shetland from the west coast began to gather momentum. Knut and his friends reached the same decision as so many more did — they would go west over sea. ''We could do virtually nothing in Norway, but if we got away we could join the Norwegian forces, and clearly every man was needed in the fight against the Germans. We well knew that escaping meant running a terrible risk, but we were young. Anything was better than life under the Germans. But we needed a boat.''

The big day came. It was 21st September, 1941. They met at an appointed spot at 11 pm, in the darkness. They were all in a state of suppressed excitement, and then they heard the familiar "tonk-tonk-tonk", and the *Fernanda* loomed out of the darkness. "The skipper asked if we were ready, and suddenly people started appearing all around us, and we got on board. There were forty-eight of us altogether." (*This figure is Knut's recollection — Ragnar Ulstein's book quotes thirty-six.*)

Their party included six women and three children, and the voyage went reasonably smoothly. They made Lerwick as planned, were well received, kept there for two days, then sent on south with the *St Magnus*. After the usual procedures in London, Knut was sent to the Royal Norwegian Air Force HQ in Kensington, where he worked for a time as a clerk. But when volunteers for wireless operators and air gunners were called for, Knut was ready. He received his wireless training near South Queensferry, and his gunnery training at Morpeth. Then he was posted to 333 Squadron at Dundee, and that remained his base HQ for the remainder of the war. But it was not from Dundee but from Sullom Voe that the bulk of his flying took place. Here, too, 330 (Norwegian) Squadron was based, equipped with Sunderlands, the massive, four-engined, British built flying-boats carrying a crew of thirteen. Catalinas were twin-engined, American built seaplanes, with an endurance of twenty-six hours compared with the Sunderland's eighteen. Knut flew in Catalinas, detached from their Dundee HQ, and attached for a time to 190 Catalina Squadron, and later for a period to 210 Catalina Squadron. "My connection with Shetland wasn't finished. I had arrived there from Norway, and now I was back in the islands. We made many trips from Sullom Voe, and I went on a total of nearly a hundred operations.''

When the Catalinas were anchored at Sullom Voe they were always at risk during bad weather. Knut recalls that some sank at Invergordon when at anchor. On that occasion the wind lifted them and turned them over, and of course they went down. At Sullom on one occasion four of the Catalinas sank, but there the cause was either the heavy seas damaging the bows, or, more probably, the mooring rings on the fuselage tearing out, along with junks of the body skin, and so allowing the sea to waterlog and sink the boats. At Sullom it was the custom to have "gale crews" on board in very rough weather conditions, the crews usually consisting of a pilot, a wireless operator and a flight engineer. When the wind got really bad they would start one engine, and keep the propeller turning at 900 – 950 revolutions, just to hold the plane steady at its moorings. Sometimes there were up to twelve or fourteen seaplanes at anchor in Sullom Voe, and in severe gale conditions that made for a dicey situation. Once a "gale crew" was on board it was often very difficult to get them off again until weather conditions moderated, and a "gale crew" turn of duty frequently extended to ten or twelve hours, and conditions were both difficult and dangerous. There was in fact one occasion when a crew was on board for three days before they could be relieved. It was later accepted that the conditions were altogether too dangerous, and the practice of posting "gale crews" was discontinued.

Knut's last sortie of the war was on 7th May, 1945. They were ordered to fly down between Denmark and Sweden, and try to find a German E-boat which would contain a large number of German officers trying to escape from Oslo to Kiel. "We flew for twelve hours, searching and patrolling in that area, and were then ordered back to Sullom. We landed, to be told that the war was over. What a feeling!" The biggest contribution to the war effort by the Sullom Voe squadrons was their patrols in support of convoys, and their never-ceasing fight against submarines. They proved very effective in preventing U-boats from surfacing, and 210 Squadron was credited with sinking seven German submarines between 1942 and 1945.

The Norwegians at Sullom Voe lost one Catalina, and they also had a man killed during a night attack over the North Sea. That plane was so badly damaged in the attack that it was scrapped. Knut remembers the occasion when Flying-Officer Cruickshank of 210 Squadron won his VC at Sullom. He also remembers an episode which was to result in the award of a VC to a Canadian pilot from 162 Squadron based at that time, he believes, in the north of Scotland. (*413 was the Canadian squadron at Sullom.*) "In June, 1944, we were out on patrol when we spotted a U-boat on the surface, and went in to attack. As we dropped six depth charges we were met by heavy and unpleasantly accurate fire from the submarine, but the depth charges were also accurate, the U-boat sank, and we returned safely to Sullom Voe. Two days later we were again patrolling away to the north of Shetland, when the alarm sounded and we all went to action stations. The gunner was sure he had seen tracers coming up from the sea some distance away, and the pilot took us over the spot from which the gunner estimated they had been coming. Suddenly we saw a dinghy in the water with what appeared to be eight men in it, apparently the crew of a seaplane which had presumably been brought down by a submarine. We couldn't tell whether the submarine had been sunk or had dived. We reported to Group, who ordered us to stand by, so we commenced endlessly circling the dinghy. We would have liked to attempt to land to pick up the men, but Group refused permission. The weather, already poor, deteriorated much further, and the poor fellows in the dinghy were having a really miserable time. We had given Group an accurate fix, between Faroe and Shetland, but no craft appeared, and we continued to circle. After about ten hours came word that a rescue boat was on the way, and we continued to go round and round. After over thirteen hours above the dinghy we were dangerously low on fuel, and we finally had to break away and return to Sullom, though there was still no sign of the rescue boat. However, when we landed at base we heard that the men had been picked up, but, sadly, the Flight Lieutenant commanding had died before he could be brought back to Shetland.''

The dinghy over which Knut's Catalina maintained its seemingly endless vigil contained eight men, the crew of a Canso seaplane which had been shot down by a U-boat. The plane belonged to 162 Squadron, Royal Canadian Air Force, which was based at Iceland. Three of the Squadron aircraft had been detached to Wick, and this particular one was commanded by Flight Lieutenant David Ernest Hornell. On 24th June, 1944, he was piloting his plane on his 60th operation since 1941. It was 7 pm and they had been airborne since 9.30 am. They were some distance north of Shetland, and Hornell was just about to set course for a return to Wick, when a U-boat was spotted on the surface about five miles away. Hornell immediately turned and commenced the run-in for an attack, and almost immediately came under fire from the submarine. The slow-moving, twin-engined aircraft was repeatedly hit, the starboard engine being completely shattered, and soon a mass of flames. Hornell pressed on through a sheer curtain of flak, and at 50 feet released his depth charges, with devastating effect on the submarine.

But the plane was also mortally wounded, and came down in the sea, the starboard engine having fallen out on the way down. The two four-man dinghies were thrown overboard, but there was an almost immediate disaster as one of them blew up. That meant there were now eight men for one four-man dinghy, and to begin with they took shifts, with four men in the dinghy and the other four in the water up to their necks hanging on to the sides. As the wind and swell increased, all eight tried to squeeze into the frail craft which proved physically impossible, one man having to hang largely in the water. By this time Knut's Catalina was overhead, and had commenced its watchful circling.

Several times the dinghy capsized, and the men's condition progressively weakened. One man died. After nearly fourteen hours the Norwegian Catalina had to leave because of shortage of fuel, and, when they had been sixteen hours in the water, an air-sea rescue Warwick appeared overhead, but the lifeboat she dropped fell 500 yards away from the men in the dinghy. Another man died. Finally a Sunderland appeared, guiding an air-sea rescue launch to the scene. The six survivors were taken on board, having been 20½ hours in the water. While still in the dinghy Hornell had become blind, and extremely weak from exposure and cold, and he died very soon afrer being taken aboard the launch. Fourteen hours later the little ship reached Lerwick, with its complement of the living and the dead. Hornell's body still lies in Lerwick Cemetery. He was posthumously awarded the Victoria Cross for his part in this epic wartime saga.

What does Knut remember of Sullom Voe? "My memories? Wind, gales, sheep — but we were very, very happy there. It was a remote and lonely spot, but there were so many of us, and there always seemed to be something to do." (*At its peak Sullom probably had about 600 Norwegians and upwards of 1200 British on station.*) When it was all over he went back to a Norway which was in a very bad way. When his mother saw him, she fainted. "It was a great experience coming back. We came back like heroes, you know." Perhaps not all returning Norwegians received such a warm welcome. With a distant look in his eyes Knut's mind goes back, spanning the years. "I'll never forget — always when we were on patrol — and we had reached the point where once again we set course for Sullom — I'll never forget the feeling when we could see Ronas Hill and the other hills of Shetland appearing on the horizon, and then gradually loom up before us — oh, it was a marvellous feeling! The Shetland Islands were definitely a very, very good home for us Norwegians."

Chapter Twenty-two

Beneath the Waves

In the middle of the First World War, in 1917, Lerwick harbour was handling more shipping than any other port in the United Kingdom. While that peak was never quite reached in the Second War, the harbour nevertheless was again an extremely busy and important place, with the constant presence of a wide variety of craft. There were naval vessels and cargo ships, troopers and "North" boats, minesweepers and escort trawlers, fishing boats and refugee boats, motor torpedo boats and motor launches, and many, many more. Among them, in increasing numbers, was a variety of submarines. Perhaps it was because they came and went so quietly, more often than not in the hours of darkness, that they have received somewhat meagre attention from historians, and yet their contribution to the overall war effort was tremendous, and Lerwick's role in their achievements was considerable. From the beginning of 1942 until the end of the war well over one hundred different submarines used Lerwick harbour, some of them coming and going on many occasions.

For the first two years of the war there was little or no indication that Lerwick was to have any submarine connection at all. The arrival of the Dutch submarine *P14* in August, 1941, and the Free French *Minerve* coming in at the beginning of September, caused a flicker of interest, but these two, along with three British submarines, were all that had arrived by the end of 1941.

Hardly had 1942 started before the picture began to change. The *P27* arrived in January, to be followed in succeeding weeks by the *Trident, Sturgeon, Tuna, Sea Wolf, Tigris, Unbending, Salmon, Sea Lion* and *P49*. The Free French *Minerve* and *Junon* were among them, along with the Dutch *P14* and the Norwegian *Uredd*. At the end of March two large armoured yachts, about the size of the *Sunniva,* arrived, one, the *Conqueror,* to act as a submarine mother ship, the other, the *White Bear,* camouflaged white and blue, and armed with batteries of rocket guns. In all probability this sudden upsurge in submarine activity was not unconnected with the fact that the German battleship *Tirpitz* had come round into the North Sea from the Baltic in January, 1942.

The increasing submarine presence was not escaping the notice of harbour watchers, and one of them recalls that, by the summer of 1942, the place "was alive with submarines", with as many as eight or so frequently in port at one time. In July eleven called briefly for supplies, on passage south from a mission in far northern waters, and by the end of the year "flocks of submarines were coming and going", while in January, 1943, a submarine which turned out to be *U570,* a German captured by aircraft, tied up at Victoria pier. In April a very large submarine came in, "longer than the troopers", said one man. It was probably the *Thames,* a sister ship to the *Severn,* and reputed to be the biggest submarine in the world at that time.

In mid-June came reports of the *Truculent* having sunk a U-boat, and it was about now that the Norwegian *Ula* first appeared in Lerwick harbour. The *Uredd* had become well-known to local people, and she had given a good account of herself, with a number of sinkings to her credit. From her eighth mission, in February, 1943, she failed to return, and it was later established that she had struck a mine, was badly damaged, and sank. Her resting place in northern Norway, in Fugleøyfjorden, near Bodø, was confirmed in 1985, and at a memorial ceremony in 1986 it was officially designated a war grave.

Many of the under-sea boats coming into Lerwick harbour were known only by a number, e.g. *P45, P48, P51, P219, P247, P615, N63, N76, N95* and so on. But there were many whose names became familiar, such as *Unison, Viking, Unshaken, Tribune, Stubborn, Thresher, Truculent, Sea Nymph, Syrtis, Sceptre, Squid, Seascout, Turpin, Totem, Trusty, Taku, Truant,* and many more. Of particular interest was the fact that a number of submarines, from a variety of Allied countries, used the port. For instance, Dutch crews manned *Zeehond, Dolfyn, Zwaardvisch, Jan Gelder, P10, P14, N10,* and *N15.* The Free French had the *Minerve, Junon, Rubus, Morse* and *Curie,* while the Poles had the famous *Sokol,* as well as the *Dzik* and *P255.* The Norwegians had firstly *P41 Uredd,* then *P66 Ula,* with *P85 Utsira* coming on the scene late in 1944. The Russians were allocated four British submarines, the *Unbroken, Unison, Ursula* and *Sunfish,* and the Americans briefly had two submarines in the harbour.

All these foreign boats belonged to the 9th Submarine Flotilla, with its base in Dundee. This was an international flotilla, and at

one time it had boats flying the flags of six different nations —
British, Dutch, Polish, French, Norwegian and Russian. Hans
Ormestad, a member of the crew of the *Ula,* explains that Lerwick
was a secondary base for the international flotilla, and he recalls an
occasion when *Ula* was one of no less than sixteen submarines in
Lerwick at the same time. Probably the biggest concentration was
in 1944, when intelligence reports suggested that the *Tirpitz* was
about to try to make her way back to Germany for repairs to the
damage inflicted by the midget submarines. A Lerwick man
remembers an occasion when there were twenty submarines in
harbour.

Submarine voyages often tended to be quite lengthy, with the
result that their crews probably spent less time in port than, say, the
men of the MTBs or the Bus boats. And with Lerwick merely a
secondary base, the men of the Norwegian submarines had less
opportunity than most of the other Norwegians in Shetland to
make friends with the local people. But *Uredd* and *Ula* seemed to
use Lerwick fairly frequently, and a few of their men did establish
close relationships. One such was Reidar Pedersen, a member of
the crew of the *Ula,* who became a frequent visitor to the home of
Dr T. M. Y. Manson, whose family made the young man warmly
welcome whenever his submarine was in port. When the *Uredd* was
lost there was a considerable period when *Ula* was the only
Norwegian submarine operating.

Reidar Pedersen was one of seven young men, all belonging to
the area around Leirvik, in Stord, who arrived in Lerwick on 6th
January, 1942, having made their escape in a 40-ft boat called the
Eli. She was not the ideal craft for a mid-winter, North Sea
crossing, being what we would call a flitboat, usually carrying
limestone in her big, open hold. She was powered by a 20-hp
Lysekil engine which had been mended on many occasions with bits
and pieces from other old engines, and while that made her maybe
just adequate for work among the islands, she was hardly suitable
for the open North Sea.

The Stord/Bømlo area was the source of many daring and
dangerous escapes west over sea to Shetland, and we have already
met a number of the people from there in the earlier pages of this
book. While most of the escape attempts were successful, we
cannot forget that it was from here that the *Blia* went to her doom
with all forty-two on board. Of the seven young men in Reidar's
group, Leiv Vallestad was the oldest at twenty-five, Pedar Nonås
the youngest at seventeen. Pedar's father owned the *Eli.* The other
four boys were Aksel Eikeland, Gideon Laukhamar, Arvid Olsen

and Erik Hollekim. They had already made one abortive escape attempt in October, 1941. That was just after the Stein organisation had been sprung, and many of its members were fleeing the Gestapo. Over twenty of them joined the boys on the *Eli,* but the engine stopped almost as soon as they started, they couldn't get it going again, and the boat drifted ashore on an island. The Stein people disappeared quickly, but the boys rowed the *Eli* round to the slip without the Germans being any the wiser.

Reidar and Arvid had been employed at the pyrites mine whose destruction by the Shetland-based Commandos has already been described. Erik had been arrested by the Germans, but had escaped, though his friend, arrested with him, failed to get away and died in a German concentration camp. Olsen, involved in the same episode, pretended to be mentally handicapped, and was allowed to go. Aksel was in bad odour with the enemy — a German had asked him the way to the cafe, and Aksel had directed him to the prison! The need to get away was urgent.

Finally they were underway again, successfully outwitting a German check soon after they left. Almost as soon as they were outside the islands they ran into extremely heavy head seas and wind, and after some hours had to return to land. They lay in the lee of an island, and camouflaged the boat as best they could with fishing nets and other gear, covering the huge hold opening with a tarpaulin. Then they were off again, the weather only a very little improved. Twice the engine stopped, but each time they managed to get it going again. The fuel tank was small, and they had to keep refilling it, for which task they really needed a siphon because of the rough seas. They didn't have one, and Aksel substituted by lying down and sucking — the taste remained in his mouth for a very long time! After twenty-nine hours they saw land. It was Out Skerries.

Back in Norway the Germans learned of their departure, and called at some of their homes, but they had suspicions only, and the parents managed to tell stories sufficiently convincing to escape arrest. In Shetland the boys proceeded to London and were soon embarked on their various wartime careers against the enemy. Vallestad and Eikeland served in the Artillery, Nonås was with the Shetland Bus and the Merchant Navy, but sadly was drowned in Scalloway in April, 1943. Gideon was an engineer on merchant ships as was Hollekim. Olsen was in the famous 332 Squadron of the Air Force, and Reidar joined submarines. All returned safely to Norway at war's end except Pedar Nonås.

Hans Ormestad, another *Ula* crew member, still lives in

Dundee. His home was in Sognefjord, but when the Germans invaded he was in Las Palmas, aged eighteen. In October, 1940, he joined the British navy, and spent eighteen months in a British minesweeper, the *Gadfly*. He transferred to the Norwegian navy in March, 1942, where he volunteered for submarines. On 19th May, 1943, he was posted to the *Ula*. Life in a submarine would hold few attractions for most of us, even in peacetime, and in wartime it was so much worse. But the *Ula* was a submarine which saw plenty of action, and Hans was part of most of it. All the submarines flew "Jolly Rogers" on which were depicted their successes, white bars denoting merchant ships sunk, red bars for warships sent to the bottom, and daggers for "special" operations. A U denoted a U-boat attacked, while a U with a line across it was a U-boat sunk. At the end of operations *Ula* had twelve white bars, two red bars and two daggers. She had also sunk a U-boat, though Hans doesn't remember them putting the special sign for a U-boat on their "Jolly Roger". Of all the submarines in the international flotilla, the *Ula* was the top scorer, though the French *Rubus* also had an impressive total, albeit some of her successes were achieved with mines rather than torpedoes.

In the summer of 1944 the Dundee evening paper carried a headline which said, "Norwegian submarine gets more than 200 depth charges in 2½ hours." Hans was on board *Ula* at the time and can vouch for the accuracy of the story, and also for the truth of the report that the submarine's commander, Lieut Valvatne, deliberately made his escape by lying under a minefield, and then, having reloaded the torpedo tubes, returned to the attack. Inevitably the boat underwent a further heavy depth-charge assault, but once more escaped and returned to the safety of Lerwick harbour.

One of Hans' most vivid memories is of a cruise off the southern tip of Norway. The *Ula* was fitted with an early form of radar, and on the set they could see a plane cruising parallel to them at some distance. When it was just abeam it did a 90° turn, and came straight for them. Of course the alarm was immediately sounded, and the *Ula* dived. Naturally, efficiency in carrying out a crash dive was something which was frequently practised, because on its speedy execution could depend the lives of all on board. The fact that the *Ula* could reach 30 ft in 14 seconds meant that, for the three men in the conning tower, there was but the briefest time span in which to get back inside the submarine, and slam tight the hatch behind them. On this occasion the whole operation was perfectly carried out, but the aeroplane was quickly overhead, bathing the water in the brilliant glare of a searchlight mounted underneath the fuselage, and quickly dropping three depth charges on the spot where the submarine had disappeared. The depth charges exploded uncomfortably close, and the *Ula* had to return to Lerwick to have the torpedo tubes checked for damage. This particular depth charge attack was one of the most dangerous which the *Ula* endured, and she endured quite a few! The fact that it was a British Coastal Command plane which dropped the charges didn't make them any less dangerous!

The special operations represented by the two daggers on the "Jolly Roger" provided a complete contrast to normal underwater trips, for on one of them they went in to a small island in northern Norway and landed three agents, one of whom was a very young man making his first landing as a secret agent and naturally somewhat apprehensive. As well as the three men they also put ashore a ton of materials, using a little rubber boat and rubber rafts, along with a great deal of hard work, for a submarine was far from ideal as a makeshift freighter. Later they repeated the operation, this time without landing any agents. Hans retired at the age of sixty-four, having spent the previous eleven years on the pilot cutter belonging to Dundee Harbour Trust.

Another member of the *Ula's* crew for a short time was Anders Petterøe. Very fortuitously he has recorded on paper much of what life was like on both the *Ula* and later the *Utsira,* and has given permission for the writer to draw on his material for this book. Anders had become interested in the submarine service soon after the occupation, when his ship was lying in Torshavn, and the *B1,* Norway's only submarine to escape the Germans, came into harbour. Somewhat enviously he watched the cook from his own ship make his way down the gangplank to join the submarine. The idea remained in his mind, and when he came down to Scotland he applied for a transfer to the submarine service. Three and a half years later, on 8th January, 1944, he was on his way by train to report to the submarine base, "HMS Ambrose", at Dundee. His posting had at last come through. But now people were beginning to feel that the war was starting to go better for the Allies, and by the time he was trained for submarines it might all be over. On arrival in Dundee he recognised some of the men as former shipmates, and there were also men who had served on the *Uredd* and the *Ula.* Experienced and inexperienced, they were to make up the crew of a new submarine which was just being built. First they had to be trained as submariners, and for that they went for a very intensive three weeks' course at Blyth.

Having absorbed everything they could learn at Blyth, they went to Gosport, where there was thorough training in how to escape from a sunken submarine. Anders gives a detailed description of the "Davis-lung", and the means for getting out via the escape hatch. He concludes wryly that, while crews might well be able to get out of the submarine and to the surface, survival in the ice-cold water of northerly winter seas was likely at best to be brief. Lieut Sars was *Ula's* commander, and he suddenly fell ill and was unfit for duty. Lieut Valvatne, who was to take over the new submarine, was posted temporarily to the *Ula*. She was to sail on the following day, and Valvatne speedily seized the opportunity to take a number of newly trained submarine men with him. The result was a welcome spell of leave for many of *Ula's* regulars, and a sudden opportunity for the new men to put into practice all that they had been learning.

Ula put to sea, and called first at Lerwick, where it was the custom to take on supplies, and to put ashore items not required when on duty patrol such as gangway, mooring ropes, etc., which could be a nuisance when the ship was in action. Anders had his duties allocated — look-out in the conning tower when on the surface, steering side rudder when submerged. The call at Lerwick was brief, then they were on their way to the Norwegian coast, carrying out parctice dives on the way. Suddenly Lieut Valvatne's voice boomed on the loudspeakers, and what he had to say was exciting news. "Agents in Norway," he said, "have reported that the *Tirpitz* has left Altafjorden, presumably in an attempt to get home to Germany to have repairs carried out to the damage inflicted by the midget submarines. All available submarines are on their way across the North Sea, and will patrol in her likely path. Our area is near Ålesund. At all costs *Tirpitz* must not be allowed to get back to Germany." For men on their first trip on a submarine this was indeed momentous news.

They did most of the journey to the Norwegian coast on the surface, and Anders found his two-hour tours of duty quite long enough, for besides having to be constantly on the alert with binoculars at his eyes, he was almost immediately saturated with sea water. However the watch was two hours on and four off, so he managed to get dried out in the four hours between watches. Having reached the patrol area the *Ula* dived and remained submerged. The only clue to what was happening on the surface would come via the asdic operator, but he was hearing nothing. After two days of fruitless patrol, word came that the *Tirpitz* had gone back into Altafjorden. There was a sudden release of tension, but while many of the submarines returned to base, *Ula* was ordered to continue on patrol. in more or less the same area, and look for suitable targets.

After some time Valvatne spotted a small convoy of two cargo ships escorted by three armed trawlers. *Ula* was positioned for an attack, but the first torpedo refused to leave the tube. Two, three and four all signalled their deadly departure by the characteristic tug felt in a submarine each time compressed air drives one out. The interval after firing torpedoes is always a tense period, with everyone waiting for the sound of the explosions as the torpedoes hit their target. This time they waited in vain, until far in the distance they heard two soft explosions as two of the torpedoes hit the land. The third had obviously sunk. The attack had been a complete failure.

Steering away from the area work immediately commenced on reloading the tubes with the spare torpedoes, but suddenly the Germans came to life, with an aircraft searching overhead, and the escort vessels also beginning to hunt. It had dawned on the Germans that there was a submarine in the area. For two hours *Ula* stayed at 80 ft, then came up for Valvatne to have a peep through the periscope, but there was nothing to be seen and reloading the torpedo tubes recommenced. With darkness they surfaced to charge their batteries. And now came the order to return to Lerwick. They had achieved precisely nothing.

In Lerwick they had much-needed baths, cleaned out the submarine, loaded a great deal of equipment and supplies for agents who had been landed in Norway, and took on replacement torpedoes, though the *Ula* was now so crowded that they had to sail with one torpedo short of full complement. Landing the supplies would need to be carried out quickly and efficiently, and they took *Ula* up to Lunna to practise the exercise. On the way out they fired a few practice rounds at a white mark on a steep cliff, but had to stop as the top of the cliff was suddenly covered by a large flock of inquisitive Shetland sheep!

Arrived on the north Norwegian coast they made their way submerged into a narrow fjord, then surfaced and went in till the submarine gently grounded. The gun on deck was manned, and all precautions taken before they began unloading their cargo. They had been submerged for twenty hours, and it was like heaven for the men to have the chance to breathe fresh air again. While the unloading went on, the captain and four men maintained a constant watch through binoculars. The supplies were ferried ashore on rubber rafts, four men having gone ahead in the little rubber dinghy to pull the rafts to the shore. Only one house could be seen, and the gun was kept trained on the house, for no one could tell what danger might lurk there. A woman suddenly appeared, carrying a lantern. The gun tracked her every movement. She went innocently to the cowshed, oblivious of what lay down at the shore.

It was a beautiful, moonlit night, with a few degrees of frost, the fjord surface like a mirror, and the "roaring" Northern Lights illuminating the sky above with every colour in the spectrum. Though they got on with their work they were clearly powerfully affected by the beauty which surrounded them. Everything was so still and quiet. "We don't speak out loud. We speak very little, but when we do it's in a whisper. In a way we feel that the scene around us is so beautifully fragile that it could burst into fragments if we spoke aloud." The rafts were pulled backwards and forwards, and when the job was completed Valvatne himself went ashore. When he returned he was carrying a small stone with him — a stone from the ground of his native Norway — which he intended to mount and use as a paperweight. Even for this hardy Norwegian naval warrior it was something special to be able to step once again on to Norwegian soil. Who could tell — maybe it would be the last chance he would have. Their job completed — it would warrant a dagger on their "Jolly Roger" — they got orders to resume patrol in the vicinity of Stadlandet. They proceeded on the surface and Anders, at his usual post in the conning-tower, enjoyed the chance to continue breathing the clean sea air.

In due course, in the early hours of a morning, with daylight coming early because it was now April, they moved in past a German fortified post on the one side and a mine field on the other, and as they lay in wait they spotted two cargo boats with two escorts. As they watched a light began to flash a challenge from the shore. They had been spotted, and immediately dived. A major handicap this morning was that the hydrophone was not working. A quick look through the periscope showed that a guard boat was almost on top of them. Down again, and the hours passed slowly and quietly, until suddenly the "Action stations" alarm went. Valvatne had spotted a convoy through the periscope, and had already selected a 9000-tonner in the middle of the convoy as the best target. The fact that there were numerous escort ships was ignored.

Anders explains in detail each man's duties when an attack is being prepared, and also notes just how little is known by the men below the waves of what is happening on top. On this occasion there came the sudden report that the hydrophone was working, and immediately up-to-date information started flowing from the instrument. "Fire one, fire two, fire three, fire four." "All tropedoes away," came the report, and this time none refused to leave its tube. Now came the period of waiting, with the tension rapidly mounting. Two and a half minutes was the expected time of the torpedoes to their target. One minute passed. Two. Two and a half. "I feel my stomach muscles tie up in a hard lump, and I realise my teeth are tightly clenched. My throat is dry." Then the crash of an exploding torpedo was heard.

Immediately they dived to 150 feet, and prepared for what they knew would inevitably follow — depth charges. Now they depended entirely on the silent electric motors. Silence was all-important at such times. No one moved around — talking was kept to a minimum and mostly in whispers. From the distance came the sound of the ore cargo in the torpedoed ship sliding around as she went down stern first. Then came the sound of steel plates tearing apart, just as one tears a sheet of paper. "No one speaks. We don't look at each other. We just wait for what is going to happen. Then we hear "ping-ping-ping". Two vessels are coming quickly nearer. Then the pings stop, and something like a fast train passes above us. Instinctively we crouch down. We don't have to wait long. Seven powerful explosions boom through the water from somewhere astern. The whole submarine is jolted upwards in the water, then everything goes quiet. I am frightened — I am not afraid to admit it. My first thought when the depth charges started exploding was: So this is what it feels like to be killed on board a submarine!"

Soon a second attack came in, this time with six depth charges, and a lot closer. *Ula* was sent flying, the instruments behaving in a totally mad fashion. The attacks kept coming — the number of depth charges reached thirty, then forty, but after they reached sixty-five there was a break, and finally it seemed the Germans had given up. Valvatne watched the position being plotted on the chart table, and suddenly gave the order to dive to 200 feet. Nobody could understand what was wrong. It was only when they were level and again under control that Valvatne said, almost to himself, "We are in the middle of the minefield." Slowly it dawned on the crew that they had been at periscope depth in the midst of mines, and the scraping noises they had heard earlier had been mine cables rubbing against the submarine's hull. When he was reasonably sure that they were on the inside of the minefield, Valvatne again took *Ula* to periscope depth. A searching aircraft had appeared overhead, and the guard-ships were still hunting not very far away. Their asdic was still in operaton, and its beam was still locating the submarine, sounding to those inside the ship like someone knocking on the hull with a small hammer.

It was far from healthy on the surface, and they dived again. Suddenly the enemy was once more overhead, and the depth charging began all over again, the explosions coming so close together that it was difficult to keep count. "They are above us and below us, and on both sides, simultaneously. We can hear the water gushing around us, and the *Ula* is tossed about more than in the worst hurricane. Nearly all the light bulbs blow, and we are left with only the glim of the emergency lighting. The electrician replaces the bulbs during a lull, but then it starts up again, and the explosions are virtually non-stop for nearly two hours." Then another attacker approached. This one was the loudest yet, and the crew visibly shrank within themselves as the roar passed overhead. The racket from the propellers was deafening, and the men felt as if it was penetrating the hull. Then the depth charges exploded, ten of them this time, and on all sides. This was certainly the worst attack so far. But it was to prove the last one, though for a time the crew could hardly believe it. It was some time before anyone spoke. Sheer exhaustion was on every face. They had undergone the longest and most concentrated underwater attack ever mounted on one submarine, and they were utterly drained. With darkness they surfaced, the conning-tower was opened, and they enjoyed once again the most precious thing in a submariner's life — fresh air.

But their cruise hadn't finished. The torpedo tubes had been reloaded, and they were once again ready for action. A day and a half of blessed calm followed, and then a target was sighted. The attack went in successfully, and a ship was sent to the bottom. The *Ula* made off at full speed. Soon two hunters started closing in, their asdic guiding them. Once more the depth charges started coming down, five in the first salvo. The next attack had ten, and *Ula* was being tossed around like a cork. "It is unbelievable how much hammering this kind of submarine can stand up to — but there must be a limit somewhere." Still the charges rained down, on and off all day, until the total this time had reached sixty-eight. But they survived, and at night they surfaced and headed for Lerwick. On this one trip the *Ula's* tough hull had stood up to the explosive force of over two hundred depth charges, and, like their ship, the men's nerve had proved equal to the ordeal.

"In Lerwick we knew of an old man who was in charge of a bathroom, with about ten baths and showers, and plenty of lovely hot water. No matter what time of day we called on him he had always the same pleasant greeting. This time he wished us welcome home again, and unlocked the door for us.'' Next in importance in a submarine man's life, after fresh air, came the opportunity to be clean again.

They stayed in Lerwick for about a week, and had a good rest and a good time. The 9th Submarine Flotilla had a camp up on the hillside (*Annsbrae Caravan Site*), but it provided little comfort, and as soon as the submarine had been thoroughly cleaned and tidied up again, they moved back on board. They were always welcome in the MTB canteen, but Anders knew none of the men, so he usually ended up in a Lerwick bar. ''The Shetland people are more free than what we Norwegians are, so it is easier to get in conversation with them. One of the asdic operators, William Adie, has his home on the outskirts of Lerwick. His mother is a Norwegian, and when we stay in port for a few days she comes on board to see us, and she has one of her home-baked cakes with her. Linge Kompani men were also based in Shetland, and we often had visits from them. One was a baker, and he usually had cakes with him when he came on board. Another was a priest (minister). After the war he was a seamen's minister for many years. So far as I know he was the only minister ordained in the Norwegian Church who trained as a parachutist.''

On 16th April *Ula* once more nosed out of Lerwick harbour. There was no action during their first day on the Norwegian coast, but next day a target presented itself. They could see a minesweeper and two other vessels escorting a U-boat, which was setting out for an Atlantic mission. The attack was successfully carried out, and the U-boat, U974, went down. The typical sounds of a vessel breaking up came through the water to the men in the *Ula*. Soon salvos of depth charges were coming down, and in an hour they had had eighteen. Surprisingly the Germans then broke off.

Ula moved farther south. Intelligence sent word that a convoy was expected to leave Stavanger, and Valvatne positioned the submarine in readiness. But the first to appear was a convoy heading north. Valvatne steered the *Ula* parallel to the convoy, on the surface. He picked his target, and altered course straight towards the convoy. Suddenly the ships of the expected Stavanger convoy appeared on the scene, heading south. ''There are ships everywhere. Cargo ships with lighted lanterns on their way north. Cargo ships, blacked out, on their way south. In the middle of the whole lot, the *Ula*.'' A target was selected, the torpedoes were fired, the German ship sank and *Ula* dived. Strangely the German escort ships did not hunt the submarine this time, and the *Ula* returned to Lerwick without further incident. On her return to Dundee news of her exploits had preceded her, and a huge crowd waited to give her a great welcome. The Flag Officer (Submarines) in a report to naval HQ commented, "It is with the greatest pleasure that I draw your attention to the particularly distinguished and successful part the Royal Norwegian submarine *Ula* has played." This was the end of Anders' brief but eventful service on the *Ula*. Now the new submarine for which they were to be the crew was nearing completion in Barrow.

"We stayed three months in Barrow. It was a lovely time. The town's whole population accepted us, and couldn't do enough for us. Even the weather couldn't have been better." While in Barrow, D-Day came and went, but submarines were not used in the great adventure. On 18th August Job J3201 became H.(Nor.)M. submarine *Utsira*. Prince Olav came from London to perform the naming ceremony. Almost immediately *Utsira* went to sea for training exercises, most of which were carried out at Larne and Scapa Flow. Then came the first official mission — anti-submarine patrol in the middle of the North Sea, on the look-out for U-boats going on or returning from missions. This first trip passed without incident, and then it was the real thing. Up to Lerwick first, then off to the Norwegian coast, where memories of their experiences in the *Ula* came surging back. Valvatne was with them again as commander. First contact was an armed trawler, which was not considered worth a torpedo. But then Anders on look-out thought there was something behind the trawler. With difficulty they established that it was a U-boat, on her way with an escort to the Atlantic. The attack was mounted, the torpedoes were fired. All missed the target and exploded when they hit the shore. *Utsira's* first attempt had ended in inglorious failure.

Utsira broke away, the torpedo tubes were laboriously reloaded, then the patrol continued. Again a target appeared — a U-boat. The two submarines came so close together that Anders could clearly see the men in the U-boat's conning-tower — two officers and two ratings. An attack was mounted, the four torpedoes were fired, and two of them homed in on the U-boat and exploded, sinking her instantly. *Utsira* immediately dived and closed off for the expected depth charge attack. Surprisingly none came, and the new submarine had carried out her first successful and profitable mission without mishap. On 21st December they were back in Dundee, where they celebrated Christmas, the last Christmas of the war. Their "Jolly Roger" already had a U with a line across it to signify a U-boat sunk.

Anders tells vividly of these submarine actions, but he also talks realistically of life on board a submarine during the last war. The *Uredd, Ula* and *Utsira* were all similar in size, about 200 feet in length. *Ula* and *Uredd* could stand a dive to 200 feet, *Utsira* to 300. They all had four torpedo tubes, and these were all loaded when they went on a mission, with a further four spare torpedoes carried on the fo'c'sle, two on each side. Each torpedo was nearly eighteen feet in length. All three ships had a complement of five officers, ten petty officers and thirty ratings. These ratings lived in the fo'c'sle along with the four torpedoes. There was far too little room for thirty hammocks, so some men had to sleep on the floor. But the floor was always wet with condensation, and wooden grids were laid down, with rubber matting on top, to form beds. Above them were two tiers of hammocks, and the result was that the men on the floor couldn't sit upright, even when eating — there was only one space for both eating and sleeping. Of course, when the first four torpedoes had been fired and the tubes reloaded with the second four, then there was a great deal more space.

It was invariably the practice to surface during the hours of darkness, primarily to charge the batteries, but almost equally importantly to allow fresh air into the submarine. It frequently happened that the submarine might be submerged for up to twenty hours or more, and the air inside the hull became completely fetid. Anders was one of the conning-tower lookouts when on the surface, and he says, "It is wonderful to come up in the conning-tower, and to fill my lungs with lovely, fresh, sea air. No one who has not experienced this — getting out of a small, stuffy submarine, and into wonderful fresh air — can have any understanding of how marvellous it is to be able to breathe properly again."

But running on the surface could be extremely unpleasant at times in rough seas. If the sea was on the beam the ship would roll terribly, the water in the ballast tanks causing a sort of double roll. If it was a stern sea, the waves tended to wash over the conning tower, and the men in the tower had to be tied down to prevent them being washed overboard. Then the hatch-cover could not be left open, or the control room would fill with water. But it couldn't be completely closed either, because the diesels were running and needed air. So a wedge was usually inserted to keep open a little space between hatch cover and frame. But the submarine was ideal when driving into a head sea.

Breakfast was served whenever the submarine surfaced. In winter this might be some hours before midnight, then dinner came about midnight and supper shortly before the submarine

57. The submarine men's camp in the golf course, Lerwick.

58. A submarine lies at the Fish Market.

59. Three submariners at a recent veterans' reunion in Horten. Left to right, John Einar Johansen, wireless operator, *Ulsira*, Anders Petterøe, *Ula* and *Utsira* and Hans Ormestad, *Ula*.

60. The war memorial in the churchyard on little Vigra, a massive boulder brought from the shore by manpower only.

61. Three MTB veterans, Sverre Syversen, Asbjørn Lie and Albert Eilertsen, with Leif Larsen and a model of the *Arthur,* Lerwick, 1985.

62. A German Junkers 52 in BEA service at Sumburgh, 1946.

63. David Howarth's yard in Scalloway builds the *Enterprise* shortly after the war.

submerged. As the shorter nights came round submarines found
that the time between meals got steadily less, as time on the surface
during the hours of darkness was steadily curtailed. The
atmosphere in the submarine was not conducive to keeping rations
in a good condition, bread, for instance, soon becoming green and
"woolly."

The toilets on a submarine were unique. They were flushed
down into a tank, which, because of the pressure of water outside
the hull, had to be emptied by using compressed air. But that would
be an immediate giveaway if an enemy craft were in the vicinity, so,
in such circumstances, when the tank was full, buckets were
brought into use. When undergoing the kind of depth charge
attacks which *Ula* suffered, when she was being tossed around like
a cork, one can imagine what happened to the buckets. So it is not
hard to understand why submarine men valued very highly both
personal cleanliness and the cleanliness of their vessel.

We have looked with admiration at the daring, courageous
exploits of the Bus men, the MTB men, the airmen, the
Commandos, the agents, the export groups — and many more. But
surely the submarine men deserve a special word. Living most of
the time beneath the waves, feeling the air they breathed hourly
becoming more difficult to take into their lungs, they enjoyed a
brief flash of excitement while the torpedoes ran towards their
target, then, perhaps for hours, waited for their last moment to
come as powerful explosions strained their eardrums, and tossed
their undersea home hither and thither at will. These prolonged
depth-charge attacks must have tested these men's nerve and
endurance to the limit, and there must have been many occasions
when they felt that their submarine would surely be their coffin.
Just how vulnerable they were was clearly shown when the *Uredd*
went down. With her went a third of Norway's submarine
personnel.

Chapter Twenty-Three

End Piece

As 1944 drew to a close it was clear to everyone that the war in Europe was approaching a climax. For the Norwegians any hope of an Allied invasion of their country had gone. Now the whole effort, both from east and west, was devoted to striking into the very heart of Germany, and exterminating the canker of Nazism at its core. But the German presence in Norway had never been greater. With the retreating German army in the far north now added to the occupation troops, the total number of German fighting men in the country amounted to approximately 450,000, and the Todt Organisation work-force accounted for 75,000 on top of that. Then there were 70,000 prisoners and slave workers, and the overall picture showed well over half-a-million incomers — or an increase of 20% in Norway's normal population. With the situation in Germany getting more difficult every day, the unwelcome visitors had little option, even if they had wished, but to live off Norwegian resources, and food, which was already in extremely short supply, became rapidly scarcer for the Norwegian people.

In the summer of 1944 Crown Prince Olav assumed command of all Norwegian armed forces, including those of the military resistance. A very full liaison was established between the Resistance forces and London, and Jens Christian Hauge became the Home Forces' leader. During the latter half of 1944 scores of instructors were sent in by both air and sea, and Home Force military bases were established in the mountains, where intensive training was carried out. The role of the Home Forces was, broadly speaking, five-fold. Firstly, to collect information of military value and transmit it to London; secondly, to organise military and industrial sabotage; thirdly, to equip, train and hold ready for action the Home Forces which were eventually to co-operate with liberating forces arriving from outside Norway; fourthly, to liquidate dangerous people; and, fifthly, to pin down the German troops in Norway, by making movement as difficult as possible.

As we saw in an earlier chapter the various sabotage operations undertaken by the Home Forces, particularly the disruption of the railway system, and the interference with port facilities, effectively prevented German troop movements on a scale which might have been of any real help to the main German defence lines in Europe. While this was of considerable help to the overall war effort, it meant an ever decreasing food supply for the Norwegian people. Though the Resistance never carried out many executions, there were one or two notable examples. The use of the parcel bomb as a reprisal against the Majavatn traitor has already been noted. But before that Lindvig, Chief of the Quisling Security Police, had been given the task of breaking up the campaign against labour mobilisation by hunting down and executing suspected ringleaders. He duly executed one suspect, but he, too, was quickly eliminated by means of another parcel bomb. Then in February, 1945, Marthisen, Chief of State Police, who was responsible along with the Quisling "Minister of Police", Jonas Lie, for organising the "Special Courts" which had sentenced fifty Norwegian patriots to death, was warned by the Resistance that he would be killed. The Gestapo took the threat very seriously, and they provided him with a continuous heavy guard. However, an attack was duly mounted, and the Chief's car had to stop when a hail of bullets punctured his tyres. As the guard faced towards the side from which the bullets had come, a man ran up to the other side and fired a number of rounds from his Sten into Marthisen, killing him instantly. As a reprisal, the Germans executed thirty-eight innocent Norwegians, who had no connection with the killing. But it was some months before a man could be found brave enough to take on Marthisen's job. These few summary executions which the Home Front did carry out were very effective in intimidating Norwegian Quislings whose earlier arrogance was now fading rapidly.

In the last six months or so of the war over sixty transmitters were sending information to London, and advances in technology were enabling agents to smuggle large quantities of information out of Norway in the minimum of space, thanks to microphotography. By early 1945 there were something like 40,000 trained men in the Home Forces, including 13,000 who were training as "police" troops in Sweden. Though all of them were lightly armed — their chief weapon was the Sten gun — and their uniforms were simply grey jackets and arm bands marked with "HS" (Hjemme-Styrkene), they had the government's full backing. On 5th May their leader received the following communication from London,

"In the case of German capitulation in Norway, the Home Front leadership is hereby authorised on behalf of the government to take the necessary steps for the maintenance of order and the establishment of Norwegian administration, based on Norwegian laws and regulations, until members of the government arrive in Oslo." Clearly London was accepting that the Home Forces were now an impressive organisation, deserving of respect.

Though at the time there must surely have been some misgivings in the minds of the Home Forces' leadership, it is now a fact of history that, during the night of 7th May, 1945, the lightly armed Home Forces took over the country from 450,000 well-armed German troops, without incident. By the time the first Norwegian and British airborne troops arrived on 8th May, the great surrender was complete. It was a surrender without parallel in history, and there had probably been few of the Allied hierarchy who had expected it to happen with so little fuss. Of course it is only fair to note that the cowed herrenvolk who laid down their arms to the tiny Norwegian Home Forces in May 1945 were vastly different from the Germans who had arrived in Norway with so much swagger in 1940. At that time they had been persuaded by Nazi propaganda before setting out that their Nordic brothers would receive them with open arms. That illusion was quickly shattered. As the months went by they had become more and more conscious of the freezing hostility — even hatred — of the whole Norwegian people. Away from towns the climate, with its endless hours of winter darkness, and its extreme cold, also proved a major burden for the young Germans to carry. Morale quickly plummeted, and as the war began to turn against Germany, and news of disasters such as Stalingrad and North Africa seeped through, gloom and despondency were quick to set in. It seems highly probable that morale among German troops in Norway deteriorated farther than in any of the other occupied countries. A German officer is quoted as saying, "In Poland we risked losing our lives, but in Norway we risk losing our souls."

Over in Shetland as 1944 ended there was the same optimism, as in Norway, that the war was nearing its end. Garrison troops left in a steady stream for employment elsewhere. In March, 1944, many Lerwegians had had a grandstand view of the destruction of a German JU88. The plane had appeared over the town to be met with an immediate barrage of ack-ack fire, and within 30 seconds it was plunging into the sea near the Baas of Beosetter in a mass of flames. Three crew members managed to get clear, and were picked by an RAF rescue launch. One of them was an elderly lieutenant, the other two young fellows not more than twenty. To the townspeople the whole episode seemed symbolic of how the military situation was changing.

But with the war seemingly on its last legs, the stream of refugees in late 1944 and early 1945 showed a marked increase. The *Hessa, Hitra* and *Vigra,* the need for absolute secrecy not now so pressing, were landing many escaping Norwegians in Lerwick, and the three sub-chasers at this time were providing the main escape channel for the dozens of Norwegians on the run from the Gestapo. On 3rd May, 1945, those in the know were awaiting the arrival of a German boat. This was a motor launch which had come over with six or seven Luftwaffe men on board from an airfield near Trondheim. A plane had spotted the boat and reported its position. MTB 711, with Sverre Syversen again a member of its crew, went out and came alongside the launch about 50-60 miles from Muckle Flugga. The Germans wanted to blow up the launch, at which 711 drew off, left the Germans on board and told them to go ahead. The Luftwaffe men changed their minds. 711 then took off the men, and one of the big Norwegian whalers towed the launch to Baltasound. There was some difficulty in getting the engine started, but the Norwegians managed to get it going, and the boat was in due course steered triumphantly into Lerwick harbour. In Lerwick the story was that the Germans' morale had been so low that they had simply packed their bags and set off. The MTB landed them at the North Ness, and they came ashore in their "new blues".

8th May duly arrived, and in Shetland as elsewhere in Britain, the celebrations to mark the end of long, hard years of war were enjoyable, lively and uninhibited. Everyone for a little while let their hair down, and the Norwegians in the islands were very much part of the widespread rejoicing. In every Norwegian mind, however, was the same question — when do we go back home? Within a day or two the MTBs were off and were home in their own country for the most important day of the year, 17th May. For the first time since the Germans arrived the National Day was once again celebrated in the traditional style, but this time its observance was marked with special pride and deep feeling. Sadly for the MTBs, both 709 and 715 were badly damaged by a heavy explosion in the engine-room of 715 on 19th May when laying at Fosnavåg, and both became total wrecks. The remainder of the MTBs returned to Lerwick, and then, on 1st June, they left for the last time. They got a tremendous send-off. Shetland people crowded the Esplanade, the Pier, the arms of the Peerie Dock and the whole front as far as South Ness. The MTB boys stood lined up on deck in regular navy fashion, in salute to the friends they were leaving on

the shore. Many who were there, both Shetlanders and Norwegians, have said that it was a very, very moving occasion. The
type of friendship forged through years of common, deadly danger
cannot be dissolved in a matter of minutes.

Over in Scalloway the Bus boys had the same mental question
— when do we go home? On 15th May the sub-chasers, too, were
off east over sea. Two went to Bergen, one to Ålesund, and to the
great joy of the crews they were able to be on home soil for
Constitution Day. Like the MTBs they, too, returned for one last
visit, and to close down the base which had been their second home
for so long. Of course that was a task that couldn't be completed in
a day or two, and when they finally left Harald Angeltveit, who
had played such a vital role in the engineering requirements of the
Moore yard, stayed behind for several months to complete the
decommissioning of the home of the Shetland Bus.

What happened to all these boats which for so long had been
part of the Shetland scene? Of the sub-chasers, the *Hessa* was
finally scrapped, though there was an attempt in 1967 to have her
preserved. Sadly this foundered through lack of interest. The *Vigra*
was sold in 1958, for conversion to a motor yacht. She later sank in
Drammens River, but was salvaged, and in 1970 her engines were
removed, after which she was scuttled in Drammensfjord. The
Hitra was found, partly sunk, in 1981 at Tjurkö, Karlskrona in
Sweden. She was brought back to Norway, to Oma Båtbyggeri A/S
at Leirvik on Stord, and there she was completely restored, at very
considerable cost. Fittingly, some of the money used in her reconstruction came from Shetland. In June, 1987, with a number of her
old crew, she returned for a moving and nostalgic visit to
Scalloway, where both crew and boat received the warmest of
welcomes. It was like a family reunion.

We have seen how two of the MTBs met their fate at
Fosnavåg. Nos. 704, 711, 713, 716, 717, 719, 722 and 723 were
taken over by the Royal Norwegian Navy, the remainder being
returned to the Royal Navy. So far as is known only one of these
craft still exists. That one is No. 618, which now lies at Shoreham
on the English south coast in a fairly sorry condition, and still in
use as a houseboat. Almost as soon as the war was over Norwegian
fishing craft re-appeared in Lerwick harbour. Some of them were
boats which had earlier escaped and were now ready to resume
where they had left off, but many of them came over from Norway
immediately after 8th May. Britain had been subjected to strict
rationing during the whole war, but short as supplies of many
things had been, conditions simply bore no comparison with what

the Norwegians had endured. The final months of the war had been particularly severe, when the extra mouths to feed numbered well over half a million, and virtually nothing in the way of supplies was coming in from Germany. The crews of MTBs, sub-chasers and fishing boats all bought whatever was available in Lerwick to take back to Norway to alleviate in some small way the critical shortages there.

And what of the men who have lent their own lustre to the pages of this book? For most of them the return to Norway, something they had looked forward to for five long years, was far from easy. Heroes they were, but many of those who had stayed at home had done their bit as well in no uncertain fashion. Now they were all in the same boat — living in a country which the Germans had stripped bare, and left desperately short of food, houses, materials and work. It was clear that the post-war years would be no picnic for anyone. Øivind Steinsvåg, for instance, back home in time for his 19th birthday, completed a three-year electrical training course in two years, then joined the merchant navy. He still makes frequent visits to Shetland by yacht, and was over with the *Hitra* in 1987. And rightly so, for he had been closely and actively involved in her reconstruction. Today he lives on the beautiful island of Bømlo. Kåre Mørk left the naval service for good in December, 1945. He got work first on coastal boats, and later on deep-water vessels. Rolf Nordhus stayed in the navy, but received back injuries when thrown from his bunk during a storm. These injuries troubled him for some time, but he regained full fitness and today lives in Bergen. He, too, was over with the *Hitra* in 1987. Kåre Iversen is still well-known in Shetland, and still a frequent visitor. "The Scalloway people knew exactly what was going on, but they never talked, they never asked — they were just good friends." Torleif Fagertun got work in the shipyard on Stord, and his wife speaks very good English, having taken her degree in the language by attending nightschool. On his wall hangs the picture of a little boat. It is from the local paper which did a feature on Torleif's marathon row up Norway's west coast. Louis Rasmussen came back to Stord on the *Vigra,* and was demobilised after a few months. He went north and took over his uncle's farm at Molde. His family had heard absolutely nothing from him from the day he left till the day he returned. "Let me tell you about Shetland," he says. "It was very good. I don't know how to tell you how good it was. It was just like a close family — it was just like being at home. I was probably closest to the Hutchison family. I found out afterwards that when we were away on a trip they would go down to the pier and look out past the islands to see if there was any sign of us. I can never forget Scalloway and Shetland.''

Hans Bakkland's war had many tough moments, and a return to north Norway after the devastation left by the Germans was equally tough. He went back to the fishing. His first boat was poor, but he got a better one, and married in 1949. "I made many friends in Scalloway, and many in other parts of Shetland. I have so many happy memories." Harald Angeltveit, as we have seen, stayed on in Scalloway for several months after the others had gone. Says Harald, "There were a lot of Norwegians in Scalloway. It had been bad times in Norway, but when we came to Scalloway it was so much better. I have to say thank you to all you Shetland people — it was fine to live with you — you were so easy to get along with. I thank you for the friendship we shared with you in Shetland." Otto Hoddevik, still active in Måløy, recalls, "We got on extremely well with the people of Lerwick. I can't remember a single MTB man being arrested. There were at least five hundred of us altogether, always with a reserve crew standing by, waiting for any emergency. I was many times ashore in Norway, and it was a very special feeling to stand on the soil of my homeland. But when we were outside the coastal islands and heading back to Shetland, I always felt I was going home." Nils Robertstad, his daring days as an agent far behind him, lives today on a hillside on Bømlo, his house windows looking down on a beautiful fjord, so symbolic of the marvellous land for which he risked so much. Reidar Nilsen returned to Leirvik on the *Vigra,* and stayed in the service for a few months. Today he lives in Ålesund, his memories of the far-off war years still vivid and fresh. Arne Melkevik (Nipen) found work very hard to get when he returned to Norway, and came back to Shetland in 1946. He fished with the *Duen* for some months, then went to work at Moore's yard in Scalloway before going home again in 1950. He became a chief engineer in the merchant navy, but was severely injured in an accident on the Aberdeen/Inverness road nearly twenty years ago.

Albert Eilertsen as we saw married in 1943. When the Commandos left Shetland in 1944, Albert became one of the crew of the *Vigra,* and got to know the legendary Larsen very well. Salvage ship, old battleship, Shetland Bus, MTBs, Commandos, sub-chasers — Albert knew them all, and he is left with a wonderfully mixed bag of memories. He was demobilised in January, 1946, and took his wife over to Norway. However, they returned to Shetland, and today they live in Lerwick. Asbjørn Lie married his Shetland wife at the end of 1944, and returned to

Norway on MTB 719, his first port of call being Måløy. He was the first of the brothers to return, and he remembers he had some real tobacco for his father. Things were very difficult, and he stayed with the navy for a time, and brought his family over to Norway. But in 1947 they returned to Shetland, and they live today in Lerwick. Sverre Syversen stayed in the navy for a time, and was demobilised in 1946, his final service being on board the king's yacht. His first civilian job was as foreman fireman at the airport, but he couldn't settle. He returned to Shetland and married Isobel in 1947. Sverre tells the story of how, some years after the war, a Norwegian doctor saw a couple coming up the path to his front door. When he answered the door the man said, "I have brought my wife to Norway to show her where I had such a wonderful time during the war." The doctor had known the man — and had also known that he was a member of the Gestapo. His reaction can be imagined. Today there are surely few Lerwegians who look on "Steve", Asbjørn and Albert as anything other than Shetlanders.

While official records credit the MTBs with sinking only 26 ships on 137 operations, their own records show that they made 161 operations and sank 42 ships, amounting to 137,000 tons, and badly damaged another 26 ships. They shot down six planes and damaged eight. They shot up numerous coastal stations, laid mines, landed and picked up agents, and were a constant thorn in the enemy's side. The boats of the Shetland Bus, both the simple fishing vessels and the sub-chasers, became a legend, and their contribution to the overall war effort was far in excess of what might have been expected of the relatively small provision of resources. The submarines — *Uredd, Ula* and *Utsira* — made their own notable contribution, and the Sunderlands and Catalinas operating from Sullom Voe with Norwegian crews were a very important part of Coastal Command. The agents who slipped quietly in and out of Shetland were a race apart, whose individual contribution to the fight for freedom must have been tremendous. No one tried to pry — no one asked questions — everyone recognised that their very existence depended on secrecy. Those with Shetland as their point of departure sometimes landed from Bus boats, sometimes from MTBs, sometimes from submarines. Whilst everyone was in danger these boys were putting their heads right into the lion's mouth, with the consequences, if caught, too horrible to contemplate. In earlier pages we have seen the vital contribution made by the Commandos.

There is always an aftermath to war, and in a land which has suffered oppressive occupation by a country such as Germany was between 1940 and 1945, that aftermath can be traumatic. In some respects Norway probably suffered less than some of the other occupied countries, but the hard fact was that between 30,000 and 40,000 Norwegians were arrested by the Germans. 162 of those met their deaths in fights with their enemy, 366 were executed, 130 died in prison camps in Norway, and 1340 in concentration camps in Germany, including 610 Jews. From those escaping west over the North Sea it is known that 93 perished — the actual number is probably significantly higher. In many cases their deaths were shrouded in mystery, on which no amount of investigation could throw any further light. For instance, in Bergen in 1945, there was an inquiry into the fate of the boat *Knut* which had set out for Shetland on 30th September, 1941. Another boat could report seeing her about 60 miles west, riding out a storm, but there was no record of her having arrived anywhere in Britain, and none of the eleven people on board had ever been seen again. But in 1943 the father of one of the boys received a letter saying his son was all right, and then the father-in-law of another of the boys received a letter, posted in Sweden, supposed to be from the boy, but not in his handwriting and not in his style. Naturally these letters had kindled new hope in the hearts of the bereaved parents, but with the lack of any real evidence to the contrary, it had to be assumed that the *Knut* and all on board had perished. The question remained — what kind of crank or sadist had been responsible for the two letters?

With the Germans beaten it would not have been surprising if there had been Norwegians ready and eager to exact a swift revenge. But it was not like that. Of course, there were a lot of guilty people, and inevitably a large number of arrests. By the end of June, 14,000 people had been pulled in. But the arrests were carried out in a quiet, orderly and lawful manner. The only people who were sometimes the subject of summary justice were the "German tarts" who were occasionally seized and had their hair shorn. Quite a few of them were taken into protective custody. Two men who clearly felt they could expect little mercy were Terboven and SS General Rediess who blew themselves up in a bunker at Skaugum, the official residence of the Crown Prince, which Terboven had used as his home. A number of the leaders of Quisling's party also committed suicide, but not Quisling himself. He was forced to give himself up, and underwent a lengthy trial, at the end of which he was found guilty, sentenced to death, and executed by firing squad on 24th October, 1945. Said the Supreme Court in passing sentence on him, "The requirement of obedience and loyalty to those who lawfully represent the nation and the people applies absolutely and unremittingly. When the nation's destiny is at stake, chaos must not prevail.''

Charges against 90,000 people in all were investigated, and of these 46,000 were found guilty. 18,000 got terms of imprisonment and/or a fine, and 28,000 were only fined. Only 600 prison sentences were for more than eight years, the majority for very much less, and in the event, no matter the length of the sentence, the time served was very much less — sometimes less than half. The last of the end-of-war prisoners was released in 1957 — in fact as early as 1951 there were only 150 still in prison.

Twenty-five Norwegians and twelve Germans suffered the death penalty, and of these only Quisling and two of his henchmen could be categorised as political. The largest number of death sentences were passed on Henry Rinnan and members of his gang, and rightly so. Rinnan and nine of his men were sentenced to death, eleven to hard labour for life, and many others to lengthy terms of imprisonment. The gang had betrayed over 1000 Norwegians to the Germans. Of that number over 100 were killed and hundreds more subjected to vicious torture. Rinnan himself was personally convicted of 13 murders. Well might Lilly Walle say, "Henry Rinnan was the most evil man in Norway." Terje Teige, who might have been expected to seek revenge on the person who betrayed him, said at war's end, "This is a time for rebuilding, not for revenge." And the people of Norway, with freedom won, behaved with dignity and restraint. An inner strength, so much a part of the Norwegian character, had stood them in good stead during the long years of oppression. Now they saw, even more clearly than before, that the basic tenet of the 1814 Constitution — that "the land must be built on law" — was of supreme importance. German oppression from 1940 to 1945 had high-lighted the relevance of that principle. Said Churchill, "In Norway there was a dignified absence of fury and mob violence."

The new government, which this time included a woman, Kirsten Hansteen, widow of Viggo Hansteen, the first labour leader to be executed by the Germans, faced up to the massive problems confronting them with courage. Few governments meet with universal acclaim. But history will perhaps accept that this government saw the promotion of the welfare and happiness of the individual as its prime concern. And perhaps history will also accept that it strove hard to achieve at least something approaching that ideal.

With the Nazis finally crushed, the circumstances which had

brought Norway and Shetland so closely together came to an end. The Norwegians returned home to be once again among their own people. The bonds which had bound the two so closely in happy friendship had to be relaxed, and, with an almost complete lack of any kind of regular transport between the islands and Norway, soon almost all that was left for many were memories. But for the fishermen of Norway's west coast, fishing the Shetland grounds was almost like taking a "home road". Still their boats continued to use Lerwick harbour. Still their crews came ashore to shop along Commercial Street. And when they needed help they called on Ruby in Universal Stores. For many years it was a common sight to see Ruby, with several Norwegians in tow, going from shop to shop, explaining and interpreting for the benefit of these friendly visitors.

While Norway's young men waged their own war against the Germans from Shetland's shores, the islands' own youth were fully engaged in a similar manner elsewhere. In the First War Shetland's casualties were higher, relative to population, than those of any part of Britain. In the Second War the number killed was less, but the islands' contribution to the overall war effort was considerable. Traditionally, large numbers of her men were to be found in the ships of the merchant navy, sailing the seas of the world and only too often at the mercy of a U-boat's torpedo. But her men — and women — were also in every branch of the armed services, and there were few big actions of the war where Shetlanders were not involved. There were men from the islands present at Britain's greatest defeat — Dunkirk. But Shetlanders were back in Normandy on D-Day, and at the heart of Germany when final victory came. They were in North Africa and Italy, in Burma and in the Middle East, in bombers over Berlin and in cargo boats at Murmansk. A Shetland pilot in the RAF was an early casualty of the war — a Shetland seaman was dragged to a watery grave aboard the tragic *Hood*. Shetland grieved for the ones who were lost, but Shetland was proud of the service which her young people gave in a war which, for once, was a people's war.

And the islands had a special pride in having provided a home and a base for the young Norwegians, so like their own sons and husbands, who daily risked their lives in the fight for freedom. The friendships which were forged during these days of common danger were warm, meaningful and abiding. But nearly half a century has passed since those heady days, and, while the survivors still have their own vivid memories, their numbers are ever more swiftly decreasing with the passage of time. For older people it is perhaps somewhat surprising to realise that over two-thirds of the present populations of Norway and Shetland have no first-hand knowledge of the war years. Their awareness comes only from hearsay, from books, or from the anecdotes of parents or grandparents. So was the Shetland/Norway relationship from 1940 to 1945 just a moment in history — a tiny episode that meant a lot to a relatively small number of people, but which will soon disappear in the aeons of time? Only history will tell. But the indications are that the relationship is of a much more enduring character. With the coming of regular summer services between Shetland and Norway, both by sea and by air, a completely new era of interchange between the two peoples has commenced. Both groups and individuals are now widely involved, and Shetlanders at last have the opportunity to savour this beautiful country and its people at first hand. And always they find that to say they are from Shetland ensures an immediate warm welcome. Time and again they are amazed at the feelings of gratitude still expressed for the part Shetland played in Norway's war. It is so easy to feel at home in each other's country.

After 126 years of peaceful neutrality, Norway was forced, for five long years, to endure a situation which was completely alien to every Norwegian's basic instincts. She suffered — but never accepted — the German occupation, and emerged at the end with her people impoverished and almost starving, but with their pride intact, and their fierce love of freedom and independence stronger than ever. We here in Shetland never had to face German occupation, and so we cannot come even near to appreciating what the people of occupied countries endured. How we would have behaved had we been placed in a similar situation to the Norwegians is probably anybody's guess. All we could do at the time was to offer sympathy, friendship and whatever help we could muster. But maybe it is some little comfort to reflect on how much we have in common with our friends across the North Sea. Would that common background and a similar outlook on life have enabled us to conduct ourselves with the same determined, hostile endurance which characterised the Norwegians during the five long years? May we never in the future have to face a situation which will provide the answer.

Appendix

The Norwegian National Anthem

"JA VI ELSKER DETTE LANDET"

Ja, vi elsker dette landet
som det stiger frem,
furet, vaerbitt over vannet
med de tusen hjem.
Elsker, elsker det og tenker,
på vår far og mor,
og den saganatt som senker
drømme på vår jord.

Norske mann i hus og hytte,
takk din store Gud!
Landet ville han beskytte,
Skjønt det mørkt så ut.
Alt hva fedrene har kjempet,
mødrene har grett,
har den Herre stille lempet,
så vi vant vår rett.

Ja, vi elsker dette landet
som det stiger frem,
furet, vaerbitt, over vannet,
med de tusen hjem.
Og some fedres kamp har hevet
det av nød til seir,
også vi, når det blir krevet,
for dets fred slår leir.

Bjørnstjerne Bjørnson, 1859. First sung 17th May, 1864.

Verse One, English version, by G. M. Gathorne-Hardy

Yes, we love with fond devotion
This, the land that looms
Rugged, storm-scarred, o'er the ocean,
With her thousand homes
Love her, in our love recalling
Those who gave us birth,
And old tales which night, in falling,
Brings as dream to earth.

The MTB Song

Langt ut i Nordsjøn,
langt ut i rom sjø'n,
seiler det båter i massevis.
Her er det norske MTB.
Daevelen, her skal du se!
Daevelen, steike meg, her skal det skje!

Først kommer Tamber,
blåser i bartene,
så kommer Ola, liten men go'!
Så kommer resten av oss;
Daevelen, her skal vi slåss!
Daevelen steike meg, her skal det skje!

Inn Mellom holmer,
inn mellom båer og skjaer,
seiler vi alle i sjøsprøyt og brått.
For imellom holmer og skjaer
er det vårt arbeid er.
Daevelen steike meg, her skal det skje!

Så ser vi tyskeren.
Han tok jo landet vårt.
Nå skal han senkes i massevis!
Si du til coxswain at han kommer —
Styrbord og babord igjen!
Daevelen steike meg, her skal det skje!

Klar med torpedoene!
Klar med kanonene!
Vi går til angrep, siktet er klart.
Der går torpedoene ut,
finner nok målet til sluttt.
Daevelen steike meg, her skal det skje!

Vi har gjort jobben,
båten er senket,
vi går tilbake, tar oss en dram.
Til vi drar over igjen,
kom og bli med oss, min venn!
Daevelen steike meg, her skal det skje!

Some Shetland/Norwegian Marriages

Edith Bruce to Asbjørn Lie
Elizabeth A. Bruce to Ole Breivik
Barbara E. M. Christie to Arne Johannes Olsen (Melkevik)
Williamina C. Fraser to Simon J. Juliussen
Helen Gray to Ludvik Smaaskjaer
Isobel M. Herculeson to Sverre Syversen
Ruby Irvine to Roald Hansen
Helen Isbister to Gunder Vinje (in London)
Maisie A. Johnston to Hans A. Nordhuus
Barbara G. Leask to Anker Olsen
Elizabeth G. Leslie to Hilmar A. Heiskel
Christina A. Moar to Aksel Rognaldsen
Williamina V. I. Moncrieff to Bjarne H. Larsen
Thomasina J. Mouat to Harald Nicolaysen
E. Wilfreda Nicolson to Albert A. Abrahamsen
Ina Pottinger to Albert B. Eilertsen
Christina C. Slater to Kåre E. Iversen
Lillian B. Smith to Bjarne Karlsen (in Inverness)
Annie D. E. Spence to Nils C. Grønneberg
Agnes H. Stewart to Trygve E. Aas
Cissie B. Sutherland to Hans Boi Boisen (in Norway)
Johanna Grace Thomson to Rudolf Sigbjørnsen
Margaret Thomson to Nils Olsen Midttyit
Ruth C. Thomson to Einar Bakken
Mary Helen Watt to Kolbjørn Kristiansen

Bibliography

Abelsen, Frank, *Marinens Fartøyer 1939-1945*

Andenaes, Riste and Skodvin, *Norway and the Second World War*

Bowyer, Charles, *For Valour*

Broch, Theodor, *The Mountains Wait*

Haga, Arfinn, *Arquebus Kaller London*

Haga, Arfinn, *Klar til Storm*

Haga, Arfinn, *Kystens partisaner*

Hauge, E. O. *Mannen som stjal Galtesund —*
        English translation — *Salt-water Thief*

Hegland, J. R., *Norske Torpedobåter 1873-1973*

Howarth, David, *The Shetland Bus*

Howarth, David, *Escape Alone (We Die Alone)*

Laker, Rosalind, *This Shining Land*

Macksey, Kenneth, *Godwin's Saga*

Nicolson, Jas. R., *Lerwick Harbour*

Olsen, Oluf Reed, *Two Eggs on my Plate*

Os, Edvard, *Selje og Vågsøy*

Riste & Nökleby, *Norway 1940-45 — The Resistance Movement*

Robson, Adam, *The Saga of a Ship*

Saelen, Fritjof, *Sjetlands Larsen*

Schofield, B. B., *The Russian Convoys*

Storm-Bjerke, H., *Klar til Kamp*

Strand, Odd, *Hitra*

Ulstein, Ragnar, *Englandsfarten 1 — Alarm i Ålesund*

Ulstein, Ragnar, *Englandsfarten 2 — Søkelys mot Bergen*

Warbey, William, *Look to Norway*

Warren and Benson, *Above Us the Waves*

Sunnhordland Årbok 1972

Lerwick Harbour Trust Arrivals' Books

Files of *Shetland Life* and *New Shetlander*

Index